PENGUIN BOOKS

I, CLAUDIUS
and
CLAUDIUS THE GOD

Robert Graves was born in 1895 at Wimbledon, son of Alfred Perceval Graves, the Irish writer, and Amalia von Ranke. He went from school to the First World War, where he became a captain in the Royal Welch Fusiliers. His principal calling was poetry, and his *Selected Poems* have been published in the Penguin Poets. Apart from a year as Professor of English Literature at Cairo University in 1926 he earned his living by writing, mostly historical novels which include: *I, Claudius*; *Claudius the God*; *Sergeant Lamb of the Ninth*; *Count Belisarius*; *Wife to Mr Milton* (all published as Penguins); *Proceed, Sergeant Lamb*; *The Golden Fleece*; *They Hanged My Saintly Billy*; and *The Isles of Unwisdom*. He wrote his autobiography, *Goodbye to All That*, in 1929. His two most discussed non-fiction books are *The White Goddess*, which presents a new view of the poetic impulse, and *The Nazarene Gospel Restored* (with Joshua Podro), a re-examination of primitive Christianity. He translated Apuleius, Lucan, and Suetonius for the Penguin Classics, and compiled the first modern dictionary of Greek mythology, *The Greek Myths*. He was elected Professor of Poetry at Oxford in 1961, and became an Honorary Fellow of St John's College, Oxford, in 1971. A new edition of his *Collected Poems* was published in 1975.

Robert Graves died on December 7th 1985 in Majorca, his home since 1929. On his death *The Times* said of him 'He will be remembered for his achievements as a prose stylist, historical novelist and memoirist, but above all as the paradigm of the dedicated poet, "the greatest lore poet in English since Donne".'

D1339156

ROBERT GRAVES

I, CLAUDIUS
and
CLAUDIUS THE GOD

PENGUIN BOOKS

PENGUIN BOOKS

Published by the Penguin Group
Penguin Books Ltd, 27 Wrights Lane, London W8 5TZ, England
Viking Penguin, a division of Penguin Books USA Inc.
375 Hudson Street, New York, New York 10014, USA
Penguin Books Australia Ltd, Ringwood, Victoria, Australia
Penguin Books Canada Ltd, 2801 John Street, Markham, Ontario, Canada L3R 1B4
Penguin Books (NZ) Ltd, 182–190 Wairau Road, Auckland 10, New Zealand

Penguin Books Ltd, Registered Offices: Harmondsworth, Middlesex, England

I, Claudius first published by Arthur Barker 1934
Published by Methuen 1939
First published in Penguin Books 1941

Claudius the God first published by Arthur Barker 1934
Published in Penguin Books 1943

I, Claudius and *Claudius the God* published in this edition 1986
5 7 9 10 8 6

Copyright 1934 © by Robert Graves
All rights reserved

Printed in England by Clays Ltd, St Ives plc
Set in Monotype Times

CONTENTS

I, CLAUDIUS

FROM THE AUTOBIOGRAPHY OF
TIBERIUS CLAUDIUS

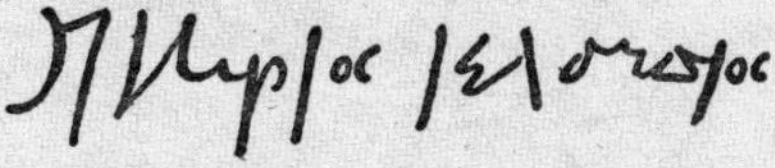

[handwritten Greek signature]

EMPEROR OF THE ROMANS

BORN 10 B.C.
MURDERED AND DEIFIED
A.D. 54

I am indebted for the Latin version of the Sibylline verses mentioned in the first chapter to Mr A. K. Smith, I.C.S. They are here first printed:

Punica centenos durabit poena per annos:
Res Romana viro parebit caesariato:
Calvus caesarie dominus dominabitur urbi:
Omnibus ille viris mulier mas ille puellis:
Rex equitabit equo bifidis equus unguibus ibit:
Filius imbelli fictus mactaverit ictu.
Imperium hinc alter ficto patre caesariato
Caesariae crinitus habet, qui marmore Romae
Mutabit lateres. Non visis vinciet Urbem
Compedibus. Fictae secreto coniugis astu
Occidet ut fictus bona filius occupet heres.
Tertius hinc sumet ficto patre caesariato
Calvus caesarie regnum cui sanguine limus
Commixtus. Victrix penes ilium et victa vicissim
Roma erit. Ille instar gladii pulvinar habebit,
Filius et fictus regni potietur iniqui.
Quartus habet solium ficto patre caesariato
Calvus caesarie invenis, cui Roma ministrae est.
Feta veneficiis Urbs impia serviet uni.
Quo puer ibat equo vectus calcatus eodem
Se iuvenem ferro cecidisse fatetur equino
Caesariatus ad hoc quintus numerabitur hirtus
Caesarie, toti genti contemptus avitae.
Imbecillus iners, aestivas addere Romae
Aptus aquas populo frumenta hiemalia praebet.
Ille tamen fictae secreto coniugis astu
Occidet ut fictus bona filius occupet heres.
Sextus habet regnum ficto patre caesariato.
Flamma pavor citharoedus eunt tria monstra per urbem.
Sanguine dextra rubet materno. Septimus heres
Nemo erit, at sexti busto cruor ibit ab imo.

R. G.

Galmpton, Brixham
1941

... A story that was the subject of every variety of misrepresentation, not only by those who then lived but likewise in succeeding times: so true is it that all transactions of pre-eminent importance are wrapt in doubt and obscurity; while some hold for certain facts the most precarious hearsays, others turn facts into falsehood; and both are exaggerated by posterity.

TACITUS

Author's Note

THE 'gold piece' here used as the regular monetary standard is the Latin *aureus*, a coin worth 100 *sestertii*, or twenty-five silver *denarii* ('silver pieces'): it may be thought of as worth roughly one pound sterling, or five American dollars at pre-war value. The 'mile' is the Roman mile, some thirty paces shorter than the English mile. The marginal dates have for convenience been given according to Christian reckoning: the Greek reckoning, used by Claudius, counted the years from the First Olympiad, which took place in 776 B.C. For convenience also, the most familiar geographical names have been used: thus 'France', not 'Transalpine Gaul', because France covers roughly the same territorial area and it would be inconsistent to call towns like Nîmes and Boulogne and Lyons by their modern names – their classical ones would not be popularly recognized – while placing them in *Gallia Transalpina* or, as the Greeks call it, *Galatia*. (Greek geographical terms are most confusing: Germany was 'the country of the Celts'.) Similarly the most familiar forms of proper names have been used – 'Livy' for Titus Livius, 'Cymbeline' for Cunobelinus, 'Mark Antony' for Marcus Antonius.

It has been difficult at times to find suitable renderings for military, legal, and other technical terms. To give a single instance, there is the word 'assegai'. Aircraftman T. E. Shaw (whom I take this opportunity of thanking for his careful reading of these proofs) questions my use of 'assegai' as an equivalent of the German *framea* or *pfreim*. He suggests 'javelin'. But I have not adopted the suggestion, as I have gratefully adopted others of his, because I needed 'javelin' for *pilum*, the regular missile weapon of the disciplined Roman infantryman; and 'assegai' is more savage-sounding. 'Assegai' has had a 300-year currency in English and acquired new vigour in the nineteenth century because of the Zulu wars. The long-shafted iron-headed *framea* was used, according to Tacitus, both as a missile and as a stabbing weapon. So was the assegai of the Ama-Zulu warriors, with whom the Germans of Claudius's day had culturally much in common. If Tacitus's statements, first as to the handiness of the *framea* at close quarters, and then as to its unmanageability among trees, are to be reconciled, the Germans probably did what the Zulus did – they broke off the end of the *framea*'s long shaft when hand-to-hand fighting started. But it seldom came to that, for the Germans

7

always preferred strike-and-run tactics when engaged with the better-armed Roman infantryman.

Suetonius in his *Twelve Caesars* refers to Claudius's histories as written 'ineptly' rather than 'inelegantly'. Yet if certain passages of the present work are not only ineptly written but somewhat inelegantly too – the sentences painfully constructed and the digressions awkwardly placed – this is not out of keeping with Claudius's literary style as exhibited in his Latin speech about the Aeduan franchise, fragments of which survive. The speech is, indeed, thickly strewn with inelegancies of this sort, but then it is probably a transcription of the official shorthand record of Claudius's exact words to the Senate – the speech of a tired man conscientiously extemporizing oratory from a paper of rough notes. *I, Claudius* is a conversational piece of writing; as Greek, indeed, is a far more conversational language than Latin. Claudius's recently discovered Greek letter to the Alexandrians, which may however be partly the work of an imperial secretary, reads much more easily than the Aeduan speech.

For help towards classical correctness I have to thank Miss Eirlys Roberts; and for criticism of the congruity of the English, Miss Laura Riding.

R. G.

1934

Chapter 1

I, TIBERIUS CLAUDIUS DRUSUS NERO GERMANICUS This-that-and-the-other (for I shall not trouble you yet with all my titles), who was once, and not so long ago either, known to my friends and relatives and associates as 'Claudius the Idiot', or 'That Claudius', or 'Claudius the Stammerer',   A.D. 41 or 'Clau-Clau-Claudius', or at best as 'Poor Uncle Claudius', am now about to write this strange history of my life; starting from my earliest childhood and continuing year by year until I reach the fateful point of change where, some eight years ago, at the age of fifty-one, I suddenly found myself caught in what I may call the 'golden predicament' from which I have never since become disentangled.

This is not by any means my first book: in fact literature, and especially the writing of history – which as a young man I studied here at Rome under the best contemporary masters – was, until the change came, my sole profession and interest for more than thirty-five years. My readers must not therefore be surprised at my practised style: it is indeed Claudius himself who is writing this book, and no mere secretary of his, and not one of those official annalists, either, to whom public men are in the habit of communicating their recollections, in the hope that elegant writing will eke out meagreness of subject-matter and flattery soften vices. In the present work, I swear by all the Gods, I am my own mere secretary, and my own official annalist: I am writing with my own hand, and what favour can I hope to win from myself by flattery? I may add that this is not the first history of my own life that I have written. I once wrote another, in eight volumes, as a contribution to the City archives. It was a dull affair, by which I set little store, and only written in response to public request. To be frank, I was extremely busy with other matters during its composition, which was two years ago. I dictated most of the first four volumes to a Greek secretary of mine and told him to alter nothing as he wrote (except, where necessary, for the balance of the sentences, or to remove contradictions or repetitions). But I admit that nearly all the second half of the work, and some chapters at least of the first, were composed by this same fellow, Polybius (whom I had named myself, when a slave-boy, after the famous historian), from material that I gave him. And he modelled his style so accurately on mine that, really, when he had done, nobody could have guessed what was mine and what was his.

It was a dull book, I repeat. I was in no position to criticize the Emperor Augustus, who was my maternal grand-uncle, or his third and last wife, Livia Augusta, who was my grandmother, because they had both been officially deified and I was connected in a priestly capacity with their cults; and though I could have pretty sharply criticized Augusta's two unworthy Imperial successors, I refrained for decency's sake. It would have been unjust to exculpate Livia, and Augustus himself in so far as he deferred to that remarkable and – let me say at once – abominable woman, while telling the truth about the other two, whose memories were not similarly protected by religious awe.

I let it be a dull book, recording merely such uncontroversial facts as, for example, that So-and-so married So-and-so, the daughter of Such-and-Such who had this or that number of public honours to his credit, but not mentioning the political reasons for the marriage or the behind-scene bargaining between the families. Or I would write that So-and-so died suddenly, after eating a dish of African figs, but say nothing of poison, or to whose advantage the death proved to be, unless the facts were supported by a verdict of the Criminal Courts. I told no lies, but neither did I tell the truth in the sense I mean to tell it here. When I consulted this book to-day in the Apollo Library on the Palatine Hill, to refresh my memory for certain particulars of date, I was interested to come across passages in the public chapters which I could have sworn I had written or dictated, the style was so peculiarly my own, and yet which I had no recollection of writing or dictating. If they were by Polybius they were a wonderfully clever piece of mimicry (he had my other histories to study, I admit), but if they were really by myself then my memory is even worse than my enemies declare it to be. Reading over what I have just put down I see that I must be rather exciting than disarming suspicion, first as to my sole authorship of what follows, next as to my integrity as an historian, and finally as to my memory for facts. But I shall let it stand; it is myself writing as I feel, and as the history proceeds the reader will be the more ready to believe that I am hiding nothing – so much being to my discredit.

This is a confidential history. But who, it may be asked, are my confidants? My answer is: it is addressed to posterity. I do not mean my great-grandchildren, or my great-great-grandchildren: I mean an extremely remote posterity. Yet my hope is that you, my eventual readers of a hundred generations ahead or more, will feel yourselves directly spoken to, as if by a contemporary: as often Herodotus and Thucydides, long dead, seem to speak to me. And why do I specify so extremely remote a posterity as that? I shall explain.

I went to Cumae, in Campania, a little less than eighteen years ago, and visited the Sibyl in her cliff cavern on Mount Gaurus. There is always a Sibyl at Cumae, for when one dies her novice-attendant succeeds; but they are not all equally famous. Some of them are never granted a prophecy by Apollo in all the long years of their service. Others prophesy, indeed, but seem more inspired by Bacchus than by Apollo, the drunken nonsense they deliver; which has brought the oracle into discredit. Before the succession of Deiphobe, whom Augustus often consulted, and Amalthea, who is still alive and most famous, there had been a run of very poor Sibyls for nearly 300 years. The cavern lies behind a pretty little Greek temple sacred to Apollo and Artemis – Cumae was an Aeolian Greek colony. There is an ancient gilt frieze above the portico ascribed to Daedalus, though this is patently absurd, for it is no older than 500 years, if as old as that, and Daedalus lived at least 1,100 years ago. It represents the story of Theseus and the minotaur whom he killed in the Labyrinth of Crete. Before being permitted to visit the Sibyl I had to sacrifice a bullock and a ewe there, to Apollo and Artemis respectively. It was cold December weather. The cavern was a terrifying place, hollowed out from the solid rock; the approach steep, tortuous, pitch-dark, and full of bats. I went disguised, but the Sibyl knew me. It must have been my stammer that betrayed me. I stammered badly as a child and though, by following the advice of specialists in elocution, I gradually learned to control my speech on set public occasions, yet on private and unpremeditated ones I am still, though less so than formerly, liable every now and then to trip nervously over my own tongue; which is what happened to me at Cumae.

I came into the inner cavern, after groping painfully on all-fours up the stairs, and saw the Sibyl, more like an ape than a woman, sitting on a chair in a cage that hung from the ceiling, her robes red and her unblinking eyes shining red in the single red shaft of light that struck down from somewhere above. Her toothless mouth was grinning. There was a smell of death about me. But I managed to force out the salutation that I had prepared. She gave me no answer. It was only some time afterwards that I learnt that this was the mummied body of Deiphobe, the previous Sibyl, who had died recently at the age of 110; her eyelids were propped up with glass marbles silvered behind to make them shine. The reigning Sibyl always lived with her predecessor. Well, I must have stood for some minutes in front of Deiphobe, shivering and making propitiatory grimaces – it seemed a lifetime. At last the living Sibyl, whose name was Amalthea, quite a young woman too, revealed herself. The red shaft of light failed, so that Deiphobe disappeared – somebody, probably the novice, had covered up the tiny red-glass window – and a new shaft, white, struck down and lit up Amalthea, seated on an ivory throne in the shadows behind. She had a beautiful mad-looking face with a high forehead and sat as motionless as Deiphobe. But her eyes were closed. My knees shook and I fell into a stammer from which I could not extricate myself.

'O Sib ... Sib ... Sib ... Sib ... Sib ...' I began. She opened her eyes, frowned, and mimicked me: 'O Clau ... Clau ... Clau ...' That shamed me and I managed to remember what I had come to ask. I said with a great effort: 'O Sibyl: I have come to question you about Rome's fate and mine.'

Gradually her face changed, the prophetic power overcame her, she struggled and gasped, and there was a rushing noise through all the galleries, doors banged, wings swished my face, the light vanished, and she uttered a Greek verse in the voice of the God:

> Who groans beneath the Punic Curse
> And strangles in the strings of purse,
> Before she mends must sicken worse.
>
> Her living mouth shall breed blue flies,
> And maggots creep about her eyes.
> No man shall mark the day she dies.

Then she tossed her arms over her head and began again:

> Ten years, fifty days and three,
> Clau – Clau – Clau shall given be
> A gift that all desire but he.

To a fawning fellowship
He shall stammer, cluck, and trip,
Dribbling always with his lip.

But when he's dumb and no more here,
Nineteen hundred years or near,
Clau – Clau – Claudius shall speak clear.

The God laughed through her mouth then, a lovely yet terrible sound – ho! ho! ho! I made obeisance, turned hurriedly and went stumbling away, sprawling headlong down the first flight of broken stairs, cutting my forehead and knees, and so painfully out, the tremendous laughter pursuing me.

Speaking now as a practised diviner, a professional historian and a priest who has had opportunities of studying the Sibylline books as regularized by Augustus, I can interpret the verses with some confidence. By the Punic Curse the Sibyl was referring plainly enough to the destruction of Carthage by us Romans. We have long been under a divine curse because of that. We swore friendship and protection to Carthage in the name of our principal Gods, Apollo included, and then, jealous of her quick recovery from the disasters of the Second Punic War, we tricked her into fighting the Third Punic War and utterly destroyed her, massacring her inhabitants and sowing her fields with salt. 'The strings of purse' are the chief instruments of this curse – a money-madness that has choked Rome ever since she destroyed her chief trade rival and made herself mistress of all the riches of the Mediterranean. With riches came sloth, greed, cruelty, dishonesty, cowardice, effeminacy, and every other un-Roman vice. What the gift was that all desired but myself – and it came exactly ten years and fifty-three days later – you shall read in due course. The lines about Claudius speaking clear puzzled me for years, but at last I think that I understand them. They are, I believe, an injunction to write the present work. When it is written, I shall treat it with a preservative fluid, seal it in a lead casket, and bury it deep in the ground somewhere for posterity to dig up and read. If my interpretation be correct it will be found again some 1,900 years hence. And then, when all other authors of to-day whose works survive will seem to shuffle and stammer, since they have written only for to-day, and guardedly, my story will speak out clearly and boldly. Perhaps on second thoughts I shall not take the trouble to seal it up in a casket. I shall merely leave it lying about. For my experience as a historian is that more documents survive by chance than by intention. Apollo has made the prophecy, so I shall let Apollo take care of the manuscript. As you see, I have chosen to write in Greek, because Greek, I believe, will always remain the chief literary language of the world, and if Rome rots away as the Sibyl has indicated, will not her language rot away with her? Besides, Greek is Apollo's own language.

I shall be careful with dates (which you see I am putting in the margin) and proper names. In compiling my histories of Etruria and Carthage I have spent more angry hours than I care to recall, puzzling out in what year this or that event happened and whether a man named So-and-so was really So-and-so or whether he was a son or grandson or great-grandson or no relation at all. I intend to spare my successors this sort of irritation. Thus, for example, of the several characters in this present history who have the name of Drusus – my father; myself; a son of mine; my first cousin; my nephew – each will be plainly distinguished wherever mentioned. And, for example again, in speaking of my tutor, Marcus Portius Cato, I must make it plain that he was neither Marcus Portius Cato, the Censor, instigator of the Third Punic War; nor his son of the same name, the well-known jurist; nor his grandson, the Consul of the same name, nor his great-grandson of the same name, Julius Caesar's enemy; nor his great-great-grandson of the same name, who fell at the Battle of Philippi; but an absolutely undistinguished great-great-great-grandson, still of the same name, who never bore any public dignity and who deserved none. Augustus made him my tutor and afterwards schoolmaster to other young Roman noblemen and sons of foreign kings, for though his name entitled him to a position of the highest dignity, his severe, stupid, pedantic nature qualified him for nothing better than that of elementary schoolmaster.

To fix the date to which these events belong I can do no better, I think, than to say that my birth occurred in the 744th year after the foundation of Rome by Romulus, and in the 767th year after the First Olympiad, and that the Emperor Augustus, whose name is unlikely to perish even in 1,900 years of history, had by then been ruling for twenty years.

10 B.C.

Before I close this introductory chapter I have something more to add about the Sibyl and her prophecies. I have already said that, at Cumae, when one Sibyl dies another succeeds, but that some are more famous than others. There was one very famous one, Demophile, whom Aeneas consulted before his descent into Hell. And there was a later one, Herophile, who came to King Tarquin and offered him a collection of prophecies at a higher price than he wished to pay. When he refused, so the story runs, she burned a part and offered what was left at the same price, which he again refused. Then she burned another part and offered what was left, still at the same price – which, for curiosity, he paid. Herophile's oracles were of two kinds, warning or hopeful prophecies of the future, and directions for the suitable propitiatory sacrifices to be made when such and such portents occurred. To these were added, in the course of time, whatever remarkable and well-attested oracles were uttered to private persons. Whenever, then, Rome has seemed threatened by strange portents or disasters the Senate orders a consultation of the books by the priests who have charge of them and a remedy is always found. Twice the books have been partially destroyed by fire and the lost prophecies restored by the combined memories of the priests in charge. The memories seem in many instances to have been extremely faulty: this is why Augustus set to work on an authoritative canon of the prophecies, rejecting obviously uninspired interpolations or restorations. He also called in and destroyed all unauthorized private collections of Sibylline oracles as well as all other books of public prediction that he could lay his hands upon, to the number of over 2,000. The revised Sibylline books he put in a locked cupboard under the pedestal of Apollo's statue in the temple which he built for the God close to his palace on the Palatine Hill. A unique book from Augustus's private historical library came into my possession some time after his death. It was called 'Sibylline Curiosities: being such prophecies found incorporated in the original canon as have been rejected as spurious by the priests of Apollo'. The verses were copied out in Augustus's own beautiful script, with the characteristic mis-spellings which, originally made from ignorance, he ever after adhered to as a point of pride. Most of these verses were obviously never spoken by the Sibyl either in ecstasy or out of it, but composed by irresponsible persons who wished to glorify themselves or their houses or to curse the houses of rivals by claiming divine authorship for their own fanciful predictions against them. The Claudian family had been particularly active, I noticed, in these forgeries. Yet I found one or two pieces whose language proved them respectably archaic and whose inspiration seemed divine, and whose plain and alarming sense had evidently decided Augustus – his word was law among the priests of Apollo – against admitting them into his canon. This little book I no longer have. But I can recall almost every word of the most memorable of these seemingly genuine prophecies, which was recorded both in the original Greek, and (like most of the early pieces in the canon) in rough Latin verse translation. It ran thus:

> A hundred years of the Punic Curse
> And Rome will be slave to a hairy man,
> A hairy man that is scant of hair.
> Every man's woman and each woman's man.
> The steed that he rides shall have toes for hooves.
> He shall die at the hand of his son, no son,
> And not on the field of war.

> The hairy one next to enslave the State
> Shall be son, no son, of this hairy last,
> He shall have hair in a generous mop.
> He shall give Rome marble in place of clay
> And fetter her fast with unseen chains,
> And shall die at the hand of his wife, no wife,
> To the gain of his son, no son.

> The hairy third to enslave the State
> Shall be son, no son, of this hairy last.
> He shall be mud well mixed with blood,
> A hairy man that is scant of hair.
> He shall give Rome victories and defeat
> And die to the gain of his son, no son –
> A pillow shall be his sword.

> The hairy fourth to enslave the State
> Shall be son, no son, of this hairy last.
> A hairy man that is scant of hair,
> He shall give Rome poisons and blasphemies
> And die from a kick of his aged horse
> That carried him as a child.

> The hairy fifth to enslave the State,
> To enslave the State, though against his will,
> Shall be that idiot whom all despised.

He shall have hair in a generous mop.
He shall give Rome water and winter bread
And die at the hand of his wife, no wife,
To the gain of his son, no son.

The hairy sixth to enslave the State
Shall be son, no son, of this hairy last.
He shall give Rome fiddlers and fear and fire.
His hand shall be red with a parent's blood.
No hairy seventh to him succeeds
And blood shall gush from his tomb.

Now it must have been plain to Augustus that the first of the hairy ones, that is, the Caesars (for Caesar means a head of hair), was his grand-uncle Julius, who adopted him. Julius was bald and he was renowned for his debaucheries with either sex; and his war charger, as is a matter of public record, was a monster which had toes instead of hooves. Julius escaped alive from many hard-fought battles only to be murdered at last, in the Senate House, by Brutus. And Brutus, though fathered on another, was believed to be Julius's natural son. 'Thou too, child!' said Julius, as Brutus came at him with a dagger. Of the Punic Curse I have already written. Augustus must have recognized in himself the second of the Caesars. Indeed, he himself at the end of his life made a boast, looking at the temples and public buildings that he had splendidly re-edified, and thinking too of his life's work in strengthening and glorifying the Empire, that he had found Rome in clay and left her in marble. But as for the manner of his death, he must have found the prophecy either unintelligible or incredible: yet some scruple kept him from destroying it. Who the hairy third and the hairy fourth and the hairy fifth were this history will plainly show; and I am indeed an idiot if, granting the oracle's unswerving accuracy in every particular up to the present, I do not recognize the hairy sixth; rejoicing on Rome's behalf that there will be no hairy seventh to succeed him.

Chapter 2

I CANNOT remember my father, who died when I was an infant, but as a young man I never lost an opportunity of gathering information of the most detailed sort about his life and character from every possible person – senator, soldier, or slave – who had known him. I began writing his biography as my apprentice-task in history, and though that was soon put a stop to by my grandmother, Livia, I continued collecting material in the hope of one day being able to finish the work. I finished it, actually, just the other day, and even now there is no sense in trying to put it into circulation. It is so republican in sentiment that the moment Agrippinilla – my present wife – came to hear of its publication every copy would be suppressed and my unfortunate copying-scribes would suffer for my indiscretions. They would be lucky to escape with their arms unbroken and their thumbs and index fingers unlopped, which would be a typical indication of Agrippinilla's pleasure. How that woman loathes me!

My father's example has guided me throughout life more strongly than that of any other person whatsoever, with the exception of my brother Germanicus. And Germanicus was, all agree, my father's very image in feature, body (but for his thin legs), courage, intellect, and nobility; so I readily combine them in my mind as a single character. If I could start this story fairly with an account of my infancy, going no farther back than my parents, I would certainly do so, for genealogies and family histories are tedious. But I shall not be able to avoid writing at some length about my grandmother Livia (the only one of my four grandparents who was alive at my birth) because unfortunately she is the chief character in the first part of my story, and unless I give a clear account of her early life her later actions will not be intelligible. I have mentioned that she was married to the Emperor Augustus: this was her second marriage, following her divorce from my grandfather. After my father's death she became the virtual head of our family, supplanting my mother Antonia, my uncle Tiberius (the legal head), and Augustus himself – to whose powerful protection my father had committed us children in his will.

Livia was of the Claudian family, one of the most ancient of Rome, and so was my grandfather. There is a popular ballad, still sometimes sung by old people, of which the refrain is that the Claudian tree bears two sorts of fruit, the sweet apple and the crab, but that the crabs outnumber the apples. Among the crab sort the balladist reckons Appius Claudius the Proud, who put all Rome in a tumult by trying to enslave and seduce a free-born girl called Virginia, and Claudius Drusus, who in Republican days tried to make himself King of all Italy, and Claudius the Fair, who, when the sacred chickens would not feed, threw them into the sea, crying 'Then let them drink,' and so lost an important sea-battle. And of the former sort the balladist mentions Appius the Blind, who dissuaded Rome from a dangerous league with King Pyrrhus, and Claudius the Tree-Trunk, who drove the Carthaginians out of Sicily, and Claudius Nero (which in the Sabine dialect means The Strong), who defeated Hasdrubal as he came out of Spain to join forces with his brother, the great Hannibal. These three were all virtuous men, besides being bold and wise. And the balladist says that of the Claudian women too, some are apples and some are crabs, but that again the crabs outnumber the apples.

My grandfather was one of the best of the Claudians. Believing that Julius Caesar was the one man powerful enough to give Rome peace and security in those difficult times, he joined the Caesarean party and fought bravely for Julius in the Egyptian War. When he suspected that Julius was aiming at personal tyranny, my grandfather would not willingly further his ambitions in Rome, though he could not risk an open breach. He therefore asked for and secured the office of pontiff and was sent in that capacity to France to found colonies of veteran soldiers there. On his return after Julius's assassination he incurred the enmity of young Augustus, Julius's adopted son, who was then known as Octavian, and of his ally, the great Mark Antony, by boldly proposing honours for the tyrannicides. He had to flee from Rome. In the disturbances that followed he sided now with this party and now with that, according as the right seemed to lie here or there. At one time he was with young Pompey, at another he fought with Mark Antony's brother against Augustus, at Perusia in Etruria. But convinced at last that Augustus, though bound by loyalty to avenge the murder of Julius, his 41 B.C.

19

adopted father – a duty which he ruthlessly performed – was not tyrant-hearted and aimed at the restoration of the ancient liberties of the people, he came over to his side and settled at Rome with my grandmother Livia, and my uncle Tiberius, then only two years old. He took no more part in the Civil Wars, contenting himself with his duties as a pontiff.

My grandmother Livia was one of the worst of the Claudians. She may well have been a re-incarnation of that Claudia, sister of Claudius the Fair, who was arraigned for high treason because once when her coach was held up by a street crowd she called out, 'If only my brother was alive! He knew how to clear crowds away. He used his whip.' When one of the Protectors of the People ('tribunes', in Latin) came up and angrily ordered her to be silent, reminding her that her brother, by his impiety, had lost a Roman fleet: 'A very good reason for wishing him alive,' she retorted. 'He might lose another fleet, and then another, God willing, and thin off this wretched crowd a little.' And she added: 'You're a Protector of the People, I see, and your person is legally inviolable, but don't forget that we Claudians have had some of you protectors well thrashed before now, and be damned to your inviolability.' That was exactly how my grandmother Livia spoke at this time of the Roman people. 'Rabble and slaves! The Republic was always a humbug. What Rome really needs is a king again.' That at least is how she talked to my grandfather, urging him that Mark Antony, and Augustus (or Octavian, I should say) and Lepidus (a rich but unenergetic nobleman), who between them now ruled the Roman world, would in time fall out; and that, if he played his hand well, he could use his dignity as a pontiff and the reputation for integrity which was conceded him by all factions as a means to becoming king himself. My grandfather replied sternly that if she spoke in this strain again he would divorce her; for in the old style of Roman marriage the husband could put his wife away without a public explanation, returning the dowry that had come with her, but keeping the children. At this my grandmother was silent and pretended to submit, but all love between them died from that moment. Unknown to my grandfather, she immediately set about engaging the passions of Augustus.

This was no difficult matter, for Augustus was young and impressionable and she had made a careful study of his tastes: besides which, she was by popular verdict one of the three most beautiful women of her day. She had picked on Augustus as a better instrument for her ambitions than Antony – Lepidus did not count – and that he would stick at nothing to gain his ends and proscriptions he had shown two years before, when 2,000 knights and 300 senators belonging to the opposing faction had been summarily put to death, by far the greatest number of these at Augustus's particular instance. When she had made sure of Augustus she urged him to put away Scribonia – a woman older than himself, whom he had married for political reasons – telling him that she had knowledge of Scribonia's adultery with a close friend of my grandfather's. Augustus was ready to believe this without pressing for detailed evidence. He divorced Scribonia, though she was quite innocent, on the very day that she bore him his daughter, Julia; whom he took from the 38 B.C. birth-chamber before Scribonia had as much as seen the little creature, and gave to the wife of one of his freedmen to nurse. My grandmother – who was still only seventeen years old, nine years younger than Augustus – then went to my grandfather and said, 'Now divorce me. I am already five months gone with child, and you are not the father. I made a vow that I would not bear another child to a coward, and I intend to keep it.' My grandfather, whatever he may have felt when he heard this confession, said no more than 'Call the adulterer here to me and let us discuss the matter together in private.' The child was really his own, but he was not to know this, and when my grandmother said that it was another's he believed her.

My grandfather was astonished to find that it was his pretended friend Augustus who had betrayed him, but concluded that Livia had tempted him and that he had not been proof against her beauty; and perhaps Augustus still bore a grudge against him for the unlucky motion that he had once introduced in the Senate for rewarding Julius Caesar's assassins. However it may have been, he did not reproach Augustus. All that he said was: 'If you love this woman and will marry her honourably, take her; only let the decencies be observed.' Augustus swore that he would marry her immediately and never cast her off while she continued faithful to him; he bound himself by the most frightful oaths. So my grandfather divorced her. I have been told that he regarded this infatuation of hers as a divine punishment on himself because once in Sicily at her instigation he had armed slaves to fight against Roman citizens; moreover, she was a Claudian, one of his own family, so for these two reasons he was unwilling to show her public dishonour. It was certainly not for fear of Augustus that he assisted in person at her marriage a few weeks later, giving her away as a father would his daughter and joining in her wedding hymn. When I consider that he had loved her dearly and that by his generosity he risked the name of coward and pander, I am filled with admiration for his conduct.

But Livia was ungrateful – angry and ashamed that he seemed to take the matter so calmly, giving her up tamely as if she were a thing of little worth. And when her child, my father, was born three months later she was deeply vexed with Augustus's sister Octavia, Mark Antony's wife – these were my two other grandparents – because of a Greek epigram to the effect that parents were fortunate who had three-months' children: such short gestation had hitherto been confined to cats and bitches. I do not know whether Octavia was truly the author of this verse, but, if she was, Livia made her pay dearly for it before she had done. It is unlikely that she was the author, for she had herself been married to Mark Antony while with child by a husband who had died; and, in the words of the proverb, cripples do not mock cripples. Octavia's was, however, a political marriage and legalized by a special decree of the Senate: it was not brought about by passion on one side and personal ambition on the other. If it be asked how it happened that the College of Pontiffs consented to admit the validity of Augustus's marriage with Livia, the answer is that my grandfather and Augustus were both pontiffs, and that the High Pontiff was Lepidus, who did exactly what Augustus told him.

As soon as my father was weaned Augustus sent him back to my grandfather's house, where he was brought up with my uncle Tiberius, the elder by four years. My grandfather, as soon as the children reached the age of understanding, took their education in hand himself, instead of entrusting it to a tutor, as was already the general custom. He never ceased to instil in them a hatred of tyranny and a devotion to ancient ideals of justice, liberty, and virtue. My grandmother Livia had long grudged that her two boys were out of her charge – though indeed they visited her daily at Augustus's palace, which was quite close to their home on the Palatine Hill – and when she found in what way they were 33 B.C. being educated she was greatly annoyed. My grandfather died suddenly while dining with some friends, and it was suspected that he had been poisoned, but the matter was hushed up because Augustus and Livia had been among the guests. In his will the boys were left to Augustus's guardianship. My uncle Tiberius, aged only nine, spoke the oration at my grandfather's funeral.

Augustus loved his sister Octavia dearly and had been much grieved on her account when, soon after her marriage, he learnt that Antony, after starting out for the East to fight a war in Parthia, had stopped on the way to renew his intimacy with Cleopatra, Queen of Egypt; and still more grieved at the slighting letter that Octavia had received from Antony when she went out to help him the next year with men and money for his campaign. The letter, which reached her when she was half-way on her journey, ordered her coldly to return home and attend to her household affairs; yet he accepted the men and money. Livia was secretly delighted at the incident, having long been assiduous in making misunderstandings and jealousies between Augustus and Antony, which Octavia had been as assiduous in smoothing out. When Octavia returned to Rome, Livia asked Augustus to invite her to leave Antony's house and stay with them. She refused to do so, partly because she did not trust Livia and partly because she did not wish to appear a cause of the impending war. Finally Antony, incited by Cleopatra, sent Octavia a bill of divorce and declared war on Augustus. This was the last of the Civil Wars, a duel to the death between the only two men left on their feet – if I may use the metaphor – after an all-against-all sword-fight in the universal amphitheatre. Lepidus was still alive, to be sure, but a prisoner in all but name, and quite harmless – he had been forced to fall at Augustus's feet and beg for his life. Young Pompey, too, the only other person of importance, whose fleet had for a long time commanded the Mediterranean, had by now been defeated by Augustus, and captured and put to death by Antony. The duel between Augustus and Antony was short. Antony was totally defeated in the sea-battle off Actium, in Greece. 31 b.c. He fled to Alexandria, and there took his own life – as did Cleopatra too. Augustus assumed Antony's Eastern conquests as his own and became, as Livia had intended, the sole ruler of the Roman world. Octavia remained true to the interests of Antony's children – not only his son by a former wife, but actually his three children by Cleopatra, a girl and two boys – bringing them up with her own two daughters, one of whom, Antonia the younger, was my mother. This nobility of mind excited general admiration at Rome.

Augustus ruled the world, but Livia ruled Augustus. And I must here explain the remarkable hold that she had over him. It was always a matter of wonder that there were no children of the marriage, seeing that my grandmother had not shown herself unfruitful and that Augustus was reported to be the father of at least four natural children, besides his daughter Julia, who there is no reason for doubting was his own daughter. He was known, moreover, to be passionately devoted to my grandmother. The truth will not easily be credited. The truth is that the marriage was never consummated. Augustus, though capable enough with other women, found himself as impotent as a child when he tried to have commerce with my grandmother. The only reasonable explanation is that Augustus was, at bottom, a pious man, though cruelty and even ill-faith had been forced on him by the dangers that followed his grand-uncle Julius Caesar's assassination. He knew that the marriage was impious: this knowledge, it seems, affected him nervously, putting an inner restraint on his flesh.

My grandmother, who had wanted Augustus as an instrument of her ambition rather than as a lover, was more glad than sorry for this impotence. She found that she could use it as a weapon for subjecting his will to hers. Her practice was to reproach him continually for having seduced her from my grandfather, whom she protested that she had loved, by assurances to her of deep passion and by secret threats to him that if she were not given up he would be arraigned as a public enemy. (This last was perfectly untrue.) Now look, she said, how she had been tricked! This passionate lover turned out to be no man at all; any poor charcoal-burner or slave was more of a man than he! Even Julia was not his real daughter, and he knew it. All that he was good for, she said, was to fondle and fumble and kiss and make eyes like a singing eunuch. It was in vain that Augustus protested that with other women he was a Hercules. Either she would refuse to believe it or she would accuse him of wasting on other women what he denied her. But that no scandal of this should go about she pretended on one occasion to be with child by him and then to have a miscarriage. Shame and unslakable passion bound Augustus closer to her than if their mutual longings had been nightly satisfied or than if she had borne him a dozen fine children. And she took the greatest care of his health and comfort, and was faithful to him, not being naturally lustful except of power; and for this he was so grateful that he let her guide and rule him in all his public and private acts. I have heard it confidently stated by old palace officials that, after marrying my grandmother, Augustus never looked at another woman. Yet all sorts of stories were current at Rome about his affairs with the wives and daughters of notables; and after his death, in explaining how it was that she had so complete a command of his affections, Livia used to say that it was not only because she was faithful to him but also because she never interfered with his passing love-affairs. It is my belief that she put all these scandals about herself in order to have something to reproach him with.

If I am challenged as to my authority for this curious history I shall give it. The first part relating to the divorce I heard from Livia's own lips in the year she died. The remainder, about Augustus's impotence, I heard from a woman called Briseis, a wardrobe-maid of my mother's, who had previously served my grandmother as a page-girl, and being then only seven years old had been allowed to overhear conversations that she was thought too young to understand. I believe my account true and will continue to do so until it is supplanted by one that fits the facts equally well. To my way of thinking, the Sibyl's verse about 'wife, no wife' confirms the matter. No, I cannot close the matter here. In writing this passage, with the idea, I suppose, of shielding Augustus's good name, I have been holding something back which I shall now after all set down. Because, as the proverb says, 'truth helps the story on'. It is this. My grandmother Livia ingeniously consolidated her hold on Augustus by secretly giving him, of her own accord, beautiful young women to sleep with whenever she noticed that passion made him restless. That she arranged this for him, and without a word said beforehand or afterwards, forbearing from the jealousy that, as a wife, he was convinced that she must feel; yet everything was done very decently and quietly, the young women (whom she picked out herself in the Syrian slave-market – he preferred Syrians) being introduced into his bedroom at night with a knock and the rattle of a chain for signal, and called away again early in the morning by a similar knock and rattle; and that they kept silence in his presence as if they were succubi who came in dreams – that she contrived all this so thoughtfully and remained faithful to him herself in spite of his impotence with her, he must have considered a perfect proof of the sincerest love. You may object that Augustus, in his position, might have had the most beautiful women in the world, bond or free, married or unmarried, to feed his appetite, without the assistance of Livia as procuress. That is true, but it is true nevertheless that after his marriage to Livia he tasted no meat, as he once said himself, though perhaps in another context, that she had not passed as fit for eating.

Of women, then, Livia had no cause to be jealous, except only of her sister-in-law, my other grandmother, Octavia, whose beauty excited as much admiration as her virtue. Livia had taken malicious pleasure in sympathizing with her over Antony's faithlessness. She had gone so far as to suggest that it had been largely Octavia's own fault in dressing in so modest a way and behaving with such decorum. Mark Antony, she pointed out, was a man of strong passions, and to hold him successfully a woman must temper the chastity of a Roman matron with the arts and extravagances of an Oriental courtesan. Octavia should have taken a leaf from Cleopatra's book: for the Egyptian, though Octavia's inferior in looks and her senior by eight or nine years, knew well how to feed his sensual appetite. 'Men such as Antony, real men, prefer the strange to the wholesome,' Livia finished sententiously. 'They find maggoty green cheese more tasty than freshly pressed curds.' 'Keep your maggots to yourself,' Octavia flared at her.

Livia herself dressed very richly and used the most expensive Asiatic perfumes; but she did not allow the least extravagance in her household, which she made a boast of running in old-fashioned Roman style. Her rules were: plain but plentiful food, regular family worship, no hot baths after meals, constant work for everyone, and no waste. 'Everyone' was not merely the slaves and freedmen but every member of the family. The unfortunate child Julia was expected to set an example of industry. She led a very weary life. She had a regular daily task of wool to card and spin, and cloth to weave, and needlework to do, and was made to rise from her hard bed at dawn, and even before dawn in the winter months, to be able to get through it. And because her stepmother believed in a liberal education for girls, she was set, among other tasks, to learn the whole of Homer's *Iliad* and *Odyssey* by heart.

Julia had also to keep a detailed diary, for Livia's benefit, of what work she did, what books she read, what conversations she had, and so on; which was a great burden to her. She was allowed no friendships with men, though her beauty was much toasted. One young man of ancient family and irreproachable morals, a Consul's son, was bold enough to introduce himself to her one day at Baiae on some polite pretext, when she was taking the half-hour's walk allowed her by the seaside, accompanied only by her duenna. Livia, who was jealous of Julia's good looks and of Augustus's affection for her, had the young man sent a very strong letter, telling him that he must never expect to hold public office under the father of the girl whose good name he had tried to besmirch by this insufferable familiarity. Julia herself was punished by being forbidden to take her walk outside the grounds of the villa. About this time Julia went quite bald. I do not know whether Livia had a hand in this: it seems not improbable, though certainly baldness was in the Caesar family. At all .events, Augustus found an Egyptian wig-maker who made her one of the most magnificent fair wigs that was ever seen, and her charms were thus rather increased than diminished by her mischance; she had not had very good hair of her own. It is said that the wig was not built, in the usual way, on a base of hair net but was the whole scalp of a German chieftain's daughter shrunk to the exact size of Julia's head and kept alive and pliant by occasional rubbing with a special ointment. But I must say that I don't believe this.

Everyone knew that Livia kept Augustus in strict order and that, if not actually frightened of her, he was at any rate very careful not to offend her. One day, in his capacity as Censor, he was lecturing some rich men about allowing their wives to bedizen themselves with jewels. 'For a woman to overdress,' he said, 'is unseemly. It is the husband's duty to restrain his wife from luxury.' Carried away by his own eloquence he unfortunately added: 'I sometimes have occasion to admonish my own wife about this.' There was a delighted cry from the culprits. 'Oh, Augustus,' they said, 'do tell us in what words you admonish Livia. It will serve as a model for us.' Augustus was embarrassed and alarmed. 'You mis-heard me,' he said, 'I do not say that I had ever had occasion to reprimand Livia. As you know well, she is a paragon of matronly modesty. But I certainly should have no hesitation in reprimanding her were she to forget her dignity by dressing, as some of your wives do, like an Alexandrian dancing-girl who has by some queer turn of fate become an Armenian queen-dowager.' That same evening Livia tried to make Augustus look small by appearing at the dinner-table in the most fantastically gorgeous finery she could lay her hands on, the foundation of which was one of Cleopatra's ceremonial dresses. But he got well out of an awkward situation by praising her for her witty and opportune parody of the very fault he had been condemning.

Livia had grown wiser since the time that she had advised my grandfather to put a diadem on his head and proclaim himself king. The title 'king' was still execrated at Rome on account of the unpopular Tarquin dynasty to which, according to legend, the first Brutus (I call him this to distinguish him from the second Brutus, who murdered Julius) had put an end – expelling the royal family from the City and becoming one of the first two Consuls of the Roman Republic. Livia realized now that the title of king could be waived so long as Augustus could control the substantial powers of kingship. By following her advice he gradually concentrated in his single person all the important Republican dignities. He was Consul at Rome, and when he passed the office to a reliable friend he took in exchange the 'High Command' – which, though nominally on a level with the consulship, ranked in practice above this or any other magistracy. He had absolute control of the provinces, too, and power to appoint the provincial governors-general, together with the command of all armies and the right of levying troops and of making peace or war. In Rome he was voted the life-office of People's Protector, which secured him against all interference with his authority, gave him the power of vetoing the decisions of other office-holders, and carried with it the inviolability of his person. The title 'Emperor', which once merely meant 'field-marshal' but has recently come to mean supreme monarch, he shared with other successful generals. He also had the Censorship, which gave him authority over the two leading social orders, those of Senators and Knights; on the pretext of moral shortcomings he could disqualify any member of either order from its dignities and privileges – a disgrace keenly felt. He had control of the Public Treasury: he was supposed to render periodic accounts, but nobody was ever bold enough to demand an audit, though it was known that there was constant juggling between the Treasury and Privy Purse.

Thus he had command of the armies, the control of the laws – for his influence on the Senate was such that they voted whatever he suggested to them – the control of public finances, the control of social behaviour, and inviolacy of person. He even had the right of summarily condemning any Roman citizen, from plough-man to senator, to death or perpetual banishment. The last dig-nity that he assumed was that of High Pontiff, which gave him control of the entire religious system. The Senate were anxious to vote him whatever title he would accept, short of King: they were afraid to vote him the kingship, for fear of the people. His real wish was to be called Romulus, but Livia advised him against this. Her argument was that Romulus had been a king and that the name was therefore dangerous, and further that he was one of the Roman tutelary deities and that to take his name would seem blasphemous. But her real feeling was that it was not a grand enough title. Romulus had been a mere bandit-chieftain and was not among the first rank of the Gods. On her advice he therefore signified to the Senate that the title Augustus would be agreeable to him. So they voted him that. 'Augustus' had a semi-divine connota-tion, and the common title of King was nothing by comparison.

How many mere kings paid tribute to Augustus! How many were marched in chains in Roman triumphs! Had not even the High King of remote India, hearing of Augustus's fame, sent am-bassadors to Rome, begging for the protection of his friendship, with propitiatory presents of remarkable silks and spices; and rubies, emeralds, and sardonyx; and tigers, then for the first time seen in Europe; and the Indian Hermes, the famous armless boy, who could do the most extraordinary things with his feet? Had not Augustus put an end to that line of kings in Egypt that went back at least 5,000 years before the foundation of Rome? And at that fateful interruption of history what monstrous portents had not been seen? Had there not been flashes of armour from the clouds and bloody rain falling? Had not a serpent of gigantic size appeared in the main street of Alexandria and uttered an incred-ibly loud hiss? Had not the ghosts of dead Pharaohs appeared? Had not their statues frowned? Had not Apis, the sacred bull of Memphis, uttered a bellow of lamentation and burst into tears? This was how my grandmother reasoned with herself.

Most women are inclined to set a modest limit to their ambitions; a few rare ones set a bold limit. But Livia was unique in setting no limit at all to hers, and yet remaining perfectly level-headed and cool in what would be judged in any other woman to be raving madness. It was only little by little that even I, with such excellent opportunities for observing her, came to guess generally what her intentions were. But even so, when the final disclosure came, it came as a shock of surprise. Perhaps I had better record her various acts in historical sequence, without dwelling on her hidden motives.

On her advice, Augustus prevailed on the Senate to create two new Divinities, namely, the Goddess Roma, who represented the female soul of the Roman Empire, and the Demi-god Julius, the warlike hero who was Julius Caesar in apotheosis. (Divine honours had been offered to Julius, in the East, while he was still alive; that he had not refused them was one of the reasons for his assassination.) Augustus knew the value of a religious bond to unite the province with the City, a bond far stronger than one based merely on fear or gratitude. It sometimes happened that after long residence in Egypt or Asia Minor even true-born Romans turned to the worship of the gods they found there and forgot their own, thereby becoming foreigners in all but name. On the other hand, Rome had imported so many religions from the cities she had conquered, giving alien deities, such as Isis and Cybele, noble temples in the City – and not merely for the convenience of visitors – that it was reasonable that she should now, in fair exchange, plant gods of her own in these cities. Roma and Julius, then, were to be worshipped by such provincials as were Roman citizens and wished to be reminded of their national heritage.

The next step that Livia took was to arrange for delegations of provincials not fortunate enough to possess full citizenship to visit Rome and beg to be given a Roman God whom they might worship loyally and without presumption. On Livia's advice Augustus told the Senate, half-jokingly, that these poor fellows, while obviously they could not be allowed to worship the superior deities, Roma and Julius, must not be denied some sort of God, however humble. At this Maecenas, one of Augustus's ministers, with whom Augustus had already discussed the advisability of taking the name of Romulus, said: 'Let us give them a God who will watch over them well. Let us give them Augustus himself.' Augustus appeared somewhat embarrassed but admitted that Maecenas's suggestion was a sound one. It was an established custom among Orientals, and one which might well be turned to Roman profit, to pay divine honours to their rulers; but since it was clearly impracticable for Eastern cities to worship the whole Senate in a body, putting up 600 statues in each of their shrines, one way out of the difficulty, certainly, was for them to worship the Senate's chief executive officer, who happened to be himself. So the Senate, feeling complimented that each member had in him at least one six-hundredth part of divinity, gladly voted Maecenas's motion, and shrines to Augustus were immediately erected in Asia Minor. The cult spread, but at first only in the frontier provinces, which were under the direct control of Augustus, not in the home provinces, which were nominally under the control of the Senate, nor in the City itself.

Augustus approved of Livia's educative methods with Julia and of her domestic arrangements and economies. He had simple tastes himself. His palate was so insensitive that he did not notice the difference between virgin olive oil and the last rank squeezings when the olive-paste has gone a third time through the press. He wore homespun clothes. It was justly said that, Fury though Livia was, but for her unwearying activity Augustus would never have been able to undertake the immense task he set himself of restoring Rome to peace and security after the long disasters of the Civil Wars – in which he himself had, of course, played so destructive a part. Augustus's work filled fourteen hours a day, but Livia's, it was said, filled twenty-four. Not only did she manage her huge household in the efficient way I have described, but she bore an equal share with him in public business. A full account of all the legal, social, administrative, religious, and military reforms which they carried out between them, to say nothing of the public works which they undertook, the temples which they re-edified, the colonies they planted, would fill many volumes. Yet there were many leading Romans of the elder generation who could not forget that this seemingly admirable reconstitution of the State had only been made possible by the military defeat, secret murder, or public execution of almost every person who had defied the power of this energetic pair. Had their sole and arbitrary power not been disguised under the forms of ancient liberty they would never have held it long. Even as it was there were no less than four conspiracies against Augustus's life by would-be Brutuses.

Chapter 3

THE name 'Livia' is connected with the Latin word which means Malignity. My grandmother was a consummate actress, and the outward purity of her conduct, the sharpness of her wit, and the graciousness of her manners deceived nearly everybody. But nobody really liked her: malignity commands respect, not liking. She had a faculty for making ordinary easy-going people feel acutely conscious in her presence of their intellectual and moral shortcomings. I must apologize for continuing to write about Livia, but it is unavoidable: like all honest Roman histories, this is written 'from egg to apple': I prefer the thorough Roman method, which misses nothing, to that of Homer and the Greeks generally, who love to jump into the middle of things and then work backwards or forwards as they feel inclined. Yes, I have often had the notion of re-writing the story of Troy in Latin prose for the benefit of our poorer citizens who cannot read Greek; beginning with the egg from which Helen was hatched and continuing, chapter by chapter, to the apples eaten for dessert at the great feast in celebration of Ulysses's home-coming and victory over his wife's suitors. Where Homer is obscure or silent on any point I would naturally draw from later poets, or from the earlier Dares whose account, though full of poetical vagaries, seems to me more reliable than Homer's, because he actually took part in the war, first with the Trojans, then with the Greeks.

I once saw a strange painting on the inside of an old cedar chest which came, I believe, from somewhere in Northern Syria. The inscription, in Greek, was 'Poison is Queen', and the face of Poison, though executed over a hundred years before Livia's birth, was unmistakably the face of Livia. And in this context I must write about Marcellus, the son of Octavia by a former husband. Augustus, who was devoted to Marcellus, had adopted him as his son, giving him administrative duties greatly in advance of his years; and had married him to Julia. The common opinion at Rome was that he intended to make Marcellus his heir. Livia did not oppose the adoption, and indeed seemed genuinely to welcome it as giving her greater facility for winning Marcellus's affection and confidence. Her devotion to him seemed beyond question. It was by her advice that Augustus advanced him so rapidly in rank; and Marcellus, who knew of this, was duly grateful to her.

Livia's motive in favouring Marcellus was thought by a few shrewd observers to be that of making Agrippa jealous. Agrippa was the most important man at Rome after Augustus: a man of low birth, but Augustus's oldest friend and most successful general and admiral. Livia had always hitherto done her best to keep Agrippa's friendship for Augustus. He was ambitious, but only to a degree; he would never have presumed to contend for sovereignty with Augustus, whom he admired exceedingly, and wanted no greater glory than that of being his most trusted minister. He was, moreover, over-conscious of his humble origin, and Livia, by playing the grand patrician lady, always had the whip-hand of him. His importance to Livia and Augustus did not, however, lie only in his services, his loyalty, and his popularity with the commons and the Senate. It was this: by a fiction which Livia herself had originally created, he was supposed to hold a watching brief for the nation on Augustus's political conduct. At the famous sham-debate staged in the Senate, after the overthrow of Antony, between Augustus and his two friends, Agrippa and Maecenas, Agrippa's part had been that of counselling him against assuming sovereign power; only to let his objections be overruled by the arguments of Maecenas and the enthusiastic demands of the Senate. Agrippa had then declared that he would faithfully serve Augustus so long as the sovereignty was wholesome and no arbitrary tyranny. He was thenceforth popularly looked to and trusted as a buttress against possible encroachments of tyranny; and what Agrippa let pass, the nation let pass. It was now thought by these same shrewd observers that Livia was playing a very dangerous game in making Agrippa jealous of Marcellus, and events were watched with great interest. Perhaps her devotion to Marcellus was a sham and her real intention was that Agrippa should be goaded into putting him out of the way. It was rumoured that a devoted member of Agrippa's family had offered to pick a quarrel with Marcellus and kill him: but that Agrippa, though he was no less jealous than Livia had intended him to be, was too honourable to accept such a base suggestion.

It was generally assumed that Augustus had made Marcellus his chief heir and that Marcellus would not only inherit his immense wealth but the monarchy – for how else can I write of it but as that? – into the bargain. Agrippa therefore let it be known that while he was devoted to Augustus and had never regretted his decision to support his authority, there was one thing that he would not permit, as a patriotic citizen, and that was that the monarchy should become hereditary. But Marcellus was now almost as popular as Agrippa, and many young men of rank and family to whom the question 'Monarchy or Republic?' seemed already an academic one, tried to ingratiate themselves with him, hoping for important honours from him when he succeeded Augustus. This general readiness to welcome a continuance of the monarchy seemed to please Livia, but she privately announced that, in the lamentable case of the death or incapacity of Augustus, the immediate conduct of State affairs, until such time as further arrangements should be made by decrees of the Senate, must be entrusted to hands more experienced than those of Marcellus. Yet Marcellus was such a favourite of Augustus that, though Livia's private announcements usually ended as public edicts, nobody paid much attention to her on this occasion: and more and more people courted Marcellus.

The shrewd observers wondered how Livia would meet this new situation; but luck seemed to be with her. Augustus caught a slight chill which took an unexpected turn, with fevers and vomiting: Livia prepared his food with her own hands during 23 B.C. this illness, but his stomach was so delicate that he could keep nothing down. He was growing weaker and weaker and felt at last that he was on the point of death. He had often been asked to name his successor, but had not done so for fear of the political consequences, and also because the thought of his own death was extremely distasteful to him. Now he felt that it was his duty to name someone, and asked Livia to advise him. He said that sickness had robbed him of all power of judgement; he would choose whatever successor, within reason, she suggested. So she made the decision for him, and he agreed to it. She then summoned to his bedside his fellow-Consul, the City magistrates, and certain representative senators and knights. He was too weak to say anything, but handed the Consul a register of the naval and military forces and a statement of the public revenues, and then beckoned to Agrippa and gave him his signet ring; which was as much as to say that Agrippa was to succeed him, though with the close co-operation of the Consuls. This came as a great surprise. Everyone had expected that Marcellus would be chosen.

And from this moment Augustus began mysteriously to recover: the fever abated and his stomach accepted food. The credit for his cure went, however, not to Livia, who continued attending to him personally, but to a certain doctor called Musa, who had a harmless fad about cold lotions and cold potions. Augustus was so grateful to Musa for his supposed services that he gave him his own weight in gold pieces, which the Senate doubled. Musa was also, though a freedman, advanced to the rank of knight, which gave him the right to wear a gold ring and become a candidate for public office; and a still more extravagant decree was passed by the Senate, granting exemption from taxes to the whole medical profession.

Marcellus was plainly mortified at not being declared Augustus's heir. He was very young, only in his twentieth year. Augustus's previous favours had given him an exaggerated sense both of his talents and of his political importance. He tried to carry the matter off by being pointedly rude to Agrippa at a public banquet. Agrippa with difficulty kept his temper; but that there was no sequel to the incident encouraged Marcellus's supporters to believe that Agrippa was afraid of him. They even told each other that if Augustus did not change his mind within a year or two Marcellus would usurp the Imperial power. They grew so rowdy and boastful, Marcellus doing little to check them, that frequent clashes occurred between them and the party of Agrippa. Agrippa was most vexed by the insolence of this young puppy, as he called him – he who had borne most of the chief offices of state and fought a number of successful campaigns. But his vexation was mixed with alarm. The impression created by these incidents was that Marcellus and he were indecently wrangling as to who should wear Augustus's signet ring after he was dead.

He was ready to make almost any sacrifice to avoid seeming to play such a part. Marcellus was the offender and Agrippa wished to put the whole burden on him. He decided to withdraw from Rome. He went to Augustus and asked to be appointed Governor of Syria. When Augustus asked him the reason for his unexpected request he explained that he thought he could, in that capacity, drive a valuable bargain with the King of Parthia. He could persuade the King to return the regimental Eagles and the prisoners captured from the Romans thirty years before, in exchange for the King's son whom Augustus was holding captive at Rome. He said nothing about the quarrel with Marcellus. Augustus, who had himself been greatly disturbed by it, torn between old friendship for Agrippa and indulgent paternal love for Marcellus, did not allow himself to consider how generously Agrippa was behaving, for that would have been a confession of his own weakness, and so made no reference to the matter either. He granted Agrippa's request with alacrity, saying how important it was to get the Eagles back, and the captives – if any of them were still alive after so long – and asked how soon he would be ready to start. Agrippa was hurt, misunderstanding his manner. He thought that Augustus wanted to get rid of him, really believing that he was quarrelling with Marcellus about the succession. He thanked him for granting his request, coldly protested his loyalty and friendship, and said that he was ready to sail the following day.

He did not go to Syria. He went no farther than the island of Lesbos, sending his lieutenant ahead to administer the province for him. He knew that his stay at Lesbos would be read as a sort of banishment incurred because of Marcellus. He did not visit the province, because if he had done so it would have given the Marcellans a handle against him: they would have said that he had gone to the East in order to gather an army together to march against Rome. But he flattered himself that Augustus would need his services before long; and fully believed that Marcellus was planning to usurp the monarchy. Lesbos was conveniently near Rome. He did not forget his commission: he opened negotiations, through intermediaries, with the King of Parthia but did not expect to conclude them for a while. It takes a deal of time and patience to drive a good bargain with an Eastern monarch.

Marcellus was elected to a City magistracy, his first official appointment, and made this the occasion for a magnificent display of public Games. He not only tented in the theatres themselves, against sun and rain, and hung them with splendid tapestries, but made a gigantic multi-coloured marquee of the whole Market Place. The effect was very gorgeous, particularly from the inside when the sun shone through. In this tent-making he used a fabulous amount of red, yellow, and green cloth which when the Games were over was cut up and distributed to the citizens for clothes and bed-linen. Huge numbers of wild beasts were imported from Africa for the combats in the amphitheatre, including many lions, and there was a fight between fifty German captives and an equal number of black warriors from Morocco. Augustus himself contributed lavishly towards the expenses; and so did Octavia, as Marcellus's mother. When Octavia appeared in the ceremonial procession she was greeted with such resounding applause that Livia could hardly restrain tears of anger and jealousy. Two days later Marcellus fell sick. His symptoms were precisely the same as those of Augustus in his recent illness, so naturally Musa was sent for again. He had become excessively rich and famous, charging as much as 1,000 gold pieces for a single professional visit, and making a favour of it at that. In all cases where sickness had not taken too strong a hold on his patients his mere name was enough to bring about an immediate cure. The credit went to the cold lotions and cold potions, the secret prescriptions for which he refused to communicate to anyone. Augustus's confidence in Musa's powers was so great that he made light of Marcellus's sickness, and the Games continued. But somehow, in spite of the unremitting attention of Livia and the very coldest lotions and potions that Musa could prescribe, Marcellus died. The grief of both Octavia and Augustus was unbounded and the death was mourned as a public calamity. There were, however, a good many level-headed people who did not regret Marcellus's disappearance. There would certainly have been civil war again between him and Agrippa if Augustus had died and he had attempted to step into his place: now Agrippa was the only possible successor. But this was reckoning without Livia, whose fixed intention it was, in the event of Augustus's death – Claudius, Claudius, you said that you would not mention Livia's motives but only record her acts – whose fixed intention it was, in the event of Augustus's death, to continue ruling the Empire through my uncle Tiberius, with my father in support. She would arrange for them to be adopted as Augustus's heirs.

Marcellus's death left Julia free for Tiberius to marry, and all would have gone well with Livia's plans had there not been a dangerous outbreak of political unrest at Rome, the mob clamouring for a restoration of the Republic. When Livia tried to address them from the Palace steps they pelted her with rotten eggs and filth. Augustus happened to be away on a tour of the Eastern provinces, in company with Maecenas, and had reached Athens when the news arrived. Livia wrote shortly and in haste that the situation in the City could not be worse and that Agrippa's help must be secured at any price. Augustus at once summoned Agrippa from Lesbos and begged him, for friendship's sake, to return with him to Rome and restore public confidence. But Agrippa had been nursing his grudge too long to be grateful for this summons. He stood on his dignity. In three years Augustus had written him only three letters and those in a hard official tone; and after Marcellus's death should certainly have recalled him. Why should he help Augustus now? It was Livia, as a matter of fact, who had been responsible for this estrangement; she had miscalculated the political situation by dropping Agrippa too soon. She had even hinted to Augustus that Agrippa, though absent in Lesbos, knew more than most people about Marcellus's mysterious and fatal illness; someone, she said, had told her that Agrippa, when he heard the news, had shown no surprise and considerable complacence. Agrippa told Augustus that he had been so long away from Rome that he was out of touch with City politics and did not feel capable of undertaking what was asked of him. Augustus, fearing that Agrippa, if he went to Rome in his present mood, would be more inclined to put himself forward as a champion of popular liberties than to support the Imperial government, dismissed him with words of gracious regret and hurriedly summoned Maecenas to ask his advice. Maecenas wanted permission to talk to Agrippa freely on Augustus's behalf and undertook to find out from him exactly on what terms he would do what was wanted of him. Augustus begged Maecenas for God's sake to do so, 'as quick as boiled asparagus' (a favourite expression of his). So Maecenas took Agrippa aside and said: 'Now, old friend, what is it that you want? I realize that you think you have been badly treated, but I assure you that Augustus has a right to think himself equally injured by you. Can't you see how badly you behaved towards him, by not being frank? It was an insult both to his justice and to his friendship for you. If you had explained that Marcellus's faction put you in a very uncomfortable position and that Marcellus himself had insulted you – I swear to you that Augustus never knew about this until just the other day – he would have done all in his power to right matters. My frank opinion is that you have behaved like a sulky child – and he has treated you like a father who won't be bullied by that sort of behaviour. You say that he wrote you very cold letters? Were your own, then, written in such affectionate language? And what sort of a good-bye had you given him? I want to mediate between the two of you now, because if this breach continues it will be the ruin of us all. You both love each other dearly, as it is only right that the two greatest living Romans should. Augustus has told me that he is ready, as soon as you show your old openness to him, to renew the friendship on the same terms as before, *or even more intimate ones.*'

'He said that?'

'His very words. May I tell him how grieved you are that you offended him, and may I explain that it was a misunderstanding – that you left Rome, thinking that he was aware of Marcellus's insult to you at the banquet? And that now you are anxious, on your side, to make up for past failures in friendship and that you rely on him to meet you half-way?'

Agrippa said: 'Maecenas, you are a fine fellow and a true friend. Tell Augustus I am his to command as always.'

Maecenas said: 'I shall tell him that with the greatest pleasure. And I shall add, as my own opinion, that it would not be safe to send you back to the City now, to restore order, without some outstanding mark of personal confidence.'

Then Maecenas went to Augustus. 'I smoothed him down nicely. He'll do anything you want. But he wants to believe that you really love him, like a child jealous of his father's love for another child. I think that the only thing that would really satisfy him would be for you to let him marry Julia.'

Augustus had to think quickly. He remembered that Agrippa and his wife, who was Marcellus's sister, had been on bad terms ever since the quarrel with Marcellus, and that Agrippa was supposed to be in love with Julia. He wished Livia were present to advise him, but there was no escape from an instant decision: if he offended Agrippa now he would never recover his support. Livia had written 'at any price': so he was free to make what arrangements he pleased. He sent for Agrippa again, and Maecenas staged a dignified scene of reconciliation. Augustus said that if Agrippa would consent to marry his daughter, it would be proof to him that the friendship which he valued before any other in the world was established on a secure foundation. Agrippa wept tears of joy and asked pardon for his shortcomings. He would try to be worthy of Augustus's loving generosity.

Agrippa returned to Rome with Augustus, and immediately divorced his wife and married Julia. The marriage was so popular and his celebration so magnificently lavish that the poli-
21 B.C. tical disturbances immediately subsided. Agrippa won great credit for Augustus, too, by carrying through the negotiations for the return of the Eagle standards, which were formally handed over to Tiberius as Augustus's personal representative. The Eagles were sacred objects, more truly sacred to Roman hearts than any marble statues of Gods. A few captives returned, too, but after thirty-two years of absence they were hardly worth welcoming back; most of them preferred to remain in Parthia, where they had settled down and married native women.

My grandmother Livia was far from pleased with the bargain made with Agrippa – the only cheerful side of which was the dishonour done to Octavia by the divorce of her daughter. But she concealed her feelings. It was nine years before Agrippa's
12 B.C. services could be spared. Then he died suddenly at his country house. Augustus was away in Greece at the time, so there was no inquest on the body. Agrippa left a large number of children behind him, three boys and two girls, as Augustus's heirs-in-law; it would be difficult for Livia to set their claims aside in favour of her own sons.

However, Tiberius married Julia, who had made things easy for Livia by falling in love with him and begging Augustus to use his influence with Tiberius on her behalf. Augustus consented only because Julia threatened suicide if he refused to help her. Tiberius himself hated having to marry Julia, but did not dare refuse. He was obliged to divorce his own wife, Vipsania, Agrippa's daughter by a former marriage, whom he passionately loved. Once when he met her accidentally afterwards in the street he followed her with his eyes in such a hopeless longing way that Augustus, when he heard of it, gave orders that, for decency's sake, this must not happen again. Special look-outs must be kept by the officers of both households to avoid an encounter. Vipsania married, not long afterwards, an ambitious young noble called Gallus. And before I forget it, I must mention my father's marriage to my mother, Antonia, the younger daughter of Mark Antony and Octavia. It had taken place in the year of Augustus's illness and Marcellus's death.

My uncle Tiberius was one of the bad Claudians. He was morose, reserved, and cruel, but there had been three people whose influence had checked these elements in his nature. First there was my father, one of the best Claudians, cheerful, open, and generous; next there was Augustus, a very honest, merry, kindly man who disliked Tiberius but treated him generously for his mother's sake; and lastly there was Vipsania. My father's influence was removed, or lessened, when they were both of an age to do their military service and were sent on campaign to different parts of the Empire. Then came the separation from Vipsania, and this was followed by a coolness with Augustus, who was offended by my uncle's ill-concealed distaste for Julia. With these three influences removed, he gradually went altogether to the bad.

I should at this point, I think, describe his personal appearance. He was a tall, dark-haired, fair-skinned, heavily-built man with a magnificent pair of shoulders, and hands so strong that he could crack a walnut, or bore a tough-skinned green apple through with thumb and forefinger. If he had not been so slow in his movements he would have made a champion boxer: he once killed a comrade in a friendly bout – bare-fisted, not with the usual metal boxing-gloves – with a blow on the side of the head that cracked his skull. He walked with his neck thrust slightly forward and his eyes on the ground. His face would have been handsome if it had not been disfigured by so many pimples, and if his eyes had not been so prominent, and if he had not worn an almost perpetual frown. His statues make him extremely handsome, because they leave out these defects. He spoke little, and that very slowly, so that in conversation with him one always felt tempted to finish his sentences for him and answer them in the same breath. But, when he pleased, he was an impressive public speaker. He went bald early in life except at the back of his head, where he grew his hair long, a fashion of the ancient nobility. He was never ill.

Tiberius, unpopular as he was in Roman society, was nevertheless an extremely successful general. He revived various ancient disciplinary severities, but since he did not spare himself when on campaign, seldom sleeping in a tent, eating and drinking no better than the men, and always charging at their head in battle, they preferred to serve under him than under some good-humoured, easy-going commander in whose leadership they did not have the same confidence. Tiberius never gave his men a smile or a word of praise, and often overmarched and overworked them. 'Let them hate me,' he once said, 'so long as they obey me.' He kept the colonels and regimental officers in as strict order as the men, so there were no complaints of his partiality. Service under Tiberius was not unprofitable: he usually contrived to capture and sack the enemy's camps and cities. He fought successful wars in Armenia, Parthia, Germany, Spain, Dalmatia, the Alps, and France.

My father was, as I say, one of the best Claudians. He was as strong as his brother, far better looking, quicker of speech and movement, and by no means less successful as a general. He treated all soldiers as Roman citizens and therefore as his equals, except in rank and education. He hated having to inflict punishment on them: he gave orders that as far as possible all offences against discipline should be dealt with by the offender's own comrades, whom he assumed to be jealous for the good name of their section or company. He gave it out that if they found that any offence was beyond their corrective powers – for he did not allow them to kill a culprit or incapacitate him for his daily military duties – it should be referred to the regimental colonel; but so far as possible he wished his men to be their own judges. The captains might flog, by permission of their regimental colonels, but only in cases where the offence, such as cowardice in battle or theft from a comrade, showed a baseness of character that made flogging appropriate; but he ordered that a man once flogged must never afterwards serve as a combatant; he must be degraded to the transport or clerical staff. Any soldier who considered that he had been unjustly sentenced by his comrades or his captain might appeal to him; but he thought it unlikely that such sentences would need to be revised. This system worked admirably, because my father was such a fine soldier that he inspired the troops to a virtue of which other commanders did not believe them capable. But it can be understood how dangerous it was for troops who had been handled in this way to be commanded afterwards by any ordinary general. The gift of independence once granted cannot be lightly taken away again. There was always trouble when troops who had served under my father happened to be drafted for service under my uncle. It happened the other way about too: troops who had served under my uncle reacted with scorn and suspicion to my father's disciplinary system. Their custom had been to shield each other's crimes and to pride themselves on their cunning in avoiding detection; and since under my uncle a man could be flogged, for example, for addressing an officer without being first addressed, or for speaking with too great frankness, or for behaving independently in any way, it was an honour rather than a disgrace for a soldier to be able to show the marks of the lash on his back.

My father's greatest victories were in the Alps, France, the Low Countries, but especially in Germany, where his name will, I think, never be forgotten. He was always in the thick of the fighting. His ambition was to perform a feat which had only been performed twice in Roman history, namely, as general to kill the opposing general with his own hands and strip him of his arms. He was many times very close to success, but his prey always escaped him. Either the fellow galloped off the field or surrendered instead of fighting, or some officious private soldier got the blow in first. Veterans telling me stories of my father have often chuckled admiringly: 'Oh, Sir, it used to do our hearts good to see your father on his black horse playing hide-and-seek in the battle with one of those German chieftains. He'd be forced to cut down nine or ten of the bodyguard sometimes, tough men too, before he got near the standard, and by then the wily bird would be flown.' The proudest boast of men who had served under my father was that he was the first Roman general who had marched the full length of the Rhine from Switzerland to the North Sea.

Chapter 4

MY father had never forgotten my grandfather's teaching about liberty. As quite a small boy he had fallen foul of Marcellus, five years his senior, to whom Augustus gave the title 'Leader of Cadets'. He had told Marcellus that the title had been awarded to him only for a specific occasion (a sham-fight called 'Greeks and Trojans' fought on Mars Field between two forces of mounted cadets the sons of knights and senators) and that it did not carry with it any of the general judicial powers which Marcellus had since assumed; and that, for himself, as a free-born Roman, he would not submit to such tyranny. He reminded Marcellus that the opposing side in the sham-fight had been led by Tiberius, and that Tiberius had won the honours of the engagement. He chal-lenged Marcellus to a duel. Augustus was very much amused when he heard the story and for a long time never referred to my father except playfully as 'the free-born Roman'.

Whenever he was in Rome now my father chafed at the growing spirit of subservience to Augustus that he everywhere encountered, and always longed to be back in arms. While acting as one of the chief City magistrates during an absence of Augustus and Tiberius in France he was disgusted by the prevalence of place-hunting and political jobbery. He privately told a friend, from whom I heard it years later, that there was more of the old Roman spirit of liberty to be found in a single company of his soldiers than in the whole senatorial order. Shortly before his death he wrote Tiberius a bitter letter to this effect from a camp in the interior of Germany. He said that he wished to heaven that Augustus would follow the glorious example of the Dictator Sulla, who, when sole master of Rome after the first Civil Wars, all his enemies being either subjugated or pacified, had only paused until he had settled a few State matters to his liking before laying down his rods of office and becoming once more a private citizen. If Augustus did not do the same pretty soon – and he had always given out that this was his ultimate intention – it would be too late. The ranks of the old nobility were sadly thinned: the proscriptions and the civil wars had carried away the boldest and best, and the survivors, lost among the new nobility – nobility indeed – tended more and more to behave like family slaves to Augustus and Livia. Soon Rome would have forgotten what freedom meant and would fall at last under a tyranny as barbarous and arbitrary as those of the East. It was not to forward such a calamity that he had fought so many wearisome campaigns under Augustus's supreme command. Even his love and deep personal admiration for Augustus, who had been a second father to him, did not prevent him from expressing these feelings. He asked Tiberius's opinion: could not the two of them together persuade, even compel, Augustus to retire? 'If he consents I shall hold him in a thousand times greater love and admiration than formerly; but I am sorry to say that the secret and illegitimate pride that our mother Livia has always derived from her exercise of supreme power through Augustus will be the greatest hindrance that we are likely to encounter in this matter.'

By ill-luck the letter was delivered to Tiberius while he was in the presence of Augustus and Livia. 'A dispatch from your noble brother!' the Imperial courier called out, handing it to him. Tiberius, not suspecting that there was anything in the letter that should not be communicated to Livia and Augustus, asked permission to open and read it at once. Augustus said: 'By all means, Tiberius, but on condition that you read it aloud to us.' He motioned the servants out of the room. 'Come, let us lose no time. What are his latest victories? I am impatient to hear. His letters are always well written and interesting, much more so than yours, my dear fellow, if you'll pardon me for making the comparison.'

Tiberius read out the first few words and then grew very red. He tried to skip over the dangerous part, but found that there was little but danger throughout the letter, except just at the end, where my father complained of giddiness from a head-wound and told of his difficult march to the Elbe. Curious portents had occurred lately, he wrote. A most extraordinary display of shooting stars, night after night; sounds like the lamenting of women from the forest; and two divine youths on white horses in Greek, not German, dress, had suddenly ridden through the middle of the camp at dawn. Finally, a German woman of more than mortal size had appeared at his tent door and spoken to him in Greek, telling him to advance no further because fate ruled against it. So Tiberius read a word here and there, stumbled, said that the writing was illegible, started again, stumbled again, and finally excused himself.

'What's this?' said Augustus. 'Surely you can make out more than that.'

Tiberius pulled himself together. 'To be honest, Sir, I can, but the letter does not deserve reading. Evidently my brother was not well at the time of writing it.'

Augustus was alarmed. 'He is not seriously ill, I hope?' But my grandmother Livia, as if her mother's anxiety for once overrode good manners – though of course she guessed at once that there was something in the letter that Tiberius was afraid to read because it reflected either on Augustus or herself – snatched it from him. She read it through, frowned grimly and handed it to Augustus, saying: 'This is a matter which only concerns you. It is not my business to punish a son, however unnatural, but yours as his guardian and as the head of the State.'

Augustus was alarmed, wondering what in the world could be amiss. He read the letter, but it seemed to call for disapproval rather as something which had outraged my grandmother than as something written against himself. Indeed, except for the ugly word 'compel' he secretly approved of the sentiments expressed in the letter, even though the insult to my grandmother reflected on himself, as having been persuaded by her against his better judgement. The Senate were certainly becoming shamefully obsequious in their manners towards him and his family and staff. He disliked the situation as much as my father, and it was true that as long ago as before the defeat and death of Antony he had publicly promised to retire when no public enemy remained in the field against him; and he had several times since referred in his speeches to the happy day when his task would be done. He was weary now of perpetual State business and perpetual honours: he wanted a rest and anonymity. But my grandmother would never allow him to give up; she would always say that his task was not half accomplished yet, that nothing but civil disorder could be expected if he retired now. Yes, he worked hard, she owned, but she worked still harder and with no direct public reward. And he must not be simple-minded: once out of office and a mere private citizen he was liable to impeachment and banishment, or worse; and what of the secret grudges that the relations of men whom he had killed or dishonoured bore against him? As a private citizen he would have to give up his bodyguard as well as his armies. Let him accept another ten years of office, and at the end of them, perhaps, things might have changed for the better. So he always gave in and continued ruling. He accepted his monarchical privileges in instalments. He was voted them for five or ten years at a stretch, usually ten.

My grandmother looked hard at Augustus when he had finished reading the unlucky letter: 'Well?' she asked.

'I agree with Tiberius,' he said mildly. 'The young man must be ill. This is the derangement of overstrain. You notice the final paragraph where he mentions the results of his head-wound and seeing those visions – well, that proves it. He needs a rest. The natural generosity of his soul has been perverted by the anxieties of campaign. Those German forests are no place for a man sick in mind, are they, Tiberius? The howling of wolves gets on one's nerves the worst, I believe: the lamenting of women he talks about was surely wolves. What about recalling him now that he has given these Germans such a shaking as they'll never forget? It would do me good to see him back here at Rome again. Yes, we must certainly have him back. You'll be glad, dearest Livia, to have your boy again, won't you?'

My grandmother did not answer directly. She said, still frowning: 'And you, Tiberius?'

My uncle was more politic than Augustus. He knew his mother's nature better. He answered: 'My brother certainly seems ill, but even illness cannot excuse such unfilial behaviour and such gross folly. I agree that he should be recalled to be reminded of the heinousness of having entertained such base thoughts about his most devoted and indefatigable mother, and of the further enormity of committing them to paper and sending them by courier through unfriendly country. Besides, the argument from the case of Sulla is childish. As soon as Sulla was out of power the Civil Wars began again and his new constitution was overturned.' So Tiberius came quite well out of the affair, but much of his severity against my father was genuine, for landing him in so embarrassing a position.

Livia was choking with rage against Augustus for allowing insults to her to go by so easily, and in her son's presence too. Her rage against my father was equally violent. She knew that when he returned he was likely to carry into execution his plan for forcing Augustus to retire. She also saw that she would never now be able to rule through Tiberius – even if she could assure the succession for him – so long as my father, a man of enormous popularity at Rome, and with all the Western regiments at his back, stood waiting to force the restoration of popular liberties. And supreme power for her had come to be more important than life or honour; she had sacrificed so much for it. Yet she was able to disguise her feelings. She pretended to take Augustus's view that my father was merely sick, and told Tiberius that she thought his censure too severe. She agreed, however, that my father should be recalled at once. She even thanked Augustus for his generous extenuation of her poor son's fault and said that she would send him out her own confidential physician with a parcel of hellebore, from Anticyra in Thessaly, which was a famous specific for cases of mental weakness.

The physician set out the next day in company with the courier who took Augustus's letter. The letter was one of friendly congratulations on his victories and sympathy for his head-wound; it permitted him to return to Rome, but in language which meant that he must return whether he wished to come or not.

My father replied a few days later with thanks for Augustus's generosity. He said that he would return as soon as his health permitted, but that the letter had reached him the day after a slight accident: his horse had fallen under him at full gallop, rolled on his leg, and crushed it against a sharp stone. He thanked his mother for her solicitude, for the gift of the hellebore and for sending her physician, of whose services he had immediately availed himself. But he feared that even his well-known skill had not kept the wound from taking a serious turn. He said finally that he would have preferred to stay at his post but that Augustus's wishes were his commands; and repeated that as soon as he was well again he would return to the City. He was at present encamped near the Thuringian Saal.

On hearing this news, Tiberius, who was with Augustus and Livia at Pavia, instantly asked leave to attend his brother's sickbed. Augustus granted it, and he mounted his cob and galloped off north, with a small escort, making for the quickest pass across the Alps. A 500-mile journey lay before him, but he could count on frequent relays of horses at the posting-houses and when he was too weary for the saddle he could commandeer a gig and snatch a few hours' sleep in it without delaying his progress. The weather favoured him. He went over the Alps and descended into Switzerland, then followed the main Rhine road, not having yet stopped for as much as a hot meal, until he reached a place called Mannheim. Here he crossed the river and struck north-east by rough roads through unfriendly country. He was alone when he reached his destination on the evening of the third day, his original escort having long fallen out, and the new escort which he had picked up at Mannheim not having been able to keep up with him either. It is claimed that on the second day and night he travelled just under 200 miles between noon and noon. He was in time to greet my father but not in time to save his life; for the leg by now was gangrened up to the thigh. My father, though on the point of death, had just sufficient presence of mind to order the
9 B.C.   camp to pay my uncle Tiberius the honours due to him as an army commander. The brothers embraced and my father

whispered, 'She read my letter?' 'Before I did myself,' groaned my uncle Tiberius. Nothing more was said except by my father, who sighed, 'Rome has a severe mother: Lucius and Gaius have a dangerous stepmother.' Those were his last words, and presently my uncle Tiberius closed his eyes.

I heard this account from Xenophon, a Greek from the island of Cos, who was quite a young man at this time. He was my father's staff-surgeon and had been most disgusted that my grandmother's physician had taken the case out of his hands. Gaius and Lucius, I should explain, were Augustus's grandchildren by Julia and Agrippa. He had adopted them as his own sons while they were still infants. There was a third boy, Postumus, so called because he was born posthumously; Augustus did not adopt him too, but left him to carry on Agrippa's name.

The camp where my father died was named 'The Accursed' and his body was carried in a marching military procession to the army's winter quarters at Mainz on the Rhine, my uncle Tiberius walking all the way as chief mourner. The army wished to bury the body there, but he brought it back for a funeral at Rome, where it was burnt on a monstrous pyre in Mars Field. Augustus himself pronounced the funeral oration, in the course of which he said, 'I pray the gods to make my sons Gaius and Lucius as noble and virtuous men as this Drusus and to vouchsafe to me as honourable a death as his.'

Livia was not sure how far she could trust Tiberius. On his return with my father's body his sympathy with her had seemed forced and insincere, and when Augustus wished himself as honourable a death as my father's she saw a brief half-smile cross his face. Tiberius, who, it appears, had long suspected that my grandfather had not died a natural death, was resolved now not to cross his mother's will in anything. Dining so often at her table he felt himself completely at her mercy. He worked hard to win her favour. Livia understood what was in his mind, and was not dissatisfied. He was the only one who suspected her of being a poisoner, and would obviously keep his suspicions to himself. She had lived down the scandal of her marriage with Augustus and was now quoted in the City as an example of virtue in its strictest and most disagreeable form. The Senate voted that four statues of her should be set up in various public places; this was by way of consoling her for her loss. They also enrolled her by a legal fiction among the 'Mothers of Three Children'. Mothers of three or more children had special privileges under Augustus's legislation, particularly as legatees – spinsters and barren women were not allowed to benefit under wills at all, and their loss was the gain of their fruitful sisters.

Claudius, you tedious old fellow, here you have come to within an inch or two of the end of the fourth roll of your autobiography and you haven't even reached your birthplace. Put it down at once or you'll never reach even the middle of your story. Write, 'My birth occurred in Lyons in France, on the first of August, a year before my father's death.' So. My parents had had six children before me, but as my mother always accompanied my father on his campaigns, a child had to be very hardy to survive. Only my brother Germanicus, five years older than myself, and my sister Livilla, a year older than myself, were living: both inherited my father's magnificent constitution. I did not. I nearly died on three occasions before my second year, and had not my father's death brought the family back to Rome it is most unlikely that this story would have been written.

Chapter 5

AT Rome we lived in the big house which had belonged to my grandfather and which he had left in his will to my grandmother. It was on the Palatine Hill, close to Augustus's palace and the temple of Apollo built by Augustus, where the library was. The Palatine Hill looked down on the Market Place. Under the steepest part of the cliff was the temple of the Twin Gods, Castor and Pollux. (This was the old temple, built of timber and sods, which sixteen years later Tiberius replaced, at his own expense, with a magnificent marble structure, the interior painted and gilded and furnished as sumptuously as a rich noblewoman's boudoir. My grandmother Livia made him do this to please Augustus, I may say. Tiberius was not religious-minded and very stingy with money.) It was healthier on that hill than down in the hollow by the river; most of the houses there belonged to senators. I was a very sickly child – 'a very battleground of diseases,' the doctors said – and perhaps only lived because the diseases could not agree as to which should have the honour of carrying me off. To begin with, I was born prematurely, at only seven months, and then my foster-nurse's milk disagreed with me, so that my skin broke out in an ugly rash, and then I had malaria, and measles, which left me slightly deaf in one ear, and erysipelas, and colitis, and finally infantile paralysis, which shortened my left leg so that I was condemned to a permanent limp. Because of one or other of these various illnesses I have all my life been so weak in the hams that to run or walk long distances has never been possible for me: a great deal of my travelling has had to be done in a sedan-chair. Then there is the appalling pain that catches me often in the pit of my stomach after eating. It has been so bad that on two or three occasions, if my friends had not intervened, I would have plunged a carving-knife (which I madly snatched up) into the place of torment. I have heard it said that this pain, which they call 'the cardiac passion', is worse than any other pain known to man except the strangury. Well, I must be thankful, I suppose, that I have never had the strangury.

It will be supposed that my mother Antonia, a beautiful and noble woman brought up to the strictest virtue by her mother Octavia, and the one passion of my father's life, would have taken the most loving care of me, her youngest child, and even made a particular favourite of me in pity for my misfortunes. But such was not the case. She did all for me that could be expected of her as a duty, but no more. She did not love me. No, she had a great aversion to me, not only because of my sickliness but also because she had had a most difficult pregnancy of me, and then a most painful delivery from which she barely escaped with her life and which left her more or less an invalid for years. My premature birth was due to a shock that she got at the feast given in honour of Augustus when he visited my father at Lyons to inaugurate the 'Altar of Rome and Augustus' there: my father was Governor of the Three Provinces of France, and Lyons was his headquarters. A crazy Sicilian slave who was acting as waiter at the feast suddenly drew a dagger and flourished it in the air behind my father's neck. Only my mother saw this happening. She caught the slave's eye and had presence of mind enough to smile at him and shake her head in deprecation, signing to him to put the dagger back. While he hesitated, two other waiters followed her glance and were in time to overpower and disarm him. Then she fainted, and immediately her pains began. It may well be because of this that I have always had a morbid fear of assassination; for they say that a pre-natal shock can be inherited. But of course there is no real reason for any pre-natal influence to be mentioned. How many of the Imperial family have died a natural death?

Since I was an affectionate child, my mother's attitude caused me much misery. I heard from my sister Livilla, a beautiful girl but cruel, vain, and ambitious – in a word a typical Claudian of the bad variety – that my mother had called me 'a human portent' and said that when I was born the Sibylline books should have been consulted. Also that Nature had begun but never finished me, throwing me aside in disgust as a hopeless start. Also that the ancients were wiser and nobler than ourselves: they exposed all weakly infants on a bare hillside for the good of the race. These may have been embroideries by Livilla on less severe remarks – for seven-months' children are very horrible objects – but I know that once when my mother grew angry on hearing that some senator had introduced a foolish motion in the House she burst out: 'That man ought to be put out of the way! He's as stupid as a donkey – what am I saying? Donkeys are sensible beings by comparison – he's as stupid as ... as ... Heavens, he's as stupid as my son Claudius!'

Germanicus was her favourite, as he was everyone's favourite, but so far from envying him for the love and admiration that he won wherever he went, I rejoiced on his behalf. Germanicus pitied me and did the most he could to make my life happier, and recommended me to my elders as a good-hearted child who would repay generous and careful treatment. Severity only frightened me, he would say, and made me more sickly than I need be. And he was right. The nervous tic of my hands, the nervous jerking of my head, my stammer, my queasy digestion, my constant dribbling at the mouth, were principally due to the terrors to which, in the name of discipline, I was subjected. When Germanicus stood up for me my mother used to laugh indulgently and say, 'Noble heart, find some better object for your overflow!' But my grandmother Livia's way of talking was: 'Don't be a fool, Germanicus. If he reacts favourably to discipline, we shall treat him with the kindness he deserves. You're putting the cart before the horse.' My grandmother seldom spoke to me, and when she did it was contemptuously and without looking at me, mostly to say

'Get out of this room, child, I want to be in it.' If she had occasion to scold me she never did so by word of mouth but sent a short, cold note. For example: 'It has come to the knowledge of the Lady Livia that the boy Claudius has been wasting his time mooning about the Apollo Library. Until he can profit from the elementary text-books provided for him by his tutors it is absurd for him to meddle with the serious works on the Library shelves. Moreover his fidgeting disturbs genuine students. This practice must cease.'

As for Augustus, though he never treated me with calculated cruelty, he disliked having me in the same room with him as much as my grandmother did. He was extraordinarily fond of little boys (remaining to the end of his life an overgrown boy himself), but only of the sort that he called 'fine manly little fellows', such as my brother Germanicus and his grandchildren, Gaius and Lucius, who were all extremely good-looking. There were a number of sons of confederate kings or chieftains, kept as hostages for their parents' good behaviour – from France, Germany, Parthia, North Africa, Syria – who were educated with his grandchildren and the sons of leading senators in the Boys' College; and he often came into the cloisters there to play at taws, or knucklebones, or tag. His chief favourites were little brown boys, the Moors and Parthians and Syrians: and those who could rattle away happily to him in boyish talk as if he were one of themselves. Only once did he try to master his repugnance to me and let me into a game of taws with his favourites: but it was so unnatural an effort that it made me more than usually nervous – and I stammered and shook like a mad thing. He never tried again. He hated dwarfs and cripples and deformities, saying that they brought bad luck and should be kept out of sight. Yet I could never find it in my heart to hate Augustus as I came to hate my grandmother, for his dislike of me was without malice and he did what he could to master it: and indeed I must have been a wretched little oddity, a disgrace to so strong and magnificent a father and so fine and stately a mother. Augustus was a fine-looking man himself, though somewhat short, with curly fair hair that went grey only very late in his life, bright eyes, merry face, and upright graceful character.

I remember once overhearing an elegiac epigram that he made about me, in Greek, for the benefit of Athenodorus, a Stoic philosopher, from Tarsus in Cilicia, whose simple serious advice he often asked. I was about seven years old, and they came upon me by the carp-pool in the garden of my mother's house. I cannot remember the epigram exactly, but the sense of it was: 'Antonia is old-fashioned: she does not buy a pet marmoset at great expense from an Eastern trader. And why? Because she breeds them herself.' Athenodorus thought for a moment and replied severely in the same metre: 'Antonia, so far from buying a pet marmoset from Eastern traders, does not even cosset and feed with sugar-plums the poor child of her noble husband.' Augustus looked somewhat abashed. I should explain that neither he nor Athenodorus, to whom I had always been represented as a half-wit, guessed that I could understand what they were saying. So Athenodorus drew me towards him and said playfully in Latin: 'And what does young Tiberius Claudius think about the matter?' I was sheltered from Augustus by Athenodorus's big body and somehow forgot my stammer. I said straight out, in Greek: 'My mother Antonia does not pamper me, but she has let me learn Greek from someone who learned it directly from Apollo.' All I meant was that I understood what they were saying. The person who had taught me Greek was a woman who had been a priestess of Apollo on one of the Greek islands but had been captured by pirates and sold to a brothel-keeper in Tyre. She had managed to escape, but was not permitted to be a priestess again because she had been a prostitute. My mother Antonia, recognizing her gifts, took her into the family as a governess. This woman used to tell me that she had learned directly from Apollo, and I was merely quoting her: but as Apollo was the God of learning and poetry, my remark sounded far wittier than I intended. Augustus was startled and Athenodorus said: 'Well spoken, little Claudius: marmosets don't understand a word of Greek, do they?' I answered: 'No, and they have long tails, and steal apples from the table.' However, when Augustus began eagerly questioning me, taking me from Athenodorus's arm, I grew self-conscious and stammered as badly as ever. But from thenceforth Athenodorus was my friend.

There is a story about Athenodorus and Augustus which does great credit to both. Athenodorus told Augustus one day that he did not take nearly enough precaution about admitting visitors to his presence: one day he would get a dagger in his vitals. Augustus replied that he was talking nonsense. The next day Augustus was told that his sister, the Lady Octavia, was outside and wished to greet him on the anniversary of their father's death. He gave orders for her immediate admittance. She was an incurable invalid when this happened – it was the year she died – and was always carried about in a covered sedan. When the sedan was brought in, the curtains parted and out sprang Athenodorus with a sword, which he pointed at Augustus's heart. Augustus, so far from being angry, thanked Athenodorus and confessed that he had been very wrong to treat his warning so casually.

One extraordinary event in my childhood I must not forget to record. One summer when I was just eight years old my mother, my brother Germanicus, my sister Livilla, and I were visiting my Aunt Julia in a beautiful country-house close to the sea at Antium. It was about six o'clock in the evening and we were out taking the cool breeze in a vineyard. Julia was not with us, but Tiberius's son – that Tiberius Drusus whom we afterwards always called 'Castor' – and Postumus and Agrippina, Julia's children, were in the party. Suddenly we heard a great screeching above us. We looked up and saw a number of eagles fighting. Feathers floated down. We tried to catch them. Germanicus and Castor each caught one before it fell and stuck it in his hair. Castor had a small wing feather, but Germanicus a splendid one from the tail. Both were stained with blood. Spots of blood fell on Postumus's upturned face and on the dresses of Livilla and Agrippina. And then something dark dropped through the air. I do not know why I did so, but I put out a fold of my gown and caught it. It was a tiny wolf-cub wounded and terrified. The eagles came swooping down to retrieve it, but I had it safe hidden, and when we shouted and threw sticks they rose baffled and flew screaming off. I was embarrassed. I didn't want the cub. Livilla grabbed at it, but my mother, who looked very grave, made her give it back to me. 'It fell to Claudius,' she said. 'He must keep it.'

She asked an old nobleman, a member of the College of Augurs, who was with us, 'Tell me what this portends.'

The old man answered, 'How can I say? It may be of great significance or none.'

'Don't be afraid. Say what it seems to mean to you.'

'First send the children away,' he said.

I do not know whether he gave her the interpretation which, when you have read my story, will be forced on you as the only possible one. All I know is that while we other children kept our distance – dear Germanicus had found another tail-feather for me, sticking in a hawthorn bush, and I was putting it proudly in my hair – Livilla crept up inquisitively behind a rose-hedge and overheard something. She interrupted, laughing noisily: 'Wretched Rome, with *him* as her protector! I hope to God I'll be dead before then!'

The Augur turned on her and pointed with his finger. 'Impudent girl,' he said, 'God will no doubt grant your wish in a way that you won't like!'

'You're going to be locked up in a room with nothing to eat, child,' said my mother. Those were ominous words too, now I come to recall them. Livilla was kept in bounds for the rest of her holidays. She revenged herself on me, in a variety of ingeniously spiteful ways. But she could not tell us what the Augur had said, because she had been bound by an oath by Vesta, and our household gods, never to refer to the portent either directly or in a roundabout way in the lifetime of anyone present. We were all made to take that oath. Since I have now for many years been the only one left alive of that party – my mother and the Augur, though so much older, surviving all the rest – I am no longer bound to silence. For some time after this I often caught my mother looking curiously at me, almost respectfully, but she treated me no better than before.

I was not allowed to go to the Boys' College, because the weakness of my legs would not let me take part in the gymnastic exercises which were a chief part of the education, and my illnesses had made me very backward in lessons, and my deafness and stammer were a handicap. So I was seldom in the company of boys of my own age and class, the sons of the household slaves being called in to play with me: two of these, Callon and Pallas, both Greeks, were later to be my secretaries, entrusted with affairs of the highest importance. Callon became the father of two other secretaries of mine, Narcissus and Polybius. I also spent much of my time with my mother's women, listening to their talk as they sat spinning or carding or weaving. Many of them, such as my governess, were women of liberal education and, I confess, I found more pleasure in their society than in that of almost any society of men in which I have since been placed: they were broadminded, shrewd, modest, and kindly.

My tutor I have already mentioned, Marcus Portius Cato, who was, in his own estimation at least, a living embodiment of that ancient Roman virtue which his ancestors had one after the other shown. He was always boasting of his ancestors, as stupid people do who are aware that they have done nothing themselves to boast about. He boasted particularly of Cato the Censor, who of all characters in Roman history is to me perhaps the most hateful, as having persistently championed the cause of 'ancient virtue' and made it identical in the popular mind with churlishness, pedantry, and harshness. I was made to read Cato the Censor's self-glorifying works as text-books, and the account that he gave in one of them of his campaign in Spain, where he destroyed more towns than he had spent days in that country, rather disgusted me with his inhumanity than impressed me with his military skill or patriotism. The poet Virgil has said that the mission of the Roman is to rule: 'To spare the conquered, and with war the proud To overbear.' Cato overbore the proud, certainly, but less with actual warfare than with clever management of inter-tribal jealousies in Spain: he even employed assassins to remove redoubtable enemies. As for sparing the conquered, he put multitudes of unarmed men to the sword even when they unconditionally surrendered their cities, and he proudly records that many hundreds of Spaniards committed suicide, with all their families, rather than taste of Roman vengeance. Was it to be wondered at that the tribes rose again as soon as they could get a few arms together, and that they have been a constant thorn in our side ever since? All that Cato wanted was plunder and a triumph: a triumph was not granted unless so-and-so many corpses – I think it was 5,000 at this time – could be counted, and he was making sure that no one would challenge him, as he had himself jealously challenged rivals, for having pretended to a triumph on an inadequate harvest of dead.

Triumphs, by the way, have been a curse to Rome. How many unnecessary wars have been fought because generals wanted the glory of riding crowned through the streets of Rome with enemy captives led in chains behind them and the spoils of war heaped on carnival wagons? Augustus realized this: on Agrippa's advice, he decreed that henceforth no general, unless a member of the Imperial family, should be awarded a public triumph. This decree, published in the year that I was born, read as though Augustus were jealous of his generals, for by that time he had finished with active campaigning himself and no members of his family were old enough to win triumphs; but all it meant was that he did not wish the boundaries of the Empire enlarged any further, and that he reckoned that his generals would not provoke the frontier tribes to commit acts of war if they could not hope to be awarded triumphs by victory over them. None the less he allowed 'triumphal ornaments' – an embroidered robe, a statue, a chaplet, and so on – to be awarded to those who would otherwise have earned a triumph; this should be a sufficient incentive to any good soldier to fight a necessary war. Triumphs, besides, are very bad for military discipline. Soldiers get drunk and out of hand and usually finish the day by breaking up the wine-shops and setting fire to the oil-shops and insulting the women and generally behaving as if Rome were the city they had conquered, not some miserable log-hut encampment in Germany or sand-burrowed village in Morocco. After a triumph celebrated by a nephew of mine, whom I shall soon be telling you about, 400 soldiers and nearly 4,000 private citizens lost their lives one way and another – five big blocks of tenements in the prostitutes' quarter of the City were burned to the ground and 300 wine-shops sacked, besides any amount of other damage.

But I was on the subject of Cato the Censor. His manual of husbandry and household economy was made my spelling-book, and every time I stumbled over a word I used to get two blows; one on my left ear for my stupidity, and one on my right for insulting the noble Cato. I remember a passage in the book which summed up the mean-souled fellow very well: 'A master of a household should sell his old oxen, and all the horned cattle that are of a delicate frame; all his sheep that are not hardy, their wool, their very pelts; he should sell his old wagons and his old instruments of husbandry; he should sell such of his slaves as are old and infirm and everything else that is worn out or useless.' For myself, when I was living as a country gentleman on my little estate at Capua, I made a point of putting my worn-out beasts first to light work and then to grass until old age seemed too much of a burden to them, when I had them knocked on the head. I never demeaned myself by selling them for a trifle to a countryman who would work them cruelly to their last gasp. As for my slaves, I have always treated them generously in sickness and health, youth and old age, and expected the highest degree of devotion from them in return. I have seldom been disappointed, though when they have abused my generosity I have had no mercy on them. I have no doubt old Cato's slaves were always falling sick, with the hope of being sold to a more humane master, and I also think it likely that he got, on the whole, less honest work and service out of them than I got out of mine. It is foolish to treat slaves like cattle. They are more intelligent than cattle, capable besides of doing more damage in a week to one's property by wilful carelessness and stupidity than the entire price you have paid for them. Cato made a boast of never spending more than a few pounds on a slave: any evil-looking cross-eyed fellow that seemed to have good muscles and teeth would do. How on earth he managed to find buyers for these beauties when he had quite finished with them I cannot say. From what I know of the character of his descendant, who was supposed to resemble him closely in looks – sandy-haired, green-eyed, harsh-voiced, and heavily built – and in character, I guess that he bullied his poor neighbours into taking all his cast-off stuff at the price of new.

My dear friend Postumus, who was a little less than two years older than myself – the truest friend, except Germanicus, that I have ever had – told me that he had read in a contemporary book that old Cato was a regular crook besides being a skinflint: he was guilty of some very sharp practice in the shipping trade, but avoided public disgrace by making one of his ex-slaves the nominal trader. As Censor, in charge of public morals, he did some mighty queer things: they were allegedly in the name of public decency but really, it seems, to satisfy his personal spites. On his own showing, he expelled one man from the order of senators because he had been 'wanting in Roman gravity' – he had kissed his wife in daylight in his daughter's presence! When challenged by a friend of the expelled man, another senator, as to the justice of his decision and asked whether he himself and his wife never embraced except during the marital act, Cato replied hotly: 'Never!' 'What, *never*?' 'Well, a couple of years ago, to be frank with you, my wife happened to throw her arms around me during a thunderstorm which scared her, but fortunately nobody was about and I assure you it will be a long time before she does it again.' 'Oh,' said the senator, pretending to misunderstand him, for Cato meant, I suppose, that he had given his wife a terrible lecture for her want of gravity, 'I'm sorry about that. Some women aren't very affectionate with plain-looking husbands, however upright and virtuous they may be. But never mind, perhaps Jove will be good enough to thunder again soon.'

Cato did not forgive that senator, who was a distant relative. A year later he was going through the roll of senators, as his duty as Censor was, asking each man in turn whether he was married. There was a law, which has since lapsed, that all senators should be honourably married. The turn came for his relative to be examined, and Cato asked him in the usual formula, which enjoined the senator to answer 'in his confidence and honesty'. 'If you have a wife, in your confidence and honesty, answer!' Cato intoned in his raucous voice. The man felt a little foolish, because after joking about Cato's wife's affection for Cato, he had found that his own wife had so far lost her affection for himself that he was now forced to divorce her. So to show goodwill and turn the joke decently against himself he replied: 'Yes, indeed, I *have* a wife, but she's not in my confidence any more, and I wouldn't give much for her honesty, either.' Cato thereupon expelled him from the Order for irreverence.

And who brought the Punic Curse on Rome? That same old Cato who, whenever he was asked his opinion in the Senate on any matter whatever, would end his speech with: 'This is my opinion; and my further opinion is that Carthage should be destroyed: she is a menace to Rome.' By harping incessantly on the menace of Carthage he brought about such popular nervousness that, as I have said, the Romans eventually violated their most solemn commitments and razed Carthage to the ground.

I have written about old Cato more than I intended, but it is to the point: he is bound up in my mind both with the ruin of Rome, for which he was just as responsible as the men whose 'unmanly luxury', he said, 'enervated the State', and with the memory of my unhappy childhood under that muleteer, his great-great-great-grandson. I am already an old man and my tutor has been dead these fifty years, yet my heart still swells with indignation and hatred when I think of him.

Germanicus stood up for me against my elders in a gentle, persuasive way, but Postumus was a lion-like champion. He seemed not to care a fig for anyone. He even dared to speak out straight to my grandmother Livia herself. Augustus made a favourite of Postumus, so for a while Livia pretended to be amused at what she called his boyish impulsiveness. Postumus trusted her at first, being himself incapable of deceit. One day when I was twelve and he was fourteen he happened to be passing by the room where Cato was giving me my lessons. He heard the sound of blows and my cries for mercy and came bursting angrily in. 'Stop beating him, at once!' he shouted.

Cato looked at him in scornful surprise and fetched me another blow that knocked me off my stool.

Postumus said: 'Those that can't beat the ass, beat the saddle.' (That was a proverb at Rome.)

'Impudence, what do you mean?' roared Cato.

'I mean,' said Postumus, 'that you're revenging yourself on Claudius for what you consider a general conspiracy to keep you down. You're really too good for the job of tutoring him, eh?' Postumus was clever: he guessed that this would make Cato angry enough to forget himself. And Cato rose to the bait, shouting out with a string of old-fashioned curses that in the days of his ancestor, whose memory this stammering imp was insulting, woe betide any child who failed in reverence to his elders; for they dealt out discipline with a heavy hand in those days. Whereas in these degenerate times the leading men of Rome gave any ignorant oafish lout (this was for Postumus) or any feeble-minded decrepit-limbed little whippersnapper (this was for me) full permission – –

Postumus interrupted with a warning smile: 'So I was right. The degenerate Augustus insults the great Censor by employing you in his degenerate family. I suppose you have told the Lady Livia just how you feel about things?'

Cato could have bitten off his tongue with vexation and alarm. If Livia should hear what he had said, that would be the end of him; he had hitherto always expressed the most profound gratitude for the honour of being entrusted with the education of her grandchild, not to mention the free return of the family estates – confiscated after the Battle of Philippi, where his father had died fighting against Augustus. Cato was wise enough or cowardly enough to take the hint, and after this my daily torments were considerably abated. Three or four months later, much to my delight, he ceased to be my tutor, on his appointment to the headmastership of the Boys' College. Postumus came under his tutelage there.

Postumus was immensely strong. At the age of not quite fourteen he could bend a bar of cold iron as thick as my thumb across his knees, and I have seen him walk around the playground with two boys on his shoulders, one on his back, and one standing on each of his hands. He was not studious, but of an intellect far superior to Cato's, to say the least of it, and in his last two years at the College the boys elected him their leader. In all the school games he was 'The King' – strange how long the word 'king' has survived with schoolboys – and kept a stern discipline over his fellows. Cato had to be very civil to Postumus if he wanted the other boys to do what he wanted; for they all took their cue from Postumus.

Cato was now required by Livia to write her out half-yearly reports on his pupils: she remarked that if she felt them to be of interest to Augustus she would communicate them to him. Cato understood from this that his reports were to be non-committal unless he had a hint from her to praise or censure any particular boy. Many marriages were arranged while the boys were still at the College, and a report might be useful to Livia as an argument for or against some contemplated match. Marriages of the nobility at Rome had to be approved by Augustus as High Pontiff and were for the most part dictated by Livia. One day Livia happened to visit the College cloisters, and there was Postumus in a chair issuing decrees as the King. Cato noticed that she frowned at the sight. He was emboldened to write in his next report: 'With great unwillingness but in the interest of virtue and justice, I am compelled to report that the boy Agrippa Postumus is inclined to display a savage, domineering and intractable temper.' After this Livia behaved to him so graciously that his next report was even stronger. Livia did not show the reports to Augustus but kept them in reserve, and Postumus himself had no knowledge of them.

Under Postumus's kingship I had the happiest two years of my youth, I may say of my life. He gave orders to the other boys that I was to be freely admitted to games in the cloisters, though not a member of the College, and that he would regard any incivility or injury to me as incivility or injury to himself. So I took part in whatever sports my health allowed and it was only when Augustus or Livia happened to come along that I slipped into the background. In place of Cato I now had good old Athenodorus for my tutor. I learned more from him in six months than I had learned from Cato in six years. Athenodorus never beat me, and used the greatest patience. He used to encourage me by saying that my lameness should be a spur to my intelligence. Vulcan, the god of all clever craftsmen, was lame too. As for my stammer, Demosthenes, the noblest orator of all time, had been born with a stammer, but had corrected it by patience and concentration. Demosthenes had used the very method that he was now teaching me. For Athenodorus made me declaim with my mouth full of pebbles: in trying to overcome the obstruction of the pebbles I forgot about the stammer and then the pebbles were removed one at a time until none remained, and I found to my surprise that I could speak as well as anyone. But only in declamations. In ordinary conversation I still stammered badly. He made it a pleasant secret between himself and me that I could declaim so well. 'One day, Cercopithecion, we shall surprise Augustus,' he would say. 'But wait a little longer.' When he called me Cercopithecion ['little marmoset'], it was for affection, not scorn, and I was proud of the name. When I did badly he would shame me by rolling out, 'Tiberius Claudius Drusus Nero Germanicus, remember who you are and what you are doing.' With Postumus and Athenodorus and Germanicus as my friends I gradually began to win self-confidence.

Athenodorus told me, the very first day of his tutorship, that he proposed to teach me not facts which I could pick up anywhere for myself, but the proper presentation of facts. And this he did. One day, for example, he asked me, kindly enough, why I was so excited; I seemed unable to concentrate on my task. I A.D. 2 told him that I had just seen a huge draft of recruits parading on Mars Field under Augustus's inspection before being sent off to Germany, where war had recently broken out again. 'Well,' said Athenodorus, still in the same kindly voice, 'since this is so much on your mind that you can't appreciate the beauties of Hesiod, Hesiod can wait until to-morrow. After all, he's waited seven hundred years or more, so he won't grudge us another day. And meanwhile, suppose you were to sit down and take your tablets and write me a letter, a short account of all that you saw on Mars Field; as if I had been five years absent from Rome and you were sending me a letter across the sea, say to my home in Tarsus. That would keep your restless hands employed and be good practice too.' So I gladly scribbled away on the wax, and then we read the letter through for faults of spelling and composition. I was forced to admit that I had told both too little and too much, and had also put my facts in the wrong order. The passage describing the lamentations of the mothers and sweethearts of the young soldiers, and how the crowd rushed to the bridgehead for a final cheer of the departing column, should have come last, not first. And I need not have mentioned that the cavalry had horses: people took that for granted. And I had twice put in the incident of Augustus's charger stumbling; once was enough if the horse only stumbled once. And what Postumus had told me, as we were going home, about the religious practices of the Jews, was interesting, but did not belong here because the recruits were Italians, not Jews. Besides, at Tarsus he would probably have more opportunities of studying Jewish customs than Postumus had at Rome. On the other hand, I had not mentioned several things that he would have been interested to hear -- how many recruits there were in the parade, how far advanced their military training was, to what garrison town they were being sent, whether they looked glad or sorry to go, what Augustus said to them in his speech.

Three days later Athenodorus made me write out a description of a brawl between a sailor and a clothes dealer which we had watched together that day as we were walking in the rag-market; and I did much better. He first applied this discipline to my writing, then to my declamations, and finally to my general conversation with him. He took endless pains with me, and gradually I grew less scatter-brained, for he never let any careless, irrelevant, or inexact phrase of mine pass without comment.

He had tried to interest me in speculative philosophy, but when he saw that I had no bent that way he did not force me to exceed the usual bounds of polite education in the subject. It was he who first inclined me to history. He had copies of the first twenty volumes of Livy's history of Rome, which he gave me to read as an example of lucid and agreeable writing. Livy's stories enchanted me and Athenodorus promised me that as soon as I had mastered my stammer I should meet Livy himself, who was a friend of his. He kept his word. Six months later he took me into the Apollo Library and introduced me to a bearded stooping man of about sixty with a yellowish complexion, a happy eye and a precise way of speaking, who greeted me cordially as the son of a father whom he had so much admired. Livy was at this time not quite half-way through his history, which was to be completed in one hundred and fifty volumes and to run from the earliest legendary times to the death of my father some twelve years previously. It was at this date that he had begun publishing his work, at the rate of five volumes a year, and he had now reached the date at which Julius Caesar was born. Livy congratulated me on having Athenodorus as my tutor. Athenodorus said that I well repaid the pains he spent on me; and then I told Livy what pleasure I had derived from reading his books since Athenodorus had recommended them to me as a model for writing. So everybody was pleased, especially Livy. 'What! are you to be an historian too, young man?' he asked. 'I should like to be worthy of that honourable name,' I replied, though I had indeed never seriously considered the matter. Then he suggested that I should write a life of my father, and offered to help me by referring me to the most reliable historical sources. I was much flattered and determined to start the book next day. But Livy said that writing was the historian's last task: first he had to gather his materials and sharpen his pen. Athenodorus would lend me his little sharp penknife, Livy joked.

Athenodorus was a stately old man with dark gentle eyes, a hooked nose and the most wonderful beard that surely ever grew on human chin. It spread in waves down to his waist and was as white as a swan's wing. I do not make this as an idle poetical comparison, for I am not the sort of historian who writes in pseudo-epic style. I mean that it was literally as white as a swan's wing. There were some tame swans on an artificial lake in the Gardens of Sallust, where Athenodorus and I once fed them with bread from a boat, and I remember noticing that his beard and their wings as he leaned over the side were of exactly the same colour. Athenodorus used to stroke his beard so slowly and rhythmically as he talked, and told me once that it was this that made it grow so luxuriantly. He said that invisible seeds of fire streamed off from his fingers, which were food for the hairs. This was a typical Stoic joke at the expense of Epicurean speculative philosophy.

Mention of Athenodorus's beard reminds me of Sulpicius, who, when I was thirteen years old, was appointed by Livia as my special history-tutor. Sulpicius had, I think, the most wretched-looking beard I have ever seen: it was white, but the white of snow in the streets of Rome after a thaw – a dirty greyish-white streaked with yellow, and very ragged. He used to twist it in his fingers when he was worried, and would even put the ends in his mouth and chew them. Livia chose him, I believe, because she thought him the most boring man in Rome and hoped by making him my tutor to discourage my historical ambitions; for she soon came to hear of them. Livia was right: Sulpicius had a genius for making the most interesting things seem utterly vapid and dead. But even Sulpicius's dryness could not turn me away from my work, and there was this about him, that he had a most exceptionally accurate memory for facts. If I ever wanted some out-of-the-way information, such for instance as the laws of succession to the chieftainship among one of the Alpine tribes against whom my father had fought, or the meaning and etymology of their outlandish battle-cry, Sulpicius would know what authority had treated of these points, in which book, and from which shelf of which case in which room of which library they were to be obtained. He had no critical sense and wrote miserably, the facts choking each other like flowers in a seed-bed that has not been thinned out. But he proved an invaluable assistant when later I learned to use him as such, instead of as a tutor; and he worked for me until his death at the age of eighty-seven, nearly thirty years later, his memory remaining unimpaired to the last, and his beard as discoloured and thin and disordered as ever.

Chapter 6

I MUST now go back a few years to write about my uncle Tiberius, whose fortunes are by no means irrelevant to this story. He was in an unhappy position, forced against his will to be continually in the public eye, now as general in some frontier-campaign, now as Consul at Rome, now as special commissioner to the provinces; when all he wanted was a long   6 B.C.
rest and privacy. Public honours meant little to him, if only because they were awarded him, as he once complained to my father, rather as being chief errand-boy to Augustus and Livia, than as one acting in his own right and on his own responsibility. Moreover, with the dignity of the Imperial family to maintain and Livia continually spying on him, he had to be very careful of his private morals. He had few friends, being, as I think I have said, of a suspicious, jealous, reserved, and melancholy temperament, and

those rather hangers-on than friends, whom he treated with the cynical contempt that they deserved. And, lastly, things had gone from bad to worse between him and Julia since his marriage with her five years before. A boy had been born but he had died; and then Tiberius had refused to sleep with her ever again; for three reasons. The first was that Julia was by now getting middle-aged and losing her slender figure – Tiberius preferred immature women, the more boyish the better, and Vipsania had been a little wisp of a thing. The second was that Julia made passionate demands on him which he was unwilling to meet and that she used to become hysterical when he repulsed her. The third was that he found, after repulsing her, that she was revenging herself by finding gallants to give her what he withheld.

Unfortunately he could get no proof of Julia's infidelities apart from the evidence of slaves, for she managed things very carefully; and slave-evidence was not good enough to offer Augustus as grounds for divorcing his beloved only daughter. Rather than tell Livia about it, however, for he mistrusted her as much as he hated her, he preferred to suffer in silence. It occurred to him that, if he could once get away from Rome and Julia, the chances were that she would grow careless and Augustus would eventually find out for himself about her behaviour. His only chance of escape lay in another war breaking out somewhere on one of the frontiers important enough for him to be sent there in command. But no signs of war appeared in any quarter and, besides, he was sick of fighting. He had succeeded my father in command of the German armies (Julia had insisted on accompanying him to the Rhine) and had now only been back in Rome for a few months: but Augustus had worked him like a slave ever since his return, giving him the difficult and unpleasant task of investigating the administration of workhouses and labour conditions generally in the poorer quarters of Rome. One day, in an unguarded moment, he had burst out to Livia: 'O mother, to be free, for only a few months even, from this intolerable life.' She frightened him by making no answer and haughtily leaving the room, but later in the same day called him to her and surprised him by saying that she had decided to grant his wish and obtain temporary leave of retirement for him from Augustus. She took the decision partly because she wanted to put him under a debt of gratitude to her, and partly because she now knew about Julia's love-affairs and had the same idea as Tiberius about giving her rope and letting her hang herself with it. But her chief reason was that Postumus's elder brothers, Gaius and Lucius, were growing up and relations between them and their stepfather Tiberius were strained.

Gaius, who was not a bad fellow at bottom (and neither was Lucius), had to some extent come to fill the place in Augustus's affections that Marcellus had once held. But he spoilt them both so shamelessly, in spite of Livia's warnings, that the wonder is that they did not turn out far worse than they did. They tended to behave insolently towards their elders, particularly men towards whom they knew Augustus would secretly like them to behave so, and to live with great extravagance. When Livia saw that it was useless trying to keep Augustus's nepotism in check she changed her policy and encouraged him to make greater favourites of them than ever. By doing so, and letting them know she was doing so, she hoped to gain their confidence. She calculated, too, that if their self-importance was increased only a little more they would forget themselves and try to seize the monarchy for themselves. Her spy-system was excellent and she would get wind of any such plot in good time to have them arrested. She encouraged Augustus to have Gaius elected Consul, for four years ahead, when he was only fifteen; though the youngest age at which a man could legally become Consul had been fixed by Sulla at forty-three, before which he had to fill three different magistral offices of ascending importance. Later, Lucius was given the same honour. She also suggested that Augustus should present them to the Senate as 'Leaders of the Cadets'. The title was not, as in the case of Marcellus, given them for a specific occasion only, but put them in a position of permanent authority over all their equals in age and rank. It seemed perfectly clear now that Augustus intended Gaius as his successor; so it was not to be wondered at that the same sort of young noblemen as had boasted the untried powers of young Marcellus against the ministerial and military reputation of the veteran Agrippa now did the same for Agrippa's son Gaius against the veteran reputation of Tiberius, whom they subjected to many slights. Livia intended Tiberius to follow the example of Agrippa. If he now retired, with so many victories and public honours to his credit, to some near-by Greek island and left the political field clear for Gaius and Lucius, this would create a better impression and win him far more popular sympathy than if he stayed behind to dispute it. (The historical parallel would become still closer if Gaius and Lucius were to die during Tiberius's retirement and Augustus were to feel the need of his services again.) So she promised to prevail on Augustus to grant him indefinite leave of absence from Rome and permission to resign from all his offices; but to give him the honorary rank of Protector of the People – which would make him secure against assassination by Gaius, should Gaius think of removing him.

Livia found it extremely difficult to keep her promise, for Tiberius was Augustus's most useful minister and most successful general, and for a long time the old man refused to treat the request seriously. But Tiberius pleaded ill-health and urged that his absence would relieve Gaius and Lucius of much embarrassment: he admitted that he did not get on well with them. Still Augustus would not listen. Gaius and Lucius were mere lads, totally inexperienced as yet in war or statecraft, and would be of no service to him at all should serious disturbances break out in the City, in the provinces, or on the frontier. He realized, perhaps for the first time, that Tiberius was now his only stand-by in any such emergency. But he was irritated at having the realization forced on him. He refused Tiberius's request and said that he would listen to no arguments. Since there was no help for it, therefore, Tiberius went to Julia and told her with studied brutality that their marriage had become such a farce that he could not bear to remain in the same house with her a day longer. He suggested that she should go to Augustus and complain that she had been ill-treated by her ruffianly husband and would not be happy until she had a divorce. Augustus, he said, was for family reasons unlikely, worse luck, to consent to the divorce, but would probably banish him from Rome. He was ready even to go into exile rather than continue to live with her.

Julia decided to forget that she had ever loved Tiberius. She had suffered much from him. Not only did he treat her with the greatest contempt whenever they were alone together, but he had by now begun cautiously experimenting in those ludicrously filthy practices which later made his name so detestable to all decent-minded people; and she had found out about it. So she took him at his word and complained to Augustus in far stronger terms than Tiberius (who was vain enough to believe that she still loved him in spite of everything) could have foreseen. Augustus had always great difficulty in concealing his dislike for Tiberius as a son-in-law – which had of course encouraged the Gaius faction – and now went storming up and down his study calling Tiberius all the names that he could lay his tongue to. But he nevertheless reminded Julia that she had only herself to blame for her disappointment in a husband about whose character he had never failed to warn her. And, much as he loved and pitied her, he could not dissolve the marriage. For his daughter and stepson to separate after a union that had been given such political importance would never do, and Livia would see the matter in the same light as himself, he was sure. So Julia begged that Tiberius should at least be sent away somewhere for a year or two, because at the moment she could not abide his presence within a hundred miles of her. To this he eventually agreed, and a few days later Tiberius was on his way to the island of Rhodes, which he had, long before this, chosen as the ideal place for retirement. But Augustus, while granting him the rank of Protector, at Livia's urgent insistence, had made it plain that if he never saw his face again it would be no grief to him.

Nobody but the principals in this curious drama knew why Tiberius was leaving Rome, and Livia used Augustus's unwillingness to discuss the matter publicly, to Tiberius's advantage. She told her friends, 'in confidence', that Tiberius had decided to retire as a protest against the scandalous behaviour of the party of Gaius and Lucius. She also said that Augustus had sympathized greatly with him, and had first refused to accept his resignation, promising to silence the offenders; Tiberius had then insisted that he did not wish to make further bad blood between himself and his wife's sons, and had demonstrated the fixity of his purpose by going without food for four days. Livia kept up the farce by accompanying Tiberius to his ship at Ostia, the port of Rome, and beseeching him, in Augustus's name and her own, to reconsider his decision. She even arranged that all members of her immediate family – Tiberius's younger son Castor, and my mother, and Germanicus, Livilla, and myself – should come along with her and increase the poignancy of the occasion by adding our pleas to hers. Julia did not appear, and her absence fitted well with the impression that Livia was trying to create – that she had been siding with her sons against her husband. It was a ridiculous but well-staged scene. My mother played up well, and the three children, who had been carefully coached, really spoke their parts as if they meant them. I was bewildered and dumb until Livilla gave me a good pinching, at which I burst into tears and so did better than any of them. I was four years old when all this happened, but I had turned twelve before Augustus was reluctantly compelled to recall my uncle to Rome, the political situation having by then greatly changed.

Now Julia deserves far greater sympathy than she has popularly won. She was, I believe, naturally a decent, good-hearted woman, though fond of pleasures and excitements, and the only one of my female relations who had a kindly word for me. I also believed that there were no grounds for the charges made against her many years later, of infidelity to Agrippa while she was married to him. Certainly all her boys resembled him closely. The true story is as follows. In her widowhood, as I have related, she fell in love with Tiberius and persuaded Augustus to let her marry him. Tiberius, enraged at having to divorce his own wife for her sake, treated her very coldly. She was then imprudent enough to approach Livia, whom she feared but trusted, and ask her advice. Livia gave her a love-philtre, which she was to drink, saying that within a year it would make her irresistible to her husband, but that she must take it once a month, at full moon, and make certain prayers to Venus, saying nothing about it to a living soul, or the drug would lose its virtue and do her a great deal of harm. What Livia very cruelly gave her was a distillation of the crushed bodies of certain little green flies, from Spain, which so stimulated her sexual appetite that she became like a demented woman. (I shall explain later how I came to learn all this.) For a while indeed she fired Tiberius's appetite by the abandoned wantonness to which the drug drove her, against her natural modesty; but soon she wearied him and he refused to have any further marital commerce with her. She was forced by the action of the drug, which I suppose became a habit with her, to satisfy her sexual cravings by adulterous intercourse with whatever young courtiers she could trust to behave with discretion. She did this in Rome, I mean: in Germany and France she seduced private soldiers of Tiberius's bodyguard and even German slaves, threatening, if they hesitated, to accuse them of offering her familiarities and to have them flogged to death. As she was still a fine-looking woman, they apparently did not hesitate long.

71

After Tiberius's banishment Julia grew careless, and all Rome soon came to know of her infidelities. Livia never said a word to Augustus, confident that in due time he would come to hear about them from some other quarter. But Augustus's blind love for Julia was a byword and nobody dared to say anything to him. After a time it was generally assumed that he could no longer be ignorant, and that his condonation of her behaviour was a further caution to silence. Julia's nocturnal orgies in the Market Place and on the Oration Platform itself had become a matter of grave public scandal, yet it was four years before so much as a rumour reached Augustus. Then he heard the whole story from none other than her sons, Gaius and Lucius, who came together into his presence and angrily asked him how long he was going to permit himself and his grandchildren to be disgraced. They understood, they said, that regard for the family's good name had made him very patient with their mother, but surely there was a limit to his long-suffering. Were they to wait until she presented them with a litter of many-fathered bastard brothers before any official notice was taken of her pranks? Augustus listened with horror and amazement and for a long time could do no more than gape and move his lips. When he found his voice it was to call in strangled tones for Livia. They repeated their story in her presence, and she pretended to sob, saying that it had been her greatest grief these three years that Augustus had deliberately shut his ears to the truth. Several times, she said, she had gathered up courage to speak to him, but it had been quite clear that he did not want to listen to a word she said. 'I was confident that you really knew all about it and that the subject was too painful for you to discuss even with me. ...' Augustus, weeping, with his head between his hands, muttered that he had never heard the slightest whisper, or entertained the faintest suspicion that his daughter was not the chastest woman at Rome. Livia asked, why then did he suppose that her son Tiberius had gone into exile. For love of exile? No, it was because he was unable to check the excesses of his wife and yet was distressed that Augustus was condoning them, for so he believed; and since he did not wish to antagonize Gaius and Lucius, her sons, by asking Augustus for leave to divorce her, there was no course open for him but to withdraw decently from the scene.

The talk about Tiberius was wasted on Augustus, who threw a

fold of his robe over his head and groped his way to the passage leading to his bedroom, where he locked himself in and was seen by nobody, not even by Livia, for four whole days, during which time he took no food or drink, nor any sleep, and what was still stronger proof – if any was required – of the violence of his grief, went all that time unshaved. Finally he pulled the string which ran through a hole in the wall and tinkled a little silver bell in Livia's room. Livia came hurrying to him with a face of loving concern, and Augustus, not yet trusting his voice, wrote down on his wax-tablet the single sentence, in Greek: 'Let her be banished for life, but do not tell me where.' He handed Livia his seal-ring so that she might write letters to the Senate by his authority, recommending the banishment. (This seal, by the way, was the great emerald cut with the helmeted head of Alexander the Great, from whose tomb it had been stolen, along with a sword and breastplate and other personal trappings of the hero. Livia insisted on his using it, in spite of his scruples – he realized how presumptuous it was – until one night he had a dream in which Alexander, frowning angrily, hacked off with his sword the finger on which he wore it. Then he had a seal of his own, a ruby from India, cut by the famous goldsmith Dioscurides, which all his successors have used as the token of their sovereignty.)

Livia wrote the recommendation for banishment in very strong terms. It was composed in Augustus's own literary style; which was easy to imitate because it always sacrificed elegance to clarity – for example, by a determined repetition of the same word, where it occurred often in a passage, instead of hunting about for a synonym or periphrasis (which is the common literary practice). And he had a tendency to over-prepositionalize his verbs. She did not show the letter to Augustus but sent it direct to the Senate, who immediately voted a decree of perpetual banishment. Livia had listed Julia's crimes in such detail and had credited Augustus with such calm expressions of detestation for them that she made it impossible for him ever afterwards to change his mind and ask the Senate to cancel their decision. She did a good piece of business on the side, too, by singling out for special mention as Julia's partners in adultery three or four men whom it was to her interest to ruin. Among them was an uncle of mine, Iulus, a son of Antony, to whom Augustus had shown great favour for Octavia's sake, raising him to the Consulship. Livia, in naming him in her letter to the Senate, strongly emphasized the ingratitude that he had shown his benefactor and hinted that he and Julia were conspiring together to seize the supreme power. Iulus committed suicide. I believe that the charge of conspiracy was groundless, but as the only surviving son of Antony, by his wife Fulvia – Augustus had put Antyllus, the eldest, to death immediately after his father's suicide, and the other two, Ptolemy and Alexander, his sons by Cleopatra, had died young – and as an ex-Consul and the husband of Marcellus's sister, whom Agrippa had divorced, he seemed dangerous. Popular discontent with Augustus often expressed itself in a wish that it had been Antony who had won the Battle of Actium. The other men whom Livia accused of adultery were banished.

A week later Augustus asked Livia whether 'a certain decree' had been duly passed – for he never mentioned Julia by name again and seldom even by a roundabout expression, though she plainly was much in his thoughts. Livia told him that 'a certain person' had been sentenced to perpetual confinement on an island and was already on her way there. At this he seemed further downcast, that Julia had not done the one honourable thing left to her to do, namely to take her own life. Livia mentioned that Phoebe, who was Julia's lady-in-waiting and chief confidant, had hanged herself as soon as the decree of banishment had been published. Augustus said: 'I wish to God I had been Phoebe's father.' He delayed his public appearance for a further fortnight. I well remember that dreadful month. We children were all, by Livia's orders, made to wear mourning and not allowed to play or make a noise or even smile. When we saw Augustus again he looked ten years older, and it was months before he had the heart to visit the playground in the Boys' College or even to resume his daily morning exercise, which consisted of a brisk walk around the Palace grounds with a run at the end over a course of low hurdles.

Tiberius had the news about Julia sent him at once by Livia. At her prompting he wrote two or three letters to Augustus, begging him to forgive Julia, as he did himself, and saying that however badly she had behaved as a wife he wished her to keep all the property that he had at any time made over to her. Augustus did not answer. He firmly believed that Tiberius's original coldness and cruelty to Julia, and the examples of immorality he had given her, were responsible for her moral degeneration. So far from recalling him from banishment he refused even to renew his Protectorate when it came to an end the following year.

There is a soldiers' marching-ballad called *The Three Griefs of Lord Augustus*, composed in the rough tragi-comic style of the camp, which was sung many years later by the regiments stationed in Germany. The theme is that Augustus grieved first for Marcellus, next for Julia, and the third time for the lost Eagles of Varus. Deeply for Marcellus's death, more deeply for Julia's disgrace, but most deeply of all for the Eagles, for with each Eagle had vanished a whole regiment of Rome's bravest men. The ballad laments in a number of verses the unhappy fate of the Seventeenth, Eighteenth, and Nineteenth Regiments which, when I was nineteen years old, were ambushed and massacred by the Germans in a remote marshy forest; and tells how, after the news of this unparalleled disaster reached him, Lord Augustus kept knocking his head against the wall: –

> Lord Augustus each time bawling
>   As he fetched his head a crack,
> 'Varus, Varus, General Varus,
>   Give me my three Eagles back!'
>
> Lord Augustus tore his bedclothes,
>   Blankets, sheet, and counterpane.
> 'Varus, Varus, General Varus,
>   Give my Regiments back again!'

The next verses say that he never afterwards formed new regiments under the numbers of the three destroyed, but kept the gap in the Army List. He is made to swear that Marcellus's life and Julia's honour had been nothing to him by comparison with the life and honour of his soldiers, and that his spirit would have 'no more rest than a flea in an oven' until all three Eagles were recovered and safely laid in the Capitol. But though since then the Germans had been thrashed again and again in battle, nobody had been able to discover where the lost Eagles were 'roosting' – the cowards kept them so closely hidden. That was how the troops belittled Augustus's grief for Julia, but it is my opinion that for every hour he grieved for the Eagles he must have grieved a full month for her.

He did not wish to know where she had been sent, because this would have meant that his mind would be continually turning there and he would hardly be able to restrain himself from taking ship and visiting her. So it was easy for Livia to treat Julia with great revengefulness. She was not allowed wine, cosmetics, fine clothes, or luxuries of any sort, and her guard consisted of eunuchs and very old men. She was allowed no visitors and was even set to work on a daily spinning task as in her schoolgirl days. The island was off the Campanian coast. It was a very small one and Livia purposely increased her sufferings by keeping the same guards there year after year without relief; they naturally blamed her for their banishment in that confined and unhealthy spot. The one person who comes well out of this ugly story is Julia's mother, Scribonia, whom it will be recalled Augustus had divorced in order to be able to marry Livia. Now a very old woman, who had lived in retirement for a number of years, she boldly went to Augustus and asked permission to share her daughter's banishment. She told him in Livia's presence that her daughter had been stolen from her as soon as born but that she had always worshipped her from a distance and, now that the whole world was against her darling, she wished to show what *true* mother's love was. And in her opinion the poor child was not to blame: things had been made very difficult for her. Livia laughed contemptuously but must have felt pretty uncomfortable. Augustus, mastering his emotion, signed that the request was granted.

Five years later, on Julia's birthday, Augustus asked Livia suddenly: 'How big is the island?'

'Which island?' asked Livia.

'The island ... where an unlucky woman is living.'

'Oh, a few minutes' walk from end to end, I believe,' Livia said with affected carelessness.

'A few minutes' walk! Are you joking?' He had thought of her as in exile on some big island, like Cyprus or Lesbos or Corfu. After a while he asked: 'What is it called?'

'It's called Pandataria!'

'What? My God, *that* desolate place? Oh, cruel! Five years on Pandataria!'

Livia looked at him severely and said: 'I suppose you want her back here at Rome?'

Augustus then went over to the map of Italy, engraved on a thin sheet of gold studded with small jewels to mark the cities, which hung on the wall of the room in which they were. He was unable to speak, but pointed to Reggio, a pleasant Greek town on the straits of Messina.

So Julia was sent to Reggio, where she was given somewhat greater liberty, and even allowed to see visitors – but a visitor had first to apply in person to Livia for permission. He had to explain what business he had with Julia, and fill in a detailed passport for Livia's signature, giving the colour of his hair and eyes and listing distinguishing marks and scars, so that only he himself could use it. Few cared to submit to these preliminaries. Julia's daughter Agrippina asked permission to go, but Livia refused out of consideration, she said, for Agrippina's morals. Julia was still kept under severe discipline and had no friend living with her, her mother having died of fever on the island.

Once or twice when Augustus was walking in the streets of Rome there were cries from the citizens: 'Bring your daughter back! She's suffered enough! Bring your daughter back!' This was very painful to Augustus. One day he made his police-guard fetch from the crowd two men who were shouting this out most loudly, and told them gravely that Jove would surely punish their folly by letting them be deceived and disgraced by their own wives and daughters. These demonstrations expressed not so much pity for Julia as hostility to Livia, whom everyone justly blamed for the severity of Julia's exile and for so playing on Augustus's pride that he could not allow himself to relent.

As for Tiberius on *his* comfortably large island, it suited him very well for a year or two. The climate was excellent, the food was good, and he had ample leisure for resuming his literary studies. His Greek prose style was not at all bad and he wrote several elegant silly elegiac Greek poems in imitation of such poets as Euphorion and Parthenius. I have a book of them somewhere. He spent much of his time in friendly disputation with the professors at the university. The study of classical mythology amused him and he made an enormous genealogical chart, in circular form, with the stems raying out from our earliest ancestor Chaos, the father of Father Time, and spreading to a confused perimeter thickly strewn with nymphs and kings and heroes. He used to delight in puzzling the mythological experts, while building up the chart, with questions like: 'What was the name of Hector's maternal grandmother?' and 'Had the Chimaera any male issue?' and then challenging them to quote the relevant verse from the ancient poets in support of their answer. It was, by the way, from a recollection of this table, now in my possession, that many years afterwards my nephew Caligula made his famous joke against Augustus: 'Oh, yes, he was my great-uncle. He stood in precisely the same relationship to me as the Dog Cerberus did to Apollo.' As a matter of fact, now that I consider the matter, Caligula made a mistake here, did he not? Apollo's great-uncle was surely the monster Typhoeus who according to some authorities was the father, and according to others the grandfather of Cerberus. But the only genealogical tree of the Gods is so confused with incestuous alliances – son with mother, brother with sister – that it may be that Caligula could have proved his case.

As a Protector of the People Tiberius was held in great awe by the Rhodians; and provincial officials sailing out to take up their posts in the East, or returning from there, always made a point of turning aside in their course and paying him their respects. But he insisted that he was merely a private citizen and deprecated any public honours paid to him. He usually dispensed with his official escort of yeomen. Only once did he exercise the judicial powers that his Protectorship carried with it: he arrested and summarily condemned to a month in gaol a young Greek who, in a grammatical debate where he was acting as chairman, tried to defy his authority as such. He kept himself in good condition by riding and taking part in the sports at the gymnasium, and was in close touch with affairs at Rome – he had monthly news-letters from Livia. Besides his house in the island capital he owned a small villa some distance from it, built on a lofty promontory overlooking the sea. There was a secret path to it up the cliff, by which a trusted freedman of his, a man of great physical strength, used to conduct the disreputable characters – prostitutes, pathics, fortunetellers, and magicians – with whom he customarily passed his evenings. It is said that very often these creatures, if they had displeased Tiberius, somehow missed their footing on the return journey and fell into the sea far below.

I have already mentioned that Augustus refused to renew Tiberius's Protectorship when the five years expired. It can be imagined that this put him in a very awkward position at Rhodes, where he was personally unpopular: the Rhodians, seeing him deprived of his yeoman escort, his magisterial powers, and the inviolateness of his person, began to treat him first with familiarity and then with contumely. For example, one famous Greek professor of philosophy to whom he applied for leave to join his classes told him that there was no vacancy but that he could come back in seven days' time and see whether one had occurred. Then news came from Livia that Gaius had been sent to the East as Governor of Asia Minor. But though not far away, at Chios, Gaius did not come and pay Tiberius the expected visit. Tiberius heard from a friend that Gaius believed the false reports circulating at Rome that he and Livia were plotting a military rebellion and that a member of Gaius's suite had even offered, at a public banquet at which everyone was somewhat drunk, to sail across to Rhodes and bring back the head of 'The Exile': Gaius had told the fellow that he had no fear of 'The Exile': let him keep his useless head on his useless shoulders. Tiberius swallowed his pride and sailed at once to Chios to make his peace with his stepson, whom he treated with a humility that was much commented upon. Tiberius, the most distinguished living Roman, after Augustus, paying court to a boy not yet out of his teens, and the son of his own disgraced wife! Gaius received him coldly but was much flattered. Tiberius begged him to have no fears, for the rumours that had reached him were as groundless as they were malicious. He said that he did not intend to resume the political career which he had interrupted out of regard for Gaius himself and his brother Lucius: all that he wanted now was to be allowed to spend the rest of his life in the peace and privacy which he had learned to prize before all public honours.

Gaius, flattered at the chance of being magnanimous, undertook to forward a letter to Rome asking Augustus's permission for Tiberius to return there, and to endorse it with his own personal recommendation. In this letter Tiberius said that he had left Rome only in order not to embarrass the young princes, his stepsons, but that, now they were grown up and firmly established, the obstacles to his living quietly at Rome were no longer present; he added that he was weary of Rhodes and longed to see his friends and relations again. Gaius forwarded the letter with the promised endorsement. Augustus replied, to Gaius not to Tiberius, that Tiberius had gone away, in spite of the strong pleas of his friends and relations, when the State had most need of him; he could not now make his own terms about coming back. The contents of this letter became generally known and Tiberius's anxiety increased.

He had heard that the people of Nîmes in France had overthrown the statues erected there in memory of his victories, and that Lucius too had now been given false information against him which he was inclined to believe. He removed from the city and lived in a small house in a remote part of the island, only occasionally visiting his villa on the promontory. He no longer took any care of his physical condition or even of his personal appearance, rarely shaving, and going about in dressing-gown and slippers. He finally wrote a private letter to Livia, explaining his dangerous situation. He pledged himself, if she managed to secure permission for him to return, to be solely guided by her in every thing so long as they both lived. He said that he addressed her not so much as his devoted mother but as the true, though so far unacknowledged, helmsman of the Ship of State.

This was just what Livia wanted; she had purposely refrained hitherto from persuading Augustus to recall Tiberius. She wanted him to become as weary of inaction and public contumely A.D. 2 as he had previously been of action and public honour. She sent back a brief message to say that she had his letter safe, and that it was a bargain. A few months later Lucius died mysteriously at Marseilles, on his way to Spain, and while Augustus was still stunned by the shock Livia began working on his feelings by saying how much she had missed the support of her dear son Tiberius all these years; for whose return she had not until now ventured to plead. He had certainly done wrong, but had also certainly learned his lesson by now and his private letters to her breathed the greatest devotion and loyalty to Augustus. Gaius, who had endorsed that petition for his return, would, she urged, need a trustworthy colleague now that his brother was dead.

One evening a fortune-teller called Thrasyllus, by birth an Arab, came to Tiberius at his house on the promontory. He had been two or three times before and had made a number of very encouraging predictions, but none of these had yet been fulfilled. Tiberius, growing sceptical, told his freedman that if Thrasyllus did not entirely satisfy him this time he was to lose his footing on his way down the cliff. When Thrasyllus arrived, the first thing that Tiberius said was, 'What is the aspect of my stars to-day?' Thrasyllus sat down and made very complicated astrological calculations with a piece of charcoal on the top of a stone table. At last he pronounced, 'They are in a most unusually favourable conjunction. The evil crisis of your life is now finally passing. Henceforth you are to enjoy nothing but good fortune.'

'Excellent,' said Tiberius, dryly, 'and now what about your own?'

Thrasyllus made another set of calculations, and then looked up in real or pretended terror. 'Great Heavens!' he exclaimed, 'an appalling danger threatens me from air and water.'

'Any chance of circumventing it?' asked Tiberius.

'I cannot say. If I could survive the next twelve hours, my fortune would be, in its degree, as happy even as yours; but nearly all the malevolent planets are in conjunction against me and the danger seems all but unavoidable. Only Venus can save me.'

'What was that you said just now about her? I forget.'

'That she is moving into Scorpio, which is your sign, portending a marvellously happy change in your fortunes. Let me venture a further deduction from this all-important movement: you are soon to be engrafted into the Julian house, which, I need hardly remind you, traces direct descent from Venus, the mother of Aeneas. Tiberius, my humble fate is curiously bound up with your illustrious one. If good news comes to you before dawn tomorrow, it is a sign that I have almost as many fortunate years before me as yourself.'

They were sitting out on the porch and suddenly a wren or some such small bird hopped on Thrasyllus's knee and, cocking its head on one side, began to chirp at him. Thrasyllus said to the bird, 'Thank you, sister! It came only just in time.' Then he turned to Tiberius: 'Heaven be praised! That ship has good news for you, the bird says, and I am saved. The danger is averted.'

Tiberius sprang up and embraced Thrasyllus, confessing what his intentions had been. And, sure enough, the ship carried Imperial dispatches from Augustus informing Tiberius of Lucius's death and saying that in the circumstances he was graciously permitted to return to Rome, though for the present only as a private citizen.

As for Gaius, Augustus had been anxious that he should have no task assigned to him for which he was not fitted, and that the East should remain quiet during his governorship. Unfortunately the King of Armenia revolted and the King of Parthia threatened to join forces with him; which put Augustus in a quandary. Though Gaius had shown himself an able peace-time governor, Augustus did not believe him capable of conducting so important a war as this; and he himself was too old to go campaigning and had too many affairs to attend to at Rome, besides. Yet he could not send out anybody else to take over the Eastern regiments from Gaius because Gaius was Consul and should never have been allowed to enter upon the office if he was incapable of high military command. There was nothing to be done but to let Gaius be and hope for the best.

Gaius was lucky at first. The danger from the Armenians was removed by an invasion of their Eastern border by a wandering tribe of barbarians. The King of Armenia was killed while chasing them away. The King of Parthia, hearing of this and also of the large army that Gaius was getting together, then came to terms with him: to the great relief of Augustus. But Augustus's new nominee to the throne of Armenia, a Mede, was not acceptable to the Armenian nobles, and when Gaius had sent home his extra forces as no longer necessary they declared war after all. Gaius reassembled his army, and marched to Armenia, where a few months later he was treacherously wounded by one of the enemy generals who had invited him to a parley. It was not a serious wound. He thought little of it at the time and concluded the campaign successfully. But somehow he was given the wrong medical treatment, and his health, which from no apparent cause had been failing him for the last two years, became seriously affected: he lost all power of mental concentration. Fianlly he wrote to Augustus for permission to retire into private life. Augustus was grieved, but granted his plea. Gaius died on his way home. Thus A.D. 4 of Julia's sons only fifteen-year-old Postumus now remained, and Augustus was so far reconciled to Tiberius that, as Thrasyllus foretold, he engrafted him into the Julian house by adopting him, jointly with Postumus, as his son and heir.

The East was quiet now for a time, but when the war that had broken out in Germany again – I mentioned it in connexion with my schoolboy composition for Athenodorus – took a serious turn, Augustus made Tiberius army-commander and showed his renewed confidence in him by awarding him a ten years' Protectorship. The campaign was a severe one and Tiberius handled it with his old force and skill. Livia, however, insisted on his making frequent visits to Rome so as not to lose touch with political events there. Tiberius was keeping his part of the bargain with her and allowed himself to be led by her in everything.

Chapter 7

I WENT back in time a few years to tell of my Uncle Tiberius, but by following that history through until his adoption by Augustus, I have come out ahead of my own story. I shall try to devote these next chapters strictly to events that happened between my ninth and sixteenth years. Mostly it is a record of the betrothals and marriages of us young nobles. First Germanicus came 1 B.C. of age – September the 30th was his fourteenth birthday, but the coming-of-age celebrations always took place in March. As the custom was, he went out garlanded from our house on the Palatine, in the early morning, wearing his purple-bordered boy's dress for the last time. Crowds of children ran ahead, singing and scattering flowers, an escort of his noble friends walked with him, and an immense throng of citizens followed behind, in their degrees. The procession went slowly down the slope of the Hill, through the Market Place, where Germanicus was greeted uproariously. He returned the greeting in a short speech. Finally the procession moved on up the slope of the Capitoline Hill. At the Capitol, Augustus and Livia were waiting to greet him, and he sacrificed a white bull in the temple there to Capitoline Jove, the Thunderer, and put on his white manly-gown for the first time. Much to my disappointment I was not allowed to come too. The walk would have been too much for me and it would have created a bad impression if I had been carried in a sedan. All I witnessed of the ceremonies was his dedication, when he returned, of his boy's dress and ornaments to the household gods; and the scattering of cakes and pence to the crowd from the steps of the house.

A year later he married. Augustus did all he could by legislation to encourage marriage among men of family. The Empire was very big and needed more officials and senior army officers than the nobility and gentry were able to supply, in spite of constant recruiting to their ranks from the populace. When there were complaints from men of family about the vulgarity of these newcomers, Augustus used to answer testily that he chose the least vulgar he could find. The remedy was in their own hands, he said: every man and woman of rank should marry young and breed as large a family as possible. The steady decrease in the number of births and marriages in the governing classes became an obsession with Augustus.

On one occasion when the Noble Order of Knights, from whom the senators were chosen, complained of the severity of his laws against bachelors, he summoned the entire order into the Market Place for a lecture. When he had them assembled there he divided them up into two groups, the married and the unmarried. The unmarried were a very much larger group than the married and he addressed separate speeches to each group. He worked himself up into a great passion with the unmarried, calling them beasts and brigands and, by a queer figure of speech, murderers of their posterity. By this time Augustus was an old man with all the petulance and crankiness of an old man who has been at the head of affairs all his life. He asked them, had they an hallucination that they were Vestal Virgins? At least a Vestal Virgin slept alone, which was more than they did. Would they, pray, explain why instead of sharing their beds with decent women of their own class and begetting healthy children on them, they squandered all their virile energy on greasy slave-girls and nasty Asiatic-Greek prostitutes? And if he were to believe what he heard, the partner of their nightly bed-play was more often one of those creatures of a loathsome profession whom he would not even name, lest the admission of their existence in the City should be construed as a condonation of it. If he had his way, a man who shirked his social obligations and at the same time lived a life of sexual debauch should be subject to the same dreadful penalties as a Vestal who forgot her vows – to be buried alive.

As for us married men, for I was among them by this time, he gave us a most splendid eulogy, spreading out his arms as if to embrace us. 'There are only a very few of you, in comparison with the huge population of the City. You are far less numerous than your fellows over there, who are unwilling to perform any of their natural social duties. Yet for this very reason I praise you the more, and am doubly grateful to you for having shown yourselves obedient to my wishes and for having done your best to man the State. It is by lives so lived that the Romans of the future will become a great nation. At first we were a mere handful, you know, but when we took to marriage and begot children we came to vie with neighbouring states not only in the manliness of our citizens but in the size of our population too. We must always remember this. We must console the mortal part of our nature with an endless succession of generations, like torch-bearers in a race, so that through one another we may immortalize the one side of our nature in which we fall short of divine happiness. It was for this reason chiefly that the first and greatest God who created us divided the human race in two: He made one half of it male and the other half female and implanted in these halves mutual desire for each other, making their intercourse fruitful so that by continual procreation He might, in a sense, make even mortality immortal. Indeed, tradition says that some of the Gods themselves are male and others female, and that they are all interrelated by sexual ties of kinship and parentage. So you see that even among those beings who have really no need of such a device, marriage and the procreation of children have been approved as a noble custom.'

I wanted to laugh, not only because I was being praised for what had been forced on me greatly against my will – I will soon tell you about Urgulanilla, to whom I was married at this time – but because the whole business was such an utter farce. What was the use of Augustus addressing us in this way, when he was perfectly well aware that it was not the men who were shirking, as he called it, but the women? If he had summoned the women it is just possible that he might have accomplished something by talking to them in the right way.

I remember once hearing two of my mother's freedwomen discussing modern marriage from the point of view of a woman of family. What did she gain by it? they asked. Morals were so loose now that nobody took marriage seriously any longer. Granted, a few old-fashioned men respected it sufficiently to have a prejudice against children being fathered on them by their friends or household servants, and a few old-fashioned women respected their husbands' feelings sufficiently to be very careful not to become pregnant to any but them. But as a rule any good-looking woman nowadays could have any man to sleep with whom she chose. If she did marry and then tired of her husband, as usually happened, and wanted someone else to amuse herself with, there might easily be her husband's pride or jealousy to contend with. Nor in general was she better off financially after marriage. Her dowry passed into the hands of her husband, or her father-in-law as master of the household, if he happened to be alive; and a husband, or father-in-law, was usually a more difficult person to manage than a father, or elder brother, whose foibles she had long come to understand. Being married just meant vexatious household responsibilities. As for children, who wanted them? They interfered with the lady's health and amusement for several months before birth and, though she had a foster-mother for them immediately afterwards, it took time to recover from the wretched business of childbirth, and it often happened that her figure was ruined after having more than a couple. Look how the beautiful Julia had changed by obediently gratifying Augustus's desire for descendants. And a lady's husband, if she was fond of him, could not be expected to keep off other women throughout the time of her pregnancy, and anyway he paid very little attention to the child when it was born. And then, as if all this were not enough, foster-mothers were shockingly careless nowadays and the child often died. What a blessing it was that those Greek doctors were so clever, if the thing had not gone too far – they could rid any lady of an unwanted child in two or three days, and nobody be any the worse or wiser. Of course some ladies, even very modern ladies, had an old-fashioned hankering for children, but they could always buy a child for adoption into their husband's family, from some man of decent birth who was hard pressed by his creditors. ...

Augustus gave the Noble Order of Knights permission to marry commoners, even freedwomen, but this did not improve things very much. Knights, if they married at all, married for rich dowries, not for children or for love, and a freedwoman was not much of a catch; and besides knights, especially those recently raised to the order, had strong feelings against marrying beneath them. In families of the ancient nobility the difficulty was still greater. Not only were there fewer women to choose from in the correct degree of kinship, but the marriage ceremony was stricter. The wife was more absolutely in the power of the master of the household into which she married. Every sensible woman thought twice before committing herself to this contract, from which there was no escape but divorce; and after divorce it was difficult to recover the property that she had brought him as dowry. In other than anciently noble families, however, a woman could marry a man legally and yet remain independent, with control of her own property – if she cared to stipulate that she should sleep three nights of the year outside her husband's house; for this condition would interrupt his right over her as a permanent chattel. Women liked this form of marriage for obvious reasons, the very reasons for which their husbands disliked it. The practice started among the lowest families of the City but worked upwards, and soon became the rule in all except the anciently noble families. Here there was a religious reason against it. From these families the State priests were chosen, and by religious law a priest had to be a married man, married in the strict form, and the child of a strict-form marriage too. As time went on suitable candidates for priesthood were increasingly difficult to find. Finally there were vacancies in the colleges of Priests that could not be filled and something had to be done about it, so the lawyers found a way out. Women of rank were allowed, on contracting strict-form marriages, to stipulate that the complete surrender of themselves and property was 'as touching sacred matters' and that otherwise they enjoyed all the benefits of free marriage.

But that came later. Meanwhile the best that Augustus could do, apart from his legal penalization of bachelors and childless married men, was to put pressure on masters of households to marry off their young people (with instructions to increase and multiply) while they were still too young to realize to what they were being committed or to do anything but obey implicitly. To show a good example, therefore, all we younger members of the families of Augustus and Livia were betrothed and married at the earliest possible age. It may sound strange, but Augustus was a great-grandfather at the age of fifty-four and a great-great-grandfather before he died at the age of seventy-six; while Julia, as a result of her second marriage too, had a marriageable granddaughter before she was herself beyond child-bearing age. The generations somewhat overlapped in this way and the genealogical tree of the Imperial family became a rival in complexity to that of Olympus. This was not only because of the frequent adoptions and the marrying of members in closer degree of kinship than religious custom really permitted – for the Imperial family was by this time getting above the law; but because as soon as a man died his widow was made to marry again and always in the same small circle of relationship. I shall do my best now to straighten the matter out at this point, without being too long-winded.

I have mentioned Julia's children, Augustus's chief heirs since Julia herself had been banished and cut out of his will, namely, her three boys, Gaius, Lucius, and Postumus, and her two daughters, Julilla and Agrippina. The younger members of Livia's family were Tiberius's son, Castor, and his three first-cousins, namely, my brother Germanicus, my sister Livilla, and myself. But I must not forget Julia's grandchild – for Julilla had in the absence of any possible husband from Livia's family married a wealthy senator called Aemilius (her first-cousin through a previous marriage of Scribonia's) and had borne him a daughter called Aemilia. Julilla's marriage was unfortunate, for Livia grudged that any granddaughter of Augustus should marry any but a grandson of her own; but as you will soon see it did not trouble her for long, and meanwhile Germanicus married Agrippina, a handsome serious girl to whom he had as a matter of fact been long devoted. Gaius married my sister Livilla but died soon afterwards, leaving no children. Lucius, who had been betrothed to Aemilia but not yet married, was already dead.

On Lucius's death the question arose of a suitable match for Aemilia. Augustus had a shrewd notion that Livia intended Aemilia's husband to be no other than myself, but he had tender feelings for the child and could not bear the idea of her marrying a sickly creature like me. He resolved to oppose the match: for once, he promised himself, Livia should not have her way. It happened shortly after the death of Lucius that Augustus was dining with Medullinus, one of his oldest generals, who traced his descent from the dictator Camillus. Medullinus told him, smiling, when the wine cups had been filled several times, that he had a young granddaughter of whom he was very fond. She had suddenly shown a surprising advance in her literary studies and he understood that he had a young relative of his most honoured guests's to thank for this improvement.

Augustus was puzzled. 'Who on earth can that be? I have heard nothing of it. What is happening? Is it a secret love affair with a literary sauce?'

'Yes, something of the sort,' said Medullinus, grinning. 'I have spoken to the young fellow, and for all his physical misfortunes and capabilities I can't help liking him. He has a frank and noble nature, and as a young scholar he impresses me considerably.'

Augustus asked incredulously: 'What, you don't mean young Tiberius Claudius?'

'Yes, that's the one,' said Medullinus.

Augustus's face lit up with a sudden resolution and he asked rather more hastily than was decent: 'Listen, Medullinus, old friend, would you have any objection to him as your granddaughter's husband? If you agree to the match I shall be only too glad to arrange it. Young Germanicus is now nominally master of the household, but in matters like this he takes the advice of his elders. Well, it certainly isn't every girl who could overcome her physical repugnance to such a poor deaf, stammering cripple, and Livia and myself have had a natural delicacy in betrothing him to anyone. But if your granddaughter of her own free will – –'

Medullinus said: 'The child has spoken to me about this marriage herself and weighed matters very carefully. She tells me that young Tiberius Claudius is modest and truthful and kind-hearted; and that his lameness will never allow him to go to the wars and be killed – –'

'Or to run after other women,' laughed Augustus.

'And that his deafness is only on the one side, and as for his general health – –'

'I suppose the little minx has it worked out that he is not crippled in that part of the body for which honest wives show the most solicitude? Yes, why shouldn't he be capable of begetting perfectly healthy children on her? My old lame, whistling stud-stallion Bucephalus has sired more chariot-race winners than any horse in Rome. But, joking apart, Medullinus, yours is a very honourable house and my wife's family will be proud to be connected with it by marriage. Do you seriously mean that you approve the match?'

Medullinus said that the girl could do very much worse; quite apart from the unlooked-for honour to the family of being allied in marriage with the Father of the Country.

Now Medullina, the granddaughter, was my first love; and never, I swear, was there such a beautiful child seen in all the world. I met her one summer afternoon in the Gardens of Sallust, where I was taken by Sulpicius in the absence of Athenodorus, who was unwell. Sulpicius's daughter was married to Medullina's uncle, Furius Camillus, a distinguished soldier who was Consul six years later. When I first saw her it was with a shock of surprise, not only at her beauty, but at her sudden appearance, for she came up on my deaf side while I was reading a book, and when I raised my eyes, there she was standing over me laughing at my preoccupation. She was slender, with rich black hair, white skin, and very dark blue eyes, and all her movements were quick and birdlike.

'What's your name?' she asked, in a friendly voice.

'Tiberius Claudius Drusus Nero Germanicus.'

'Ye gods, all that! Mine's Medullina Camilla. How old are you?'

'Thirteen,' I said, mastering my stammer well.

'I'm only eleven, but I bet I can race you to that cedar tree and back.'

'Are you a champion runner, then?'

'I can beat any girl in Rome, and my elder brothers too.'

'Well, I'm afraid you win by default. I can't run at all, I'm lame.'

'Oh, you poor fellow. How did you come here, then? Hobble-hobbling all the way?'

'No, Camilla, in a sedan-chair, like a lazy old man.'

'Why do you call me by my last name?'

'Because it's the more appropriate one.'

'How do you make that out, clever?'

'Because among the Etruscans "Camilla" is what they call the young hunting priestesses dedicated to Diana. With a name like Camilla one is bound to be a champion runner.'

'That's nice. I never heard that. I shall make all my friends call me Camilla now.'

'And call me Claudius, will you? That's my appropriate name. It means a cripple. My family usually call me Tiberius, and that's inappropriate because the Tiber runs very fast.'

She laughed. 'Well then, Claudius, tell me what do you do all day if you can't run about with the other boys?'

'I read, mostly, and write. I have read scores of books this year already and it's only June. This one's Greek.'

'I can't read Greek yet. I only just know the alphabet. My grandfather is cross with me – I have no father, you know – he calls me lazy. Of course, I understand Greek when I hear it talked: we always have to talk Greek at meals and whenever visitors come. What's the book about?'

'It's part of Thucydides's history. This passage is about how a politician, a tanner called Cleon, began criticizing the generals who were blockading the Spartans in an island. He said that they were not doing their best and that if he were general he would bring back the whole Spartan force as captives within twenty days. The Athenians were so sick of his talk that they appointed him to command the forces himself.'

'That was a funny idea. What happened?'

'He kept his promise. He chose a good staff-officer and told him to fight in any way he liked so long as he won the battle, and the man knew his job; so within twenty days Cleon brought back to Athens a hundred and twenty Spartans of the highest rank.'

Camilla said: 'I've heard my uncle Furius say that the cleverest leader is one who chooses clever people to think for him.' Then she said: 'You must be very wise by now, Claudius.'

'I am supposed to be an utter fool and the more I read the more of a fool they think me.'

'I think you're very sensible. You tell things so nicely.'

'But I stammer. My tongue's a Claudian too.'

'Perhaps that's just nervousness. You don't know many girls, do you?'

'No,' I said, 'and you're the first one I have met who hasn't laughed at me. Couldn't we see each other now and then, Camilla? You couldn't teach me to run, but I could teach you to read Greek. Would you like that?'

'Oh, I'd love it. But will you teach me from interesting books?'

'From any book you like. Do you like history?'

'I think I like poetry best; there are so many names and dates to remember in history. My eldest sister raves about the love-poetry of Parthenius. Have you read any of it?'

'Some of it, but I don't like it. It's so artificial. I like *real* books.'

'So do I. But is there any Greek love-poetry that isn't artificial?'

'There's Theocritus. I like him very much. Get your aunt to bring you here to-morrow at the same time and I'll bring Theocritus and we'll begin at once.'

'You promise he's not boring?'

'No, he's very good.'

After this we used to meet in the garden nearly every day and sit in the shade together and read Theocritus and talk. I made Sulpicius promise not to tell anybody about it, for fear Livia should hear of it and stop my going. Camilla said one day that I was the kindest boy she had ever met and that she liked me better than all her brother's friends. Then I told her how much I liked her and she was very pleased and we kissed shyly. She asked whether there was any possible chance of our getting married. She said that her grandfather would do anything for her and that she would bring him along one day to the gardens and introduce us; but would my father approve? When I told her that I had no father and that it all rested with Augustus and Livia she became depressed. We had not talked much about families until then. She had never heard any good of Livia, but I said that it was possible she might consent, because she disliked me so much that I didn't think she cared very much what I did, so long as I didn't disgrace her.

Medullinus was a straight dignified old man and something of an historian, which made conversation between us easy. He had been my father's superior officer in his first campaign and was full of anecdotes of him, many of which I noted down gratefully for my biography. One day we began talking about Camilla's ancestor Camillus, and when he asked me what action of Camillus's I most admired I said: 'When the treacherous schoolmaster of Falerii decoyed the children under his charge to the walls of Rome, saying that the Falerians would offer any terms to get them back, Camillus disdained the offer. He had him stripped naked and tied his hands behind his back and gave the boys rods and scourges to whip the traitor back home. Wasn't that magnificent?' In reading this story I had pictured the schoolmaster as Cato, the boys as Postumus and myself, and so my enthusiasm for Camillus was a little mixed. But Medullinus was pleased.

When Germanicus was asked for his approval of our marriage he gave it gladly, for I had told him of my love for Camilla; and my uncle Tiberius raised no objection; and my grandmother Livia hid her anger as usual and congratulated Augustus on having been so quick to take Medullinus at his word – he must have been drunk, she said, to have approved the match, though indeed the dowry was small, and the honour of the alliance great for a man of his family. The house of Camillus had bred no men of outstanding capacity or reputation for many generations.

Germanicus told me that everything had been arranged and that the betrothal ceremony was to take place on the next lucky day – we Romans are very superstitious about days; nobody would dream, for instance, of fighting a battle or A.D. 3 marrying or buying a house on July 16, the day of the Allia disaster in Camillus's time. I could hardly believe my good fortune. I too had feared that I would be made to marry Aemilia, an ill-tempered affected little girl who copied my sister Livilla in teasing and making a fool of me whenever she came to us on a visit, which was often. The betrothal ceremony, Livia insisted, was to be as private as possible, because she could not trust me not to make a fool of myself if there was a crowd. I preferred it that way: I hated ceremonies. Only the necessary witnesses would attend, and there would be no feast, merely the usual ritual sacrifice of a ram whose entrails would then be examined to see whether the auspices were favourable. Of course they would be; Augustus, officiating as priest, in compliment to Livia, would see to that. Then a contract would be signed for the second ceremony to take place as soon as I came of age, with stipulations about the dowry. Camilla and I would join hands and kiss and then I would give her a gold ring and she would return to her grandfather's house – quietly, as she had come, without any train of singing attendants.

It hurts me even now to write about that day. I stood, very nervously, in my chaplet and clean robe waiting with Germanicus by the family altar for Camilla to appear. She was late. She was very late. The witnesses began to grow impatient and criticize the bad manners of old Medullinus in keeping them waiting on a ceremonial occasion like this. At last the porter announced Camilla's uncle Furius and he came in, ashy-white and wearing mourning garments. After a short speech of greeting and apology to Augustus and the rest of the company for his tardiness and ill-omened appearance he said: 'A great calamity has happened. My niece is dead.'

'Dead!' cried Augustus. 'What joke is this? We had a message only half an hour ago that she was already on her way here.'

'She died by poison. A crowd gathered at the door, as crowds will, when they heard that the daughter of the house was about to go to her betrothal. When my niece came out, the women all pressed admiringly around her. She gave a little cry as if someone had trod on her foot, but nobody thought anything of it, and she stepped into the sedan. We had not gone the length of the street before my wife, Sulpicia, who was with her, saw her lose colour and asked whether she felt frightened. "Oh, aunt," she said, "that woman stuck a needle into my arm and I feel faint." Those were her last words, my friends. She died a few minutes later. I hurried here as soon as I had changed my clothes. You will forgive me.'

I burst into tears and began to sob hysterically. My mother, furious at my disgraceful conduct, told one of the freedmen to lead me away to my room; where I remained for days, in a nervous fever, unable to eat or sleep. But for the comfort that dear Postumus gave me, I believe I should have lost my wits altogether. The murderess was never found and nobody was able to explain what motive she could have had. Livia reported to Augustus a few days later that according to reports which seemed reliable one of the women in the crowd had been a Greek girl who considered herself, no doubt groundlessly, to have been wronged by the girl's uncle and may have decided to revenge herself in this monstrous way.

When I was well again, or no iller than usual, Livia complained to Augustus that the death of young Medullina Camilla had happened most unfortunately. In spite of Augustus's pardonable sentiment against such a match, she feared that young Aemilia would, after all, now have to be betrothed to her impossible grandson: everybody, she said, had been surprised that she had not been matched with him before. So, as usual, Livia had her way. I was betrothed to Aemilia a few weeks later; and went through the ceremony without disgrace, because grief for Camilla had made me quite indifferent. But Aemilia's eyes were red when she arrived, from tears not of grief but of rage.

Now as to Postumus, poor fellow, he was in love with my sister Livilla, of whom he saw much because she had gone to live in the Palace when she married his brother Gaius, and was still there. It was generally expected that he would marry her, to renew the family connexion broken by his brother's death. Livilla was flattered by his passionate devotion. She flirted with him constantly, but had no love for him. Castor was her choice – a cruel, dissolute, handsome fellow who seemed made for her. I knew of the understanding between Livilla and Castor, which I had discovered accidentally, and this made me very unhappy on Postumus's behalf, the more so because Postumus had no suspicion of her character and I did not dare to tell him of it. Whenever Livilla and I and he were together she used to show me pretended affection, which touched Postumus as much as it angered me. I knew that as soon as he had gone she would begin her spiteful tricks again. Livia got wind of the intrigue between Livilla and Castor and kept a careful watch on them: one night she was rewarded by a message from a trusted servant that Castor had just climbed in at Livilla's window by the balcony. She put an armed guard on the balcony and then knocked at Livilla's door, calling her by name. After a minute or so Livilla opened the door, pretending to have been sound asleep; but Livia went inside and found Castor behind the curtain. She talked very plainly to them and appears to have made them understand that the matter would not be reported to Augustus, who would certainly banish them if it was, only on certain conditions; and that if these same conditions were strictly observed she would even arrange that they should marry. Not long after my betrothal to Aemilia, Livia so settled matters with Augustus that Postumus was betrothed, much to his grief, to a   A.D. 4 girl called Domitia, a first-cousin of mine on my mother's side; and Castor married Livilla. This was the year that Tiberius and Postumus were adopted as Augustus's sons.

Livia considered Julilla and her husband Aemilius as a possible obstacle to her designs. She was lucky enough to get evidence that Aemilius and Cornelius, a grandson of Pompey the Great, were plotting to remove Augustus from power and to divide up his offices between themselves and certain ex-Consuls, among them Tiberius, though Tiberius had not yet been sounded for his opinion. The plot never gathered much way, because the first ex-Consul whom Aemilius and Cornelius approached refused to have anything to do with it. Augustus did not punish either Aemilius or Cornelius by death or banishment. It had been a welcome proof of the strength of his own position that they could get so little support for their plot, and by sparing them he proved it still stronger. He merely called them to his presence and lectured them on their folly and ingratitude. Cornelius fell at his feet and thanked him abjectly for his clemency; and Augustus begged him not to make a further fool of himself. He was not a tyrant, he said, either to conspire against, or to worship for showing a tyrant's clemency: he was merely a State-official of the Roman Republic who had been temporarily granted wide powers for the better maintenance of order. Aemilius had evidently led him astray by misrepresentations. The best cure for this nonsense was for Cornelius to become Consul next year in due course and so satisfy his ambitions by attaining equal honour with himself; for there was no higher rank than Consul in Rome. (Theoretically this was true.) Aemilius was proud and remained standing; and Augustus told him that as his relative by marriage he ought to have shown more decency, and as an ex-Consul he ought to have shown more sense. He thereupon deprived him of all his honours.

An amusing feature of this case was that Livia won all the credit for Augustus's clemency by claiming to have pleaded, with a woman's tenderness, for the lives of the two conspirators; of whom, she said, Augustus had practically decided to make an example. She got his consent to the publication of a little book which she had written called *A Pillow Debate on Force and Gentleness*, full of intimate touches. Augustus is represented as restless and worried and unable to sleep. Livia begs him prettily to speak his mind and they go together over the question of the proper treatment of Aemilius and Cornelius.

Augustus explains that he does not wish to put them to death, yet he fears that he must do so, for if he lets them off it will be thought that he is afraid of them, and others will be tempted to conspire against him. 'To be always under the necessity of taking vengeance and inflicting punishments is a very painful position for any honourable man to be in, my dearest wife.'

Livia answers: 'You are quite right and I have a piece of advice to give you – that is, if you are willing to accept it and will not blame me for daring, though a woman, to suggest to you something which nobody else, even of your most intimate friends, would dare to suggest.'

Augustus says: 'Out with it, whatever it is.'

Livia answers: 'I shall tell you without hesitation, because I have an equal share in your good fortune and ill fortune and as long as you are safe I also have my part in reigning; whereas if you came to any harm, which the Gods forbid, that is the end of me too. ...' She advises forgiveness. 'Soft words turn away wrath, as harsh words excite wrath even in a gentle spirit: forgiveness will melt the most arrogant heart, as punishment will harden even the humblest. ... I do not mean by this that we must spare all criminals without distinction: for there is such a thing as an incurable and persistent depravity on which kindness is wasted. A man who offends in this way should be removed at once as a cancer in the body politic. But in the case of the rest, whose errors, committed wilfully or otherwise, are due to youth or ignorance or misapprehension, we should, I believe, merely rebuke them, or punish them in the mildest possible way. Let us make the experiment, therefore, starting with these very men.' Augustus applauds her wisdom and confesses himself persuaded. But note the reassurance to the world that on Augustus's death Livia's rule would end, and further note and remember the phrase 'incurable and persistent depravity'. My grandmother Livia was a sly one!

Livia now told Augustus that the proposed marriage between Aemilia and myself must be cancelled as a sign of Imperial displeasure with her parents; and Augustus was delighted to agree to this, because Aemilia had been complaining bitterly to him of her misfortune in having to marry me. Livia had little to fear from Julilla now, whom Augustus suspected of being an accomplice in her husband's schemes: but she would make sure of her too, before she had done. Meanwhile she had to pay a debt of honour to her friend Urgulania, a woman whom I have not yet mentioned but who is one of the most unpleasant characters in my story.

Chapter 8

URGULANIA was Livia's only confidante and bound to her by the strongest ties of interest and gratitude. She had lost her husband, a partisan of Young Pompey's, in the Civil Wars and with her infant son had been sheltered by Livia, then still married to my grandfather, from the brutality of Augustus's soldiers. Livia, on marrying Augustus, insisted that he should restore to Urgulania her husband's confiscated estates, and invite her to live with them as a member of the family. By Livia's influence – for in Augustus's name Livia could force Lepidus, the High Pontiff, to make whatever appointments she pleased – she was set in a position of spiritual authority over all the married noblewomen of Rome. I must explain that. Every year, early in December, these women had to attend an important sacrifice to the Good Goddess presided over by the Vestal Virgins, on the proper conduct of which would depend the wealth and security of Rome for the ensuing twelve months. No man was allowed to profane these mysteries on pain of death. Livia, who had put herself into the good graces of the Vestals by rebuilding their Convent, furnishing it in luxurious style, and winning them, through Augustus, many privileges from the Senate, suggested to the Chief Vestal that the chastity of some of the women who attended these sacrifices was not beyond suspicion. She said that the troubles of Rome during the Civil Wars might well have been due to the Good Goddess's anger at the lewdness of those who attended her mysteries. She suggested further that if a solemn oath were to be given to any woman who confessed to a lapse from moral strictness that her confession would not be reported to any ear of man, and thus not involve her in public disgrace, there would be a greater chance of the Goddess being served only by the chaste, and her anger appeased.

The Chief Vestal, a religiously-minded woman, approved of the idea but asked Livia's authority for this innovation. Livia told her that she had seen the Goddess in a dream only the night before, and that she had asked that, since the Vestals themselves were not experienced in matters of sex, a widow of good family should be appointed Mother Confessor for this very purpose. The Chief Vestal asked whether the sins confessed should pass unpunished. Livia replied that she could not have expressed an opinion had not the Goddess fortunately made a pronouncement on this point in the same dream: that the Mother Confessor would be empowered to prescribe expiatory penances and that the penances should be a matter of holy confidence between the criminal and the Mother Confessor. The Chief Vestal, she said, would be informed merely that such-and-such a woman was unfit to take part in the mysteries of this year; or that such-and-such had now performed her penance. This suited the Chief Vestal well, but she was afraid to suggest a name for fear that Livia would turn it down. Livia then said that the High Pontiff was obviously the man to make the appointment, and that if the Chief Vestal permitted her, she would explain matters to him and ask him to name a suitable person, after performing the necessary ceremonies to ensure a choice favourable to the Goddess. So Urgulania was appointed, and of course Livia did not tell Lepidus or Augustus the powers that the appointment carried. She spoke of it casually as a position of advisory assistant to the Chief Vestal in moral matters, 'the Chief Vestal, poor woman, being so unworldly'.

The sacrifice was customarily held at the house of a Consul, but now always at Augustus's palace, because he ranked above the Consuls. This was convenient for Urgulania, who made the women come into her room there (which was arranged in a way to inspire fear and truthfulness), bound them to tell the truth by the most frightful oaths, and when they had confessed, dismissed them while she considered the appropriate penance. Livia, who was in the room concealed behind a curtain, would then suggest one. The two got a great deal of amusement out of this game and Livia plenty of useful information and assistance in her plans.

As Mother Confessor in the service of the Good Goddess, Urgulania considered herself above the law. Later I shall tell how once, when summoned by a senator to whom she owed a large sum of money to appear before the magistrate in the Debtors' Court, she refused to obey the summons; and how, to avoid the scandal, Livia paid up. On another occasion she was subpoenaed as a witness in a Senatorial inquiry: having no intention of being cross-examined she excused herself from attending and a magistrate was sent to take her deposition down in writing instead. She was a dreadful old woman with a cleft chin and hair kept black with lamp-soot (the grey showing plainly at the roots), and she lived to a great age. Her son, Silvanus, had recently been Consul and was one of those whom Aemilius approached at the time of his plot. Silvanus went straight to Urgulania and told her about Aemilius's intentions. She passed the news on to Livia and Livia promised to reward them for this valuable information by marrying Silvanus's daughter Urgulanilla to me and so allying them with the Imperial family. Urgulania was in Livia's confidence and was pretty sure that my uncle Tiberius – not Postumus, though he was Augustus's nearest heir – would be the next Emperor: so this marriage was even more honourable than it seemed.

I had never seen Urgulanilla. Nobody had. We knew that she lived with an aunt at Herculaneum, a town on the slopes of Vesuvius, where old Urgulania had property, but she never came to Rome even on a visit. We concluded that she must be delicate. But when Livia wrote me one of her curt cruel notes, to the effect that it had just been decided at a family council that I should marry the daughter of Silvanus Plautius, and that this was a more appropriate match for me, considering my infirmities, than the two previously projected, I suspected that there was something much more seriously wrong with this Urgulanilla than mere ill-health. A cleft palate, perhaps, or a strawberry-mark across half her face? Something at any rate that made her quite unpresentable. Perhaps she was a cripple like myself. I wouldn't mind that. Perhaps she was a very nice girl really, but misunderstood. We might have a lot in common. Of course, it would not be like marrying Camilla, but it might at least be better than marrying Aemilia.

The day was chosen for our betrothal. I asked Germanicus about Urgulanilla, but he was as much in the dark as I was, and seemed a little ashamed of having consented to the marriage without making careful inquiries beforehand. He was very happy with Agrippina and wanted me to be happy too. Well, the day came, a 'lucky' one, and there I was again in my chaplet and clean gown again waiting at the family-altar for the bride to arrive. 'The third time's lucky,' said Germanicus. 'I am sure she's a beauty, really, and kind and sensible and just the sort for you.' But was she? Well, in my life I have had many cruel bad jokes played on me, but I think that this was the cruellest and worst. Urgulanilla was – well, in brief, she lived up to her name, which is the Latin form of Herculanilla. A young female Hercules she indeed was. Though only fifteen years old, she was over six foot three inches in height and still growing, and broad and strong in proportion, with the largest feet and hands I have ever seen on any human being in my life with the single exception of the gigantic Parthian hostage who walked in a certain triumphal procession many years later. Her features were regular but heavy and she wore an almost perpetual scowl. She stooped. She talked as slowly as my uncle Tiberius (whom, by the way, she resembled closely – there was even talk of her being really his daughter). She had no learning, wit, accomplishments, or any endearing qualities. And it is strange, but the first thoughts that struck me when I saw her were: 'This woman is capable of murder by violence' and 'I shall be very careful from the first to hide my repugnance to her, and give her no just cause to harbour resentment against me. For if once she comes to hate me, my life is not safe.' I am a pretty good actor, and though the solemnity of the ceremony was broken by smirks, whispered jokes, and repressed titters from the company, Urgulanilla had no cause to blame me for this indecorousness. After it was over the two of us were summoned into the presence of Livia and Urgulania. When the door was shut and we stood there facing them – myself nervous and fidgety, Urgulanilla massive and expressionless and clenching and unclenching her great fists – the solemnity of these two evil old grandmothers gave way, and they burst into uncontrollable laughter. I had never heard either of them laugh like that before and the effect was frightening. It was not decent healthy laughter but a hellish sobbing and screeching, like that of two old drunken prostitutes watching a torture or crucifixion. 'Oh, you two beauties!' sobbed Livia at last, wiping her eyes. 'What wouldn't I give to see you in bed together on your wedding night! It would be the funniest scene since Deucalion's Flood!'

'And what happened particularly funny on that famous occasion, my dear?' asked Urgulania.

'Why, don't you know? God destroyed the whole world with a flood, except Deucalion and his family, and a few animals that took refuge on the mountain tops. Haven't you read Aristophanes's *Flood*? It's my favourite play of his. The scene is laid on Mount Parnassus. Various animals are assembled, unfortunately only one of each kind, and each thinks himself the sole survivor of his species. So in order to replenish the earth somehow with animals they have to mate with one another in spite of moral scruples and obvious difficulties. The Camel is betrothed by Deucalion to the She-Elephant.'

'Camel and Elephant! That's a fine one!' cackled Urgulania. 'Look at Tiberius Claudius's long neck and skinny body and long silly face. And my Urgulanilla's great feet and great flapping ears, and little pig-eyes! Ha, Ha, Ha, Ha! And what was their offspring? Giraffe? Ha, Ha, Ha, Ha!'

'The play doesn't get that far. Iris comes on the stage for the messenger speech and reports another refuge of animals on Mount Atlas. Iris breaks off the nuptials just in time.'

'Was the Camel disappointed?'

'Oh, most bitterly.'

'And the Elephant?'

'The Elephant just scowled.'

'Did they kiss on parting?'

'Aristophanes does not tell. But I'm sure they did. Come on, Beasts. Kiss!'

I smiled foolishly, Urgulanilla scowled.

'Kiss, I say,' Livia insisted in a voice that meant that we had to obey.

So we kissed, and started the old women on their hysterics again. When we were outside the room again I whispered to Urgulanilla: 'I'm sorry. It's not my fault.' But she did not answer except to scowl more deeply than before.

There was still a year before we were actually to marry, for the family had decided that I should not come of age until I was fifteen and a half, and much might happen in that time. If only Iris would come!

But she didn't. Postumus had his troubles too: he had already come of age now and it was only a few months before Domitia would be of marriageable age. My poor Postumus, he was still in love with Livilla, though she was married. But before I continue with the story of Postumus I must tell of my meeting with the 'Last of the Romans'.

Chapter 9

HIS name was Pollio and I shall recall the exact circumstances of our meeting, which took place just a week after my betrothal to Urgulanilla. I was reading in the Apollo Library when along came Livy and a little brisk old man in the robe of a senator. Livy was saying: 'It seems, then, that we may as well abandon all hopes of finding it, unless perhaps ... Why, there's Sulpicius! *He'll* know if anyone does. Good morning, Sulpicius. I want you to do a favour for Asinius Pollio and myself. There's a book we want to look at, a commentary by a Greek called Polemocles on Polybius's *Military Tactics*. I seem to remember coming across it here once, but the catalogue does not mention it and the librarians here are perfectly useless.' Sulpicius gnawed his beard for a while and then said: 'You've got the name wrong. Polemocrates was the name and he wasn't a Greek, in spite of his name, but a Jew. Fifteen years ago I remember seeing it on that top shelf, the fourth from the window, right at the back, and the title tag had just "A Dissertation on Tactics" on it. Let me get it for you. I don't expect it's been moved since then.'

Then Livy saw me. 'Hullo, my friend, how goes it? Do you know the famous Asinius Pollio?'

I saluted them and Pollio said: 'What's that you're reading, boy? Trash, I'll be bound, by the shamefaced way you hide it. Young fellows nowadays read only trash.' He turned to Livy: 'I'll bet you ten gold pieces that it's some wretched "Art of Love", or Arcadian pastoral nonsense, or something of that sort.'

'I'll take the bet,' said Livy. 'Young Claudius is not that sort of young man at all. Well, Claudius, which of us wins?'

I said, stammering, to Pollio: 'I'm glad to say, sir, that you lose.'

Pollio frowned angrily at me: 'What's that you say? Glad that I *lose*, eh? Is that a proper way to speak to an old man like me, and a senator too?'

I said: 'I said it in all respect, sir. I am glad that you lose. I should not like to hear this book called trash. It's your own history of the Civil Wars and, if I may venture to praise it, a very fine book indeed.'

Pollio's face changed. He beamed and chuckled and pulled out his purse, pressing the coins on Livy. Livy, with whom he seemed on terms of friendly animosity – if you know what I mean – refused them with mock-serious insistence. 'My dear Pollio, I couldn't possibly take the money. You were quite right: these young fellows nowadays read the most wretched stuff. Not another word, please: I agree that I've lost the bet. Here are ten gold pieces of my own and I'm glad to pay them.'

Pollio appealed to me. 'Now, sir – I don't know who you are but you seem to be a lad of sense – have you read our friend Livy's work? I appeal to you, isn't that at least trashier writing than mine?'

I smiled. 'Well, at least it's easier to read.'

'Easier, eh? How's that?'

'He makes the people of Ancient Rome behave and talk as if they were alive now.'

Pollio was delighted. 'He has you there, Livy, on your weakest spot. You credit the Romans of seven centuries ago with impossibly modern motives and habits and speeches. Yes, it's readable all right, but it's not history.'

Before I record more of this conversation I must say a few words about old Pollio, perhaps the most gifted man of his day, not even excepting Augustus. He was now nearly eighty years old but in full possession of his mental powers and seemingly in better physical health than many a man of sixty. He had crossed the Rubicon with Julius Caesar and fought with him against Pompey, and served under my grandfather Antony, before his quarrel with Augustus, and had been Consul and Governor of Further Spain and of Lombardy, and had won a triumph for a victory in the

Balkans and had been a personal friend of Cicero's until he grew disgusted with him, and a patron of the poets, Virgil and Horace. Besides all this he was a distinguished orator and writer of tragedies. But he was a better historian than he was either tragedian or orator, because he had a love of literal truth, amounting to pedantry, which he could not square with the conventions of these other literary forms. With the spoils of the Balkan campaign he had founded a public library, the first public library at Rome. There were now two others: the one we were in and another called after my grandmother Octavia; but Pollio's was much better organized for reading purposes than either.

Sulpicius had now found the book, and after a word of thanks to him, they renewed their argument.

Livy said: 'The trouble with Pollio is that when he writes history he feels obliged to suppress all his finer, more poetical feelings, and make his characters behave with conscientious dullness, and when he puts a speech into their mouths he denies them the least oratorical ability.'

Pollio said: 'Yes, Poetry is Poetry, and Oratory is Oratory, and History is History, and you can't mix them.'

'Can't I? Indeed I can,' said Livy. 'Do you mean to say that I mustn't write a history with an epic theme because that's a prerogative of poetry, or put worthy eve-of-battle speeches in the mouths of my generals because to compose such speeches is the prerogative of oratory?'

'That is precisely what I do mean. History is a true record of what happened, how people lived and died, what they did and said; an epic theme merely distorts the record. As for your generals' speeches they are admirable as oratory but damnably unhistorical: not only is there no particle of evidence for any one of them, but they are inappropriate. I have heard more eve-of-battle speeches than most men and though the generals that made them, Caesar and Antony especially, were remarkably fine platform orators, they were all too good soldiers to try any platform business on the troops. They *spoke* to them in a conversational way, they did not orate. What sort of speech did Caesar make before the Battle of Pharsalia? Did he beg us to remember our wives and children and the sacred temples of Rome and the glories of our past campaigns? By God, he didn't! He climbed up on the stump of a pine-tree with one of those monster-radishes in one hand and a lump of hard soldiers' bread in the other, and joked, between mouthfuls. Not dainty jokes but the real stuff told with the straightest face: about how chaste Pompey's life was compared with his own reprobate one. The things he did with that radish would have made an ox laugh. I remember one broad anecdote about how Pompey won his surname The Great – oh, that radish! – and another still worse one about how he himself had lost his hair in the Bazaar at Alexandria. I'd tell you them both now but for this boy here, and but for your being certain to miss the point, not having been educated in Caesar's camp. Not a word about the approaching battle except just at the close: "Poor old Pompey! Up against Julius Caesar and his men! What a chance he has"!'

'You didn't put any of this in your history,' said Livy.

'Not in the public editions,' said Pollio. 'I'm not a fool. Still, if you like to borrow the private *Supplement* which I have just finished writing, you'll find it there. But perhaps you'll never bother. I'll tell you the rest: Caesar was a wonderful mimic, you know, and he gave them Pompey's dying speech, preparatory to falling on his sword (the radish again – with the end bitten off). He railed, in Pompey's name, at the Immortal Gods for always allowing vice to triumph over virtue. How they laughed! Then he bellowed: "And isn't it true, though Pompey says it? Deny it if you can, you damned fornicating dogs, you!" And he flung the half-radish at them. The roar that went up! Never were there soldiers like Caesar's. Do you remember the song they sang at his French triumph?

> "Home we bring the bald whoremonger,
> Romans, lock your wives away." '

Livy said: 'Pollio, my dear fellow, we were not discussing Caesar's morals, but the proper way to write history.'

Pollio said: 'Yes, that's right. Our intelligent young friend was criticizing your method, under the respectful disguise of praising your readability. Boy, have you any further charges to bring against the noble Livy?'

I said: 'Please, sir, don't make me blush. I admire Livy's work greatly.'

'The truth, boy! Have you ever caught him out in any historical inaccuracies? You seem to be a fellow who reads a good deal.'

'I would rather not venture ...'

'Out with it. There must be something.'

So I said: 'There *is* one thing that puzzles me, I confess. That is the story of Lars Porsena. According to Livy, Porsena failed to capture Rome, being first prevented by the heroic behaviour of Horatius at the bridge and then dismayed by the astounding daring of Scaevola; Livy relates that Scaevola, captured after an attempt at assassinating Porsena, thrust his hand into the flame on the altar and swore that three hundred Romans like himself had bound themselves by an oath to take Porsena's life. And so Lars Porsena made peace. But I have seen the labyrinth tomb of Lars Porsena at Clusium and there is a frieze on it of Romans emerging from the City gate and being led under a yoke. There's an Etruscan priest with a pair of shears cutting off the beards of the Fathers. And even Dionysius of Halicarnassus, who was very favourably disposed towards us, states that the Senate voted Porsena an ivory throne, a sceptre, a golden crown, and a triumphal robe; which can only mean that they paid him sovereign honours. So perhaps Lars Porsena *did* capture Rome, in spite of Horatius and Scaevola. And Aruns the priest at Capua (he's supposed to be the last man who can read Etruscan inscriptions) told me last summer that according to Etruscan records the man who expelled the Tarquins from Rome was not Brutus but Porsena, and that Brutus and Collatinus, the first two Consuls at Rome, were merely the City Stewards appointed to collect his taxes.'

Livy grew quite angry. 'I am surprised at you, Claudius. Have you no reverence for Roman tradition that you should believe the lies told by our ancient enemies to diminish our greatness?'

'I only asked,' I said humbly, 'what really happened then.'

'Come on, Livy,' said Pollio. 'Answer the young student. What really happened?'

Livy said: 'Another time. Let's keep to the matter in hand now, which is a general discussion of the proper way to write history. Claudius, my friend, you have ambitions that way. Which of us two old worthies will you choose as a model?'

'You make it very difficult for the boy, you jealous fellows,' put in Sulpicius. 'What do you expect him to answer?'

'The truth will offend neither of us,' answered Pollio.

I looked from one face to the other. At last I said, 'I think I would choose Pollio. As I am sure that I can never hope to attain

Livy's inspired literary elegance, I shall do my best to imitate Pollio's accuracy and diligence.'

Livy grunted and was about to walk off, but Pollio restrained him. Bottling down his glee as well as he could he said: 'Come, Livy, you won't grudge me one little disciple, will you, when you have them in regiments all over the world? Boy, did you ever hear about the old man from Cadiz? No, it's not dirty. In fact, it's rather sad. He came on foot to Rome, what to see? Not the temples or the theatres or the statues or the crowds or the shops or the Senate House. But a Man. What man? The man whose head is on the coins? No, no. A greater than he. He came to see none other than our friend Livy, whose works, it seems, he knew by heart. He saw him and saluted him and went straight back to Cadiz – where he immediately died; the disillusion and the long walk had been too much for him.'

Livy said: 'At any rate my readers are genuine readers. Boy, do you know how Pollio has built up his reputation? Well, he's rich and has a very large, beautiful house and a surprisingly good cook. He invites a great crowd of literary people to dinner, gives them a perfect meal and afterwards casually picks up the latest volume of his history. He says humbly, "Gentlemen, there are a few passages here that I am not quite sure about. I have worked very hard at them but they still need the final polish which I am counting on you to give them. By your leave. ...." Then he begins to read. Nobody listens very carefully. Everyone's belly is stuffed. "The cook's a genius," they are all thinking. "The mullet with piquant sauce, and those fat stuffed thrushes and the wild-boar with truffles – when did I eat so well last? Not since Pollio's last reading, I believe. Ah, here comes the slave with the wine again. That excellent Cyprian wine. Pollio's right: it's better than any Greek wine on the market." Meanwhile Pollio's voice – and it's a nice voice to listen to, like a priest's at evening sacrifice in summer – goes smoothly on and every now and then he asks humbly, "Is that all right, do you think?" And everyone says, thinking of the thrushes again, or perhaps of the little simnel cakes: "Admirable. Admirable, Pollio." Now and then he will pause and ask: "Now which is the right word to use here? Shall I say that the returning envoys *persuaded* or *excited* this tribe to revolt? Or shall I say that the account they gave of the situation *influenced* the tribe in its decision to revolt? Actually, I think, they gave an impartial account of what they had seen." Then a murmur goes up from the couches, "*Influenced*, Pollio. Use *influenced*!" "Thank you, friends," he says, "you are very kind. Slave, my penknife and pen! I'll change the sentence at once if you'll forgive me." Then he publishes the book and sends each of the diners a free copy. They say to their friends, chatting at the Public Baths: "Admirable book, this. Have you read it? Pollio's the greatest historian of our age; and not above asking advice in small points of style from men of taste, either. Why, this word *influenced* I gave him myself."'

Pollio said: 'That's right. My cook's too good. Next time I'll borrow yours and a few dozen bottles of your so-called Falernian wine and then I'll get really honest criticism.'

Sulpicius made a gesture of deprecation: 'Gentlemen, gentlemen, this is becoming personal.'

Livy was already going away. But Pollio grinned at the retreating back and said in a loud voice for his benefit:

'A decent fellow, Livy is, but there's one thing wrong with him. It's a disease called Paduanity.'

This made Livy stop and turn round. 'What's wrong with Padua? I won't hear a word against the place.'

Pollio explained to me. 'It's where he was born, you know. Somewhere in the Northern Provinces. There's a famous hotspring there, of extraordinary properties. You can always tell a Paduan. By bathing in the water of the spring or drinking it – and I'm told that they do both things simultaneously – Paduans are able to believe whatever they like and believe it so strongly that they can make anyone else believe it. That's how the city has got such a wonderful commercial reputation. The blankets and rugs they make there are really no better than any other sort, in fact rather inferior, because the local sheep are yellow and coarse-fleeced, but to the Paduans they are soft and white as goose-feathers. And they have persuaded the rest of the world that it's so.'

I said, playing up to him: 'Yellow sheep! That's a rarity. How do they get that colour, sir?'

'Why, by drinking the spring water. There's sulphur in it. All Paduans are yellow. Look at Livy.'

Livy came slowly towards us. 'A joke is a joke, Pollio, and I can take it in good part. But there's also a serious matter in question and that is, the proper writing of history. It may be that I have made mistakes. What historian is free from them? I have not, at least, told deliberate falsehoods: you'll not accuse me of that. Any legendary episode from early historical writings which bears on my theme of the ancient greatness of Rome I gladly incorporate in the story: though it may not be true in factual detail, it is true in spirit. If I come across two versions of the same episode I choose the one nearest my theme, and you won't find me grubbing around Etruscan cemeteries in search of any third account which may flatly contradict both – what good would that do?'

'It would serve the cause of the truth,' said Pollio gently. 'Wouldn't that be something?'

'And if by serving the cause of truth we admit our revered ancestors to have been cowards, liars, and traitors? What then?'

'I'll leave this boy to answer the question. He's just starting in life. Come on, boy, answer it!'

I said at random: 'Livy begins his history by lamenting modern wickedness and promising to trace the gradual decline of ancient virtue as conquests made Rome wealthy. He says that he will most enjoy writing the early chapters because he will be able, in doing so, to close his eyes to the wickedness of modern times. But in closing his eyes to modern wickedness hasn't he sometimes closed his eyes to ancient wickedness as well?'

'Well?' asked Livy, narrowing his eyes.

'Well,' I fumbled. 'Perhaps there isn't so much difference really between their wickedness and ours. It may be just a matter of scope and opportunity.'

Pollio said: 'In fact, boy, the Paduan hasn't made you see his sulphur fleeces as snow-white?'

I was very uncomfortable. 'I have got more pleasure from reading Livy than from any other author,' I repeated.

'Oh, yes,' Pollio grinned, 'that's just what the old man of Cadiz said. But like the old man of Cadiz you feel a little disillusioned now, eh? Lars Porsena and Scaevola and Brutus and company stick in your throat?'

'It's not disillusion, sir. I see now, though I hadn't considered the matter before, that there are two different ways of writing history: one is to persuade men to virtue and the other is to compel men to truth. The first is Livy's way and the other is yours: and perhaps they are not irreconcilable.'

'Why, boy, you're an orator,' said Pollio delightedly.

Sulpicius, who had been standing on one leg with his foot held in his hand, as his habit was when excited or impatient, and twisting his beard in knots, now summed up: 'Yes, Livy will never lack readers. People love being "persuaded to ancient virtue" by a charming writer, particularly when they are told in the same breath that modern civilization has made such virtue impossible of attainment. But mere truth-tellers – "undertakers who lay out the corpse of history" (to quote poor Catullus's epigram on the noble Pollio) – people who record no more than actually occurred – such men can only hold an audience while they have a good cook and a cellar of Cyprian wine.'

This made Livy really furious. He said, 'Pollio, this talk is idle. Young Claudius here has always been considered dull-witted by his family and friends, but I didn't agree with the general verdict until to-day. You're welcome to your disciple. And Sulpicius can perfect his dullness: there's no better teacher of dullness in Rome.' Then he gave us his Parthian shot: *Et apud Apollinem istum Pollionis Pollinctorem diutissime polleat.* Which means, though the pun is lost in Greek, 'And may he flourish long at the shrine of that Undertaker Apollo of Pollio's!' Then off he went, snorting.

Pollio shouted cheerfully after him: '*Quod certe pollicitur Pollio. Pollucibiliter pollebit puer.*' ('Pollio promises you he will; the boy will flourish mightily.')

When we two were alone, Sulpicius having gone off to find a book, Pollio began questioning me.

'Who are you, boy? Claudius is your name, isn't it? You obviously come of good family, but I don't know you.'

'I am Tiberius Claudius Drusus Nero Germanicus.'

'My God! But Livy's right. You're supposed to be a half-wit.'

'Yes. My family is ashamed of me because I stammer, and I'm lame and usually ill, so I go about very little in society.'

'But dull-witted? You're one of the brightest young fellows I have met for years.'

'You are very kind, sir.'

'Not at all. By God, that was a nasty hit at old Livy about Lars Porsena. Livy has no conscience, that's the truth. I'm always catching him out. I asked him once if he always had the same trouble in finding the brass tablets he wanted among the litter of the Public Record Office. He said, "Oh, no trouble at all." And it turned out that he has never once been there to confirm a single fact! Tell me, why were you reading my history?'

'I was reading your account of the siege of Perusia. My grandfather – Livia's first husband, you know – was there. I'm interested in that period and I'm getting together materials for a life of my father. My tutor Athenodorus referred me to your book: he said it was honest. My former tutor, Marcus Porcius Cato, had once told me that it was a tissue of lies, so I was the more ready to believe Athenodorus.'

'Yes, Cato wouldn't like the book. The Catos fought on the wrong side. I helped to drive his grandfather out of Sicily. But I think you are the first youthful historian I have ever met. History is an old man's game. When are you going to win battles like your father and grandfather?'

'Perhaps in my old age.'

He laughed. 'I don't see why an historian who has made a life-study of military tactics shouldn't be invincible as a commander, given good troops and courage – –'

'And good staff-officers,' I put in, remembering Cleon.

'*And* good staff-officers, certainly – though he's never actually handled a sword or shield in his life.'

I was bold enough to ask Pollio why he was often called 'The Last of the Romans'. He looked pleased at the question and replied: 'Augustus gave me the name. It was when he invited me to join him in his war against your grandfather Antony. I asked him what sort of a man he took me for: Antony had been one of my best friends. "Asinius Pollio," he said, "I believe that you're the last of the Romans. The title is wasted on that assassin, Cassius." "And if I'm the last of the Romans," I answered, "whose fault is that? And whose fault will it be when you've destroyed Antony, that nobody but myself will ever dare hold his head up in your presence or speak out of turn?" "Not mine, Asinius," he said apologetically, "it is Antony who has declared war, not I. And as soon as Antony is beaten I shall of course restore Republican government." "If the Lady Livia does not interpose her veto," I said.'

The old man then took me by the shoulders. 'By the way, I'll tell you something, Claudius. I'm a very old man, and though I look brisk enough I have reached the end. In three days I shall be dead; and I know it. Just before one dies there comes a strange lucidity. One speaks prophetically. Now listen! Do you want to live a long busy life, with honour at the end of it?'

'Yes.'

'Then exaggerate your limp, stammer deliberately, sham sickness frequently, let your wits wander, jerk your head, and twitch with your hands on all public or semi-public occasions. If you could see as much as I can see you would know that this was your only hope of safety and eventual glory.'

I said: 'Livy's story of Brutus – the first Brutus, I mean – may be unhistorical, but it's apt. Brutus pretended to be a half-wit, too, to be better able to restore popular liberty.'

'What's that? Popular liberty? You believe in that? I thought the phrase had died out among the younger generation.'

'My father and grandfather both believed in it – –'

'Yes,' Pollio interrupted sharply, 'that's why they died.'

'What do you mean?'

'I mean, that's why they were poisoned.'

'*Poisoned!* By whom?'

'Hm! Not so loud, boy. No, I'll not mention names. But I'll give you a sure token that I'm not just repeating groundless scandal. You're writing a life of your father, you say?'

'Yes.'

'Well, you'll see that you won't be allowed to get beyond a certain point in it. And the person who stops you – –'

Sulpicius came shuffling back at this point and nothing more was said of any interest except when I took my leave of Pollio and he drew me aside and muttered: 'Little Claudius, good-bye! But don't be a fool about popular liberty. That cannot come yet. Things must be far worse before they can be better.' Then he raised his voice: 'And one thing more. If, when I'm dead, you ever come across any important point in my histories that you find unhistorical I give you permission – I'll stipulate that you have the authority – to put the corrections in a supplement. Keep them up to date. Books when they grow out of date only serve as wrappings for fish.' I said that this would be an honourable duty.

Three days later Pollio died. He left me in his will a collection of early Latin histories, but they were withheld from me. My uncle Tiberius said that it was a mistake: that they were intended for him, our names being so similar. His stipulation about my having the authority to make corrections everyone treated as a joke; but I kept my promise to Pollio some twenty years later. I found that he had written very severely on the character of Cicero – a vain, vacillating, timorous fellow – and while not disagreeing with this verdict I felt it necessary to point out that he was not a traitor too, as Pollio had made him out. Pollio was relying on some correspondence of Cicero's which I was able to prove a forgery by Clodius Pulcher. Cicero had incurred Clodius's enmity by witnessing against him when he was accused of attending the sacrifice of the Good Goddess disguised as a woman-musician. This Clodius was another of the bad Claudians.

Chapter 10

WHEN I came of age, Tiberius had lately been ordered by Augustus to adopt Germanicus as his son, though he already had Castor as an heir, thus bringing him over from the Claudian into the Julian family. I now found myself head of the senior branch of the Claudians and in indisputable possession A.D. 6 of the money and estates inherited from my father. I became my mother's guardian – for she had never married again – which she felt as a humiliation. She treated me with rather more severity than before, though all business documents had to come to me for signature and I was the family priest. My coming of age ceremony contrasted curiously with that of Germanicus. I put on my manly-gown at midnight and without any attendants or procession was carried into the Capitol in a sedan, where I sacrificed and was then carried back to bed. Germanicus and Postumus would have come, but in order to call as little attention to me as possible Livia had arranged a banquet that night at the Palace which they could not be excused from attending.

When I married Urgulanilla, the same sort of thing happened. Very few people were aware of our marriage until the day after it had been solemnized. There was nothing irregular about the ceremony. Urgulanilla's saffron-coloured shoes and flame-coloured veil, the taking of the auspices, the eating of holy cake, the two stools covered with sheepskin, the libation I poured, the anointing by her of the doorposts, the three coins, my present to her of fire and water – everything was in order, except that the torchlight procession was omitted and that the whole performance was carried through perfunctorily and hurriedly and with bad grace. In order not to stumble over her husband's threshold the first time she enters, a Roman bride is always lifted over it. The two Claudians who had to do the lifting were both elderly men and unequal to Urgulanilla's weight. One of them slipped on the marble and Urgulanilla came down with a bump, pulling them with her in a sprawling heap. There is no wedding omen worse than that. And yet it would be untrue to say that it turned out an unhappy marriage; there was not enough strain between us to justify the term unhappy. We slept together at first because that seemed expected of us, and even occasionally had sexual relations – my first experience of sex – because that too seemed part of marriage, and not from either lust or affection. I was always as considerate and courteous to her as possible and she rewarded me by indifference, which was the best that I could hope from a woman of her character. She became pregnant three months after our marriage and bore me a son called Drusillus, for whom I found it impossible to have any fatherly feeling. He took after my sister Livilla in spitefulness and after Urgulanilla's brother Plautius in the rest of his character. Soon I shall tell you about Plautius, who was my moral exemplar and paragon, appointed by Augustus.

Augustus and Livia had a methodical habit of never coming to any decision on any important matter relating to the family or the State without recording in writing both the decision and the deliberations that led up to it, usually in the form of letters exchanged between each other. From the mass of correspondence left behind them on their deaths I have made transcripts of several which illustrate Augustus's attitude to me at this time. My first extract is dated three years before my marriage.

My dear Livia,

I wish to put on record a strange thing that happened to-day. I hardly know what to make of it. I was talking to Athenodorus and happened to say to him: 'I fear that tutoring young Tiberius Claudius must be rather a weary task. He seems to me to grow daily more miserable-looking and nervous and incapable.' Athenodorus said: 'Don't judge the boy too harshly. He feels most keenly the family's disappointment in him and the slights that he everywhere meets. But he's very far from incapable and, believe it or not, I get great pleasure from his society. You never heard him declaim, did you!' 'Declaim!' I said, laughing. 'Yes, declaim,' Athenodorus repeated. 'Now let me make a suggestion. You set a subject for declamation and in half an hour's time come and hear what he makes of it. But hide behind a curtain or you'll hear nothing worth listening to.' I set for a subject 'Roman Conquests in Germany' and, listening half an hour later behind that curtain, I have never been so astonished before in my life. He had his facts at his fingers' ends, his main headings were well chosen, and his detail set in proper relation and proportion to them; more than this, his voice was under control and *he did not stammer*. God strike me dead if it wasn't positively pleasant and instructive to listen to him! But how a fellow whose daily conversation is so hopelessly foolish can make a set speech, at short notice too, in so perfectly rational and even learned a style is beyond me. I slipped away, telling Athenodorus not to mention that I had been there or how surprised I had been, but feel obliged to tell you of the matter, and even to suggest that we might henceforth occasionally allow him to dine with us at night, when there are few guests there, on the understanding that he keeps his mouth shut and his ears open. If there is, after all, as I am inclined to think, some hope that he will eventually turn out a responsible member of the family, he ought to be gradually accustomed to mix with his social equals. We can't keep him shut away with his tutors and freedmen for ever. There is, of course, great division of opinion on the question of his mental capacities. His uncle Tiberius, his mother Antonia and his sister Livilla are unanimous in regarding him as an idiot. On the other side, Athenodorus, Sulpicius, Postumus, and Germanicus swear that he's as sensible, when he wishes, as any man, but that he's easily put off his balance by nervousness. As for myself, I repeat that I cannot make up my mind on the matter yet.

To which Livia replied:

My dear Augustus,

The surprise that you had behind that curtain was no greater and no less than the surprise we once had when the Indian Ambassador took the silk cloth off the gold cage which his master the High King had sent us, and we saw the bird Parrot for the first time with his emerald feathers and ruby necklet and heard him say, 'Hail Caesar, Father of the Country!' It was not the remarkableness of the phrase, for any little lisping child can say as much, but that a *bird* spoke it astonished us. And nobody but a fool would praise Parrot for his wit in coming out with the appropriate words, for he did not know the meaning of any one of them. The credit goes to the man who trained the bird, by incredible patience, to repeat the phrase, for, as you know, on other occasions he is trained to say other things; and in general conversation he talks the most arrant nonsense and we have to keep his cage covered to silence him. So with

Claudius, though it is hardly complimentary to Parrot, an undeniably handsome bird, to compare my grandson to him: what you heard was without the least doubt a speech that he had happened to learn by heart. After all, 'Roman Conquests in Germany' is a very obvious subject, and Athenodorus may well have made him word-perfect in half a dozen or more model declamations of the same sort. Mind you, I don't say that I'm not pleased to hear that he is so amenable to training: I am extremely pleased. It means, for instance, that we shall be able to coach him through his marriage-ceremony. But your suggestion about his supping with us is ridiculous. I refuse ever to eat in the same room as that fellow: it would give me indigestion.

As for the testimony in favour of his mental soundness, examine it. Germanicus as a child swore to his dying father to love and protect his infant brother: you know Germanicus's nobility of soul and that rather than betray this sacred trust he would make out the best case possible for his brother's wits, hoping that they might happen one day to improve. It is equally clear why Athenodorus and Sulpicius pretend to consider him improvable: they are very well paid to improve him and their appointments give them an excuse for hanging about the Palace and giving themselves airs as privy counsellors. As for Postumus, I have been complaining now for some months past, haven't I, that I cannot understand that young man at all. I consider that Death has been extremely unkind to take off his two talented brothers and leave us only him. He delights in starting an argument with his seniors, where no argument is necessary, the facts being clearly beyond dispute, merely to exasperate us and show his own importance as your single surviving grandson. His championship of Claudius's intelligence is a case in point. He was positively insolent to me the other day when I happened to remark that Sulpicius was wasting his time in tutoring the boy: he actually said that in his opinion Claudius had more penetration than most of his immediate relatives – which I suppose was intended to include me! But Postumus is another problem. For the moment the question is about Claudius; and I cannot, I repeat, have him dining in my company – for physical reasons, which I hope you will appreciate.

Livia.

He wrote to Livia a year later, when she was away for a few days in the country:

... As for young Claudius I shall take the advantage of your absence to invite him to supper every night. I admit that his presence still embarrasses me, but I do not think it good for him always to sup alone with his Sulpicius and Athenodorus. The talk he has with them is too purely bookish and, excellent fellows though they both are, they are not

ideal companions for a boy of his age and station. I do sincerely wish
that he would choose some young man of rank on whose bearing and
dress and behaviour he might model his own. But his timidity and diffi-
dence prevent this. He has a hero-worship for our dear Germanicus, but
he feels his own shortcomings so keenly that he would no more dare to
imitate him than I would go about in lion's skin and club and call myself Hercules. The poor creature is unfortunate; for in matters of importance (when his mind is not wool-gathering) the nobility of his heart
is clearly shown. ....

A third letter written shortly after my marriage, when I had just
been nominated as a priest of Mars, is also of interest:

My dear Livia,
    As you advised me, I have discussed with our Tiberius what we are
to do about young Claudius when these Games in honour of Mars are
held. Now that he has come of age and been appointed to the vacancy
in the College of the Priests of Mars we cannot put off our decision with
regard to his future much longer: we agree about that, do we not? If he
is sufficiently sound in mind and body to be eventually recognized as a
reputable member of the family – as I believe he is, or I would not have
adopted both Tiberius and Germanicus and left him as head of the senior
branch of the Claudian house – then obviously he should be taken in
hand and given the same opportunities for advancement as Germanicus.
I admit that I may still be mistaken – his recent improvement has not
been striking. But if we decide that, after all, the infirmities of his body
are bound up with a settled infirmity of mind, we must not give malicious
people a chance of making fun of him and us. I repeat, we must decide
pretty quickly once and for all about the lad – if only because we would
find it a continual trouble and embarrassment if we had to decide afresh
on every occasion that presented itself whether or not we considered
him able to undertake those duties of State for which his birth befits
him.
    Well, the immediate question is, what to do about him at these
Games. I would have no objection to his being put in charge of the
priests' mess-room, but on the strict understanding that he leaves everything to his brother-in-law, young Plautius Silvanus, and merely does
what he is told. He could learn a good deal in this way and there is no
reason for him to disgrace himself if he learns his lesson well. But of
course it is out of the question for him to sit with me in the President's
Box, along with the sacred Statue, for everybody in the theatre will constantly be looking in that direction and any oddities in his behaviour will
be commented upon.

Another problem is what to do with him at the Latin Festival. Germanicus is going to the Alban Hill with the Consuls to take part in the sacrifice and Claudius wishes, I understand, to go with him. But there again I am not sure whether he can be trusted not to make a fool of himself: Germanicus will be busy with his duties and unable to look after him all the time. And if he does go people will want to know what he's doing there in any case; they will ask why we have not appointed him to act as City Warden at Rome for the duration of the festival, in the absence of the magistrates – an honour which, you will recall, we have granted in turn to Gaius, Lucius, Germanicus, young Tiberius, and Postumus, as soon as they came of age, as their first taste of office. The best way out of the difficulty is to report him sick, because, of course, the City Wardenship is out of the question for him.

If you care to show Antonia this letter I have no objection: assure her that we shall soon decide one way or the other about her son. It is an incongruous position for her to be legally under his guardianship.

Augustus.

Except that it was my first public duty there is nothing remarkable to record about my management of the priests' mess. Plautius, a vain, natty little cock-sparrow of a man, did all the work for me and did not even trouble to explain the catering system and the rules of priestly precedence; even refused to answer my questions about such matters. All he did was to drill me in certain formal gestures and phrases which I was to use on welcoming the priests and at various stages of the meal; and forbade me to say another word. This was extremely uncomfortable for me because frequently I could have taken a useful part in the conversation, and my dumbness and subservience to Plautius gave a bad impression. The games themselves I did not see.

You will have noticed Livia's disparaging remarks about Postumus. From this time on they grow more and more frequent in her letters and Augustus, though at first he tries to stand up for his grandson, gradually admits disappointment in him. I think that Livia must have told Augustus a good deal more than appears in their correspondence for Postumus to have forfeited his favour so easily; but certain definite things appear. First, Tiberius is reported by Livia as complaining of an impudent reference by Postumus to the University of Rhodes. Then Cato is reported by her as complaining of Postumus's bad influence on the younger scholars in defying his discipline; then Livia produces Cato's confidential reports, saying that she has held them back so long in hope of a change. Next come worried references to his moroseness and sullenness – this was the time of Postumus's disappointment over Livilla and his grief for the death of his brother Gaius. Then there is a recommendation, when he comes of age, that the whole of his inheritance from his father Agrippa shall not be made over to him for a few years, because that 'might give him opportunities for even greater profligacy than he now indulges in!' When he is enrolled among the young men of military age he is posted to the Guards as a simple staff-lieutenant and given none of the extraordinary honours awarded to Gaius and Lucius. Augustus himself is of opinion that this is the safest course to take, for Postumus is ambitious: the same sort of uncomfortable situation must not arise as when the young nobles supported Marcellus against Agrippa or Gaius against Tiberius. Soon we read that Postumus takes this ill, telling Augustus that he does not want the honours on their own account but that their being withheld has been misinterpreted by his friends, who believe him under a cloud at the Palace.

Then follow more serious notes. Postumus has lost his temper with Plautius – but neither of the two will tell Livia later what the circumstances of their quarrel were – and has picked him up and thrown him into a fountain, in the presence of several men of rank and their lackeys. He is then called to account by Augustus, and shows no contrition, insisting that Plautius deserved his ducking for speaking in an insulting way to me; at the same time he complains to Augustus that his inheritance is being unjustly withheld. Soon he is reprimanded by Livia for his changed manner and for his surliness towards her. 'What's poisoned you?' she asks. He replies, grinning, 'Maybe you've been putting something in my soup.' When she demands an explanation of this extraordinary joke he replies, grinning still more vulgarly: 'Putting things in soup is an old trick among stepmothers.' Augustus soon after this has a complaint from Postumus's general that he does not mix with the other young officers but spends all his leisure time at the sea, fishing. He has earned the nickname 'Neptune' for this.

My duties as priest of Mars were not arduous and Plautius, who was a priest of the same college, was detailed to watch me whenever there was a ceremony. I was coming to hate Plautius. The insulting remark for which Postumus had thrown him into the fountain was one of many. He had called me a Lemur and said that it was only loyalty to Augustus and Livia that prevented him from spitting at me every time I asked him foolish and superfluous questions.

Chapter 11

THE year before I came of age and married had been a bad year for Rome. There was a series of earthquakes in the south of Italy which destroyed several cities. Little rain fell in the spring and the crops looked miserable all over the country: then just before harvest time there were torrential storms which beat down and spoilt what little corn had come to ear. The down- A.D. 5 pour was so violent that the Tiber carried away the bridge and made the lower part of the City navigable by boats for seven days. A famine seemed threatening and Augustus sent commissioners to Egypt and other parts to buy huge quantities of corn. The public granaries had been depleted because of a bad harvest the year before – though not so bad as this. The commissioners succeeded in buying a certain amount of corn, but at a high price and not really enough. There was great distress that winter, the more because Rome was overcrowded – its population had been doubled in the last twenty years; and Ostia, the port, was unsafe for shipping in the winter, so that grain-convoys from the East were unable to discharge their cargoes for weeks on end. Augustus did what he could to limit the famine. He temporarily banished all but householders and their families to country districts not nearer than 100 miles from the City, appointing a rationing-board composed of ex-Consuls, and prohibited public banquets, even on his own birthday. Much of the grain he imported at his own expense and distributed free to the needy. As usual, famine brought rioting, and rioting brought arson: whole streets of shops were set on fire at night by half-starved looters from the workers' quarters. Augustus organized a brigade of night-watchmen, in seven divisions, to prevent this sort of thing: this brigade proved so useful that it has never since been disbanded. But enormous damage had been done by the rioters. A new tax was imposed about this time to provide money for the German wars, and what with the famine, the fires, and the taxes, the commons began to get restless and openly discuss revolution. Threatening manifestos were pinned at night on the doors of public buildings. A huge conspiracy was said to be on foot. The Senate offered a reward for all information which would lead to the arrest of a ringleader and many men came forward to win it, informing against their neighbours; but this only made the confusion worse. Apparently no real conspiracy existed, only hopeful talk of conspiracies. Eventually corn began to come in from Egypt, where the harvest is much earlier than ours, and the tension relaxed.

Among the people removed from Rome during the famine were the sword-fighters. They were not numerous, but Augustus thought that if there were any civil disturbances they would be likely to play a dangerous part in them. For they were a desperate crew, some of them being men of rank who had been sold as slaves for debt – to purchasers who had agreed to let them earn the price of their freedom by sword-fighting. If a young gentleman ran into debt, as sometimes happened, through no fault of his own or from youthful thoughtlessness, his distant relations would save him from slavery, or Augustus himself would intervene. So these gentlemen sword-fighters were men whom nobody had regarded as worth saving from their fate, and who, becoming the natural leaders of the Gladiatorial Guild, were just the sort to head an armed rebellion.

When things improved they were recalled and it was decided to put everybody in a good humour by exhibiting a big public sword-fight and wild-beast hunt in the names of Germanicus and myself, in memory of our father. Livia wished to remind Rome of his great exploits with a view to calling attention to Germanicus, who resembled him so closely and who would soon, it was expected, be sent to Germany to help his uncle Tiberius, another famous soldier, win fresh conquests there. My mother and Livia contributed to the expenses of the show, the main burden of which, however, fell on Germanicus and me. It was considered, however, that Germanicus in his position needed more money than I did, so my mother explained to me that it would be only right for me to contribute twice as much as he did. I was only too glad to do what I could for Germanicus. But when I found out when it was all over what had been spent I was staggered; the show was planned regardless of cost, and besides the usual expenses of a sword-fight and wild-beast hunt we threw showers of silver to the populace.

In the procession to the amphitheatre Germanicus and I rode, by special decree of the Senate, in our father's old war-chariot. We had just offered a sacrifice to his memory, at the great tomb which Augustus had built for himself when he should come to die – and where he had interred our father's ashes, alongside those of Marcellus. We went down the Appian Way and under our father's memorial arch, with the colossal equestrian figure of him on it, which had been decorated with laurel in honour of the occasion. There was a north-east wind blowing and the doctors would not allow me to come without a cloak, so with one exception I was the only person present at the sword-fight – where I sat next to Germanicus as joint-president with him – who was wearing one. The exception was Augustus himself, who was sitting on the other side of Germanicus. He felt extremes of heat and cold severely and in the winter wore no less than four coats besides a very thick gown and a long waistcoat. There were some present who saw an omen in this similarity between my dress and Augustus's, further remarking that I had been born on the first day of the month named after him, and at Lyons, too, on the very day that he had dedicated an altar there to himself. Or at any rate, that was what they said they had said, many years after. Livia was in the Box too – a peculiar honour paid her as my father's mother. Normally she sat with the Vestal Virgins. The rule was for women and men to sit apart.

It was the first sword-fight I had been permitted to attend, and to find myself in the President's Box was all the more embarrassing for me on this account. Germanicus did all the work, though pretending to consult me when a decision had to be made, and carried it through with great assurance and dignity. It was my luck that this fight was the best that had ever been exhibited at the amphitheatre. As it was my first, however, I could not appreciate its excellence, having no background of previous displays to use for purposes of comparison. But certainly I have never seen a better since, and I must have seen nearly a thousand important ones. Livia wanted Germanicus to gain popularity as his father's son and had spared no expense in hiring the best performers in Rome to fight all out. Usually professional sword-fighters were very careful about hurting themselves and each other, and spent most of their energy on feints and parries and blows which looked and sounded Homeric but which were really quite harmless, like the thwacks that slaves give each other with stage-clubs in low-comedy. It was only occasionally, when they lost their temper with each other or had an old score to settle, that they were worth watching. This time Livia had got the heads of the Gladiatorial Guild together and told them that she wanted her money's worth. Unless every bout was a real one she would have the guild broken up: there had been too many managed fights in the previous summer. So the fighters were warned by the guild-masters that this time they were not to play kiss-in-the-ring or they would be dismissed from the guild.

In the first six combats one man was killed, one so seriously wounded that he died the same day, and a third had his shield-arm lopped off close to the shoulder, which caused roars of laughter. In each of the other three combats one of the men disarmed the other, but not before he had given such a good account of himself that Germanicus and I, when appealed to, were able to confirm the approval of the audience by raising our thumbs in token that his life should be spared. One of the victors had been a rich knight a year or two before. In all these combats the rule was that the antagonists should not fight with the same sort of weapon. It was sword against spear, or sword against battle-axe, or spear against mace. The seventh combat was between a man armed with a regulation army sword and an old-fashioned round brass-bound shield and a man armed with a three-pronged trout-spear and a short net. The sword-man or 'chaser' was a soldier of the Guards who had recently been condemned to death for getting drunk and striking his captain. His sentence had been commuted to a fight against this net-and-trident man – a professional from Thessaly, very highly paid, who had killed more than twenty opponents in the previous five years, so Germanicus told me.

My sympathies were with the soldier, who came into the arena looking very white and shaky – he had been in prison for some days and the strong light bothered him. But his entire company, who it appears sympathized very much with him, for the captain was a bully and a beast, shouted in unison for him to pull himself together and defend the company's honour. He straightened up and shouted, 'I'll do my best, lads!' His camp nickname, as it happened, was 'Roach', and this was enough to put the greater part of the audience on his side, though the Guards were pretty unpopular in the City. If a roach were to kill a fisherman that would be a good joke. To have the amphitheatre on one's side is half the battle to a man fighting for his life. The Thessalian, a wiry, long-armed, long-legged fellow, came swaggering in close behind him, dressed only in a leather tunic and a hard round leather cap. He was in a good humour, cracking jokes with the front-benches, for his opponent was an amateur, and Livia was paying him 1,000 gold pieces for the afternoon and 500 more if he killed his man after a good fight. They came together in front of the Box and saluted first Augustus and Livia and then Germanicus and me as joint-presidents, with the usual formula: 'Greetings, Sirs. We salute you in Death's shadow!' We returned the greetings with a formal gesture, but Germanicus said to Augustus: 'Why, sir, that chaser's one of my father's veterans. I know him well. He won a crown in Germany for being the first man over an enemy stockade.' Augustus was interested. 'Good,' he said, 'this should be a good fight, then. But in that case the net-man must be ten years younger, and years count in this game.' Then Germanicus signalled for the trumpets to sound and the fight began.

Roach stood his ground, while the Thessalian danced around him. Roach was not such a fool as to waste his strength running after his lightly armed opponent or yet to be paralysed into immobility. The Thessalian tried to make him lose his temper by taunting him, but Roach was not to be drawn. Only once when the Thessalian came almost within lunging distance did he show any readiness to take the offensive, and the quickness of his thrust drew a roar of delight from the benches. But the Thessalian was away in time. Soon the fight grew more lively; the Thessalian made stabs, high and low, with his long trident, which Roach parried easily, but with one eye on the net, weighted with small lead pellets, which the Thessalian managed with his left hand.

'Beautiful work!' I heard Livia say to Augustus. 'The best net-man in Rome. He's been playing with the soldier. Did you see that? He could have entangled him and got his stroke in then if he had wished. But he's spinning out the fight.'

'Yes,' said Augustus. 'I'm afraid the soldier is done for. He should have kept off drink.'

Augustus had hardly spoken when Roach knocked up the trident and jumped forward, ripping the Thessalian's leather tunic between arm and body. The Thessalian was away in a flash and as he ran he swung the net across Roach's face. By ill-luck a pellet struck Roach in the eye, momentarily blinding him. He checked his pace and the Thessalian, seeing his advantage, turned and knocked the sword spinning out of his hand. Roach sprang to retrieve it but the Thessalian got there first, ran with it to the barrier and tossed it across to a rich patron sitting in the front rank of the seats reserved for the Knights. Then he returned to the pleasant task of goading and dispatching an unarmed man. The net whistled round Roach's head and the trident jabbed here and there; but Roach was still undismayed, and once made a snatch at the trident and nearly got possession of it. The Thessalian had now worked him towards our Box to make a spectacular killing.

'That's enough!' said Livia in a matter-of-fact voice, 'he's done enough playing about. He ought to finish him now.' The Thessalian needed no prompting. He made a simultaneous sweep of his net round Roach's head and a stab at his belly with the trident. And then what a roar went up! Roach had caught the net with his right hand and, flinging his body back, kicked with all his strength at the shaft of the trident a foot or two from his enemy's hand. The weapon flew up and over the Thessalian's head, turned in the air and stuck quivering into the wooden barrier. The Thessalian stood astonished for a moment, then left the net in Roach's hands and dashed past him to recover the trident. Roach threw himself forward and sideways and caught him in the ribs, as he ran, with the spiked boss of his shield. The Thessalian fell, gasping, on allfours. Roach recovered himself quickly and with a sharp downward swing of the shield caught him on the back of his neck.

'The rabbit-blow!' said Augustus. 'I've never seen that done in an arena before, have you, my dear Livia? Eh? Killed him too, I swear.'

The Thessalian was dead. I expected Livia to be greatly displeased but all she said was: 'And served him right. That's what comes of underrating one's opponent. I'm disappointed in that net-man. Still, it has saved me that five hundred in gold, so I can't complain, I suppose.'

To crown the afternoon's enjoyment there was a fight between two German hostages who happened to belong to rival clans and had voluntarily engaged each other to a death-duel. It was not pretty fighting, but savage hacking with long sword and halberd: each wore a small highly ornamented shield strapped on the left forearm. This was an unusual manner of fighting, for the ordinary

German soldier does all his work with the slim-shafted, narrow-headed assegai: the broad-headed halberd and the long sword are marks of high rank. One of the combatants, a yellow-headed man over six feet tall, made short work of the other, cutting him about terribly before he gave him his final smashing blow on the side of the neck. The crowd gave him a great cheer, which went to his head, for he made a speech in a mixture of German and camp-Latin, saying that he was a renowned warrior in his country and had killed six Romans in battle, including an officer, before he had been given up as hostage by his jealous uncle, the tribal chief. He now challenged any Roman of rank to meet him, sword to sword, and make the lucky seventh for him.

The first champion who sprang into the ring was a young staff-officer of an old but impoverished family, called Cassius Chaerea. He came running to the Box for permission to take up the challenge. His father, he said, had been killed in Germany under that glorious general in whose memory this display was being held: might he piously sacrifice this boastful fellow to his father's ghost? Cassius was a finer fencer. I had often watched him on Mars Field. Germanicus consulted with Augustus and then with me; when Augustus gave his consent and I mumbled mine Cassius was told to arm himself. He went to the dressing-rooms and borrowed Roach's sword, shield, and body armour, for good luck and out of compliment to Roach.

Soon there began a far grander fight than any that the professionals had shown, the German swinging his great sword and Cassius parrying with his shield and always trying to get in under the German's guard – but the fellow was as agile as he was strong and twice beat Cassius to his knees. The crowd was perfectly silent, as if it were a religious performance they were watching, and nothing was heard but the clash of steel on steel and the rattle of shields. Augustus said, 'The German's too strong for him, I'm afraid. We shouldn't have permitted this. If Cassius gets killed it will create a bad impression on the frontier when the news gets there.'

Then Cassius's foot slipped in a blood pool and he fell over on his back. The German straddled over him with a triumphant smile on his face and then ... and then there was a roaring in my ears and a blackness before my eyes and I fainted away. The emotion of seeing men killed for the first time in my life, and then the combat between Roach and the Thessalian, in which I felt so strongly for Roach, and now this fight in which it seemed that it was I myself who was desperately battling for life with the German – it was too much for me. So I did not witness Cassius's wonderful recovery as the German lifted that ugly sword to crash in his skull, the quick upward thrust with the shield-boss at the German's loins, the sideways roll, and the quick decisive stab under the arm-pit. Yes, Cassius killed his man all right. Do not forget this Cassius, for he twice and three times plays an important part in this story. As for me, nobody noticed that I had fainted for some time, and when they did I was already coming to. They propped me up again in my place until the show had formally ended. To have been carried out would have been a disgrace for everyone.

The next day the Games continued, but I was not there. It was announced that I was ill. I missed one of the most spectacular contests ever witnessed in the amphitheatre, between an Indian elephant – they are much bigger than the African breed – and a rhinoceros. Experts betted on the rhinoceros, for although it was by far the smaller animal its hide was much thicker than the elephant's and it was expected to make short work of the elephant with its long sharp horn. In Africa, they were saying, elephants had learned to avoid the haunts of the rhinoceros, which holds undisputed sway in its own territory. This Indian elephant however – as Postumus described the fight to me afterwards – showed no anxiety or fear when the rhinoceros came charging into the arena, meeting him each time with his tusks and lumbering after him with clumsy speed when he retired discomfited. But finding himself unable to penetrate the thick armour of the beast's neck as he charged, this fantastic creature had recourse to cunning. He picked up with his trunk a rough broom made of a thorn bush which a sweeper had left on the sand and darted it in his enemy's face the next time he charged: he succeeded in blinding first one eye and then the other. The rhinoceros, distracted with rage and pain, dashed here and there in pursuit of the elephant and finally ran full tilt against the wooden barrier, going right through it and shattering his horn and stunning himself on the marble barrier behind. Then up came the elephant with his mouth open as if he were laughing and, first enlarging the breach in the wooden barrier, began trampling on his fallen enemy's skull, which he crushed in. He then nodded his head as if in time to music and presently walked quietly away. His Indian driver came running out with a huge bowl full of sweetmeats, which the elephant poured into his mouth while the audience roared applause. Then the beast helped the driver up on his neck, offering his trunk as a ladder, and trotted over to Augustus; where he trumpeted the royal salute – which these elephants are taught only to utter for monarchs – and knelt in homage. But, as I say, I missed this performance.

That evening Livia wrote to Augustus:

My dear Augustus,

Claudius's unmanly behaviour yesterday in fainting at the sight of two men fighting, to say nothing of the grotesque twitching of his hands and head, which at a solemn festival in commemoration of his father's victories were all the more shameful and unfortunate, has at least had this advantage, that we can now definitely decide once and for all that except in the dignity of priest – for the vacancies in the colleges must be filled *somehow* and Plautius has managed to coach him well enough in his duties – Claudius is perfectly unfit to appear in public. We must be content to write him off as a loss, except perhaps for breeding purposes, for I hear he has now done his duty by Urgulanilla – but I shan't be sure of that until I see the child, which may well be a monster like him.

Antonia has to-day abstracted from his study what appears to be a note-book of historical material which he has been collecting for a life of his father; with it she found a painfully composed introduction to the projected work, which I send you herewith. You will observe that Claudius has singled out for praise his dear father's one intellectual foible – that wilful blindness of his to the march of time, the absurd delusion that the political forms that suited Rome when Rome was a small town at war with neighbouring small towns could be re-established after Rome had become the greatest kingdom known since the days of Alexander. Look what happened when Alexander died and nobody could be found strong enough to succeed him as supreme monarch – why, the Empire simply fell to pieces. But I should not waste my time and yours in making historical platitudes.

Athenodorus and Sulpicius, with whom I have just had a conference, say that they had not seen this introduction until I showed it them and agree on its extreme inadvisability. They swear that they have never put any subversive ideas into his head, and suggest that he must have got them from old books. Personally I think that he inherited them – his grandfather had the same curious infirmity, you remember – and it is just like Claudius to have chosen that one weakness to inherit and to have refused any legacy of physical or moral soundness! Thank God for

Tiberius and Germanicus! There's no republican nonsense about *them*, so far as I know.

Naturally I am instructing Claudius that he must desist from his biographical labours, saying that if he disgraces his father's memory by fainting at the solemn Games given in his honour, he is obviously unfit to write his life: let him find some other employment for his pen.

Livia.

Ever since Pollio had told me about the poisoning of my father and grandfather I had been greatly perplexed. I could not make up my mind whether the old man had been talking senile nonsense, or joking, or whether he really knew something. Who but Augustus himself was sufficiently interested in the monarchy to have poisoned a nobleman merely because he believed in republican government? Yet I could not believe Augustus the murderer: poison was a mean way of killing, a slave's way, and Augustus would never have stooped to it. Besides, he was not a hypocrite and when he talked about my father it was always with admiration and affection. I consulted two or three recent histories, but they told me nothing that I had not already heard from Germanicus of the circumstances of my father's death.

It was only a couple of days before the Games that I happened to be talking to our porter, who had been my father's orderly throughout his campaigns. The honest fellow had been drinking rather too much, because my father's name was on everyone's lips at the time and his veterans had come in for a good deal of reflected glory. 'Tell me what you know of my father's death,' I said boldly. 'Were there any stories current in the camp that he met his death other than by accident?' He replied: 'I wouldn't say it to anybody, sir, but yourself, but I can trust you, sir. You're the son of your father and I never knew a man who didn't trust *him*. Yes, sir, there was a rumour going about and there was more in it than in most camp rumours. Your brave and noble father, sir, was poisoned, it's my sure belief. A certain Person, whose name I won't mention because you'll know it without my saying, was jealous of your father's victories and sent him an order of recall. That's not a story, or rumour, that's history. The order came when your father had broken his leg; not much of a damage either, and it was coming along well enough until that doctor fellow arrives from Rome, at the same time as the message, with his little bag of poisons in his hand. Who sent that doctor fellow? The same person who sent the message. Two and two's four, isn't it, sir? We orderlies wanted to kill that doctor fellow but he got back safe to Rome under special escort.'

When I read my grandmother Livia's note telling me to desist from writing my father's life, my perplexity increased. Pollio could surely not have meant to point to my grandmother as the murderess of her former husband and her son? It was unthinkable. And what could have been her motive? Yet when I came to consider the matter I could more easily believe that it was Livia than that it was Augustus.

That summer Tiberius needed men for his East German war, and levies were called for from Dalmatia, a province that had lately been quiet and docile. But when the contingent assembled it happened that the tax-collector was making his annual visit to those parts and exacting from the province not more than the sum fixed by Augustus, but more than it could easily pay. There were loud protests of poverty. The tax-collector exercised his right of seizing good-looking children from the villages which could not pay and carrying them off to be sold as slaves. The fathers of some of the children thus seized were members of the contingent and naturally made a great outcry. The entire force revolted, kill-their Roman captains. A Bosnian tribe rose in sympathy and soon the whole of our frontier provinces between Macedonia and the Alps were in a blaze. Fortunately Tiberius was able to conclude a peace with the Germans, at their instance not his own – and march against the rebels. The Dalmatians would not meet him in a pitched battle but broke up into small columns and carried on a skilful guerrilla warfare. They were lightly armed and knew the country well and when winter came even dared to raid Macedonia.

Augustus at Rome could not appreciate the difficulties with which Tiberius had to contend and suspected him of purposely delaying operations for some secret private ends which he could not fathom. He decided to send out Germanicus, with an army of his own, to spur Tiberius to action.

Germanicus, who was now in his twenty-third year, had just entered, five years before the customary age, on his first City magistracy. The military appointment caused surprise: everyone expected Postumus to be chosen. Postumus had no magisterial appointment, but was busy on Mars Field training the recruits

for this new army: he now bore the rank of regimental commander. He was three years younger than Germanicus, but his brother
Gaius had been sent to govern Asia at the age of nineteen and had
become a Consul in the year following. Postumus was by no
means less capable than Gaius, it was agreed, and, after all, he
was Augustus's single surviving grandson.

My own feelings on hearing the news, which had not yet been
made public, were torn between joy on Germanicus's account and
sorrow on Postumus's. I went to find Postumus and arrived at his
quarters in the Palace at the same time as Germanicus. Postumus
greeted us both affectionately and congratulated Germanicus on
his command.

Germanicus said: 'It is because of this that I have come, dear
Postumus. You know well enough that I am very proud and glad
to have been chosen, but military reputation is nothing to me if I
injure you by it. You are as capable a soldier as I am and as Augustus's heir you should obviously have been chosen. With your
consent I propose to go to him now and offer to resign in your
favour. I'll point out the misconstruction that the City will be sure
to put on his preference of me to you. It is not too late yet to make
the alteration.'

Postumus answered: 'Dear Germanicus, you are very generous
and noble, and for that reason I shall speak frankly. You are right
in saying that the City will treat this as a slight on me. The fact
that your duties as a magistrate are being interrupted by the appointment, while I am perfectly free to be sent, aggravates the
matter. But, believe me, the disappointment that I feel is amply
recompensed by this further proof you have given me of your
friendship; and I wish you a speedy recovery and every possible
success.'

Then I said: 'If you will both forgive me for expressing an
opinion, I think that Augustus has considered the situation more
carefully than you give him credit for having done. From something I overheard my mother saying this morning, I gather that he
suspects my uncle Tiberius of purposely prolonging the war. If he
were to send Postumus out with the new forces, after that old history of misunderstanding between my uncle and Postumus's
brothers, my uncle might be suspicious and offended. Postumus
would seem like a spy and a rival. But Germanicus is his adopted
son and would seem to be sent out merely as a reinforcement. I

don't think that there is more to be said than that Postumus will get his chance elsewhere, no doubt, and soon enough.'

They were both very pleased with this new view of the matter, which did credit to them both, and we all parted on the most friendly terms.

That same night, or rather in the early hours of the following morning, I was working late in my room on the upper storey of our house when I heard distant shouting and presently a slight scuffling noise from the balcony outside. I went to the door and saw a head appear over the top of the balcony and then an arm. It was a man in military dress, who threw his leg over the balcony and pulled himself up. I was paralysed for the moment, and the first wild thought that came into my head was: 'It's an assassin sent by Livia.' I was just going to shout for help when he said in a low voice: 'Hush! It's all right! I'm Postumus.'

'O Postumus! What a fright you gave me. Why do you come climbing in at this time of night like a burglar? And what's wrong with you? Your face is bleeding and your cloak's torn.'

'I've come to say good-bye, Claudius.'

'I don't understand. Has Augustus changed his mind? I thought the appointment had already been made public.'

'Give me a drink, I'm thirsty. No, I'm not going to the wars. Far from it. I've been sent fishing.'

'Don't talk in riddles. Here's the wine. Drink it quick and tell me what's wrong. Where are you going fishing?'

'Oh, to some small island. I don't think they've chosen it yet.'

'You mean ...?' My heart sank and my head swam.

'Yes, I'm being banished; like my poor mother.'

'But why? What crime have you committed?'

'No crime that can be officially mentioned to the Senate. I expect the phrase will be "incurable and persistent depravity". You remember that *Pillow Debate*?'

'O Postumus! Has my grandmother ...?'

'Listen carefully, Claudius, for time is short. I am under close arrest, but just now I managed to knock down two of my escort and break away. The Palace guard has been called out and every possible way of escape is blocked. They know I am somewhere in these buildings and they'll search every room. I felt I had to see you, because I want you to know the truth and not believe the charges that they have trumped up against me. And I want you to tell Germanicus everything. Send him my most loving greeting and tell him everything, exactly as I tell it you now. I don't care what anybody else thinks of me, but I want Germanicus and you to know the truth and think well of me.'

'I'll not forget a word, Postumus. Quick, tell it me from the beginning.'

'Well, you know that I've been out of favour with Augustus lately. I couldn't make out why, at first, but soon it was obvious that Livia was poisoning his mind against me. He is extraordinarily weak where she is concerned. Imagine living with her for nearly fifty years and still believing every word she says! But Livia was not the only one in this plot. Livilla was in it too.'

'Livilla! Oh, I am so sorry!'

'Yes. You know how much I loved her and how much I have suffered on her account. You hinted once, about a year ago, that she wasn't worth my troubling about and you remember how angry I was with you. I wouldn't talk to you for days. I am sorry now that I was angry, Claudius. But you know how it is when one is hopelessly in love with someone. I didn't explain to you then that just before she married Castor she told me that Livia had forced the marriage on her and that really she loved only me. I believed her. Why shouldn't I have believed her? I hoped that one day something would happen to Castor and she and I would be free to marry. That's been in my mind day and night ever since. This afternoon, just after seeing you, I was sitting with her and Castor in the grape-arbour by the big carp-pool. He began taunting me. I realize now that the whole thing had been carefully rehearsed beforehand between them. The first thing he said was: "So Germanicus has been preferred to you, eh?" I told him that I considered it a wise appointment and that I had just congratulated Germanicus. Then he said in a jeering way: "So it has your princely approval, has it? By the way, do you still expect to succeed your grandfather as Emperor?" I kept my temper for Livilla's sake, but said that I did not think it decent to discuss the succession while Augustus was still alive and in full possession of his faculties. Then I asked him ironically whether he was offering himself as a rival candidate. He said, with an unpleasant smile: "Well, if I did, I expect I would have more chance of success than you. I usually get what I want. I use my brains. I won Livilla by using my brains. It makes me laugh when I think how easily I persuaded Augustus that you weren't a suitable husband for her. Perhaps I'll get other things I want too, that way. Who knows?" This made me really hot. I asked him whether he meant that he had been telling lies about me. He said, "Why not? I wanted Livilla, and that's how I got her." Then I turned to Livilla and asked her whether she had known about this. She pretended to be indignant and said that she knew nothing about it at all, but that she believed Castor capable of any crooked dealing. She forced out a tear or two and said that Castor was rotten through and through and that nobody could guess how much she had suffered from him, and that she wished she were dead.'

'Yes, that's an old trick of hers. She can cry whenever it suits her. It takes everyone in. If I'd told you all that I knew of her, you'd have hated me perhaps for a time, but it would have saved you all this. Then what happened?'

'This evening she sent me a verbal message by her lady-in-waiting that Castor would probably be out all night on one of his usual debauches and that when I saw a light at her window shortly after midnight I was to come to her. A window would be left open immediately underneath the light and I was to climb in quietly. She wanted to tell me something very important. Of course, that could only mean one thing and it set my heart pounding. I waited in the garden for hours until I saw the light appear for a moment at her window. Then I found the window open below and climbed in. Livilla's maid was there and guided me upstairs. She showed me how to get into Livilla's room by climbing across from one balcony to another until I reached her window; this was to avoid the guard posted in the passage near her door. Well, I found Livilla waiting for me in her dressing-gown, with her hair down and looking infernally beautiful. She told me how cruelly Castor had behaved to her. She said that she owed him nothing as a wife, because on his own confession he had married her by fraud, and he had behaved most brutally to her. She flung her arms around me and I picked her up and carried her over to the bed. I was mad with desire for her. Then suddenly she began to scream and pummel me. I thought for the moment that she had gone mad, and put my hand over her mouth to quiet her. She struggled free, knocking over a little table with a lamp and a glass jar on it. Then she screamed 'Rape! Rape!' and then the door was battered down and in came the Palace guard with torches. Guess who was at their head?'

'Castor?'

'Livia. She brought us just as we were into Augustus's presence. Castor was with him, though Livilla had told me that he was dining at the other side of the City. Augustus dismissed the guard, and Livia, who had hardly said a word until then, began her attack on me. She told him that on his suggestion she had gone to my quarters to acquaint me privately with Aemilia's charges and ask me what explanation I had to offer.'

'Aemilia! Which Aemilia?'

'My niece.'

'I didn't know she had anything against you.'

'She hasn't. She was in the plot too. So Livia said that, not finding me in my quarters, she had made inquiries and had been told that the patrol had seen me sitting in the garden under a pear-tree on the south side. She sent a soldier to find me but he came back and said that I wasn't there but that he had something suspicious to report: a man climbing from one upper balcony to another just above the sundial. She knew whose rooms those were and was greatly alarmed. By good luck she arrived just in time. She had heard Livilla's screams for help: I had broken into her bedroom by way of the balcony and was on the point of raping her. The guards had burst down the door and pulled me away from "the terrified and half-naked young woman". She had brought me here at once, and Livilla as a witness. While Livia was telling her story that whore Livilla was sobbing and hiding her face. Her dressing-gown was ripped across – she must have torn it herself deliberately. Augustus called me a beast and a satyr and asked me whether I had gone mad. Of course, I couldn't deny that I had been in her bedroom or even that I had been making love to her. I said that I had come by invitation, and tried to explain things from the beginning, but Livilla began screaming, "It's a lie. It's a lie. I was asleep and he came in by the window and tried to rape me." Then Livia said, "And I suppose your niece Aemilia invited you to assault her too? You seem very popular with the young women." That was clever of Livia. I had to justify myself about Aemilia and leave the Livilla story. I told Augustus that I had dined with my sister Julilla the night before and that Aemilia was there, but that this was the first time I had seen the girl for six months. I asked on what occasion I was supposed to have assaulted her and Augustus said that I knew very well when it was – after dinner in the temporary absence of her parents, who were called away by an alarm of thieves – and that I had only been prevented by the return of her parents. The story was so ridiculous that, furious as I was, I could not help laughing; but this increased Augustus's rage. He was about to rise from his ivory chair and strike me.'

I said: 'I don't understand? Was there really an alarm of thieves?'

'Yes, and Aemilia and I were left alone for a few minutes, but the conversation was most blameless and her governess was there! We were discussing fruit-trees and garden-pests until Julilla and Aemilius came back and said that it was a false alarm. Julilla and Aemilius aren't in Livia's pay, you may be sure – they hate her – so Aemilia must have arranged it. I began to think quickly what spite she held against me, but I could remember nothing. Suddenly the explanation occurred to me. Julilla had told me as a secret that Aemilia was at last getting what she wanted: she was to marry Appius Silanus. You know that young dandy, don't you?'

'Yes. But I don't follow.'

'It's quite simple. I said to Livia: "Aemilia's reward for this lie is to be marriage to Silanus, isn't it? And what does Livilla get? Did you promise to poison her present husband and provide her with a handsomer one?" Once I had mentioned poison I knew that I was doomed. So I decided to say as much as I could while I had the opportunity. I asked Livia just how she had arranged the poisoning of my father and brothers and whether she favoured slow poisons or quick ones. Claudius, do you think that she killed them? I'm sure of it.'

'You dared ask her that? It's very probable. I think she poisoned my father and my grandfather, too,' I said, 'and I don't suppose they were her only victims. But I have no proof.'

'Neither have I, but I enjoyed accusing her of it. I shouted at the top of my voice so that half the Palace must have heard. Livia hurried from the room and called the guard. I saw Livilla smiling. I made a grab at her throat but Castor got between us and she escaped. Then I grappled with Castor and broke his arm and knocked out two of his front teeth on the marble floor. But I did not struggle with the soldiers. It would have been undignified. Besides, they were armed. Two of them held each of my arms as Augustus thundered abuse and threats at me. He said that I am to be banished for life to the most desolate island in his dominions and that only his unnatural daughter could have borne him so unnatural a grandson. I told him that in name he was Emperor of the Romans but that in fact he was less free than the girl slave of a drunken bawdmaster, and that one day his eyes would be opened to the unnatural crimes and deceits of his abominable wife. But meanwhile, I said, my love and loyalty to him remained unchanged.'

The hue and cry was now sounding through the lower storey of our house. Postumus said: 'I don't want to compromise you, dear Claudius. I must not be found in your room. If I had a sword now I'd use it. Better to die fighting than to rot away on an island.'

'Patience, Postumus. Yield now and your chance will come later. I promise you it will come. When Germanicus knows the truth he'll not rest until you're free again, and neither will I. If you get yourself killed it will only be a cheap triumph for Livia.'

'You and Germanicus can't explain away all that evidence against me. You'd only get yourself into trouble if you tried.'

'The opportunity will come, I say. Livia has had things her own way too long and she'll grow careless. She's bound to make a slip soon. She wouldn't be human if she didn't.'

'I don't think she *is* human,' Postumus said.

'And when Augustus suddenly realizes how he has been deceived, don't you think he'll be as merciless towards her as he was towards your mother?'

'She'll poison him first.'

'Germanicus and I will see that she doesn't. We'll warn him. Don't despair, Postumus. Everything will be all right in the end. I'll write you letters as often as I can, and send you books to read. I'm not afraid of Livia. If you don't get my letters you'll know that they are being held back. Look carefully at the seventh page of any sewn-sheet book that reaches you from me. If I have a private message for you I'll write in milk there. It's a trick that the Egyptians use. The writing is invisible until you warm it in front of a fire. Oh, listen to those doors banging. You must go now. They're at the end of the next corridor.'

Tears were in his eyes. He embraced me tenderly without another word and walked quickly to the balcony. He climbed over the edge, waved his hand in farewell, and slid down the old vine up which he had climbed. I heard him running away through the garden and a moment later cries and shouts from the guard.

*   *   *

I have no recollection at all of anything that happened for the next month or more. I was ill again: so ill that they talked of me as already dead. By the time that I began to recover, Germanicus was already at the wars and Postumus had been disinherited and banished for life. The island chosen for him was Planasia. It lay about twelve miles from Elba in the direction of Corsica and had not been inhabited within human memory. But there were some prehistoric stone huts on it which were converted into living quarters for Postumus and a barracks for the guard. Planasia was roughly triangular in shape, the longest side being about five miles long. It was treeless and rocky and only visited by the Elba boatmen in the summer when they·came to bait lobster-pots. By Augustus's orders this practice was discontinued, for fear Postumus might bribe someone and escape.

Tiberius was now Augustus's sole heir, with Germanicus and Castor to carry on the line after him – Livia's line.

A.D. 7

Chapter 12

IF I were to confine my account of the events of the next twenty-five years or more merely to my own performances it would not cost me much in paper and make very dull reading; but the later part of this autobiography, in which I figure more prominently, will only be intelligible if I continue here with the personal histories of Livia, Tiberius, Germanicus, Postumus, Castor, Livilla, and the rest, which are far from dull, I promise you.

Postumus was in exile, and Germanicus was at the wars, and only Athenodorus remained of my true friends. Soon he left me too, returning to his native Tarsus. I did not grudge his going because he went at the urgent appeal of two of his nephews there who begged him to help them free the city from the tyranny of its governor. They wrote that this governor had insinuated himself so cleverly into their God Augustus's good graces that it would need the testimony of a man like Athenodorus, in whose integrity their God Augustus had complete confidence, to persuade their God Augustus that the fellow's expulsion was justified. Athenodorus succeeded in ridding the city of this blood-sucker, but afterwards found it impossible to return to Rome as he had intended. He was needed by his nephews to help them rebuild the city administration on a firm foundation. Augustus, to whom he wrote a detailed report of his actions, showed his gratitude and confidence by granting Tarsus, as a personal favour to him, a five years' remission from the Imperial tribute. I corresponded regularly with the good old man until his death two years later at the age of eighty-two. Tarsus honoured his memory with an annual festival and sacrifice; at which the leading citizens took turns to read his *Short History of Tarsus* through from beginning to end, starting at sunrise and finishing after sunset.

Germanicus wrote to me occasionally but his letters were as brief as they were affectionate: a really good commander has no time for writing letters home to his family, his entire time between campaigns being spent in getting to know his men and officers, in studying their comfort, in increasing their military efficiency, and in gathering information about the disposition and plans of his enemy. Germanicus was one of the most conscientious commanders who ever served in the Roman army – and more beloved even than our father. I was very proud when he wrote asking me to make for him, as quickly and thoroughly as I could, a digest of all reliable reports that I could find in the libraries on the domestic customs of the various Balkan tribes against whom he was fighting, the strength and geographical situation of their cities, and their traditional military tactics and ruses, particularly in guerrilla warfare. He said that he could not get enough reliable information locally: Tiberius had been most uncommunicative. With Sulpicius's help and a small group of professional research-men and copyists working night and day I managed to get together exactly what he wanted and sent off a copy to him within a month of his asking for it. I was prouder than ever when he wrote to me not long afterwards for an edition of twenty copies of the book for circulation among his senior officers, for it had already proved of the greatest service to him. He said that every paragraph was clear and relevant, the most useful sections being those giving particulars of the secret extra-tribal military brotherhood against which, rather than against the tribes themselves, the war was being fought; and of the various sacred trees and bushes – a different sort was reverenced by each tribe – under whose protective shade the tribesmen were accustomed to bury their stores of corn, money, and weapons when they had to abandon their villages in a hurry. He promised to tell Tiberius and Augustus of my valuable services.

No public mention of this book was made, perhaps because if the enemy had heard of its existence they would have modified their tactics and dispositions. As it was, they believed that they were being constantly betrayed by informers. Augustus rewarded me unofficially by appointing me to a vacancy in the Augurs' College, but it was clear that he gave all the credit for the compilation to Sulpicius, though Sulpicius did not write a word – he merely found me some of the books. One of my chief authorities was Pollio, whose Dalmatian campaign had been a model of military thoroughness combined with brilliant intelligence-work. Though his account of local customs and conditions seemed nearly fifty years out of date, Germanicus found my extracts from it more helpful than any more recent campaign-history. I wished Pollio had been alive to hear that. I told Livy instead, who said rather crossly that he had never denied Pollio credit for writing competent military text-books; he had merely denied him the title of historian in the higher sense.

I must add to this, that if I had been more tactful I am pretty sure that Augustus would have commended me in his speech to the Senate at the conclusion of the war. But my references to his own Balkan campaigns had been fewer than they might have been had he written a detailed account of it, as Pollio did of his; or if the official historians had been less concerned with flattering their Emperor, and more with recording his successes and reverses in an unprejudiced, technical way. I could extract little or no useful matter from these eulogies, and Augustus in reading my book must have felt himself slighted. He identified himself so closely with the success of the war that during the last two campaigning seasons he moved from Rome to a town on the North-East frontier of Italy, to be as near as he could to the fighting; and as Commander-in-Chief of the Roman Armies he was continually sending Tiberius not very helpful military advice.

I was now working on an account of my grandfather's part in the Civil Wars: but I had not gone very far before I was once more stopped by Livia. I had only managed to complete two volumes. She told me that I was no more capable of writing a life of my grandfather than a life of my father and that I had behaved dishonestly in starting it behind her back. If I wanted a useful employment for my pen, I had better choose a subject that did not allow of so much misrepresentation. She offered me one: the reorganization of religion by Augustus since the Pacification. It was not an exciting subject, but had not been treated before in any detail and I was quite willing to undertake it. Augustus's religious reforms had been almost without exception excellent: he had revived several ancient societies of priests, built and endowed eighty-two new temples in Rome and its environs, re-edified numerous old ones that were falling into decay, introduced foreign cults for the benefit of visiting provincials, and reinstituted a number of interesting old public festivals that had been allowed to lapse one after the other during the civil disturbances of the previous half-century. I went into the subject very closely and completed my survey within a few days of the death of Augustus six years later. It was in forty-one volumes, averaging five thousand words apiece, but a great deal of this consisted of transcripts of religious decrees, nominal lists of priests, catalogues of gifts made to temple treasuries, and so on. The most valuable volume was the introductory one dealing with primitive ritual at Rome. Here I found myself in difficulties, because Augustus's ritualistic reforms were based on the findings of a religious commission which had not done its work properly. There had apparently been no antiquarian expert among the commissioners, so that a number of gross misunderstandings of ancient religious formulas had been embodied in the new official liturgies. Nobody who has not made a study of the Etruscan and Sabine languages is capable of interpreting the more ancient of our religious incantations; and I devoted a great deal of time to mastering the rudiments of both. At this time there were a few countrymen who still talked nothing but Sabine in the home and I persuaded two of them to come to Rome and provide Pallas, who was now acting as my secretary, with material for a short Sabine dictionary. I paid them well for this. Callon, the best of my other secretaries, I sent to Capua to collect material for a similar dictionary of the Etruscan language from

Aruns, the priest who had given me the information about Lars Porsena which had so pleased Pollio and so disgusted Livy. These two dictionaries, which later I enlarged and published, enabled me to clear up, to my own satisfaction, a number of outstanding problems of ancient religious worships; but I had learned to be careful and nothing that I wrote reflected on Augustus's scholarship or judgement.

I shall not spend any time on an account of the Balkan War, beyond saying that in spite of the wise generalship of my uncle Tiberius, the able assistance given him by my father-in-law Silvanus, and the dashing exploits of Germanicus it dragged on for three years. In the end the whole country was reduced, and practically made into a desert, because these tribes, men and women, fought with extraordinary desperation and only acknowledged defeat when fire, famine, and plague had more than halved the population. When the rebel leaders came to Tiberius to treat for peace he questioned them closely. He wanted to know why they had taken it into their heads to revolt in the first instance and then to offer so desperate a resistance. The chief rebel, a man called Bato, answered: 'You yourselves are to blame. You send as guardians of your flocks neither shepherds nor watch-dogs, but wolves.'

This was not exactly true. Augustus chose the governors of his frontier provinces himself and paid them a substantial salary and saw to it that they did not divert any of the Imperial revenues into their own pockets. Taxes were paid directly to them, no longer farmed out to unprincipled tax-collecting companies. Augustus's governors were never wolves, as had been most of the Republican governors, whose only interest in their provinces was how much they could squeeze out of them. Many of them were good watch-dogs and some were even honest shepherds. But it often happened that Augustus would unintentionally put the tax at too high a rate, discounting the distress caused by a bad harvest or a cattle plague or an earthquake; and rather than complain to him that the assessment was too high the governors would collect it to the last penny, even at the risk of revolt. Few of them took any personal interest in the people they were supposed to govern. A governor would settle in the Romanized capital town, where there were fine houses and theatres and temples and public baths and markets, and never think of visiting the outlying districts of his province. The real governing was done by deputies and by deputies of deputies, and there must have been a great deal of petty jack-in-office oppression by the smaller men: perhaps it was these whom Bato called wolves, though 'fleas' would have been a better word. There can be no doubt that under Augustus the provinces were infinitely more prosperous than under the Republic, and further that the home-provinces, which were governed by nominees of the Senate, were not nearly so well off as the frontier-provinces governed by Augustus's nominees. This comparison provided one of the few plausible arguments that I ever heard advanced against republican government; though based on the untenable hypothesis that the standard of personal morality among the leading men of an average republic is likely to be lower than the personal morality of an average absolute monarch and his chosen subordinates; and on the fallacy that the question of how the provinces are governed is more important than the question of what happens in the City. To recommend a monarchy on account of the prosperity it gives the provinces seems to me like recommending that a man should have liberty to treat his children as slaves, if at the same time he treats his slaves with reasonable consideration.

For this costly and wasteful war a great triumph was decreed by the Senate for Augustus and Tiberius. It will be recalled that now only Augustus himself or members of his family were to be permitted a proper triumph, other generals being awarded what were called 'triumphal ornaments'. Germanicus, though a Caesar, was granted only these ornaments, on technical A.D. 9 grounds. Augustus might have stretched the point, but he was so grateful to Tiberius for his successful conduct of the war that he did not wish to antagonize him by giving Germanicus equal honours with him. Germanicus was also raised a degree in magisterial rank, and allowed to become Consul several years before the customary age. Castor, though he had taken no part in the war, was granted the privilege of attending meetings of the Senate before becoming a member of it, and was also advanced a degree in magisterial rank.

At Rome the populace was looking forward with excitement to the triumph, which would mean largesse in corn and money and all sorts of good things: but a great disappointment was in store for them. A month before the date fixed for the triumph a terrible omen was observed – in Mars Field the temple of the War God was struck by lightning and nearly destroyed – and a few days later news came through from Germany of the heaviest military reverse suffered by Roman arms since Carrhae, I might even say since The Allia, not quite 400 years before. Three regiments had been massacred and all the conquests east of the Rhine had been lost at a stroke; it seemed that there was nothing to prevent the Germans crossing the river and laying waste the three settled and prosperous provinces of France.

I have already told of the crushing effect that this news had on Augustus. He felt it so strongly because he was not only officially responsible for the disaster, as the man charged by the Roman Senate and people with the security of all frontiers, but morally responsible as well. The disaster had been due to his imprudence in trying to force civilization on the barbarians too rapidly. The Germans conquered by my father had been gradually adapting themselves to Roman ways, learning the use of coinage, holding regular markets, building and furnishing houses in civilized style, and even meeting in assemblies that did not end, as their former assemblies had always ended, in armed battles. They were allies in name and if they had been allowed to forget their old barbarous ways gradually and to rely on the Roman garrison to protect them from their still uncivilized neighbours while they enjoyed the luxuries of provincial peace, they might perhaps in a couple of generations or less have grown as peaceful and docile as the French of Provence. But Varus, a connexion of mine, whom Augustus appointed Governor of Germany Across the Rhine, began treating them not as allies but as a subject race: he was a vicious man and showed little regard for the extraordinarily strong feelings that Germans have about the chastity of their womenfolk. Then Augustus needed money for the military treasury which the Balkan War had emptied. He imposed a number of new taxes from which the Across-Rhine Germans were not exempted. Varus advised him as to the paying capacity of the province and in his zeal assessed it too high.

There were in Varus's camp two German chieftains, Hermann and Siegmyrgth, who spoke Latin fluently and appeared to be completely Romanized. Hermann had commanded German auxiliaries in the previous war and his loyalty was unquestioned. He had spent some time in Rome and had actually been enrolled among the noble knights. These two often ate at Varus's table and were on terms of the most intimate friendship with him. They encouraged him to suppose that their compatriots were no less loyal and grateful to Rome for the benefits of civilization than they themselves were. But they were in constant secret communication with malcontent fellow-chieftains whom they persuaded for the time being to make no armed resistance to the Roman power and to pay their taxes with the greatest possible show of willingness. Soon they would be given the signal for mass-revolt. Hermann, whose name means 'warrior', and Siegmyrgth – or let us call him Segimerus – whose name means 'joyful victory', were too clever for Varus. Members of his staff were constantly warning him that the Germans were unnaturally well-behaved of recent months and that they were trying to disarm his suspicions before making a sudden rising; but he laughed at the suggestion. He said that the Germans were a very stupid race and incapable either of thinking out any such plan or of executing it without giving the secret away long before the time was ripe. Their docility was mere cowardice; the harder you hit a German the more he respected you: he was arrogant in prosperity and independence, but once defeated came crawling to your feet like a dog and kept to heel ever afterwards. He refused even to heed warnings given him by another German chieftain who had a grudge against Hermann and saw far into his designs. Instead of keeping his forces concentrated as he should have done in an only partially subdued country, he broke them up.

On the secret instructions of Hermann and Segimerus, outlying communities sent Varus requests for military protection against bandits and for escorts to convoys of merchandise from France. Next came an armed uprising at the Eastern extremity of the province. A tax-collector and his staff were murdered. When Varus gathered his available forces for a punitive expedition, Hermann and Segimerus escorted him for part of his journey and then excused themselves from further attendance, promising to assemble their auxiliary forces and come to his help, if needed, as soon as he sent for them. These auxiliaries were already under arms and in ambush a few days' journey ahead of Varus on his line of march. The two chieftains now sent word to the outlying communities to fall upon the Roman detachments sent for their protection and not to let a man escape.

No news came to Varus about this massacre because there were no survivors, and he was, in any case, out of touch with his head-quarters. The road he was following was a mere forest track. But he did not take the precaution of putting out an advance guard of skirmishers or flank-guards, but let the whole force – which con-tained a large number of non-combatants – string out in a dis-orderly column with as little precaution as if he had been within fifty miles of Rome. The march was very slow because he had con-stantly to be felling trees and bridging streams to enable the com-missariat carts to get across; and this gave time for huge numbers of tribesmen to join the ambushing forces. The weather suddenly broke, a downpour of rain lasting for twenty-four hours or more soaked the men's leather shields, making them too heavy for fighting, and putting the archers' bows out of commission. The clay track became so slippery that it was difficult to keep one's footing and the carts were constantly getting stuck. The distance between the head and the tail of the column increased. Then a smoke signal went up from a neighbouring hill and the Germans suddenly attacked from front, rear, and both flanks.

The Germans were no match for the Romans in fair fight and Varus had not much exaggerated their cowardice. At first they only dared to attack stragglers and transport drivers, avoiding hand-to-hand fighting but flinging volleys of assegais and darts from behind cover, and running back into the forest if a Roman so much as shook a sword and shouted. But they caused many casualties by these tactics. Parties led by Hermann, Segimerus, and other chieftains made blocks on the road by wheeling cap-tured carts together, breaking their wheels, and felling trees across the wreckage. They made several of these blocks and left tribes-men behind them to harass the soldiers when they tried to clear them away. This so delayed the men at the tail of the column that, afraid of losing touch, they abandoned all the carts which were still in their possession and hurried forward, hoping that the Ger-mans would be so busy plundering that they would not return to the attack for some time.

The leading regiment had reached a hill where there were not many trees because of a recent forest fire and here they formed up in safety and waited for the other two. They still had their trans-port and had only lost a few hundred men. The other two regi-ments were suffering much more heavily. Men got separated from their companies, and new units were formed of from fifty to 200 men apiece, each with a rear-guard, an advance-guard, and flank guards. The flank guards could only go forward very slowly because of the denseness and marshiness of the forest and frequently lost touch with their little units; the advance-guards lost heavily at the barricades and the rear-guards were constantly being assegaied from behind. When the roll was called that night Varus found that nearly a third of his force was killed or missing. The next day he fought his way into open country, but he had been obliged to abandon the remainder of his transport. Food was scarce and on the third day he had to plunge into the forest again. The casualties on the second day had not been severe, for a large number of the enemy were occupied plundering the wagons and carrying the loot away with them, but when the roll was called on the evening of the third day only a quarter of the original force was present to answer their names. On the fourth day Varus was still advancing, for he was too wrong-headed to admit defeat and abandon his original objective, but the weather, which had improved somewhat, now became worse than ever, and the Germans, who were accustomed to heavy rain, grew bolder and bolder as they saw resistance weakening. They came to closer quarters.

About noon Varus saw that all was over and killed himself rather than fall alive into the hands of the enemy. Most of the senior officers surviving followed his example, and many of the men. Only one officer kept his head – the same Cassius Chaerea who fought that day in the amphitheatre. He was commanding the rear-guard, composed of mountaineers from Savoy, who were more at home in a forest than most; and when news came by a fugitive that Varus was dead, the Eagles captured, and not 300 men of the main body left on their feet, he determined to save what he could from the slaughter. He turned his force about and broke through the enemy with a sudden charge. Cassius's great courage, something of which he managed to convey to his men, awed the Germans. They left this small resolute body of men alone and ran forward to make easier conquests. It stands as perhaps the finest soldiering feat of modern times that of the 120 men whom Cassius had with him when he turned about he managed after eight days' march through hostile country to bring eighty safely back, under the company banner, to the fortress from which he had set out twenty days previously.

It is difficult to convey an impression of the panic that reigned at Rome when the rumours of the disaster were confirmed. People started packing up their belongings and loading them on carts as if the Germans were already at the City gates. And indeed there was good reason for anxiety. The losses in the Balkan War had been so heavy that nearly all the available reserves of fighting men in Italy had been used up. Augustus was at his wits' end to find an army to send out under Tiberius to secure the Rhine bridge-heads, which apparently the Germans had not yet seized. Of Roman citizens who were liable for service few came forward willingly on the publication of the order calling them up; to march against the Germans seemed like going to certain death. Augustus then issued a second order that of those who did not offer themselves within three days every fifth man would be disenfranchised and deprived of all his property. Many hung back even after this, so he executed a few as an example and forced the remainder into the ranks, where some of them, as a matter of fact, made quite good soldiers. He also called up a class of men over thirty-five years of age and re-enlisted a number of veterans who had completed their sixteen years with the colours. With these and a regiment or two composed of freedmen, who were not normally liable for service (though Germanicus's reinforcements in the Balkan War had consisted largely of such), he built up quite an imposing force and sent each company off North on its own as soon as it was armed and equipped.

It was the greatest shame and grief to me that in this hour of Rome's supreme need I was incapable of serving as a soldier in her defence. I went to Augustus and begged to be sent out in some capacity where my bodily weakness would not be a disability: I suggested going as intelligence-officer to Tiberius and undertaking such useful tasks as collecting and collating reports on enemy movements, questioning prisoners, making maps, and giving special instructions to spies. Failing this appointment (for which I considered myself qualified because I had made a close study of the campaigns in Germany and I had learned to think in an orderly way and to direct clerks) I volunteered to act as Tiberius's Quartermaster-General: I would indent to Rome for necessary military supplies, and check and distribute them on their arrival at the base. Augustus seemed pleased that I had come forward so willingly and said that he would speak to Tiberius about my offer.

But nothing came of it. Perhaps Tiberius believed me incapable of any useful service; perhaps he was merely annoyed at my coming forward with this request when his son Castor had hung back and had persuaded Augustus to send him to raise and train troops in the South of Italy. However, Germanicus was in the same case as myself, which was some comfort. He had volunteered for service in Germany, but Augustus needed him at Rome, where he was very popular, to help him quell the civil disturbances which he feared might break out as soon as the troops had left the City.

Meanwhile the Germans hunted down all the fugitives from Varus's army and sacrificed scores of them to their forest-gods, burning them alive in wicker cages. The remainder they held as captives. (Some of them were later ransomed by their relatives at an extravagantly high price, but Augustus forbade them ever to enter Italy again.) The Germans also enjoyed a long succession of tremendous drinking-bouts on the captured wine, and quarrelled bloodily over the glory and plunder. It was a long time before they became active again and realized how little opposition they would meet if they marched to the Rhine. But as soon as the wine began to give out they attacked the weakly-held frontier-fortresses and one by one captured and sacked them. Only a single fortress put up a decent resistance: it was the one held by Cassius. The Germans would have occupied this as easily as the rest because the garrison was small, but Hermann and Segimerus were elsewhere and none of the rest understood the Roman art of siege-warfare with catapults, mangonels, the tortoise, and sapping. Cassius had a big supply of bows and arrows in his fortress and taught everyone, even the women and slaves, to use them. He successfully beat off several wild attacks on the gates and had great pots of boiling water always ready to pour on any Germans who attempted to scale the walls with ladders. The Germans were so busy trying to capture this place, where they expected to find rich plunder, that they did not push on to the Rhine bridge-heads which were held by inadequate guards.

News came of Tiberius's rapid approach at the head of his new army. Hermann at once rallied his forces, determined to capture the bridges before Tiberius could reach them. A detachment was left to invest the fortress, which was known to be badly supplied with provisions. Cassius, who got wind of Hermann's plans, decided to get away while there was still time. One stormy night he slipped out with the whole garrison, and managed to get past the first two enemy outposts before the crying of some of the children who were with him gave the alarm. At the third outpost there was hand-to-hand fighting and if the Germans had not been so anxious to get into the town to plunder it Cassius's party would have had no chance of survival. But he got clear somehow and half an hour later told his trumpeters to sound the 'advance at the double' to make the Germans believe that a relief force was coming up; so there was no pursuit. The troops at the nearest bridge heard the distant sound of Roman trumpets, for the wind was blowing from the east, and guessing what was happening sent out a detachment to escort the garrison back to safety. Cassius two days later succesfully held the bridge against a mass-attack of Segimerus's men; after which Tiberius's vanguard came up and the situation was saved.

The close of the year was marked by the banishment of Julilla, on the charge of promiscuous adultery – just like her mother Julia – to Tremerus, a small island off the coast of Apulia. The real reason for her banishment was that she was just about to bear another child, which if it were a boy would be a great-grandson of Augustus, and unrelated to Livia; Livia was taking no risks now. Julilla had one son already, but he was a delicate, timorous, slack-twisted fellow and could be disregarded. Aemilius himself provided Livia with grounds for the accusation. He had quarrelled with Julilla and now charged her in the presence of their daughter Aemilia with trying to father another man's child on him. He named Decimus, a nobleman of the Silanus family, as the adulterer. Aemilia, who was clever enough to realize that her own life and safety depended on keeping in Livia's good books, went straight to her and told what she had heard. Livia made her repeat the story in Augustus's presence. Augustus then summoned Aemilius and asked him whether it was true that he was not the father of Julia's child. It did not occur to Aemilius that Aemilia could have betrayed her mother and himself, so he assumed that the intimacy which he suspected between Julilla and Decimus was a matter of common scandal. He therefore held by his accusation, though it was founded rather on jealousy than on knowledge. Augustus took the child as soon as it was born and had it exposed on the mountain-side. Decimus went into voluntary exile and several other men accused of having been Julilla's lovers at one time or another followed him: among them was the poet Ovid whom Augustus, curiously enough, made the principal scapegoat as having also written (many years before) *The Art of Love*. It was this poem, Augustus said, that had debauched his granddaughter's mind. He ordered all copies of it found to be burned.

Chapter 13

AUGUSTUS was over seventy years of age. Until recently nobody had thought of him as an old man. But these new public and private calamities made a great change in him. His temper grew uncertain and he found it increasingly difficult to welcome chance visitors with his usual affability or to keep his patience at public banquets. He was even inclined to be short-tempered with Livia. Nevertheless he continued his work conscientiously as ever and even accepted another ten years' instalment of the monarchy. Tiberius and Germanicus when they were in the City undertook many tasks for him that normally he would have undertaken himself, and Livia worked harder than ever. During the Balkan War she had remained at Rome while Augustus was away and, armed with a duplicate seal of his and in close touch with him by dispatch-riders, had managed everything herself. Augustus was becoming more or less reconciled to the prospect of Tiberius's succeeding him. He judged him capable of ruling reasonably well, with Livia's help, and of carrying on his own policies, but he also flattered himself that everyone would miss the Father of the Country when he was dead and would speak of the Augustan Age as they spoke of the Golden Age of King Numa. In spite of his signal services to Rome, Tiberius was personally unpopular and would surely not gain in popularity when he was Emperor. It was a satisfaction to Augustus that Germanicus, being older than Castor, his brother by adoption, was Tiberius's natural successor, and tha Germanicus's infant sons, Nero and Drusus, were his own great-grandsons. Though Fate had decreed against his grandsons succeeding him he would surely one day reign again, as it were, in the persons of his great-grandchildren. For by this time Augustus had forgotten about the Republic, as almost everybody else had, and accepted the view that his forty years of hard and anxious service on Rome's behalf had earned him the right of appointing his Imperial successors, to the third generation, even, if it so pleased him.

When Germanicus was in Dalmatia I did not write to him about Postumus for fear of some agent of Livia's intercepting my letter, but I told him everything as soon as he returned from the war. He was greatly troubled and said that he did not know what to believe. I should explain that Germanicus's way was always to refuse to think evil of any person until positive proof of such evil should be forced on him, and, on the contrary, to credit everyone with the highest motives. This extreme simplicity was generally of service to him. Most people with whom he came in contact were flattered by his high estimate of their moral character and tended in their dealings with him to live up to it. If he were ever to find himself at the mercy of a downright wicked character, this generosity of heart would of course be his undoing; but on the other hand if any man had any good in him Germanicus always seemed to bring it out. So now he told me that he would not willingly believe either Livilla or Aemilia capable of such criminal baseness, though lately, he owned, he had been disappointed in Livilla. He also said that I had not made their possible motives clear except by dragging our grandmother Livia into it, which was plainly ridiculous. Who in his senses, he asked, suddenly indignant, could suspect Livia of inciting them to such evil? One might as easily suspect the Good Goddess of poisoning the City wells. But when I asked in reply whether he really believed Postumus guilty of two attempted rapes on successive nights, both excessively imprudent, or capable of lying to Augustus and us about them even if he had been guilty, he was silent. He had always loved and trusted Postumus. I pursued my advantage and made him swear by the ghost of our dead father that if ever he found the least piece of evidence to show that Postumus had been unjustly sentenced he would tell Augustus all that he knew about the case and force him to bring Postumus back and punish the liars as they deserved.

In Germany nothing much was happening. Tiberius held the bridges but did not attempt to cross the Rhine, not having confidence yet in his troops, whom he was busy knocking into shape. The Germans did not attempt to cross either. Augustus grew impatient again with Tiberius, and urged him to avenge Varus without further delay and win back the lost Eagles. Tiberius answered that nothing was nearer to his own heart but that his troops were not yet fit to attempt the task. Augustus sent out Germanicus when he had finished his term of magistracy, and Tiberius then had to show some activity; he was not really lazy, or a coward, only extremely cautious. He crossed the Rhine and over-ran parts of the lost province, but the Germans avoided a   A.D. 11 pitched battle; and Tiberius and Germanicus, both very careful not to fall into any ambush, did not do much more than burn a few enemy encampments near the Rhine and parade their military strength. There were a few skirmishes in which they came off well – some hundreds of prisoners were taken. They remained in this region until the autumn, when they recrossed the Rhine; and in the next spring the long-delayed triumph over the Dalmatians was celebrated at Rome, to which was added another for this German expedition, just to restore confidence. I must not fail here to award Tiberius credit for a generous action, to which Germanicus persuaded him: after displaying Bato, the captured Dalmatian rebel, in his triumph, he gave him his freedom and a large present of money and settled him comfortably at Ravenna. Bato deserved it: he had once chivalrously allowed Tiberius to escape from a valley where he was trapped with most of his army.

Germanicus was Consul now and Augustus wrote a special letter commending him to the Senate and the Senate to Tiberius. (By thus commending the Senate to Tiberius, instead of the other way about, Augustus showed both that he intended Tiberius as his Imperial successor, in authority over the Senate, and that he did not wish to utter any eulogy on him as he did on Germanicus.) Agrippina always accompanied Germanicus when he went to the wars, as my mother had accompanied my father. She did this chiefly for love of him but also because she did not want to stay alone in Rome and perhaps be summoned before Augustus on a trumped-up charge of adultery. She could not be sure how she stood with Livia. She was the typical Roman matron of ancient legend – strong, courageous, modest, witty, pious, fertile, and chaste. She already had borne four children to Germanicus and was to bear him five more.

Germanicus, though Livia's rule against my presence at her table still held, and though my mother showed no change of heart towards me either, brought me into the company of his noble friends whenever occasion offered. For his sake I was treated with a certain respect; but the family opinion of my capacities was known and Tiberius was understood to share it, so nobody took the trouble to cultivate my acquaintance. On Germanicus's advice I advertised that I would give a reading of my recent historical work and invited a number of prominent literary people to attend it. The book I had chosen to read was one at which I had worked very hard, and one which should have been very interesting to my audience – an account of the formulas used during ritual washing by the Etruscan priests, with a Latin translation in each case which threw light on many of our own lustral rites, the exact significance of which had been obscured by time. Germanicus read it through beforehand and showed it to my mother and Livia, who approved it, and then was generous enough to sit with me through a rehearsal of my reading. He congratulated me both on the work and on my delivery and I think must have spoken about it widely, for the room in which I was to give the reading was packed. Livia was not there, nor Augustus, but my mother attended, and Germanicus himself and Livilla.

I was in high spirits and not nervous at all. Germanicus had suggested that I should fortify myself with a cup of wine beforehand and I thought this good advice. There was a chair put for Augustus in case he should arrive and one for Livia, both very splendid ones – the chairs which were always reserved for them when they visited our house. When everyone had arrived and sat down the doors were shut and I began reading. I was getting along splendidly, conscious that I was not reading too fast or too slow or too loud or too soft, but just right, and that the audience, which had not expected much of me, was interested in spite of itself, when a most unlucky thing happened. A loud knock came at the door and then, when nobody opened it, another. Then there was a great rattle of the handle and in walked the fattest man I had ever seen in my life, dressed in a knight's robe, and carrying in his hand a large embroidered cushion. I stopped reading because I had come to a difficult and important passage and nobody was listening – all eyes were fixed on the knight. He recognized Livy and greeted him in a sing-song accent, which I learned later was that of Padua, and then made a general salutation to the rest of the company; which caused a lot of titters. He paid no especial attention to Germanicus as Consul or to my mother and myself as hosts. Then he looked round for a seat and saw Augustus's, but it seemed rather too narrow for him, so he took possession of Livia's. He put his cushion on it, gathered his gown about his knees and sat down with a grunt. And of course the chair, which was an ancient one from Egypt, part of the spoil of Cleopatra's palace, and of very delicate workmanship, collapsed with a crash.

Everyone except Germanicus and Livy and my mother and the graver members of the audience laughed very loudly; but when the knight had picked himself up and groaned and sworn and rubbed himself and had been escorted from the room by a freedman, there was an attentive silence and I tried to go on again. But I was almost hysterical with laughter. Perhaps it was the wine I had drunk, or perhaps it was because I had seen the expression on the fellow's face when the chair was giving under him, which nobody else had, because he was in the front row and I was the only person facing him; but at any rate I found concentration on the lustral rites of the Etruscans impossible. At first the audience sympathized with my amusement and even laughed with me, but when, struggling through another paragraph, very badly, I happened with the corner of my eye to see the chair which the knight had broken propped up insecurely on its splintered legs, I broke down again and the audience began to get impatient. To make matters still worse, when I had just fought hard with myself and got into my stride again, to the evident relief of Germanicus, the doors were thrown open and who should come in but Augustus and Livia! They walked grandly between the rows of chairs and Augustus sat down. Livia was about to do the same when she saw that something was amiss. She asked in a loud ringing voice: 'Who's been sitting in *my* chair?' Germanicus did his best to explain matters but she decided that she was being insulted. She went out. Augustus, looking uncomfortable, followed. Can anyone blame me for making a mull of the rest of my reading? The cruel god Momus must have been in that chair, for five minutes later the legs slid apart and once more the thing collapsed, a little gold lion's head breaking off from one arm, skidding across the floor and sliding under my right foot, which was slightly raised. I broke down again, choking and wheezing and guffawing.

Germanicus came over to me and implored me to control myself, but I could only pick up the lion's head and point helplessly at the chair. If I ever saw Germanicus annoyed with me it was then. It upset me very much to see him annoyed and sobered me instantly. But I had lost all self-confidence and began to stammer so badly that the reading came to a dismal end. Germanicus did his best by moving a vote of thanks for my interesting paper – regretting that an untoward accident had disturbed me half-way through and that in consequence of the same accident the Father of the country and the Lady Livia his wife had withdrawn their presences, and hoping that on a more auspicious day in the near future I might give a further reading. There was never so considerate a brother as Germanicus, or so noble a man. But I have not given a single public reading of my works since.

Germanicus came to me one day looking very grave. It was a long time before he could make up his mind to speak, but at last he said: 'I was talking to Aemilius this morning and the subject of poor Postumus happened to come up. He introduced it first by asking me what the precise charges against Postumus had been; and said, apparently quite ingenuously, that he understood that Postumus had attempted to violate two noblewomen, but that nobody seemed to know who they were. I looked hard at him when he said this, but could see that he was speaking the truth. So I offered to exchange my knowledge with his, but only if he promised to keep what I told him to himself. When I said that it was his own daughter who had charged Postumus with trying to outrage her, and in his own house, he was astonished and refused to believe it. He got very angry. He said Aemilia's governess had surely been with them all the time. He wanted to go to Aemilia and ask her if the story was true and if so, why this was the first he had heard of it; but I restrained him, reminding him of his promise. I mistrusted Aemilia. Instead I suggested that we should question the governess, but not so as to alarm her. So he sent for her and asked what conversation Aemilia and Postumus had had, during that alarm of thieves, on the last occasion he had dined with them. She looked blank at first, but when I asked "Wasn't it about fruit-trees?" she said "Yes, of course, about pests on fruit-trees." Aemilius then wanted to know whether any other conversation had taken place during his absence and she said that she believed not. She recalled that Postumus had been explaining new Greek methods for dealing with the pest called "blackamoor" and that she had been extremely interested because she knew about gardens. No, she said, she had not left the room for a moment. So next I went to Castor and casually introduced the subject of Postumus. You remember that Postumus's estate was confiscated and sold while I was away in Dalmatia and that the proceeds were devoted to the military treasury? Well, I asked him what had happened to certain pieces of plate of mine that Postumus had borrowed from me for a banquet; and he told me how to recover them. Then we discussed his banishment. Castor talked quite freely and I am glad to say that I am now quite satisfied in my mind that he was not in the plot.'

'You admit now that it was a plot?' I asked eagerly.

'I'm afraid, after all, that is the only explanation. But Castor himself was innocent, I am convinced. He told me, without being prompted, that on Livilla's suggestion he had teased Postumus in the garden, as Postumus told you he had. He explained that it was only because Postumus had been making sheep's eyes at Livilla and as her husband he did not like it. But he said that he did not regret having done so – though it was perhaps not a joke in the best of taste – because Postumus's attempt to outrage Livilla and his own serious injuries at that madman's hands made any regrets foolish.'

'He believed that Postumus tried to outrage Livilla?'

'Yes. I did not undeceive him. I did not want Livilla to know what you and I suspect. Because, if she did, Livia would hear of it.'

'Germanicus, you believe now that Livia arranged the whole thing?'

He did not answer.

'You will go to Augustus?'

'I gave you my word. I always keep my word.'

'When are you going to him?'

'Now.'

What happened at the interview I do not know and shall never know. But Germanicus seemed much happier that evening at dinner and the manner in which he later evaded my questions suggested that Augustus had believed him and had sworn him to secrecy for the present. It was a long time before I learned as much of the sequel as I can tell now. Augustus wrote to the Corsicans, who had been complaining for some years A.D. 13 of pirate raids on their coasts, that he would soon come in person to investigate the matter; he would stop on his way to Marseilles where he intended to dedicate a temple. Shortly afterwards he set sail, but broke his journey at Elba for two days. On the first day he ordered Postumus's guards at Planasia to be relieved at once by an entirely new set. This was done. The same night he sailed secretly across to the island in a small fishing-boat, accompanied only by Fabius Maximus, a close friend, and one Clement, who had once been a slave of Postumus's and bore a remarkably close resemblance to his former master. I have heard that Clement was a natural son of Agrippa's. They were lucky enough to meet Postumus as soon as they landed. He had been setting night-lines for fish and had seen the sail of the boat from some distance away in the light of a strong moon; he was alone. Augustus revealed himself, and stretched out his hand crying, 'Forgive me, my son!' Postumus took the hand and kissed it. Then the two went apart while Fabius and Clement kept watch. What was said between them nobody knows; but Augustus was weeping when they came back together. Then Postumus and Clement changed clothes and names, Postumus sailing back to Elba with Augustus and Fabius, and Clement taking Postumus's place at Planasia until the word should come for his release, which Augustus said would not be long delayed. Clement was promised his freedom and a large sum of money if he played his part well. He was to feign sick for the next few days and grow his hair and beard long, so that nobody would notice the imposture, especially since that afternoon he had not been seen by the new guard for more than a few minutes.

Livia suspected that Augustus was doing something behind her back. She knew his dislike of the sea and that he never went by ship when he could go by land, even if it meant losing valuable time. It is true that he could not have gone to Corsica except by sea, but the pirates were not a serious menace and he could easily have sent Castor or any one of several other subordinates to investigate the matter on his behalf. So she began to make inquiries and eventually heard that when Augustus stopped at Elba he had ordered Postumus's guards to be changed, and that he and Fabius had gone out catching cuttle-fish the same night in a small boat, accompanied only by a slave.

Fabius had a wife called Marcia who shared all his secrets, and Livia, who had paid little attention to her, now began to cultivate her acquaintance. Marcia was a simple woman and easily deceived. When Livia was sure that she was completely in Marcia's confidence she took her aside one day and asked: 'Come, my dear, tell me, was Augustus very much affected when he met Postumus again after all those years? He's much more tender-hearted than he makes out.' Now Fabius had told Marcia that the story of the voyage to Planasia was a secret which she must not reveal to anyone in the world, or the consequences might be fatal to him. So she would not answer at first. Livia laughed and said, 'Oh, you *are* cautious. You're like that sentry of Tiberius's in Dalmatia who wouldn't let Tiberius himself into the camp one evening when he came back from a ride because he couldn't give the watchword. "Orders are orders, General," the idiot said. My dear Marcia, Augustus has no secrets from me, nor I from Augustus. But I commend your prudence.' So Marcia apologized and said: 'Fabius said he wept and wept.' Livia said, 'Of course he did. But, Marcia, perhaps it would be wiser not to let Fabius know that we've talked about it – Augustus doesn't like people to know how much he confides in me. I suppose Fabius told you about the slave?'

This was a shot in the dark. The slave may have been of no importance, but it was a question worth asking. Marcia said: 'Yes. Fabius said that he was extraordinarily like Postumus, only a little shorter.'

'You don't think the guards will notice the difference?'

'Fabius said he thought they wouldn't. Clement was one of Postumus's household staff, so if he's careful he won't betray himself by ignorance and, as you know, the guard was changed.'

So Livia now only had to find out the whereabouts of Postumus, whom she assumed to be hidden somewhere under the name of Clement. She thought that Augustus was planning to restore him to favour and might even pass over Tiberius and appoint him his immediate successor in the monarchy, by way of making amends. She now took Tiberius into her confidence, more or less, and warned him of her suspicions. Trouble had started again in the Balkans and Augustus was proposing to send Tiberius to suppress it before it took a serious turn. Germanicus was in France collecting tribute. Augustus spoke of sending Castor away too, to Germany; and he had been having frequent conversations with Fabius, who Livia concluded was acting as his go-between with Postumus. As soon as the coast was clear Augustus would no doubt suddenly introduce Postumus into the Senate, get the decree against him reversed and have him appointed his colleague in place of Tiberius. With Postumus restored her own life would not be safe: Postumus had accused her of poisoning his father and brothers and Augustus would not be taking him back into favour unless he believed that these accusations were well grounded. She set her most trusted agents to spy on Fabius's movements with a view to tracing a slave called Clement; but they could discover nothing. She decided at any rate to lose no time in removing Fabius. He was waylaid in the street one night on his way to the Palace and stabbed in twelve places: his masked assailants escaped. At the funeral a scandalous thing happened. Marcia threw herself on her husband's corpse and begged his pardon, saying that she alone had been responsible for his death by her thoughtlessness and disobedience. However, nobody understood what she meant and it was thought that grief had crazed her.

Livia told Tiberius to keep in constant communication with her on his way to the Balkans and to travel as slowly as possible: he might be sent for at any moment. Augustus, who had accompanied him as far as Naples, cruising easily along the coast, now fell sick: his stomach was disordered. Livia prepared to nurse him but he thanked her and told her that it was A.D. 14 nothing; he could cure himself. He went to his own medicine-cabinet and chose a strong purge, then fasted for a day. He positively forbade her to worry about his health; she had enough cares without that. He laughingly refused to eat anything but bread from the common table and water from the pitcher which she used herself and green figs which he picked from the tree with his own hands. Nothing in his manner to Livia seemed altered, nor was hers altered towards him, but each read the other's mind.

In spite of all precautions his stomach grew worse again. He had to break his journey at Nola; from there Livia sent a message recalling Tiberius. When he arrived Augustus was reported to be sinking and to be earnestly calling for him. He had already taken his farewell of certain ex-Consuls who had hurried from Rome at the news of his illness. He had asked them with a smile whether they thought he had acted well in the farce; which is the question that actors in comedies put to the audience at the conclusion of the piece. And smiling back, though many of them had tears in their eyes, they answered: 'No man better, Augustus.' 'Then send me off with a good clap,' he said. Tiberius went to his bedside, where he remained for some three hours, and then emerged to announce in sorrowful tones that the Father of the Country had just passed away, in Livia's arms, with a final loving salutation to himself, to the Senate, and to the people of Rome. He thanked the Gods that he had returned in time to close the eyes of his father and benefactor. As a matter of fact, Augustus had been dead a whole day, but Livia had concealed this, giving out reassuring or discouraging bulletins every few hours. By a strange coincidence he died in the very room in which his father had died, seventy-five years before. I remember well how the news came to me. It was on the 20th of August. I was sleeping late after working nearly all night on my history; I found it easier in the summer to work by night and sleep by day. I was awakened by the arrival of two old knights who excused themselves for disturbing me but said that the matter was urgent. Augustus was dead and the Noble Order of Knights had met hurriedly and elected me their representative to go to the Senate. I was to ask that they might be honoured by the permission to bring Augustus's dead body back to the City on their shoulders. I was still half-asleep and did not think what I was saying. I shouted, 'Poison is Queen, Poison is Queen!' They glanced anxiously and uncomfortably at each other and I recalled myself and apologized, saying that I had been dreaming a fearful dream and was repeating words that I heard in it. I asked them to repeat their message and when they did so thanked them for the honour and undertook to do what was asked of me. It was not altogether an honour, of course, to be singled out as a distinguished knight. Everyone was a knight who was free-born, and had not disgraced himself in any way, and owned property above a certain value; and, with my family connexions, if I had shown even average ability I should by now have been an honoured member of the Senate like my contemporary Castor. I was chosen in fact as being the only member of the Imperial family who still belonged to the lower order, and to avoid jealousy among the other knights. This was the first time that I had ever visited the Senate during a session. I made the plea without stammering or forgetting my words or otherwise disgracing myself.

Chapter 14

ALTHOUGH it had been clear that Augustus's powers were failing and that he had not many more years to live, Rome could not accustom itself to the idea of his death. It is not an idle comparison to say that the City felt much as a boy feels when he loses his father. Whether the father has been a brave man or a coward, just or unjust, generous or mean, signifies little: he has been that boy's father, and no uncle or elder brother can ever take his place. For Augustus's rule had been a very long one and a man had to be already past middle age to remember back behind it. It was therefore not altogether unnatural that the Senate met to deliberate whether the divine honours which had, even in his lifetime, been paid him by the provinces should now be voted him in the City itself.

Pollio's son, Gallus – hated by Tiberius because he had married Vipsania (Tiberius's first wife, you will recall, whom he had been forced to divorce on Julia's account), and because he had never given a public denial of the rumour which made him the real father of Castor, and because he had a witty tongue – this Gallus was the only senator who had dared to question the propriety of the motion. He rose to ask what divine portent had occurred to suggest that Augustus would be welcomed in the Heavenly Mansions – merely at the recommendation of his mortal friends and admirers?

There followed an uncomfortable silence, but at last Tiberius rose slowly and said: 'One hundred days ago, it will be recalled, the pediment of my father Augustus's statue was struck by lightning. The first letter of his name was blotted out, which left the words AESAR AUGUSTUS. What is the meaning of the letter C? It is the sign for one hundred. What does AESAR mean? I shall tell you. It means God, in the Etruscan tongue. Clearly, in a hundred days from that lightning stroke Augustus is to become a God in Rome. What clearer portent than this can you require?' Though Tiberius took the sole credit for this interpretation it was I who had first given meaning to AESAR (the queer word had been much discussed), being the only person at Rome who was acquainted with the Etruscan language. I told my mother about it and she called me a fanciful fool; but she must have been sufficiently impressed to repeat what I said to Tiberius, for I told nobody but her.

Gallus asked why Jove should give his messages in Etruscan rather than in Greek or Latin? Could nobody swear to having observed any other more conclusive omen? It was all very well to decree new gods to ignorant Asiatic provincials, but the honourable House ought to pause before ordering educated citizens to worship one of their own number, however distinguished. It is possible that Gallus would have succeeded in blocking the decree by this appeal to Roman pride and sanity had it not been for a man called Atticus, a senior magistrate. He solemnly rose to say that when Augustus's corpse had been burned on Mars Field he had seen a cloud descending from heaven and the dead man's spirit then ascending on it, precisely in the way in which tradition relates that the spirits of Romulus and Hercules ascended. He would swear by all the Gods that he was testifying the truth.

This speech was greeted with resounding applause and Tiberius triumphantly asked whether Gallus had any further remarks to make. Gallus said that he had. He recalled, he said, another early tradition about the sudden death and disappearance of Romulus, which appeared in the works of even the gravest historians as an alternative to the one quoted by his honourable and veracious friend Atticus: namely, that Romulus was so hated for his tyranny over a free people that one day, taking advantage of a sudden fog, the Senate murdered him, cut him up, and carried the pieces away under their robes.

'But what about Hercules?' someone hurriedly asked.

Gallus said: 'Tiberius himself in his eloquent oration at the funeral repudiated the comparison between Augustus and Hercules. His words were: "Hercules in his childhood dealt only with serpents, and even when a man only with a stag or two, and a wild boar which he killed, and a lion; and even this he did reluctantly and at somebody's command; whereas Augustus fought not with beasts but with men and of his own free will" – and so forth and so forth. But *my* reason for repudiating the comparison lies in the circumstances of Hercules's death.' Then he sat down. The reference was perfectly clear to anybody who considered the matter; for the legend was that Hercules died of poison administered by his wife.

But the motion for Augustus's deification was carried. Shrines were built to him in Rome and the neighbouring cities. An order of priests was formed for administering his rites and Livia, who had at the same time been granted the titles of Julia and Augusta, was made his High Priestess. Atticus was rewarded by Livia with a gift of ten thousand gold pieces, and was appointed one of the new priests of Augustus, being even excused the heavy initiation fee. I was also appointed a priest, but had to pay a higher initiation fee than anyone, because I was Livia's grandson. Nobody dared ask why this vision of Augustus's ascent had only been seen by Atticus. And the joke was that on the night before the funeral Livia had concealed an eagle in a cage at the top of the pyre, which was to be opened as soon as the pyre was lit by someone secretly pulling a string from below. The eagle would then fly up and was intended to be taken for Augustus's spirit. Unfortunately the miracle had not come off. The cage door refused to open. Instead of saying nothing and letting the eagle burn, the officer who was in charge clambered up the pyre and opened the cage door with his hands. Livia had to say that the eagle had been thus released at her orders, as a symbolic act.

I shall not write more about Augustus's funeral, though a more magnificent one has never been seen at Rome, for I must now begin to omit all things in my story except those of the first importance: I have already filled more than thirteen rolls of the best paper – from the new paper-making factory I have recently equipped – and not reached a third of the way through it. But I must not fail to tell about the contents of Augustus's will, the reading of which was awaited with general interest and impatience. Nobody was more anxious to know what it contained than I was, and I shall explain why.

A month before his death Augustus had suddenly appeared at the door of my study – he had been visiting my mother who was just convalescent after a long illness – and after dismissing his attendants had begun to talk to me in a rambling way, not looking directly at me, but behaving as shyly as though he were Claudius and I were Augustus. He picked up a book of his history and read a passage. 'Excellent writing!' he said. 'And how soon will the work be finished?'

I told him, 'In a month or less', and he congratulated me and said that he would then give orders to have a public reading of it at his own expense, inviting his friends to attend. I was perfectly astonished at this, but he went on in a friendly way to ask if I would not prefer a professional reciter to do justice to it rather than read myself: he said that public reading of one's own work must be very embarrassing – even tough old Pollio had confessed that he was always nervous on such occasions. I thanked him most sincerely and heartily and said that a professional would obviously be more suitable, if my work indeed deserved such an honour.

Then he suddenly held out his hand to me: 'Claudius, do you bear me any ill-will?'

What could I say to that? Tears came to my eyes and I muttered that I reverenced him and that he had never done anything to deserve my ill-will. He said with a sigh: 'No, but on the other hand little to earn your love. Wait a few months longer, Claudius, and I hope to be able to earn both your love and your gratitude. Germanicus has told me about you. He says that you are loyal to three things – to your friends, to Rome, and to the truth. I should be very proud if Germanicus thought the same of me.'

'Germanicus's love for you falls only a little short of outright worship,' I said. 'He has often told me so.'

His face brightened. 'You swear it? I am very happy. So now, Claudius, there's a strong bond between us – the good opinion of Germanicus. And what I came to tell you was this: I have treated you very badly all these years and I'm sincerely sorry and from now on you'll see that things will change.' He quoted in Greek: 'Who wounded thee, shall make thee whole,' and with that he embraced me. As he turned to go he said over his shoulder: 'I have just paid a visit to the Vestal Virgins and made some important alterations in a document of mine in their charge: and since you yourself are partly responsible for these I have given your name greater prominence there than it had before. But not a word!'

'You can trust me,' I said.

He could only have meant one thing by this: that he had believed Postumus's story as I had reported it to Germanicus and was now restoring him in his will (which was in charge of the Vestals) as his heir; and that I was to benefit too as a reward for my loyalty to him. I did not then, of course, know of Augustus's visit to Planasia but confidently expected that Postumus would be brought back and treated with honour. Well, I was disappointed. Since Augustus had been so secretive about the new will, which had been witnessed by Fabius Maximus and a few decrepit old priests, it was easy to suppress it in favour of one which had been made six years before at the time of the disinheriting of Postumus. The opening sentence was: 'Forasmuch as a sinister fate has bereft me of Gaius and Lucius, my sons, it is now my will that Tiberius Claudius Nero Caesar become heir, in the first range, of two-thirds of my estate; and of the remaining third, in the first range also, it is now my will that my beloved wife Livia shall become my heir, if so be that the Senate will graciously permit her to inherit this much (for it is in excess of the statutory allowance for a widow's legacy), making an exception in her case as having deserved so well of the State.' In the second range – that is, in the event of the first-mentioned legatees dying or becoming otherwise incapable to inherit – he put such of his grandchildren and great-grandchildren as were members of the Julian house and had incurred no public disgrace; but Postumus had been disinherited, so this meant Germanicus, as Tiberius's adopted son and Agrippina's husband, and Agrippina herself and her children, and Castor, Livilla, and their children. In this second range Castor was to inherit a third, and Germanicus and his family two-thirds of the estate. In the third range the will named various senators and distant connexions; but as a mark of favour rather than as likely to benefit. Augustus cannot have expected to outlive so many heirs of the first and second ranges. The third range heirs were grouped in three categories: the most favoured ten were set down to be joint-heirs of half the estate, the next most favoured fifty were set down to share a third of the estate, and the third class contained the names of fifty more who were to inherit the remaining sixth. The last name in this last list of the last range was Tiberius Claudius Drusus Nero Germanicus, which meant Clau-Clau-Claudius, or Claudius the Idiot, or as Germanicus's little boys were already learning to call him: 'Poor Uncle Claudius' – in fact, myself. There was no mention of Julia or Julilla except a clause forbidding their ashes to be interred in the mausoleum beside his own when they came to die.

Now, although Augustus had in the previous twenty years benefited under the wills of the old friends he had outlived, to the extent of no less than 140 million gold pieces, and had lived a most parsimonious life, he had spent so much on temples and public works, on doles and entertainments for the populace, on frontier wars (when there was no money left in the military treasury), and on similar State expenses, that of those 140 millions and a great mass of private treasure besides, accumulated from various sources, a mere fifteen million remained for bequest, much of this not easily realizable in cash. This did not, however, include certain important sums of money, not reckoned in the estate and ready tied up in sacks in the vaults of the Capitol, which had been set aside as particular bequests to confederate kings, to senators and knights, to his soldiers, and to the citizens of Rome. These amounted to two million more. There was also a sum set aside for the expenses of his funeral. Everyone was surprised at the smallness of the estate, and all sorts of ugly rumours went round until Augustus's accounts were produced and it was clear that there was no fraud on the part of the executors. The citizens were most discontented with their meagre bequests, and when a memorial play was exhibited in Augustus's honour at the public expense there was a riot in the theatre: the Senate had so stinted the grant that one of the actors in the play refused to appear for the fee offered him. Of the discontent in the Army I shall tell shortly. But first about Tiberius.

Augustus had made Tiberius his colleague and his heir but could not bequeath him the monarchy, or not in so many words. He could only recommend him to the Senate to whom all the powers he had exercised now reverted. The Senate did not like Tiberius or wish him to be Emperor, but Germanicus, whom they would have chosen if they had been given the chance, was away. And Tiberius's claims could not be disregarded.

So nobody dared to mention any name but that of Tiberius, and there were no dissentients from the motion, introduced by the Consuls, inviting him to take over Augustus's task where he had laid it down. He gave an evasive answer, emphasizing the immense responsibility that they were trying to put on him and his own unaspiring disposition. He said that the God Augustus alone had been capable of this mighty charge, and that in his opinion it would be best to divide up Augustus's offices into three parts and so divide the responsibility.

Senators anxious to curry favour with him pleaded that the triumvirate, or three-man rule, had been tried more than once in the preceding century and that a monarchy had been found the only remedy for the resulting civil wars. A disgraceful scene followed. Senators pretended to weep and lament, and embraced Tiberius's knees, imploring him to do as they asked. Tiberius, to cut this business short, said that he did not wish to shirk any charge laid upon him, but held by his assertion that he was not equal to the whole burden. He was no longer a young man: he was fifty-six years old, and his eyesight was not good. But he would undertake any particular part entrusted to him. All this was done so that nobody would be able to accuse him of seizing power too eagerly: and especially so that Germanicus and Postumus (wherever he happened to be) might be impressed by the strength of his position in the City. For he was afraid of Germanicus, whose popularity with the Army was infinitely greater than his own. He did not believe Germanicus capable of seizing the power for his own selfish ends but thought that if he knew of the suppressed will he might try to restore Postumus to his rightful inheritance and even to make him the third – Tiberius, Germanicus, and Postumus – in the new triumvirate. Agrippina was devoted to Postumus, and Germanicus took her advice as consistently as Augustus had taken Livia's. If Germanicus marched on Rome the Senate would go out in a body to welcome him: Tiberius knew that. And, at the worst, by behaving modestly now he would be able to escape with his life and live in honourable retirement.

The Senate realized that Tiberius really wanted what he was so modestly refusing and were about to renew their pleas when Gallus interposed in a practical voice: 'Very well, then, Tiberius, which part of the government do you want to be entrusted to you?'

Tiberius was confounded by this awkward and unforeseen question. He was silent for some time and at last said: 'The same man cannot both make the division and choose; and even if this were possible it would be immodest for me to choose or reject any particular branch of the administration when, as I have explained, I really want to be excused the whole of it.'

Gallus pressed his advantage: 'The only possible division of the Empire would be: first, Rome and all Italy; second, the armies; and third, the provinces. Which of these would you choose?'

When Tiberius was silent Gallus continued: 'Good. I know there's no answer. That's why I asked the question. I wanted you to admit by your silence that it was nonsense to speak of splitting into three an administrative system that has been built up and centrally co-ordinated by a single individual. Either we must return to the republican form of government or we must continue with the monarchy. It is wasting the time of the House, which appears to have decided in favour of the monarchy, to go on talking about triumvirates. You have been offered the monarchy. Take it or leave it.'

Another senator, a friend of Gallus's, said: 'As Protector of the People you have the power of vetoing the motion of the Consuls offering you the monarchy. If you really don't want it you should have used your veto half an hour ago.'

So Tiberius was forced to beg the Senate's pardon and to say that the suddenness and unexpectedness of the honour had overcome him: he begged leave to consider his answer a little longer.

The Senate then adjourned, and in succeeding sessions Tiberius gradually allowed himself to be voted, one by one, all Augustus's offices. But he never used the name Augustus, which had been bequeathed him, except when writing letters to foreign kings; and was careful to discourage any tendency to pay him divine honours. There was another explanation of this cautious behaviour of his, namely that Livia had boasted in public that he was receiving the monarchy as a gift from her hands. She made the boast not only to strengthen her position as Augustus's widow but to warn Tiberius that if her crimes ever came to light he would be regarded as her accomplice, being the person who principally benefited from them. Naturally he wished to appear under no obligation to her but as having had the monarchy forced on him against his will by the Senate.

The Senate were profuse in their flattery of Livia and wanted to confer many unheard-of honours on her. But Livia as a woman could not attend the debates in the Senate and was legally now under Tiberius's guardianship – he had become head of the Julian house. So having himself refused the title 'Father of the Country', he had refused, on her behalf, the title 'Mother of the Country' which had been offered her, on the ground that modesty would not allow her to accept it. Nevertheless, he was greatly afraid of Livia and at first wholly dependent on her for learning the inner secrets of the Imperial system. It was not merely a matter of understanding the routine. The criminal dossiers of every man of importance in the two Orders and of most of the important women, secret service reports of various sorts, Augustus's private correspondence with confederate kings and their relatives, copies of treasonable letters intercepted but duly forwarded – all these were in Livia's keeping and written in cipher, and Tiberius could not read them without her help. But he also knew that she was extremely dependent on him. There was an understanding between them of guarded co-operation. She even thanked him for refusing the title offered her, saying that he had been right to do so; and in return he promised to have her voted whatever titles she wished as soon as their position seemed secure. As proof of his good faith he put her own name alongside his own in all letters of State. As a proof of hers she gave him the key of the common cipher, though not that of the cipher extraordinary, the secret of which, she pretended, had died with Augustus. It was in the cipher extraordinary that the dossiers were written.

Now about Germanicus. When, at Lyons, he heard of Augustus's death and of the terms of his will, and of Tiberius's succession, he felt it his duty to stand loyally by the new régime. He was Tiberius's nephew and adopted son, and though there was no true affection between the two they had been able to work together without friction both at home and on campaign. He did not suspect Tiberius of complicity in the plot that had brought about Postumus's banishment; and he knew nothing of the suppressed will, and further, he still believed Postumus to be on Planasia – for Augustus had told nobody but Fabius either of the visit or of the substitution. He decided, however, to return to Rome as soon as he could and frankly discuss the case of Postumus with Tiberius. He would explain that Augustus had told him privately that he intended to restore Postumus to favour as soon as he had evidence of his innocence to offer the Senate; and that though death had prevented him from putting his intentions into execution, they should be respected. He would insist on Postumus's immediate recall, the restoration of his confiscated estates and his elevation to honourable office; and lastly on Livia's compulsory retirement from State affairs as having unjustly engineered his banishment. But before he could do anything in the matter news came from Mainz of an army mutiny on the Rhine, and then, as he was hurrying to put it down, news of Postumus's death. Postumus, it was reported, had been killed by the captain of the guard, who was under orders from Augustus not to let his grandson survive him. Germanicus was shocked and grieved that Postumus had been executed but had no leisure for the moment to think of anything but the mutiny. You may be sure, though, that it caused poor Claudius the greatest possible grief, for poor Claudius at this time never wanted for leisure. On the contrary poor Claudius was hard put to it often to find occupation for his mind. Nobody can write history for more than five or six hours a day, especially when there is little hope of anyone ever reading it. So I gave myself up to my misery. How was I to know that it was Clement who had been killed, and that not only was the murder not ordered by Augustus but that Livia and Tiberius were also innocent of it?

For the man really responsible for Clement's murder was an old knight called Crispus, the owner of the Gardens of Sallust and a close friend of Augustus. At Rome, as soon as he heard of Augustus's death, he had not waited to consult Livia and Tiberius at Nola but immediately dispatched the warrant for Postumus's execution to the captain of the guard at Planasia, attaching Tiberius's seal to it. Tiberius had entrusted him with this duplicate seal for the signing of some business papers which he had not been able to deal with before being sent to the Balkans. Crispus knew that Tiberius would be angry or pretend to be angry, but explained to Livia, whose protection he at once claimed, that he had put Postumus out of the way on learning of a plot among some of the Guards officers to send a ship to rescue Julia and Postumus and carry them off to the regiments at Cologne; there Germanicus and Agrippina could hardly fail to welcome and shelter them and the officers would then force Germanicus and Postumus to march on Rome. Tiberius was furious that his name had been used in this way, but Livia made the best of things and pretended that it really *was* Postumus who had been killed. Crispus was not prosecuted and the Senate was unofficially informed that Postumus had died by the orders of his deified grandfather who had wisely foreseen that the savage-tempered young man would attempt to usurp supreme power as soon as news came of his grandfather's death; as indeed he had done. Crispus's motive in having Postumus murdered was not a wish to curry favour with Tiberius and Livia or to prevent civil war. He was revenging an insult. For Crispus, who was as lazy as he was rich, had once boasted that he had never stood for office, content to be a simple Roman knight. Postumus had replied: 'A simple Roman knight, Crispus? Then you had better take a few simple Roman riding-lessons.'

Tiberius had not yet heard of the mutiny. He wrote Germanicus a friendly letter condoling with him on the loss of Augustus and saying that Rome now looked to him and his adoptive brother Castor for the defence of the frontiers, himself being now too old for foreign service and required by the Senate to manage affairs at Rome. Writing of Postumus's death, he said that he deplored its violence but could not question the wisdom of Augustus in the matter. He did not mention Crispus. Germanicus could only conclude that Augustus had once more changed his mind about Postumus on the strength of some information of which he himself knew nothing; and was content for awhile to let the matter rest there.

Chapter 15

THE Rhine mutiny had broken out in sympathy with a mutiny among the Balkan forces. The soldiers' disappointment with their bequests under Augustus's will – a mere four months' bounty of pay, three gold pieces a man – aggravated certain long-standing grievances; and they reckoned that the insecurity of Tiberius's position would force him to meet any reasonable demands they made, in order to win their favour. These demands included a rise in pay, service limited to sixteen years, and a relaxation of camp discipline. The pay was certainly insufficient: the soldiers had to arm and equip themselves out of it, and prices had risen. And certainly the exhaustion of military reserves had kept thousands of soldiers with the Colours who should have been discharged years before, and veterans had been recalled to the Colours who were quite unfit for service. And, certainly too, the detachments formed from recently liberated slaves were such poor fighting material that Tiberius had considered it necessary to tighten up discipline, choosing martinets for his captains, and giving them instructions to keep the men constantly employed on fatigue duty and to keep the vine-branch saplings – their badges of rank – constantly employed on the men's backs.

When the news of Augustus's death reached the Balkan forces, three regiments were together in a summer camp, and the General gave them a few days' holiday from parades and fatigues. This experience of ease and idleness unsettled them and they refused to obey their captains when called out on parade again. They formulated certain demands. The General told them that he had no authority to grant these demands and warned them of the danger of a mutinous attitude. They offered him no violence but refused to be awed into obedience and finally obliged him to send his son to Rome to convey their demands to Tiberius. After the son had left the camp on this mission the disorder increased. The less-disciplined men began plundering the camp and the neighbouring villages, and when the General arrested the ringleaders, the rest broke open the guard-room and released them, finally murdering a captain who tried to oppose them. This captain was nicknamed 'Old Give-me-Another' because after breaking one sapling over a man's back, he would call for a second and a third. When the General's son arrived at Rome, Tiberius sent Castor to the General's support at the head of two battalions of Guards, a squadron of Guards cavalry, and most of the Household Battalion, who were Germans; a staff-officer called Sejanus, the son of the Commander of the Guards and one of Tiberius's few intimates, went with Castor as his lieutenant. Of this Sejanus I shall later have more to write. Castor on arrival addressed the mob of soldiers in a dignified and fearless way and read them a letter from his father, promising to take care of the invincible regiments with whom he had shared the hardships of so many wars, and to negotiate with the Senate about their demands as soon as he had recovered from his grief for Augustus's death. Meanwhile, he wrote, his son had come to them to make whatever immediate concessions might be practicable – the rest must be reserved for the Senate.

The mutineers made one of their captains act as their spokesman and present their demands, for no soldier would risk doing so for fear of being singled out later as a ringleader. Castor said that he was very sorry, but that the sixteen-year limit of service, the discharge of veterans, and the increase of pay to a full silver piece a day were demands which he had no authority to grant. Only his father and the Senate could make such concessions.

This put the men into an ugly temper. They asked why in Hell's name had he come then if he had no power to do anything for them. His father Tiberius, they said, used always to play the same trick on them when they presented their grievances: he used to shelter behind Augustus and the Senate. What was the Senate, anyhow? A pack of rich good-for-nothing lazybones, most of whom would die of fear if they ever caught sight of an enemy shield or saw a sword drawn in anger! They began throwing stones at Castor's staff and the situation became dangerous. But it was saved that night by a fortunate chance. The moon was eclipsed, which affected the army – all soldiers are superstitious – in a surprising way. They took the eclipse for a sign that Heaven was angry with them for their murder of Old Give-me-Another and for their defiance of authority. There were a number of secret loyalists among the mutineers, and one of these came to Castor suggesting that he should get hold of others like himself and send them around the tents in parties of two or three to try to bring the disaffected men to their senses. This was done. By morning there was a very different atmosphere in the camp and Castor, though he consented to send the General's son again to Tiberius with the same demands endorsed by himself, arrested the two men who appeared to have started the mutiny and publicly executed them. The rest made no protest and even voluntarily handed over the five murderers of the captain as a proof of their own fidelity. But there was still a firm refusal to attend parades, or do any but the most necessary fatigues until an answer came from Rome. The weather broke and incessant rain flooded the camp and made it impossible for the men to keep communication between tent and tent. This was taken as a fresh warning from Heaven, and before the messenger had time to return the mutiny was at an end, the regiments marching obediently back to winter quarters under their officers.

But the mutiny on the Rhine was a far more serious affair. Roman Germany was now bounded on the east by the Rhine and divided into two provinces, the Upper and the Lower. The capital of the Upper Province, which extended up into Switzerland, was Mainz, and that of the Lower, which reached north to the Scheldt and Sambre, was Cologne. An army of four regiments manned each of the provinces and Germanicus was Commander-in-Chief. Disorders broke out in a summer camp of the Lower Army. The grievances were the same here as in the Balkan army, but the conduct of the mutineers was more violent because of the greater proportion of newly-recruited City freedmen in the ranks. These freedmen were still slaves by nature and accustomed to a far more idle and luxurious life than the freeborn citizens, mostly poor peasants, who formed the backbone of the army. They made thoroughly bad soldiers and their badness went unchecked by any regimental *esprit-de-corps*. For these were not the regiments which had been under the command of Germanicus in the recent campaign; they were Tiberius's men.

The General lost his head and was unable to check the insolence of the mutineers who came crowding round him with complaints and threats. His nervousness encouraged them to fall on their most hated captains, about twenty of whom they beat to death with their own vine-saplings, throwing their bodies into the Rhine. The remainder they jeered at and insulted and drove from the camp. Cassius Chaerea was the only senior officer who made any attempt to oppose this monstrous and unheard-of behaviour. He was set upon by a large party, but instead of running away or begging for mercy rushed straight into the thick of them with his sword drawn, stabbing right and left, and broke through to the sacred tribunal-platform where he knew that no soldier would dare to touch him.

Germanicus had no battalions of Guards to support him but rode at once to the mutinous camp with only a small staff behind him. He did not yet know of the massacre. The men surged about him in a mob, as they had done about their General, but Germanicus calmly refused to say anything to them until they had formed up decently in companies and battalions under their proper banners so that he should know whom he was addressing. It seemed a small concession to authority; and they wanted to hear what he had to tell them. Once they were back in military formation a certain sense of discipline returned, and though by the murder of their officers they had put themselves beyond hope of his trust or forgiveness, their hearts suddenly went out to him as a brave and humane and honourable man. One old veteran – there were many there who had been serving in Germany twenty-five and thirty years before this – called out: 'How like he is to his father!' And another: 'He's got to be cursed good to be as cursed good as him.' Germanicus began in a voice of ordinary conversational pitch, to command more attention. He first spoke of the death of Augustus and the great grief it had inspired, but assured them that Augustus had left behind him an indestructible work and a successor capable of carrying on the government and commanding the armies in the way that he himself would have wished. 'Of my father's glorious victories in Germany you are not unaware. Many of you have shared in them.'

'Never was there a better general or a better man,' shouted a veteran. 'Hurrah for Germanicus, father and son!'

It is a comment on my brother's extreme simplicity that he did not realize the effect his words were having. By his father, he meant Tiberius (who also was often styled Germanicus), but the veterans thought he meant his real father; and by Augustus's successor he meant Tiberius again, but the veterans thought that he meant himself. Unaware of these cross-purposes he went on to speak of the harmony that prevailed in Italy and of the fidelity of the French, from whose territory he had just come, and said that he could not understand the sudden feeling of pessimism that had overcome them. What ailed them? What had they done with their captains and their colonels and their generals? Why weren't these officers on parade? Had they really been expelled from the camp, as he had heard?

'A few of us are still alive and about, Caesar,' someone said, and Cassius came limping through the ranks and saluted Germanicus. 'Not many! They pulled me off the tribunal and have kept me tied up in the guardroom without food for the last four days. An old soldier has just been good enough to release me.'

'*You*, Cassius! They did that to *you*! The man who brought back the eighty from the Teutoburger Forest? The man who saved the Rhine bridge?'

'Well, at least they spared my life,' said Cassius.

Germanicus asked with horror in his voice: 'Men, is this true?'

'They brought it on themselves,' someone shouted, and then a fearful hubbub arose. Men stripped themselves to the skin to show the clean silver scars of honourable wounds on their breasts and the ragged discoloured marks of flogging on their backs. One decrepit old man broke from the ranks, and running forward pulled his mouth open with his fingers to show his bare gums. Then he shouted, 'I can't eat hard tack without teeth, General, and I can't march and fight on slops. I served under your father in his first campaign in the Alps and I'd done six years' service even then. I've two grandsons serving in the same company as myself. Give me my discharge, General. I dandled you on my knees when you were a baby! And look, General, I've got a rupture and they expect me to march twenty miles with a hundred pounds' weight on my back.'

'Back to the ranks, Pomponius,' ordered Germanicus, who recognized the old man and was shocked to find him still under arms. 'You forget yourself. I'll look into your case later. For Heaven's sake show a good example to the young soldiers!'

Pomponius saluted and returned to the ranks. Germanicus held up his hand for silence, but the men went on shouting about their pay and the unecessary fatigues put on them so that they hardly had a moment to themselves from reveille to lights out, and that the only discharge a man got from the Army now was to drop dead from old age. Germanicus made no attempt to speak until he had complete quiet again. Then he said: 'In the name of my father Tiberius I promise you justice. He has your welfare at heart as deeply as I have and whatever can be done for you without danger to the Empire he will do. I'll answer for that.'

'Oh, to hell with Tiberius!' someone shouted, and the cry was picked up on all sides with groans and catcalls. And then suddenly they all began to shout: 'Up, Germanicus! You're the Emperor for us. Chuck Tiberius into the Tiber! Up, Germanicus! Germanicus for Emperor! To hell with Tiberius! To hell with that bitch Livia! Up, Germanicus! March on Rome! We're your men! Up, Germanicus, son of Germanicus! Germanicus for Emperor!'

Germanicus was thunderstruck. He shouted: 'You're mad, men, to talk like that. What do you think I am? A traitor?'

A veteran shouted: 'None of that, General! You said just now that you'd take on Augustus's job. Don't back out!'

Germanicus then realized his mistake, and when the cheers of 'Up, Germanicus' continued he jumped off the tribunal and hurried to where his horse was standing tied to a post, intending to mount and gallop wildly away from this accursed camp. But the men drew their swords and barred his way.

Germanicus, beside himself, cried: 'Let me pass, or by God, I'll kill myself.'

'You're the Emperor for us,' they answered.

Germanicus drew his sword, but someone caught at his arm. It was clear to any decent man that Germanicus was in earnest, but a good many of the ex-slaves thought that he was just making a hypocritical gesture of modesty and virtue. One of them laughed and called out: 'Here, take my sword. It's sharper!' Old Pomponius, who was standing next to this fellow, flared up and struck him on the mouth. Germanicus was hurried away by his friends to the General's tent. The General was lying in bed half-dead with dismay, hiding his head under a coverlet. It was a long time before he could get up and pay his respects to Germanicus. His life and that of his staff had been saved by his bodyguard, mercenaries from the Swiss border.

A hurried council was held. Cassius told Germanicus that from a conversation which he had overheard while lying in the guard-room the mutineers were about to send a deputation to the regiments in the Upper Province, to secure their co-operation in a general military revolt. There was talk of leaving the Rhine unguarded and marching into France, sacking cities, carrying off the women, and setting up an independent military kingdom in the south-west, protected in the rear by the Pyrenees. Rome would be paralysed by this move and they would remain undisturbed long enough to be able to make their kingdom impregnable.

Germanicus decided to go at once to the Upper Province and make the regiments there swear allegiance to Tiberius. These were the troops who had recently served directly under his command and he believed that they would remain loyal if he reached them before the deputation of mutineers. They had the same grievance about pay and service, he was aware, but their captains were a better set of men, chosen by himself for their patience and soldierly qualities rather than for their reputation. But first something had to be done to quiet the mutinous regiments here. There was only one course to take. He committed the first and only crime in his life: he forged a letter purporting to come from Tiberius and had it delivered to him at his tent door the next morning. The courier had been secretly sent out at night with instructions to steal a horse from the horse-lines, ride twenty miles south-west and then gallop back at top speed by another route.

The letter was to the effect that Tiberius had heard that the regiments in Germany had voiced certain legitimate grievances, and was anxious to remove them at once. He would see that Augustus's legacy was promptly paid to them and as a mark of his confidence in their loyalty would double it from his own purse. He would negotiate with the Senate about the rise in pay. He would give an immediate and unqualified discharge to all men of twenty years' service and a qualified discharge to all who had completed sixteen years – these would be called on for no military duty whatsoever except garrison duty.

Germanicus was not as clever a liar as his uncle Tiberius or his grandmother Livia or his sister Livilla. The courier's horse was recognized by its owner and so was the courier, one of Germanicus's own grooms. Word went round that the letter was a forgery. But the veterans were in favour of treating it as authentic and asking for the promised discharge and the legacy at once. They did so, and Germanicus replied that the Emperor was a man of his word and that the discharges could be granted that very day. But he asked them to have patience about the legacy, which could only be paid in full when they marched back to their winter quarters. There was not sufficient coin in the camp, he said, for every man to have his six gold pieces, but he would see that the General would hand over as much as there was. This quieted them, though opinion had somewhat turned against Germanicus as not being the man they had taken him to be: he was afraid of Tiberius, they said, and not above committing forgery. They sent parties out to look for their captains and undertook to obey orders from their General again. Germanicus had told the General that he would have him impeached before the Senate for cowardice if he did not immediately take himself in hand.

So having seen that the discharges were made in due form and all the available money distributed, Germanicus rode off to the Upper Province. He found the regiments standing by waiting for news of what was happening in the Lower Province; but not yet in open mutiny, for Silius, their General, was a strong-minded man. Germanicus read them the same forged letter and made them swear allegiance to Tiberius; which they did at once.

There was great emotion at Rome when news arrived of the Rhine mutiny. Tiberius, who had been strongly criticized for sending Castor out to the Balkan mutiny – which had not yet been put down – instead of going there himself, was now booed in the streets and asked why it was that the troops who mutinied were the ones whom he had personally commanded, while the others remained loyal. (For the regiments that Germanicus had commanded in Dalmatia had not mutinied either.) He was called on to go to Germany at once and do his own dirty work on the Rhine instead of leaving it to Germanicus. He therefore told the Senate that he would go to Germany, and began slowly to make preparations, choosing his staff and fitting out a small fleet. But by the time he was ready the approach of winter made navigation dangerous and the news from Germany was more hopeful. So he did not go. He had not intended to go.

Meanwhile, I had had a hasty letter from Germanicus, begging me to raise 200,000 gold pieces at once from his estate, but with the greatest secrecy; they were needed for the safety of Rome. He said no more but sent me a signed warrant which enabled me to act for him. I went to his chief steward, who said that he could only raise half that amount without selling property, and that to sell property would make talk, which was what Germanicus evidently wanted to avoid. So I had to find the rest myself – 50,000 from my strong-box, which left me with only 10,000 after I had paid my initiation fee to the new priesthood – and another 50,000 from the sale of some City property which had been left me by my father – luckily I had already had an offer for it – and such of my slaves as I could spare, but only men and women whom I considered not particularly devoted to my service. I sent the money out within two days of getting the letter asking for it. My mother was extremely angry when she heard that the property had been sold, but I was pledged not to tell her why the money was needed, so I said that I had been playing dice for too high stakes lately and in trying to recoup my heavy losses had lost twice as much again. She believed me, and 'gambler' was another stick to beat me with. But the thought that I had not failed Germanicus or Rome was ample compensation for her taunts.

I was gambling a good deal at this time, I must say, but never either lost or gained much. I used to play as a relaxation from my work. After finishing my history of Augustus's religious reforms I wrote a short humorous book about Dice, dedicated to the divinity of Augustus; which was to tease my mother. I quoted a letter that Augustus, who had been very fond of dice, had once written to my father: in which he said how much he had enjoyed their game on the previous night, for my father was the best loser he had ever met. My father, he wrote, always made a great laughing outcry against fate whenever he threw the Dog, but if a fellow-gambler threw Venus he seemed as pleased as if he had thrown her himself. 'It is, indeed, a pleasure to win from you, my dear fellow, and to say this is the highest praise I can bestow on a man, for usually I hate winning because of the insight it gives me into the hearts of my supposedly most devoted friends. All but the very best grudge losing to me, because I am the Emperor and, they think, of infinite wealth, and obviously the Gods should not give more to a man who already has too much. It is my policy therefore – perhaps you have noticed it – always to make a mistake in the reckoning after a round of throws. Either I claim less than I have won, as if by mistake, or I pay more than I owe, and hardly anyone but yourself, I find, is honest enough to put me right.' (I should have liked to quote a further passage in which there was a reference to Tiberius's bad sportsmanship, but of course I could not.)

In this book I began with a mock-serious inquiry into the antiquity of dice, quoting a number of non-existent authors, and describing various fanciful ways of shaking the dice-cup. But the main subject was, naturally, that of winning and losing, and the title was *How to Win at Dice*. Augustus had written in another letter that the more he tried to lose, the more he seemed to win, and even by cheating himself in the reckoning it was seldom that he rose from the table poorer than he sat down. I quoted an opposite statement attributed by Pollio to my grandfather Antony to the effect that the more he tried to win at dice-play the more he seemed to lose. Putting these statements together I deduced that the fundamental law of dice was that the Gods, unless they had a grudge against him on another score, always let the man win who cared least about winning. The only way to win at dice therefore was to cultivate a genuine desire to lose. Written in a heavy style, parodying that of my bugbear Cato, it was, I flatter myself, a very funny book, the argument being so perfectly paradoxical. I quoted the old proverb which promises a man 1,000 gold pieces every time he meets a stranger riding on a piebald mule, but only on condition that he does not think of the mule's tail until he gets the money. I had hoped that this squib would please people who found my histories indigestible. It did not. It was not read as a humorous work at all. I should have realized that old-fashioned readers who had been brought up on the works of Cato were hardly the sort to enjoy a parody of their hero and that the younger generation, who had not been brought up on Cato, would not recognize it as a parody. The book was therefore dismissed as a

fantastically dull and stupid production written in painful seriousness and proving my rumoured mental incapacity beyond further
dispute.

But this has been a very ill-judged digression, leaving Germanicus, as it were, waiting anxiously for his money while I write a
book about dice. Old Athenodorus would criticize me pretty
severely, I think, if he were alive now.

Chapter 16

GERMANICUS was met at Bonn by a deputation of senators sent
by Tiberius. They really came to see whether Germanicus had
been either exaggerating or minimizing the seriousness of the
mutiny. They also brought a private letter from Tiberius approving the promises made to the men on his behalf with the exception
of the doubled bequest, which would now have to be promised to
the entire Army, not merely the regiments in Germany. Tiberius
congratulated Germanicus on the apparent success of the ruse but
deplored the necessity of forgery. He added that whether he fulfilled the promises depended on the behaviour of the men. (By this
he did not mean, as Germanicus supposed, that if the men returned to obedience he would fulfil the promises, but exactly the
reverse.) Germanicus wrote back at once apologizing for the expense involved in the doubling of the bequest, but explained that
the money was being paid from his own purse and the men would
not know that it was not Tiberius who was their benefactor: and
that in the forged letter he had made it plain that only the German
regiments were to benefit, making the payment a reward for their
recent successful campaign across the Rhine. As for the other
specific promises, the veterans of twenty years' service had already
been discharged and were only remaining with the Colours until
the bounty-money arrived for them.

Germanicus could ill afford this heavy charge on his estate and
wrote asking me not to press him for repayment of my 50,000 for
awhile. I answered that it had not been a loan but a gift, which I
was proud to have been able to make. But to return to the order
of events. Two of the regiments were in their winter quarters at
Bonn when the deputation arrived. Their march back under their

General had been a disgraceful display: the bags which had contained the money were tied to long poles and carried mouth downwards, between the standards. The other two regiments had refused to leave the summer camp until the whole bequest was paid them. The Bonn regiments, the First and Twentieth, suspected that the deputation had been sent to cancel the concessions and began to riot again. Some of them were for marching to their new kingdom at once and at midnight a party broke into Germanicus's quarters where the Eagle of the Twentieth Regiment was kept in a locked shrine and, pulling him out of bed, tore the key of the shrine from the thin gold chain which he wore round his neck, unlocked the shrine, and seized the Eagle. As they marched shouting down the streets, calling on their comrades to 'follow the Eagle', they met the senators of the deputation, who had heard the noise and came running for protection to Germanicus. The soldiers cursed and drew their swords. The senators changed their direction and darted into the headquarters of the First Regiment, where they took sanctuary with its Eagle. But their pursuers were mad with rage and drink, and if the Eagle-bearer had not been a man of courage, and a good swordsman too, the leader of the deputation would have had his skull split open – a crime which would have outlawed the regiment beyond pardon and been the signal for civil war throughout the country.

The disorders continued all night, but fortunately without bloodshed except as the result of drunken brawls between rival companies of soldiers. When dawn came Germanicus told the trumpeter to blow the Assembly, and stepped on the tribunal, putting the leader of the senatorial deputation beside him. The men were in a nervous, guilty, irritable mood, but Germanicus's courage fascinated them. He stood up, commanded silence, and then gave a great yawn. He covered his mouth with his hand and apologized, saying that he had not slept well because of the scuffling mice in his quarters. The men liked that joke and laughed. He did not laugh with them. 'Heaven be praised that dawn is here. Never have I known such an evil night. At one moment I dreamed that the Eagle of the Twentieth flew away. What a delight to see it on parade this morning! There were destructive spirits hovering in the camp, sent beyond doubt by some God whom we have offended. You all felt the madness and it was only by a miracle that you were prevented from committing a crime unparalleled in the history of Rome – the unprovoked murder of an ambassador of your own City who had taken sanctuary from your swords with your own regimental Deities!' He then explained that the deputation had come merely to confirm Tiberius's original promises on behalf of the Senate and to report whether they were being faithfully executed by himself.

'Well, what about it, then? Where's the rest of the bounty?' someone shouted, and the cry was taken up. 'We want our bounty.' But by a lucky chance the money-wagons were sighted at that moment, driving into camp under convoy of a troop of auxiliary horse. Germanicus took advantage of the situation to send the senators hurriedly back to Rome under escort of these same auxiliaries; then he supervised the distribution of the coin, having difficulty in restraining some of the men from plundering the money intended for the other regiments.

The disorder increased that afternoon; so much gold in the men's purses meant heavy drinking and reckless gambling. Germanicus decided that it was not safe for Agrippina, who was now with him, to remain in the camp. She was pregnant again; and though her young sons, my nephews Nero and Drusus, were here at Rome staying with my mother and myself, she had little Gaius there with her. This pretty child had become the army mascot and someone had made him a miniature soldier-suit, complete with tin breastplate and sword and helmet and shield. Everyone spoilt him. When his mother put on his ordinary clothes and sandals he used to cry and plead for his sword and his little boots to go visiting the tents. So he was nicknamed Caligula, or Little Boot.

Germanicus insisted on Agrippina's going away, though she swore that she was afraid of nothing and would far rather die with him there than have news from safety of his murder by the mutineers. But he asked her whether she thought that Livia would make a good mother for their orphaned children, and this decided her to do as he wished. With her went several officers' wives, with their children, all weeping and wearing mourning clothes. They passed on foot slowly through the camp, without their usual attendants, like fugitives from a doomed city. A single rough cart, drawn by a mule, was all their transport. Cassius Chaerea went with them as guide and sole protector. Caligula rode on Cassius's back as if on a charger, shouting and making the regulation sword-cuts and parries in the air with his sword, as the cavalrymen had taught him. They left the camp very early in the morning, and hardly anyone saw them go; for there was no guard at the gate and nobody now took the trouble to blow the reveille, most of the men sleeping like pigs till ten or eleven o'clock. A few old soldiers who woke early from long habit were outside the camp gathering firewood for their breakfasts and called to ask where the ladies were off to. 'To Treves,' shouted Cassius. 'The Commander-in-Chief is sending his wife and child away to the protection of the uncivilized but loyal French allies of Treves rather than risk their murder by the famous First Regiment. Tell your comrades that.'

The old soldiers hurried back to the camp and one of them, the old man Pomponius, got hold of a trumpet and blew the alarm. The men came tumbling out of their tents half-asleep with their swords in their hands. 'What's wrong? What's happened?'

'He's been sent away from us. That's the end of our luck and we'll never see him again.'

'Who's that? Who's been sent away?'

'Our boy has. Little Boot. His father says he can't trust the First Regiment with him, so he's sent him away to the damned French allies. God knows what will happen to him there. You know what the French are. His mother's been sent off too. Seven months gone with her latest, and walking on foot, like a slave woman, poor lady. O lads! Germanicus's wife and the daughter of old Agrippa whom we used to call the Soldier's Friend! And our Little Boot.'

Soldiers really are an extraordinary race of men, as tough as shield-leather, as superstitious as Egyptians, and as sentimental as Sabine grandmothers. Ten minutes later there were about 2,000 men besieging Germanicus's tent in a drunken ecstasy of sorrow and repentance and imploring him to let his lady come back with their darling little boy.

Germanicus came out to them with a pale angry face and told them to trouble him no more. They had disgraced themselves and him and the name of Rome and he could never trust them so long as he lived; they had done him no kindness in wresting his sword from him when he was on the point of plunging it into his breast.

'Tell us what to do, General! We'll do anything you say. We swear we'll never mutiny again. Forgive us. We'll follow you to the world's end. But give us back our little playfellow.'

Germanicus said: 'These are my conditions. Swear allegiance to my father Tiberius, and sort out from among yourselves the men responsible for the death of your captains, the insult to the deputation, and the stealing of the Eagle. If you do this you will so far have my forgiveness that I shall let you have your play-fellow back. My wife, however, must not be brought to bed in this camp until it has been purged of guilt. Her time is near now and I want no evil influence to cloud the life of the child. But I can send her to Cologne instead of Treves if you do not wish it said that I confided her to the protection of barbarians. My full pardon will only be given when you have wiped out the memory of your bloody crimes by a bloodier victory over your country's enemies, the Germans.'

They swore to abide by his conditions. So he sent a messenger to overtake Agrippina and Cassius; he was to explain matters and fetch Caligula back. The men ran to the tents and called on every loyal comrade to join them and arrest the ringleaders of the mutiny. About 100 men were seized and frog-marched to the tribunal, about which the remainder of the two regiments formed a hollow square with drawn swords. A colonel made each prisoner in turn mount a rough scaffold which had been put up beside the tribunal, and if the men of his company judged him guilty he was thrown down and beheaded by them. Germanicus said nothing throughout the two hours of this informal trial, sitting with folded arms and an impassive face. All but a few of the prisoners were found guilty.

When the last head had fallen and the bodies had been taken out of camp to be burned, Germanicus called up every captain in turn to the tribunal and asked him to give particulars of his service. If he had a good record and had evidently not been appointed by favouritism, Germanicus appealed to the company veterans for their opinion of him. If they gave him a good name and the battalion colonel had nothing against him the man was confirmed in his rank. But if his record was bad or if there were complaints from his company he was degraded, and Germanicus called on the company to choose the best man they had among them to succeed him. Germanicus then thanked the men for their co-operation and called on them to take the oath of allegiance to Tiberius. They took it solemnly; and a moment later a great cheer went up. They saw Germanicus's messenger galloping back; and there was Caligula on the crupper in front of him shouting in his shrill voice and waving his toy sword.

Germanicus embraced the child and said that he had one more thing to add. Fifteen hundred time-expired veterans had been discharged from the two regiments in accordance with instructions from Tiberius. But if any of them, he said, wanted his full pardon, which their fellows were soon going to earn by crossing the Rhine and avenging Varus's defeat, they could still win it. He would permit the more active men to re-enlist in their old companies; while those who were only fit for garrison duty could enlist in a special force for service in the Tyrol, where dangerous raids from Germany had lately been reported. Would you believe it? – every man stepped forward and more than half volunteered for active service across the Rhine. Among these active volunteers was Pomponius, who protested that he was as fit as any man in the army, in spite of his bare gums and his rupture. Germanicus made him his tent-orderly and put his grandsons into the bodyguard. So everything was all right again at Bonn, and Caligula was told by the men that he had put down the mutiny single-handed and that one day he'd be a great emperor and win wonderful victories; which was very bad for the child, who was already, as I say, disgracefully spoilt.

But there remained the two other regiments who were at a place called Xanten to bring to their senses. They had continued to behave mutinously even after the payment of their bounty and their General could do nothing with them. When news came of the change of heart in the Bonn regiments the chief mutineers became seriously alarmed for their own safety and stirred up their comrades to fresh acts of violence and depredation. Germanicus sent their General word that he was coming down the Rhine at once at the head of a powerful force and that if such loyal men as remained under his command did not quickly follow the example of the Bonn regiments and execute the troublemakers he would put the whole lot to the sword indiscriminately. The General read the letter privately to the standard-bearers, non-commissioned officers, and a few trustworthy old soldiers and told them that there was little time for delay; for Germanicus might be on them any moment. They promised him to do what they could and, letting a few more loyalists into the secret, which was well kept, they rushed into the tents at midnight on a given signal and began to massacre the mutineers. These defended themselves as best they could and killed a number of the loyalists, but they were soon overpowered. Five hundred men were killed or wounded that night. The rest, leaving only sentries in the camp, marched out to meet Germanicus, begging him to lead them at once across the Rhine against the enemy.

Although the campaigning season was nearly at an end, the fine weather still held and Germanicus promised to do what they asked. He threw a pontoon bridge over the river and marched across at the head of 12,000 Roman infantry, twenty-six battalions of allies, and eight squadrons of cavalry. From his agents in enemy territory he knew of a large concentration of the enemy in the villages of Münster, where an annual autumn festival in honour of the German Hercules was being held. News of the mutiny had reached the Germans – the mutineers had actually been in treaty with Hermann and had exchanged presents with him – and they were only waiting for the regiments to march away to their new kingdom in the south-west before crossing the Rhine and marching direct for Italy. Germanicus followed a rarely used forest-route and surprised the Germans completely, catching them at their beer-drinking. (Beer is a fermented drink made from steeped grain and they drink it to extraordinary excess at their feasts.) He divided his forces into four columns and wasted the country on a fifty-mile frontage, burning the villages and slaughtering the inhabitants without respect for age or sex. On his return he found detachments of various neighbouring tribes posted to dispute his passage through the forest; but he advanced in skirmishing order and was pressing the enemy back well when there was a sudden alarm from the Twentieth Regiment, which was acting as rearguard, and Germanicus found that a huge force of Germans under the personal command of Hermann was upon him. Fortunately the trees at this point were not dense and allowed room for manoeuvre. Germanicus rode back to the position of most danger and cried out 'Break their line, Twentieth, and everything will be forgiven and forgotten'. The Twentieth fought like madmen and threw the Germans back with huge slaughter, pursuing them far into the open country at the back of the wood. Germanicus caught sight of Hermann and challenged him to combat, but Hermann's men were running away: it would have been death for him to have accepted the challenge. He galloped off. Germanicus was as unlucky as our father had been in his pursuit of enemy chieftains; but he won his victories in the same style, and the name 'Germanicus' which he had inherited he bore now in his own right. He marched the exultant army back to safety in their camps across the Rhine.

Tiberius never understood Germanicus, nor Germanicus Tiberius. Tiberius, as I have said, was one of the bad Claudians. Yet he was, at times, easily tempted to virtue, and in a noble age might well have passed for a noble character: for he was a man of no mean capacity. But the age was not a noble one and his heart had been hardened, and for that hardening Livia must, you will agree, bear the chief blame. Germanicus, on the other hand, was wholly inclined to virtue and, however evil the age into which he had been born, could never have behaved any differently from the way he did. So it was that when he refused the monarchy offered him by the German regiments, and made them swear allegiance to Tiberius, Tiberius could not make out why he should have done so. He decided that he must be even more subtle than himself and playing some very deep game indeed. The simple explanation, that Germanicus put honour above all other considerations and that he was bound to Tiberius by military allegiance and by having been adopted as his son, never occurred to him. But Germanicus, since he did not suspect Tiberius of complicity in Livia's designs and since Tiberius never offered him any slights or injuries, but on the contrary praised him greatly for his handling of the mutiny and decreed him a full triumph for his campaign in Münster, believed him to be as honourably-intentioned as himself, only a little simple-minded not to have seen through Livia's designs yet. He determined to have a frank talk with Tiberius as soon as he went home for the triumph. But Varus's death was not yet avenged; it was three years before Germanicus came back. The tone of the letters exchanged between Germanicus and Tiberius during this period was set by Germanicus, who wrote with dutiful affection. Tiberius replied in the same friendly strain because he thought that by so doing he was beating Germanicus at his own clever game. He undertook to repay him the amount of the doubled bequest and to extend the bounty to the Balkan regiments too. As a matter of policy he did pay the Balkan regiments this extra three gold pieces a man – there were threats of another mutiny – but excused himself from repaying Germanicus for a few months on the grounds of financial embarrassment. Naturally

Germanicus did not press him for the money and naturally Tiberius never gave it him. Germanicus wrote again to ask me whether he might wait to repay me until Tiberius repaid him, and I wrote back that I really meant the money as a gift.

Shortly after Tiberius's accession I wrote to him and said that I had been studying law and administration – as was the case – for some time, in the hope that I would at last be given an opportunity of serving my country in some responsible capacity. He wrote back to say that it certainly was an anomaly for a man who was the brother of Germanicus and his own nephew to go about as a mere knight, and that since I was now being made a priest of Augustus I must certainly be allowed to wear the dress of a senator: in fact, if I could undertake not to make a fool of myself in it he should ask permission for me to adopt the brocaded gown now worn by Consuls and ex-Consuls. I wrote back at once to say that I would even prefer office without dress to dress without office; but his only answer to this was to send me a present of forty golden pieces 'to buy toys with next All Fools' Day'. The Senate did vote me the brocaded gown, and as a mark of honour to Germanicus, who was now in the middle of a new successful campaign in Germany, proposed to decree me a seat in the House among the ex-Consuls. But Tiberius here interposed his veto, telling them that I was in his opinion incapable of delivering a speech on matters of State which would not be a trial of his fellow-members' patience.

There was another decree proposed at the same time, which he also vetoed. The circumstances were as follows: Agrippina had been delivered of her child, a girl called Agrippinilla, at Cologne; and I must say at once that this Agrippinilla turned out one of the very worst of the Claudians – in fact, I may say that she shows signs of outdoing all her ancestors and ancestresses in arrogance and vice. Agrippina was ill for some months after her delivery, and unable to keep Caligula in hand properly, so he was sent away on a visit to Rome as soon as Germanicus began his spring campaign. The child became a sort of national hero. Whenever he went out for a walk with his brothers he was cheered and stared at and made much of. Not yet three years old but marvellously precocious, he was a most difficult case, only pleasant when flattered and only docile when treated firmly. He came to stay with his great-grandmother Livia, but she had no time to look after him properly, and because he was always getting into mischief and quarrelling with his elder brothers, he came from her to live with my mother and me. My mother never flattered him, but neither did she treat him with enough firmness, until one day he spat at her in a fit of temper and she gave him a good spanking. 'You horrid old German woman,' he said, 'I'll burn your German house down!' He used 'German' as the worst insult he knew. And that afternoon he sneaked away into a lumber-room, which was next to the slaves' attic and full of old furniture and rubbish, and there set fire to a heap of worn-out straw mattresses. The fire soon swept the whole upper storey, and since it was an old house with dry-rot in the beams and draught-holes in the flooring there was no putting it out even with an endless bucket-chain to the carp pool. I managed to save all my papers and valuables and some of the furniture, and no lives were lost except two old slaves who were lying sick in bed, but nothing was left of the house except the bare walls and the cellars. Caligula was not punished, because the fire had given him such a great fright. He nearly got caught in it himself, hiding guiltily under his bed until the smoke drove him screaming out.

Well, the Senate wanted to decree that my house should be rebuilt at the expense of the State, on the ground that it had been the home of so many distinguished members of my family: but Tiberius would not allow this. He said that the outbreak of fire had been due to my negligence and that the damage could easily have been confined to the attics if I had acted in a responsible way; and rather than that the State should pay he undertook to rebuild and refurnish the house himself. Loud applause from the House. This was most unjust and dishonest, particularly as he had no intention of keeping his undertaking. I was forced to sell my last important piece of property in Rome, a block of houses near the Cattle Market and a large building site adjoining, to rebuild the house at my own expense. I never told Germanicus that Caligula had been the incendiary, because he would have felt obliged to make good the damage himself; and I suppose it was, in a way, an accident, because one couldn't hold so young a child responsible.

When Germanicus's men went out to fight the Germans again they had a new addition to that ballad of Augustus's Three Griefs, of which I recall two or three verses and odd lines of others, most of them ridiculous:

>   Six gold bits a man he left us
>   For to buy us pork and beans,
>   For to buy us cheese and cracknels
>   In the German dry canteens.

and

>   God Augustus walks in Heaven,
>   Ghost Marcellus swims in Styx,
>   Julia's dead and gone to join him –
>   That's the end of Julia's tricks.

>   But our Eagles still are straying
>   And by shame and sorrow stirred
>   To the tomb of God Augustus
>   We'll bring back each wandering bird.

There was another which began:

>   German Hermann lost his sweetheart
>   And his little pot of beer,

but I can't remember the finish, and the verse is not important except as reminding me to tell of Hermann's 'sweetheart'. She was the daughter of a chieftain called, in German, Siegstoss or something of the sort; but his Roman name was Segestes. He had been to Rome, like Hermann, and enrolled among the Knights, and unlike Hermann had felt morally bound by the oath of friendship he had sworn to Augustus. It was this Segestes who had warned Varus about Hermann and Segimerus and suggested that Varus should arrest them at the banquet to which he had invited them just before his unfortunate expedition started. Segestes had a favourite daughter whom Hermann had carried off and married and Segestes never forgave him for this injury. He could not, however, come out openly on the side of the Romans against Hermann, who was a national hero; all that he had been able to do as yet was to maintain a secret correspondence with Germanicus, giving him intelligence of military movements and constantly assuring him that he had never wavered in his loyalty to Rome and was only waiting for an opportunity to make proof of it. But now he wrote to Germanicus that he was being besieged in his stockaded village by Hermann, who had sworn to give no quarter; and that he could not hold out much longer. Germanicus made a forced march, defeated the besieging force, which was not numerous – Hermann himself was away, wounded – and rescued

Segestes: when he found that he had a valuable prize awaiting him – Hermann's wife, who had been visiting her father when the quarrel broke out between them and her husband, and who was far gone in pregnancy. Germanicus treated Segestes and his household very kindly, giving them an estate on the western side of the Rhine. Hermann, who was enraged at his wife's capture, feared that Germanicus's clemency might induce other German chieftains to make overtures of peace. He built up a strong new confederation of tribes, including some which had always hitherto been friendly to Rome. Germanicus was undaunted. The more Germans he had in the field openly against him, the better he was pleased. He had never trusted them as allies.

And before the summer was out he had beaten them in a series of battles, forced Segimerus to surrender, and won back the first of the three lost Eagles, that of the Nineteenth Regiment. He also visited the scene of Varus's defeat and gave the bones of his comrades-in-arms a decent burial, laying the first sod of their tomb with his own hands. The General who had behaved so supinely in the mutiny fought bravely at the head of his corps, and on one occasion turned what had seemed a hopeless defeat into a creditable victory. Premature news that this battle was lost and that the conquering Germans were marching towards the Rhine caused such consternation at the nearest bridge that the captain of the guard gave his men orders to retreat across it and then break it down: which would have meant abandoning everyone on the other side to their fate. But Agrippina was there and countermanded the order. She told the men that she was captain of the guard now and would remain so until her husband returned to relieve her of her command. When eventually the victorious troops came marching back she was at her post to welcome them. Her popularity now almost equalled that of her husband. She had organized a hospital for the wounded as Germanicus sent them back after each battle and had given them the best available medical treatment. Ordinarily, wounded soldiers remained with their units until they either died or recovered. The hospital she paid for out of her own purse.

But I mentioned the death of Julia. When Tiberius became Emperor, Julia's daily supply of food at Reggio was reduced to four ounces of bread a day and one ounce of cheese. She was already in a consumption from the unhealthiness of her quarters and this starvation diet soon carried her off. But there was still no news of Postumus, and Livia, until she was certain of his death, could not be easy in her mind.

Chapter 17

TIBERIUS continued to rule with moderation and consulted the Senate before taking any step of the least political importance. But the Senate had been voting according to direction for so long that they seemed to have lost the power of independent decision; and Tiberius never made it plain which way he wanted them to vote even when he was very anxious for them to vote one way or another. He wanted to avoid all appearance of tyranny and yet to keep his position at the head of affairs. The Senate soon found that if he spoke with studied elegance in favour of a motion he meant that he wanted it voted against, and that if he spoke with studied elegance against it this meant that he wanted it passed; and that on the very few occasions when he spoke briefly and without any rhetoric he meant to be taken literally. Gallus and an old wag called Haterius used to delight in making speeches in warm agreement with Tiberius, enlarging his arguments to a point only just short of absurdity and then voting the way he really wanted them to vote; thus showing that they understood his tricks perfectly. This Haterius in the debate about Tiberius's accession had cried out: 'O Tiberius, how long will you allow unhappy Rome to remain without a head?' – which had offended him because he knew that Haterius saw through his intentions. The next day Haterius pursued the joke by falling at Tiberius's feet and pleading for pardon for not having been warm enough. Tiberius started back in disgust, but Haterius grabbed at his knees and Tiberius went over, catching the back of his head a bang on the marble floor. Tiberius's German bodyguard did not understand what was happening and sprang forward to slaughter their master's assailant; Tiberius only just stopped them in time.

Haterius excelled in parody. He had an enormous voice, a comic face, and great fertility of invention. Whenever Tiberius in his speeches introduced any painfully far-fetched or archaic phrase Haterius would pick it up and make it the key-word of his reply.

(Augustus had always said that the wheels of Haterius's eloquence needed a drag-chain even when he was driving uphill.) The slow-witted Tiberius was no match for Haterius. Gallus's gift was for mock zeal. Tiberius was extremely careful not to appear a candidate for any divine honours and refused to allow himself to be spoken about as if he had any superhuman attributes: he did not even allow the provincials to build him temples. Gallus was therefore fond of referring, as if accidentally, to Tiberius as 'His Sacred Majesty'. When Haterius, who was always ready to carry on the gag, rose to rebuke him for this incorrect way of speaking he would apologize profusely and say that nothing was farther from his mind than to do anything in disobedience of the orders of His Sacred ... oh, dear, it was so easy to fall into that mistaken way of speaking, a thousand apologies once more ... he meant, contrary to the wishes of his honoured friend and fellow-senator Tiberius Nero Caesar Augustus.

'*Not* Augustus, fool,' Haterius would say in a stage whisper. 'He's refused that title a dozen times. He only uses it *when he writes letters to other monarchs*.'

They had one trick which annoyed Tiberius more than any other. If he made a show of modesty when thanked by the Senate for performing some national service – such as undertaking to complete the temples which Augustus had left unfinished – they would praise his honesty in not taking credit for his mother's work, and congratulate Livia on having so dutiful a son. When they saw that there was nothing that Tiberius hated so much as hearing Livia praised they kept it up. Haterius even suggested that just as the Greeks were called by their father's names, so Tiberius should be named after his mother and that it should be a crime to call him other than Tiberius Liviades – or perhaps Livigena would be the more correct Latin form. Gallus found another weak spot in Tiberius's armour, and that was his hatred of any mention of his stay at Rhodes. The most daring thing he did was to praise Tiberius one day for his clemency – it was the very day that news reached the city of Julia's death – and to tell the story of the teacher of rhetoric at Rhodes who had refused Tiberius's modest application to join his classes, on the ground that there was no vacancy at present, saying that he must come back in seven days. Gallus added, 'And what do you think His Sacred ... I beg your pardon, I should say, what do you think my honoured friend and fellow-senator Tiberius Nero Caesar did on his recent accession to the monarchy, when the same impertinent fellow arrived to pay his respects to the new divinity? Did he cut off that impudent head and give it as a football to his German bodyguard? Not at all: with a wit only equalled by his clemency he told him that he had no vacancies at present in his corps of flatterers and that he must come back in seven years.' This was an invention, I think, but the Senate had no reason to disbelieve it and applauded so heartily that Tiberius had to let it go by as the truth.

Tiberius at last silenced Haterius by saying very slowly one day: 'You will please forgive me, Haterius, if I speak rather more frankly than it is usual for one senator to speak to another, but I must say that I think you are a dreadful bore and not in the least witty.' Then he turned to the House: 'You will forgive me, my lords, but I have always said and will say again that since you have been good enough to entrust such absolute power to me I ought not to be ashamed to use it for the common good. If I use it now to silence buffoons who insult you as well as myself by their silly performances, I trust that I will earn your approval. You have always been kind and patient with me.' Without Haterius, Gallus had to play a lone game.

Though Tiberius hated his mother more than ever, he continued to let her rule him. All the appointments which he made to Consulships or provincial governorships were really hers: and they were very sensible ones, the men being chosen for merit, not for family influence or because they had flattered her or done her some private service. For I must make it plain, if I have not already done so, that however criminal the means used by Livia to win the direction of affairs for herself, first through Augustus and then through Tiberius, she was an exceptionally able and just ruler; and it was only when she ceased to direct the system that she had built up that it went wrong.

I have spoken of Sejanus, the son of the Commander of the Guards. He now succeeded to his father's command and was one of the only three men to whom Tiberius in any way opened his mind. Thrasyllus was another; he had come to Rome with Tiberius and never lost his hold on him. The third was a senator called Nerva. Thrasyllus never discussed State policy with Tiberius and never asked for any official position; and when Tiberius gave him large sums of money he accepted them casually, as if money were something of little importance to him. He had a big observatory in a dome-shaped room in the Palace which had windows of glass so clear and transparent that you hardly knew they were there. Tiberius used to spend a great deal of his time here with Thrasyllus, who taught him the rudiments of astrology and many other magic arts, including that of interpreting dreams in the Chaldean style. Sejanus and Nerva Tiberius seems to have chosen for their totally opposite characters. Nerva never made an enemy and never lost a friend. His one fault, if you may call it so, was that he kept silent in the presence of evil when speech would not remedy it. He was sweet-tempered, generous, courageous, utterly truthful, and was never known to stoop to the least fraud, even if good promised to come from so doing. If he had been in Germanicus's position, for instance, he would never have forged that letter, though his own safety and that of the Empire had hung upon it. Tiberius made Nerva superintendent of the City aqueducts and kept him constantly by him; I suppose by way of providing himself with a handy yardstick of virtue – as Sejanus certainly served as a handy yardstick of wickedness. Sejanus had as a young man been a friend of Gaius, on whose staff he had served in the East, and had been clever enough to foresee Tiberius's return to favour: he had contributed to it by reassuring Gaius that Tiberius meant what he said when he disclaimed any ambition to rule, and by urging him to write that letter of recommendation to Augustus. He let Tiberius know at the time that he had done this and Tiberius wrote him a letter, still in his possession, promising never to forget his services. Sejanus was a liar but so fine a general of lies that he knew how to marshal them into an alert and disciplined formation – this was a clever remark of Gallus's, it is not mine – which would come off best in any skirmish with suspicions or any general engagement with truth. Tiberius envied him this talent as he envied Nerva his honesty: for though he had progressed far in the direction of evil, he still felt hampered by unaccountable impulses towards the good.

It was Sejanus who first began poisoning his mind against Germanicus, telling him that a man who could forge a letter from his father in whatever circumstances was not to be trusted; and that Germanicus was really aiming at the monarchy but was acting with caution – first winning the men's affection by bribery and then making sure of their fighting capacities and his own leadership by this unnecessary campaign across the Rhine. As for Agrippina, Sejanus said, she was a dangerously ambitious woman: look how she had behaved – styled herself captain of the bridge and welcomed the regiments on their return as if she were Heaven knows who! That the bridge was in danger of being destroyed was probably an invention of her own. Sejanus also said that he knew from a freedman of his who had once been a slave in Germanicus's household that Agrippina somehow believed Livia and Tiberius responsible for the death of her three brothers and the banishment of her sister, and had sworn to be revenged. Sejanus also began discovering all kinds of plots against Tiberius and kept him in constant fear of assassination while assuring him that he need not have the least anxiety with himself on guard. He encouraged Tiberius to cross Livia in trifling ways, to show her that she over-estimated the strength of her position. It was he who, a few years later, organized the Guards into a disciplined body. Hitherto the three battalions stationed at Rome had been billeted by sections in various parts of the City, in inns and such-like places, and were difficult to fetch out on parade in a hurry and slovenly in their dress and movements. He suggested to Tiberius that if he built a single permanent camp for them outside the City it would give them a strong corporate sense, prevent them from being influenced by the rumours and waves of political feeling which were always running through the City, and attach them more closely to his person as their Emperor. Tiberius improved on his advice by recalling the remaining six battalions from their stations in other parts of Italy and making the new camp big enough to house them all – 9,000 infantry and 2,000 cavalry. Apart from the four City battalions, one of which he now sent to Lyons, and various colonies of discharged veterans, these were the only soldiers in Italy. The German bodyguard did not count as soldiers, being technically slaves. But they were picked men and more fanatically loyal to their Emperor than any true-born Roman. There was not a man of them who really wanted to return to his cold, rude, barbarous land, though they were always singing sad choruses about it; they had too good a time here.

As for the criminal dossiers, to which Tiberius, because of his fear of plots against his life, was most anxious now to have access, Livia still pretended that the key to the cipher was lost. Tiberius, at Sejanus's suggestion, told her that since they were of no use to anyone he would burn them. She said that he could do so if he liked, but surely it would be better to keep them, just in case the key turned up? Perhaps she might even suddenly remember the key. 'Very well, mother,' he answered, 'I'll take charge of them until you do; and meanwhile I'll spend my evenings trying to work the cipher out myself.' So he took them off to his own room and locked them in a cupboard. He tried his hardest to find the key to that cipher but it beat him. The common cipher was simply writing Latin E for Greek Alpha, Latin F for Greek Beta, G for Gamma, H for Delta, and so on. The key of the high cipher was next to impossible to discover. It was provided by the first hundred lines of the first book of the *Iliad*, which had to be read concurrently with the writing of the cipher, each letter in the writing being represented by the number of letters of the alphabet intervening between it and the corresponding letter in Homer. Thus the first letter of the first word of the first line of the first book of the *Iliad* is Mu. Suppose the first letter of the first word of an entry in the dossier to be Upsilon. There are seven letters in the Greek alphabet intervening between Mu and Upsilon, so Upsilon would be written as 7. In this plan the alphabet would be thought of as circular, Omega, the last letter, following Alpha, the first, so that the distance between Upsilon and Alpha would be 4, but the distance between Alpha and Upsilon would be 18. It was Augustus's invention and must have taken rather a long time to write and decode, but I suppose by practice they came to know the distance between any two letters in the alphabet without having to count up, which saved a lot of time. And how do I know about all this? Because many many years later when the dossiers came into my possession I worked the cipher out myself. I happened to find a roll of the first book of Homer, written on sheepskin, filed among the other rolls. It was clear that the first hundred lines only had been studied; because the sheepskin was badly soiled and inked at the beginning and quite clear at the end. When I looked closer and saw tiny figures – 6, 23, 12 – faintly scratched under the letters of the first line, it was not difficult to connect them with the cipher. I was surprised that Tiberius had overlooked this clue.

Speaking of the alphabet, I was interested at this time in a simple plan for making Latin truly phonetic. It seemed to me that three letters were missing. These three were consonantal u to distinguish it from u the vowel; a letter to correspond to the Greek

Upsilon (which is a vowel between Latin I and U) for use in Greek words which have become Latinized; and a letter to denote the double consonant which we now write in Latin as BS but pronounce like the Greek Psi. It was important, I wrote, for provincials learning Latin to learn it correctly; if the letters did not correspond to the sound how could they avoid mistakes in pronunciation? So I suggested, for consonantal U, the upside-down F (which is used for that purpose in Etruscan): thus LAꟼINIA instead of LAUINIA; and a broken H for Greek Upsilon: thus BꞀBLIOTHECA instead of BIBLIOTHECA; and an upside-down C for BS: thus AꓛQUE for ABSQUE. The last letter was not so important, but the other two seemed to me essential. I suggested the broken H and the upside-down F and C because these would cause the least trouble to the men who use letter-punches for metal or clay: they would not have to make any new punches. I published the book and one or two people said that my suggestions were sensible; but of course it had absolutely no result. My mother told me that there were three impossible things in the world: that shops should stretch across the bay from Baiae to Puteoli, that I should subdue the island of Britain, and that any one of these absurd new letters would ever appear on public inscriptions in Rome. I have always remembered this remark of hers, for it had a sequel.

My mother was extremely short-tempered with me these days because our house took such a long time to rebuild and the new furniture I bought was not equal to the old, and because her income was greatly reduced by the share she took in these expenses – I could not have found all the money myself. We lived for two years in quarters at the Palace (not very good ones) and she vented her irritation on me so constantly that in the end I could not bear it any longer and moved out of Rome to my villa near Capua, only visiting the City when my priestly functions demanded it, which was not often. You will ask about Urgulanilla. She never came to Capua; in Rome we had little to do with each other. She scarcely greeted me when we met and took no notice of me except, for appearances sake, when guests were present; and we always slept apart. She seemed fond enough of our boy, Drusillus, but did little for him in any practical way. His bringing-up was left to my mother, who managed the household, and never called on Urgulanilla for any help. My mother treated Drusillus as if he were her own child, and somehow contrived to forget who his parents were. I never learned to like Drusillus myself; he was a surly, stolid, insolent child, and my mother scolded me so often in his presence that he learned to have no respect for me.

I don't know how Urgulanilla got through her days. But she never seemed bored and ate enormously and, so far as I know, entertained no secret lovers. This strange creature had one passion, though – Numantina, the wife of my brother-in-law Silvanus, a little fair-haired elf-like creature who had once done or said something (I don't know what) which had penetrated through that thick hide and muscular bulging body and touched what served Urgulanilla for a heart. Urgulanilla had a life-size portrait of Numantina in her boudoir: she used, I believe, to sit gazing at it for hours whenever there was no opportunity for gazing at Numantina herself. When I moved to Capua, Urgulanilla stayed at Rome with my mother and Drusillus.

The only inconvenience of Capua as a home for me was the absence of a good library. However, I began a book for which a library was not needed – a history of Etruria. I had by now made some progress in Etruscan, and Aruns, with whom I spent a few hours every day, was most helpful in giving me access to the archives of his half-ruined temple. He told me that he had been born on the day that the comet appeared which had announced the beginning of the tenth and last cycle of the Etruscan race. A cycle is a period reckoned by the longest life: that is to say, a cycle does not close until the death of everyone who was alive at the festival celebrating the close of the previous cycle. The Etruscans reckoned it at 110 years. This was the last cycle and it would end with the total disappearance of Etruscan as a spoken language. The prophecy was already as good as fulfilled because he had no successors in his priestly office, and the country-people now talked Latin even in the home; so he was glad to help me to write my history, he said, as a mausoleum for the traditions of a once great race. I started it in the second year of Tiberius's reign and I finished it twenty-one years later. I consider it my best work: certainly I worked hardest at it. So far as I know, there is no other book on the subject of the Etruscans at all and they were a very interesting race indeed; so I think that historians of the future will be grateful to me.

I had Callon and Pallas with me and lived a quiet orderly life. I took an interest in the farm attached to my villa and enjoyed occasional visits from friends in Rome who came out for a holiday. There was a woman permanently living with me, called Actë, a professional prostitute and a very decent woman. I never had any trouble with her in the fifteen years she was with me. Our relationship was a purely business one. She had deliberately chosen prostitution as her profession; I paid her well; there was no nonsense about her. We were quite fond of each other in a way. At last she told me that she wanted to retire on her earnings. She would marry a decent man, an old soldier for choice, and settle down in one of the colonies and have children before it was too late. She had always wanted to have a houseful of children. So I kissed her and said good-bye and gave her enough dowry-money to make things very easy for her. She did not go away, though, until she had found me a successor whom she could trust to treat me properly. She found me Calpurnia, who was so like her that I have often thought she must have been her daughter. Actë did once mention having had a daughter whom she had put out to nurse because one couldn't be a prostitute and a mother at the same time. Well, so Actë married an ex-Guardsman who treated her quite well and had five children by her. I have always kept an eye on that family. I mention her only because my readers will wonder what sort of sexual life I led when living apart from Urgulanilla. I do not think it is natural for an ordinary man to live long without a woman, and since Urgulanilla was impossible as a wife I do not think that I can be blamed for living with Actë. Actë and I had an understanding that while we were together we would neither of us have to do with anyone else. This was not sentiment but a medical precaution: there was so much venereal disease now in Rome – another fatal legacy, by the way, of the Punic War.

Here I wish to put it on record that I have never at any time of my life practised homosexuality. I do not use Augustus's argument against it, that it prevents men having children to support the State, but I have always thought it at once pitiful and disgusting to see a full-grown man, a magistrate, perhaps, with a family of his own, slobbering luxuriously over a plump little boy with a painted face and bangles; or an ancient senator playing Queen Venus to some tall young Adonis of the Guards cavalry who tolerates the old fool only because he has money.

When I had to go up to Rome I stayed there for as short a time as possible. I felt something uncomfortable in the atmosphere on the Palatine Hill, which may well have been the growing tension between Tiberius and Livia. He had begun building a huge palace for himself on the north-west of the hill, and now moved into the lower rooms, before the upper ones were finished, leaving her in sole possession of Augustus's palace. Livia, as if to show that Tiberius's new building, though three times the size, would never have the prestige of the old one, put a magnificent gold statue of Augustus in her hall and proposed, as High-Priestess of his cult, to invite all the senators and their wives to the dedicatory banquet. But Tiberius pointed out that he must first ask the Senate to vote on the matter: it was a State occasion, not a private entertainment. He so managed the debate that the banquet was held in two parts simultaneously: the senators in the hall with himself as host, and their wives in a big room leading off it with Livia as hostess. She swallowed the insult by not treating it as such, only as a sensible arrangement more in keeping with what Augustus would have wished himself; but gave orders to the Palace cooks that the women were to be served first with the best joints and sweetmeats and wine. She also appropriated the most costly dishes and drinking-vessels for her feast. She got the better of him on that occasion and the senators' wives all had a good laugh at the expense of Tiberius and their husbands.

Another uncomfortable thing about coming to Rome was that I never seemed to be able to avoid meeting Sejanus. I disliked having anything to do with him, though he was always studiously polite to me and never did me any direct injury. I was astonished that a man with a face and manner like his and not well-born or a famous fighter, or even particularly rich, could have made such a huge success in the City: he was now the next most important man after Tiberius, and extremely popular with the Guards. It was a completely untrustworthy face – sly, cruel, and irregular-featured – and the one thing that held it together was a certain animal hardiness and resolution. What was stranger still to me, several women of good family were said to be rivals in love for him. He and Castor got on badly together, which was only natural, for there were rumours that Livilla and Sejanus had some sort of understanding. But Tiberius seemed to have complete confidence in him.

I have mentioned Briseis, my mother's old freedwoman. When I told her that I was leaving Rome and settling at Capua she said how much she would miss me, but that I was wise to go. 'I had a funny dream about you last night, Master Claudius, if you'll forgive me. You were a little lame boy; and thieves broke into his father's house and murdered his father and a whole lot of relations and friends; but he squeezed through the pantry-window and went hobbling into the neighbouring wood. He climbed up a tree and waited. The thieves came out of the house and sat down under the tree where he was hiding, to divide the plunder. Soon they began to quarrel about who should have what, and one of the thieves got killed, and then two more, and then the rest began drinking wine and pretended to be great friends; but the wine had been poisoned by one of the murdered thieves, so they all died in agony. The lame boy climbed down the tree and collected the valuables and found a lot of gold and jewels among them that had been stolen from other families: but he took it all home with him and became quite rich.'

I smiled. 'That's a funny dream, Briseis. But he was still as lame as ever and all that wealth could not buy his father and family back to life again, could it?'

'No, my dear, but perhaps he married and had a family of his own. So choose a good tree, Master Claudius, and don't come down till the last of the thieves are dead. That's what my dream said.'

'I'll not come down even then, if I can help it, Briseis. I don't want to be the receiver of stolen goods.'

'You can always give them back, Master Claudius.'

This was all very remarkable in the light of what happened later. I have no great faith in dreams. Athenodorus once dreamed that there was treasure in a badger's den in a wood near Rome. He found his way to the exact spot, which he had never visited before, and there in a bank was the hole leading to the den. He fetched a couple of countrymen to dig away the bank until they came to the den at the end of the hole – where they found a rotten old purse containing six mouldy coppers and a bad shilling, which was not enough to pay the countrymen for their work. And one of my tenants, a shopkeeper, dreamed once that a flight of eagles wheeled round his head and one settled on his shoulder. He took it for a sign that he would one day be Emperor, but all that happened was that a piquet of Guards visited him the next morning (they had eagles on their shields) and the corporal arrested him for some offence that brought him under military jursidiction.

Chapter 18

ONE summer afternoon at Capua I was sitting on a stone bench behind the stables of my villa, thinking out some problem of Etruscan history and idly shooting dice, left hand against right, on the rough plank table in front of me. A raggedly-dressed man came up and asked whether I was Tiberius A.D. 16 Claudius Drusus Nero Germanicus: he had been directed here from Rome, he said.

'I have a message for you, sir. I don't know whether it's worth delivering, but I'm an old soldier on the tramp – one of your father's veterans, sir – and you know what it is, I'm glad of having an excuse for taking one road rather than another.'

'Who gave you the message?'

'A fellow I met in the woods near Cape Cosa. Curious sort of fellow. He was dressed like a slave, but he spoke like a Caesar. A big thick-set fellow and looked half starved.'

'What name did he give?'

'No name at all. He said you'd know who he was by the message, and be surprised to hear from him. He made me repeat the message twice to make sure I had it right. I was to say that he was still fishing, but that a man couldn't live wholly on fish, and that you were to pass the word to his brother-in-law, and that if the milk was sent it never reached him, and that he wanted a little book to read, at least seven pages long. And that you were not to do anything until you heard from him again. Does that make sense, sir, or was the fellow cracked?'

When he said that, I could not believe my ears. Postumus! But Postumus was dead. 'Has he a big jaw, blue eyes, and a way of tilting his head on one side when he asks you a question?'

'That's the man, sir.'

I poured him out a drink with a hand so shaky that I spilt as much as I poured. Then, signing that he was to wait there for me, I went into the house. I found two good plain gowns and some underclothes and sandals and a pair of razors and some soap. Then I took the first sewn-sheet book that came to hand – it happened to be a copy of some recent speeches of Tiberius to the Senate – and on the seventh page I wrote in milk: *What joy ! I shall write to G. at once. Be careful. Send for whatever you need. Where can I see you? My dearest love to you. Here are twenty gold pieces, all I have at the moment, but quick gifts are double gifts, I hope.*

I waited for the page to dry and then gave the man the book and clothes wrapped in a bundle, and a purse. I said: 'Take these thirty gold pieces. Ten are for yourself. Twenty are for the man in the woods. Bring back a message from him and you shall have ten more. But keep your mouth shut and be back soon.'

'Good enough, sir,' he said. 'I'll not fail you. But what's to prevent me from going off with this bundle and all the money?'

I said: 'If you were a dishonest man you wouldn't ask that question. So let us have another drink together and off you go.'

To cut a long story short, he went away with the bundle and money and a few days later brought me back a verbal answer from Postumus, which was thanks for the money and clothes and that I was not to seek him out, but that the Crocodile's mother would know where he was and that his name was now Pantherus and would I forward him his brother-in-law's answer as soon as possible. I paid the old soldier the ten pieces I had promised him and ten more for his faithfulness. I understood whom Postumus meant by the Crocodile's mother. The Crocodile was an old freedman of Agrippa's whom we called that because of his torpidity and greed and his enormous jaws. He had a mother living at Perusia, where she kept an inn. I knew the place well. I sent off a letter to Germanicus at once to tell him the news; I sent it by Pallas to Rome telling him to send it off with the next post to Germany. In the letter I merely said that Postumus was alive and in hiding – I did not say where – and begged Germanicus to acknowledge the receipt of the letter at once. Then I waited and waited for an answer, but none came. I wrote again, rather more fully; but still no answer. I sent a message to the Crocodile's mother by a country-carrier that no message had yet arrived for Pantherus from his brother-in-law.

I did not hear again from Postumus. He did not wish to compromise me further, and now that he had money and was able to move about without being arrested on suspicion as a runaway slave he was not dependent on my help. Somebody at the inn recognized him and he had to move from there for safety's sake. Very soon the rumour that he was alive was all over Italy. Everyone was talking about it at Rome. A dozen people, including three senators, came out to me from the City to ask me privately if it were true. I told them that I had not seen him but that I had met someone who had, and that there was no doubt that it was Postumus. In return I asked them what they intended to do if he came to Rome and won the support of the populace. But the directness of my question embarrassed and hurt them, and I got no answer.

Postumus was reported to have visited various country towns in the neighbourhood of Rome, but apparently he took the precaution of not entering them before nightfall and always going away, in disguise, before dawn. He was never seen publicly but would lodge at some inn and leave behind a message of thanks for the kindness shown him – signed with his real name. At last one day he landed at Ostia from a small coasting vessel. The port knew, a few hours beforehand, that he was coming, and he had a tremendous ovation at the quay as he stepped ashore. He chose to land at Ostia because it was the summer headquarters of the Fleet, of which his father Agrippa had been Admiral. His vessel flew a green pennant which Augustus had given Agrippa the right to fly whenever he was at sea (and his sons after him) in memory of his sea victory off Actium. Agrippa's memory was honoured at Ostia almost beyond that of Augustus.

Postumus was in great danger of his life, being still under sentence of banishment and therefore outlawed by his public reappearance in Italy. He made a short speech of thanks to the crowd for their welcome. He said that if Fortune was kind to him and if he won back the esteem of the Roman Senate and people which he had forfeited because of certain lying accusations brought against him by his enemies – accusations which his grandfather, the God Augustus, had realized too late were untrue – he would reward the loyalty of the men and women of Ostia in no niggardly fashion. A company of Guards was there with orders to arrest him, for Livia and Tiberius had got the news too, somehow. But the men would have had no chance against that crowd of sailors. The captain wisely made no attempt to carry out his commission; he ordered two men to change into sailors' slops and not lose sight of Postumus. But by the time they had changed he had disappeared and they could find no trace of him.

The next day Rome was full of sailors who picketed the principal streets: whenever they met a knight or senator or public official they asked him the pass-word. The pass-word was 'Neptune', and if he did not already know it he was given it and made to repeat it three times unless he wanted a beating. Nobody wanted a beating, and popular feeling now ran so strongly in sympathy with Postumus and against Tiberius and Livia that if a single favourable word had come from Germanicus the whole City, including the Guards and the City battalions, would have come over to him at once. But without Germanicus's support any rising in favour of Postumus would have meant civil war; and nobody had much confidence in Postumus's chances if it came to a struggle with Germanicus.

In this crisis the same Crispus who had antagonized Tiberius two years before by sending Clement to his death on the island (but had been forgiven) came forward and offered to redeem his fault by this time making sure of Postumus. Tiberius gave him a free hand. He found out somehow where Postumus's headquarters were and, going to him with a large sum of money which he said was for the payment of his sailors, who had already lost two working-days by this picketing work, he undertook to bring over the German bodyguard to Postumus's side as soon as he gave the signal. He had, he said, already given them enormous bribes. Postumus believed him. They arranged a meeting for two hours after midnight at a certain street corner where Postumus's sailors were also to assemble in force. They would march to Tiberius's Palace. Crispus would order the bodyguard to admit Postumus. Tiberius, Castor, and Livia would be arrested, and Crispus said that Sejanus, while not active in the plot, had undertaken to bring the Guards over in support of the new régime as soon as the first blow had been successfully struck: on condition that he retained his command.

The sailors were punctual at the rendezvous but Postumus did not arrive. At that hour no citizens were in the street; so when a combined force of Germans from the bodyguard and picked men of Sejanus's suddenly fell on the sailors – who were mostly drunk and not in any regular formation – the pass-word 'Neptune' lost its power. Many of them were killed on the spot, many more as they broke and ran, and the rest never once slowed down, it is said, before they reached Ostia again. Crispus and two soldiers had waylaid Postumus in a narrow alley between his headquarters and the rendezvous, stunned him with a sandbag, gagged and bound him, put him into a covered sedan, and carried him off to the Palace. The next day Tiberius made a statement to the Senate. A certain slave of Postumus Agrippa's called Clement, he said, had caused a deal of unnecessary alarm in the City by impersonating his dead former master. This bold fellow had run away from the provincial knight who had bought him when Postumus's estate was sold and had hidden in a wood on the coast of Tuscany until his beard grew long enough to hide his receding chin – the chief point of dissimilarity between himself and Postumus. Some rowdy sailors at Ostia had pretended to believe in him, but only as an excuse for marching to Rome and creating a disturbance there. They had assembled in the suburbs a little before dawn that morning under his leadership with the object of marching to the centre of the City and plundering shops and private houses. When challenged by a force of Watchmen they had dispersed and deserted their leader, who had since been put to death: so the House need have no further anxiety about the matter.

I heard later that Tiberius pretended not to recognize Postumus when he was brought before him at the Palace and asked him, mockingly: 'How did you happen to become one of the Caesars?' To which Postumus answered: 'In the same way and on the same day as you did. Have you forgotten?' Tiberius told a slave to strike Postumus on the mouth for his insolence, and he was then put on the rack and asked to reveal his fellow-conspirators. But he would only tell scandalous anecdotes of the private life of Tiberius, which were so disgusting and so circumstantial that Tiberius lost his temper and battered his face in with his great bony fists. The soldiers finished the bloody work by beheading him and hacking him into pieces in the cellar of the Palace.

What greater sorrow can there be than to mourn a beloved friend as murdered – at the close of a long and undeserved exile, too – and then, after the brief joy and astonishment of hearing that he has somehow cheated his executioners, to have to mourn him a second time – this time without hope of error and without even seeing him in the interval – as treacherously recaptured and shamefully tortured and killed? My one consolation was that when Germanicus heard what had happened – and I would at once write him the whole story so far as I knew it – he would leave his campaigns in Germany and march back to Rome at the head of as many regiments as could be spared from the Rhine and avenge Postumus's death on Livia and Tiberius. I wrote, but he did not answer; I wrote again, and still no answer. But eventually a long affectionate letter came in which there was a wondering reference to the success which Clement had had in impersonating Postumus – how in the world had he managed to do it? From this sentence it was quite clear that none of my important letters had arrived: the only one to arrive had been sent off by the same post as the second. In this I had merely given him particulars of a business matter which he had asked me to look into for him: he now thanked me for the information, which he said was exactly what he wanted. I realized with a sudden feeling of dread that Livia or Tiberius must have intercepted all the rest.

My digestion had always been bad and fear of poison in every dish did not improve it. My stammer returned and I had attacks of aphasia – sudden blanks in the mind which brought me into great ridicule: if they caught me in the middle of a sentence I would finish it anyhow. The most unfortunate result of this weakness was that I made a mess of my duties as priest of Augustus, which hitherto I had carried out without cause for complaint from anyone. There is an old custom at Rome that if any mistake is made in the ritual of a sacrifice or other service the whole thing has to be gone over again from the beginning. It now often happened when I was officiating that I would lose my way in a prayer and perhaps go on repeating the same sequence of sentences two or three times before I realized what I was doing, or that I would take up the flint knife for cutting the victim's throat before sprinkling its head with the ritual flour and salt – and this sort of thing meant going back to the beginning again. It was tedious to make three or four attempts at a service before I could get through it perfectly, and the congregation used to get very restless. At last I wrote to Tiberius as High Pontiff and asked to be relieved from all my religious duties for a year on the ground of ill-health. He granted the request without comment.

Chapter 19

GERMANICUS's third year of war against the Germans was more successful even than the first two. He had worked out a new plan of campaign, by which he would take the Germans by surprise

and save his men a lot of dangerous and weary marching.
This was to build on the Rhine a fleet of nearly a thousand A.D. 16
transports, embark with most of his forces, and sail down
the river and, by way of the canal that our father had once cut,
through the Dutch lakes and by sea to the mouth of the Ems.
Here he would anchor his transports on the near bank, except for
a few which would serve for making a pontoon bridge. He would
then attack the tribes across the Weser, a river, fordable in places,
which runs parallel to the Ems about fifty miles beyond. The plan
worked well in every detail.

When the advance-guard reached the Weser they found Hermann and some allied chieftains waiting on the further bank.
Hermann shouted across to ask whether Germanicus was in command. When they answered yes, he asked whether they would
take him a message? The message was: 'Hermann's courteous
greetings to Germanicus, and might he be permitted speech with
his brother?' This was a brother of Hermann's called, in German,
something like Goldkopf, or at any rate a name so barbarous that
it was impossible to transliterate it into Latin – as 'Hermann' had
been made into 'Arminius', or as 'Siegmyrgth' into 'Segimerus',
so it was translated as Flavius, meaning the golden-headed.
Flavius had been in the Roman Army for years, and being at
Lyons at the time of the disaster of Varus had there made a de-
claration of his continued loyalty to Rome, repudiating all the
family ties which bound him to his treacherous brother Hermann.
In the next year's campaign of Tiberius and Germanicus he had
fought bravely and lost an eye.

Germanicus asked Flavius whether he wished to address his
brother. Flavius said he didn't much want to but that it might be
an offer to surrender. So the two brothers started shouting at each
other across the river. Hermann began talking German, but
Flavius said that unless he talked Latin the conversation was at an
end. Hermann did not want to talk Latin, which the other chiefs
did not understand, for fear of being thought a traitor, and Flavius did not want to be thought a traitor by the Romans, who did
not understand German. On the other hand, Hermann wanted to
make an impression on the Romans, and Flavius on the Germans.
Hermann tried to keep to German, and Flavius to Latin, but as
they grew more and more heated they fell into such a dreadful
mixture of both languages that, as Germanicus wrote to me, it

was as good as a comedy to hear them. I quote from Germanicus's account of the dialogue.

Hermann: Hullo, brother. What's happened to your face? That scar's an awful deformity. Lost an eye?

Flavius: Yes, brother. Did you happen to pick one up? I lost it that day you galloped away out of the wood with mud smeared on your shield so that Germanicus wouldn't recognize you.

Hermann: You're wrong, brother. That wasn't me. You must have been drinking again. You were always like that before a battle: a bit nervous unless you had drunk at least a gallon of beer, and had to be strapped to the saddle by the time the warhorns sounded.

Flavius: That's a lie, of course, but it reminds me what a barbarous gut-rotting drink your German beer is. I never drink it now even when there's a great consignment come into the camp from one of your captured villages. The men only drink it when they have to: they say that it's better than swamp water spoilt by German corpses.

Hermann: Yes, I like Roman wine myself. I have a few hundred jars left of what I captured from Varus. This summer I'll be getting in another good supply, if Germanicus doesn't look out. By the way, what reward did you get for losing your eye?

Flavius (with great dignity): The personal thanks of the Commander-in-Chief, and three decorations, including the Crown and the Chain.

Hermann: Ho, ho! The Chain! Do you wear it round your ankles, you Roman slave?

Flavius: I'd rather any day be a slave to the Romans than a traitor to them. By the way, your dear Thrusnelda's very well and so's your boy. When are you coming to Rome to visit them?

Hermann: At the end of this campaign, brother. Ho, ho!

Flavius: You mean when you walk behind Germanicus's car in the triumph and the crowd pelts you with rotten eggs? How I'll laugh!

Hermann: You had better do all your laughing in advance, because if you still have any throat left to laugh through in three days from now my name's not Hermann. But enough of this. I have a message to you from your mother.

Flavius (suddenly serious and fetching a deep sigh): Ah, my dear,

dear mother! What message does my mother send me? Have I her sacred blessing still, brother?

Hermann: Brother, you have wounded our wise and noble and prolific mother to the soul. She says that she will turn her blessing into a curse if you continue to be a traitor to your family and tribe and race, and do not instantly come over to us again and act as joint-General with me.

Flavius (*in German, bursting into tears of rage*)*:* Oh, she never said that, Hermann. She couldn't have said that. It's a lie you made up yourself just to make me unhappy. Confess it's a lie, Hermann!

Hermann: She gave you two days to make up your mind.

Flavius (*to his groom*)*:* Hi, you ugly-faced pig, give me my horse and arms! I'm going over the stream to fight my brother. Hermann, you foul thing, I'm coming to fight you!

Hermann: Come on then, you one-eyed bean-eating slave, you!

Flavius jumped on his horse and was about to swim it across the river when a Roman colonel caught at his leg and pulled him off the saddle: he knew German and he knew the absurd veneration that Germans have for their wives and mothers. Suppose Flavius really meant to desert? So he told him not to bother about Hermann or believe his lies. But Flavius couldn't resist having the last word. He dried his eyes and shouted across: 'I saw your father-in-law last week. He'd got a nice place near Lyons. He told me that Thrusnelda came to him because she couldn't bear the disgrace of being married to a man who broke his solemn oath as an ally of Rome and betrayed a friend at whose table he had eaten She said that the only way you can ever win back her esteem is by not using the arms which she gave you on your wedding-day against your sworn friends. She has not been unfaithful to you yet, but that won't last long if you don't instantly come to your senses.'

Then it was Hermann's turn to weep and storm and accuse Flavius of telling lies. Germanicus privately detailed a captain to watch Flavius very carefully during the next battle and at the least sign of treachery to run him through.

Germanicus wrote seldom, but when he did they were long letters and he put into them, he said, all the interesting and amusing things that did not seem quite suitable for his official dispatches to Tiberius: I lived for those letters. I was never anxious about

Germanicus's safety when he was fighting the Germans: he had the same sort of confidence with them as an experienced bee-keeper has with bees, who can go boldly to a hive and remove the honey, and the bees somehow never sting him as they would you or me if we tried to do the same thing. Two days after fording the Weser he fought a decisive battle with Hermann. I have always been interested in speeches made before a battle: there is nothing that throws such light on the character of a general. Germanicus neither harangued his men in an oratorical way nor joked obscenely with them like Julius Caesar. He was always very serious, very precise, and very practical. His speech on this occasion was about what he really thought of the Germans. He said that they were not soldiers. They had a certain bravado and fought well in a mob, as wild cattle fight, and they had a certain animal cunning too which made it unwise to neglect ordinary precautions in fighting them. But they soon tired after their first furious charge and they had no discipline in any true military sense, only a spirit of mutual rivalry. Their chiefs could never count on them to do what was wanted: either they did too much or not enough. 'The Germans,' he said, 'are the most insolent and boastful nation in the world when things go well with them, but once they are defeated they are the most cowardly and abject. Never trust a German out of your sight, but never be afraid of him when you have him face to face. And that's all that need be said except this: most of the fighting to-morrow will be in among those woods, where from all accounts the enemy will be so tightly packed that they will have no room for manoeuvre. Go straight at them, never mind their assegais, and get to close quarters at once. Stab at their faces: that is what they hate most.'

Hermann had chosen his battle-ground carefully: a narrowing plain lying between the Weser and a range of wooded hills. He would fight at the narrow end of this plain with a big oak and birch forest at his back, the river on his right and the hills on his left. The Germans were in three detachments. The first of these, young assegai-men of local tribes, were to advance into the plain against the leading Roman regiments, who would probably be French auxiliaries, and drive them back. Then when the Roman supports came up they were to break off the fight and pretend to fly in panic. The Romans would press on towards the wood and at this point the second detachment, consisting of Hermann's own tribe, would charge down from an ambush on the hill and take them in the flank. This would cause great confusion and the first detachment would then return, closely supported by the third – the experienced elder men of the local tribes – and drive the Romans into the river. The German cavalry by this time would have come round from behind the hill and taken the Romans in the rear.

It would have been a good plan if Hermann had been in command of disciplined troops, But it went ludicrously wrong. Germanicus's order of battle was as follows: first, two regiments of French heavy infantry on the river flank, and two of the auxiliary Germans on the mountain flank, then the foot archers, then four regular regiments, then Germanicus with two Guards battalions and the regular cavalry, then four more regular regiments, then the French mounted archers, then the French light infantry. As the German auxiliaries advanced along the spurs of the mountain, Hermann, who was watching events from the top of a pine tree, called out excitedly to his nephew who was standing by for orders below: 'There goes my traitor brother! He must never leave this battle alive.' The stupid nephew sprang forward shouting, 'Hermann's orders are to charge at once!' He rushed down into the plain with about half the tribe. Hermann with difficulty managed to restrain the rest. Germanicus sent the regular cavalry out at once to charge the fools in the flank before they could reach Flavius's men, and the French mounted archers to cut off their retreat.

The German skirmishing detachment had meanwhile advanced from the wood, but the Roman cavalry charge sent the men under Hermann's nephew rushing back on top of them and they caught the panic and ran back too. The German third detachment, the main body, then came out of the wood, expecting the skirmishers to halt and turn back with them as arranged. But the skirmishers' only thought was to get away from the cavalry: they ran back through the main body. At this moment there came a most cheering omen for the Romans – eight eagles, who had been frightened from the hill by the sortie and were wheeling about the plain, uttering loud shrieks, now flew all together towards the wood. Germanicus called out: 'Follow the Eagles! Follow the Roman Eagles!' The whole army took up the cry: 'Follow the Eagles!' Meanwhile Hermann had charged with the rest of his men and taken the foot-archers by surprise, killing a number of them; but the rear regiment of French heavy infantry wheeled round to the archers' assistance. Hermann's force, which consisted of some 15,000 men, might still have saved the battle by crushing the French infantry and thus driving a formidable wedge between the Roman advance guard and the main body. But the sun flashed in their faces from the weapons and breast-plates and shields and helmets of the long ranks of advancing regular infantry, and the Germans lost courage. Most of them rushed back to the hill. Hermann rallied a thousand or two, but not enough, and by this time two squadrons of regular cavalry had come charging back among the fugitives, and cut off his retreat to the hill. How he got away is a mystery, but it is generally believed that he spurred his horse towards the wood and overtook the German auxiliaries who were advancing to attack it. Then he shouted: 'Make way, cattle! I'm Hermann!' Nobody dared to kill him because he was Flavius's brother and Flavius would feel bound in family honour to avenge his death.

It was no longer a battle but a slaughter. The German main body was outflanked and forced towards the river, which many managed to swim, but not all. Germanicus pushed his second line of regular infantry into the wood and routed the skirmishers who were waiting there in the vague hope of the battle suddenly turning in their favour. (The archers had good sport shooting down Germans who had climbed trees and were hiding in the foliage at the top.) All resistance was now over. From nine o'clock in the morning until seven o'clock in the evening, when it began to get dark, the killing went on. For ten miles beyond the battlefield the woods and plains were scattered with German corpses. Among the captives was the mother of Hermann and Flavius. She begged for life, saying that she had always tried to persuade Hermann to abandon his futile resistance to the Roman conquerors. So Flavius's loyalty was now assured.

A month later another battle was fought, in thick forest-land on the banks of the Elbe. Hermann had chosen an ambush and made dispositions which might have been most effective if Germanicus had not heard all about them a few hours beforehand from deserters. As it was, instead of the Romans being driven into the river, the Germans were forced back through the wood, in which they were packed too closely for their usual strike-and-run tactics

– back into a quaking bog which surrounded it, where thousands slowly sank out of sight, yelling with rage and despair. Hermann, who had been disabled by an arrow wound in the previous battle, was not much to the fore this time. But he carried on the fight in the wood as stubbornly as he could and, meeting by chance with his brother Flavius, thrust him through with an assegai. He escaped across the bog, jumping from tussock to tussock with extraordinary nimbleness and good luck.

Germanicus raised a huge trophy-heap of German weapons and put on it the following inscription: 'The Forces of Tiberius Caesar having subdued the tribes between Rhine and Elbe consecrate these memorials of their victory to Jove, to Mars, and to Augustus.' No mention of himself. His total casualties in these two battles were not above 2,500 men killed and seriously wounded. The Germans must have lost at least 25,000.

Germanicus considered that he had done enough this year and sent some of his men back to the Rhine by land and embarked the rest on transports. But then came misfortune: a sudden storm from the south-west caught the fleet soon after it weighed anchor and scattered it in all directions. Many vessels went to the bottom and only Germanicus's own ship managed to reach the mouth of the Weser, where he reproached himself as a second Varus with the loss of a whole Roman army. He was with difficulty prevented by his friends from leaping into the sea to join the dead. However, a few days later the wind veered round to the north and one by one the scattered ships came back, almost all oarless and some with cloaks spread instead of sails, the less disabled taking turns to tow the ones that could barely keep afloat.

Germanicus hurried set to work repairing the damaged hulls and sent off as many of the fit vessels as he could to search the desolate neighbouring islands for survivors. Many were found there, but in a half-starved state, kept alive only by shell-fish and the carcases of horses thrown up on the beach. Many more came in from points further up the coast; they had been respectfully treated by the inhabitants, who had lately been forced to swear alliance with Rome. About twenty ship-loads returned from as far away as Britain, which had been paying a nominal tribute since its conquest seventy years before by Julius Caesar, sent back by the petty kings of Kent and Sussex. In the end not more than a quarter of the lost men were unaccounted for, and nearly 200 of these were found, years later, in Central Britain. They were rescued from the lead-mines, where they had been put to forced labour.

The inland Germans, when they first heard of this disaster, thought that their gods had avenged them. They overthrew the battlefield trophy and even began talking of a march to the Rhine. But Germanicus suddenly struck again, sending an expedition of sixty infantry battalions and 100 cavalry squadrons against the tribes of the upper Weser, while he himself marched with eighty more infantry battalions and another 100 cavalry squadrons against the tribes between the lower Rhine and the Ems. Both expeditions were completely successful and, what was better than the killing of many thousand Germans, the Eagle of the Eighteenth Regiment was found in an underground temple in a wood and triumphantly borne away. Only the Eagle of the Seventeenth now remained unredeemed, and Germanicus promised his men that next year, if he was still in command, they would rescue that too. Meanwhile he marched them back to winter quarters.

Then Tiberius wrote pressing him to come home for the triumph which had been decreed him, for he had surely done enough. Germanicus wrote back that he would not be content until he had altogether broken the power of the Germans, for which not many more battles were now needed, and recovered the third Eagle. Tiberius wrote again that Rome could not afford such high casualties even at the reward of such splendid victories: he was not criticizing Germanicus's skill as a general, for his battles had been most economical in men, but between battle casualties and the sea-disaster he had lost the equivalent of two whole regiments, which was more than Rome could afford. He reminded Germanicus that he had himself been sent nine times into Germany by Augustus and so was not talking without experience. His opinion was that it was not worth the life of a single Roman to kill even as many as ten Germans. Germany was like a Hydra: the more heads you lopped off the more it grew. The best way of managing Germans was to play on their inter-tribal jealousies and foment war between neighbouring chieftains: encouraging them to kill each other without outside help. Germanicus wrote back begging for one year more in which to complete his work of subjugation. But Tiberius told him that he was wanted at Rome as Consul again, and touched him on his most tender spot by saying that he should remember his brother Castor. Germany was the only country now where any important war was being fought and if he insisted on finishing it himself, Castor would have no opportunity of winning a triumph or the title of field-marshal. Germanicus persisted no longer but said that Tiberius's wishes were his law and that he would return as soon as relieved.

He came back in the early spring and celebrated his triumph. The whole population of Rome streamed out to welcome him twenty miles from the City. A great arch to com- _{A.D. 17} memorate the recovery of the Eagles was dedicated near the temple of Saturn. The triumphal procession passed under it. There were cars heaped with the spoil of German temples, and with enemy shields and weapons; others carried tableaux representing battles or German river-gods and mountain-gods dominated by Roman soldiers. Thrusnelda and her child were on one car, with halters about their necks, followed by an enormous train of manacled German prisoners. Germanicus rode, crowned, in his chariot with Agrippina seated beside him and his five children – Nero, Drusus, Caligula, Agrippinilla, and Drusilla – seated behind. He won more applause than any other triumphant general had won since Augustus's triumph after Actium.

But I was not there. Of all places in the world I was in Carthage! Only a month before Germanicus's return I had been sent a note by Livia instructing me to prepare for a journey to Africa. A representative of the Imperial family was needed to dedicate a new temple to Augustus at Carthage, and I was the only one who could be spared for the task. I would be given ample advice on how to conduct myself and how to perform the ceremony, and it was to be hoped I would not once more make a fool of myself, even before African provincials. I guessed at once why I was being sent. There was no reason for anyone to go yet, because the temple would not be completed for at least another three months. I was being got out of the way. While Germanicus was in the City I would not be allowed to return, and all my letters home would be opened. So I never had an opportunity of telling Germanicus what I had been saving up for him so long. On the other hand, Germanicus had his talk with Tiberius. He told him that he knew that Postumus's banishment had been due to a cruel plot on Livia's part – he had positive proof of it. Livia certainly ought to be removed from public affairs. Her actions could not be justified by any subsequent misbehaviour of Postumus's. It was only natural for him to try to escape from undeserved confinement. Tiberius professed to be shocked by Germanicus's revelations; but said that he could not create a public scandal by suddenly dishonouring his mother: he would charge her privately with the crime and gradually take away her powers.

What he really did was to go to Livia and tell her exactly what Germanicus had said to him, adding that Germanicus was a credulous fool, but seemed to be in earnest and was so popular at Rome and in the Army that perhaps it would be advisable for Livia to convince him that she was not guilty of what he charged her, unless she thought this beneath her dignity. He added that he would send Germanicus away somewhere as soon as possible, probably to the East, and would raise the question again in the Senate of her being called Mother of the Country, a title which she had well deserved. He had taken exactly the right line with her. She was pleased that he still feared her sufficiently to tell her so much, and called him a dutiful son. She swore that she had not arranged false charges against Postumus: this story was probably invented by Agrippina, whom Germanicus followed blindly and who was trying to persuade him to usurp the monarchy. Agrippina's plan, she said, was no doubt to make trouble between Tiberius and his loving mother. Tiberius, embracing her, said that though little disagreements might occasionally occur nothing could break the ties that bound them. Livia then sighed, she was getting to be an old woman now – she was well on in her seventies – and was beginning to find her work too much for her: perhaps he would anyhow relieve her of the more tedious part and only consult her on important questions of appointments and decrees? She would not even be offended if he discontinued his practice of putting her name above his on all official documents: she did not want it said that he was under her tutelage. But, she said, the sooner he persuaded the Senate to give her that title the more pleased she would be. So there was a show of reconciliation: but neither trusted the other.

Tiberius now named Germanicus as his colleague in the Consulship and told him that he had persuaded Livia to retire from public business, though as a matter of form he would still pretend to consult her. This seemed to satisfy Germanicus. But Tiberius did not feel at all comfortable. Agrippina would hardly speak to him, and knowing that Germanicus and she had only one soul between them, he could not believe in their continued loyalty. Besides, things were going on at Rome which a man of Germanicus's character would naturally detest. First of all, the informers. Since Livia would not give him access to the criminal dossiers or let him share the control of her very efficient spy-system – she had a paid agent in almost every important household or institution – he had to adopt another method. He made a decree that if anyone was found guilty of plotting against the State or blaspheming the God Augustus his confiscated estates would be divided among his loyal accusers. Plots against the State were less easy to prove than blasphemies against Augustus. The first case of blasphemy against Augustus was that of a wag, a young shopkeeper, who happened to be standing near Tiberius in the Market Place as a funeral passed. He sprang forward and whispered something in the ear of the corpse. Tiberius was curious to know what it was. The man explained that he was asking the dead man to tell Augustus when he met him down below that his legacies to the people of Rome had not yet been paid. Tiberius had the man arrested and executed for speaking of Augustus as if he were a mere ghost, not an immortal God, and said that he was sending him down below to convince him of his mistake. A month or two later, by the way, he did pay the legacies in full. In a case like this Tiberius had some justification, but later the most harmless abuses of Augustus's name were enough to put a man on trial for his life.

A class of professional informers sprang up who could be counted on to make out a case against any man who was indicated to them as having incurred Tiberius's displeasure. Thus criminal dossiers based on a record of real delinquency were superfluous. Sejanus was Tiberius's go-between with these scoundrels. In the year before Germanicus's return Tiberius had put the informers to work on a young man called Libo who was a A.D. 16 great-grandson of Pompey and a cousin of Agrippina's through their grandmother Scribonia. Sejanus had warned Tiberius that Libo was dangerous and had been making disrespectful remarks about him: but Tiberius was careful at this stage not to make disrespect to himself an indictable offence, so he had to invent other charges. Now, Tiberius, to cover his own association with Thrasyllus, had expelled from Rome all astrologers, magicians, fortune-tellers, and interpreters of dreams, and forbidden anyone to consult such of them as secretly stayed on. A few stayed with Tiberius's connivance, on condition that they gave séances only with an Imperial agent concealed in the room. Libo was persuaded by a senator who had turned professional informer to visit one of these decoys and have his fortune told. His questions were noted down by the hidden agent. In themselves they were not treasonable, only foolish: he wanted to know how rich he would become and whether he would ever be the leading man at Rome, and so on. But a forged document was produced at his trial which was said to have been discovered by slaves in his bedroom – a list, in what appeared to be his handwriting, of names of all the members of the Imperial family and of the leading senators, with curious Chaldean and Egyptian characters written against each name in the margin. The penalty for consulting a magician was banishment, but the penalty for practising magic oneself was death. Libo denied authorship of the document, and the evidence of slaves, even under torture, would not be sufficient to condemn him: slave-evidence was accepted only when the accusation was that of incest. There was no freedman evidence, because Libo's freedman could not be persuaded to testify against him nor might a freedman be put to torture to force a confession from him. On Sejanus's advice, however, Tiberius made a new legal ruling that when a man was charged with a capital crime his slaves could be bought at a fair valuation by the Public Steward and thus enabled to give evidence under torture. Libo, who had not been able to get a lawyer brave enough to defend him, saw that he was caught and asked for an adjournment of the trial until the next day. When this was granted he went home and killed himself. The charge against him was nevertheless gone through with in the Senate with the same formality as if he had been alive, and he was found guilty on all charges. Tiberius said that it was unfortunate that the foolish young man had killed himself, because he would have interceded for his life. Libo's estate was divided among his accusers, among whom were four senators. Such a disgraceful farce could never have been played when Augustus was Emperor, but under Tiberius it was played, with variations, over and over again. Only one man made a public protest, and that was a certain Calpurnius Piso, who rose in the Senate to say that he was so disgusted with the atmosphere of political intrigue in the City, the corruption of justice, and the disgraceful spectacle of his fellow-senators acting as paid informers, that he was leaving Rome for good and retiring to some village in a remote part of Italy. Having said this he walked out. The speech made a powerful impression on the House. Tiberius sent someone to call Calpurnius back, and when he was once more in his seat told him that if there were miscarriages of justice any senator was at liberty to call attention to them at question-time. He said, too, that a certain amount of political intrigue was inevitable in the capital city of the greatest Empire the world had ever known. Did Calpurnius suggest that the senators would not have come forward with their accusations if they had had no hopes of reward? He said that he admired Calpurnius's earnestness and independence and envied his talents; but would it not be better to employ these noble qualities for the improvement of social and political morality at Rome than to bury them in some wretched hamlet of the Apennines, among shepherds and bandits? So Calpurnius had to stay. But soon after he showed his earnestness and independence by summoning old Urgulania to appear in court for non-payment of a large sum of money which she owed him for some pictures and statuary: Calpurnius's sister had died and there had been a sale. When Urgulania read the summons, which was for her immediate attendance at the Debtor's Court, she told her chair-men to take her straight to Livia's Palace. Calpurnius followed her and was met in the hall by Livia, who told him to be off. Calpurnius courteously but firmly excused himself, saying that Urgulania must obey the summons without fail unless too ill to attend, which clearly she was not. Even Vestal Virgins were not exempt from attendance at court when subpoenaed. Livia said that his behaviour was personally insulting to her and that her son, the Emperor, would know how to avenge her. Tiberius was sent for and tried to smooth things over, telling Calpurnius that Urgulania surely meant to come as soon as she had composed herself after the sudden shock of the summons, and telling Livia that it was no doubt a mistake, that Calpurnius certainly meant no disrespect, and that he himself would attend the trial and see that Urgulania had a capable counsel and a fair trial. He left the Palace, walking beside Calpurnius towards the courts and talking with him of this and that. Calpurnius's friends tried to persuade him to drop the charge, but he replied that he was old-fashioned: he liked being paid money that was owed him. The trial never came off. Livia sent a mounted messenger after them with the whole amount of the debt in gold in his saddle-bags: he overtook Calpurnius and Tiberius before they arrived at the door of the Court.

But I am writing about informers and the demoralizing effect they had on life at Rome, and about judicial corruption. I was about to record that while Germanicus was at Rome there was not a single charge heard in the courts of blaspheming Augustus or of plotting against the State, and the informers were warned to keep absolutely quiet. Tiberius was on his best behaviour and his speeches in the Senate were models of frankness. Sejanus retired into the background, Thrasyllus was removed from Rome to the shelter of Tiberius's village on the island of Capri, and Tiberius appeared to have no intimate friend but the honest Nerva, whose advice he was always asking.

Castor I never could learn to like. He was a foul-mouthed, bloody-minded, violent-tempered, dissolute fellow. His character showed up most clearly at a sword-fight, where he took more delight in seeing blood spurting from a wound than in any act of skill or courage on the part of the combatants. But I must say that he behaved very finely towards Germanicus and seemed to undergo a real change of heart in his company. City factions tried to force the two into the wretched position of rivals for succession to the monarchy, but they never on any occasion encouraged this view. Castor treated Germanicus with the same brotherly consideration that Germanicus gave him. Castor was not exactly a coward, but he was a politician rather than a soldier. When he was sent across the Danube in answer to an appeal for help by the tribes of East Germany who were fighting a defensive and bloody war against Hermann's Western confederacy, he managed by clever intrigue to bring into the war the tribes of Bohemia, and of Bavaria too. He was carrying out Tiberius's policy of encouraging the Germans to exterminate each other. Maroboduus ('He who walks on the lake bottom'), the priest-king of the East Germans, fled for protection to Castor's camp. Maroboduus was given a safe retreat in Italy; and since the East Germans had sworn an oath of perpetual allegiance he remained for eighteen years a hostage for their good behaviour. These East Germans were a fiercer and more powerful race than the West Germans and Germanicus was lucky not to have had them at war with him too. But Hermann had become a national hero by his defeat of Varus, and

Maroboduus was jealous of his success. Rather than that Hermann should become High King of all the German nations, which was his ambition, Maroboduus had refused to give him any help in his campaign against Germanicus, even by making a diversion on another frontier.

I have often thought about Hermann. He was a remarkable man in his way, and though it is difficult to forget his treachery to Varus, Varus had done much to provoke the revolt and Hermann and his men were certainly fighting for liberty. They had a genuine contempt for the Romans. They could not understand in what sense the extremely severe discipline in the Roman army under Varus, Tiberius, and almost every other general but my father and my brother, differed from downright slavery. They were shocked at the disciplinary floggings and regarded the system of paying soldiers at so much a day, instead of engaging them by promises of glory and plunder, as most base. The Germans have always been very chaste in their morals, and Roman officers openly practised vices which in Germany, if they ever came to light – but this was seldom – were punished by smothering both culprits in mud under a hurdle. As for German cowardice, all barbarous people are cowards. If Germans ever become civilized it will then be time to judge whether they are cowards or not. They seem, however, to be an exceptionally nervous and quarrelsome people, and I cannot make up my mind whether there is any immediate chance of their becoming really civilized. Germanicus thought that there was none. Whether his policy of extermination was justified or not (certainly it was not the usual Roman policy with frontier tribes) depends on the answer to the first question. Of course, the captured Eagles had to be won back, and Hermann had shown no mercy, after the defeat of Varus, when he overran the province; and Germanicus, who was a most gentle and humane man, disliked general massacre so much that he must have had very good reasons for ordering it.

Hermann did not die in battle. When Maroboduus was forced to fly from the country, Hermann thought that his way was now clear to a monarchy over all the nations of Germany. But he was mistaken: he was not even able to make himself monarch of his own tribe, which was a free tribe, the chieftain having no power to command, only to lead and advise and persuade. One day, a year or two later, he tried to issue orders like a king. His family, which had hitherto been greatly devoted to him, were so scandalized that, without even first discussing the matter together, they all rushed at him with their weapons and hacked him to pieces. He was thirty-seven when he died, having been born the year before my brother Germanicus, his greatest enemy.

Chapter 20

I WAS nearly a year in Carthage. (It was the year that Livy died, at Padua, where his heart had always been.) Old Carthage had been razed to the ground and this was a new city, built by Augustus on the south-east of the peninsula and destined to A.D. 18 become the first city of Africa. It was the first time I had been out of Italy since my babyhood. I found the climate very trying, the African natives savage, diseased, and overworked; the resident Romans dull, quarrelsome, mercenary, and behind the times; the swarms of unfamiliar creeping and flying insects most horrible. What I missed most was the absence of any wild wooded countryside. In Tripoli there is nothing to mediate between the regularly planted land – fig and olive orchards, or cornfields – and the bare, stony, thorny desert. I stayed at the house of the Governor, who was that Furius Camillus, my dear Camilla's uncle, of whom I have already written; he was very kind to me. Almost the first thing he told me was how useful my *Balkan Summary* had been to him in that campaign and that I should certainly have been publicly rewarded for compiling it so well. He did everything he could to make my dedication ceremony a success and to exact from the provincials the respect due to my rank. He was also most assiduous in showing me the sights. The town did a flourishing trade with Rome, exporting not only vast quantities of grain and oil, but slaves, purple dye, sponges, gold, ivory, ebony, and wild beasts for the Games. But I had little occupation here and Furius suggested that it would be a good thing for me, while I was here, to collect materials for a complete history of Carthage. There was no such book to be found in the libraries at Rome. The archives of the old town had recently come into his hands, discovered by natives quarrying in the ruins for hidden treasure, and if I cared to use them they were mine. I told him that I had no knowledge of the Phoenician language; but he undertook, if I was sufficiently interested, to set one of his freedmen the task of translating the more important manuscripts into Greek.

The idea of writing the history pleased me very much: I felt that historical justice had never been done to the Carthaginians. I spent my leisure time in making a study of the ruins of the Old City, with the help of a contemporary survey, and familiarizing myself with the geography of the country in general. I also learned the rudiments of the language well enough to be able to read simple inscriptions and understand the few Phoenician words used by authors who have written about the Punic Wars from the Roman side. When I returned to Italy I began to write the book concurrently with my Etruscan history. I like having two tasks going at the same time: when I tire of one I turn to the other. But I am perhaps too careful a writer. I am not satisfied merely with copying from ancient authorities while there is any possible means of checking their statements by consulting other sources of information on the same subject, particularly accounts by writers of rival political parties. So these two histories, each of which I could have written in a year or two if I had been less conscientious, kept me busy between them for some twenty-five years. For every word I wrote I must have read many hundreds; and in the end I became a very good scholar both of Etruscan and Phoenician, and had a working knowledge of several other languages and dialects too, such as Numidian, Egyptian, Oscan, and Faliscan. I finished the *History of Carthage* first.

Shortly after my dedication of the temple, which went off without a hitch, Furius had suddenly to take the field against Tacfarinas with the only forces available in the province – a single regular regiment, the Third, together with a few battalions of auxiliaries and two cavalry squadrons. Tacfarinas was a Numidian chief, originally a deserter from the ranks of the Roman auxiliaries, and a remarkably successful bandit. He had recently built up a sort of army on the Roman model in the interior of his own country and had allied himself with the Moors for an invasion of the province from the West. The two armies together outnumbered Furius's force by at least five to one. They met in open country about fifty miles from the City and Furius had to decide whether to attack Tacfarinas's two semi-disciplined regiments which were in the centre of the undisciplined Moorish forces on the flank. He sent the cavalry and auxiliaries, mostly archers, to keep the Moors in play and with his regular regiment marched straight at Tacfarinas's Numidians. I was watching the battle from a hill some 500 paces away – I had ridden out on a mule – and never before or since, I think, have I been so proud of being a Roman. The Third kept perfect formation: it might have been a ceremonial parade on Mars Field. They advanced in three lines at fifty paces' distance. Each line consisted of 150 files, eight men deep. The Numidians halted in a defensive posture. They were in six lines, with a frontage the same as ours. The Third did not halt but marched straight at them without pausing a moment, and it was only when they were ten paces off that the leading line discharged their javelins in a shining shower. Then they drew their swords and charged, shield to shield. They rolled the enemy's first line, who were pike-men, back on the second. The new line they broke with a fresh discharge of javelins – every soldier carried a pair. Then the Roman support-line passed through them, to give them a chance to reorganize. Soon I saw still another shower of javelins, simultaneously thrown, fly shining at the Numidians' third line. The Moors on the flanks, who were greatly bothered by the arrows of the auxiliaries, saw the Romans cutting their way deep into the centre. They began howling, as if the battle was lost, and scattered in all directions. Tacfarinas had to fight a costly rear-guard action back to his camp. The only unpleasant memory I have of this victory was the banquet with which it was celebrated: in the course of which Furius's son, who was called Scribonianus, made satiric references to the moral support I had given the troops. He did this chiefly to call attention to his own gallantry, which he thought had not been sufficiently praised. Furius afterwards made him beg my pardon. Furius was voted triumphal ornaments by the Senate – the first member of his family to win military distinction since his ancestor Camillus saved Rome more than 400 years previously.

When I was finally recalled to Rome, Germanicus had already gone to the East, where the Senate had voted him supreme command of all the provinces. With him went Agrippina, and Caligula, who was now aged eight. The elder children remained at Rome with my mother. Though Germanicus was greatly disappointed at having to leave the German War unfinished, he decided to make the most of things and improve his education by visiting places famous in history or literature. He visited the Bay of Actium, and there saw the memorial chapel dedicated to Apollo by Augustus, and the camp of Antony.

As Antony's grandson the place had a melancholy fascination for him. He was explaining the plan of the battle to young Caligula, when the child interrupted with a silly laugh: 'Yes, father, my grandfather Agrippa and my great-grandfather Augustus gave your grandfather Antony a pretty good beating. I wonder you're not ashamed to tell me the story.' This was only one of many recent occasions on which Caligula had spoken insolently to Germanicus, and Germanicus now decided that it was no use treating him in the gentle, friendly way he treated other children – that the only course with Caligula was strict discipline and severe punishments.

He visited Boeotian Thebes, to see Pindar's birth-chamber, and the island of Lesbos, to see Sappho's tomb. Here another of my nieces was born, who was given the unlucky name of Julia. We always called her Lesbia, though. Then he visited Byzantium, Troy, and the famous Greek cities of Asia Minor. From Miletus he wrote me a long letter describing his journey in terms of such delighted interest that it was clear that he no longer greatly regretted his recall from Germany.

Meanwhile affairs at Rome relapsed into the condition in which they had been before Germanicus's Consulship; and Sejanus revived Tiberius's old fears about Germanicus. He reported a remark of Germanicus's made at a private dinner-party at which one of his agents had been present, to the effect that the Eastern regiments probably needed the same sort of overhauling as he had given the ones on the Rhine. This remark had actually been made, but meant no more than that these troops were probably being mishandled by the inferior officers in much the same way as the others had been: and that he would review all appointments at the first opportunity. Sejanus made Tiberius understand the remark as meaning that the reason why Germanicus had delayed his usurpation of power so long was that he could not count on the affection of the Eastern regiments: which he was now going to win by letting the men choose their own captains, and giving them presents and relaxing the severity of their discipline – just as he had done on the Rhine.

Tiberius was alarmed and thought it wise to consult Livia: he counted on her to work with him. She knew what to do at once.

They appointed a man called Gnaeus Piso to the governorship of the province of Syria – an appointment which would give him command, under Germanicus, of the greater part of the Eastern regiments – and told him in private that he could count on their support if Germanicus tried to interfere with any of his political or military arrangements. It was a clever choice. Gnaeus Piso, an uncle of that Lucius Piso who had offended Livia, was a haughty old man who twenty-five years before had earned the bitter hatred of the Spanish, when sent to them by Augustus as Governor, for his cruelty and avarice. He was deeply in debt and the hint that he could behave how he liked in Syria, so long as he provoked Germanicus, seemed an invitation to make another fortune to replace the one he had made in Spain and had long since run through. He disliked Germanicus for his seriousness and piety and used to call him a superstitious old woman; and he was also extremely jealous of him.

Germanicus, when he had visited Athens, had shown his respect for her ancient glories by appearing at the city gates with only a single yeoman as escort. He had also made a long and earnest speech in eulogy of Athenian poets, soldiers, and philosophers, at a festival which was organized in his honour. Now Piso came through Athens on his way to Syria and, since it was not part of his province and he did not take any pains to be civil to them as Germanicus had done, the Athenians did not take any pains to be civil to him. A man called Theophilus, the brother of one of Piso's creditors, had just been condemned for forgery by a vote of the City Assembly. Piso asked as a personal favour that the man should be pardoned, but his request was refused, which made Piso very angry: if Theophilus had been pardoned, the brother would have certainly cancelled the debt. He made a violent speech in which he said that the latter-day Athenians had no right to identify themselves with the great Athenians of the days of Pericles, Demosthenes, Aeschylus, Plato. The ancient Athenians had been extirpated by repeated wars and massacres and these were mere mongrels, degenerates, and the descendants of slaves. He said that any Roman who flattered them as if they were the legitimate heirs of those ancient heroes was lowering the dignity of the Roman name; and that for his part he could not forget that in the last Civil War they had declared against the great Augustus and supported that cowardly traitor Antony.

Piso then left Athens and sailed for Rhodes on his way to Syria. Germanicus was at Rhodes too, visiting the University, and news of the speech, which was plainly directed at himself, reached him just before Piso's ships were sighted. A sudden squall rose and Piso's ships were seen to be in difficulties. Two smaller vessels went down before Germanicus's eyes, and the third, which was Piso's, was dismasted and was being driven on the rocks of the northern headland. Who but Germanicus would not have abandoned Piso to his fate? But Germanicus sent out a couple of well-manned galleys which succeeded by desperate rowing in reaching the wreck just before it struck and towing it safely to port. Or who but a man as depraved as Piso would not have rewarded his rescuer with lifelong gratitude and devotion? But Piso actually complained that Germanicus had delayed the rescue until the last moment, in the hope that it would come too late; and without stopping a day at Rhodes, he sailed away again while the sea was still rough in order to reach Syria before Germanicus.

As soon as he arrived at Antioch he began to overhaul the regiments in just the opposite sense to that intended by Germanicus. Instead of removing slack, bullying captains, he reduced to the ranks every officer who had a good record and appointed scoundrelly favourites of his own in their places – with the understanding that a commission of half whatever they succeeded in making out of their appointments should be paid to him, and no questions asked. So a bad year began for the Syrians. Shopkeepers in the towns and farmers in the country had to pay secret 'protection-money' to the local captains; if they refused to pay there would be a raid at night by masked men, their houses would be burned down, and their families murdered. At first there were many appeals made to Piso against this terrorism by city guilds, farmers' associations, and so forth. He always promised an immediate inquiry but never made one; and the complainers were usually found beaten to death on the road home. A delegation was sent to Rome to enquire privately from Sejanus whether Tiberius was aware of what was going on and, if so, whether he countenanced it. Sejanus told the provincials that Tiberius knew nothing officially; and though he would, no doubt, promise an inquiry, Piso had done as much for them as that, had he not? Perhaps the best course for them to take, he said, would be to pay whatever protection-money was demanded with as little fuss as possible.

Meanwhile the standard of camp-discipline in the Syrian regiments had sunk so low that Tacfarinas's bandit-army would by comparison have seemed a model of efficiency and devotion to duty.

Delegates also came to Germanicus at Rhodes, and he was disgusted and amazed at their revelations. In his recent progress through Asia Minor he had made it his task to enquire personally into all complaints of maladministration and to remove all magistrates who had acted in an illegal or oppressive way. He now wrote to Tiberius telling him of the reports that had reached him of Piso's behaviour, saying that he was setting out for Syria at once; and asking for permission to remove Piso and put a better man in his place if even a few of the complaints were justified. Tiberius wrote back that he had also heard certain complaints, but they appeared to be unfounded and malicious; he had confidence in Piso as a capable and just Governor. Germanicus did not suspect Tiberius of dishonesty and was confirmed in the opinion he had already had of him as simple-minded and easily imposed upon. He regretted having written for permission to do what he should have done at once on his own responsibility. He now heard another serious charge against Piso, namely, that he was plotting with Vonones, the deposed king of Armenia, who was in refuge in Syria, to restore him to his throne. Vonones was immensely wealthy, having fled to Syria with most of the contents of the Armenian treasury, so Piso hoped to do well out of the business. Germanicus went at once to Armenia, called a conference of nobles and, with his own hands, but in Tiberius's name, put the diadem on the head of the man they had chosen for king. He then ordered Piso to visit Armenia at the head of two regiments to pay his neighbourly respects to the new monarch: or, if he was held by more important business, to send his son. Piso neither sent his son nor went himself. Germanicus, having visited other outlying provinces and allied kingdoms and settled affairs there to his satisfaction, came down into Syria and met Piso at the winter quarters of the Tenth Regiment.

There were several officers present as witnesses of this meeting, because Germanicus did not wish Tiberius to be misinformed as to what was said. He began, in as gentle a voice as he could command, by asking Piso to explain disobedience of orders. He said that if there was no explanation of it but the same personal animosity and discourtesy which he had shown in his speech at Athens, in his ungrateful remarks at Rhodes, and on several occasions since, a strong report would have to be forwarded to the Emperor. He went on to complain that, for troops living under peace-time conditions in a healthy and popular station, he found the Tenth Regiment in a most shockingly undisciplined and dirty condition.

Piso said, grinning: 'Yes, they *are* a dirty lot, aren't they? What would the people of Armenia have thought if I had sent them there as representatives of the power and majesty of Rome?' ('The power and majesty of Rome' was a favourite phrase of my brother's.)

Germanicus, keeping his temper with difficulty, said that the deterioration seemed to date only from Piso's arrival in the province, and that he would write to Tiberius to that effect.

Piso made an ironical plea for forgiveness, coupled with an insulting remark about the high ideals of youth which often have to yield, in this hard world, to less exalted but more practical policies.

Germanicus interrupted with flashing eyes: 'Often, Piso, but not always. To-morrow, for instance, I shall sit with you on the appeal tribunal and we shall see whether the high ideals of youth are controlled by any obstacle at all: and whether justice to the provincials can be denied them by any incompetent, avaricious, bloody-minded sexagenarian debauchee.'

This ended the interview. Piso at once wrote to Tiberius and Livia, telling what had happened. He quoted Germanicus's last sentence in such a way that Tiberius believed that the 'incompetent, avaricious, bloody-minded sexagenarian debauchee' was himself. Tiberius replied that he had the fullest confidence in Piso, and that if a certain influential person continued to speak and act in this disloyal way, any steps, however daring, taken by a subordinate to check this disloyalty would doubtless be pleasing to the Senate and people of Rome. Meanwhile Germanicus sat on the tribunal and heard appeals from the provincials against unjust sentences in the courts. Piso did his best at first to embarrass him by legal obstructionism, but when Germanicus kept his patience and continued the hearing of the cases without any respite for meals or siestas, he gave up that policy and excused himself from attendance altogether on the grounds of ill-health.

Piso's wife, Plancina, was jealous of Agrippina because, as

Germanicus's wife, she took precedence over her at all official functions. She thought out various petty insults to annoy her, chiefly discourtesies by subordinates which could be explained away as due to accident or ignorance. When Agrippina retaliated by snubbing her in public, she went still further. One morning in the absence of both Piso and Germanicus she appeared on parade with the cavalry and put them through a burlesque series of movements in front of Germanicus's headquarters. She wheeled them through a cornfield, charged a line of empty tents, which were slashed to ribbons, had every possible call sounded from 'Lights Out!' to the fire-alarm, and arranged collisions between squadrons. She finally galloped the whole force round and round in a gradually dwindling circle, and then, when she had narrowed the centre space to only a few paces across, gave the order, 'Right about wheel,' as if to reverse the movement. Many horses went down, throwing their riders. There never was such a mess-up seen in the whole history of cavalry manoeuvre. The rowdier men increased it by sticking daggers into their neighbours' horses to make them buck, or wrestling from the saddle. Several men were badly kicked, or had legs broken, their horses falling on them. One man was picked up dead. Agrippina sent a young staff-officer to request Plancina to stop making a fool of herself and the Army. Plancina sent back the answer, in parody of Agrippina's own brave words at the Rhine bridge: 'Until my husband returns *I* am in command of the cavalry. I am preparing them for the expected Parthian invasion.' Some Parthian ambassadors had, as a matter of fact, just arrived in camp, and were watching this display in astonishment and contempt.

Now Vonones, before he had been king of Armenia, had been king of Parthia, from which he had been quickly expelled. His successor had sent these ambassadors to Germanicus to propose that the alliance between Rome and Parthia should be renewed and to say that in honour of Germanicus he would come to the River Euphrates (the boundary between Syria and Parthia) to greet him. In the meantime he requested that Vonones might not be allowed to remain in Syria, where it was easy for him to carry on a treasonable correspondence with certain Parthian nobles. Germanicus replied that as representative of his father, the Emperor, he would be pleased to meet the king, and renew the alliance, and that he would remove Vonones to some other province. So Vonones was sent to Cilicia, and Piso's hope of a fortune vanished. Plancina was as angry as her husband; Vonones had been giving her almost daily presents of beautiful jewels.

Early the next year news reached Germanicus of great scarcity in Egypt. The last harvest had not been good, but there was plenty of corn from two years before, stored in granaries. The big corn-brokers kept up the price by putting only very small supplies on the market. Germanicus sailed at once to Alexandria and forced the brokers to sell at a reasonable price all the A.D. 19 corn that was needed. He was glad of this excuse for visiting Egypt, which interested him even more than Greece. Alexandria was then, as it is now, the true cultural centre of the world, as Rome was, and is, the political centre, and he showed his respect for its traditions by entering the city in simple Greek costume, with bare feet and no bodyguard. From Alexandria he sailed up the Nile, visiting the pyramids and the Sphinx and the gigantic ruins of Egyptian Thebes, a former capital, and the great stone statue of Memnon, the breast of which is hollow, and which shortly after the sun rises begins to sing, because the air in the hollow becomes warm and rises in a current through the pipe-shaped throat. He went as far as the ruins of Elephantis, keeping a careful diary of his travels. At Memphis he visited the pleasure-ground of the great God Apis, incarnate as a bull with peculiar markings; but Apis gave him no encouraging sign, walking away from him the moment that they met and entering the 'malevolent stall'. Agrippina was with him but Caligula had been left behind at Antioch in the charge of a tutor, as a punishment for his continued disobedience.

Germanicus could do nothing now that did not encourage Tiberius's suspicions of him; but going to Egypt was the worst mistake he had yet made. I shall explain why. Augustus, realizing early in his reign that Rome was now chiefly dependent on Egypt for her corn supply and that Egypt, if it fell into the hands of an adventurer, could be successfully defended by a quite small army, had laid it down as a precept of government that no Roman knight or senator should henceforth be allowed to visit the province without express permission from himself. It was generally understood that the same rule held under Tiberius. But Germanicus, alarmed by reports of the corn famine in Egypt, had not wasted time by waiting to get permission to go there. Tiberius was certain now that Germanicus was about to strike the blow that he had withheld so long; he had certainly gone to Egypt to bring the garrison there over to his side; the sight-seeing up the Nile was merely an excuse for visiting the frontier-guards; it had been a great mistake to send him to the East at all. He made a public complaint in the Senate against so daring a breach of Augustus's strict injunctions.

When Germanicus returned to Syria, feeling much hurt by Tiberius's reprimand, he found that all his orders to the regiments and to the cities had either been neglected or superseded by contradictory ones from Piso. He re-issued them and now for the first time gave public notice of his displeasure by issuing a proclamation that all orders issued by Piso during his own absence in Egypt were hereby declared cancelled and that, until further notice, no order signed by Piso would be valid in the province unless endorsed by himself. He had hardly signed this proclamation when he fell ill. His stomach was so disordered that he could keep nothing down. He suspected that his food was being poisoned and took every possible precaution against this. Agrippina prepared all his meals herself and none of the household staff had any opportunity of handling the food either before or after she cooked it. But it was some time before he was sufficiently recovered to leave his bed and sit propped in a chair. Hunger made his sense of smell abnormally acute and he said that there was a stench of death in the house. Nobody else smelt it and Agrippina at first dismissed the complaint as a sick fancy. But he persisted in it. He said that the stench grew daily worse. At last Agrippina herself became aware of it. It seemed to be in every room. She burned incense to cleanse the air but the smell persisted. The household grew alarmed and whispered that witches were at work.

Germanicus had always been extremely superstitious, like every member of our family but myself: I am only somewhat superstitious. Germanicus not only believed in the luckiness or unluckiness of certain days or omens, but had found himself in a whole network of superstitions of his own. The number seventeen and the midnight crowing of cocks were the two things which distressed him most. He took it as a most unlucky sign that, having been able to recover the lost Eagles of the Eighteenth and Nineteenth Regiments, he had been recalled from Germany before he could recover that of the Seventeenth. And he was terrified of black magic of the sort that Thessalian witches use, and always slept with a talisman under his pillow which was proof against them: a green jasper figure of the Goddess Hecate (who alone has power over witches and phantoms) represented with a torch in one hand and the keys of the Underworld in another.

Suspecting that Plancina was practising witchcraft against him – for she had the reputation of being a witch – he made a propitiatory sacrifice of nine black puppies to Hecate; which was the proper course to take when so victimized. The next day a slave reported with a face of terror that as he had been washing the floor in the hall he had noticed a loose tile and, lifting it up, had found underneath what appeared to be the naked and decaying corpse of a baby, the belly painted red and horns tied to the forehead. An immediate search was made in every room and a dozen equally gruesome finds were made under the tiles or in niches scooped in the walls behind hangings. They included the corpse of a cat with rudimentary wings growing from its back, and the head of a negro with a child's hand protruding from its mouth. With each of these dreadful relics was a lead tablet in which was Germanicus's name. The house was ritually cleansed and Germanicus began to be more cheerful, though his stomach continued troublesome.

Soon after this hauntings began in the house. Cocks' feathers smeared in blood were found among the cushions and unlucky signs were scrawled on the walls in charcoal, sometimes low down, as if a dwarf had written them, sometimes high up, as if written by a giant – a man hanging, the word Rome upside down, a weasel; and, though only Agrippina knew of his private superstition about the number seventeen, this number was constantly recurring. Then appeared the name Germanicus, upside down, every day shortened by a letter. It would have been possible for Plancina to hide charms in his house during his absence in Egypt, but for this continued haunting there was no explanation. The servants were not suspected, because the words and signs were written in rooms to which they had no access, and in one locked room, with a window too small for a man to squeeze through, they covered the walls from floor to ceiling. Germanicus's one consolation was the courage with which Agrippina and little Caligula behaved. Agrippina did her best to make light of the hauntings, and Caligula said that *he* felt safe because a great-grandson of the God Augustus couldn't be hurt by witches, and that if he met a witch he would run her through with his sword. But Germanicus had to take to his bed again. In the middle of the night following the day when only three letters remained of his name, Germanicus was awakened by the noise of crowing. Weak as he was, he leaped out of bed, snatched up his sword and rushed into the adjoining room where Caligula and the baby Lesbia slept. There he saw a cock, a big black one with a gold ring around its neck, crowing as if to wake the dead. He tried to strike off its head but it flew out of the window. He fell down in a faint. Agrippina somehow got him back to his bed again, but when he recovered consciousness he told her that he was doomed. 'Not while you have your Hecate with you,' she said. He felt under his pillow for the charm and his courage returned.

When morning came he wrote a letter to Piso, in the old Roman manner, declaring private war between them; ordering him to leave the Province, and defying him to do his worst. Piso had, however, already sailed and was now at Chios waiting for news of Germanicus's death and ready to return to govern the Province as soon as it reached him. My poor brother was growing hourly weaker. The next day while Agrippina was out of the room and he was lying half insensible he felt a movement under his pillow. He turned on his side and fumbled in terror for the charm. It was gone; and there was nobody in the room.

The next day he called his friends together and told them that he was dying and that Piso and Plancina were his murderers. He charged them to tell Tiberius and Castor what had been done to him and implored them to avenge his cruel death. 'And tell the people of Rome,' he said, 'that I entrust my dear wife and my six children to their charge, and that they must not believe Piso and Plancina if they pretend to have had instructions to kill me; or, if they do believe it, that they must not on that account pardon them.' He died on the ninth of October, the day that the single letter G appeared on the wall of his room facing his bed, and on the seventeenth day of his illness. His wasted body was laid out in the market-place of Antioch so that everyone could see the red rash on his belly and the blueness of his nails. His slaves were put to torture. His freedmen, too, were cross-examined in turn, each for twenty-four hours on end and always by fresh questioners, and they were so broken in spirit at the end of this that if they had known anything they would certainly have revealed it, only to be left in peace. The most that could be discovered, however, either from freedmen or slaves, was that a notable witch, one Martina, had been frequently seen in Plancina's company and that she had actually been in the house one day with Plancina when nobody was there but Caligula. And that one afternoon, just before Germanicus's return, the house had been left unattended except by a single deaf old janitor, all the remaining staff having gone out to see a sword-fight exhibited by Piso in the local amphitheatre. No natural explanations could, however, be offered for the cock, or for the writing on the wall, or for the disappearance of the talisman.

There was a meeting of regimental commanders and all the other Romans of rank in the Province, to appoint a temporary Governor. The Commander of the Sixth Regiment was chosen. He immediately arrested Martina and had her sent under escort to Rome. If Piso came up for trial she would be one of the most important witnesses.

When he heard that Germanicus was dead, Piso, so far from concealing his joy, offered up sacrifices of thanksgiving in the temples. Plancina, who had recently lost a sister, actually threw off her mourning and put on her gayest clothes again. Piso wrote to Tiberius saying that he had only been dismissed from his governorship, to which he had been personally appointed by Tiberius, because of his bold opposition to Germanicus's treasonable designs against the State; he was now returning to Syria to resume his command. He also referred to Germanicus's 'luxury and insolence'. He did try to return to Syria and even got some troops to support him, but the new Governor besieged the castle in Cilicia which he had made his stronghold, forced him to surrender, and sent him to Rome to answer the charges that would surely be brought against him there.

Meanwhile Agrippina had sailed for Italy with the two children and the ashes of her husband in an urn. At Rome the news of his death had brought such grief that it was as though every single household in the City had lost its most beloved member. Three whole days, though there was no decree of the Senate or order of the magistrates for it, were consecrated to public sorrow: shops shut, law-courts were deserted, no business of any sort was transacted, everyone wore mourning. I heard a man in the street say that it was as though the sun had set, and would never rise again. Of my own sorrow I cannot trust myself to write.

Chapter 21

LIVIA and Tiberius shut themselves in their palaces and pretended to be so grief-stricken that they could not show their faces abroad. Agrippina should have come by the overland route, because the winter had already begun and the sailing season was over. But she put to sea in spite of storms and a few days A.D. 20 later reached Corfu, from where it is only a day's sail, with a good breeze, to the port of Brindisi. Here she rested for a while, sending messengers ahead to say that she was coming to throw herself on the protection of the people of Italy. Castor, who was now back at Rome, her four other children and myself went out from Rome to meet her. Tiberius had immediately sent two Guards battalions forward to the port with directions that the magistrates of the country districts through which the ashes passed should pay his dead son the last offices of respect. When Agrippina disembarked, greeted with respectful silence by an enormous crowd, the urn was put in a catafalque and carried towards Rome on the shoulders of the Guards' officers. The battalion standards were undecorated, as a sign of public calamity, and the axes and rods were borne reversed. As the procession, many thousands strong, passed through Calabria, Apulia, and Campania, everyone came flocking, the country people dressed in black, the knights in purple robes, with tears and loud lamentations, and burned offerings of perfumes for their dead hero's ghost.

We met the procession at Terracina, about sixty miles southeast of Rome, where Agrippina, who had walked dry-eyed and marble-faced, without a word to anyone all the way from Brindisi, let her grief break out afresh at the sight of her four fatherless children. She cried to Castor: 'By the love you had for my dear husband swear that you will defend the lives of his children with your own, and avenge his death! It was his last charge to you.' Castor, weeping, for the first time perhaps since his childhood, swore that he would accept the charge.

If you ask why Livilla did not come with us, the answer is that she had just been delivered of twin boys: of which, by the way, Sejanus seems to have been the father. If you ask why my mother did not come, the answer is that Tiberius and Livia did not allow her even to attend the funeral. If overwhelming grief prevented their own attendance, as grandmother and adoptive father of the dead man, it was clearly quite impossible for her, as his mother, to attend. And they were wise not to show themselves. If they had done so, even with a pretence of grief, they would certainly have been assaulted by the populace; and I think that the Guards would have stood by and not raised a finger to protect them. Tiberius had neglected to make even such preparations as were customary at the funeral of far less distinguished persons: the family masks of the Claudians and Julians did not appear nor the usual effigy of the dead man himself, laid on a bed; no funeral speech was made from the Oration Platform; no funeral hymns sung. Tiberius's excuse was that the funeral had already been celebrated in Syria and that the Gods would be offended if the rites were repeated. But never was such unanimous and sincere grief shown in Rome as on that night. Mars Field was ablaze with torches, and the crowd about Augustus's tomb, in which the urn was reverently placed by Castor, was so dense that many people were crushed to death. Everywhere people were saying that Rome was lost, and that no hope remained: for Germanicus had been their last bulwark against oppression, and Germanicus was now foully murdered. And everywhere Agrippina was praised and pitied, and prayers were offered for the safety of her children.

Tiberius published a proclamation a few days later saying that though many illustrious Romans had died for the commonwealth, none had been so universally and vehemently regretted as his dear son. But it was now time for the people to compose their minds and return to their daily business: princes were mortal, but the commonwealth eternal. In spite of this, All Fools' Festival at the end of December passed without any of the usual jokes and jollity, and it was not until the Festival of the Great Mother in April that mourning ended and normal public business was resumed. Tiberius's suspicions were now concentrated on Agrippina. She visited him at the Palace on the morning after the funeral and fearlessly told him that she would hold him responsible for her husband's death until he had proved his innocence and taken vengeance on Piso and Plancina. He cut short the interview at once by quoting at her the Greek lines:

> And if you are not queen, my dear,
> Think you that you are wronged?

Piso did not return to Rome for some time. He sent his son ahead to intercede for him with Tiberius while he himself went to visit Castor, who was now back with the legions on the Danube. He expected Castor to be grateful to him for his removal of a rival heir to the monarchy and willing to believe the story of Germanicus's treason. Castor refused to receive him and publicly told Piso's messenger that, if current rumours were true, it was on Piso that he would have to inflict the vengeance that he had sworn for his dear brother's death, and that Piso would be advised to keep away until he had plainly established his innocence. Tiberius received Piso's son without either particular graciousness or particular disfavour, as if to show that he would remain unprejudiced until a public enquiry had been made into Germanicus's death.

Eventually Piso appeared at Rome with Plancina. They came sailing down the Tiber and disembarked with a number of retainers at the tomb of Augustus, where they nearly created a riot by strutting with broad smiles through the hostile crowd which soon gathered, and stepping into a decorated carriage drawn by a pair of well-matched white French cobs which was waiting for them on the Flaminian road. Piso had a house overlooking the Market Place and this was decorated too. He invited all his friends and relations to a banquet celebrating his return and made a great deal of disturbance: merely to show the people of Rome that he was not afraid of them and that he counted on the support of Tiberius and Livia. Tiberius had planned for Piso to be prosecuted in the ordinary Criminal Court by a certain senator who could be trusted to do it so clumsily, contradicting himself and neglecting to produce proper evidence in support of his charges, that the proceedings could only end in an acquittal. But Germanicus's friends, especially the three senators who had been on his staff in Syria and had returned with Agrippina, opposed Tiberius's choice. Tiberius was forced in the end to judge the case himself, and in the Senate too, where Germanicus's friends could count on all the support they needed. The Senate had voted a number of exceptional honours to Germanicus's memory – cenotaphs, memorial arches, semi-divine rites – which Tiberius had not dared to veto.

Castor now returned once more from the Danube and, though an ovation (or lesser triumph) had been decreed him for his management of the Maroboduus affair, he entered the City on foot as a private citizen instead of on horseback with a chaplet on his head. After visiting his father he went straight to Agrippina and swore to her that she could count on him to see that justice was done.

Piso asked four senators to defend him; three of them excused themselves on the ground of sickness or incapacity; the fourth, Gallus, said that he never defended anyone on a murder charge of which he seemed guilty unless there was at least a chance of pleasing the Imperial family. Calpurnius Piso, though he had not attended his uncle's banquet, volunteered to defend him for the honour of the family, and three others afterwards joined him because they were sure that Tiberius would acquit Piso, whatever the evidence, and that they would later be rewarded for their part in the trial. Piso was pleased to be judged by Tiberius himself, because Sejanus had assured him that it would be all properly managed, that Tiberius would pretend to be very severe but finally adjourn the court *sine die* for fresh evidence. Martina, the principal witness, had already been put out of the way – smothered by Sejanus's agents – and the prosecutors now had a poor case.

Two days only were allowed for the prosecution, and the man who had been originally commissioned to bungle it for Piso's benefit came forward and did his best to talk the time out by bringing stale charges against him of misgovernment and corruption in Spain under Augustus. Tiberius let him continue with this irrelevant matter for some hours, until the Senate, by scuffling feet, coughing and clattering writing-tablets together, warned him that the principal witnesses must be heard or there would be trouble. Germanicus's four friends had their case well prepared and each in turn rose and testified to Piso's corruption of military discipline in Syria, his insulting behaviour to Germanicus and themselves, his disobedience of orders, his intrigues with Vonones, his oppression of the provincials. They accused him of murdering Germanicus by poison and witchcraft, of offering thanksgiving sacrifices at his death, and finally of having made an armed attack on the Province with private forces illegally raised.

Piso did not deny the charges of corrupting military discipline, of insulting and disobeying Germanicus, or of oppressing the provincials; he merely said that they were exaggerated. But he indignantly denied the charge of poison and witchcraft. The accusers did not mention the supernatural events at Antioch for fear of encouraging sceptical laughter, nor could they accuse Piso of interfering with Germanicus's household servants and slaves, because it had already been shown that they had nothing to do with the murder. So Piso was accused of poisoning Germanicus's food while he sat next to him at a banquet in Germanicus's own house. Piso ridiculed this charge: how could he possibly have done such a thing without someone noticing it, when the whole table, not to mention the waiters, were watching every movement he made? By magic perhaps?

He had a bundle of letters in his hand which everyone knew, by the size and colour and the way they were tied, were from Tiberius. Germanicus's friends moved that any instructions that Piso had had sent from Rome should be read. Piso refused to read the letters on the ground that they were sealed as with the Sphinx seal (originally Augustus's), which made them 'secret and confidential': it would be treasonable to read them. Tiberius ruled against the motion, saying that it would be a waste of time to read the letters, which contained nothing of importance. The Senate could not press the point. Piso handed the letters to Tiberius as a sign that he trusted him to save his life.

Angry noises were now heard from the crowd outside, which was being kept informed of the progress of the trial, and a man with a huge raucous voice shouted through a window: 'He may escape you, my Lords, but he won't escape us!' A messenger came to tell Tiberius that some statues of Piso had been seized by the crowd and were being dragged to the Wailing Stairs to be broken up. The Wailing Stairs were a flight of steps at the foot of the Capitoline Hill where the corpses of criminals were customarily exposed before being dragged by a hook in the throat to the Tiber and thrown in. Tiberius ordered the statues to be rescued and replaced on their pedestals. But he complained that he could not continue to judge a case under such conditions and adjourned it until the evening. Piso was conveyed away under escort.

Plancina, who had hitherto boasted that she would share her husband's fate whatever it might be, and if necessary die with him, now grew alarmed. She decided to make a separate defence and counted on Livia, with whom she had been on intimate terms, to get her off. Piso knew nothing of this treachery. When the trial was resumed Tiberius gave him no sign of sympathy, and though he told the accusers that they should have provided more conclusive evidence of poisoning, he warned Piso that his armed attempt to win back his province could never be forgiven. At home that evening Piso shut himself in his room and was found the next morning stabbed to death with his sword beside him. It was not, as a matter of fact, suicide.

For Piso had retained the most incriminating letter of all, one written to him by Livia but in the names of Tiberius and herself, and not stamped with the Sphinx seal (which Tiberius reserved for his own use). He told Plancina to bargain for their lives with it. Plancina went to Livia. Livia told her to wait while she consulted Tiberius. Livia and Tiberius then had their first open quarrel. Tiberius was furious with Livia for having written the letter, and Livia said that it was his own fault for not allowing her to use the Sphinx seal and complained that he had been behaving very insolently to her lately. Tiberius asked, who was Emperor, he or she? Livia said that if he was, it was by her connivance and that it was foolish of him to be rude to her, because as she had found means to make him, she could find means to break him. She took a letter from her purse and began reading it: it was an old letter written to her by Augustus during Tiberius's absence in Rhodes, accusing him of treachery, cruelty, and bestiality, and saying that if he were not her son he would not live another day. 'This is only a copy,' she said. 'But I have the original in safe keeping. It's only one of many letters in the same strain. You wouldn't like them handed about the Senate, would you?'

Tiberius controlled himself and apologized for his bad temper: he said that it was clear that he and she were each able to ruin the other and that therefore it was absurd for them to quarrel. But how could be spare Piso's life, especially after having said that, if the charge of raising private forces and trying to win back Syria with them was proved, this would mean the death penalty, beyond hope of pardon?

'Plancina didn't raise any forces, though, did she?'

'I don't see what that has to do with it. I can't get the letter back from Piso merely by promising to spare Plancina.'

'If you promise to spare Plancina, I'll get the letter from Piso: leave that to me. If Piso's killed that will satisfy public opinion. And if you are afraid of sparing Plancina on your own responsibility you can say that it was I who pleaded for her. That's fair enough, because I admit that it is a letter I wrote that all the trouble is about.'

So Livia went to Plancina and told her that Tiberius refused to listen to reason, and that he would rather sacrifice his own mother to popular hatred than risk his own skin in standing by his friends. All that she had been able to get from him, she said, was a grudging promise of pardon for her if the letter were given up. So Plancina went to Piso with a letter in Tiberius's name, forged by Livia, and said that she had arranged everything so beautifully and here was the promise of acquittal. As Piso handed her the letter in exchange she suddenly stabbed him in the throat with a dagger. As he lay dying she dipped the point of his sword in blood, clasped his sword-hand around the pommel and left him. She took the letter, and the forged promise, back to Livia as arranged.

In the Senate next day Tiberius read a statement which he said that Piso had made before his suicide, pleading complete innocence of the crimes charged against him, protesting his loyalty to Livia and himself, and imploring their protection for his sons as having taken no part in the events which had been made the subject of his impeachment. Plancina's trial then began. She was proved to have been seen in the society of Martina, and Martina's reputation as a poisoner was sworn to, and it came out that when Martina's corpse was prepared for burial a phial of poison was found knotted in her hair. Old Pomponius, Germanicus's orderly, testified to the horrible putrid relics planted in the house and to Plancina's visit there with Martina in Germanicus's absence; and when questioned by Tiberius he gave detailed evidence of the hauntings. Nobody came forward to defend Plancina. She protested her innocence with tears and oaths and said that she knew nothing of Martina's reputation as a poisoner and that her only business with her had been to buy perfumes. She said that the woman who had come with her to the house was not Martina but the wife of one of the colonels. And that surely it was an innocent thing to go calling and find nobody at home but a little boy. As for her insults to Agrippina, she was heartily sorry for them and begged Agrippina's pardon most humbly; but she had been obeying her husband's orders, as a wife was bound to do, and moreover her husband had told her that Agrippina was plotting with Germanicus against the Senate, so she had the more willingly done what was expected of her.

Tiberius summed up. He said that there seemed to be a certain doubt as to Plancina's guilt. Her connexion with Martina seemed proved, and so did Martina's reputation as a poisoner. But that it was a guilty connexion remained open to question.The prosecution had not even produced in court the phial found in Martina's hair nor any evidence that the contents were poisonous: it might well have been a sleeping draught or aphrodisiac. His mother Livia had a high opinion of Plancina's character and wished the Senate to give her the benefit of the doubt if the evidence of guilt was not conclusive; for the ghost of her beloved grandson had appeared to her in a dream and begged her not to allow the innocent to suffer for the crimes of a husband or father.

So Plancina was acquitted, and of Piso's two sons, one was allowed to inherit his father's estate and the other, who had taken part in the fighting in Cilicia, was merely banished for a few years. A senator proposed that public thanks be paid to the dead hero's family – to Tiberius, Livia, my mother Antonia, Agrippina, and Castor – for having avenged his death. This motion was just about to be voted upon when a friend of mine, an ex-Consul who had been Governor of Africa before Furius, rose to make an amendment. The motion was, he objected, not in order: one important name had been omitted, that of the dead hero's brother Claudius, who had done more than anyone to prepare the case for the prosecution and to protect the witnesses from molestation. Tiberius shrugged his shoulders and said that he was surprised to hear that I had been called upon for any assistance and that perhaps if I had not been, the charges against Piso would have been more clearly presented. (It was quite true that I had presided at the meeting of my brother's friends and decided what evidence each witness was to bring; and I had, as a matter of fact, advised them against accusing Piso of administering poison at the banquet with his own hands, but they had overruled me. And I had kept Pomponius and his grandsons and three of my brother's freedmen safely hidden in a farmhouse near my villa at Capua until the day of the trial. I had also tried to hide Martina away at the house of a merchant I knew at Brindisi, but Sejanus traced her.) Well, Tiberius let my name be included in the vote of thanks; but that meant little to me compared with the thanks that Agrippina gave me: she said that she understood now what Germanicus had meant when he told her, just before his death, that the truest friend he had ever had was his poor brother Claudius.

Feeling against Livia was so strong that Tiberius made it an excuse for her again not asking the Senate to vote her the title that he had so often promised. Everyone was wanting to know what it meant when a grandmother gave gracious interviews to the murderess of her grandson and rescued her from the vengeance of the Senate. The answer could only be that the grandmother had instigated the murder herself and was so utterly ashamed of herself that the wife and children of the victim would not survive him long.

Chapter 22

GERMANICUS was dead, but Tiberius did not feel much more secure than before. Sejanus came to him with stories of what this or that prominent man had whispered against him during Piso's trial. Instead of saying, as he had once said of his soldiers, 'let them fear me, so long as they obey me,' he now told Sejanus, 'Let them hate me, so long as they fear me.' Three knights and two senators who had been most outspoken in their recent criticism of him he put to death on the absurd charge of having expressed pleasure on hearing of the death of Germanicus. The informers divided up their estates between them.

About this time Germanicus's eldest boy Nero * came of age, and though he showed little promise of being as capable a soldier or as talented an administrator as his father, he had much of his father's good looks and sweetness of character and the City hoped much from him. There was great popular rejoicing when he married the daughter of Castor and Livilla, whom at first we called Helen because of her surprising beauty (her real name was Julia), but afterwards Heluo, which means Glutton, because she spoilt her beauty by over-eating. Nero was Agrippina's favourite. The family was divided, being of Claudian stock, into good and bad; or, in the words of the ballad, 'crabs and apples'. The crabs outnumbered the apples. Of the nine children whom Agrippina bore Germanicus three died young – two girls and a boy – and from what I saw of them this boy and the elder girl were the best of the nine. The boy, who died on his eighth birthday, had been such a favourite with Augustus that the old man kept a picture of him,

* This Nero is not to be confused with the Nero who became Emperor. – R. G.

dressed in Cupid's costume, in his bedroom and used to kiss it every morning as soon as he got out of bed. But of the surviving children only Nero had a wholly good character. Drusus was morose and nervous and easily inclined to evil. Drusilla was like him. Caligula, Agrippinilla, and the youngest, whom we called Lesbia, were wholly bad, as the younger of the girls who died seemed also to be. But the City judged the whole family by Nero because, so far, he was the only one old enough to make a strong public impression. Caligula was still only nine years old.

Agrippina visited me in great distress one day when I was in Rome and asked my advice. She said that wherever she went she felt that she was being followed and spied on, and it was making her ill. Did I know anyone beside Sejanus who had any influence over Tiberius? She was sure that he had decided to kill or banish her if he could get the slightest handle against her. I said that I only knew two people who had any influence for good over Tiberius. One was Cocceius Nerva, and the other was Vipsania. Tiberius had never been able to root his love for Vipsania out of his heart. When a granddaughter was born to her and Gallus, who at the age of fifteen exactly resembled Vipsania as she had been when Tiberius's wife, Tiberius could not bear the thought of anyone marrying her but himself; and was only prevented from doing so by her being Castor's niece, which would have made the marriage technically incestuous. So he appointed her the Chief Vestal in succession to old Occia who had just died. I told Agrippina that if she made friends with Cocceius and Vipsania (who as Castor's mother would do all in her power to help her) she was safe, and so were her children. She took my advice. Vipsania and Gallus, who were very sorry for her, made her free of their house and their three country villas and took a great deal of trouble with the children. Gallus, for instance, choose new tutors for the boys because Agrippina suspected the old ones of being agents of Sejanus. Nerva was not so much help. He was a jurist and the greatest living authority on the laws of contract, about which he had written several books: but in all other respects he was so absent-minded and unobservant as to be almost a simpleton. He was kind to her, as he was to everyone, but did not realise what she expected from him.

Unfortunately Vipsania died soon afterwards and the effect on Tiberius was apparent at once. He no longer made any serious attempt to conceal his sexual depravity, the rumours of which everyone had shrunk from taking literally. For some of his perversities were so preposterous and horrible that nobody could seriously reconcile them with the dignity of an Emperor of Rome, Augustus's chosen successor. No women or boys were safe in his presence now, even the wives and children of senators; and if they valued their own lives or those of their husbands and fathers they willingly did what he expected of them. But one woman, a Consul's wife, committed suicide afterwards in the presence of her friends, telling them that she had been forced to save her young daughter from Tiberius's lust by consenting to prostitute herself to him, which was shameful enough; but then the Old He-Goat had taken advantage of her complaisance by forcing her to such abominable acts of filthiness with him that she preferred to die rather than to live on with the memory of them.

There was a popular song circulated about this time which began with the words: 'Why, oh, why, did the Old He-Goat ...?' I should be ashamed to quote more of it, but it was as witty as it was obscene and was supposed to have been written by Livia herself. Livia was the author of a number of similar satires against Tiberius which she circulated anonymously through Urgulania. She knew that they would reach him sooner or later and that he was extremely sensitive to satires, and thought that while he felt his position insecure because of them, he would not dare to break with her. She also now went out of her way to be pleasant to Agrippina, and even told her in confidence that Tiberius alone had given Piso the instructions about baiting Germanicus. Agrippina did not trust her, but it was clear that Livia and Tiberius were at enmity, and she felt, she told me, that if she had to choose between the protection of one or the other she would prefer to be under Livia's. I was inclined to agree with Agrippina. I had observed that no favourite of Livia had yet been made the victim of Tiberius's informers. But I had forebodings of what might happen when Livia died.

What had begun to impress me as particularly ominous, though I could not altogether account for my feelings, was the strong bond between Livia and Caligula. Caligula had in general only two ways of behaving: he was either insolent or servile. To Agrippina and my mother and myself and his brothers and Castor, for instance, he was insolent. To Sejanus and Tiberius and Livilla he was servile. But to Livia he was something else, difficult to express. He was almost like her lover. It was not the usual tender tie that binds little boys to indulgent grandmothers or great-grandmothers, though it is true that he once took great pains over a copy of affectionate verses for her seventy-fifth birthday and that she was always giving him presents. I mean that there was a strong impression of some unpleasant secret between them – but I don't mean to suggest that there was any indecent relationship between them. Agrippina felt this too, she told me, but could find out nothing definite about it.

One day I began to understand why Sejanus had been so polite to me. He suggested the betrothal of his daughter to my son Drusillus. My personal feelings against the marriage were that the girl, who seemed a nice little thing, was unlucky to be matched to Drusillus, who seemed more of a lubber every time I saw him. But I could not say so. Still less could I say that I loathed the thought of being even remotely related in marriage with a scoundrel like Sejanus. He noticed my hesitation in answering and wanted to know whether I considered the match beneath the dignity of my family. I stammered and said no, certainly I did not: his branch of the Aelian family was a very honourable one. For Sejanus, though the son of a mere country knight, had been adopted in early manhood by a rich senator of the Aelian family, a Consul, who had left him all his money; there was a scandal connected with this adoption, but the fact remained that Sejanus was an Aelian. He anxiously pressed me to explain my hesitation and said that if I had any feeling against the marriage, he was sorry he had mentioned it, but of course he had only done so on Tiberius's suggestion. So I told him that if Tiberius proposed the match I would be glad to give my consent: that my chief feeling had been that four years old was rather young for a girl to be betrothed to a boy of thirteen, who would be twenty-one before he could legally consummate the marriage and by that time might have formed other entanglements. Sejanus smiled and said that he trusted me to keep the lad out of serious mischief.

There was great alarm in the City when it was known that Sejanus was to become related with the Imperial family, but everyone hastened to congratulate him, and me too. A few days later Drusillus was dead. He was found lying behind a   A.D. 23 bush in the garden of a house at Pompeii where he had been invited, from Herculaneum, by some friends of Urgula-nilla's. A small pear was found stuck in his throat. It was said at the inquest that he had been seen throwing fruit up in the air and trying to catch it in his mouth: his death was unquestionably due to an accident. But nobody believed this. It was clear that Livia, not having been consulted about the marriage of one of her own great-grandchildren, had arranged for the child to be strangled and the pear crammed down his throat afterwards. As was the custom in such cases, the pear tree was charged with murder and sentenced to be uprooted and burned.

Tiberius asked the Senate to decree Castor Protector of the People, which was as much as pointing him out as heir to the monarchy. This request caused general relief. It was taken as a sign that Tiberius was aware of Sejanus's ambitions and intended to check them. When the decree was passed someone proposed that it should be printed on the walls of the House in letters of gold. Nobody realized that it was at Sejanus's own suggestion that Castor was so honoured; he had hinted to Tiberius that Castor, Agrippina, Livia, and Gallus were in league together and pro-posed this as the best way to see who else belonged to their party. It was a friend of his own who had made the proposal about the gold inscription, and the names of senators who supported this extravagant motion were carefully noted. Castor was more popu-lar now among the better citizens than he had been. He had given up his drunken habits – the death of Germanicus seemed to have sobered him – and though he still had an inordinate love of blood-shed at sword-fights and dressed extravagantly and betted enor-mous sums on the chariot races, he was a conscientious magistrate and a loyal friend. I had little to do with him, but when we met he treated me with far greater consideration than before Germani-cus's death.

The bitter hatred between him and Sejanus always threatened to blaze up into a quarrel, but Sejanus was careful not to provoke Castor until the quarrel could be turned to account. The time had now come. Sejanus went to the Palace to congratulate Castor on his protectorship and found him in his study with Livilla. There were no slaves or freedmen present, so Sejanus could say what he pleased. By this time Livilla was so much in love with him that he could count on her to betray Castor as she had once betrayed Pos-tumus – somehow he knew that story – and there had even been talk between them in which they had regretted that they were not Emperor and Empress, to do as they pleased. Sejanus said, 'Well, Castor, I've worked it for you all right! Congratulations?'

Castor scowled. He was only 'Castor' to a few intimates. He had won the name, as I think I have explained, because of his resemblance to a well-known sword-fighter, but it had stuck because one day he had lost his temper in an argument with a knight. The knight had told him bluntly at a banquet that he was drunk and incapable, and Castor, shouting 'Drunk and incapable, am I? I'll show you if I'm drunk and incapable,' staggered from his couch and hit the knight such a terrific blow in the belly that he vomited up the whole meal. Castor now said to Sejanus: 'I don't allow anyone to address me by a nickname except a friend or an equal, and you're neither. To you I'm Tiberius Drusus Caesar. And I don't know what you claim to have "worked" for me. And I don't want your congratulations on it, whatever it is. So get out.'

Livilla said: 'If you ask *me*, I call it pretty cowardly of you to insult Sejanus like this, not to mention the ingratitude of kicking him out like a dog when he comes to congratulate you on your protectorship. You know that your father would never have given it you except on Sejanus's recommendation.'

Castor said: 'You're talking nonsense, Livilla. This filthy spy has had no more to do with the appointment than my eunuch Lygdus. He's just pretending to be important. And tell me, Sejanus, what's this about cowardice?'

Sejanus said: 'Your wife is quite right. You're a coward. You wouldn't have dared to talk to me like this before I got you appointed Protector and so made your person sacrosanct. You know perfectly well that I'd have thrashed you.'

'And serve you right,' said Livilla.

Castor looked from one face to the other and said slowly: 'So there's something between you two, is there?'

Livilla smiled scornfully: 'And suppose there is? Who's the better man?'

Castor shouted: 'All right, my girl, we'll see. Just forget for a moment that I'm a Protector of the People, Sejanus, and put your fists up.'

Sejanus folded his arms.

'Put them up, I say, you coward.'

Sejanus said nothing, so Castor struck him hard across the face with his open palm. 'Now get out!'

Sejanus went out with an ironical obeisance and Livilla followed him.

This blow settled Castor's fate. The account that Tiberius heard from Sejanus, who came to him with the mark of Castor's slap still red on his cheek, was that Castor had been drunk when Sejanus had congratulated him on his protectorship and had struck him across the face saying: 'Yes, it's good to feel that I can do this now without fear of being hit back. And you can tell my father that I'll do the same to every other dirty spy of his.' Livilla confirmed this the next day when she came to complain that Castor had beaten her; she said that he had beaten her because she told him how disgusted she was with him for striking a man who could not strike back and for insulting his father. Tiberius believed them. He said nothing to Castor but put up a bronze statue of Sejanus in the theatre of Pompey, an extraordinary honour to be paid to any man in his lifetime. This was understood to mean that Castor was out of favour with Tiberius in spite of his protectorship (for Sejanus and Livilla had circulated their version of the quarrel) and that Sejanus was now the one person whose favour was worth courting. Many replicas of the statue were therefore made, which his partisans put in a place of honour in their halls on the right hand of Tiberius's statue: but statues of Castor were rarely seen. Castor's face showed his resentment so clearly now whenever he met his father that Sejanus's task was made easy. He told Tiberius that Castor was sounding various senators as to their willingness to support him if he usurped the monarchy and that some of them had already promised their help. The ones who seemed most dangerous to Tiberius were therefore arrested on the familiar charge of blaspheming against Augustus. One man was condemned to death for having gone into a privy with a gold coin of Augustus's in his hand. Another was accused of having included a statue of Augustus in a list of furniture for sale in a country villa. He would have been condemned to death if the Consul who was judging the case had not asked Tiberius to give his vote first. Tiberius was ashamed to vote for the death-penalty, so the man was acquitted, but condemned soon after on another charge.

Castor became alarmed and asked Livia for her help against Sejanus. Livia told him not to be afraid: she would soon bring

Tiberius to his senses. But she had no confidence in Castor as an ally. She went to Tiberius and told him that Castor had accused Sejanus of debauching Livilla, of abusing his position of confidence by levying blackmail on rich men in Tiberius's name, and of aiming at the monarchy; that he had said that unless Tiberius dismissed the rascal soon he would take the matter into his own hands; and that he had then asked for her co-operation. By putting the case like this to Tiberius she hoped to make him as mistrustful of Sejanus as he was of Castor and thus to cause him to fall back into his old habit of dependence on her. For a time at least she succeeded. But then an accident suddenly convinced Tiberius that Sejanus was as loyally devoted as he pretended to be and as all his actions had hitherto shown him. They were picnicking together one day with three or four friends in a natural cave by the sea-shore, when there was a sudden rattle and roar and part of the roof fell in, killing some of the attendants and burying others, and blocking up the entrance. Sejanus crouched with arched back over Tiberius – they were both unhurt – to shield him from a further fall. When the soldiers dug them out an hour later he was found still in the same position. Thrasyllus, too, by the way, increased his reputation on this occasion: he had told Tiberius that there would be an hour of darkness about noon that day. Tiberius had Thrasyllus's assurance that he would outlive Sejanus by a great many years, and that Sejanus was not dangerous to him. I think that Sejanus had arranged this with Thrasyllus, but I have no proof: Thrasyllus was not altogether incorruptible, but when he made prophecies to suit his clients' wishes they seemed to come off just as well as his ordinary ones. Tiberius did outlive Sejanus, as it happens, by a number of years.

Tiberius gave a further public sign that Castor was out of favour by censuring him in the Senate for a letter he had written. Castor had excused himself from attending the sacrifice when the House opened after the summer recess, explaining that he was prevented by other public business from returning to the City in time. Tiberius said scornfully that anyone would think that the young fellow was on campaign in Germany or on a diplomatic visit to Armenia: when all the 'public business' that kept him was boating and bathing at Terracina. He said that he himself, now in the decline of life, might be excused for an occasional absence from the City: he might plead that his energies had been exhausted by prolonged public service with the sword and the pen. But what except insolence could detain his son? This was most unjust: Castor had been commissioned to make a report on coastal defence during the recess and had not been able to collect all the evidence in time: rather than waste time by a journey to Rome and then back again to Terracina he was finishing his task.

When Castor returned he almost immediately fell ill. The symptoms were those of rapid consumption. He lost colour and weight and began coughing blood. He wrote to his father and asked him to come and visit him in his room – he lived at the other end of the Palace – because he believed that he was dying, and to forgive him if he had in any way offended. Sejanus advised Tiberius against the visit: the illness might be real, but on the other hand it might easily be a trick for assassinating him. So Tiberius did not visit him and a few days later Castor died.

There was not much sorrow at the death of Castor. The violence of his temper and his reputation for cruelty had made the City apprehensive of what would happen if he succeeded his father. Few believed in his recent reformation. Most people A.D. 23 thought it had merely been a trick to win popular affection, and that he would have been just as bad as his father as soon as he found himself in his father's place. And now Germanicus's three sons were growing up – Drusus, too, had just come of age – and were unquestionably Tiberius's heirs. But the Senate, out of respect for Tiberius, mourned for Castor as noisily as it could and voted the same honours in his memory as it had voted Germanicus. Tiberius made no pretence of sorrow on this occasion but pronounced the panegyric he had prepared for Castor in a firm resonant voice. When he saw tears rolling down the faces of several senators he remarked in an audible aside to Sejanus at his elbow: 'Faugh! The place smells of onions!' Gallus afterwards rose to compliment Tiberius on his mastery over his grief. He recalled that even the God Augustus, during his presence among them in mortal shape, had so far given way to his feelings at the death of Marcellus, his adopted son (not even his real son), that when he was thanking the House for its sympathy he had to break off in the middle, unable to go on for emotion. Whereas the speech they had just heard was a masterpiece of restraint. (I may mention here that when four or five months later deputies arrived from Troy to condole with Tiberius on the death of his only son,

Tiberius thanked them: 'And I condole with you, gentlemen, on the death of Hector.' Tiberius then sent for Nero and Drusus, and when they arrived at the House he took them by the hand and introduced them: 'My Lords, three years ago I committed these fatherless children to their uncle, my dear son whom today we are all so bitterly mourning, desiring him to adopt them as his sons, though he already had sons of his own, and bring them up as worthy inheritors of the family tradition. (Hear, hear! from Gallus, and general applause.) But now that he has been snatched from us by cruel fate (groans and lamentations) I make the same request of *you*. In the presence of the Gods, in the face of your beloved Country, I beseech you, receive into your protection, take under your tuition, these noble great-grandchildren of Augustus, descended from ancestors whose names resound in Roman history: see that your duty and mine is honourably fulfilled towards them. Grandsons, these senators are now in the place of fathers to you, and your birth is such that whatever good or evil may befall you will spell the good or evil of the entire State.' (Resounding applause, tears, benedictions, shouts of loyalty.)

But instead of leaving off there he spoilt the whole effect by ending on a familiar note with his old stale phrases about presently retiring and restoring the Republic – when 'the Consuls or someone else' would 'take the burden of government off' his 'aged shoulders'. If he did not intend Nero and Drusus (or one or other of them) as his Imperial successors, what did he mean by identifying their fortune so closely with that of the State?

Castor's funeral was less impressive than Germanicus's, being marked by very few genuine expressions of grief, but on the other hand far more magnificent. Every one of the family masks of the Caesars and Claudians was worn in the procession, beginning with those of Aeneas, the founder of the Julian family, and Romulus, the founder of Rome, and ending with those of Gaius, Lucius, and Germanicus. Julius Caesar's mask appeared because, like Romulus, he was only a demi-god, but Augustus's did not appear, because he was a major Deity.

Sejanus and Livilla had now to consider how to achieve their ambition of becoming Emperor and Empress. Nero, Drusus, and Caligula stood in the way and would have to be removed. Three seemed rather many to get rid of safely, but, as Livilla pointed out, her grandmother had apparently managed to get rid of

Gaius, Lucius, and Postumus when she wanted to put Tiberius into power. And Sejanus was clearly in a much better position than Livia had been for carrying their plans through. To show Livilla that he really intended to marry her, as he had promised, Sejanus divorced his wife Apicata, by whom he had three children. He charged her with adultery and said that she was about to become the mother of a child which was not his own. He did not publicly name her lover but told Tiberius in private that he suspected Nero. Nero, he said, was getting a bad reputation for his affairs with the wives of prominent men and seemed to think that, as heir-presumptive to the monarchy, he could behave how he liked. Livilla meanwhile did her best to detach Agrippina from Livia's protection, by warning Agrippina that Livia was only using her as a weapon in her conflict with Tiberius – which happened to be true – and by warning Livia, through one of her ladies-in-waiting, that Agrippina was only using *her* as a weapon in her conflict with Tiberius – which was also true. She made each believe that the other had sworn to kill her as soon as her usefulness ended.

The twelve pontiffs now began to include Nero and Drusus in the customary prayers they offered for the health and prosperity of the Emperor, and the other priests followed their example. Tiberius as High Pontiff sent a letter of complaint to them, saying that they had made no difference between these boys and himself, a man who had honourably held most of the highest offices of the State twenty years before they were born, and all the rest since: it was not decent. He called them into his presence and there asked them whether Agrippina had merely coaxed them to make this addition to the prayer or whether she had frightened them into making it by using threats. They denied, of course, that she had done either, but he was not convinced; four of the twelve, including Gallus, were in some way connected with her by marriage and five others were on very friendly terms with her and her sons. He reprimanded them severely. In his next speech he warned the Senate to 'award no further premature distinctions that might encourage the giddy minds of young men to indulge in presumptuous aspirations'.

Agrippina found an unexpected ally in Calpurnius Piso. He told her that he had defended his uncle Gnaeus Piso merely out of regard for family honours and that he must not be thought of as her enemy; he would do all that he could to protect her and her children. But Calpurnius did not live long after this. He was charged in the Senate with 'treasonable words spoken in private', and of keeping poison in his house, and of coming into the Senate armed with a dagger. These two last articles were so absurd that they were dropped, but a day was fixed for his trial on the 'treasonable words' charge. He killed himself before the trial came off.

Tiberius believed Sejanus's story that there was a secret party, called the Leek Green party, now being formed by Agrippina, the sign of which was an extravagant partisanship of the Leek Green faction in the chariot-races in the Circus. In these races there were four colours – scarlet, white, sea blue, and leek green. The Leek Green faction happened to be most in favour at this time and the Scarlet the most unpopular. So now when Tiberius went to watch the races on public holidays, as he was bound to do in his official position – though he had not hitherto been at all interested in them and discouraged idle racing-talk at the Palace or at banquets to which he was invited – and began for the first time to notice what sort of support the different colours were being given he was greatly disturbed to hear the Leek Green so cried up. He had been also told by Sejanus that Scarlet was the secret symbol used by Leek Greens when they wished to refer to his own supporters, and he noticed that whenever a Scarlet chariot won, which was seldom, it came in for loud groans and hisses. Sejanus was clever: he knew that Germanicus had always backed the Leek Green and that Agrippina, Nero, and Drusus, for sentimental reasons, continued to favour the colour.

There was a nobleman called Silius who had been for many years a corps-commander on the Rhine. I think I have mentioned him as the General of the four regiments in the Upper Province of Germany which did not take part in the great mutiny. He had been my brother's most capable lieutenant and had been granted triumphal ornaments for his successes against Hermann. Recently, at the head of the combined forces of the Upper and Lower Provinces he had put down a dangerous revolt of the French tribes in the neighbourhood of my birthplace, Lyons. He was not a modest man but not particularly boastful and if he had really said in public, as was reported, that but for his tactful handling of those four regiments in the mutiny they would have joined the other mutineers, and that therefore, but for him, Tiberius would not have had any Empire at all to rule over – well, that was not far from the truth. But naturally Tiberius did not like it, if only because the mutinous regiments were, as I explained, the ones with which he himself had most to do. Silius's wife Sosia was Agrippina's best woman friend. It so happened that Silius at the great Roman Games, which were held early in September, was betting very heavily on the Leek Green. Sejanus shouted across to him: 'I'll take you up to any amount. My money's on Scarlet.' Silius shouted back: 'You're backing the wrong colour, my friend. The Scarlet charioteer hasn't the least idea of managing his reins. He tries to do it all with the whip. I'll bet you an even thousand that Leek Green wins. Young Nero here says he'll make it fifteen hundred; he's an enthusiastic Leek Greener.' Sejanus looked significantly at Tiberius, who had heard the whole exchange and was astonished at Silius's boldness. He took it as a good omen when the leader of the Leek Green chariot fell in rounding the mark on the last lap but one, and Scarlet came in an easy winner.

Ten days later Silius was impeached before the Senate. The charge was high treason. He was accused of having connived at the French revolt during its earlier stages and having taken a third part of the plunder as payment for non-intervention, of making his victory the excuse for further plunder of loyal provincials, and of afterwards imposing excessive emergency taxes on the province for the expenses of the campaign. Sosia was accused of complicity in the same offences. Silius had been unpopular at the Palace ever since the French rebellion. Tiberius had come in for a good deal of criticism for not having taken the field against the rebels, and for having shown more interest in the treason trials that were going on at the time than in the campaign. He had excused himself to the Senate on the ground of age – and Castor had been engaged in important business – and explained that he had been keeping in touch with Silius's headquarters all along, giving him valuable advice. Tiberius was very sensitive about the whole French revolt. When the French were beaten he had been made ridiculous by the motion of a waggish senator, an imitator of Gallus's tricks, that he should be awarded a triumph for being the man really responsible for victory. He was so displeased by this, taking the line that in any case the victory was not worth talking about, that nobody dared to vote Silius the triumphal ornaments which he thoroughly well deserved. Silius had been disappointed and what he had said about the Rhine mutiny had been said in resentment of Tiberius's ingratitude.

Silius disdained to reply to the charges of treason. He was not guilty of any understanding with the rebels and if the soldiers under his command had in some cases failed to distinguish between the property of rebels and the property of loyalists that was only to be expected: many pretended loyalists-were secretly financing the rebellion. As for the taxation, the fact was that Tiberius had promised him a special grant from the Treasury to cover the expenses of the campaign and to indemnify Roman citizens for their loss of houses, crops, and cattle. In anticipation of the payment of this grant Silius had imposed a tax on certain Northern tribes, promising to refund the money when it was paid him by Tiberius: which it never was. Silius was a poorer man by 20,000 gold pieces after the revolt than before it, because he had raised a troop of volunteer horse which he armed and paid at his own expense. His chief accuser, who was one of the Consuls of the year, pressed the charges of extortion with great malice. He was a friend of Sejanus and was also the son of the military governor of the Lower Province who had wished to take supreme command of the Roman forces against the French and had been forced to stand aside in Silius's favour. Silius could not even produce evidence of Tiberius's promised grant, because the letter in which it was contained was sealed with the Sphinx. And the charges of extortion were in any case irrelevant, because the trial was for treason, not for extortion.

He finally burst out: 'My Lords, I could say much in my defence but shall say nothing, because this trial is not being conducted in a constitutional manner and the verdict has been long ago decided. I understand that my real crime is having said that, but for my handling of them, the regiments in Upper Germany would have mutinied. I shall now put my culpability in this matter beyond question. I shall say that, but for Tiberius's previous handling of them, the troops in Lower Germany would *not* have mutinied. My Lords, I am the victim of an avaricious, jealous, bloodthirsty, tyrannical ...' The rest of his speech was drowned in a roar of horrified protest from the House. Silius saluted Tiberius and walked out with his head high in the air. When he arrived at his house he embraced Sosia and his children, gave an affectionate message of farewell to Agrippina, Nero, Gallus, and his other friends, and going to his bedroom drove his sword into his throat.

His guilt was held to be proved by his insults to Tiberius. His entire estate was confiscated, with a promise that the provincials should have the unjust tax repaid them out of it, and that his accusers should be given the fourth part of what remained, as the law required, and that the money which had been left him under Augustus's will as an earnest of loyalty should return to the Treasury as paid him under a misapprehension. The provincials did not dare to press for the tax to be refunded, so Tiberius kept three-quarters of the estate: for there was no longer any real distinction between the Military Treasury, the Public Treasury, and the Privy Purse. This was the first time that he had benefited directly from the confiscation of an estate or that he had let a spoken insult to himself be construed as a proof of treason.

Sosia had property of her own and, to save her life and keep the children from becoming paupers, Gallus moved that she should be banished and that half of her effects should be forfeited to her accusers, half left to the children. But a cousin by marriage of Agrippina's, who was a confederate of Gallus, proposed that the accusers should only be paid one-fourth, which was the legal minimum, saying that Gallus was more loyal to the Emperor than just to Sosia; for Sosia was known, at least, to have reproved her husband, as he lay dying, for his treasonable and ungrateful utterances. So Sosia was only banished – she went to live in Marseilles; and since Silius as soon as he knew that he would be tried for his life had secretly given Gallus and certain other friends most of his money in cash to hold in trust for the children, the family came off quite well. His eldest son lived to cause me much distress.

From now onward Tiberius, who had hitherto made his accusations of treason hang on supposed blasphemies of Augustus, enforced more and more strongly the edict which had been passed in the first year of his monarchy, making it treason for anyone to assail his own honour and reputation in any way. He accused a senator, whom he suspected to be of Agrippina's party, of having recited a scurrilous epigram aimed against him. The fact was that the senator's wife one morning noticed a sheet of paper posted high up on the gate of the house. She asked her husband to read out what was on it – he was taller. He slowly spelt out,

> He is no drunkard now of wine
>   As he was drunkard then:
> He warms him up with a richer cup –
>   The blood of murdered men.

She asked innocently what the verse meant and he said, 'It's unsafe to explain in public, my dear.' A professional informer was hanging about the gate on the chance that when the senator read the epigram, which was Livia's work, he would say something worth reporting. He went straight to Sejanus. Tiberius himself cross-examined the senator, asking what he meant by 'unsafe', and to whom, in his opinion, the epigram referred. The senator shuffled and would not give direct answers. Tiberius then said that many libels had been current when he was a younger man, all accusing him of being a drunkard, and that in recent years he had been ordered by his doctors to abstain from wine because of a tendency to gout, and that several libels had lately been published accusing him of bloodthirstiness. He asked the accused whether he was not aware of these facts, and whether he thought that the epigram could refer to anyone but his Emperor. The wretched man agreed that he had heard the libels on Tiberius's drunkenness but he knew them to have no foundation in truth and had not made any connexion in his mind between them and the one on his gate. He was then asked why he had not reported the former libels to the Senate as it was his duty to do. He answered that when he had heard them it was not yet a punishable offence to utter or repeat any epigram, however scurrilous, written against anyone, however virtuous; nor treason to utter or repeat scurrilities directed even against Augustus so long as one did not publish them in writing. Tiberius asked to what time he referred, for Augustus had late in life made an edict against spoken scurrilities too. The senator answered: 'It was during your third year at Rhodes.' Tiberius cried out, 'My Lords, how can you permit this fellow to insult me so?' So the Senate actually condemned him to be thrown down the Tarpeian cliff, a punishment ordinarily reserved for the worst traitors – generals who sold battles to the enemy, and such-like.

Another man, a knight, was put to death for writing a tragedy about King Agamemnon in which Agamemnon's queen, who murdered him in his bath, cried as she swung the axe:

> Know, bloody tyrant, 'tis no crime
> T' avenge my wrongs like this.

Tiberius said that he was intended by the character Agamemnon and that the line quoted was an incitement to assassinate him. So the tragedy, which everyone had laughed at because it was so lamely and wretchedly composed, won a sort of dignity by having all its copies called in and burned and its author executed.

This prosecution was followed two years later – but I put it down here because the Agamemnon story reminds me of it – by that of Cremutius Cordus, an old man who had come into collision with Sejanus some time before over a trifle. Sejanus entering the House one wet day had hung his cloak on the peg which had always been Cremutius's, and Cremutius, when he came in, not knowing that it was Sejanus's cloak, had moved it to another peg to make room for his own. Sejanus's cloak had fallen down from this new peg and somebody with muddy sandals had trampled on it. Sejanus retaliated in a variety of malicious ways, and Cremutius came so to loathe the sight of his face and the sound of his name that when he heard that Sejanus's statue had been set up on the Theatre of Pompey he exclaimed: 'That just about ruins the Theatre.' So now he was named to Tiberius as one of Agrippina's principal adherents. But as he was a venerable, mild old man who had no enemy in the world but Sejanus and never a spoke a word more than necessary, it was difficult to support any accusation against him with evidence that even a brow-beaten Senate could decently accept. In the end Cremutius was charged with having written in praise of Brutus and Cassius, the murderers of Julius Caesar. The evidence produced was an historical work which he had written thirty years before and which Augustus himself, Julius's adopted son, was known to have included in his private library and occasionally consulted.

Cremutius made a spirited defence against this absurd charge, saying that Brutus and Cassius had been dead so long and had been so frequently praised for their deed by subsequent historians that he could not believe that the trial was not a hoax – such a hoax as a young traveller recently suffered in the city of Larissa. This young man was publicly accused of having murdered three men, though they were no more than wineskins, hanging outside a shop, which he had slashed at in the dark, mistaking them for robbers. But this Larissan trial had taken place on the annual festival of Laughter, which gave some point to the proceedings, and the young man was a drunkard and much too ready with his sword and perhaps deserved a lesson. But he, Cremutius Cordus, was too old and too sober to be made a fool of in this way, and this was no festival of Laughter but, on the contrary, the four hundred and seventy-sixth anniversary of the solemn promulgation of the Laws of the Twelve Tables, that glorious monument to the legislative genius and the moral rectitude of our forefathers. He went home and starved himself to death. All copies of his book were called in and burned except for two or three which his daughter hid away somewhere and republished them many years later when Tiberius was dead. It was not very good writing; it got more fame than it really deserved.

I had been all this time saying to myself, 'Claudius, you're a poor fellow and not much use in this world, and you have led a pretty miserable life with one thing and another, but at least your life is safe.' So when old Cremutius whom I knew very well – we had often met and chatted in the Library – lost his life on a charge like this it was a great shock to me. I felt like a man living on the slopes of a volcano when it suddenly throws up a warning shower of ash and red-hot stones. I had written far more treasonable things in my time than Cremutius. My history of Augustus's religious reforms contained several phrases that could easily be made the subject of an accusation. And though my estate was so small that it would hardly be worth an accuser's while to impeach me for the sake of a fourth share, I realized well enough that all the recent victims of treason-trials were friends of Agrippina, whom I continued to visit whenever I went to Rome. I was not at all sure how far my being a brother-in-law of Sejanus would be sufficient protection to me.

Yes, I had lately become Sejanus's brother-in-law, and now I shall tell how it came about.

Chapter 23

ONE day Sejanus had told me that I ought to marry again, as I did not seem to get on well with my wife. I said that Urgulanilla had been the choice of my grandmother Livia and that I could not divorce her without Livia's permission.

'Oh, no, of course not,' he said. 'I quite understand that, but it must be very unhappy for you without a wife.'

'Thank you,' I said, 'I manage all right.'

He pretended to find this a good joke and laughed loudly, calling me a very wise man, but afterwards said that if by any chance I found it possible to divorce my wife I was to come to him. He had just the woman for me in mind – well-born, young, and intelligent. I thanked him but felt uncomfortable. As I was going away he said: 'My friend Claudius, I have a word of advice to you. Back Scarlet to-morrow in every race and don't mind losing a bit of money at first: you'll not lose in the long run. And *don't back Green Leek*: it's an unlucky colour these days. And don't tell anyone that I gave you the tip.' I felt much relieved that Sejanus thought me still worth cultivating, but I couldn't make sense of what he told me. However, at the chariot-race next day – it was the festival of Augustus – Tiberius saw me take my seat in the Circus and, being in an affable mood, sent for me and asked, 'What are you doing these days, nephew?'

I stammered that I was writing a history of the ancient Etruscans, if it pleased him.

He said: 'Oh, really? That does credit to your judgement. There's no ancient Etruscan left to protest and no modern Etruscan who cares: so you can write as you please. What else are you doing?'

'Wr-r-riting a history of the ancient C-C-C-C-C-Carthaginians, if you please.'

'Splendid! And what else? Hurry up with that stammer. I'm a busy man.'

'At the m-m-moment I'm b-b-b-b – –'

'Beginning a history of C-C-C-Cloud C-C-C-Cuckoo Land?'

'N-no, sir, b-b-b-backing Scarlet.'

He looked at me very shrewdly and said: 'I see, nephew, that you are not altogether a fool. What makes you back Scarlet?'

I was in difficulties, because I couldn't say that Sejanus had given me the tip. So I said: 'I dreamed that Leek Green was d-disqualified for using his whip on his c-c-c-competitors and Scarlet c-c-came in first with Sea-b-b-blue and White nowhere.'

He gave me a purse of money and muttered in my ear: 'Tell nobody that I'm staking you, but put this on Scarlet and let's see what happens.'

It proved to be Scarlet's day, and by betting with young Nero on every race I won close on 2,000 gold pieces. That evening I thought it wise to visit Tiberius at the Palace and to say: 'Here's the lucky purse, sir, with a family of little purses which it littered during the day.'

'All mine?' he exclaimed. 'Well, I *am* in luck. Scarlet's the colour, eh?'

This was just like my uncle Tiberius. He hadn't made it clear who was to keep the winnings and I had supposed that I was. But if I had lost all the money he would have said something to make me feel in his debt to that amount. He might at least have given me a commission.

The next time I came up to Rome I found my mother in such a distracted state that I did not dare at first utter a word in her presence for fear of her flying into a temper and boxing my ears. I gathered that her trouble was connected with Caligula, then aged twelve, and Drusilla, then aged thirteen, who were staying with her. Drusilla was confined to her room without food and Caligula was at liberty but looking thoroughly frightened. He visited me that evening and said: 'Uncle Claudius. Beg your mother not to tell the Emperor. We were doing no wrong, I swear. It was just a game. You can't believe it of us. Say you can't.'

When he explained what he did not want told to the Emperor, and swore by his father's honour that he and Drusilla were entirely innocent, I felt bound to do what I could for the children. I went to my mother and said: 'Caligula swears you are mistaken. He swears by his father's honour, and if there is the least possible doubt in your mind about his guilt you ought to respect that oath. For my part, I can't believe that a boy of twelve – –'

'Caligula's a monster and Drusilla's a she-monster, and you're a blockhead, and I believe my eyes more than their oaths or your nonsense. I shall go to Tiberius the first thing tomorrow.'

'But, Mother, if you tell the Emperor, it will not be only those two who will suffer. For once let's talk frankly, and be damned to informers! I may be a blockhead, but you know as well as I do that Tiberius suspects Agrippina of having poisoned Castor to get her elder boys made heirs to the monarchy, and that he lives in terror of a sudden rising in their favour. If you, as their grandmother, accuse these children of incest, do you suppose that he won't find a way of involving the elder members of the family in the charge?'

'You're a blockhead, I say. I can't bear the way your head twitches and your Adam's apple goes up and down.' But I could see that I had made an impression on her, and decided that if I kept out of her sight for the rest of my visit to Rome, so that my presence was not a reminder to her of my advice, it was likely that Tiberius would hear nothing from her about the matter. I packed up a few things and went to my brother-in-law Plautius's house, to ask him to put me up. (By now Plautius was well advanced in his career and in four years he would be Consul.) Supper was long over by the time I called and he was reading legal documents in his study. His wife had gone to bed, he said. I asked, 'How is she? She looked rather worried when I saw her last.'

He laughed. 'Why, you rustic fellow, haven't you heard? I divorced Numantina a month ago or more. When I said "my wife" I meant my new one, Apronia, daughter of the man who gave Tacfarinas such a beating recently!'

I apologized and said that I supposed I ought to offer my congratulations. 'But why did you divorce Numantina? I thought you two got on very well together.'

'Not badly at all. But, to tell the truth, I've been in rather a fix lately with debts. I had bad luck some years ago as a junior magistrate. You know how much one is expected to spend out of one's own pocket on Games. Well, to begin with, I spent more than I could afford and had extremely bad luck besides, you may remember. Twice there was a mistake made in procedure half-way through the Games and I had to start all over again the next day. The first time it was my own fault: I used a form of prayer which had been altered by statute two years previously. The next time a trumpeter who was blowing a long call had not taken a deep enough breath: he broke off short and that was enough to end things a second time. So I had to pay the sword-fighters and charioteers three times over. I have never been out of debt since. I had to do something about it at last, because my creditors were getting nasty. Numantina's dowry was spent long ago, but I managed to arrange matters with her uncle. He has taken her back without it on condition that I let him adopt our younger son. He wants an heir and has taken a fancy to the boy. And Apronia's very rich, so now I'm all right. Of course, Numantina didn't like leaving me at all. I had to tell her that I was only doing this because I had a hint from a Certain Friend of a Certain Personage that if I didn't marry Apronia, who has been in love with me and has interest at Court, I'd be charged with blasphemy against Augustus. You see, the other day one of my slaves tripped and dropped an alabaster bowl full of wine in the middle of the hall. I had a riding whip with me and when I heard the crash I rushed at the fellow and fairly laced into him. I was blind with fury. He said, "Steady on, Master, look where we are!" And the brute had one foot within that holy white square of marble around Augustus's statue. I dropped my whip at once but half a dozen freedmen must have seen me. I am confident that I can trust them not to inform against me, but Numantina was worried by the incident, so I used it to reconcile her to the divorce. By the way, this is entirely confidential. I trust you not to pass it on to Urgulanilla. I don't mind telling you she's rather annoyed about the Numantina business.'

'I never see her now.'

'Well, if you see her, you won't tell her what I've told you? Swear you won't.'

'I swear by Augustus's Godhead.'

'That's good enough. You know the bedroom that you used last time you were here?'

'Yes, thanks. If you're busy, I'll go to bed now. I've had a long journey from the country to-day and worries at home too. My mother practically threw me out of the house.'

So we said good night and I went upstairs. A freedman gave me a lamp, with rather a queer look, and I went into the bedroom which was on the corridor nearly opposite Plautius's, and after shutting myself in began undressing. The bed was behind a curtain. I took off my clothes and washed my hands and feet in the little washplace at the other end of the room. Suddenly there was a heavy step behind me and my lamp was blown out. I told myself: 'You're done for now, Claudius. Here's someone with a dagger.' But I said aloud as calmly as I could: 'Please light the lamp, whoever you may be, and see if we can't talk things over quietly. And if you decide to kill me you'll be able to see better with the lamp lit.'

A deep voice answered: 'Stay where you are.'

There was shuffling and grunting and the sound of someone dressing and then of flint and steel struck together and at last the lamp was lit. It was Urgulanilla. I had not seen her since Drusillus's funeral and she had not grown any prettier in those five years. She was stouter than ever, colossally stout, and bloated faced: there was enough strength in this female Hercules to have overpowered a thousand Claudiuses. I am pretty strong in the arms; but she had only to throw herself on me and she would have crushed me to death.

She came towards me and said slowly: 'What are you doing in my bedroom?'

I explained myself as well as I could, and said that it was a bad joke of Plautius's, sending me into her room without telling me that she was there. I had the greatest respect for her, I said, and apologized sincerely for my intrusion and would leave her at once and sleep on a couch in the Baths.

'No, my dear, now you're here you stay! It isn't often that I have the pleasure of my husband's company. Please understand that once you're here you can't escape. Get into bed and go to sleep and I'll join you later. I'm going to read a book until I feel sleepy. I've not been able to sleep properly for nights.'

'I am very sorry indeed if I woke you up just now. ...'

'Get into bed.'

'I am very sorry indeed about Numantina's divorce. I knew nothing about it until the freedman told me a moment ago.'

'Get into bed and stop talking.'

'Good night, Urgulanilla. I really am very ...'

'Shut up.' She came over and drew the curtain.

Although I was dead tired and could hardly keep my eyes open I did my best to stay awake. I was convinced that Urgulanilla would wait until I went to sleep and then strangle me. Meanwhile she was reading to herself very slowly from a very dull book, a Greek love-story of the most idiotic sort, rustling the pages and spelling out each syllable slowly to herself in a hoarse whisper:

'*O schol-ar,*' she said, '*you have tast-ed now both hon-ey and gall. Be care-ful that the sweet-ness of your pleas-ure does not turn to-morr-ow in-to the bit-ter-ness of re-pen-tance!*' '*Pshaw,*' *I re-turned.* '*My sweet-heart, I am read-y, if you give me an-oth-er kiss like that last one, to be roast-ed up-on a slow fire like a-ny chick-en or duck-ling.*'

She chuckled at this and then said aloud, 'Go to sleep, husband. I'm waiting until I hear you snore.'

I protested, 'Then you shouldn't read such exciting stories.'

I heard Plautius go to bed after a time. 'O Heavens,' I thought. 'He'll be asleep in a few minutes and with two doors between us he won't hear my cries when Urgulanilla throttles me.' Urgulanilla stopped reading and I had no muttering and crackling of paper to help me fight against my sleepiness. I felt myself falling asleep. I was asleep. I knew that I was asleep and I simply must wake up. I struggled frantically to be awake. At last I was awake. There was a thud and a rustle of paper. The book had blown off the table on to the floor. The lamp had gone out; I was aware of a strong draught in the room. The door must be open. I listened attentively for about three minutes. Urgulanilla was certainly not in the room.

As I was trying to make up my mind what to do I heard the most dreadful shriek ring out – from quite close it seemed. A woman screamed, 'Spare me! Spare me! This is Numantina's doing! O! O!' Then came the bump of a heavy metal object falling, then the crash of splintering glass, another shriek, a distant thud, then hurried footsteps across the corridor. Somebody was in my room again. The door was softly closed and barred. I recognized Urgulanilla's panting breath. I heard her clothes being taken off and laid on a chair, and soon she was lying beside me. I pretended to be asleep. She groped for my throat in the dark. I said, as if half-waking: 'Don't do that, darling. It tickles. And I've got to go to Rome to-morrow to buy some cosmetics for you.' Then in a more wakeful voice: 'O Urgulanilla! Is that you? What's all the noise? What's the time? Have we been asleep long?'

She said, 'I don't know. I must have been asleep about three hours. It's just before dawn. It sounds as though something dreadful has happened. Let's go and see.'

So we got up and put on our clothes in a hurry and unlocked the door. Plautius, naked except for a coverlet hastily wrapped round him, stood in the middle of an excited crowd armed with torches. He was quite distracted and kept saying, 'I didn't do it. I was asleep. I felt her torn from my arms and heard her borne through the air screaming for help, and then a crash of something falling and another crash as she went through the window. It was pitch dark. She called out: "Spare me! It's Numantina's doing."'

'Tell that to the judges,' said Apronia's brother, striding up, 'and see whether they'll believe you. You've killed her all right. Her skull's smashed in.'

'I didn't do it,' said Plautius. 'How could I have done? I was asleep. It was witchcraft. Numantina's a witch.'

At dawn he was taken before the Emperor by Apronia's father. Tiberius cross-examined him severely. He said now that while he was sound asleep she had torn herself from his arms and leaped across the room, shrieking, and crashed through the window into the courtyard below. Tiberius made Plautius accompany him at once to the scene of the murder. The first thing he noticed in the bedroom was his own wedding-gift to Plautius, a beautiful Egyptian bronze-and-gold candelabra taken from the tomb of a queen, now lying broken on the ground. He glanced up and saw that it had been wrenched from the ceiling. He said: 'She clung to it and it came down. She was being carried towards the window on somebody's shoulders. And look how high up in the window the hole is! She was pitched through, she did not jump through.'

'It was witchcraft,' said Plautius. 'She was carried through the air by an unseen power. She shrieked and blamed my former wife Numantina.'

Tiberius scoffed. Plautius's friends realized that he would be convicted of murder and executed, and his property confiscated. His grandmother Urgulania therefore sent him a dagger, telling him to think of his heirs, who would be allowed to keep the property if he anticipated the verdict by immediate suicide. He was a coward and could not bring himself to drive the dagger home. Eventually he got into a hot bath and ordered a surgeon to open his veins for him; he slowly and painlessly bled to death. I felt very badly about his death. I had not accused Urgulanilla of the murder at once because I would have been asked why when I heard the first shrieks I had not jumped up and rescued Apronia. I had decided to wait until the trial and only come forward if Plautius seemed likely to be condemned. I knew nothing about the dagger until it was too late. I comforted myself by the thought that he had treated Numantina very cruelly and had been a bad friend to me, besides. To clear Plautius's memory his brother brought a charge against Numantina of having disordered Plautius's wits by witchcraft. But Tiberius intervened and said that he was satisfied that Plautius had been in full possession of his faculties at the time. Numantina was discharged.

There was not another word spoken between Urgulanilla and myself. But a month later Sejanus paid me a surprise visit as he was passing through Capua. He was in Tiberius's company, on the way to Capri, an island near Naples, where Tiberius had twelve villas and frequently went for amusement. Sejanus said: 'You'll be able to divorce Urgulanilla now. She's due to have a child in about five months' time, so my agents inform me. You have me to thank for this. I knew Urgulanilla's obsession about Numantina. I happened to see a young slave, a Greek, who might have been Numantina's male twin. I made her a present of him and she fell in love with him at once. His name's Boter.'

What could I do but thank him? Then I said, 'And who's my new wife to be?'

'So you remember our conversation? Well, the lady I have in mind is my sister by adoption – Aelia. You know her, of course?'

I did, but I hid my disappointment, and merely asked whether anyone so young, beautiful, and intelligent would be content to marry an old, lame, sick, stammering fool like myself.

'Oh,' he answered brutally, 'she won't mind in the least. She'll be marrying Tiberius's nephew and Nero's uncle, that's all she thinks about. Don't imagine that she's in love with you. She might bring herself to have a child by you for the sake of its ancestry, but as for any sentiment – –'

'In fact, apart from the honour of becoming your brother-in-law, I might just as well not divorce Urgulanilla for all the improvement it will make to my life?'

'Oh, you'll manage,' he laughed. 'You don't live too lonely a life here, by the look of this room. There's a nice woman about somewhere, I can see. Gloves, a hand-mirror, an embroidery frame, that box of sweets, flowers carefully arranged. And Aelia won't be jealous. She has her own men friends, probably, though I don't pry into her affairs.'

'All right,' I said. 'I'll do it.'

'You don't sound very grateful.'

'It's not ingratitude. You have taken great trouble on my account, and I don't know how to thank you properly. I was only feeling rather nervous. From what I know of Aelia she's rather critical, if you understand what I mean.'

He burst out laughing. 'She has a tongue like a sacking-needle. But surely by now you're hardened against mere scolding?

Your mother has given you a good enough training, hasn't she?'

'I am still a little thin-skinned,' I said, 'in places.'

'Well, I mustn't stay here any longer, my dear Claudius. Tiberius will be wondering where I've gone. So it's a bargain?'

'Yes, and I thank you very much.'

'Oh, by the way, it *was* Urgulanilla, wasn't it, who killed poor Apronia? I rather expected a tragedy. Urgulanilla had a letter from Numantina begging her to avenge her. Numantina didn't really write it, you understand.'

'I know nothing. I was sound asleep at the time.'

'Like Plautius?'

'Sounder even than Plautius.'

'Sensible fellow! Well, good-bye, Claudius.'

'Good-bye, Aelius Sejanus.' He rode off.

I divorced Urgulanilla, after first writing to my grandmother for permission. Livia wrote that the child should be exposed as soon as born; this was her wish and the wish of Urgulania.

I sent a reliable freedman to Urgulanilla at Herculaneum to tell her the orders I had been given, warning her that if she wanted the child to live she must exchange it, as soon as born, for a dead baby; I had to have a baby of sorts to expose, and so long as it wasn't too long dead, any dead baby would serve the purpose. So the child was saved that way and later Urgulanilla took it back from its foster parents, from whom she had got the dead baby. I don't know what happened to Boter, but the child, who was a girl, grew up the living image of Numantina, they say. Urgulanilla has been dead many years now. When she died they had to break down a wall to get her enormous body out of the house – and it was all honest bulk, not dropsy. In her will she paid a curious tribute to me: 'I don't care what people say, but Claudius is no fool.' She left me a collection of Greek gems, some Persian embroideries, and her portrait of Numantina.

Chapter 24

TIBERIUS and Livia never met now. Livia had offended Tiberius by dedicating a statue to Augustus in their joint names and putting her name first. He retaliated by doing the one thing that she could not even pretend to forgive – when ambassadors came to A.D. 25 him from Spain asking that they might erect a temple to him and his mother he refused on behalf of both. He told the Senate that he had, perhaps in a moment of weakness, allowed the dedication of a temple in Asia to the Senate and its leader (namely, himself) – together symbolizing the paternal government of Rome. His mother's name also occurred in the dedicatory inscription as High-Priestess of the cult of Augustus. But to assent to the deification of himself and his mother would be carrying indulgence too far.

'For myself, my lords, that I am a mortal man, that I am bound by the trammels of human nature, and that I fill the principal place among you to your satisfaction – if I do – I solemnly assure you is quite enough for me: this is how I prefer to be remembered by posterity. If posterity believes me to have been worthy of my ancestors, watchful of your interest, unmoved in dangers, and, in defence of the commonwealth, fearless of private enmities, I shall be sufficiently remembered. The loving gratitude of the Senate and the people of Rome and of our allies is the fairest temple I would raise – a temple not of marble but more enduring than marble, a temple of the heart. Marble temples, when the hallowed beings to whom they are raised fall into disrepute, are despised as mere sepulchres. I therefore invoke Heaven to grant me until the end of my life an untroubled spirit and the power of clear discernment in all duties human and sacred: and therefore too I implore our citizens and allies that whenever dissolution comes to this mortal body of mine, they will celebrate my life and deeds (if they are so worthy) with inward thankfulness and praise rather than with outward pomp and temple-building and annual sacrifice. The true love that Rome felt for my father Augustus when he was among us as a man is already obscured both by the awe which his Godhead excites in the religious-minded and by the indiscriminate use of his name as a market-place oath. And while we are on the subject, my Lords, I propose that we henceforth make it a criminal offence to use the sacred name of Augustus for any but the most solemn occasions and that we enforce this law vigorously.' No mention of Livia's feelings in the matter. And the day before he had refused to appoint one of her nominees to a vacant judgeship, unless he were permitted to qualify the appointment with: 'This person is the choice of my mother, Livia Augusta, to whose importunities in his interest I have been forced to give way, against my better knowledge of his character and capacities.'

Soon after this Livia invited all the noblewomen of Rome to an all-day entertainment. There were jugglers and acrobats and recitations from the poets and marvellous cakes and sweetmeats and liqueurs and a beautiful jewel for each guest as a memento of the occasion. To conclude the proceedings Livia gave a reading of Augustus's letters. She was now eighty-three years old and her voice was weak and she whistled a good deal on her s's, but for an hour and a half she held her audience spellbound. The first letters she read contained pronouncements on public policy, all of which seemed especially written as warnings against the present state of affairs at Rome. There were some very apposite remarks about treason trials, including the following paragraph:

Though I have been bound to protect myself legally against all sorts of libel I shall exert myself to the utmost, my dear Livia, to avoid staging so unpleasant a spectacle as a trial for treason for any foolish historian, caricaturist, or epigram-maker who has made me a target of his wit or eloquence. My father Julius Caesar forgave the poet Catullus the most filthy lampoons imaginable: he wrote to Catullus that if he were trying to show that he was no servile flatterer like most of his fellow-poets, he had now fully proved his case and could return to other more poetical subjects than the sexual abnormalities of a middle-aged statesman: and would he come to dinner the next day and bring any friend he liked? Catullus came and thenceforward the two were fast friends. To use the majesty of the law for revenging any petty act of private spite is to make a public confession of weakness, cowardice, and an ignoble spirit.

There was a notable paragraph about informers:

Except where I am convinced that an informer does not expect to benefit directly or indirectly by his accusations, but brings them from a sense of true patriotism and public decency, I not only discount their importance as evidence but I put a black mark against that informer's name and never afterwards employ him in any position of trust. ...

And, to finish up, she read a series of very illuminating letters. Livia had tens of thousands of Augustus's letters, written over a stretch of fifty-two years, carefully sewn into book-form and indexed. She chose from these thousands the fifteen most damaging ones she could find. The series began with complaints against Tiberius's disgusting behaviour as a little boy, his unpopularity with his schoolfellows as a big boy, his close-fistedness and haughtiness as a young man, and so on, with signs of growing irritation and the phrase, often repeated, 'and if it were not that he was your son, my dearest Livia, I should say – –' Then came complaints of his brutal severity with the troops under his command – 'almost an encouragement to mutiny' – and his dilatoriness in pressing his attacks on the enemy, with unfavourable comparisons between his methods and my father's. Then an angry refusal to consider him as a son-in-law, and a detailed list of his moral shortcomings. Then more letters relating to the painful Julia story, written for the most part in terms of almost insane loathing and disgust for Tiberius. She read one important letter written on the occasion of Tiberius's recall from Rhodes:

Dearest Livia:
I take advantage of this forty-second anniversary of our marriage to thank you with all my heart for the extraordinary services you have rendered the State ever since we joined forces. If I am styled the Father of the Country it seems absurd to me that you should not be styled the Mother of the Country: I swear you have done twice as much as I have in our great work of public reconstruction. Why do you ask me to wait another few years before asking the Senate to vote you this honour? The only way that I can show my absolute confidence in your disinterested loyalty and profound judgement is to give way at last to your repeated pleas for the recall of Tiberius, a man to whose character I confess I continue to feel the greatest repugnance, and I pray to Heaven that by giving way to you now I do not inflict lasting damage on the commonwealth.

Livia's last choice was a letter written about a year before Augustus's death:

I had a sudden feeling of profoundest regret and despair, my dearest wife, when discussing State policy with Tiberius yesterday, that the people of Rome should be fated to be glared at by those protruding eyes of his and pounded by that bony fist of his and chewed by those dreadfully slow jaws of his and stamped on by those huge feet of his. But I was for the moment reckoning without yourself and our dear Germanicus. If I did not believe that when I am dead he will both be guided by you in all matters of State and shamed by Germanicus's example into at least a semblance of decent living, I would even now, I swear, disinherit him and ask the Senate to revoke all his titles of honour. The man's a beast and needs keepers.

When she had finished she rose and said: 'Perhaps, ladies, it would be best to say nothing to your husbands about these peculiar letters. I did not realize, in fact, when I began to read, how – how peculiar they were. I am not asking you this on my own account but for the sake of the Empire.'

Tiberius heard the whole story from Sejanus just as he was about to take his seat in the Senate, and he was overcome with shame and rage and alarm. It so happened that his business that afternoon was to hear a charge of treason brought against Lentulus, one of the pontiffs who had incurred his suspicion in the matter of the prayer for Nero and Drusus, and also because he had voted for the mitigation of Sosia's sentence. When Lentulus, a simple old man, distinguished equally for his birth, his victories in Africa under Augustus, and his unassuming mildness – his nickname was 'The Bell-Wether' – heard that he was accused of plotting against the State, he burst out laughing. Tiberius, already distracted, lost all self-control and said, nearly weeping, to the House: 'If Lentulus too hates me, I am unworthy to live.'

Gallus replied: 'Cheer up, Your Majesty – I beg your pardon, I had forgotten that you dislike the title – I should say, cheer up, Tiberius Caesar! Lentulus was not laughing *at* you, he was laughing *with* you. He was rejoicing with you that for once there should come before the Senate a charge of treason that was absolutely unfounded.' So the charge against Lentulus was dropped. But Tiberius had already been the cause of Lentulus's father's death. He was immensely rich and was so frightened by Tiberius's suspicions of him that he had killed himself, and as a proof of loyalty had left his entire fortune to Tiberius, who thereafter could not believe that Lentulus, now left very poor, harboured no resentment against him.

Tiberius did not enter the Senate again for two whole months: he could not look the senators in the face with the knowledge that their wives had heard Augustus's letters about him. Sejanus suggested that it would be good for his health to leave Rome for a while and stay a few miles away at one of his villas, where he would escape from the daily throng of Palace visitors and the noise and bustle of the City. He followed this advice. The action that he took against his mother was to superannuate her, to omit her name from all public documents, to discontinue her customary birthday honours, and to make it clear that any coupling of her name with his or any praise of her in the Senate would be regarded as little short of treason. More active vengeance he did not dare take. He knew that she still had the letter which he had written from Rhodes promising her his lifelong obedience and that she was quite capable of reading it, even though it might incriminate her as the murderess of Gaius and Lucius.

But this wonderful old woman was not defeated yet, as you shall read. One day I had a note from her. 'The Lady Livia Augusta expects her dear grandson Tiberius Claudius to visit and dine with her on the occasion of her birthday: she hopes that he is in good health.' I could not make it out. I her dear grandson! Tender enquiries after my health! I did not know whether to laugh or be afraid. I had never in my life been allowed to visit her on her birthday. I had never even dined with her. I had not spoken to her, except ceremonially at the Augustan festival, for ten years. What could her motive be? Well, I should know in three days, and meanwhile I must buy her a really magnificent present. I finally bought her something which I was sure she would appreciate – a gracefully-shaped wine-vase in bronze, with serpent-head handles and a complicated design of gold and silver inlay. It was, in my opinion, of far finer workmanship than any of the Corinthian vessels that collectors give such absurd prices for nowadays. It came from China! In the centre of the design had been sunk a gold medallion of Augustus which had somehow strayed to that wonderfully distant land. That vase cost me 500 gold pieces, though it stood no more than eighteen inches high.

But before I tell of my visit and my long interview with her I must clear up a point on which I may perhaps have misled you. From my accounts of the treason-trials and similar atrocities it will probably be deduced that the Empire under Tiberius was intolerably misgoverned in all departments. This was far from being the case. Though he undertook no new public works worth speaking of, merely contenting himself with completing those begun by Augustus, he kept the Army and the Fleet efficient and up to strength, paid his officials regularly and made them send in detailed reports four times a year, encouraged trade, assured a regular supply of corn for Italy, kept the roads and aqueducts in repair, limited public and private extravagance in a variety of ways, stabilized food prices, put down piracy and banditry and built up a considerable reserve of public money in case of any national emergency. He maintained his provincial governors in office for many years at a time, if they were any good, so as not to unsettle matters, keeping a careful watch on them, however. One governor, to show his efficiency and loyalty, sent Tiberius more tribute than was due. Tiberius gave him a reprimand: 'I want my sheep shorn, not shaved.' As a result there were few frontier wars after the German trouble was settled by Maroboduus's welcome to Rome and Hermann's death. Tacfarinas was the chief enemy. He was for a long time known as the 'Laurel-giver' because three generals – my friend Furius, and Apronius, the father of Apronia, and a third, Blaesus, Sejanus's maternal uncle, had each in turn defeated him and been awarded triumphal ornaments. Blaesus, who scattered Tacfarinas's army and captured his brother, was given the unusual honour of being made a field-marshal, an honour reserved in general only for the Imperial family. Tiberius told the Senate that he was glad to honour Blaesus in this way because of his kinship with his trusted friend Sejanus; and when, three years later, a fourth general, Dolabella, put a final end to the African War, which had broken out again with redoubled force, by not only defeating Tacfarinas but killing him, Dolabella was granted only triumphal ornaments 'lest the laurels of Blaesus, uncle of my trusted friend Sejanus, should thereby lose their lustre'.

But I was talking of Tiberius's good deeds, not his weaknesses: and really, from the point of view of the Empire as a whole, he had been for the last twelve years a wise and just ruler. That nobody can deny. The canker in the core of the apple – if the metaphor may be forgiven – did not show on the skin or impair the wholesomeness of the flesh. Of the 5,000,000 Roman citizens, a mere 200 or 300 suffered for Tiberius's jealous fears. A.D. 26 And I do not know how many scores of millions of slaves and provincials, and allies who were subjects in all but name, benefited solidly by the Imperial system as perfected by Augustus and Livia and carried on in this tradition by Tiberius. But I was living in the apple's core, so to speak, and I can be pardoned if I write more about the central canker than about the still unblemished and fragrant outer part.

Once you give way to a metaphor, Claudius, which is rare, you pursue it too far. Surely you remember Athenodorus's injunctions against this sort of thing? Well, call Sejanus the maggot and get it done with; then return to your usual homely style!

Sejanus decided to use Tiberius's sense of shame as a means of keeping him away from the City for a longer time than a mere two months. He encouraged one of his Guards officers to accuse a celebrated wit called Montanus of blackening Tiberius's private character. Whereas hitherto the accusers had been restrained from reporting any but the most general abuse of Tiberius – as haughty, or cruel or domineering – this soldier came forward and credited Montanus with libels of a most particular and substantial kind. Sejanus took care that the libels were as true as they were disgusting; though Montanus, not having Sejanus's knowledge of what went on in the Palace, had not uttered them. The witness, who was the best drill-instructor in the Guards, bawled out Montanus's alleged obscenities at the top of his voice, not slurring over the most obscene words or phrases, and refusing to let himself be cried down by the shocked protests of the senators. 'I swore to tell the whole truth,' he bellowed, 'and for the honour of Tiberius Caesar I shall not omit a single article of the accused's loathsome conversation overheard by me on the said date and in the said circumstances. Accused further declared that our gracious Emperor is fast becoming impotent from said alleged debauches and said over-indulgence in aphrodisiac medicines, and that in order to rally his waning sexual powers he holds private exhibitions every three days or so in a specially decorated underground room of the Palace. Accused declared that the performers at these exhibitions, Spintrians as they are called, come prancing in, three at a time, stark naked ...'

He went on in that strain for half an hour and Tiberius did not dare to stop him – or perhaps he wanted to find out just how much was known – until the witness said one thing too many (never mind what it was). Tiberius, forgetting himself, leaped up suddenly, his face crimson, and declared that he would instantly clear himself of these monstrous charges or establish a judicial investigation. Sejanus tried to calm him down, but he remained on his feet glaring angrily about him, until Gallus rose and gently reminded him that it was Montanus, not he, who was the accused party; that his private character was beyond suspicion; and that if news that such an investigation was about to be held reached the frontier provinces and the allied states, it would be completely misunderstood.

Shortly afterwards Tiberius was warned by Thrasyllus – whether this was arranged by Sejanus I do not know – that he would shortly leave the City and that it would be death for him to re-enter it. Tiberius told Sejanus that he would move to Capri and leave him to look after things at Rome. He attended one more treason-trial – that of my cousin Claudia Pulchra, Varus's widow, who, now that Sosia was banished, was Agrippina's most intimate friend. She was charged with adultery, prostituting her daughters, and witchcraft against Tiberius. She was, I think, completely innocent of all these charges. As soon as Agrippina heard about it she hurried to the Palace and by chance found Tiberius sacrificing to Augustus. Almost before the ceremony was over she came close up to him and said:

'Tiberius, this is illogical behaviour. You sacrifice flamingoes and peacocks to Augustus and you persecute his grandchildren.'

He said slowly: 'I do not understand you. Which grandchildren of Augustus have I persecuted that he did not himself persecute?'

'I am not talking about Postumus and Julilla. I mean myself. You banished Sosia because she was my friend. You forced Silius to kill himself because he was my friend. And Calpurnius because he was my friend. And now my dear Pulchra is doomed too, though her only crime is her foolish fondness for me. People are beginning to avoid me, saying that I am unlucky.'

Tiberius took her by the shoulders and said once more:

> And if you are not queen, my dear,
> Think you that you are wronged?

Pulchra was condemned and executed. The Crown Prosecutor was a man called Afer, engaged because of his eloquence. A few days later Agrippina happened to see him outside the theatre. He appeared ashamed of himself and avoided meeting her eye. She went up to him and said: 'There is no occasion for you to hide from me, Afer.' Then she quoted from Homer, but with alterations to suit the context, Achilles's reassuring answer to the embarrassed heralds who came to him with a humiliating message from Agamemnon. She said:

> He forced you to it. Though you were well fee'd
> It was not yours but Agamemnon's deed.

This was reported to Tiberius (though not by Afer); the word 'Agamemnon' caused him fresh alarm.

Agrippina fell ill and thought that she was being poisoned. She went in her sedan to the Palace to make a last appeal to Tiberius for mercy. She looked so thin and pale that Tiberius was charmed: perhaps she would die soon. He said: 'My poor Agrippina, you look seriously ill. What's wrong with you?'

She answered in a weak voice: 'It may be that I have done you a wrong in thinking that you persecute my friends just because they are my friends. It may be that I am unlucky in my choice of them, or that my judgement is often at fault. But I swear you have done me equal wrong in thinking that I have the least feeling of disloyalty towards you or that I have any ambition to rule either directly or indirectly. All that I ask is to be left alone, and your forgiveness for any injuries that I have unintentionally done you, and ... and ...' She ended in sobs.

'And what else?'

'O Tiberius, be good to my children! And be good to me! Let me marry again. I am so lonely. Since Germanicus died I have never been able to forget my troubles. I can't sleep at night. If you let me marry I'll settle down and lose all my restlessness and be quite a different person, and then perhaps you won't suspect me of plotting against you. I am sure it's only because I look so unhappy that you think I have bad feelings towards you.'

'Who's the man you want to marry?'

'A good, generous, unambitious man, past middle age, and one of your most loyal ministers.'

'What's his name?'

'Gallus. He says that he is ready to marry me at once.'

Tiberius turned on his heel and walked out of the room without another word.

A few days later he invited her to a banquet. He used often to invite people to dine with him whom he particularly mistrusted and stare at them throughout the meal as if trying to read their secret thoughts: which shook the self-possession of all but very few. If they looked alarmed he read it as a proof of guilt. If they met his eye steadily he read it as an even stronger proof of guilt, with insolence added. On this occasion Agrippina, still ill and unable to eat any but the lightest food without nausea, and stared constantly at by Tiberius, had a miserable time. She was not a talkative person, and the conversation, which was about the relative merits of music and philosophy, did not interest her in the least and she found it impossible to contribute anything to it. She made a pretence of eating, but Tiberius, who was watching her attentively, saw that she sent away plate after plate untouched. He thought that she suspected him of trying to poison her, and to test this he carefully picked an apple from the dish in front of him and said: 'My dear Agrippina, you haven't made much of a meal. At any rate, try this apple. It's a splendid one. I had a present of young trees from the King of Parthia three years ago and this is the first time they have borne fruit.'

Now almost everyone has a certain 'natural enemy' – if I may call it that. To some people honey is a violent poison. Others are made ill by touching a horse or entering a stable or even by lying on a couch stuffed with horse-hair. Others again are most uncomfortably affected by the presence of a cat, and going into a room will sometimes say, 'There has been a cat here, excuse me if I retire.' I myself feel an overpowering repugnance to the smell of hawthorn in bloom. Agrippina's natural enemy was the apple. She took the present from Tiberius and thanked him, but with an ill-concealed shudder, and said that she would keep it, if she might, to eat when she reached home.

'Just one bit now, to taste how good it is.'

'Please forgive me, but really I could not.' She handed the apple to a servant and told him to wrap it carefully in a napkin for her.

Why did Tiberius not immediately try her on a treason-charge, as Sejanus urged? Because Agrippina was still under Livia's protection.

Chapter 25

AND so I come to the account of my dinner with Livia. She greeted me very graciously, seeming genuinely delighted with my gift. During the meal, at which nobody else was present but old Urgulania and Caligula, now aged fourteen – a tall, pale boy with a blotched complexion and sunken eyes – she surprised me by the sharpness of her mind and the clearness of her memory. She asked me about my work, and when I began talking about the First Punic War and discrediting certain particulars given by the poet Naevius (he had served in this war) she agreed with my conclusions but caught me out in a misquotation. She said: 'You're grateful to me now, grandson, aren't you, for not letting you write that biography of your father! Do you think that you'd be dining here to-day if I hadn't intervened?'

Every time the slave filled my cup I had drunk it straight up, and now at the tenth or twelfth draught I felt like a lion. I answered boldly: 'Extremely grateful, Grandmother, to be safe among the Carthaginians and Etruscans. But will you tell me just *why* I'm dining here to-day?'

She smiled: 'Well, I admit that your presence at table still causes me a certain amount of ... But never mind. If I have broken one of my oldest rules that is my affair, not yours. Do you dislike me, Claudius? Be frank.'

'Probably as much as you dislike me, Grandmother.' (Could this be my own voice speaking?)

Caligula sniggered, Urgulania tittered, Livia laughed: 'Frank enough! By the way, have you noticed that monster there? He's been keeping unusually quiet during the meal.'

'Who, Grandmother?'

'That nephew of yours.'

'Is he a monster?'

'Don't pretend you don't know it. You *are* a monster, aren't you, Caligula?'

'Whatever you say, Great-grandmother,' Caligula said, with downcast eyes.

'Well, Claudius, that monster there, your nephew – I'll tell you about him. *He's going to be the next Emperor.*'

I thought it was a joke. I said smilingly: 'If you tell me so, Grandmother, it is so. But what are his recommendations? He's the youngest of the family and though he has given evidences of great natural talent ...'

'You mean that they won't any of them stand a chance against Sejanus and your sister Livilla?'

I was astounded at the freedom of the conversation. 'I didn't mean anything of the sort. I never concern myself with high politics. I only meant that he's young yet, much too young to be Emperor; and that as a prophecy it seems rather a long shot.'

'Not a long shot at all. Tiberius will make him his successor. No question of it. Why? Because Tiberius is like that. He has the same vanity as poor Augustus had: he can't bear the idea of a successor who will be more popular than himself. But at the same time he does all he can to make himself hated and feared. So, when he feels that his time's nearly up, he'll search for someone just a little worse than himself to succeed him. And he'll find Caligula. There is one deed that Caligula has already done which puts him in a far higher rank of criminality than Tiberius can ever now attain.'

'Please, Great-grandmother ...' Caligula pleaded.

'All right, monster, your secret's safe with me so long as you behave.'

'Does Urgulania know the secret?' I asked.

'No. It's between the monster and myself.'

'Did he confess it voluntarily?'

'Certainly not. He's not the confessing sort. I found out about it by accident. I was searching his bedroom one night to see if he was trying any schoolboy tricks on me – whether he was doing any amateur black magic, for instance, or distilling poisons or anything of the sort. I came across ...'

'*Please*, Great-grandmother.'

'A green object that told me a very remarkable story. But I gave it back to him.'

Urgulania said, grinning: 'Thrasyllus said I'm going to die this year, so I won't have the pleasure of living in your reign, Caligula, unless you hurry up and murder Tiberius!'

I turned to Livia: 'Is he going to do that, Grandmother?'

Caligula said: 'Is it safe for Uncle Claudius to be told things? Or are you going to poison him?'

She answered: 'Oh, he's quite safe, without any poison. I want you two to know each other better than you do. That's one reason for this dinner. Listen, Caligula. Your uncle Claudius is a phenomenon. He's so old-fashioned that because he's sworn an oath to love and protect his brother's children you can always impose on him – as long as you live. Listen, Claudius. Your nephew Caligula is a phenomenon. He's treacherous, cowardly, lustful, vain, de-

286

ceitful, and he'll play some very dirty tricks on you before he's done: but remember one thing, he'll never kill you.'

'Why's that?' I asked, draining my cup again. The conversation was like the sort one has in dreams – mad but interesting.

'Because you're the man who's going to avenge his death.'

'I? Who said so?'

'Thrasyllus.'

'Does Thrasyllus never make mistakes?'

'No. Never. Caligula's going to be murdered and you're to avenge his death.'

A gloomy silence suddenly fell and continued until dessert, when Livia said: 'Come, Claudius, the rest of our talk shall be in private.' The other two rose and left us alone.

I said: 'That seemed to me a very odd conversation, Grandmother. Was it my fault? Had I been drinking too much? I mean, some jokes aren't safe, nowadays. It was rather dangerous fooling. I hope the servants ...'

'Oh, they're deaf-mutes. No, don't blame the wine. There's truth in wine, and the conversation was perfectly serious so far as I was concerned.'

'But ... but if you really think him a monster, why do you encourage him? Why not give Nero your support? He's a fine fellow.'

'Because Caligula, not Nero, is to be the next Emperor.'

'But he'll make a marvellously bad one if he's what you say he is. And you, who have devoted your whole life to the service of Rome ...'

'Yes. But you can't fight against Fate. And now that Rome has been ungrateful and mad enough to allow my blackguardly son to put me on the shelf, and insult me – *me*, can you imagine it, perhaps the greatest ruler that the world has ever known, and his mother, too ...' Her voice grew shrill.

I was anxious to change the subject. I said, 'Please calm yourself, Grandmother. As you say, you can't fight against Fate. But isn't there something particular that you want to tell me, Grandmother, connected with all this?'

'Yes, it's about Thrasyllus. I consult him frequently. Tiberius doesn't know that I do, that Thrasyllus has been here often. He told me some years ago what would happen between Tiberius and me – that he'd eventually rebel against my authority and take the Empire wholly into his own hands. I didn't believe it then. He also told me another thing: that though I would die a disappointed old woman I would be acknowledged a Goddess many years after my death. And previously he had said that one who must die in the year which I know now is the year in which I must die will become the greatest Deity the world has ever known and that, finally, no temples at Rome or anywhere in the Empire will be dedicated to anyone else. Not even to Augustus.'

'When are you to die?'

'Three years hence, in the spring. I know the very day.'

'But are you so anxious to become a Goddess? My uncle Tiberius isn't at all anxious, it seems.'

'It is all I think about, now that my work is over. And why not? If Augustus is a God, it's absurd for me to be merely his priestess. I did all the work, didn't I? He no more had it in him to be a great ruler than Tiberius has.'

'Yes, Grandmother. But isn't it enough for you to *know* what you have done without wanting to be worshipped by the ignorant rabble?'

'Claudius, let me explain. I quite agree about the ignorant rabble. It's not so much my fame on earth that I'm thinking about as the position I am to occupy in Heaven. I have done many impious things – no great ruler can do otherwise. I have put the good of the Empire before all human considerations. To keep the Empire free from factions I have had to commit many crimes. Augustus did his best to wreck the Empire by his ridiculous favouritism: Marcellus against Agrippa, Gaius against Tiberius. Who saved Rome from renewed Civil War? I did. The unpleasant and difficult task of removing Marcellus and Gaius fell on me. Yes, don't pretend you haven't ever suspected me of poisoning them. And what is the proper reward for a ruler who commits such crimes for the good of his subjects? The proper reward, obviously, is to be deified. Do you believe that the souls of criminals are eternally tormented?'

'I have always been taught to believe that they are.'

'But the Immortal Gods are free from any fear of punishment, however many crimes they commit?'

'Well, Jove deposed his father and killed one of his grandsons and incestuously married his sister, and ... yes, I agree. ... They none of them have a good moral reputation. And certainly the Judges of the Mortal Dead have no jurisdiction over them.'

'Exactly. You see now why it's all-important for me to become a Goddess. And this, if you must know, is the reason why I tolerate Caligula. He has sworn that if I keep his secret he will make a Goddess of me as soon as he's Emperor. And I want you to swear that you'll do all in your power to see that I become a Goddess as soon as possible, because – oh, don't you see? – until he makes me a Goddess I'll be in Hell, suffering the most frightful torments, the most exquisite ineluctable torments.'

The sudden change in her voice, from cool Imperial arrogance to terrified pleading astonished me more than anything I had yet heard. I had to say something, so I said: 'I don't see what influence poor Uncle Claudius is ever likely to have, either on the Emperor or on the Senate.'

'Never mind about what you see or don't see, idiot! Will you swear to do as I ask? Will you swear by your own head?'

I said: 'Grandmother, I'll swear by my head – for what that's worth now – on one condition.'

'You dare to make conditions to *me*?'

'Yes, after the twentieth cup; and it's a simple condition. After thirty-six years of neglect and aversion you surely don't expect me to do anything for you without making conditions, do you?'

She smiled. 'And what is this one simple condition?'

'There are a lot of things that I'd like to know about. I want to know, in the first place, who killed my father, and who killed Agrippa, and who killed my brother Germanicus, and who killed my son Drusillus. ...'

'Why do you want to know all this? Some imbecile hope of avenging their deaths on me?'

'No, not even if you were the murderess. I never take vengeance unless I am forced to do so by an oath or in self-protection. I believe that evil is its own punishment. All I want now is just to know the truth. I am a professional historian and the one thing that really interests me is to find out how things happen and why. For instance, I write histories more to inform myself than to inform my readers.'

'Old Athenodorus has had a great influence on you, I see.'

'He was kind to me and I was grateful, so I became a Stoic. I never meddled with philosophical argument – that never appealed to me – but I adopted the Stoic way of looking at things. You can trust me not to repeat a word of what you tell me.'

I convinced her that I meant what I said, and so for four hours or more I asked her the most searching questions; and each questions she answered without evasion and as calmly as if she had been some country steward relating the minor casualties of the farm-yard to the visiting owner. Yes, she had poisoned my grand-father, and no, she had not poisoned my father in spite of Tiberius's suspicions – it was a natural gangrene; and yes, she had poisoned Augustus by smearing poison on the figs while they were still on the tree; and she told me the whole Julia story as I have related it, and the whole Postumus story – the details of which I was able to check; and yes, she had poisoned Agrippa and Lucius, as well as Marcellus and Gaius, and yes, she had intercepted my letters to Germanicus, but no, she had not poisoned him – Plancina had done that on her own initiative – but she had marked him out for death as she had marked out my father, and for the same reason.

'What reason was that, Grandmother?'

'He had decided to restore the Republic. No, don't mistake me: not in a way which violated his oath of allegiance to Tiberius, though it meant removing me. He was going to make Tiberius take the step himself voluntarily, and allow him all the credit for it, keeping in the background himself. He nearly persuaded Tiberius. You know what a coward Tiberius is. I had to work hard and forge a lot of documents and tell a lot of lies to keep Tiberius from making a fool of Sejanus. This republicanism is a persistent taint in himself. I even had to come to an understanding with the family. Your grandfather had it.'

'I have it.'

'Still? That's amusing. Nero has it too, I understand. It won't bring him much luck. And it's no use arguing with you republicans. You refuse to see that one can no more reintroduce republican government at this stage than one can reimpose primitive feelings of chastity on modern wives and husbands. It's like trying to turn the shadow back on a sundial: it can't be done.'

She confessed to having had Drusillus throttled. She told me how close I was to death when I first wrote to Germanicus about Postumus. The only reason that she had spared me was that there was a possibility of my writing him information as to Postumus's whereabouts. The most interesting account she gave me was of her poisoning methods. I asked her Postumus's question – whether she favoured slow poisons or quick ones – and she answered without the least embarrassment that she preferred repeated doses of slow tasteless poisons which gave the effect of consumption. I asked how she managed to cover up her traces so well and how she managed to strike at such long distances: for Gaius had been murdered in Asia Minor and Lucius at Marseilles.

She reminded me that she had never contrived a murder which might be held to benefit her directly and immediately. She had not, for instance, poisoned my grandfather until some time after being divorced from him, nor had she poisoned any of her female rivals – Octavia, or Julia, or Scribonia. Her victims were mostly people by whose removal her sons and grand-children were brought closer to the succession. Urgulania had been her only confidant, and she was so discreet and skilful and so devoted that not only was it most unlikely that the crimes they planned together would ever be detected but, even if they were, they would never have been brought home to *her*. The annual confessions made to Urgulania in preparation for the festival of the Good Goddess had been a useful means of removing several people who stood in the way of her plans. She explained this fully. It happened sometimes that confession was made not merely to adultery but to incest with a brother or son. Urgulania would declare that the only possible penance was the death of the man. The woman then pleaded, was there no other possible penance? Urgulania would then say that there was perhaps an alternative that the Goddess would permit. The woman could purify herself by assisting the Goddess's vengeance – with the help of the man who had caused her shame. For, Urgulania would tell her, a similarly detestable confession had been made some time before by another woman, who had however shrunk from killing her ravisher, and so the wretch was still alive, though the woman herself had suffered. The 'wretch' was successively Agrippa, Lucius, and Gaius. Agrippa was accused of incest with his daughter Marcellina – whose unexplained suicide gave colour to the story; Gaius and Lucius of incest with their mother before her banishment – and Julia's reputation gave colour to this story too. In each case the woman was only too glad to plan the murder and the man to execute it. Urgulania assisted with advice and suitable poisons. Livia's safety lay in the remoteness of the agent, who if he were to be suspected or even taken red-handed could not explain his motive for the murder without further incriminating himself. I asked whether she had had no compunction about murdering Augustus and either murdering or banishing so many of his descendants. She said: 'I never for a moment forgot whose daughter I was.' And that explained a great deal. Livia's father, Claudian, had been proscribed by Augustus after the Battle of Philippi and had committed suicide rather than fall into his hands.

In short, she told me everything that I wanted to know except about the haunting of Germanicus's house at Antioch. She repeated that she had not ordered it and that neither Plancina nor Piso had told her anything about it and that I was in as good a position to clear up the mystery as she was. I saw that it was useless to press her further, so I thanked her for her patience with me and at last took the oath by my head to do all in my power to make her a Goddess.

As I was going she handed me a small volume and told me to read it when I was in Capua. It was the collection of rejected Sibylline verses that I have written about in the first pages of this story, and when I came across the prophecy called 'The Succession of Hairy Ones' I thought I knew why Livia had invited me to dinner and made me swear that oath. If I had sworn it. It all seemed like a drunken dream.

Chapter 26

SEJANUS composed a memorial to Tiberius, begging to be remembered if a husband for Livilla was being looked for; saying that he was only a knight, he was aware, but Augustus had once spoken of marrying his only daughter to a knight, and Tiberius at least had no more loyal subordinate than himself. He did not aim at senatorial rank but was content to continue in his present station as sleepless sentinel for his noble Emperor's safety. He added that such a marriage would be a serious blow to Agrippina's party, who recognized him as their most active opponent. They would be afraid to offer violence to Castor's surviving son by Livilla – young Tiberius Gemellus. The recent death of the other twin must be laid at Agrippina's door.

Tiberius answered graciously that he could not yet give a favourable answer to the request, in spite of his great sense of obligation to Sejanus. He thought it unlikely that Livilla, both of whose previous husbands had been men of the highest birth, would be content for him to remain a knight; but if he were advanced in rank as well as being married into the Imperial family this would cause a great deal of jealousy, and so strengthen the party of Agrippina. He said that it was precisely to avoid such jealousies that Augustus had thought of marrying his daughter to a knight, a retired man who was not mixed up with politics in any way.

But he ended on a hopeful note: 'I shall forbear to tell you yet precisely what plans I have for binding you closer to me in affinity. But I shall say this much, that no recompense that I could pay you for your devotion would be too high, and that when the opportunity presents itself I shall have great pleasure in doing what I propose to do.'

Sejanus knew Tiberius too well not to realize that he had made the request prematurely – he had only written at all because Livilla had pressed him – and had given considerable offence. He decided that Tiberius must be persuaded to leave Rome at once, and must appoint him permanent City Warden – a magistrate from whose decisions the only appeal was to the Emperor. As Commander of the Guards he was also in charge of the Corps of Orderlies, the Imperial couriers, so he would have the handling of all Tiberius's correspondence. Tiberius would depend on him, too, for deciding what people to admit to his presence; and the fewer people he had to see the better he would be pleased. Little by little the City Warden would have all the real power, and could act as he pleased without danger of interference by the Emperor.

At last Tiberius left Rome. His pretext was the dedication of a temple at Capua to Jove, and one at Nola to Augustus. But he did not intend ever to return. It was known that he had taken this decision because of Thrasyllus's warning; and what Thrasyllus prophesied was accepted without question as bound to come to pass. It was assumed that Tiberius, now sixty-seven years of age – and an ugly sight he was, thin, stooping, bald, stiff-jointed, with an ulcered face patched with plasters – was to die within a very short time. Nobody could possibly have guessed that he was fated to live eleven years longer. This may have been because he never came nearer the City again than the suburbs. Well, anyway it was how it turned out.

Tiberius took with him to Capri a number of learned Greek professors, and a picked force of soldiers, including his German bodyguard, and Thrasyllus, and a number of painted strange-looking creatures of doubtful sex and, the most curious choice of all, Cocceius Nerva. Capri is an island in the Bay of Naples about three miles from the coast. Its climate is mild in winter and cool in summer. There is only one possible landing-place, the rest of the island being protected by steep cliffs and impassable thickets. How Tiberius spent his leisure time here – when he was not discussing poetry and mythology with the Greeks, or law and politics with Nerva – is too revolting a story even for history. I shall say no more than that he had brought with him a complete set of the famous books of Elephantis, the most copious encyclopaedia of pornography ever gathered together. In Capri he could do what he was unable to do at Rome – practise obscenities in the open air among the trees and flowers or down at the water's edge, and make as much noise as he liked. As some of his field-sports were extremely cruel, the sufferings of his playmates being a great part of his pleasure, he considered that the advantage of Capri's remoteness greatly outweighed the disadvantages. He did not live wholly there: he used to go for visits to Capua, Baiae, and Antium. But Capri was his headquarters.

After a while he gave Sejanus authority to remove the leaders of Agrippina's party by whatever means seemed most convenient. He was in daily touch with Sejanus and approved all his acts in letters to the Senate. One New Year's Festival he celebrated at Capua by speaking the customary prayer of A.D. 28 blessing, as High Pontiff, and then suddenly turning on a knight called Sabinus, who was standing near, and accusing him of trying to seduce the loyalty of his freedmen. One of Sejanus's men at once pulled Sabinus's gown up, muffled his head with it, and then threw a noose round his neck, and dragged him away. Sabinus called out in a choking voice: 'Help, friends, help!' But nobody stirred, and Sabinus, whose only crime was that he had been Germanicus's friend and had been tricked by a tool of Sejanus's into privately expressing sympathy for Agrippina, was summarily executed. A letter from Tiberius was read the next day in the Senate, reporting the death of Sabinus and mentioning Sejanus's discovery of a dangerous conspiracy. 'My Lords, pity an unhappy old man, living a life of constant apprehension, with members of his own family plotting wickedly against his life.' It was clear that Agrippina and Nero were meant by this. Gallus rose and moved that the Emperor should be desired to explain his fears to the Senate, and to allow them to be set at rest: as no doubt they could easily be. But Tiberius did not yet feel himself strong enough to revenge himself on Gallus.

In the summer of this year there was an accidental meeting between Livia in a sedan-chair and Tiberius on a cob in the main street of Naples. Tiberius had just landed from Capri and Livia was returning from a visit to Herculaneum. Tiberius wanted to ride past without a greeting but force of habit made him rein up and salute her with formal enquiries after her health. She said: 'I'm all the better for your kind enquiries, my boy. And as a mother my advice to you is: *be very careful of the barbel you eat on your island.* Some of the ones they catch there are highly poisonous.'

'Thank you, Mother,' he said. 'As the warning comes from you I shall in future stick religiously to tunny and mullet.'

Livia snorted and, turning to Caligula, who was with her, said in a loud voice: 'Well, as I was saying, my husband (your great-grandfather, my dear) and I came hurrying along this street one dark night sixty-five years ago, wasn't it, on our way to the docks where our ship was secretly waiting. We were expecting any moment to be arrested and killed by Augustus's men – how strange it seems! My elder boy – we had had only one child so far – was riding on his father's back. Then what should that little beast do but set up a terrific yowl: "Oh, father, I want to go back to Peru-u-u-sia." That gave the show away. Two soldiers came out of a tavern and called after us. We dodged into a dark doorway to let them pass. But Tiberius kept on yowling, "I want to go back to Peru-u-u-sia." I said, "Kill him! Kill the brat! It's our only hope." But my husband was a tender-hearted fool and refused. It was only by the merest chance we escaped.'

Tiberius, who had stopped to hear the end of the story, dug his spurs into his cob and clattered off in a fury. They never saw each other again.

Livia's warning about fish was only intended to make him

uncomfortable, to make him think that she had his fishermen or his cooks in her pay. She knew Tiberius's fondness for barbel, and that he would now have a constant conflict between his appetite and his fear of assassination. There was a painful sequel. One day Tiberius was sitting under a tree on a western slope of the island, enjoying the breeze and planning a verse-dialogue in Greek between the hare and the pheasant, in which each in turn claimed gastronomic pre-eminence. It was not an original idea: he had recently rewarded one of his court-poets with 2,000 gold pieces for a similar poem, in which the rivals were a mushroom, a titlark, an oyster, and a thrush. In his introduction to the present piece he brushed all these claims aside as trifling, saying that the hare and pheasant alone had the right to dispute the parsley-crown – their flesh alone had dignity without heaviness, delicacy without paltriness.

He was just searching for a discourteous adjective with which to qualify the oyster when he heard a sudden rustling from the thorn-bushes below him and a tousle-headed, wild-looking man appeared. His clothes were wet and torn to rags, his face bleeding, and an open knife was in his hand. He burst through the thicket, shouting: 'Here you are, Caesar; isn't it a beauty?' From the sack he was carrying over his shoulder he pulled out a monstrous barbel and threw it, still kicking, on the turf at Tiberius's feet. He was only a simple fisherman who had just made this remarkable catch and, seeing Tiberius at the cliff-top, had decided to present it to him. He had moored his boat to a rock, swum to the cliff, struggled up a precipice path to the belt of thorn-bushes, and hacked himself a path through them with his clasp-knife.

But Tiberius had been startled nearly out of his senses. He blew a whistle and shouted out in German: 'Help, help! Come at once! Wolfgang! Siegfried! Adelstan! An assassin! *Schnell!*'

'Coming, all-highest, noblest-born, gift-bestowing Chief,' the Germans instantly replied. They had been on sentry-duty to his left and right and behind him, but there was nobody posted in front, naturally. They came bounding along, brandishing their assegais.

The man did not understand German, and shutting his clasp-knife said cheerfully: 'I caught him by the grotto yonder. What do you guess he weighs? A regular whale, eh? Nearly pulled me out of the boat.'

Tiberius, somewhat reassured, but with his imagination now running on poisoned fish, shouted to the Germans: 'No, don't spear him. Cut that thing in two and rub the pieces in his face.'

Burly Wolfgang from behind clasped the fisherman around the middle so that he could not move his arms, while the other two scrubbed his face with raw fish. The unfortunate fellow called out: 'Hey, stop it! That's no joke! What luck that I didn't first offer the Emperor the other thing in my sack.'

'See what it is,' Tiberius ordered.

Edelstein opened the sack and found in it an enormous lobster. 'Rub his face with that,' said Tiberius. 'Rub it well in!'

The wretched man lost both his eyes. Then Tiberius said: 'That's enough, men. You may let him go!' The fisherman stumbled about screaming and raving with pain, and there was nothing to be done but toss him into the sea from the nearest crag.

I am glad to say that I was never invited to visit Tiberius on his island and have carefully avoided going there since, though all evidences of his vile practices have long ago been removed and his twelve villas are said to be very beautiful.

I had asked Livia's permission to marry Aelia and she had given it with malicious good wishes. She even attended the wedding. It was a very splendid wedding – Sejanus saw to that – and one effect of it was to alienate me from Agrippina and Nero and their friends. It was thought that I would not be able to keep any secrets from Aelia and that Aelia would tell Sejanus all that she found out. This saddened me a great deal, but I saw that it was useless trying to reassure Agrippina (who was now in mourning for her sister Julilla, who had just died after a twenty-years' exile in that wretched little island of Tremerus). So gradually I stopped visiting her house, to avoid embarrassment. I and Aelia were man and wife only in name. The first thing she said to me when we went into our bridal-chamber was: 'Now understand, Claudius, that I don't want you to touch me and that if we ever have to sleep together again in one bed, like to-night, there'll be a coverlet between us, and the least movement you make – out you go. And another thing: you mind your own business, and I'll mind mine. ...'

I said: 'Thank you: you have taken a great load off my mind.'

She was a dreadful woman. She had the loud, persistent eloquence of an auctioneer in the slave-market. I soon gave up trying to answer her back. Of course I still lived at Capua, and Aelia never came to see me there, but Sejanus insisted that whenever I visited Rome I should be seen in her company as much as possible.

Nero had no chance against Sejanus and Livilla. Though Agrippina constantly warned him to weigh every word he spoke, he was of far too open a nature to conceal his thoughts. Among the young noblemen whom he trusted as his friends there were several secret agents of Sejanus, and these kept a register of the opinions he expressed on all public events. Worse still, his wife, whom we called Helen, or Heluo, was Livilla's daughter and reported all his confidences to her. But the worst of all was his own brother, Drusus, to whom he confided even more than to his wife, and who was jealous because Nero was the elder son, and Agrippina's favourite. Drusus went to Sejanus and said that Nero had asked him to sail secretly to Germany with him on the next dark night, where they would throw themselves on the protection of the regiments, as Germanicus's sons, and call for a march on Rome; that he had of course indignantly refused. Sejanus told him to wait a little longer and he would then be called on to tell the story to Tiberius: but the right moment had not yet come.

Meanwhile, Sejanus sent the rumour flying around that Tiberius was about to charge Nero with treason. Nero's friends began to desert him. As soon as two or three of them began excusing themselves from attending his dinners, and returning his greeting coldly when they met him in public, the rest followed their example. After a few months only his real friends remained. Among them was Gallus, who now that Tiberius himself did not visit the Senate any more, concentrated on teasing Sejanus. His method with Sejanus was constantly to propose votes of thanks for his services, and the granting of exceptional honours – statues and arches and titles and prayers and the public celebration of his birthday. The Senate did not dare to oppose these motions, and Sejanus, not being a senator, had no say in the matter; and Tiberius did not wish to go against the Senate by vetoing their vote for fear of antagonizing Sejanus or seeming to have lost confidence in him. Whenever the Senate now wanted anything done they would first send representatives to Sejanus asking for permission to apply to Tiberius about it: and if Sejanus discouraged them the matter would be dropped. Gallus one day proposed that, as the descendants of Torquatus had a golden torque and those of Cincinnatus a curled lock of hair, granted by the Senate as family badges in commemoration of their ancestors' services to the State, so Sejanus and his descendants should be awarded as their badge a golden key, in token of his faithful services as the Emperor's doorkeeper. The Senate unanimously voted this motion and Sejanus, growing alarmed, wrote to Tiberius and complained that Gallus had maliciously proposed all the previous honours in the hope of making the Senate jealous of him, and even perhaps of making the Emperor suspect him of insolent ambitions. The present motion had been still more malicious – a suggestion to the Emperor that access to the Imperial presence was in the hands of someone who had made use of it for his own private enrichment. He begged that the Emperor would find a technical reason for vetoing the decree, and a way to silence Gallus. Tiberius answered that he could not veto the decree without damaging Sejanus's credit, but that he would very soon take steps to silence Gallus: Sejanus need not be anxious about the matter and his letter had shown true loyalty and a fine delicacy of judgement. But Gallus's hint had struck home. Tiberius suddenly realized that while all the goings and comings at Capri were known to Sejanus and could to a great extent be controlled by him, he himself only knew as much as Sejanus cared to tell him about the comings and goings by Sejanus's front door.

And now I have come to a turning-point in my story – the death of my grandmother Livia at the age of eighty-six. She might well have lived many years longer, for she kept her eyesight and hearing and the use of her limbs – not to mention her A.D. 29 mind and memory – unimpaired. But recently she had suffered from repeated colds owing to some infection of the nose, and at last one of these settled on her lungs. She summoned me to her bedside at the Palace. I happened to be in Rome and came immediately. I could see that she was dying. She reminded me of my oath again.

'I'll not rest until it's fulfilled, Grandmother,' I said. When a very old woman lies dying, one's grandmother too, one says whatever one can to please her. 'But I thought Caligula was going to arrange it for you?'

She did not answer for a time. Then she said, raging weakly:

'He was here ten minutes ago! He stood and laughed at me. He said that I could go to Hell and stew there for ever and ever for all he cared. He said that now I was dying he had no need to keep in with me any longer, and that he did not consider himself bound by the oath, because it was forced on him. He said that *he* was going to be the Almighty God that has been prophesied, not I. He said ...'

'That's all right, Grandmother. You'll have the laugh of him in the end. When you're the Queen of Heaven and he's being slowly broken on an eternal wheel by Minos's men in Hell ...'

'And to think that I ever called you a fool,' she said. 'I'm going now, Claudius. Close my eyes and put the coin in my mouth that you'll find under the pillow. The Ferryman will recognize it. He'll pay proper respect. ...'

Then she died and I closed her eyes and put the coin in her mouth. It was a gold coin of a type I had never seen before, with Augustus's head and her own facing each other on the obverse, and a triumphant chariot on the reverse.

Nothing had been said between us about Tiberius. I soon heard that he had been warned about her condition in plenty of time to pay her the last offices. He now wrote to the Senate excusing himself for not having visited her but saying that he had been exceedingly busy and would at all events come to Rome for the funeral. Meanwhile the Senate had decreed various extraordinary honours in her memory, including the title Mother of the Country, and had even proposed to make her a demi-goddess. But Tiberius reversed nearly all these decrees, explaining in a letter that Livia was a singularly modest woman, averse to all public recognition of her services, and with a peculiar sentiment against having any religious worship paid to her after death. The letter ended with reflexions on the unsuitability of women's meddling in politics 'for which they are not fitted, and which rouse in them all those worst feelings of arrogance and petulance to which the female sex is naturally prone'.

He did not of course come to the City for the funeral, though, solely with the object of limiting its magnificence, he made all arrangements for it. And he took so long over them that the corpse, old and withered as it was, had reached an advanced stage of putrefaction before it was put on the pyre. To the general surprise, Caligula spoke the funeral oration, which Tiberius himself should have done, and if not Tiberius, then Nero, as his heir. The Senate had decreed an arch in Livia's memory – the first time in the history of Rome that a woman had been so honoured. Tiberius allowed this decree to stand but promised to build the arch at his own expense: and then neglected to build it. As for Livia's will, he inherited the greater part of her fortune as her natural heir, but she had left as much of it as she was legally permitted to members of her own household and other trusted dependants. He did not pay anybody a single one of her bequests. I was to have benefited to the extent of 20,000 gold pieces.

Chapter 27

I COULD never have thought it possible that I would miss Livia when she died. When I was a child I used secretly, night after night, to pray to the Infernal Gods to carry her off. And now I would have offered the richest sacrifices I could find – unblemished white bulls and desert antelopes and ibises and flamingoes by the dozen – to have had her back again. For it was clear that it had long been only the fear of his mother that had kept Tiberius within bounds. A few days after her death he struck at Agrippina and Nero. Agrippina had by now recovered from her illness. He did not charge them with treason. He wrote to the Senate complaining of Nero's gross sexual depravity, of Agrippina's 'haughty bearing and mischief-making tongue', and suggested that severe steps should be taken for keeping both of them in order.

When the letter was read in the Senate nobody said a word for a long time. Everyone was wondering on just how much popular support Germanicus's family could count now that Tiberius was preparing to victimize them; and whether it would not be safer to go against Tiberius than against the populace. At last a friend of Sejanus's rose to suggest that the Emperor's wishes should be respected and that some decree or other should be passed against the two persons mentioned. There was a senator who acted as official recorder of the Senate's transactions, and what he said carried great weight. He had hitherto voted without question whatever had been suggested in any letter of Tiberius's, and Sejanus had reported that he could always be counted upon to do what he was told. Yet it was this Recorder who rose to oppose the motion. He said that the question of Nero's morals and

Agrippina's bearing should not be raised at present. It was his opinion that the Emperor had been misinformed and had written hastily, and that in his own interest therefore, as well as that of Nero and Agrippina, no decree should be passed until he had been allowed time to reconsider such grave charges against his near relatives. The news of the letter had meanwhile spread all over the City, though all transactions in the Senate were supposed to be secret until officially published by the Emperor's orders, and huge crowds gathered around the Senate House, making demonstrations in favour of Agrippina and Nero, and crying out, 'Long live Tiberius! The letter is forged! Long live Tiberius! It's Sejanus's doing!'

Sejanus sent a messenger at great speed to Tiberius, who had moved for the occasion to a villa only a few miles outside the City, in case of trouble. He reported that the Senate had, on the motion of the Recorder, refused to pay any attention to the letter; that the people were on the point of revolt, calling Agrippina the true Mother of the Country and Nero their Saviour; and that unless Tiberius acted firmly and decisively there would be bloodshed before the day was out.

Tiberius was frightened, but he took Sejanus's advice and wrote a menacing letter to the Senate, putting the blame on the Recorder for this unparalleled insult to the Imperial dignity, and demanding that the whole affair should be left entirely to him to settle since they were so half-hearted in his interests. The Senate gave way. Tiberius, after having the Guards marched through the City with swords drawn and trumpets blowing, threatened to halve the free ration of corn if any further seditious demonstrations were made. He then banished Agrippina to Pandataria, the very island where her mother Julia had been first confined, and Nero to Ponza, another tiny rocky island, half-way between Capri and Rome but far out of sight of the coast. He told the Senate that the two prisoners had been on the point of escaping from the City in the hope of seducing the loyalty of the regiments on the Rhine.

Before Agrippina went to her island he had her before him and asked her mocking questions about how she proposed to govern the mighty kingdom which she had just inherited from her mother (his virtuous late wife), and whether she would send ambassadors to her son, Nero, in *his* new kingdom, and enter into a grand military alliance with him. She did not answer a word. He grew angry and roared at her to answer, and when she still kept silent he told a captain of the guard to strike her over the shoulders. Then at last she spoke. 'Blood-soaked Mud is your name. That's what Theodorus the Gadarene called you, I'm told, when you attended his rhetoric classes at Rhodes.' Tiberius seized the vine branch from the captain and thrashed her about the body and head until she was insensible. She lost the sight of an eye as a result of this dreadful beating.

Soon Drusus too was accused of intriguing with the Rhine regiments. Sejanus produced letters in proof, which he said that he had intercepted, but which were really forged, and also the written testimony of Lepida, Drusus's wife (with whom he had a secret affair), that Drusus had asked her to get in touch with the sailors of Ostia, who, he hoped, would remember that Nero and he were Agrippa's grandsons. Drusus was handed over by the Senate to Tiberius to deal with and Tiberius had him confined in a remote attic of the Palace under Sejanus's supervision.

Gallus was the next victim. Tiberius wrote to the Senate that Gallus was jealous of Sejanus and had done all that he could to bring him into disfavour with his Emperor by ironical praises and other malicious methods. The Senate were so upset by the news of the suicide of the Recorder, which reached them the same day, that they immediately sent a magistrate to arrest Gallus. When the magistrate went to Gallus's house he was told that Gallus was out of the City, at Baiae. At Baiae he was directed to Tiberius's villa and, sure enough, he came on him there at dinner with Tiberius. Tiberius was pledging Gallus in a cup of wine and Gallus was responding loyally, and there seemed such an air of good humour and jollity in the dining-hall that the magistrate was embarrassed and did not know what to say. Tiberius asked him why he had come. 'To arrest one of your guests, Caesar, by order of the Senate.' 'Which guest?' asked Tiberius. 'Asinius Gallus,' replied the magistrate, 'but it seems to be a mistake.' Tiberius pretended to look grave: 'If the Senate have anything against you, Gallus, and have sent this officer to arrest you, I'm afraid our pleasant evening must come to an end. I can't go against the Senate, you know. But I'll tell you what I'll do, now that you and I have come to such a friendly understanding: I'll write to ask the Senate, as a personal favour, not to take any action in your case until they hear from me. That will mean that you will be under simple arrest, in the charge of the Consuls – no fetters or anything degrading. I'll arrange to secure your acquittal as soon as I can.'

Gallus felt bound to thank Tiberius for his magnanimity, but was sure that there was a catch somewhere, that Tiberius was paying back irony with irony; and he was right. He was taken to Rome and put in an underground room in the Senate House. He was not allowed to see anyone, not even a servant, or send any messages to his friends or family. Food was given him every day through a grille. The room was dark except for the poor light coming through the grille and unfurnished except for a mattress. He was told that these quarters were only temporary ones and that Tiberius would soon come to settle his case. But the days drew on into months, and months into years, and still he stayed there. The food was very poor – carefully calculated by Tiberius to keep him always hungry but never actually starving. He was allowed no knife to cut it up with, for fear he might use it to kill himself, or any other sharp weapon, or anything to distract himself with, such as writing materials or books or dice. He was given very little water to drink, none to wash in. If ever there was talk about him in Tiberius's presence the old man would say, grinning: 'I have not yet made my peace with Gallus.'

When I heard of Gallus's arrest I was sorry that I had just quarrelled with him. It was only a literary quarrel. He had written a silly book called: *A Comparison between my Father, Asinius Pollio, and his Friend Marcus Tullius Cicero, as Orators*. If the ground of the comparison had been moral character or political ability or even learning, Pollio would have easily come off the best. But Gallus was trying to make out that his father was the more polished orator. That was absurd, and I wrote a little book to say so; which, coming shortly after my criticism of Pollio's own remarks about Cicero, greatly annoyed Gallus. I would willingly have recalled my book from publication if by doing so I could have lightened Gallus's miserable prison life in the least degree. It was foolish of me, I suppose, to think in this way.

Sejanus was at last able to report to Tiberius that the power of the Leek Green Party was broken and that he need have no further anxieties. Tiberius rewarded him by saying that he had decided to marry him to his granddaughter Helen (whose marriage with Nero he had dissolved) and hinting at even greater favours. It was at this point that my mother, who, you must remember, was Livilla's mother too, interposed. Since Castor's death Livilla had been living with her, and was now careless enough to let her find out about a secret correspondence which she was carrying on with Sejanus. My mother had always been very economical, and in her old age her chief delight was saving candle-ends and melting them down into candles again, and selling the kitchen refuse to pig-keepers, and mixing charcoal-dust with some liquid or other and kneading it into cakes which, when dried, burned almost as well as charcoal. Livilla, on the other hand, was very extravagant and my mother was always scolding her for it. One day my mother happened to pass Livilla's room and saw a slave coming out of it with a basket of waste-paper. 'Where are you going, boy?' she asked.

'To the furnace, Mistress; the Lady Livilla's orders.'

My mother said: 'It's most *wasteful* to stoke the furnace wth perfectly good pieces of paper; do you know what paper costs? Why, three times as much as parchment, even. Some of those pieces seem hardly written on at all.'

'The Lady Livilla ordered most particularly ...'

'The Lady Livilla must have been very preoccupied when she ordered you to destroy valuable paper. Give me the basket. The clean parts will be useful for household lists, and all sorts of things. Waste not, want not.'

So she took the papers to her room and was about to clip the good pieces off one of them when it struck her that she might as well try to remove the ink from the whole thing. Until now she had honourably refrained from reading the writing; but when she began rubbing away at it, it was impossible to avoid doing so. She suddenly realized that these were rough drafts, or unsatisfactory beginnings, of a letter to Sejanus; and once she began reading she could not stop, and before she had done she knew the whole story. Livilla was clearly angry and jealous that Sejanus had consented to marry someone else – her own daughter too! But she was trying to conceal her feelings – each draft of the letter was toned down a little more. She wrote that he must act quickly before Tiberius suspected that he really had no intention of marrying Helen: and if he was not yet ready to assassinate Tiberius and usurp the monarchy had she not better poison Helen herself?

My mother sent for Pallas, who was working for me at the Library, looking up some historical point about the Etruscans, and told him to go to Sejanus and, in my name and as if sent by me, ask his permission to see Tiberius at Capri, in order to present him with my 'History of Carthage'. (I had just finished this work and sent a fair copy to my mother before having it published.) At Capri he was to beg the Emperor, in my name again, to accept the dedication of the work. Sejanus gave permission readily; he knew Pallas as one of our family slaves and suspected nothing. But in the twelfth volume of the history my mother had pasted Livilla's letters and a letter of her own in explanation, and told Pallas not to let anybody handle the volumes (which were all sealed up) but to give them to Tiberius with his own hands. He was to add to my supposed greetings and my request for permission to dedicate the book the following message: 'The Lady Antonia, too, sends her devoted greetings, but is of opinion that these books by her son are of no interest at all to the Emperor, except the twelfth volume which contains a very curious digression which will, she trusts, immediately interest him.'

Pallas stopped at Capua to tell me where he was going. He said that it was strictly against my mother's orders that he was telling me about his errand, but after that all I was his real master, not my mother, though she pretended to own him; and that he would do nothing willingly to get me into trouble; and that he was sure that I had no intention myself of offering the Emperor the dedication. I was mystified, at first, especially when he mentioned the twelfth volume, so while he was washing and changing his clothes I broke the seal. When I saw what had been inserted I was so frightened that for the moment I thought of burning the whole thing. But that was as dangerous as letting it go, so eventually I sealed it up again. My mother had used a duplicate seal of my own, which I had given her for business uses, so nobody would know that I had opened the book, not even Pallas. Pallas then hurried on to Capri and on his way back told me that Tiberius had picked up the twelfth volume and taken it out into the woods to look at. I might dedicate the book to him if I wished, he had said, but I must abstain from extravagant phrases in doing so. This reassured me somewhat, but one could never trust Tiberius when he seemed friendly. Naturally I was in the deepest anxiety as to what would happen and felt very bitter against my mother for having put my life into such terrible danger by mixing me up in a quarrel between Tiberius and Sejanus. I thought of running away, but there was nowhere to run to.

The first thing that happened was that Helen became an invalid – we know now that there was nothing wrong with her, but Livilla had given her the choice of taking to her bed as if she were ill or of taking to her bed because she was ill. She was moved from Rome to Naples, where the climate was supposed to be healthier. Tiberius gave leave for the marriage to be postponed indefinitely, but addressed Sejanus as his son-in-law as if it had already taken place. He elevated him to senatorial rank and made him his colleague in the Consulship and a pontiff. But he then A.D. 31 did something else which quite cancelled these favours: he invited Caligula to Capri for a few days and then sent him back armed with a most important letter to the Senate. In the letter he said that he had examined the young man, who was now his heir, and found him of a very different temper and character from his brothers and would, indeed, refuse to believe any accusations that might be brought against his morals or loyalty. He now entrusted Caligula to the care of Aelius Sejanus, his fellow-Consul, begging him to guard the young man from all harm. He appointed him a pontiff too, and a priest to Augustus.

When the City heard about this letter there was great rejoicing. By making Sejanus responsible for Caligula's safety Tiberius was understood to be warning him that his feud with Germanicus's family had now been carried far enough. Sejanus's Consulship was regarded as a bad omen for him: this was Tiberius's fifth time in office and every one of his previous colleagues had died in unlucky circumstances: Varus, Gnaeus Piso, Germanicus, Castor. So new hopes arose that the nation's troubles would soon be over: a son of Germanicus would rule over them. Tiberius might perhaps kill Nero and Drusus but he had clearly decided to save Caligula: Sejanus would not be the next Emperor. Everyone whom Tiberius now sounded on the subject seemed so genuinely relieved at his choice of a successor – for somehow they had persuaded themselves that Caligula had inherited all his father's virtues – that Tiberius, who recognized real evil whenever he saw it and had told Caligula frankly that he knew he was a poisonous snake and had spared him for that very reason, was much amused, and thoroughly pleased. He could use Caligula's rising popularity as a check to Sejanus and Livilla.

He now took Caligula somewhat into his confidence and gave him a mission: to find out by intimate talks with Guardsmen which of their captains had the greatest personal influence in the Guards' camp, next to Sejanus; and then to make sure that he was equally bloody-minded and fearless. Caligula dressed up in a woman's wig and clothes and, picking up with a couple of young prostitutes, began frequenting the suburban taverns where the soldiers drank in the evening. With a heavily made up face and padded figure he passed for a woman, a tall and not very attractive one, but still, a woman. The account that he gave of himself in the taverns was that he was being kept by a rich shop-keeper who gave him plenty of money – on the strength of which he used to stand drinks all round. This generosity made him very popular. He soon came to know a great deal of camp gossip, and the name that was constantly coming up in conversation was that of a captain called Macro. Macro was the son of one of Tiberius's freedmen, and from all accounts was the toughest fellow in Rome. The soldiers all spoke admiringly of his drinking feats and his wenching and his domination of the other captains and his presence of mind in difficult situations. Even Sejanus was afraid of him, they said: Macro was the only man who ever stood up to him. So Caligula picked up with Macro one evening and secretly introduced himself: the two went off for a stroll together and had a long talk.

Tiberius then began writing a queer series of letters to the Senate, now saying that he was in a bad state of health and almost dying, and now that he had suddenly recovered and would arrive in Rome any moment. He wrote very queerly too about Sejanus, mixing extravagant praises with petulant rebukes; and the general impression conveyed was that he had become senile and was losing his senses. Sejanus was so puzzled by these letters that he could not make up his mind whether to attempt a revolution at once or to hold on to his position, which was still very strong, until Tiberius died or could be removed from power on the grounds of imbecility. He wanted to visit Capri and find out for himself just how things stood with Tiberius. He wrote asking permission to visit him on his birthday, but Tiberius answered that as Consul he should stay at Rome; it was irregular enough for himself to be permanently absent. Sejanus then wrote that Helen was seriously ill at Naples and had begged him to visit her: could he not be permitted to do so, just for a day? and from Naples it was only an hour's row to Capri. Tiberius answered that Helen had the best doctors and must be patient; and that he himself was really coming to Rome now and wanted Sejanus to be there to welcome him. At about the same time he quashed an indictment against an ex-Governor of Spain, whom Sejanus was accusing of extortion, on the grounds that the evidence was conflicting. He had never before failed to support Sejanus in a case of the sort. Sejanus began to be alarmed. The term of his Consulship expired.

On the day set by Tiberius for his arrival in Rome, Sejanus was waiting, at the head of a battalion of Guards, outside the temple of Apollo, where the Senate happened to be sitting because of repairs that were being done at the time to the Senate House. Suddenly Macro rode up and saluted him. Sejanus asked him why he had left the Camp. Macro replied that Tiberius had sent him a letter to deliver to the Senate.

'Why *you*?' Sejanus asked suspiciously.

'Why not?'

'But why not me?'

'Because the letter is about you!' Then Macro whispered in his ear, 'My heartiest congratulations, General. There's a surprise for you in the letter. You're to be made Protector of the People. That means you're to be our next Emperor.' Sejanus had not really expected Tiberius to appear, but he had been made very anxious by his recent silence. He now rushed, elated, into the Senate House.

Macro then called the Guards to attention. He said: 'Boys, the Emperor has just appointed me your General in Sejanus's place. Here's my commission. You are to go straight back to the Camp now, excused all guard duties. When you get there tell the other fellows that Macro's in charge now and that there's thirty gold pieces coming to every man who knows how to obey orders. Who's the senior captain? You? March the men off! But don't make too much row about it.'

So the Guards went off and Macro called on the Commander of the Watchmen, who had already been warned, to furnish a guard in their place. Then he went in after Sejanus, handed the letter to the Consuls and came out at once before a word had been read. He satisfied himself that the Watchmen were properly posted and then hurried after the returning Guards to make sure that no disturbance arose in the Camp.

Meanwhile the news of Sejanus's Protectorship had gone round the House and everyone began to cheer him and offer their congratulations. The senior Consul called for order and began reading the letter. It began with Tiberius's usual excuses for not attending the meeting – pressure of work and ill-health – and went on to discuss general topics, then to complain slightly of Sejanus's hastiness in preparing the indictment of the ex-Governor without proper evidence. Here Sejanus smiled because this petulance of Tiberius had always hitherto been a prelude to the granting of some new honour. But the letter continued in the same strain of reproach, paragraph after paragraph, with gradually increasing severity, and the smile slowly left Sejanus's face. The senators who had been cheering him grew silent and perplexed, and one or two who were sitting near him made some excuse and walked across to the other side of the House. The letter ended by saying that Sejanus had been guilty of grave irregularities, that two of his friends, his uncle Junius Blaesus who had triumphed over Tacfarinas, and another, should, in his opinion, be punished and that Sejanus himself should be arrested. The Consul, who had been warned by Macro the night before what Tiberius wanted him to do, then called out 'Sejanus, come here!' Sejanus could not believe his ears. He was waiting for the end of the letter and his appointment to the Protectorship. The Consul had to call him twice before he understood. He said: 'Me? You mean me?'

As soon as his enemies realized that Sejanus had at last fallen they began loudly booing and hissing him; and his friends and relatives, anxious for their own safety, joined in. He suddenly found himself without a single supporter. The Consul asked the question, whether the Emperor's advice should be followed. 'Ay, ay!' the whole House shouted. The Commander of the Watchmen was summoned, and when Sejanus saw that his own Guards had disappeared and that Watchmen had taken their places, he knew that he was beaten. He was marched off to prison. and the populace, who had got wind of what was happening, crowded round him and shouted and groaned and pelted him with filth. He muffled his face with his gown, but they threatened to kill him if he did not show it; and when he obeyed they pelted him all the harder. The same afternoon the Senate, seeing that no Guards were about and that the crowd was threatening to break into the gaol to lynch Sejanus, decided to keep the credit for themselves and condemned him to death.

Caligula sent Tiberius the news at once by beacon signal. Tiberius had a fleet standing by prepared to take him to Egypt if his plans went astray. Sejanus was executed and his body thrown down the Weeping Stairs, where the rabble abused it for three whole days. When the time came for it to be dragged to the Tiber with a hook through the throat, the skull had been carried off to the Public Baths and used as a ball, and there was only half the trunk left. The streets of Rome were littered, too, with the broken limbs of his innumerable statues.

His children by Apicata were put to death by decree. There was a boy who had come of age, and a boy under age, and the girl who had been betrothed to my son Drusillus – she was now fourteen years old. The boy under age could not legally be executed, so, following a Civil War precedent, they made him put on his manly-gown for the occasion. The girl being a virgin was still more strongly protected by law. There was no precedent for executing a virgin whose only crime was being her father's daughter. When she was carried off to prison she did not understand what was happening and called out: 'Don't take me to prison! Whip me if you like and I won't do it again!' She apparently had some girlish naughtiness on her conscience. Macro gave orders that, to avoid the ill-luck that would befall the City if they executed her while still a virgin, the public executioner should outrage her. As soon as I heard of this, I said to myself: 'Rome, you are ruined; there can be no expiation for a crime so horrible,' and I called the Gods to witness that though a relative of the Emperor I had taken no part in the government of my country and that I detested the crime as much as they did, though powerless to avenge it.

When Apicata was told what had happened to her children and saw the crowd insulting their bodies on the Stairs she killed herself. But first she wrote a letter to Tiberius telling him that Castor had been poisoned by Livilla and that Livilla and Sejanus had intended to usurp the monarchy. She blamed Livilla for everything. My mother had not known about the murder of Castor. Tiberius now called my mother to Capri, thanked her for her great services, and showed her Apicata's letter. He told her that any reward within reason was hers for the asking. My mother said that the only reward that she would ask was that the family name should not be disgraced: that her daughter should not be executed and her body thrown down the Stairs. 'How is she to be punished, then?' Tiberius asked sharply. 'Give her to me,' said my mother. '*I* will punish her.'

So Livilla was not publicly proceeded against. My mother locked her up in the room next to her own and starved her to death. She could hear her despairing cries and curses, day after day, night after night, gradually weakening; but she kept her there, instead of in some cellar out of earshot, until she died. She did this not from a delight in torture, for it was inexpressibly painful to her, but as a punishment to herself for having brought up so abominable a daughter.

A whole crop of executions followed as a result of Sejanus's death – all his friends who had not been quick in making the change-over, and a great many of those who had. The ones who did not anticipate death by suicide were hurled from the Tarpeian cliff of the Capitoline Hill. Their estates were confiscated. Tiberius paid the accusers very little; he was becoming economical. On Caligula's advice he framed charges against those accusers who were entitled to benefit most heavily and so was able to confiscate their estates too. About sixty senators, 200 knights, and 1,000 or more of the commons died at this time. My alliance by marriage with Sejanus's family might easily have cost me my life, had I not been my mother's son. I was now allowed to divorce Aelia and to retain an eighth part of her dowry. As a matter of fact I returned it all to her. She must have thought me a fool. But I did this as some compensation for taking our little child Antonia away from her as soon as she was born. For Aelia had allowed herself to become pregnant by me as soon as she felt that Sejanus's position was becoming insecure. She thought that this would be some protection to her if he fell from power: Tiberius could hardly have her executed while she was with child to his nephew. I welcomed my divorce from Aelia, but would not have robbed her of the child if my mother had not insisted on it: my mother wanted Antonia for herself as something to mother of her very own – grandmother-hunger, as it is called.

The only member of Sejanus's family who escaped was his brother, and he escaped for the strange reason that he had publicly made fun of Tiberius's baldness. At the last annual festival in honour of Flora, at which he happened to be presiding, he employed only bald-headed men to perform the ceremonies, which were prolonged to the evening, and the spectators were lighted out of the theatre by 5,000 children with torches in their hands and their heads shaved. Tiberius was informed of this in Nerva's presence by a visiting senator and just to create a good impression on Nerva he said, 'I forgive the fellow. If Julius Caesar did not resent jokes about his baldness, how much less should I?' I suppose that when Sejanus fell Tiberius decided, by the same kind of whim, to renew his magnanimity.

But Helen was punished, merely for having pretended to be ill, by being married to Blandus, a very vulgar fellow whose grandfather, a provincial knight, had come to Rome as a teacher of rhetoric. This was considered very base behaviour on Tiberius's part, because Helen was his granddaughter and he was dishonouring his own house by this alliance. It was said that one had not to go far back in the Blandus line before one came to slaves.

Tiberius realized now that the Guards, to whom he paid a bounty of fifty gold pieces each, not thirty, as Macro had promised, were his one certain defence against the people and the Senate. He told Caligula: 'There's not a man in Rome who would not gladly eat my flesh.' The Guards, to show their loyalty to Tiberius, complained that they had been wronged by having the Watchmen preferred to them as Sejanus's prison escort, and as a protest marched out of Camp to plunder the suburbs. Macro let them have a good night out, but when the Assembly-call was blown at dawn the next day, the men who were not back within two hours he flogged nearly to death.

After a time Tiberius declared an amnesty. Nobody could now be tried for having been politically connected with Sejanus, and if anyone cared to go into mourning for him, remembering his noble deeds now that his evil ones had been fully punished, there would be no objection to this. A good many A.D. 32 men did so, guessing that this was what Tiberius wanted, but they guessed wrong. They were soon on trial for their lives, faced with perfectly groundless charges, the commonest being incest. They were all executed. It may be wondered how it happened that there were any senators or knights left after all this slaughter: but the answer is that Tiberius kept the Orders up to strength by constant promotion. Free birth, a clean record, and so many thousands of gold pieces, were the only qualifications for admission into the Noble Order of Knights, and there were always plenty of candidates, though the initiation fee was heavy. Tiberius was becoming more grasping than ever: he expected rich men to leave him at least half their estates in their wills, and if they were found not to have done so he declared the wills technically invalid because of some legal flaw or other, and took charge of the entire estate himself; the heirs getting nothing. He spent practically no money on public works, not even completing the Temple of Augustus, and stinted the corn-dole and the allowance for public entertainments. He paid the armies regularly, that was all. As for the provinces, he did nothing at all about them any more, so long as the taxes and tribute came in regularly; he did not even trouble to appoint new governors when the old ones died. A deputation of Spaniards once came to complain to him that they had been four years now without a governor and that the staff of the last one were pillaging the province shamefully. Tiberius said: 'You aren't asking for a new governor, are you? But a new governor would only bring a new staff, and then you'd be worse off than before. I'll tell you a story. There was once a badly wounded man lying on the battle-field waiting for the surgeon to dress his wound, which was covered with flies. A lightly wounded comrade saw the flies and was going to drive them away. "Oh, no," cried the wounded man, "don't do that! These flies are almost gorged with my blood now and aren't hurting me nearly so much as they did at first: if you drive them away their place will be taken at once by hungrier ones, and that will be the end of me." '

He allowed the Parthians to overrun Armenia, and the trans-Danube tribes to invade the Balkans, and the Germans to make raids across the Rhine into France. He confiscated the estates of a number of allied chiefs and petty kings in France, Spain, Syria, and Greece, using the most flimsy pretexts. He relieved Vonones of his treasure – you will recall that Vonones was the former king of Armenia, about whom my brother Germanicus had quarrelled with Gnaeus Piso – by sending agents to help him escape from the city in Cilicia where Germanicus had him put under guard and then having him pursued and killed.

The informers about this time began to accuse wealthy men of charging more than the legal interest on loans – one and a half per cent was all that they were allowed to charge. The statute about it had long fallen into abeyance and hardly a single senator was innocent of infringing it. But Tiberius upheld its validity. A deputation went to him and pleaded that everyone should be allowed a year and a half to adjust his private finances to conform with the letter of the law, and Tiberius as a great favour granted the request. The result was that all debts were at once called in, and this caused a great shortage of current coin. Tiberius's great idle hoards of gold and silver in the Treasury had been responsible for forcing up the rate of interest in the first place, and now there was a financial panic and land-values fell to nothing. Tiberius was eventually forced to relieve the situation by lending the bankers 1,000,000 gold pieces of public money, without interest, to pay out to borrowers in exchange for securities in land. He would not even have done this much but for Cocceius Nerva's advice. He still used occasionally to consult Nerva, who, living at Capri, where he was kept carefully away from the scene of Tiberius's debauches and allowed little news from Rome, was perhaps the only man in the world who still believed in Tiberius's goodness. To Nerva (Caligula told me some years later) Tiberius explained his painted favourites as poor orphans on whom he had taken pity, most of them a little queer in the head, which accounted for the funny way they dressed and behaved. But could Nerva really have been so simple as to have believed this, and so short-sighted?

Chapter 28

OF the last five years of Tiberius's reign the less told the better. I cannot bear to write in detail of Nero, slowly starved to death; or of Agrippina, who was cheered by news of Sejanus's fall, but when she saw that it made matters no better for her refused to eat, and was forcibly fed for awhile, and then at last left to die as she wished; or of Gallus, who died of a consumption; or of Drusus, who, removed some time before from his attic in the Palace to a dark cellar, was found dead with his mouth full of the flock from his mattress, which he had been gnawing in his starvation. But I must record at least that Tiberius wrote letters to the Senate rejoicing in the death of Agrippina and Nero – he accused her now of treason and of adultery with Gallus – and regretting, in the case of Gallus, that 'the press of public business had constantly postponed his trial so that he had died before his guilt could be proved'. As for Drusus, he wrote that this young man was the lewdest and most treacherous rascal he had ever encountered. He ordered a record to be publicly read, by the Guards' captain who had been in charge of him, of the treasonable remarks which Drusus had uttered while in prison. Never had such a painful document been read in the House before. It was clear from Drusus's remarks that he had been beaten and tortured and insulted by the captain himself, by common soldiers, and even by slaves, and that he had very cruelly been given every day less and less food and drink, crumb by crumb, and drop by drop. Tiberius even ordered the captain to read Drusus's dying curse. It was a wild but well-composed imprecation, accusing Tiberius of miserliness, treachery, obscene filthiness, and delight in torture, of murdering Germanicus and Postumus, and of a whole series of other crimes (most of which he had committed but none of which had ever been publicly mentioned before); he prayed the Gods that all the immeasurable suffering and distress that Tiberius had caused others should weigh upon him with increasing strength, waking or sleeping, night and day, for as long as he lived, should overwhelm him in the hour of his death, and should commit him to everlasting torture in the day of infernal Judgement. The senators interrupted the reading with exclamations of pretended horror at Drusus's treason, but these 'oh, oh's' and groans covered their amazement that Tiberius should voluntarily provide such a revelation of his own wickedness. Tiberius was very sorry for himself at the time (I heard afterwards from Caligula), tormented by insomnia and superstitious fears; and actually counted on the Senate's sympathy. He told Caligula with tears in his eyes that the killing of his relatives had been forced on him by their own ambition and by the policy that he had inherited from Augustus (he said Augustus, not Livia) of putting the tranquillity of the realm before private sentiment. Caligula, who had never shown the slightest signs of grief or anger at Tiberius's treatment of his mother or brothers, condoled with the old man; and then quickly began telling him of a new sort of vice that he had heard about recently from some Syrians. Such talk was the only way to cheer Tiberius up when he had attacks of remorse. Lepida, who had betrayed Drusus, did not long survive him. She was accused of adultery with a slave, and not being able to deny the charge (for she was found in bed with him), took her own life.

Caligula spent most of his time at Capri but occasionally went to Rome on Tiberius's behalf to keep an eye on Macro. Macro did all Sejanus's work now, and very efficiently, but was sensible enough to let the Senate know that he wanted no honours voted to him and that any senator who proposed any such would soon find himself on trial for his life on some charge of treason, incest, or forgery. Tiberius had indicated Caligula as his successor for several reasons. The first was that Caligula's popularity as Germanicus's son kept the people on their best behaviour for fear that any disturbance on their part would be punished by his death. The next was that Caligula was an excellent servant and one of the few people wicked enough to make Tiberius feel, by comparison, a virtuous man. The third was that he did not believe that Caligula would, as a matter of fact, ever become Emperor. For Thrasyllus, whom he still trusted absolutely (since no event had ever happened contrary to his predictions), had told him 'Caligula can no more become Emperor than he could gallop across yonder bay from Baiae to Puteoli'. Thrasyllus also said:

'Ten years from now Tiberius Caesar will still be Emperor.' This was true, as it turned out, but it was another Tiberius Caesar.

Tiberius knew a great deal, but some things Thrasyllus kept from him. He knew, for instance, the fate of his grandson Gemellus, who was not really his grandson because Castor was not the father, but Sejanus. He said to Caligula one day: 'I am making you my principal heir. I am making Gemellus my second heir in case you die before him, but this is only a formality. I know that you'll kill Gemellus; but then, others will kill you.' He said this expecting to outlive them both. Then he added, quoting from some Greek tragedian or other: 'When I am dead, let Fire the Earth confound.'

But Tiberius was not dead yet. The informers were still busy and every year more and more people were executed. There was hardly a senator left who had kept his seat since the days of Augustus. Macro had a far greater appetite for blood and far less compunction in shedding it than Sejanus. Sejanus was at any rate the son of a knight; Macro's father had been born a slave. Among the new victims was Plancina, who, now that Livia had died, had nobody to protect her. She was accused once more of poisoning Germanicus; for she was quite wealthy. Tiberius had not allowed her to be prosecuted until Agrippina was dead, because if Agrippina had heard the news it would have pleased her greatly. I was not sorry when I heard that Plancina's body had been thrown on the Stairs, though she had anticipated execution by suicide.

One day at dinner with Tiberius, Nerva asked Tiberius's pardon, explaining that he was not feeling hungry and wanted no food. Nerva had been in perfect health and spirits all this time and apparently quite contented with his sheltered life at Capri. Tiberius thought at first that Nerva had taken a purge the night before and was resting his stomach, but when he carried his fast through into the second and third day, Tiberius began to fear that he had decided to commit suicide by starvation. He sat down at Nerva's side and begged him to tell him why he was not eating. But all Nerva would do was apologize again and say that he was not hungry. Tiberius thought that perhaps Nerva was annoyed with him for not having taken his advice sooner about averting the financial crisis. He asked, 'Would you eat with a better appetite if I repealed all laws limiting the interest on loans to a figure which you consider too low?'

Nerva said: 'No, it isn't that. I'm just not hungry.'

The next day Tiberius said to Nerva: 'I have written to the Senate. Someone has told me that two or three men actually make a living by acting as professional informers against wrongdoers. It never occurred to me that by rewarding loyalty to the State I should encourage men to tempt their friends into crime and then betray them, but this seems to have happened in more than one instance. I am telling the Senate immediately to execute any person who can be proved to have made a living by such infamous conduct. Perhaps now you'll take something?'

When Nerva thanked him and praised his decision but said that he had still no appetite at all, Tiberius became most depressed. 'You'll die if you don't eat, Nerva, and then what will I do? You know how much I value your friendship and your political advice. Please, please eat, I beseech you. If you were to die the world would think that it was my doing, or at least that you were starving yourself out of hatred for me. Oh, don't die, Nerva! You're my only real friend left.'

Nerva said: 'It's no use asking me to eat, Caesar. My stomach would refuse anything I gave it. And surely nobody could possibly say such ill-natured things as you suggest? They know what a wise ruler and kind-hearted man you are and I am sure they have no reason for supposing me ungrateful, have they? If I must die, I must die, and that's all there is to it. Death is the common fate of all and at least I shall have the satisfaction of not out-living you.'

Tiberius was not to be convinced, but soon Nerva was too weak to answer his questions: he died on the ninth day.

Thrasyllus died. His death was announced by a lizard. It was a very small lizard and ran across the stone table where Thrasyllus was at breakfast with Tiberius in the sun and straddled across his forefinger. Thrasyllus asked, 'You have come to summon me, brother? I expected you at this very hour.' A.D. 36 Then, turning to Tiberius, he said: 'My life is at an end, Caesar, so farewell! I never told you a lie. You told me many. But beware when *your* lizard gives you a warning.' He closed his eyes and a few moments later was dead.

Now Tiberius had made a pet of the most extraordinary animal ever seen at Rome. Giraffes excited great admiration when first seen, and so did the rhinoceros, but this, though not so large, was far more fabulous. It came from an island beyond India called Java, and it was like a scaly lizard nine feet long with an ugly head and a long darting tongue. When Tiberius first looked at it he said that he would now no longer be sceptical about the monsters said to have been slain by Hercules and Theseus. It was called the Wingless Dragon and Tiberius fed it himself every day with cockroaches and dead mice and such-like vermin. It had a disgusting smell, dirty habits, and a vicious temper. The dragon and Tiberius understood each other perfectly. He thought that Thrasyllus meant the dragon would bite him one day, so he put it in a cage with bars too small for it to poke its ugly head through.

Tiberius was now seventy-eight years old, and constant use of myrrh and similar aphrodisiacs had made him very feeble; but he dressed sprucely and tried to behave like a man not yet past middle age. He had grown tired of Capri, now that Nerva and Thrasyllus were gone, and early in March the next year determined to defy Fate and visit Rome. He went there by easy stages, his last stopping place being a villa on the Appian A.D. 37 Road, within sight of the City walls. But the day after he arrived there the dragon gave him the prophesied warning. Tiberius went to feed it at noon and found it lying in the cage, dead, and a huge swarm of large black ants running all over it, trying to pull away bits of soft flesh. He took this as a sign that if he went any further towards the City he would die like the dragon and the crowd would tear his body to pieces. So he hurriedly turned back. He caught a chill by travelling in an east wind, which he made worse by attending some Games exhibited by the soldiers of a garrison town through which he passed. A wild boar was released in the arena and he was asked to throw a javelin at it from his box. He threw one and missed, and was annoyed with himself for missing, and called for another. He had always prided himself on his skill with the javelin and did not want the soldiers to think that old age had beaten him. So he got hot and excited, hurling javelin after javelin, trying to hit the boar from an impossible distance, and finally had to stop from exhaustion. The boar was untouched and Tiberius ordered it to be released as a reward for its skill in avoiding his shots.

The chill settled on his liver, but he continued travelling back to Capri. He reached Misenum: it lies at the nearer end of the bay of Naples. The Western fleet has its headquarters here. Tiberius was annoyed to find the sea so rough that he could not cross. He had a splendid villa, however, on the promontory of Misenum – it had once belonged to the famous epicure Lucullus. He moved into it with his train. Caligula had accompanied him and so had Macro, and to show that there was nothing seriously amiss with him Tiberius gave a great banquet to all the local officials. The feasting had gone on for some time when Tiberius's private physician asked permission to leave the table and attend to some medical business: certain herbs, you know, have greater virtue when they are picked at midnight or when the moon is in such and such a position, and Tiberius was accustomed to the physician's rising during the meal to see to things of this sort. He took up Tiberius's hand to kiss it, but held it rather longer than necessary. Tiberius thought, quite rightly, that the physician was feeling his pulse to see how weak he was, so he made him sit down again as a punishment and kept the banquet going all night, just to prove that he wasn't ill. The next day Tiberius was in a state of prostration, and the word went round Misenum, and spread from there to Rome, that he was about to die.

Now, Tiberius had told Macro that he wished evidence of treason found against certain leading senators whom he disliked and had given him orders to secure their conviction by whatever means he pleased. Macro wrote them all down as accomplices in a charge that he was preparing against a woman he had a grudge against, the wife of a former agent of Sejanus: she had repelled his advances. They were all accused of adultery with her and of taking

Tiberius's name in vain. By browbeating freedmen and torturing slaves Macro got the evidence that was needed – freedmen and slaves had by now all lost the tradition of fidelity towards their masters. The trial began. But the friends of the accused noticed that though Macro himself had conducted the examination of witnesses and the torture of slaves, the usual Imperial letter approving his actions was not laid on the table: so they concluded that perhaps Macro had added one or two private enemies of his own to the list given him by Tiberius. The chief victim of these obviously absurd charges was Arruntius, the oldest and most dignified member of the Senate. Augustus, a year before his death, had said that he was the only possible choice for Emperor, failing Tiberius; Tiberius had already once tried to convict him of treason, but unsuccessfully. Old Arruntius was the only remaining link with the Augustan age. On the previous occasion sentiment had been so strong against his accusers, though it was believed that they were acting on Tiberius's instigation, that they were themselves tried, convicted of perjury, and put to death. It was known now that Macro had recently had a dispute with Arruntius about money, so the trial was adjourned until Tiberius should have confirmed Macro's commission. Tiberius neglected to reply to the Senate's enquiry, so Arruntius and the rest had been in prison for some time. At last Tiberius sent the necessary confirmation, and the day for the new trial was fixed. Arruntius had determined to kill himself before the trial came off so that his estate should not be confiscated and his grandchildren pauperized. He was saying goodbye to a few old friends when the news arrived of Tiberius's severe illness. His friends begged him to postpone suicide until the last moment, because if the news was true he had a very good chance of surviving Tiberius and being pardoned by his successor. Arruntius said: 'No, I have lived too long. My life was difficult enough in the days when Tiberius shared his power with Livia. It was well-nigh intolerable when he shared it with Sejanus. But Macro has shown himself more of a villain even than Sejanus and, mark my words, Caligula with his Capri education will make a worse Emperor even than Tiberius. I cannot in my old age become the slave of a new master like him.' He took a penknife and severed an artery of his wrist. Everyone was greatly shocked, for Caligula was a popular hero, and was expected to be a second and better Augustus. Nobody thought of blaming him for his pretended loyalty to Tiberius: he was on the contrary greatly admired for his cleverness in surviving his brothers and for concealing so well what were supposed to be his real feelings.

Meanwhile, Tiberius's pulse nearly stopped and he lapsed into a coma. The physician told Macro that two days more, at the outside, were all that he had to live. So the whole Court was in a great bustle. Macro and Caligula were in perfect accord. Caligula respected Macro's popularity with the Guards, and Macro respected Caligula's popularity with the nation as a whole: each counted on the other's support. Besides, Macro was indebted to Caligula for his rise to power, and Caligula was carrying on an affair with Macro's wife, which Macro had been good enough to overlook. Tiberius had already commented sourly on Macro's cultivation of Caligula, saying, 'You do well to desert the setting for the rising sun.' Macro and Caligula began sending off messages to the commanders of different regiments and armies to tell them that the Emperor was sinking fast and had appointed Caligula as his successor: he had given him his signet ring. It was true that Tiberius in a lucid interval had called for Caligula and drawn the ring off his finger. But he had changed his mind and put the ring back on again and then clasped his hands tightly together as if to prevent anyone from robbing him of it. When he relapsed into unconsciousness and gave no further signs of life Caligula had quietly pulled the ring off and was now strutting about, flashing it in the faces of everyone he met and accepting congratulations and homage.

But Tiberius was not dead yet even now. He groaned, stirred, sat up, and called for his valets. He was weak because of his long fast, but otherwise quite himself. It was a trick that he had played before, to seem dead and then to come to life again. He called once more. Nobody heard him. The valets were all in the buttery, drinking Caligula's health. But soon an enterprising slave happened to come along to see what he could steal from the death-chamber in their absence. The room was dark and Tiberius frightened him nearly out of his senses by suddenly shouting: 'Where in Hell's name are the valets? Didn't they hear me call? I want bread and cheese, an omelette, a couple of beef-cutlets, and a drink of Chian wine *at once*! And a thousand Furies! Who's stolen my ring?' The slave dashed out of the room and nearly ran into Macro, who was passing. 'The Emperor's alive, sir, and calling for food and his ring.' The news ran through the Palace and a ludicrous scene followed. The crowd around Caligula scattered in all directions. Cries went up. 'Thank God, the news was false. Long live Tiberius!' Caligula was in a miserable state of shame and terror. He pulled the ring off his finger and looked around for somewhere to hide it.

Only Macro kept his head. 'It's a nonsensical lie,' he shouted. 'The slave must have lost his wits. Have him crucified, Caesar! We left the old Emperor dead an hour ago.' He whispered something to Caligula, who was seen to nod in grateful relief. Then he hurried into Tiberius's room. Tiberius was on his feet, cursing and groaning and tottering feebly towards the door. Macro picked him up in his arms, threw him back on the bed, and smothered him with a pillow. Caligula was standing by.

So Arruntius's fellow-prisoners were released, though most of them later wished that they had followed Arruntius's example. There were, besides, about fifty men and women who had been accused of treason in a separate batch from this. They had no influence in the Senate, being mostly shopkeepers who had baulked at paying the 'protection money' that Macro's captains now levied on all the City wards. They were tried and condemned and were to be executed on the 16th of March. This was the very day that news came of Tiberius's death, and they and their friends went nearly mad with joy to think that now they would be saved. But Caligula was away at Misenum and could not be appealed to in time, and the prison governor was afraid of losing his job if he took the responsibility of postponing the executions. So they were killed and their bodies thrown on the Stairs in the usual way.

This was the signal for an outburst of popular anger against Tiberius. 'He stings like a dead wasp,' someone shouted. Crowds gathered at the street corners for solemn commination-services under the ward-masters, beseeching Mother Earth and the Judges of the Dead to grant the corpse and the ghost of that monster no rest or peace until the day of universal dissolution. Tiberius's body was brought to Rome under a strong escort of Guards. Caligula walked in the procession as a mourner and the whole countryside came flocking to meet him, not in mourning for Tiberius but in holiday clothes, weeping with gratitude that Heaven had preserved a son of Germanicus to rule over them. Old country women cried out, 'O sweet darling, Caligula! Our chicken! Our baby! Our star!' A few miles from Rome he rode ahead to make preparations for the solemn entry of the corpse into the City. But when he had passed, a big crowd gathered and barricaded the Appian Road with planks and blocks of building-stone. When the outriders of the escort appeared there was booing and groaning and cries of 'Into the Tiber with Tiberius!' 'Throw him down the Stairs!' 'Eternal damnation to Tiberius!' The leader shouted: 'Soldiers, we Romans won't allow that evil corpse into the City. It will bring us bad luck. Take it back to Atella and half-burn it in the amphitheatre there!' Half-burning, I should explain, was the usual fate of paupers and unfortunates, and Atella was a town celebrated for a kind of rough country masque or farce which had been performed there at the harvest festival every year from the very earliest times. Tiberius had a villa at Atella and used to attend the festival nearly every year. He had converted the innocent rural bawdry of the masque into a sophisticated vileness. He made the men of Atella build an amphitheatre to present the revised show, which was produced by himself.

Macro ordered his men to charge the barricade, and a number of citizens were killed and wounded, and three or four soldiers were knocked unconscious with paving-stones. Caligula prevented further disorders and Tiberius's body was duly burned on Mars Field. Caligula spoke the funeral oration. It was a very formal and ironical one and much appreciated because there was a good deal in it about Augustus and Germanicus, but very little about Tiberius.

At a banquet that night Caligula told a story which made the whole company weep and gained him great credit. He said that early one morning at Misenum, being as usual sleepless with grief for the fate of his mother and brothers, he had determined, come what might, to be avenged at last on their murderer. He seized the dagger that had been his father's and went boldly into Tiberius's room. The Emperor lay groaning and tossing in nightmare on his bed. Caligula slowly lifted the dagger to strike but a Divine Voice sounded in his ears: 'Great-grandson, hold your hand! To kill him would be impious.' Caligula answered, 'O God Augustus, he killed my mother and my brothers, your descendants. Should I not avenge them even at the price of being shunned by all men as a parricide?' Augustus answered, 'Magnanimous son, who art to be Emperor hereafter, there is no need to do what you would do.

By My orders the Furies nightly avenge your dear ones, while he dreams.' And so he had laid his dagger on the table beside the bed and walked out. Caligula did not explain what had happened next morning when Tiberius woke and saw the dagger on the table; the presumption was that Tiberius had not dared to mention the incident.

Chapter 29

CALIGULA was twenty-five years old when he became Emperor. Seldom, if ever, in the history of the world has a prince been more enthusiastically acclaimed on his accession or had an easier task offered him of gratifying the modest wishes of his people, which were only for peace and security. With a bulging treasury, well-trained armies, an excellent administrative system that needed only a little care to get it into perfect order again – for in spite of Tiberius's neglect the Empire was still running along fairly well under the impetus given it by Livia – with all these advantages, added to the legacy of love and confidence he enjoyed as Germanicus's son, and the immense relief felt by Tiberius's removal, what a splendid chance he had of being remembered in history as 'Caligula the Good', or 'Caligula the Wise', or 'Caligula the Saviour!' But it is idle to write in this way. For if he had been the sort of man that the people took him for, he would never have survived his brothers or been chosen by Tiberius as his successor. Claudius, remember what scorn old Athenodorus had for such *impossible contingencies*: he used to say, 'If the Wooden Horse of Troy had foaled, horses to-day would cost far less to feed.'

It amused Caligula at first to encourage the absurd misconception that everyone but myself and my mother and Macro and one or two others had of his character, and even to perform a number of acts in keeping with it. He wanted also to make sure of his position. There were two obstacles to his complete freedom of action. One was Macro, whose power made him dangerous. The other was Gemellus. For when Tiberius's will was read (which for secrecy's sake he had had witnessed by a few freedmen and illiterate fishermen) it was found that the old man, just to make trouble, had not appointed Caligula his first heir, with Gemellus as a second choice in case of accidents: he had made them joint-heirs, to rule alternate years. However, Gemellus had not come of age and so was not even allowed yet to enter the Senate, while Caligula was already a magistrate of the second rank, some years before the legal age, and a pontiff. The Senate was therefore very ready to accept Caligula's view that Tiberius had not been of sound mind when he made the will and to give the whole power to Caligula without encumbrance. Except for this matter of Gemellus, from whom he also withheld his share in the Privy Purse, on the ground that the Privy Purse was an integral part of the sovereignty, Caligula observed all the terms of the will and paid every legacy promptly.

The Guards were to receive a bounty of fifty gold pieces a man; Caligula, to ensure their loyalty when the time came for Macro's removal, doubled the amount. He paid the people of Rome the 450,000 gold pieces bequeathed them and added three gold pieces a head; he said that he had intended to give them this when he came of age, but the old Emperor had forbidden it. The armies were awarded the same bounty as under Augustus's will, but this time it was paid promptly. What was more, he paid all the sums owing under Livia's will, which we legatees had long ago written off as bad debts. To me the two most interesting items in Tiberius's will were: the specific bequest to me of the historical books which Pollio had left me but which I had been cheated of, together with a number of other valuable volumes, and the sum of 20,000 gold pieces; and a bequest to the Chief Vestal, the granddaughter of Vipsania, of 100,000 gold pieces to be spent as she pleased, either on herself or on the College. The Chief Vestal, as the granddaughter of the murdered Gallus, melted the coin down and made it into a great golden casket for his ashes.

With these bequests from Livia and Tiberius I was now quite well off. Caligula astonished me by further paying me back the 50,000 that I had found for Germanicus at the time of the mutiny: he had heard the story from his mother. He did not allow me to refuse it and said that if I made any further protest he would insist on paying me the accumulated interest too: it was a debt he owed his father's memory. When I told Calpurnia about my new wealth she seemed more sorry than pleased. 'It won't bring you any luck,' she said. 'Much better be modestly well off, as you have been, than run the risk of having your whole fortune stripped from you by informers on a charge of treason.' Calpurnia was Actë's successor, you remember. She was very shrewd for her years – seventeen.

I said, 'What do you mean, Calpurnia? Informers? There are no such things in Rome now, and no treason-trials.'

She said: 'I didn't hear that the informers were packed off in the same boat with the Spintrians.' (For Tiberius's painted 'orphans' had been banished by Caligula. As a public gesture of pure-mindedness he had sent the whole crew of them off to Sardinia, a most unhealthy island, and told them to labour honestly for their living as road-makers. Some of them just lay down and died when picks and shovels were put into their hands, but the rest were whipped into work, even the daintiest of them. Soon they had a stroke of luck. A pirate vessel made a sudden raid, captured them, and carried them off to Tyre, where they were sold as slaves to rich Eastern profligates.)

'But they wouldn't dare to try their old tricks again, Calpurnia?'

She put down her embroidery. 'Claudius, I'm no politician or scholar, but I can at least use my prostitute's wit and do simple sums. How much money did the old Emperor leave?'

'About twenty-seven million gold pieces. That's a lot of money.'

'And how much has the new one paid out in legacies and bounties?'

'About three million and a half. Yes, at least that amount.'

'And since he has been Emperor how many panthers and bears and lions and tigers and wild bulls and things has he imported for the huntsmen to kill in the amphitheatres and the Circus?'

'About twenty thousand, perhaps. Probably more.'

'And how many other animals have been sacrificed in the temples?'

.'I don't know. I should guess between one and two hundred thousand.'

'Those flamingoes and desert antelopes and zebras and British beavers must have cost him something! So what with buying all those animals and paying the huntsmen in the amphitheatres, and then the sword-fighters, of course – sword-fighters get four times what they got under Augustus, I'm told – and all the State banquets and decorated cars and the theatre shows – they say that when he recalled the actors whom the old Emperor banished he paid them for all the years they were out of work – handsome, eh? – and my goodness, the money he has spent on racehorses! Well, what with one thing and the other he can't have much change left out of twenty million, can he?'

'I think you're right there, Calpurnia.'

'Well, seven million in three months! How is the money going to last at that rate, even if all the rich men who die leave him all their money? The Imperial revenue is less now than it used to be when your old grandmother ran the business and went over the accounts.'

'Perhaps he'll be more economical after the first excitement of having money to spend. He's got a good excuse for spending: he says that the stagnation of money in the Treasury under Tiberius had a most disastrous effect on trade. He wants to put a few million into circulation again.'

'Well, you're better acquainted with him than I am. Perhaps he'll know just when to stop. But if he goes on at this rate he won't have a penny left in a couple of years, and then who's going to pay? That's why I spoke of informers and treason-trials.'

I said: 'Calpurnia. I'm going to buy you a pearl necklace while I still have the money. You're as clever as you are beautiful. And I only hope you are as discreet.'

'I'd prefer cash,' she said, 'if you don't mind.' And I gave her 500 gold pieces the next day. Calpurnia, a prostitute and the daughter of a prostitute, was more intelligent and loyal and kind-hearted and straightforward than any of the four noblewomen I have married. I soon began to take her into my confidence about my private affairs and I may say at once that I never regretted having done so.

The moment that Tiberius's funeral was over, Caligula had taken ship, in spite of very bad weather, to the islands where his mother and his brother Nero had been buried; he gathered up their remains, half-burned, and brought them back, burned them properly, and piously interred them in Augustus's tomb. He instituted a new annual festival, with sword-fighting and horse races, in his mother's memory and annual sacrifices to her ghost and that of his brothers. He called the month of September 'Germanicus', as the previous month had been called after Augustus. He also heaped on my mother by a single decree as many honours as

Livia had been given in her lifetime, and appointed her High-Priestess of Augustus.

He next pronounced a general amnesty, recalling all banished men and women and releasing all political prisoners. He even brought together a large batch of criminal records covering the cases of his mother and brothers and publicly burned them in the Market Place, swearing that he had not read them and that any-one who had acted as informer or contributed in any other way to the deplorable fate of his loved ones need have no fear: all record of those evil days was destroyed. As a matter of fact what he burned were only copies: he kept the originals. He followed Au-gustus's example by making a strict scrutiny of the Orders and re-jecting all unworthy members of either, and Tiberius's example in refusing all titles of honour except those of Emperor and Protec-tor of the People and in forbidding statues of himself to be set up. I wondered how long this mood of his would last, and how long he would keep by the promise he had made to the Senate on the occasion that they had voted him the Imperial power, to share it with them and be their faithful servant.

After six months of his monarchy, in September, the Consuls in office finished their term and he undertook a Consulship for him-self for a while. Whom do you suppose he chose as a colleague? He actually chose me! And I who had twenty-three years before begged Tiberius to be given real honours, not empty ones, would now willingly have resigned my appointment in anyone's favour. It was not that I wanted to go back to my writing (for I had just completed and revised my Etruscan history and had begun on no new work), but that I had quite forgotten all the rules of procedure and legal formulas and precedents that I had once studied so pain-fully, and that I felt thoroughly ill at ease in the Senate. From being so little at Rome, too, I knew nothing about how to pull strings and get things done quickly, or who were the men with real power. I got into great trouble with Caligula almost at once. He entrusted me with the task of having statues made of Nero and Drusus, to be set up and consecrated in the Market Place, and the Greek firm from whom I commissioned them promised faithfully to have them ready on the day fixed for the ceremony early in December. Three days before I went along to see how the statues looked. The rogues hadn't begun on them. They made some ex-cuse about the right coloured marble having only just come in. I flew into a temper (as I often do on occasions of this sort, but my anger doesn't last long) and told them that if they didn't get workmen busy on the blocks and keep them at the job night and day I would have the whole firm – owner, managers, and men – thrown out of the City. Perhaps I made them nervous, because though Nero was done on the afternoon before the ceremony – it was a good likeness too – a careless sculptor somehow broke Drusus's hand off at the wrist. There are ways of repairing a break of this sort, but the join always shows, and I couldn't present Caligula with a botched piece of work on so important an occasion. All that I could do was to go at once and tell him that Drusus wouldn't be ready. Heavens, how angry he was! He threatened to degrade me from my Consulship and wouldn't listen to any explanation. Fortunately he had decided to resign his own Consulship the next day, and ask me to resign mine, in favour of the men who had originally been chosen for it; so nothing came of his threat and I was even chosen again as Consul with him for four years ahead.

I was expected to occupy a suite of rooms at the Palace and because of Caligula's stern speeches against all sorts of immorality (in the manner of Augustus) I could not have Calpurnia there with me, though I was unmarried. She had to remain at Capua, much to my annoyance, and I was only able to get away occasionally to visit her. His own morals seemed not to come into the scope of his strictures. He was growing tired of Macro's wife, Ennia, whom Macro had divorced at his request and whom he had promised to marry, and used to go out at night in search of gallant adventures with a party of jolly fellows whom he called 'The Scouts'. They consisted usually of three young staff-officers, two famous sword-fighters, Apelles the actor, and Eutychus, the best charioteer in Rome, who won nearly every race in which he competed. Caligula had now come out strong as a partisan of the Leek Greens and sent all over the world in search of the fastest horses. He found a religious excuse for public chariot-racing, with twenty heats a day, almost whenever the sun shone. He made a lot of money by challenging rich men to take his bets against the other colours, which for politeness they did. But what he got by this was a mere drop, as the saying is, in the ocean of his expenses. At all events with these jolly 'Scouts' he used to go out at night, disguised, and visit the lowest haunts of the City, usually coming into conflict with the night-watchmen and having riotous escapades which the Commander of the Watchmen was careful to hush up.

Caligula's three sisters, Drusilla, Agrippinilla, and Lesbia, had all been married to noblemen; but he insisted on their coming to the Palace and living there. Agrippinilla and Lesbia were told to bring their husbands with them, but Drusilla had to leave hers behind; his name was Cassius Longinus and he was sent to govern Asia Minor. Caligula demanded that the three of them should be treated with the greatest respect and gave them all the privileges enjoyed by the Vestal Virgins. He had their names joined with his own in the public prayers for his health and safety, and even in the public oath that officials and priests swore in his name on their consecration ... 'neither shall I value my own life or the lives of my children more highly than His life and the lives of His sisters'. He behaved towards them in a way that puzzled people – rather as if they were his wives than his sisters.

Drusilla was his favourite. Although she was well rid of her husband, she always seemed unhappy now, and the unhappier she grew the more solicitous were Caligula's attentions. He now married her, for appearances only, to a cousin of his, Aemilius Lepidus, whom I have already mentioned as a slack-twisted younger brother of that Aemilia, Julilla's daughter, to whom I was nearly married when I was a boy. This Aemilius Lepidus, who was known as Ganymede because of his effeminate appearance and his obsequiousness to Caligula, was a valued member of the Scouts. He was seven years older than Caligula but Caligula treated him like a boy of thirteen, and he seemed to like it. Drusilla could not bear him. But Agrippinilla and Lesbia were always in and out of his bedroom laughing and joking and playing pranks. Their husbands did not seem to mind. Life at the Palace I found extremely disorderly. I don't mean that I wasn't made very comfortable or that the servants were not well trained or that the ordinary formalities and courtesies were not observed towards visitors. But I never quite knew what tender relations existed between this person and that: Agrippinilla and Lesbia seemed to have exchanged husbands at one time, and at another Apelles seemed somehow intimately connected with Lesbia and the charioteer with Agrippinilla. As for Caligula and Ganymede – but I have said enough to show what I mean by 'disorderly'. I was the only one among them past middle-age, and did not understand the ways of the new generation at all. Gemellus also lived in the Palace: he was a frightened, delicate boy who bit his nails to the quick and was usually to be found sitting in a corner and drawing designs of nymphs and satyrs and that sort of thing for vases. I can't tell you much more about Gemellus than that I got into talk with him once or twice, feeling sorry for him because he was not really one of the party, any more than I was; but perhaps he thought that I was trying to draw him out and force him into saying something against Caligula, for he would only answer in monosyllables. On the day that he put on his manly-gown Caligula adopted him as his son and heir, and appointed him Leader of Cadets; but that wasn't the same thing by any means as sharing the monarchy with him.

Caligula fell ill and for a whole month his life was despaired of. The doctors called it brain-fever. The popular consternation at Rome was so great that a crowd of never less than 10,000 people stood day and night around the Palace, waiting A.D. 38 for a favourable bulletin. They kept up a quiet muttering and whispering together; the noise, as it reached my window, was like that of a distant stream running over pebbles. There were a number of most remarkable manifestations of anxiety. Some men even pasted up placards on their house-doors, to say that if Death held his hand and spared the Emperor, they vowed to give him their own lives in compensation. By universal consent all traffic noises and street cries and music ceased within half a mile or more of the Palace. That had never happened before, even during Augustus's illness, the one of which Musa was supposed to have cured him. The bulletin always read: 'No change'.

One evening Drusilla knocked at my door and said, 'Uncle Claudius! The Emperor wants to see you urgently. Come at once. Don't stop for anything.'

'What does he want me for?'

'I don't know. But for Heaven's sake humour him. He's got a sword there. He'll kill you if you don't say what he wants you to say He had the point at my throat this morning. He told me that I didn't love him. I had to swear and swear that I did love him. "Kill me, if you like, my darling," I said. O Uncle Claudius, why was I ever born? He's mad. He always was. But he's worse than mad now. He's possessed.'

I went along to Caligula's bedroom, which was heavily curtained and thickly carpeted. One feeble oil-lamp was burning by the bedside. The air smelt stale. His querulous voice greeted me. 'Late again? I told you to hurry.' He didn't look ill, only unhealthy. Two powerful deaf-mutes with axes stood as guards, one on each side of his bed.

I said, saluting him, 'Oh, how I hurried! If I hadn't had a lame leg I'd have been here almost before I started. What joy to see you alive and to hear your voice again, Caesar! Can I dare to hope that you're better?'

'I have never really been ill. Only resting. And undergoing a metamorphosis. It's the most important religious event in history. No wonder the City keeps so quiet.'

I felt that he expected me to be sympathetic, nevertheless. 'Has the metamorphosis been painful, Emperor? I trust not.'

'As painful as if I were my own mother. I had a very difficult delivery. Mercifully, I have forgotten all about it. Or nearly all. For I was a very precocious child and distinctly remember the midwives' faces of admiration as they washed me after my emergence into this world, and the taste of the wine they put between my lips to refresh me after my struggles.'

'An astounding memory, Emperor. But may I humbly enquire precisely what is the character of this glorious change that has come over you?'

'Isn't it immediately apparent?' he asked angrily.

Drusilla's word 'possessed' and the conversation I had had with my grandmother Livia as she lay dying gave me the clue. I fell on my face and adored him as a God.

After a minute or two I asked from the floor whether I was the first man privileged to worship him. He said that I was and I burst out into gratitude. He was thoughtfully prodding me with the point of his sword in the back of my neck. I thought I was done for.

He said: 'I admit I am still in mortal disguise, so it is not remarkable that you did not notice my Divinity at once.'

'I don't know how I could have been so blind. Your face shines in this dim light like a lamp.'

'Does it?' he asked with interest. 'Get up and give me that mirror.'

I handed him a polished steel mirror and he agreed that it shone very brightly. In this fit of good humour he began to tell me a good deal about himself.

'I always knew that it would happen,' he said. 'I never felt anything but divine. Think of it. At two years old I put down a mutiny of my father's army and so saved Rome. That was prodigious, like the stories told about the God Mercury when a child, or about Hercules, who strangled the snakes in his cradle.'

'And Mercury only stole a few oxen,' I said, 'and twanged a note or two on the lyre. That was nothing by comparison.'

'And what's more, by the age of eight I had killed my father. Jove himself never did that. He merely banished the old fellow.'

I took this as raving on the same level, but I asked in a matter-of-fact voice, 'Why did you do that?'

'He stood in my way. He tried to discipline me – me, a young God, imagine it! So I frightened him to death. I smuggled dead things into our house at Antioch and hid them under loose tiles; and I scrawled charms on the walls; and I got a cock in my bedroom to give him his marching orders. And I robbed him of his Hecate. Look, here she is! I always keep her under my pillow.' He held up the green jasper charm.

My heart went as cold as ice when I recognized it. I said in a horrified voice: '*You* were the one, then? And it was you who climbed into the bolted room by that tiny window and drew your devices there too?'

He nodded proudly and went rattling on: 'Not only did I kill my natural father but I killed my father by adoption too – Tiberius, you know. And whereas Jupiter only lay with one sister of his, Juno, I have lain with all three of mine. Martina told me it was the right thing to do if I wanted to be like Jove.'

'You knew Martina well, then?'

'Indeed I did. When my parents were in Egypt I used to visit her every night. She was a very wise woman. I'll tell you another thing. Drusilla's divine too. I'm going to announce it at the same time as I make the announcement about myself. How I love Drusilla! Almost as much as she loves me.'

'May I ask what are your sacred intentions? This metamorphosis will surely affect Rome profoundly.'

'Certainly. First, I'm going to put the whole world in awe of me. I won't allow myself to be governed by a lot of fussy old men any longer. I'm going to show ... but you remember your old grandmother, Livia? That was a joke. Somehow she had got the notion that it was she who was to be the everlasting God about whom everyone has been prophesying in the East for the last thousand years. I think it was Thrasyllus who tricked her into believing that she was meant. Thrasyllus never told lies but he loved misleading people. You see, Livia didn't know the precise terms of the prophecy. The God is to be a man not a woman, and not born in Rome, though he is to reign at Rome (I was born at Antium), and born at a time of profound peace (as I was), but destined to be the cause of innumerable wars after his death. He is to die young and to be at first loved by his people and then hated, and finally to die miserably, forsaken of all. "His servants shall drink his blood." Then after his death he is to rule over all the other Gods of the world, in lands not yet known to us. That can only be myself. Martina told me that many prodigies had been seen lately in the near East, which proved conclusively that the God had been born at last. The Jews were the most excited. They somehow felt themselves peculiarly concerned. I suppose that this was because I once visited their city Jerusalem with my father and gave my first divine manifestation there.' He paused.

'It would greatly interest me to know about that,' I said.

'Oh, it was nothing much. Just for a joke I went into a house where some of their priests and doctors were talking theology together and suddenly shouted out: "You're a lot of ignorant old frauds. You know nothing at all about it." That caused a great sensation and one old white-bearded man said: "Oh? And who are you, Child? Are you the prophesied one?" "Yes," I answered boldly. He said, weeping for rapture: "Then teach us!" I answered: "Certainly not! It's beneath my dignity," and ran out again. You should have seen their faces! No, Livia was a clever and capable woman in her way – a female Ulysses, as I called her once to her face – and one day perhaps I shall deify her as I promised, but there's no hurry about that. She will never make an important deity. Perhaps we'll make her the patron goddess of clerks and accountants, because she had a good head for figures. Yes, and we'll add poisoners, as Mercury has thieves under his protection as well as merchants and travellers.'

'That's only justice,' I said. 'But what I am anxious to know at once is this: in what name am I to adore you? Is it incorrect, for instance, to call you Jove? Aren't you someone greater than Jove?'

He said: 'Oh, greater than Jove, certainly, but anonymous as yet. For the moment, I think though, I'll call myself Jove – the Latin Jove to distinguish myself from that Greek fellow. I'll have to settle with him one of these days. He's had his own way too long.'

I asked: 'How does it happen that your father wasn't a God too? I never heard of a God without a divine father.'

'That's simple. The God Augustus was my father.'

'But he never adopted you, did he? He only adopted your elder brothers and left you to carry on your father's line.'

'I don't mean that he was my father by adoption. I mean that I am his son by his incest with Julia. I must be. That's the only possible solution. I'm certainly no son of Agrippina: her father was a nobody. It's ridiculous.'

I was not such a fool as to point out that in this case Germanicus wasn't his father and therefore his sisters were only his nieces. I humoured him as Drusilla advised and said: 'This is the most glorious hour of my life. Allow me to retire and sacrifice to you at once, with my remaining strength. The divine air you exhale is too strong for my mortal nostrils. I am nearly fainting.' The room was dreadfully stuffy. Caligula hadn't allowed the windows to be opened ever since he took to his bed.

He said: 'Go in peace. I thought of killing you, but I won't now. Tell the Scouts about my being a God and about my face shining, but don't tell them any more. I impose holy silence on you for the rest.'

I grovelled on the floor again and retired, backwards. Ganymede stopped me in the corridor and asked for the news. I said: 'He's just become a God and a very important one, he says. His face shines.'

'That's bad news for us mortals,' said Ganymede. 'But I saw it coming. Thanks for the tip. I'll pass it on to the other fellows. Does Drusilla know? No? Then I'll tell her.'

'Tell her that she's a Goddess too,' I said, 'in case she hasn't noticed it.'

I went back to my room and thought to myself, 'This has happened for the best. Everyone will soon see that he's mad, and lock him up. And there are no other descendants of Augustus left now of an age to become Emperor, except Ganymede, and he's not got the popularity or the necessary force of character. The Republic will be restored. Caligula's father-in-law is the man for that. He has the most influence of any man in the Senate. I'll back him up. If only we could get rid of Macro, and have a decent commander of the Guards in his place, everything would be easy. The Guards are the greatest obstacle. They know very well that they'd never get bounties of fifty and a hundred gold pieces a man voted them by a Republican Senate. Yes, it was Sejanus's idea of turning them into a sort of private army for my uncle Tiberius that gave monarchy its oriental absoluteness. We ought to break up the Camp and billet the men in private houses again as we used to do.'

But – would you believe it? – Caligula's divinity was accepted by everyone without question. For awhile he was content to let the news of it circulate privately, and to remain officially a mortal still. It would have spoilt his free and easy relations with the Scouts and curtailed most of his pleasure if everyone had had to lie face-down on the floor whenever he appeared. But within ten days of his recovery, which was greeted with inexpressible jubilation, he had taken on himself all the mortal honours that Augustus had accepted in a lifetime and one or two more besides. He was Caesar the Good, Caesar the Father of the Armies, and the Most Gracious and Mighty Caesar, and Father of the Country, a title which Tiberius had steadfastly refused all his life.

Gemellus was the first victim of the terror. Caligula sent for a colonel of the Guards and told him, 'Kill that traitor, my son, at once.' The colonel went straight to Gemellus's rooms and struck his head off. The next victim was Caligula's father-in-law. He was one of the Silanus family – Caligula had married his daughter Junia but she had died in childbirth a year before he became Emperor. Silanus enjoyed the distinction of being the only Senator whom Tiberius had never suspected of disloyalty: Tiberius had always refused to listen to any appeal from his judicial sentences. Caligula now sent him a message, 'By dawn to-morrow you must be dead.' The unfortunate man thereupon said good-bye to his family and cut his throat with a razor. Caligula explained in a letter to the Senate that Gemellus had died a traitor's death: during his own dangerous illness the lad had offered no prayer for his recovery but had tried to ingratiate himself with the officers of the bodyguard. He had moreover taken antidotes against poison whenever he came to dine at the Palace, so his whole person smelt of them. 'But is there any antidote against Caesar?' His father-in-law, Caligula wrote, was another traitor: he had refused to come to sea with him that stormy day when he had sailed to Pandataria and Ponza to collect the remains of his mother and brother, and had stayed behind in the hope of seizing the monarchy if tempests wrecked the ship.

These explanations were accepted by the Senate. The truth of the matter was that Silanus was so bad a sailor that he nearly died of sea-sickness every time he went out in a boat, even in fine weather, and it was Caligula himself who kindly refused his offer to accompany him on that voyage. As for Gemellus he had an obstinate cough and smelt of the medicine that he took to soothe his throat, so as not to be a nuisance at table.

Chapter 30

WHEN my mother heard of Gemellus's murder she was very grieved and came to the Palace asking to see Caligula, who received her sulkily, for he felt that she was about to scold him. She said: 'Grandson, may I speak to you in private? It is about the death of Gemellus.'

'No, certainly not in private,' he answered. 'Say what you wish to say in Macro's presence. I must have a witness by me if what you have to say is as important as all that.'

'Then I prefer to keep silent. It is a family matter, not for the ears of the sons of slaves. That fellow's father was the son of one of my vine-dressers. I sold him to my brother-in-law for forty-five gold pieces.'

'You will please tell me at once what it was you were about to say, without insulting my ministers. Don't you know that I have the power to make anyone in the world do just what I please?'

'It is nothing that you will be glad to hear.'

'Say it.'

'As you wish. I came to say that your killing of my poor Gemellus was wanton murder and I wish to resign all the honours I have had from your wicked hands.'

Caligula laughed and said to Macro: 'I think the best thing that this old lady can do now is to go home and borrow a pruning-knife from one of her vine-dressers and cut her vocal cords with it.'

Macro said: 'I always gave the same sort of advice to *my* grand-mother, but the old witch refused to take it.'

My mother came to see me. 'I am about to kill myself, Claudius,' she said. 'You will find all my affairs in order. There will be a few small debts outstanding: pay them punctually. Be good to my household staff; they have been loyal workers, every one of them. I am sorry that your little daughter will have nobody now to look after her: I think that you had better marry again to give her a mother. She's a good child.'

I said: 'What, Mother! Kill yourself? Why? Oh, don't do that!'

She smiled sourly. 'My life's my own, isn't it? And why should you dissuade me from taking it? Surely you won't miss me, will you?'

'You are my mother,' I said. 'A man has only one mother.'

'I am surprised that you speak so dutifully. I have been no very loving mother to you. How could I have been expected to be so? You were always a great disappointment to me – a sick, feeble, timorous, woolly-witted thing. Well, I have been prettily punished by the Gods for my neglect of you. My splendid son Germanicus murdered, and my poor grandsons Nero and Drusus and Gemellus murdered, and my daughter Livilla punished for her wickedness, her abominable wickedness, by my own hand – that was the worst pain I suffered, no mother ever suffered a worse – and my four granddaughters all gone to the bad, and this filthy, impious Caligula. ... But you'll survive him. You'd survive a Universal Deluge, I believe.' Her voice, calm at first, had risen to its usual angry scolding tone.

I said: 'Mother, have you no kindly word to give me even at a time like this? How did I ever intentionally wrong you or disobey you?'

But she did not seem to hear. 'I have been prettily punished,' she repeated. Then: 'I wish you to come to my house in five hours' time. By that time I shall have completed my arrangements. I count on you to pay me the last rites. I don't want you to catch my dying breath. If I am not dead when you arrive, wait in the ante-room until you get the word from my maid Briseis. Don't make a muddle of the valedictory: that would be just like you. You will find full instructions written out for the funeral. You are to be chief mourner. I want no funeral oration. Remember to cut off my hand for separate burial: because this will be a suicide. I want no perfumes on the pyre; it's often done but it's strictly against the law and I have always regarded it as a most *wasteful* practice. I am giving Pallas his freedom, so he'll wear the cap of liberty in the procession, don't forget. And just for once in your life try to carry one ceremony through without a mistake.' That was all, except a formal 'Good-bye.' No kiss, no tears, no blessing. As a dutiful son I carried out her last wishes, to the letter. It was odd her giving my own slave Pallas his freedom. She did the same with Briseis.

Watching her pyre burning, from his dining-room window, a few days later, Caligula said to Macro: 'You stood by me well against that old woman. I'm going to reward you. I'm going to give you the most honourable appointment in the whole Empire. It's an appointment which, as Augustus laid down as a principle of State, must never fall into the hands of an adventurer. I am going to make you Governor of Egypt.' Macro was delighted: he did not quite know, these days, how he stood with Caligula, and if he went to Egypt he would be safe. As Caligula had said, the appointment was an important one: the Governor of Egypt had the power of starving Rome by cutting off the corn-supply, and the garrison could be strengthened by local levies until it was big enough to hold the province against any invading army that could be brought against it.

So Macro was relieved of his command of the Guards. Caligula appointed nobody in his place for a time, but let the nine colonels of battalions each command for a month in turn. He gave out that at the end of this time the most loyal and efficient of them would be given the appointment permanently. But the man to whom he secretly promised it was the colonel of the battalion which found the Palace Guard – none other than the same brave Cassius Chaerea whose name you cannot have forgotten if you have read this story with any attention – the man who killed the German in the amphitheatre, the man who led his company back from the massacre of Varus's army, and who afterwards saved the bridgehead; the man too who cut his way through the mutineers in the camp at Bonn and who carried Caligula on his back that early morning when Agrippina and her friends had to trudge on foot from the camp under his protection. Cassius was white-haired now, though not yet sixty years of age, and stooped a little, and his hands trembled because of a fever that had nearly killed him in Germany, but he was still a fine swordsman and reputedly the bravest man in Rome. One day an old soldier of the Guards went mad and ran amok with his spear in the courtyard of the Palace. He thought he was killing French rebels. Everyone fled but Cassius, who though unarmed stood his ground until the madman charged him, when he calmly gave the parade-ground order, 'Company, halt! Ground arms!' and the crazy fellow, to whom obedience to orders had become second nature, halted and laid his spear flat along the ground. 'Company about turn,' Cassius ordered again. 'Quick march!' So he disarmed him. Cassius, then, was the first temporary commander of the Guards and kept them in order while Macro was being tried for his life.

For Macro's appointment to the governorship of Egypt was only a trick of Caligula's, the same sort of trick that Tiberius had played on Sejanus. Macro was arrested as he went aboard his ship at Ostia and brought back to Rome in chains. He was accused of having brought about the deaths of Arruntius and several other innocent men and women. To this charge Caligula added another, namely that Macro had played the pander, trying to make him fall in love with his wife Ennia – a temptation to which in his youthful inexperience, he admitted, he had nearly succumbed. Macro and Ennia were both forced to kill themselves. I was surprised how easily he got rid of Macro.

One day Caligula as High Pontiff went to solemnize a marriage between one of the Piso family and a woman called Orestilla. He took a fancy to Orestilla, and when the ceremony was completed and most of the high nobility of Rome were gathered at the wedding feast, having great fun, as one does on these occasions, he suddenly called out to the bridegroom: 'Hey, there, Sir, stop kissing that woman! She's my wife.' He then rose and, in the hush of surprise that followed, ordered the guards to seize Orestilla and carry her off to the Palace. Nobody dared to protest. The next day he married Orestilla: her husband was forced to attend the ceremony and give her away. He sent a letter to the Senate to inform them that he had celebrated a marriage in the style of Romulus and Augustus – referring, I suppose, to Romulus's rape of the Sabine women and Augustus's marriage with my grandmother (when my grandfather was present). Within two months he had divorced Orestilla and banished her, and her former husband too, on the grounds that they had been committing adultery when his back was turned. She was sent to Spain and he to Rhodes. He was only allowed to take ten slaves with him: when he asked as a favour to be allowed double that number Caligula said: 'As many as you like, but for every extra slave you take you'll have to have an extra soldier to guard you.'

Drusilla died. I am certain in my own mind that Caligula killed her, but I have no proof. Whenever he kissed a woman now, I am told, he used to say: 'As white and lovely a neck as this is, I have only to give the word, and slash! it will be cut clean through.' If the neck was particularly white and lovely he could sometimes not resist the temptation of giving the word and seeing his boast proved true. In the case of Drusilla I think that he struck the blow himself. At all events nobody was allowed to see her corpse. He gave out that she died of a consumption and gave her a most extraordinarily rich funeral. She was deified under the name of Panthea and had temples built to her, and noblemen and noble-women appointed her priests, and a great annual festival insti-tuted in her honour, more splendid than any other in the Calen-dar. A man earned 10,000 gold pieces for seeing her spirit being received into Heaven by Augustus. During the days of public mourning that Caligula ordered in her honour, it was a capital crime for any citizen to laugh, sing, shave, go to the baths, or even have dinner with his family. The law-courts were closed, no marriages were celebrated, no troops performed military exer-cises. Caligula had one man put to death for selling hot water in the streets, and another for exposing razors for sale. The resulting gloom was so profound and widespread that he could not himself bear it (or it may have been remorse), so one night he left the City and travelled down towards Syracuse, alone except for a guard of honour. He had no business there, but the journey was a distrac-tion. He got no further than Messina, where Etna happened to be in slight eruption. The sight frightened him so much that he turned back at once. When he reached Rome again he soon set things going as usual, particularly sword-fighting, chariot-racing, and wild-beast hunting. He suddenly remembered that the men who had vowed their lives in exchange for his during his illness had not yet committed suicide; and made them do it, not only on general principles to keep them from the sin of perjury, but more particularly to prevent Death from going back on the bargain they had struck with him.

A few days later at supper I happened to be laying down the law, rather drunkenly, about the inheritance of female beauty, and quoting examples of my contention that it usually missed a generation, going from the grandmother to the granddaughter. Unfortunately I wound up by saying, 'The most beautiful woman in Rome when I was a boy has reappeared, feature for feature, and limb for limb, in the person of her granddaughter and namesake Lollia, the wife of the present Governor of Greece. With the sole exception of a certain lady whom I shall not name, because she is present in this room, Lollia is in my opinion the most beautiful woman alive to-day.' I made this exception merely for tactfulness. Lollia was far and away more beautiful than my nieces, Agrippinilla or Lesbia, or than any other member of the company. I was not in love with her, I may say: I had merely noticed one day that she was perfect, and remembered having made exactly the same observation about her grandmother when I was a boy. Caligula grew interested and questioned me about Lollia. I did not realize that I had said too much, and said more. That evening Caligula wrote to Lollia's husband telling him to return to Rome and accept a signal honour. The signal honour turned out to be that of divorcing Lollia and marrying her to the Emperor.

Another chance remark that I made at supper about this time had an unexpected effect on Caligula. Someone mentioned epilepsy and I said that Carthaginian records showed Hannibal to have been an epileptic, and that Alexander and Julius Caesar were both subject to this mysterious disease, which seemed to be an almost inevitable accompaniment of superlative military genius. Caligula pricked up his ears at this, and a few days later he gave a very good imitation of an epileptic fit, falling on the floor in the Senate House and screaming at the top of his voice, his lips white with foam – soap-suds, probably.

The people of Rome were still happy enough. Caligula continued giving them a good time with theatrical shows and swordfights and wild-beast hunts and chariot-races and largesse thrown from the Oration Platform or from the upper windows of the Palace. What marriages he contracted or dissolved, or what courtiers he murdered, they did not much care. He was never satisfied unless every seat in the theatre or Circus was occupied and all the gangways crowded; so whenever there was a performance he postponed all lawsuits and suspended all mourning to give nobody any excuse for not attending. He made several other innovations. He allowed people to bring cushions to sit on, and in hot weather to wear straw hats, and to come barefooted – even senators, who were supposed to set an example of austerity.

When I eventually managed to visit Capua for a few days, for the first time for nearly a year, almost the first thing Calpurnia asked me was: 'How much is left in the Privy Purse, Claudius, of that twenty million?'

'Less than five million, I believe. But he's been building pleasure-barges of cedar-wood and overlaying them with gold and studding them with jewels and putting baths and flower-gardens in them, and he's started work on sixty new temples and talks of cutting a canal across the isthmus of Corinth. He takes baths in spikenard and oil of violet. Two days ago he gave Eutychus, the Leek Green charioteer, a present of twenty thousand in gold for winning a close race.'

'Does Leek Green always win?'

'Always. Or almost always. Scarlet happened to come in first the other day and the people gave it a big cheer. They were tiring of the monotony of Leek Green. The Emperor was furious. Next day the Scarlet charioteer and his winning team were all dead. Poisoned. The same sort of thing has happened before.'

'By this time next year things will be going badly with you, my poor Claudius. By the way, would you like to look at your accounts? It's been an unlucky year, as I wrote to you. Those valuable cattle dying, and the slaves stealing right and left, and the corn-ricks burned. You're the poorer by two thousand or more gold pieces. It's not the steward's fault, either. He does his best and at least he's honest. It's because you are not here to act as overseer that these things happen.'

'It can't be helped,' I said. 'To be frank, I am more anxious about my life than about money these days.'

'Are you badly treated?'

'Yes. They make a fool of me all the time. I don't like it. The Emperor is my chief tormentor.'

'What do they do to you?'

'Oh, practical jokes. Booby traps with buckets of water suspended over doors. And frogs in my bed. Or nasty pathics smelling of myrrh: you know how I loathe frogs and pathics. If I happen to take a nap after my dinner they flip date-stones at me or tie shoes on my hands or ring the fire-bell in my ears. And I never get time to do any work. If I ever start they upset my inkpot all over it. And nothing that I say is ever treated seriously.'

'Are you the only butt they have?'

'The favourite one. The official one.'

'Claudius, you're luckier than you realize. Guard your appointment jealously. Don't let anyone usurp it.'

'What do you mean, girl?'

'I mean that people don't kill their butts. They are cruel to them, they frighten them, they rob them, but they don't kill them.'

I said: 'Calpurnia, you are very clever. Listen to me now. I still have money. I shall buy you a beautiful silk dress and a gold cosmetic box and a marmoset and a parcel of cinnamon sticks.'

She smiled. 'I should prefer the present in cash. How much were you going to spend?'

'About seven hundred.'

'Good. It will come in handy one of these days. Thank you, kind Claudius.'

When I returned to Rome I heard that there had been trouble. Caligula had been disturbed one night by the distant noise of the people crowding to the amphitheatre just before dawn, and pushing and struggling to get near the gates, so that when these opened they could get into the front rows of the free seats. Caligula sent a company of Guards with truncheons to restore order. The Guards were ill-tempered at being pulled from their beds for this duty and struck out right and left, killing a number of people, including some quite substantial citizens. To show his displeasure at having had his sleep disturbed by the original commotion and by the far louder noise that the people made when they scattered screaming before the truncheon-charge, Caligula did not appear in the amphitheatre until well on in the afternoon when everyone was worn out by waiting for him, and hungry too. When the Leek Greens gave an equestrian display they were hissed and booed. Caligula leaped angrily from his seat: 'I wish you had only a single neck. I'd hack it through!'

The next day there was to be a sword-fight and a wild-beast hunt. Caligula cancelled all the arrangements that had been made and sent in the most wretched set of animals that he could buy up in the wholesale market – mangy lions and panthers and sick bears and old worn-out wild bulls, the sort that are sent to out-of-the-way garrison towns in the provinces where audiences are not particular and amateur huntsmen don't welcome animals of too good quality. The huntsmen whom Caligula substituted for the performers advertised to appear were in keeping with the animals: fat, stiff-jointed, wheezy veterans. Some of them had perhaps been good men in their day – back in Augustus's golden age. The crowd jeered and booed them. This was what Caligula had been waiting for. He sent his officers to arrest the men who were making most noise and put them into the arena to see if they would do any better. The mangy lions and panthers and sick bears and worn-out bulls made short work of them.

He was beginning to be unpopular. That the crowd always likes a holiday is a common saying, but when the whole year becomes one long holiday, and nobody has time for attending to his business, and pleasure becomes compulsory, then it is a different matter. Chariot-races grew wearisome. It was all very well for Caligula, who had a personal interest in the teams and drivers and even used sometimes to drive a car himself. He was not a bad hand with the reins and whip and the competing charioteers took care not to win from him. Theatrical shows grew rather wearisome too. All theatre-pieces are much the same except to connoisseurs: or they are to me at all events. Caligula fancied himself a connoisseur and was also sentimentally attached to Apelles, the Philistine tragic actor, who wrote many of the pieces in which he played. One piece which Caligula admired particuarly – because he had made suggestions which Apelles had incorporated in his part – was played over and over again until everyone hated the sight and sound of it. He had an even stronger liking for Mnester, the principal dancer of the mythological ballets then in fashion. He used to kiss Mnester in full view of the audience whenever he had done anything particularly well. A knight began coughing once during a performance, couldn't stop, and at last had to leave. The noise he made by squeezing along past people's knees, and apologizing and coughing and pushing his way through the crowded aisles to the exit disturbed Mnester, who stopped in the middle of one of his most exquisite dances to soft flute-music and waited for everyone to settle down again. Caligula was furious with the knight, had him brought before him and gave him a good beating with his own hands. Then he sent him off post-haste on a journey to Tangier, with a sealed message for the King of Morocco. (The King, a relative of mine – his mother was my Aunt Selene, Antony's daughter by Cleopatra – was greatly mystified by the message. It read: 'Kindly send bearer back to Rome.') The other knights resented this incident very much: Mnester was only a freedman and gave himself airs like a triumphant general. Caligula took private lessons in elocution and dancing from Apelles and Mnester and after a time frequently appeared on the stage in their parts. After delivering a speech in some tragedy, he used sometimes to turn and shout to Apelles in the wings: 'That was perfect, wasn't it? You couldn't have done better yourself.' And after a graceful hop, skip, and jump or two in the ballet he would stop the orchestra, hold up his hand for absolute silence, and then go through the movement again unaccompanied.

As Tiberius had a pet dragon, so Caligula had a favourite stallion. This horse's original stable name was Porcellus (meaning 'little pig') but Caligula did not consider that grand enough and renamed him 'Incitatus', which means 'swift-speeding'. Incitatus never lost a race and Caligula was so extravagantly fond of him that he made him first a citizen and then a senator and at last put him on the list of his nominees for the Consulship four years in advance. Incitatus was given a house and servants. He had a marble bedroom with a big straw mat for a bed, a new one every day, also an ivory manger, a gold bucket to drink from, and pictures by famous artists on the walls. He used to be invited to dinner with us whenever he won a race, but preferred a bowl of barley to the meat and fish that Caligula always offered him. We had to drink his health twenty times over.

The money went faster and faster and at last Caligula decided to make economies. He said one day, for instance, 'What is the use of putting men in prison for forgery and theft and breaches of the peace? They don't enjoy themselves there and they are a great expense for me to feed and guard; yet if I were to let them go they would only start their career of crime again. I'll visit the prisons to-day and look into the matter.' He did. He weeded out the men whom he considered the most hardened criminals, and had them executed. Their bodies were cut up and used as meat for the wild beasts waiting to be killed in the amphitheatre: which made it a double economy. Every month now he made his round of the prisons. Crime decreased slightly. One day his Treasurer, Callistus, reported only a million gold pieces left in the Treasury and only half a million in the Privy Purse. He realized that economy was not enough: revenue had to be increased. So first he began selling priesthoods and magistracies and monopolies, and that brought him in a great deal, but not enough; and then, as Calpurnia had foreseen, he began using informers to convict rich men of real or imaginary crimes, in order to get their estates. He had abolished the capital charge for treason as soon as he became Emperor, but there were plenty of other crimes punishable with death.

He celebrated his first batch of convictions with a particularly splendid wild-beast hunt. But the crowd was in an ugly temper. They booed and groaned and refused to pay any attention to the proceedings. Then a cry began at the other end of the amphitheatre from the President's Box where Caligula sat: 'Give up the informers! Give up the informers!' Caligula rose to command silence, but they howled him down. He sent Guards with truncheons along to the part where noise was loudest and they whacked a few men on the head, but it began again more violently elsewhere. Caligula grew alarmed. He hurriedly left the amphitheatre, calling on me to take on the presidency from him. I did not welcome this at all and was much relieved, when I rose to speak, that the crowd gave me a courteous hearing and even shouted 'Feliciter' which means 'Good luck to you!' My voice is not strong. Caligula's was very strong: he could make himself heard from one end of Mars Field to the other. I had to find someone to repeat my speech after me. Mnester volunteered, and made it sound much better than it was.

I announced that the Emperor had unfortunately been called away on important State business. That made everyone laugh; Mnester did some beautiful gestures illustrative of the importance and urgency of this State business. Then I said that the President's duties had devolved on my unfortunate and unworthy self. Mnester's hopeless shrug and the little twiddle with a forefinger at his temples expressed this excellently. Then I said: 'Let us go on with the Games, my friends.' But at once the shout rose again, 'Give up the informers!' But I asked, and Mnester repeated the question willingly: 'And if the Emperor does consent to give them up, what then? Will someone inform against them?' There was no answer to this but a confused buzzing. I asked them a further question. I asked them which was the worst sort of criminal – an informer? or an informer against an informer? or an informer against an informer against an informer? I said that the further you took the offence the more heinous it became, and the more people it polluted. The best policy was to do nothing which might give informers any ground for action. If everyone, I said, lived a life of the strictest virtue, the cursed breed would die out for want of nourishment, like mice in a miser's kitchen. You would never believe what a tempest of laughter this sally provoked. The simpler and sillier the joke, the better a big crowd likes it. (The greatest applause I ever won for a joke was once in the Circus when I happened to be presiding in Caligula's absence. The people called out angrily for a sword-fighter called Pigeon who was advertised to perform but had not turned up, so I said, 'Patience, friends! First catch your Pigeon and then pluck him!' Whereas really witty jokes of mine have been quite lost on them.)

'Let's get on with the Games, my friends,' I repeated, and this time the shouting stopped. The Games turned out very good ones. Two sword-fighters killed each other, with simultaneous thrusts in the belly: this is a very rare happening. I ordered the weapons to be brought to me and had little knives made of them; such little knives are the most effective charms known for use in cases of epilepsy. Caligula would appreciate the gift – if he forgave me for quieting the crowd where he had failed. For he had been in such a fright that he had driven out of Rome at full speed in the direction of Antium; and did not reappear for several days.

It turned out all right. He was pleased with the little knives, which gave him an opportunity of enlarging on the splendour of his disease; and when he asked what had happened at the amphitheatre I said that I had warned the crowd of what he would do if they did not repent of their disloyalty and ingratitude. I said that they had then changed their rebellious cries into howls of guilty fear and pleas for forgiveness. 'Yes,' he said, 'I was too gentle with them. I am determined now not to yield an inch. "Immovable rigour" is the watchword from henceforward.' And to keep himself reminded of this decision, he used every morning now to practise frightful faces before a mirror in his bedroom and terrible shouts in his private bathroom, which had a fine echo.

I asked him: 'Why don't you publicly announce your God-head? That would awe them as nothing else would!'

He answered: 'I have still a few acts to perform in my human disguise.'

The first of these acts was to order harbourmasters throughout Italy and Sicily to detain all vessels that were over a certain tonnage, put their cargoes in bond, and send them empty under the convoy of warships to the Bay of Naples. Nobody understood what this order meant. It was supposed that he contemplated an invasion of Britain and wanted the vessels for use as transports. But nothing of the sort. He was merely about to justify Thrasyllus's statement that he could no more become Emperor than ride a horse across the Bay of Baiae. He collected about 4,000 vessels, including 1,000 built especially for the occasion, and anchored them across the bay, thwart to thwart in a double line from the docks of Puteoli to his villa at Bauli. The prows were outward, and the sterns interlocked. The sterns stuck up too high for his purpose, so he had them trimmed flat, sawing off the helmsman's seat and the figurehead from every one; which made the crews very unhappy, because the figurehead was the guardian deity of the ship. Then he boarded the double line across and threw earth on the boards and had the earth watered and rammed flat; and the result was a broad firm road, some 6,000 paces long from end to end. When more ships arrived, just back from voyages to the East, he lashed them together into five islands which he linked to the road, one at every 1,000 paces. He had a row of shops built all the way across and ordered the ward-masters of Rome to have them stocked and staffed within ten days. He installed a drinking-water system and planted gardens. The islands he made into villages.

Fortunately the weather was fine throughout these preparations and the sea glassy smooth. When everything was ready he put on the breastplate of Alexander (Augustus was unworthy to use Alexander's ring, but Caligula wore his very breastplate) and over it a purple silk cloak stiff with jewel-encrusted gold embroidery; then he took Julius Caesar's sword and the reputed battle-axe of Romulus and the reputed shield of Aeneas which were stored in the Capitol (both forgeries in my opinion, but such early forgeries as to be practically genuine) and crowned himself with a garland of oak-leaves. After a propitiatory sacrifice to Neptune – a seal, because that is an amphibious beast – and another, a peacock, to Envy, in case, as he said, any God should be jealous of him, he mounted on Incitatus and began trotting across the bridge from the Bauli end. The whole of the Guards cavalry was at his back, and behind that a great force of cavalry brought from France, followed by 20,000 infantry. When he reached the last island, close to Puteoli, he made his trumpeters blow the charge and dashed into the city as fiercely as if he were pursuing a beaten enemy.

He remained in Puteoli that night and most of the next day, as if resting from battle. In the evening he returned in a triumphal chariot with gold-plated wheels and sides. Incitatus and the mare Penelope to whom Caligula had ritually married him were in the shafts. Caligula was wearing the same splendid clothes as before, except that he had a garland of bay-leaves instead of oak-leaves. A long wagon-train followed heaped high with what were supposed to be battle-spoils – furniture and statues and ornaments robbed from the houses of rich Puteoli merchants. For prisoners he used the hostages which the petty kings of the East were required to send to Rome as earnest of good behaviour and whatever foreign slaves he could lay his hands upon, dressed in their national costumes and loaded with chains. His friends followed in decorated chariots, wearing embroidered gowns and chanting his praises. Then came the army, and last a procession of about 200,000 people in holiday dress. Countless bonfires were alight on the whole circle of hills around the bay and every soldier and citizen in the procession carried a torch. It was the most impressive theatrical spectacle, I should think, that the world has ever seen, and I am sure it was the most pointless. But how everybody enjoyed it! A pine-wood went on fire at Cape Misenum to the southwest and blazed magnificently. As soon as Caligula reached Bauli again he dismounted and called for his gold-pronged trident and his other purple cloak worked over with silver fish and dolphins. With these he entered the biggest of his five cedar-built pleasure-barges which were waiting on the shore-side of the bridge, and was rowed out in it to the middle island of the five, which was by far the biggest, followed by most of his troops in war-vessels.

Here he disembarked, mounted a silk-hung platform and harangued the crowds as they passed along the bridge. There were watchmen to keep them on the move, so nobody heard more than a few sentences, except his friends around the platform – among whom I found myself – and the soldiers in the nearest war-vessels, who had not been permitted to land. Among other things, he called Neptune a coward for allowing himself to be put in fetters without a struggle, and promised, one day soon, to teach the old God an even sharper lesson. (He seemed to forget the propitiatory sacrifice he had made.) As for the Emperor Xerxes who had once bridged the Hellespont in the course of his unlucky expedition against Greece, Caligula laughed at him like anything. He said that Xerxes's famous bridge had been only half the length of the present one and not nearly so solid. Then he announced that he was about to give every soldier two gold pieces to drink his health with, and every member of the crowd five silver pieces.

The cheering lasted for half an hour; which seemed to satisfy him. He stopped it and had the money paid out on the spot. The whole procession had to file past again and bag after bag of coin was brought up and emptied. After a couple of hours the money-supply failed and Caligula told the disappointed late-comers to revenge themselves on the greedy first-comers. This, of course, started a free fight.

There followed one of the most remarkable nights of drinking and singing and horse-play and violence and merry-making that was ever known. The effect of drink on Caligula was always to make him a little mischievous. At the head of the Scouts and the German bodyguard he charged about the island and along the line of shops, pushing people into the sea. The water was so calm that it was only the dead-drunk, the decrepit, the aged, and little children who failed to save themselves. Not more than 200 or 300 were drowned.

About midnight he made a naval attack on one of the smaller islands, breaking the bridge on either side of it and then ramming ship after ship of the island until the inhabitants whom he had cut off were crowded together in a very small space in the middle. The finsl assault was reserved for Caligula's flag-ship. He stood waving his trident in the forecastle top, swept down on the terrified survivors, and sent them all under. Among the victims of this sea-battle was the most remarkable exhibit of Caligula's triumphal procession – Eleazar, the Parthian hostage, who was the tallest man in the world. He was over eleven foot high. He was not, however, strong in proportion to his height: he had a voice like the bleat of a camel and a weak back, and was considered to be of feeble intellect. He was a Jew by birth. Caligula had the body stuffed and dressed in armour and put Eleazar outside the door of his bed-chamber to frighten away would-be assassins.

Chapter 31

THE expense of this two days' entertainment drained the Treasury and the Privy Purse completely dry. To make things worse Caligula, instead of returning the vessels to their masters and crew, ordered the breach in the bridge to be repaired and then, riding back to Rome, busied himself with other affairs. Neptune, to prove himself no coward, sent a heavy storm at the bridge from the west and sank about 1,000 ships. Most of the rest dragged their anchors and were driven ashore. About 2,000 rode the storm or were hauled in on the beach for safety, but the loss of the rest caused a great shortage of ships for the carriage of corn from Egypt and Africa, and so a serious food-shortage in the City. Caligula swore to be revenged on Neptune. His new ways of raising money were most ingenious and amused all but the victims and their friends or dependants. For instance, any young men whom he put so deeply in his debt by fines or confiscations that they became his slaves he sent to the sword-fighting schools. When they were trained he put them into the amphitheatre to fight for their lives. His only expense in this was their board and lodgings: being his slaves they were given no payment. If they were killed, there was an end of them. If they were victorious he auctioned them off to the magistrates whose duty it was to give similar contests – lots were drawn for this distinction – and to anyone else who cared to bid. He ran up the prices to an absurd height by pretending that people had made bids when they had done no more than scratch their heads or rub their noses. My nervous toss of the head got me into great trouble: I was saddled with three sword-fighters at an average of 2,000 gold pieces each. But I was luckier than a magistrate called Aponius who fell asleep during the auction. Caligula sold him sword-fighters whom nobody else seemed to fancy, raising the bid every time his head nodded on his breast: when he woke up he found that he had no less than 90,000 gold pieces to pay for thirteen sword-fighters whom he did not in the least want. One of the sword-fighters I had bought was a very good performer, but Caligula betted against him heavily with me. When the day came for him to fight he could hardly stand and was easily beaten. It appears that Caligula had drugged his food. Many rich men came to these auctions and willingly bid large sums, not because they wanted sword-fighters but because if they loosened their purse-strings now Caligula would be less likely to bring some charge against them later and rob them of their lives as well as of their money.

An amusing thing happened on the day that my sword-fighter was beaten. Caligula had betted heavily with me against five net-and-trident men who were matched against an equal number of chasers armed with sword and shield. I was resigned to losing the 1,000 gold pieces that he had made me bet against 5,000 of his own; for as soon as the fight began I could see that the net-men had been bribed to give the fight away. I was sitting next to Caligula and said: 'Well, you seem likely to win, but it's my opinion that those net-men aren't doing their best.' One by one the chasers rounded up the net-men, who surrendered, and finally all five were lying with their faces in the sand and each with a chaser standing over him with a raised sword. The audience turned their thumbs downwards as a signal that they should be killed. Caligula, as the President, had a right to take this advice or not, as he pleased. He took it. 'Kill them!' he shouted. 'They didn't try to win!' This was hard luck on the net-men, to whom he had secretly promised their lives if they allowed themselves to be beaten; for I wasn't by any means the only man who had been forced to bet on them – he stood to win 80,000 if they lost. Well, one of them felt so sore at being cheated that he suddenly grappled with his chaser, overturned him and managed to pick up a trident, which was lying not far off, and a net, and dash away. You wouldn't believe it, but I won my 5,000 after all! First that angry net-man killed two chasers who had their backs to him, and were busy acknowledging the cheers of the audience after dispatching their victims, and then he killed the other three, one by one, as they came running at him, each a few paces behind the other. Caligula wept for vexation and exclaimed, 'Oh, the monster! Look, he's killed five promising young swordsmen with that horrible trout-spear of his!' When I say that I won my 5,000, I mean that I would have won it if I hadn't been tactful enough to call the bet off. 'For one man to kill five isn't fair fighting,' I said.

Up to this time Caligula had always spoken of Tiberius as a thorough scoundrel and encouraged everyone else to do the same. But one day he entered the Senate and delivered a long eulogy on him, saying that he had been a much misunderstood man and that nobody must speak a word against him. 'In my capacity as Emperor I have the right to criticize him if I please, but you have no right. In fact you are guilty of treason. The other day a senator said in a speech that my brothers Nero and Drusus were murdered by Tiberius after having been imprisoned on false charges. What an amazing thing to say!' Then he produced the records which he had pretended to burn, and read lengthy extracts. He showed that the Senate had not questioned the evidence collected against his brothers by Tiberius, but had unanimously voted for them to be handed over to him for punishment. Some had even volunteered testimony against them. Caligula said: 'If you knew that the evidence which Tiberius laid before you (in all good faith) was false, then you are the murderers, not he; and it is only since he has been dead that you have dared to blame your cruelty and treachery on him. Or if you thought at the time that the evidence was true, then he was no murderer and you are treasonably defaming his character. Or if you thought that it was false and that he knew it was false, then you were as guilty of murder as he was, and cowards too.' He frowned heavily in imitation of Tiberius and made Tiberius's sharp chopping motion of the hand, which brought back frightening memories of treason-trials, and said in Tiberius's harsh voice, 'Well spoken, my Son! You can't trust any one of these curs farther than you can kick him. Look what a little God they made of Sejanus before they turned and tore him to pieces! They'll do the same to you if they get half a chance. They all hate you and pray for your death. My advice to you is, consult no interest but your own and put pleasure before everything. Nobody likes being ruled over, and the only way that I kept my place was by making this trash afraid of me. Do the same. The worse you treat them, the more they'll honour you.'

Caligula then reintroduced treason as a capital crime, ordered his speech to be at once engraved on a bronze tablet and posted on the wall of the House above the seats of the Consuls, and rushed away. No more business was transacted that day: we were all too dejected. But the next day we lavished praise on Caligula as a sincere and pious ruler and voted annual sacrifices to his Clemency. What else could we do? He had the Army at his back, and power of life and death over us, and until someone was bold and clever enough to make a successful conspiracy against his life all that we could do was to humour him and hope for the best. At a banquet a few nights later he suddenly burst into a most extraordinary howl of laughter. Nobody knew what the joke was. The two Consuls, who sat next to him, asked whether they might be graciously permitted to share in it. At this Caligula laughed even louder, the tears starting from his eyes. 'No,' he choked, 'that's just the point. It's a joke that you wouldn't think at all funny. I was laughing to think that with one nod of my head I could have both your throats cut on the spot.'

Charges of treason were now brought against the twenty reputedly wealthiest men in Rome. They were given no chance of committing suicide before trial and all condemned to death. One of them, a senior magistrate, proved to have been quite poor. Caligula said: 'The idiot! Why did he pretend to have money? I was quite taken in. He need not have died at all.' I can only remember a single man who escaped with his life from a charge of treason. That was Afer, the man who had prosecuted my cousin Pulchra, a lawyer famous for his eloquence. His crime was having put an inscription on a statue of Caligula in the hall of his house, to the effect that the Emperor in his twenty-seventh year was already Consul for the second time. Caligula found this treasonable – a sneer at his youth and a reproach against him for having held the office before he was legally capable of doing so. He composed a long, careful speech against Afer and delivered it in the Senate with all the oratorical force at his command, every gesture and tone carefully rehearsed beforehand. Caligula used to boast that he was the best lawyer and orator in the world, and was even more anxious to outshine Afer in eloquence than to secure his condemnation and confiscate his money. Afer realized this and pretended to be astonished and overcome by Caligula's genius as a prosecutor. He repeated the counts against himself, point by point, praising them with a professional detachment and muttering 'Yes, that's quite unanswerable' and 'He's got the last ounce of weight out of that argument' and 'A very real dilemma' and 'What extraordinary command of language!' When Caligula had finished and sat down with a triumphant grin, Afer was asked if he had anything to say. He answered: 'Nothing except that I consider myself most unlucky. I had counted on using my oratorical gifts as some slight offset against the Emperor's anger with me for my inexcusable thoughtlessness in the matter of that cursed inscription. But Fate has weighted the dice far too heavily against me. The Emperor has absolute power, a clear case against me, and a thousand times more eloquence than I could ever hope to achieve even if I escaped sentence and studied until I was a centenarian.' He was condemned to death, but reprieved the next day.

Speaking of weighted dice – when rich provincials came to the City they were always invited to dinner at the Palace and a friendy gamble afterwards. They were astonished and dismayed by the Emperor's luck: he threw Venus every time and skinned them of all they had. Yes, Caligula always played with weighted dice. For instance, he now removed the Consuls from office and fined them heavily on the ground that they had celebrated the usual festival in honour of Augustus's victory over Antony at Actium. He said that it was an insult to his ancestor Antony. (By the way, he appointed Afer to one of the vacant Consulships.) He had told us at dinner a few days before the festival that whatever the Consuls did he would punish them: for if they refrained from celebrating the festival they would be insulting his ancestor Augustus. It was on this occasion that Ganymede made a fatal mistake. He cried: 'You *are* clever, my dear! You catch them every way. But the poor idiots will celebrate the festival, if they have any sense; because Agrippa did most of the work at Actium and he was your ancestor too, so they will at least be honouring two of your ancestors out of three.'

Caligula said: 'Ganymede, we are no longer friends.'

'Oh,' said Ganymede, 'don't tell me that, my dear! I said nothing to offend you, did I?'

'Leave the table,' ordered Caligula.

I knew at once what Ganymede's mistake was. It was a double one. Ganymede, as Caligula's cousin on the maternal side, was descended from Augustus and Agrippa, but not from Antony. All his ancestors had been of Augustus's party. So he should have been careful to avoid the subject. And Caligula disliked any reminder of his descent from Agrippa, a man of undistinguished family. But he took no action against Ganymede yet.

He divorced Lollia, saying that she was barren, and married a woman called Caesonia. She was neither young nor good-looking and was the daughter of a captain of the Watchmen, and married to a baker, or some such person, by whom she already had three children. But there was something about her that attracted Caligula in a way that nobody could explain, himself least of all. He used often to say that he would fetch the secret out of her, even if he had to do it with the fiddle-string torture, why it was that he loved her so entirely. It was said that she won him with a love-philtre, and further that it sent him mad. But the love-philtre is only a guess, and he had begun to go mad long before he met her. In any case, she was with child by him, and he was so excited at the thought of being a parent that, as I say, he married her. It was shortly after his marriage with Caesonia that he first publicly declared his own Divinity. He visited the temple of Jove on the Capitoline Hill. Apelles was with him. He asked Apelles, 'Who's the greater God – Jove or myself?' Apelles hesitated, thinking that Caligula was joking, and not wishing to blaspheme Jove in Jove's own temple. Caligula whistled two Germans up and had Apelles stripped and whipped in sight of Jove's statue. 'Not so fast,' Caligula told the Germans. 'Slowly, so that he feels it more.' They whipped him until he fainted, and then revived him with holy water and whipped him until he died. Caligula then sent letters to the Senate announcing his divinity and ordered the immediate building of a great shrine next door to the temple of Jove, 'in order that I may dwell with my brother Jove'. Here he set up an image of himself, three times the size of life, made of solid gold and dressed every day in new clothes.

But he soon quarrelled with Jove and was heard to threaten him angrily: 'If you can't realize who's master here I'll pack you off to Greece.' Jove was understood to apologize, and Caligula said: 'Oh, keep your wretched Capitoline Hill. I'll go to the Palatine. It's a much finer situation. I'll build a temple there worthy of myself, you shabby old belly-rumbling fraud.' Another curious thing happened when he visited the temple of Diana in company with a former governor of Syria called Vitellius. Vitellius had done very well out there, having surprised the King of Parthia, who was about to invade the province, by a forced march across the Euphrates. Caught on ground unfavourable for battle, the Parthian king was obliged to sign a humiliating peace and give his sons up as hostages. I should have mentioned that Caligula had the eldest son as a prisoner with him in his chariot when he drove across the bridge. Well, Caligula was jealous of Vitellius and would have put him to death if Vitellius had not been warned by me (he was a friend of mine) what to do. A letter from me was waiting for him at Brindisi when he arrived, and as soon as he reached Rome and was admitted to Caligula's presence he fell prostrate and worshipped him as a God. This was before the news of Caligula's divinity was officially known, so Caligula thought it was a genuine tribute. Vitellius became his intimate friend and showed his gratitude to me in many ways. As I was saying, Caligula was in Diana's temple talking to the Goddess – not the statue but an invisible presence. He asked Vitellius whether he could see her too, or only the moonlight. Vitellius trembled violently, as if in awe, and keeping his eyes fixed on the ground said: 'Only you Gods, my Lord, are privileged to behold one another.'

Caligula was pleased. 'She's very beautiful, Vitellius, and often comes to sleep with me at the Palace.'

It was about this time that I got into trouble again. I thought at first that it was a plot of Caligula's to get rid of me. I am still not so sure that it was not. An acquaintance of mine, a man I used to play dice with a good deal, forged a will and took the trouble to forge my seal to it as witness. Luckily for me he had not noticed a tiny chip on the edge of the agate seal-gem, which always left its mark on the wax. When I was suddenly arrested for conspiracy to defraud and brought to Court, I bribed a soldier to carry a secret plea to my friend Vitellius, begging him to save my life as I had saved his. I asked him to hint about the chip to Caligula, who was judging the case, and to have a genuine seal of mine ready for Caligula to compare with the forged one. But Caligula must be encouraged to find the difference for himself and to take all the credit. Vitellius managed the affair very tactfully. Caligula noticed the chip, boasted of his quickness of eye, and absolved me with a stern warning to be more careful in future about my associates. The forger had his hands cut off and hung around his neck as a warning. If I had been found guilty I would have lost my head. Caligula told me so at supper that night.

I replied: 'Most merciful God, I really don't understand why you trouble so much about my life.'

It is the nature of nephews to enjoy an uncle's flattery. He unbent a little and asked me, with a wink to the rest of the table, 'And what precise valuation would you put on your life to-night, may I ask?'

'I have worked it out already: one farthing.'

'And how do you arrive at so modest a figure?'

'Every life has an assessable value. The ransom that Julius Caesar's family actually paid the pirates who had captured him and threatened to kill him – though they asked a great deal more than this at first – was no more than twenty thousand in gold. So Julius Caesar's life was actually worth no more than twenty thousand. My wife Aelia was once attacked by footpads, but persuaded them to spare her life by handing over an amethyst brooch worth only fifty. So Aelia was worth only fifty. *My* life has just been saved by a chip of agate weighing, I should judge, no more than the fortieth part of a scruple. That quality of agate is worth perhaps as much as a silver-piece a scruple. The chip, if one could find it, which would be difficult, or find a buyer, which would be still more difficult, would therefore be worth one fortieth part of a silver piece or exactly one farthing. So my life is also worth exactly one farthing – –'

'– *If you could find a buyer*,' he roared, delighted with his own wit. How everybody cheered, myself included! For a long time after this was I was called 'Teruncius' Claudius at the Palace, instead of Tiberius Claudius. Teruncius is Latin for farthing.

For his worship he had to have priests. He was his own High Priest and his subordinates were myself, Caesonia, Vitellius, Ganymede, fourteen ex-Consuls, and his noble friend the horse Incitatus. Each of these subordinates had to pay 80,000 gold pieces for the honour. He helped Incitatus to raise the money by imposing a yearly tribute in his name on all the horses in Italy: if they did not pay they would be sent to the knackers. He helped Caesonia to raise the money by imposing a tax in her name on all married men for the privilege of sleeping with their wives. Ganymede, Vitellius, and the others were rich men; though in some instances they had to sell property at a loss to get the 80,000 in cash at short notice, they still remained comfortably off. Not so poor Claudius. Caligula's previous tricks in selling me sword-fighters, and charging me heavily for the privilege of sleeping and boarding at the Palace, had left me with a mere 30,000 in cash, and no property to sell except my small estate at Capua and the house left me by my mother. I paid Caligula the 30,000 and told him the same night at dinner that I was putting up all my property for sale at once to enable me to pay him the remainder when I found a buyer. 'I've nothing else to sell,' I said. Caligula thought this a great joke. 'Nothing at all to sell? Why, what about the clothes you're wearing?'

By this time I had found it wisest to pretend I was quite half-witted. 'By heaven,' I said, 'I forgot all about them. Will you be good enough to auction them for me to the company? You're the most wonderful auctioneer in the world.' I began stripping off all my clothes until I had on nothing but a table-napkin which he hastily wrapped round my loins. He sold my sandals to someone for 100 gold pieces each, and my gown for 1,000, and so on, and each time I expressed my boisterous delight. He then wanted to auction the napkin. I said, 'My natural modesty would not prevent me from sacrificing my last rag, if the money it brought in helped me to pay the rest of the fee. But in this case, alas, something more powerful even than modesty prevents me from selling.'

Caligula frowned. 'What's that? What's stronger than modesty?'

'My veneration for yourself, Caesar. It's your own napkin. One that you had graciously set for my use at this excellent meal.'

This little play only reduced my debt by 3,000. But it did convince Caligula of my poverty.

I had to give up my rooms and my place at table and lodged for a time with old Briseis, my mother's former maid, who was caretaker of the house until it found a buyer. Calpurnia came to live with me there, and would you believe it, the dear girl still had the money which I had given her instead of necklaces and marmosets and silk dresses, and offered to lend it to me. And what was more, my cattle hadn't really died as she pretended, nor had the ricks burned. It was just a trick to sell them secretly at a good price and put the money aside for an emergency. She paid it all over to me – 2,000 gold pieces – together with an exact account of the transactions signed by my steward. So we managed pretty well. But to keep up the pretence of absolute poverty I used to go out with a jug every night, using a crutch instead of a sedan chair, and buy wine from the taverns.

Old Briseis used to say, 'Master Claudius, people all think that I was your mother's freedwoman. It isn't so. I became your slave when you first grew up to be Master, and it was you who gave me my freedom, not she, wasn't it?'

I would answer, 'Of course, Briseis. One day I'll nail that lie in public.' She was a dear old thing and entirely devoted to me. We lived in four rooms together, with an old slave to do the porter's work, and had a very happy time, all considered.

Caesonia's child, a girl, was born a month after Caligula married her. Caligula said that this was a prodigy. He took the child and laid her on the knees of the statue of Jove – this was before his quarrel with Jove – as if to make Jove his honorary colleague in fatherhood, and then put her in the arms of Minerva's statue and allowed her to suck at the Goddess's marble breast for awhile. He called her Drusilla, the name that his dead sister had discarded when she became the Goddess Panthea. This child was made a priestess too. He raised the money for the initiation fee by making a pathetic appeal to the public, complaining of his poverty and the heavy expenses of fatherhood, and opening a fund, called the Drusilla Fund. He put collecting boxes in every street marked 'Drusilla's Food', 'Drusilla's Drink', and 'Drusilla's Dowry', and nobody dared pass by the Guards posted there without dropping in a copper or two.

Caligula dearly loved his little Drusilla, who turned out as precocious a child as he had himself been. He took delight in teaching her his own 'immovable rigour', beginning the lessons when she was only just able to walk and talk. He encouraged her to torture kittens and puppies and to fly with her sharp nails at the eyes of her little playmates. 'There can be no reasonable doubt as to your paternity, my pretty one,' he used to chuckle when she showed particular promise. And once in my presence he bent down and said slyly to her: 'And the first full-sized murder you commit, Precious, if it's only your poor old granduncle Claudius, I'll make a Goddess of you.'

'Will you make me a Goddess if I kill Mamma?' the little fiend lisped. 'I hate Mamma.'

The gold statue for his temple was another expense. He paid for it by publishing an edict that he would receive New Year's gifts at the main gate of the Palace. When the day came he sent parties of Guards out to herd the City crowds up the Palatine Hill at the sword-point and make them shed every coin they had on them into great tubs put out for the purpose. They were warned that if they tried to dodge the Guards or hold back a single farthing of money they would be liable to instant death. By evening 2,000 huge tubs had been filled.

It was about this time that he said to Ganymede and Agrippinilla and Lesbia: 'You ought to be ashamed of yourselves, you idle drones. What do you do for your living? You're mere parasites. Are you aware that every man and woman in Rome works hard to support me? Every wretched baggage-porter gladly pays me one-eighth of his wage, and every poor prostitute the same.'

Agrippinilla said: 'Well, brother, you have stripped us of practically all our money on one pretext or another. Isn't that enough?'

'Enough? Indeed it isn't. Money inherited is not the same as money honestly earned. I'm going to make you girls and boys work.'

So he advertised in the Senate, by distributing leaflets, that on such and such a night a most exclusive and exquisite brothel would be opened at the Palace, with entertainment to suit all tastes provided by persons of the most illustrious birth. Admission, only 1,000 gold pieces. Drinks free. Agrippinilla and Lesbia, I am sorry to say, did not protest very strongly against Caligula's disgraceful proposal, and indeed thought that it would be great fun. But they insisted that they should have the right of choosing their own customers and that Caligula should not take too high a commission on the money earned. Much to my disgust I was dragged into this business, by being dressed up as the comic porter. Caligula, wearing a mask and disguising his voice, was the bawd-master, and played all the usual bawd-master tricks for cheating his guests of their pleasure and their money. When they protested, I was called upon to act as chucker-out. I am strong enough in the arms, stronger than most men, I may say, though my legs are very little use to me: so I caused a great deal of amusement by my clumsy hobbling and by the unexpectedly heavy drubbing I gave the guests when I managed to get hold of them. Caligula declaimed in a theatrical voice the lines from Homer:

> Vulcan with awkward grace his office plies
> And unextinguished laughter shakes the skies.

This was the passage in the First Book of the *Iliad* where the lame God goes hobbling about Olympus and the other Gods all laugh at him. I was lying on the floor pounding Lesbia's husband with my fists – it wasn't often that I got such a chance of paying back old scores – and raising myself up I said:

> Then from his anvil the lame craftsman rose.
> Wide, with distorted legs, oblique he goes,

and staggered over to the refreshment table. Caligula was delighted and quoted another couple of lines which occur just before the 'unextinguished laughter' passage:

> If you submit, the Thunderer stands appeased,
> The Gracious God is willing to be pleased.

This was how he came to call me Vulcan, a title that I was glad to win, because it gave me a certain protection against his caprices.

Caligula then quietly left us, removed his disguise, and reappeared as himself, coming in from the Palace courtyard by the door where he had posted me. He pretended to be utterly surprised and shocked at what was going on and stood declaiming Homer again – Ulysses's shame and anger at the behaviour of the palace-women:

> As thus pavilioned in the porch he lay,
> Scenes of lewd loves his wakeful eyes survey,
> Whilst to nocturnal joys impure repair
> With wanton glee, the prostituted fair.
> His heart with rage this new dishonour stung,
> Wavering his thought in dubious balance hung.
> Or, instant should he quench the guilty flame
> With their own blood, and intercept the shame;
> Or to their lust indulge a last embrace,
> And let the peers consummate the disgrace;
> Round his swoln heart the murmurous fury rolls;
> As o'er her young the mother-mastiff growls,
> And bays the stranger groom: so wrath compress'd
> Recoiling, mutter'd thunder in his breast.
> 'Poor, suffering heart,' he cried, 'support the pain
> Of wounded honour and thy rage restrain!
> Not fiercer woes thy fortitude could foil
> When the brave partners of thy ten-year toil
> Dire Polypheme devoured: I then was freed
> By patient prudence from the death decreed.'

'For "Polypheme" read "Tiberius",' he explained. Then he clapped his hands for the Guard, who came running up at the double. 'Send Cassius Chaerea here at once!' Cassius was sent for and Caligula said: 'Cassius, old hero, you who acted as my war-horse when I was a child, my oldest and most faithful family-friend, did you ever see such a sad and degrading sight as this? My two sisters prostituting their bodies to senators in my very Palace, my uncle Claudius standing at the gate selling tickets of admission! Oh, what would my poor mother and father have said if they had lived to see this day!'

'Shall I arrest them all, Caesar?' asked Cassius eagerly.

> No, to their lust indulge a last embrace
> And let the peers consummate the disgrace,

Caligula replied resignedly, and made mother-mastiff noises in his throat. Cassius was told to march the Guard off again.

It was not the last orgy of this sort at the Palace and thereafter Caligula made the senators who had attended the show bring their wives and daughters to assist Agrippinilla and Lesbia. But the problem of raising money was becoming acute again and Caligula decided to visit France and see what he could do there.

He first gathered an enormous number of troops, sending for detachments from all the regular regiments, and forming new regiments, and raising levies from every possible quarter. He marched out of Italy at the head of 150,000 men and increased them, in France, to 250,000. The expense of arming and equipping this immense force fell on the cities through which he passed: and he commandeered the necessary food supplies from them too. Sometimes he went forward at a gallop and made the army march forty-eight hours or more on end to catch up with him, sometimes he went forward at the rate of only a mile or two a day, admiring the scenery from a sedan-chair carried on eight men's shoulders and frequently stopping to pick flowers.

He sent letters ahead ordering the presence at Lyons, where he proposed to concentrate his forces, of all officials in France and the Rhine provinces who were over the rank of captain. Among those who obeyed the summons was Gaetulicus, one of my dear brother Germanicus's most valued officers, who had been in command of the four regiments of the Upper Province for the last few years. He was very popular among the troops because he kept up the tradition of mild punishments and of discipline based on love rather than on fear. He was popular with the regiments in the

Lower Province too, commanded by his father-in-law Apronius – for Gaetulicus had married a sister of that Apronia whom my brother-in-law Plautius was supposed to have thrown out of the window. At the fall of Sejanus he would have been put to death by Tiberius because he had promised his daughter in marriage to Sejanus's son, but he escaped by writing the Emperor a bold letter. He said that *so long as he was allowed to retain his command* his allegiance could be counted on, and so could that of the troops. Tiberius wisely let him alone. But Caligula envied him his popularity and almost as soon as he arrived had him arrested.

Caligula had not invited me on this expedition, so I missed what followed and cannot write about it in detail. All I know is that Ganymede and Gaetulicus were accused of conspiracy – Ganymede with designs on the monarchy, Gaetulicus with abetting him, and that both were put to death without trial. Lesbia and Agrippinilla (the latter's husband had lately died of dropsy) were also supposed to be in the plot. They were banished to an island off the coast of Africa near Carthage. It was a very hot, very arid island where sponge-fishing was the only industry, and Caligula ordered them to learn the trade of diving for sponges, for he said that he could not afford to support them longer. But before being sent to their island they had a task laid on them: they had to walk to Rome, all the way from Lyons, under an armed escort, and take turns at carrying in their arms the urn in which Ganymede's ashes had been put. This was a punishment for their persistent adultery with Ganymede, as Caligula explained in a loftily styled letter he sent the Senate. He enlarged on his own great clemency in not putting them to death. Why, they had proved themselves worse than common prostitutes: no honest prostitute would have had the face to ask the prices they asked, and got, for their debaucheries!

I had no reason to feel sorry for my nieces. They were as bad as Caligula, in their way, and treated me very spitefully. When Agrippinilla's baby was born three years before, she had asked Caligula to suggest a name for it. Caligula said, 'Call it Claudius and it will be sure to turn out a beauty.' Agrippinilla was so furious that she nearly struck Caligula; instead she turned quickly round and spat towards me – and then burst into tears. The baby was called Lucius Domitius.* Lesbia was too proud to pay attention to me or acknowledge my presence in any way. If I happened

* Afterwards the Emperor Nero. – R. G.

to meet her in a narrow passage she used to walk straight on down the middle without slackening her pace, making me squeeze against the wall. It was difficult for me to remember that they were the children of my dear brother and that I had promised Agrippina to do my very best to protect them.

I had the embarrassing duty assigned to me of going to France, at the head of an embassy of four ex-Consuls, to congratulate Caligula on his suppression of the conspiracy. This was my first visit to France since my infancy and I wished I was not making it. I had to take money from Calpurnia for travelling expenses, for my estate and home had not yet found a buyer, and I could not count on Caligula's being pleased to see me. I went by sea from Ostia, landing at Marseilles. It appears that after banishing my nieces Caligula had auctioned the jewellery and ornaments and clothes they had brought with them. These fetched such high prices that he also sold their slaves and then their freedmen, pretending that these were slaves too. The bids were made by rich provincials who wanted the glory of saying, 'Yes, such and such belonged to the Emperor's sister. I bought it from him personally!' This gave Caligula a new idea. The old Palace where Livia had lived was now shut up. It was full of valuable furniture and pictures and relics of Augustus. Caligula sent for all this stuff to Rome and made me responsible for its safe and prompt arrival at Lyons. He wrote 'Sent it by road, not by sea. I have a quarrel with Neptune.' The letter arrived only the day before I sailed, so I put Pallas in charge of the job. The difficulty was that all the surplus horses and carts had already been commandeered for the transport of Caligula's army. But Caligula had given the order, and horses and conveyances had somehow to be found. Pallas went to the Consuls and showed them Caligula's orders. They were forced to commandeer public mail-coaches and bakers' vans and the horses that turned the corn-mills, which was a great inconvenience to the public.

So it happened that one evening in May just before sunset, Caligula, sitting on the bridge at Lyons engaged in imaginary conversation with the local river-god, saw me coming along the road in the distance. He recognized my sedan A.D. 40 by the dice-board I have fitted across it: I beguile long journeys by throwing dice with myself. He called out angrily: 'Hey, you sir, where are the carts? Why haven't you brought the carts?'

I called back: 'Heaven bless your Majesty! The carts won't be here for a few days yet, I fear. They are coming by land, through Genoa. My colleagues and I have come by water.'

'Then back by water you'll go, my man,' he said. 'Come here!'

When I reached the bridge I was pulled out of my sedan by two German soldiers and carried to the parapet above the middle arch, where they sat me with my back to the river. Caligula rushed forward and pushed me over. I turned two back-somersaults and fell what seemed like 1,000 feet before I struck the water. I remember saying to myself: 'Born at Lyons, died at Lyons!' The river Rhône is very cold, very deep, and very swift. My heavy robe entangled my arms and legs, but somehow I managed to keep afloat, and to clamber ashore behind some boats about half a mile downstream, out of sight of the bridge. I am a much better swimmer than I am a walker: I am strong in the arms and being rather fat from not being able to take exercise and from liking my meals I float like a cork. By the way, Caligula couldn't swim a stroke.

He was surprised, a few minutes later, to see me come hobbling up the road, and laughed hugely at the stinking, muddy mess I was in. 'Where have you been, my dear Vulcan?' he called.

I had the answer pat:

> 'I felt the Thunderer's might,
> Hurled headlong downward from th' ethereal height.
> Tost all the day in rapid circles round
> Nor till the sun descended touch'd the ground.
> Breathless I fell, in giddy motions lost;
> The Sinthians raised me on the Lemnian coast.

'For "Lemnian" read "Lyonian",' I said.

He was sitting on the parapet with my three fellow-envoys lying on the ground face-downwards in a row before him. He had his feet on the necks of two and his swordpoint balanced between the shoulders of the third, Lesbia's husband, who was sobbing for mercy. 'Claudius,' he groaned, hearing my voice, 'beseech the Emperor to set us free: we only came to offer him our loving congraulations.'

'I want carts, not congratulations,' said Caligula.

It seemed as if Homer had written the passage from which I had just quoted on purpose for this occasion. I said to Lesbia's husband:

> 'Be patient and obey,
> Dear as you are, if Jove his arm extend,
> I can but grieve, unable to defend.
> What soul so daring in your aid to move
> Or lift his hand against the might of Jove?'

Caligula was delighted. He said to the three suppliants: 'What are your lives worth to you? Fifty thousand gold pieces each?'

'Whatever you say, Caesar,' they answered faintly.

'Then pay poor Claudius that sum as soon as you get back to Rome. He's saved your lives by his ready tongue.' So they were allowed to rise and Caligula made them sign a promise then and there, to pay me 150,000 gold pieces in three months' time. I said to Caligula: 'Most gracious Caesar, your need is greater than mine. Will you accept one hundred thousand gold pieces from me, when they pay me, in gratitude for my own salvation? If you condescend to take that gift, I would still have fifty thousand left, which would enable me to pay my initiation fee in full. I have worried a great deal about that debt.'

He said, 'Anything that I can do that will contribute to your peace of mind!' and called me his Golden Farthing.

So Homer saved me. But Caligula a few days later warned me not to quote Homer again. 'He's a most overrated author. I am going to have his poems called in and burned. Why shouldn't I put Plato's philosophical recommendations into practice? You know *The Republic*? An admirable piece of argument. Plato was for keeping all poets whatsoever out of his ideal state: he said that they were all liars, and so they are.'

I asked: 'Is your Sacred Majesty going to burn any other poets beside Homer?'

'Oh, indeed, yes. All the overrated ones. Virgil for a start. He's a dull fellow. Tries to be a Homer and can't do it.'

'And any historians?'

'Yes, Livy. Still duller. Tries to be a Virgil and can't do it.'

Chapter 32

HE called for the most recent official property-census and after examining it summoned all the richest men in France to Lyons, so that when the Palace-stuff arrived there from Rome he would be sure to get good prices for it. Just before the auction started, he made a speech. He said that he was a poor bankrupt with enormous liabilities, but trusted that, for the sake of the Empire, his affectionate provincial friends and grateful allies would not take advantage of his financial plight. He begged them not to offer less than the true value of the family heirlooms which, much to his grief, he was being forced to put up for sale.

There was no ordinary auctioneer's trick that he had not learned, and he invented a great many new ones, too, beyond the scope of the market-place cheap-jacks from whom he borrowed so much of his patter. For instance, he sold the same article several times over to different buyers with each time a different account of its quality and usefulness and history. And by 'true value' he expected bidders to understand 'sentimental value' which always turned out to be a hundred times greater than the intrinsic value. For instance he would say: 'This was the favourite easy-chair of my great-grandfather Mark Antony' – 'the God Augustus drank out of this wine-cup at his marriage feast' – 'this dress was worn by my sister, the Goddess Panthea, at a reception given to King Herod Agrippa in celebration of his release from prison' – and so forth. And he sold what he called 'blind bargains', small articles wrapped up in cloth. When he had inveigled a man into buying an old sandal or a piece of cheese for 2,000 gold pieces, he was tremendously pleased with himself.

Bidding always started at the reserve price; for he would nod at some rich Frenchman and say, 'I think you said forty thousand gold pieces for that alabaster casket? Thank you. But let's see if we can't do better. Who'll say forty-five thousand?' You can imagine that fear made the bidding brisk. He skinned the whole lot of all they had and celebrated the skinning by a magnificent ten-day festival.

He then continued his progress to the Rhine Provinces. He swore that he was about to fight a war against the Germans that would only end in their total extermination. He would piously complete the task begun by his grandfather and father. He sent a couple of regiments over the river to locate the nearest enemy. About 1,000 prisoners were brought back. Caligula reviewed them and after picking out 300 fine young men for his bodyguard he lined up the remainder against a cliff. A bald-headed man was at either end of the line. Caligula gave Cassius the order: 'Kill them, from bald head to bald head, in vengeance for the death of Varus.' The news of this massacre reached the Germans and they withdrew into their thickest forests. Caligula then crossed the river with his entire army and found the entire countryside deserted. The first day of his march, just to make things more exciting, he ordered some of his German bodyguard into a neighbouring wood, and then had news brought to him at supper that the enemy was at hand. At the head of his 'Scouts' and a troop of Guards Cavalry he then dashed out to the attack. He brought back the men as prisoners, loaded with chains, and announced a crushing victory against overwhelming odds. He rewarded his comrades-in-arms with a new sort of military decoration called 'The Scouts' Crown', a golden coronet decorated with the Sun, Moon, and stars in precious stones.

On the third day the road lay through a narrow pass. The army had to move in column instead of in skirmishing order. Cassius said to Caligula, 'It was in a place rather like this, Caesar, that Varus got ambushed. I shall never forget that day so long as I live. I was marching at the head of my company and had just reached a bend in the road, as it might be this one we are coming to, when suddenly there was a tremendous war-cry, as it might be from that clump of firs yonder, and three or four hundred assegais came whizzing down on us. ...'

'Quick, my mare!' called Caligula in a panic. 'Clear the road.' He sprang from his sedan, mounted Penelope (Incitatus was at Rome, winning races) and galloped back down the column. In four hours' time he was at the bridge again, but found it so choked with baggage-wagons and was in such a hurry to cross that he dismounted and made soldiers hand him in a chair from wagon to wagon until he was safely on the other side. He recalled his arms at once, announcing that the enemy were too cowardly to meet him in battle, and that he would therefore seek new conquests elsewhere. When the whole force had reassembled at Cologne he marched down the Rhine and then across to Boulogne, the nearest port to Britain. It so happened that the heir of Cymbeline, the King of Britain, had quarrelled with his father and, hearing of Caligula's approach, he fled across the Channel with a few followers and put himself under Roman protection. Caligula, who had already informed the Senate of his total subjugation of Germany, now wrote to say that King Cymbeline had sent his son to acknowledge Roman suzerainty over the entire British archipelago from the Scilly Islands to the Orkneys.

I was with Caligula throughout this expedition and had a very difficult time trying to humour him. He complained of sleeplessness and said that his enemy Neptune was plaguing him all the time with sea-noises in his ears, and used to come by night and threaten him with a trident. I said: 'Neptune? I wouldn't allow myself to be browbeaten by that saucy fellow if I were you. Why don't you punish him as you punished the Germans? You threatened him once before, I remember, and if he continues to flout you, it would be wrong to stretch your clemency any further.'

He looked at me, uncomfortably, through narrowed eyelids. 'Do you think I'm mad?' he asked, after a time.

I laughed nervously. '*Mad*, Caesar? You ask whether I think you *mad*? Why, you set the standard of sanity for the whole habitable world.'

'It's a very difficult thing, you know, Claudius,' he said confidentially, 'to be a God in human disguise. I've often thought I was going mad. They say that the hellebore cure at Anticyra is very good. What do you think of it?'

I said: 'One of the greatest Greek philosophers, but I can't remember now which of them it was, took the hellebore cure just to make his clear brain still clearer. But if you are asking me to advise you, I should say, "Don't take it! Your brain is as clear as a pool of rock-water."'

'Yes,' he said, 'but I wish I could get more than three hours' sleep at night.'

'Those three hours are because of your mortal disguise,' I said. 'Undisguised Gods never sleep at all.'

So he was comforted and the next day drew up his army in order of battle on the sea-front: archers and slingers in front, then the auxiliary Germans armed with assegais, then the main Roman forces, with the French in the rear. The cavalry were on the wings and the siege-engines, mangonels, and catapults planted on sand-dunes. Nobody knew what on earth was going to happen. He rode forward into the sea as far as Penelope's knees and cried: 'Neptune, old enemy, defend yourself. I challenge you to mortal fight. You treacherously wrecked my father's fleet, did you? Try your might on me, if you dare.' Then he quoted from Ajax's wrestling match with Ulysses, in Homer:

> Or let me lift thee, Chief, or lift thou me.
> Prove we our force ...

A little wave came rolling past. He cut at it with his sword and laughed contemptuously. Then he coolly retired and ordered the 'general engagement' to be sounded. The archers shot, the slingers slung, the javelin-men threw their javelins; the regular infantry waded into the waters as far as their arm-pits and hacked at the little waves, the cavalry charged on either flank and swam out some way, slashing with their sabres, the mangonels hurled rocks, and the catapults huge javelins and iron-tipped beams. Caligula then put to sea in a war-vessel and anchored just out of range of the missiles, uttering absurd challenges to Neptune and spitting far out over the vessel's side. Neptune made no attempt to defend himself or to reply, except that one man was nipped by a lobster, and another stung by a jelly-fish.

Caligula finally had the rally blown and told his men to wipe the blood off their swords and gather the spoil. The spoil was the sea-shells on the beach. Each man was expected to collect a helmet-full, which was added to a general heap. The shells were then sorted and packed in boxes to be sent to Rome in proof of this unheard-of victory. The troops thought it great fun, and when he rewarded them with four gold pieces a man cheered him tremendously. As a trophy of victory he built a very high lighthouse, on the model of the famous one at Alexandria, which has since proved a great blessing to sailors in those dangerous waters.

He then marched us up the Rhine again. When we reached Bonn Caligula took me aside and whispered darkly: 'The regiments have never been punished for the insult they once paid me by mutinying against my father, during my absence from this Camp. You remember, I had to come back and restore order for him.'

'I remember perfectly,' I said. 'But that's rather long ago, isn't

it? After twenty-six years there can't be many men still serving it
the ranks who were then there. You and Cassius Chaerea are
probably the only two veteran survivors of that dreadful day.'

'Perhaps I shall only decimate them, then,' he said.

The men of the First and Twentieth Regiments were ordered to
attend a special assembly and told that they might leave their
arms behind, because of the hot weather. The Guards cavalry
were also ordered to attend but instructed to bring their lances as
well as their sabres. I found a sergeant who looked as though he
might have fought at Philippi, he was so old and scarred. I said,
'Sergeant, do you know who I am?'

'No, sir. Can't say that I do, sir. You seem to be an ex-Consul,
sir.'

'I am the brother of Germanicus.'

'Indeed, sir. Never knew that there was such a person, sir.'

'No, I'm not a soldier or anyone important. But I've got an important message for you fellows. *Don't leave your swords too far
away when you go to this afternoon's assembly !*'

'Why, sir, if I may ask?'

'Because you may need them. Perhaps there will be an attack
by the Germans. Perhaps by someone else.'

He stared hard at me and then saw that I really meant it.

'Much obliged to you, sir; I'll pass the word around,' he
answered.

The infantry were massed in front of the tribunal platform and
Caligula spoke to them with an angry, scowling face, stamping his
feet and sawing with his hands. He began reminding them of a
certain night in early autumn, many years before, when under a
starless and bewitched sky. ... Here some of the men began sneaking away through a gap between two troops of cavalry. They were
going to fetch their swords. Others boldly pulled theirs out from
under their military cloaks where they had been hiding them.
Caligula must have noticed what was happening, for he suddenly
changed his tone, in the middle of a sentence. He began drawing a
happy contrast between those bad days, happily forgotten, and the
present reign of glory, wealth, and victory. 'Your little playfellow
grew to manhood,' he said, 'and became the mightiest Emperor
this world has ever known. No foeman, however fierce, dares
challenge his unconquerable arms.'

My old sergeant rushed forward. 'All is lost, Caesar,' he shouted. 'The enemy has crossed the river at Cologne – three hundred thousand strong. They're out to sack Lyons – then they'll cross the Alps, and sack Rome!'

Nobody believed this nonsensical story but Caligula. He turned yellow with fear, dived from the platform, grabbed hold of a horse, tumbled into the saddle, and was out of the camp like a flash. A groom galloped after him and Caligula called back to him, 'Thank God I still hold Egypt. I'll be safe there at least. The Germans aren't sailors.'

How everyone laughed! But a colonel went after him on a good horse and caught him before very long. He assured Caligula that the news was exaggerated. Only a small force, he said, had crossed the river and had been beaten back: the Roman bank was now quite clear of the enemy. Caligula stopped at the next town and wrote a dispatch to the Senate, informing them that all his wars were now successfully over and that he was coming back at once with his laurel-garlanded troops. He blamed those cowardly stay-at-homes most severely for having, from all accounts, lived life in the City just as usual – theatres, baths, supper-parties – while he had been undergoing the severest hardships of campaign. He had eaten, drunk, and slept no better than a private soldier.

The Senate was puzzled how to pacify him, being under strict orders from him to vote him no honours on their own initiative. They sent him an embassy, however, congratulating him on his magnificent victories and begging him to hasten back to Rome where his presence was so sadly missed. He was dreadfully angry that no triumph had been decreed him even in spite of his orders, and that he was not referred to as Jove in the message but merely as the Emperor Gaius Caesar. He rapped his hand on his sword-pommel and shouted: 'Hasten back? Indeed I will, and with this in my hand.'

He had made preparations for a triple triumph: over Germany, over Britain, and over Neptune. For British captives he had Cymbeline's son and his followers, to which were added the crews of some British trading vessels whom he had detained at Boulogne. For German captives he had 300 real ones and all the tallest men he could find in France, wearing yellow wigs and German clothes and talking together in a jargon supposed to be German. But, as I say, the Senate had been afraid to vote him a formal triumph, so he had to be content with an informal one. He rode into the

City in the same style as he had ridden across the bridge at Baiae, and it was only on the intercession of Caesonia, who was a sensible woman, that he refrained from putting the entire Senate to the sword. He rewarded the people for their alms-giving generosity to him in the past by showering gold and silver from the Palace roof. But he mixed red-hot discs of iron with this largesse, to remind them that he had not yet forgiven them for their behaviour in the amphitheatre. His soldiers were told that they could make as much disturbance as they pleased and get as drunk as they liked at the public expense. They took full advantage of this licence, sacking whole streets of shops and burning down the prostitutes' quarter. Order was not restored for ten days.

This was in September. While he was away the workmen had been busy on the new temple on the Palatine Hill at the other side of the Temple of Castor and Pollux from the New Palace. An extension had been made as far as the Market Place. Caligula now turned the Temple of Castor and Pollux into a vestibule for the new temple, cutting a passage between the statues of the Gods. 'The Heavenly Twins are my doorkeepers,' he boasted. Then he sent a message to the Governor of Greece to see that all the most famous statues of Gods were removed from the temples there and sent to him at Rome. He proposed to take off their heads and substitute his own. The statue he most coveted was the colossal one of Olympian Jove. He had a special ship built for its conveyance to Rome. But the ship was struck by lightning just before it was launched. Or this, at least, was the report – I believe, really, that the superstitious crew burned it on purpose. However, Capitoline Jove then repented of his quarrel with Caligula (or so Caligula told us) and begged him to return and live next to him again. Caligula replied that he had now practically completed a new temple; but since Capitoline Jove had apologized so humbly he would make a compromise – he would build a bridge over the valley and join the two hills. He did this: the bridge passed over the roof of the Temple of Augustus.

Caligula was now publicly Jove. He was not only Latin Jove but Olympian Jove, and not only that but all the other Gods and Goddesses, too, whom he had decapitated and re-headed. Sometimes he was Apollo and sometimes Mercury and sometimes Pluto, in each case wearing the appropriate dress and demanding the appropriate sacrifices. I have seen him go about as Venus in a long gauzy silk robe with face painted, a red wig, padded bosom, and high-heeled slippers. He was present as the Good Goddess at her December festival: *that* was a scandal. Mars was a favourite character with him, too. But most of the time he was Jove: he wore an olive-wreath, a beard of fine gold wires, and a bright blue silk cloak, and carried a jagged piece of electrum in his hand to represent lightning. One day he was on the Oration Platform in the Market Place dressed as Jove and making a speech. 'I intend shortly,' he said, 'to build a city for my occupation on the top of the Alps. We Gods prefer mountain-tops to unhealthy river-valleys. From the Alps I shall have a wide view of my Empire – France, Italy, Switzerland, the Tyrol, and Germany. If I see any treason hatching anywhere below me, I shall give a warning growl of thunder so! [He growled in his throat.] If the warning is disregarded I shall blast the traitor with this lightning of mine, so!' [He hurled his piece of lightning at the crowd. It hit a statue and bounced off harmlessly.] A stranger in the crowd, a shoemaker from Marseilles on a sight-seeing visit to Rome, burst out laughing. Caligula had the fellow arrested and brought nearer to the platform, then bending down he asked, frowning: 'Who do I seem to you to be?' 'A big humbug,' said the shoemaker. Caligula was puzzled. 'Humbug?' he repeated. '*I* a humbug!' 'Yes,' said the Frenchman. 'I'm only a poor French shoemaker and this is my first visit to Rome. And I don't know any better. If anyone at home did what you're doing he'd be a big humbug.'

Caligula began to laugh too. 'You poor half-wit,' he said. 'Of course he would be. That's just the difference.'

The whole crowd laughed like mad, but whether at Caligula or at the shoemaker was not clear. Soon after this he had a thunder-and-lightning machine made. He lit a fuse and it made a roar and a flash and catapulted stones in whatever direction he wanted. But I have it on good authority that whenever there was a real thunderstorm at night he used to creep under the bed. There is a good story about that. One day a storm burst when he was parading about dressed as Venus. He began to cry: 'Father, Father, spare your pretty daughter!'

The money he had won in France was soon spent and he invented new ways of increasing the revenue. His favourite one now was to examine judicially the wills of men who had just died and had left him no money: he would then give evidence of the benefits

that the testators had received from him and declare that they
had been either ungrateful or of unsound mind at the time of
drawing their wills and that he preferred to think that they had
been of unsound mind. He cancelled the wills and appointed himself principal heir. He used to come into Court in the early morning and write up on a blackboard the sum of money that he intended to win that day, usually 200,000 gold pieces. When he had
won it, he closed the Court. He made a new edict one morning
about the hours of business permitted in various sorts of shops.
He had it written in very small letters on a tiny placard posted
high on a pillar in the Market Place where nobody troubled to
read it, not realizing its importance. That afternoon his officers
took the names of several hundred tradesmen who had unwittingly
infringed the edict. When they were brought to trial he allowed
any of them who could do so to plead in mitigation of sentence
that they had named him as co-heir with their children. Few of
them could. It now became customary for men with money to
notify the Imperial Treasurer that Caligula was named in their
wills as the principal heir. But in several cases this proved unwise.
For Caligula made use of the medicine chest that he had inherited
from my grandmother Livia. One day he sent round presents of
honied fruits to some recent testators. They all died at once. He
also summoned my cousin, the King of Morocco, to Rome and
put him to death, saying simply: 'I need your fortune, Ptolemy.'

During his absence in France there had been comparatively
few convictions at Rome and the prisons were nearly empty: this
meant a shortage of victims for throwing to the wild beasts. He
made the shortage up by using members of the audience, first cutting out their tongues so that they could not call out to their
friends for rescue. He was becoming more and more capricious.
One day a priest was about to sacrifice a young bull to him in his
aspect of Apollo. The usual sacrificial procedure was for a deacon
to stun the bull with a stone axe, and for the priest then to cut its
throat. Caligula came in dressed as a deacon and asked the usual
question: 'Shall I?' When the priest answered 'Do so,' he brought
the axe down smash on the priest's head.

I was still living in poverty with Briseis and Calpurnia, for
though I had no debts, neither had I any money except what little
income came to me from the farm. I was careful to let Caligula
know how poor I was and he graciously permitted me to remain in

the Senatorial Order though I no longer had the necessary financial qualifications. But I felt my position daily more insecure. One midnight early in October I was awakened by loud knocking at the front door. I put my head out of the window. 'Who's there?' I asked.

'You're wanted at the Palace immediately.'

I said: 'Is that you, Cassius Chaerea? Am I going to be killed, do you know?'

'My orders are to fetch you to him immediately.'

Calpurnia cried and Briseis cried and both kissed me good-bye very tenderly. As they helped me to dress I hurriedly told them how to dispose of my few remaining possessions, and what to do with little Antonia, and about my funeral, and so on. It was a most affecting scene for all of us, but I did not dare prolong it. Soon I was hopping along at Cassius's side to the Palace. He said gruffly, 'Two more ex-Consuls have been summoned to appear with you.' He told me their names and I was still more alarmed. They were rich men, just the sort whom Caligula would accuse of a plot against him. But why me? I was the first to arrive. The two others came rushing in almost immediately after, breathless with haste and fear. We were taken into the Hall of Justice and made to sit on chairs on a sort of scaffold looking down on the tribunal platform. A guard of German soldiers stood behind us, muttering together in their own language. The room was in complete darkness but for two tiny oil lamps on the tribunal. The windows behind were draped, we noticed, with black hangings embroidered with silver stars. My companions and I silently clasped hands in farewell. They were men from whom I had had many insults at one time or another, but in the shadow of death such trifles are forgotten. We sat there waiting for something to happen until just before daybreak.

Suddenly we heard a clash of cymbals and the gay music of oboes and fiddles. Slaves filed in from a door at the side of the tribunal, each carrying two lamps, which they put on tables at the side; and then the powerful voice of a eunuch began singing the well-known song *When the long watches of the night*. The slaves retired. A shuffling sound was heard and presently in danced a tall ungainly figure in a woman's pink silk gown with a crown of imitation roses on its head. It was Caligula.

> The rosy-fingered Goddess then
> Will roll away the night of stars ...

Here he drew away the draperies from the window and disclosed the first streaks of dawn, and then, when the eunuch reached the part about the rosy-fingered Goddess, blowing out the lamps one by one, brought this incident into the dance too. Puff. Puff. Puff.

> And where clandestine lovers lie
> Entangled in sweet passion's toils ...

From a bed which we had not noticed, because it was in an alcove, the Goddess Dawn then pulled out a girl and a man, neither of them with any clothes on, and in dumb show indicated that it was the time for them to part. The girl was very beautiful. The man was the eunuch who was singing. They parted in opposite directions as if profoundly distressed. When the last verse came:

> O Dawn, of Goddesses most fair,
> Who with thy slow and lovely tread
> Dost give relief to every care ...

I had the sense to prostrate myself on the ground. My companions were not slow in following my example. Caligula capered off the stage and soon afterwards we were summoned to breakfast with him. I said, 'O God of Gods, I have never in my life witnessed any dance that gave me such profound spiritual joy as the one I have just witnessed. I have no words for its loveliness.'

My companions agreed with me and said that it was a million pities that so matchless a performance had been given to so tiny an audience. He said, complacently, that it was only a rehearsal. He would give it one night soon in the amphitheatre to the whole City. I didn't see how he would manage the curtain-drawing effect in an open-air amphitheatre hundreds of yards long, but I said nothing about that. We had a very tasty breakfast, the senior ex-Consul sitting on the floor alternately eating thrush-pie and kissing Caligula's foot. I was just thinking how pleased Calpurnia and Briseis would be to see me back when Caligula, who was in a very pleasant humour, suddenly said: 'Pretty girl, wasn't she, Claudius, you old lecher?'

'Very pretty indeed, God.'

'And still a virgin, so far as I know. Would you like to marry her? You can if you like. I took a fancy to her for a moment, but it's a funny thing, I don't really like immature women any more. ... Or any mature woman, for that matter, except Caesonia. Did your recognize the girl?'

'No, Lord, I was only watching you, to tell the truth.'

'She's your cousin Messalina, Barbatus's daughter. The old pander didn't utter a word of protest when I asked for her to be sent along to me. What cowards they are, after all, Claudius!'

'Yes, Lord God.'

'All right, then, I'll marry you two to-morrow. I'm going to bed now, I think.'

'A thousand thanks and homages, Lord.'

He gave me his other foot to kiss. Next day he kept his promise and married us. He accepted a tenth of Messalina's dowry as a fee but otherwise behaved courteously enough. Calpurnia had been delighted to see me alive again and had pretended not to mind about my marriage. She said in a businesslike way: 'Very well, my dear, I'll go back to the farm and look after things for you there again. You won't miss me, with that pretty wife of yours. And now you have money you'll have to live at the Palace again.'

I told her that the marriage was forced on me and that I would miss her very much indeed. But she pooh-poohed that: Messalina had twice her looks, three times her brains, and birth and money into the bargain. I was in love with her already, Calpurnia said.

I felt uncomfortable. Calpurnia had been my only true friend in all those four years of misery. What had she not done for me? And yet she was right: I *was* in love with Messalina, and Messalina was to be my wife now. There would be no place for Calpurnia with Messalina about.

She was in tears as she went away. So was I. I was not in love with her, but she was my truest friend and I knew that if ever I needed her she would be there to help me. I need not say that when I received the dowry money I did not forget her.

Chapter 33

MESSALINA was an extremely beautiful girl, slim and quick moving, with eyes as black as jet and masses of curly black hair. She hardly spoke a word and had a mysterious smile which drove me nearly crazy with love for her. She was so glad to have escaped from Caligula and so quick to realize the advantages that marriage with me gave her, that she behaved in a way which made me quite sure that she loved me as much as I loved her. This was practically the first time I had been in love with anyone since my boyhood; and when a not very clever, not very attractive man of fifty falls in love with a very attractive and very clever girl of fifteen it is usually a poor look-out for him. We were married in October. By December she was pregnant by me. She appeared very fond of my little Antonia, who was aged about ten, and it was a relief to me that the child now had someone whom she could call mother, someone who was near enough to her in age to be a friend and could explain the ways of society to her and take her about, as Calpurnia had not been able to do.

Messalina and I were invited to live at the Palace again. We arrived at an unfortunate time. A merchant called Bassus had been asking questions of a captain of the Palace Guards about Caligula's daily habits – was it true that he walked about the cloisters at night because he could not sleep? At what time did he do this? Which cloisters did he usually choose? What Guard did he have with him? The captain reported the incident to Cassius and Cassius reported it to Caligula. Bassus was arrested and cross-examined. He was forced to admit that he had intended to kill Caligula but denied even under torture that he had any associates. Caligula then sent a message to Bassus's old father, ordering him to attend his son's execution. The old man, who had no notion that Bassus had been planning to assassinate Caligula or even that he had been arrested, was greatly shocked to find his son groaning on the Palace floor, his body broken by torture. But he controlled himself and thanked Caligula for his graciousness in summoning him to close his son's eyes. Caligula laughed. 'Close his eyes indeed! He's going to have no eyes to close, the assassin! I'm going to poke them out in a moment. And yours too.'

Bassus's father said: 'Spare our lives. We are only tools in the hands of powerful men. I'll give you all the names.'

This impressed Caligula, and when the old man mentioned the Guards' Commander, the Commander of the Germans, Callistus the Treasurer, Caesonia, Mnester, and three or four others, he grew pale with alarm. 'And whom would they make Emperor in my place?' he asked.

'Your uncle Claudius.'

'Is he in the plot too?'

'No, they were merely going to use him as a figure-head.'

Caligula hurried away and summoned the Guards' Commander, the Commander of the Germans, the Treasurer, and myself to a private room. He asked the others, pointing to me: 'Is that creature fit to be Emperor?'

They answered in surprised tones, 'Not unless you say so, Jove.'

Then he gave them a pathetic smile and exclaimed, 'I am one and you are three. Two of you are armed and I am defenceless. If you hate me and want to kill me, do so at once and put that poor idiot into my place as Emperor.'

We all fell on our faces and the two soldiers handed him their swords from the floor, saying, 'We are innocent of any such treacherous thought, Lord. If you disbelieve us, kill us!'

Do you know, he was actually about to kill us! But while he hesitated I said: 'Almighty God, the colonel who summoned me here told me of the charge brought against these loyal men by Bassus's father. Its falsity is evident. If Bassus had really been employed by them, would it have been necessary for him to question the captain about your movements? Would he not have been able to get all the necessary information from these generals themselves? No, Bassus's father has tried to save his own life and Bassus's by a clumsy lie.'

Caligula appeared to be convinced by my argument. He gave me his hand to kiss, made us all rise, and handed the swords back. Bassus and his father were thereupon hewn to pieces by the Germans. But Caligula could not rid his mind of the dread of assassination, which was presently increased by a number of unlucky omens. First the porter's lodge at the Palace was struck by lightning. Then Incitatus, when he was brought in to dinner one evening, reared up and cast a shoe which broke an alabaster cup that had belonged to Julius Caesar, spilling the wine on the floor. The worst omen of all was what happened at Olympus, when, in accordance with Caligula's orders, the temple workmen began to take the statue of Jove to pieces for conveyance to Rome. The head was to come off first, to be used as a measure for the new head of Caligula that would be substituted when the statue was reassembled. They had got the pulley fixed to the temple roof and a rope knotted around the neck and were just about to haul, when suddenly a thunderous peal of laughter roared out through the whole building. The workmen rushed away in panic. Nobody could be found bold enough to take their places.

Caesonia now advised him, since by his immovable rigour he had made everyone tremble at the very sound of his name, to rule mildly and earn the people's love instead of their fear. For Caesonia realized how dangerously he was placed and that if anything happened to him she would certainly lose her life too, unless she was known to have done her best to dissuade him from his cruelties. He was behaving in a most imprudent way now. He went in turn to the Guards' Commander, the Treasurer, and the Commander of the Germans and pretended to take each of them into his confidence, saying, 'I trust *you*, but the others are plotting against me and I want you to regard them as my deadliest enemies.' They compared notes; and that is why when a real plot was formed they shut their eyes to it. Caligula said that he approved Caesonia's advice and thanked her for it; he would certainly follow it when he had made his peace with his enemies. He called the Senate together and addressed us in this strain: 'Soon I shall grant you all an amnesty, my enemies, and reign with love and peace a thousand years. That is the prophecy. But before that golden time comes heads must roll along the floor of this House and blood spurt up to the beams. A wild five minutes that will be.' If the 1,000 years of peace had come first, and then the wild five minutes, we should have preferred it.

The plot was formed by Cassius Chaerea. He was an old-fashioned soldier, accustomed to blind obedience to the orders of his superiors. Things have to be extraordinarily bad before a man of this stamp can think of plotting against the life of his Commander-in-Chief, to whom he has sworn allegiance in the most solemn terms imaginable. Caligula had treated Cassius extremely badly. He had definitely promised him the command of the Guards and then without a word of explanation or apology had given it to a captain of short service and no military distinction as a reward for a remarkable drinking feat at the Palace: he had volunteered to drain a three-gallon jar of wine without removing it from his lips, and had really done so – I was watching – and kept the wine down into the bargain. Caligula had also made this man a senator. And Caligula employed Cassius on all his most unpleasant errands and tasks – collection of taxes that were not really due, the seizure of property for offences never committed, the execution of innocent men. Recently he had made him torture a beautiful girl, well born too, called Quintilia. The story was as follows. Several young men had wanted to marry her, but the one whom her guardian had proposed, a member of the Scouts, she did not like at all. She begged him to let her choose one of the others; he consented, and the day for the marriage was fixed. The rejected Scout went to Caligula and brought an accusation against his rival, saying that he had blasphemed, speaking of his August Sovereign as 'that bald-headed madame'. He cited Quintilia as a witness. Quintilia and her betrothed were brought before Caligula. Both denied the charge. Both were sentenced to the rack. Cassius's face revealed his disgust, for only slaves could legally be put to torture. So Caligula ordered him to supervise Quintilia's racking and turn the screws with his own hands. Quintilia did not utter a word or a cry throughout her ordeal and afterwards said to Cassius, who was so affected that he was weeping, 'Poor Colonel, I bear you no grudge. Sometimes it must be hard to obey orders.' Cassius said bitterly: 'I wish I had died that day with Varus in the Teutoburger Forest.'

She was taken again into Caligula's presence, and Cassius reported that she had made no confession and not allowed a cry to escape her. Caesonia said to Caligula, 'That was because she was in love with the man. Love conquers all. You might cut her in pieces but she would never betray him.'

Caligula said: 'And would you too be so gloriously brave on my account, Caesonia?'

'You know that I would,' she said.

So Quintilia's betrothed was not tortured but given a free pardon, and Quintilia was awarded a dowry of 8,000 gold pieces from the estate of the Scout, who was executed for perjury. But Caligula heard that Cassius had wept during Quintilia's torture and jeered at him for an old cry-baby. 'Cry-baby' was not the worst name he found. He pretended that Cassius was an effeminate old pathic, and was always making dirty jokes about him to the other Guards officers, who were obliged to laugh heartily at them. Cassius used to come to Caligula for the watchword every day at noon. It had always been 'Rome' or 'Augustus' or 'Jove' or 'victory' or something of the sort; but now to annoy Cassius, Caligula would give him absurd words like 'Staylaces' or 'Lots of Love' or 'Curling-irons' or 'Kiss me, Sergeant', and Cassius had to take them back to his brother-officers and stand their chaff. He decided to kill Caligula.

Caligula was madder than ever. He came into my room one day and said without any introductory remark: 'I shall have three Imperial cities, and Rome won't be one of them. I shall have my city on the Alps, and I shall rebuild Rome at Antium because that's where I was born and it deserves the honour, and because it's on the sea, and then I shall have Alexandria in case the Germans capture the other two. Alexandria is a very cultivated place.'

'Yes, God,' I said humbly.

He then suddenly remembered that he had been called a bald-headed madame – his hair was certainly very thin on top now – and shouted out, 'How dare you go about with a great ugly bush of hair in my presence? It's blasphemy.' He turned to his German guard. 'Cut his head off!'

Once more I thought I was done for. But I had the presence of mind to say sharply to the Guard who was running at me with his sword, 'What are you doing, idiot? The God didn't say "head", he said "hair"! Run off and fetch the shears at once!' Caligula was taken aback and perhaps really thought that he had said 'hair'. He allowed the German to fetch the shears. My crown was shorn clean. I asked permission to dedicate the clippings to his Deity and he graciously gave consent. So now he had everyone in the Palace shorn, except the Germans. When it came to Cassius's turn Caligula said, 'Oh, what a pity! Those darling little ringlets that the Sergeant loves so much!'

That evening Cassius met Lesbia's husband. He had been Ganymede's best friend and from something that Caligula had said that morning was not likely to live much longer. He said, 'Good evening, Cassius Chaerea, my friend. What's the watchword to-day?'

Cassius had never been called 'my friend' before by Lesbia's husband and looked intently at him.

Lesbia's husband – his name was Marcus Vinicius – said again, 'Cassius, we have much in common and when I call you "friend", I mean it. What's the watchword?'

Cassius answered, 'The watchword to-night is "Little Ringlets". But, my friend Marcus Vinicius, if I may indeed call you friend, give me the watchword "Liberty" and my sword is at your service.'

Vinicius embraced him. 'We are not the only two who are ready to strike for Liberty. The Tiger is also with me.' The Tiger – his real name was Cornelius Sabinus – was another Guards colonel, who relieved Cassius whenever he went off duty.

The great Palatine Festival started the next day. This festival in honour of Augustus had been instituted by Livia at the beginning of Tiberius's monarchy and was held annually in the Southern Court of the Old Palace. It began with sacrifices to Augustus and a symbolic procession, and continued for three days with theatrical pieces, dancing, singing, juggling, and the like. Wooden stands were erected with seating for 60,000 people. When the festival ended the stands were taken down and stored away until the following year. This year Caligula had prolonged the three days to eight, interspersing the performances with chariot-races in the Circus and sham naval-fights in the Basin. He wanted to be continuously amused until the day he sailed for Alexandria, which was to be the twenty-fifth of January. For he was going to Egypt to see the sights, to raise money by immovable rigour and the same sort of trickery he had used in France, to make plans for the rebuilding of Alexandria and, lastly, so he boasted, to put a new head on the Sphinx.

The Festival started. Caligula sacrificed to Augustus, but in a somewhat perfunctory and disdainful way – like a master who in some emergency or other has to perform some menial service for one of his slaves. When this was over he proclaimed that if any citizen present asked a boon that it was in his power to grant he would graciously grant it. He had been angry with the people lately for their lack of enthusiasm at the last wild-beast show and had punished them by shutting the city granaries for ten days; but perhaps he had forgiven them now, because he had just scattered largesse from the Palace roof. So a glad shout went up. 'More bread, less taxes, Caesar! More bread, less taxes!' Caligula was very angry. He sent a platoon of Germans along the benches and 100 heads were chopped off. This incident disturbed the conspirators; it was a reminder of the barbarity of the Germans and the marvellous devotion that they paid Caligula. By this time, there can hardly have been a citizen in Rome who did not long for the death of Caligula, or would not willingly have eaten his flesh, as the saying is; but to these Germans he was the most glorious hero the world had ever known. And if he dressed as a woman; or galloped suddenly away from his army on the march; or made Caesonia appear naked before them and boasted of her beauty; or burned down his most beautiful villa at Herculaneum on the ground that his mother Agrippina had been imprisoned there for two days on her way to the island where she died – this inexplicable sort of behaviour only made him the more worthy of their worship as a divine being. They used to nod wisely to each other and say, 'Yes, the Gods are like that. You can't tell what they are going to do next. Tuisco and Mann, at home, in our dear, dear Fatherland, are just the same.'

Cassius was reckless and did not care what happened to him personally, so long as Caligula was assassinated, but the other conspirators, who did not feel so strongly, began to wonder what vengeance the Germans would take on the murderers of their wonderful hero. They began making excuses and Cassius could not get them to agree on a proper plan of action. They suggested leaving it to chance. Cassius grew anxious. He called them cowards and accused them of playing for time. He said that they really wanted Caligula to get safe away to Egypt. The last day of the festival came, and Cassius had with great difficulty persuaded them to agree to a workable plan, when Caligula suddenly gave out that the festival would go on for another three days. He said that he wanted to act and sing in a masque which he had himself composed for the benefit of the Alexandrians, but which he thought it only fair to show his own countrymen first.

This change of plans gave the more timorous of the conspirators a new opportunity for hedging. 'Oh, but Cassius, this quite alters matters. It makes everything much easier for us. We can kill him on the last day, just as he comes off the stage. That's a far better plan. Or as he goes on. Whichever you prefer.'

Cassius answered: 'We've made a plan and sworn to keep it, and keep it we must. It's a very good plan too. Not a flaw in it.'

'But we have plenty of time now. Why not wait another three days?'

Cassius said: 'If you won't carry that plan out to-day as you all swore you would, I shall have to work single-handed. I won't have much of a chance against the Germans – but I'll do my best. If they are too strong for me I'll call out, "Vinicius, Asprenas, Bubo, Aquila, Tiger, why aren't you here as you promised?"'

So they agreed to carry out the original plan. Caligula was to be persuaded by Vinicius and Asprenas to leave the theatre at noon for a plunge in the swimming pool and a quick lunch. Just before this Cassius, The Tiger, and the other captains who were in the plot were to slip out unobtrusively by the stage-door. They were to go round to the entrance of the covered passage which was the short cut from the theatre to the New Palace. Asprenas and Vinicius would persuade Caligula to take this short cut.

The play that day had been announced as *Ulysses and Circe* and Caligula had promised to scatter fruit and cakes and money at the end of it. He would naturally do this from the end nearest the gate, where his seat was, so everyone came as early as possible to the theatre to secure seats at that end. When the gates were opened the crowd rushed in and raced for the nearest seats. Usually all the women sat together in one part, and there were seats reserved for knights, and for senators, and for distinguished foreigners, and so on. But to-day everyone was muddled up together. I saw a senator who had come in late forced to sit between an African slave and a woman with saffron-dyed hair and the dark-coloured gown that common prostitutes wear as their professional dress. 'So much the better,' said Cassius to The Tiger. 'The more confusion there is, the better chance we have.'

Apart from the Germans and Caligula himself almost the only person at the Palace who had not by now heard of the plot was poor Claudius. This was because poor Claudius was going to be killed too, as Caligula's uncle. All Caligula's family were to be killed. The conspirators were afraid, I suppose, that I would make myself Emperor and avenge his death. They had determined to restore the Republic. If only the idiots had taken me into their confidence this story would have had a very different ending. For I was a better Republican than any of them. But they mistrusted me, and very cruelly doomed me to death. Even Caligula knew more about the plot than I did, in a sense, for he had just been sent a warning oracle from the Temple of Fortune at Antium: 'Beware of Cassius.' He misunderstood it, and recalled Drusilla's first husband, Cassius Longinus, from Asia Minor, where he was Governor. He thought that Longinus was angry with him for murdering Drusilla and remembered that he was a descendant of that Cassius who helped to assassinate Julius Caesar.

I came into the theatre that morning at eight o'clock and found that a place had been reserved for me by the ushers. I was between the Guards' Commander and the Commander of the Germans.

The Guards' Commander leant across me and asked: 'Have you heard the news?'

'What news?' asked the Commander of the Germans.

'They are playing a new drama to-day.'

'What is it?'

'*The Tyrant's Death.*'

The Commander of the Germans gave him a quick look and quoted frowning:

> 'Brave comrade, hold thy peace
> Lest someone hear thee, of the men of Greece.'

I said: 'Yes, there is a change in the programme. Mnester is to give us *The Tyrant's Death*. It hasn't been played for years. It's about King Cinyras, who wouldn't come into the war against Troy, and got killed for his cowardice.'

The play began and Mnester was at the top of his form. When he died at the hands of Apollo he spurted blood all over his clothes from a little bladder concealed in his mouth. Caligula sent for him and kissed him on both cheeks. Cassius and The Tiger escorted him to his dressing-room as if to protect him from his admirers. Then they went out by the stage-door. The captains followed during the confusion of the largesse-throwing. Asprenas said to Caligula: 'That was marvellous. Now what about a plunge in the bath and a little light luncheon?'

'No,' said Caligula. 'I want to see those girl acrobats. They're said to be pretty good. I think I'll sit the show out. It's the last day.' He was in an extremely affable mood.

So Vinicius rose. He was going to tell Cassius, The Tiger, and the rest, not to wait. Caligula pulled at his cloak. 'My dear fellow, don't run away. You must see those girls. One does a dance called the fish-dance which makes you feel as if you were ten fathoms under water.'

Vinicius sat down and saw the fish-dance. But first he had to sit through a short melodramatic interlude called *Laureolus*, or *The Robber Chief*. There was a lot of slaughter in it and the actors, a second-rate lot, had all found blood-bladders to put in their mouths in imitation of Mnester. You never saw such an ill-omened mess as they made of the stage! When the fish-dance was over Vinicius rose again: 'To tell the truth, Lord, I would love to stay but Cloacina calls me. It's some confounded thing I ate.

'Soft but cohesive let my offerings flow,
Not roughly swift, nor impudently slow ...'

Caligula laughed. 'Don't blame it on me, my dear fellow. You're one of my best friends. I wouldn't doctor your food for the world.'

Vinicius went out by the stage-door and found Cassius and The Tiger in the court. 'You'd better come back,' he said. 'He's sitting it out to the end.'

Cassius said: 'Very well. Let's go back. I'm going to kill him where he sits. I expect you to stand by me.'

Just then a Guardsman came up to Cassius and said, 'The boys are here at last, sir.'

Now, Caligula had lately sent letters to the Greek cities of Asia Minor ordering them each to send him ten boys of the noblest blood to dance the national sword-dance at the festival and sing a hymn in his honour. This was only an excuse for getting the boys in his power: they would be useful hostages when he turned his fury against Asia Minor. They should have arrived several days before this, but rough weather in the Adriatic had held them up at Corfu. The Tiger said, 'Inform the Emperor at once.' The Guardsman hurried to the theatre.

Meanwhile I was beginning to feel very hungry. I whispered to Vitellius who was sitting behind me, 'I do wish that the Emperor would set us the example of going out for a little luncheon.' Then the Guardsman came up with the message about the boys' arrival and Caligula said to Asprenas: 'Splendid! They'll be able to perform this afternoon. I must see them at once and have a short rehearsal of the hymn. Come on, friends! The rehearsal first, then a bathe, luncheon, and back again!'

We went out. Caligula stopped at the gate to give orders about the afternoon performance. I walked ahead with Vitellius, a senator named Sentius, and the two generals. We went by the covered passage. I noticed Cassius and The Tiger at the entrance. They did not salute me, which I thought strange, for they saluted the others. We reached the Palace. I said, 'I *am* hungry. I smell venison cooking. I hope that rehearsal won't take too long.' We were in the ante-room to the banqueting-hall. 'This is odd,' I thought. 'No captains here, only sergeants.' I turned questioningly to my companions but – another odd thing – found that they had all silently vanished. Just then I heard distant shouting and screams, then more shouting. I wondered what on earth was happening. Someone ran past the window shouting, 'It's all over. He's dead!' Two minutes later there came a most awful roar from the theatre, as if the whole audience was being massacred. It went on and on but after a time there was a lull followed by tremendous cheering. I stumbled upstairs to my little reading-room where I collapsed trembling on a chair.

The pillared portrait-busts of Herodotus, Polybius, Thucydides, and Asinius Pollio stood facing me. Their impassive features seemed to say: 'A true historian will always rise superior to the political disturbances of his day.' I determined to comport myself as a true historian.

Chapter 34

WHAT had happened was this. Caligula had come out of the theatre. A sedan was waiting to take him the long way round to the New Palace between double ranks of Guards. But Vinicius said: 'Let's go by the short cut. The Greek boys are waiting there at the entrance, I believe.' 'All right, then, come along,' said Caligula. The people tried to follow him out but Asprenas dropped behind and forced them back. 'The Emperor doesn't want to be bothered with you,' he said. 'Get back!' He told the gate-keepers to close the gates again.

Caligula went towards the covered passage. Cassius stepped forward and saluted. 'The watchword, Caesar?'

Caligula said, 'Eh? Oh, yes, the watchword, Cassius. I'll give you a nice one to-day – "Old Man's Petticoat".'

The Tiger called from behind Caligula, 'Shall I?' It was the agreed signal.

'*Do so!*' bellowed Cassius, drawing his sword, and striking at Caligula with all his strength.

He had intended to split his skull to the chin, but in his rage he missed his aim and struck him between the neck and the shoulders. The upper breastbone took the chief force of the blow. Caligula was staggered with pain and astonishment. He looked wildly around him, turned, and ran. As he turned Cassius struck at him again, severing his jaw. The Tiger then felled him with a badly-aimed blow on the side of his head. He slowly rose to his knees. 'Strike again!' Cassius shouted.

Caligula looked up to Heaven with a face of agony. 'O Jove,' he prayed.

'Granted,' shouted The Tiger, and hacked off one of his hands.

A captain called Auila gave the finishing stroke, a deep thrust in the groin, but ten more swords were plunged into his breast and belly afterwards, just to make sure of him. A captain called Bubo dipped his hand in a wound in Caligula's side and then licked his fingers, shrieking, 'I swore to drink his blood!'

A crowd had collected and the alarm went round, 'The Germans are coming.' The assassins had no chance against a whole battalion of Germans. They rushed into the nearest building, which happened to be my old home, lately borrowed from me by Caligula as guest-apartments for foreign ambassadors whom he did not want to have about in the Palace. They went in at the front door and out at the back door. All got away in time but The Tiger and Asprenas. The Tiger had to pretend that he was not one of the assassins and joined the Germans in their cries for vengeance. Asprenas ran into the covered passage, where the Germans caught him and killed him. They killed two other senators whom they happened to meet. This was only a small party of Germans. The rest of the battalion marched into the theatre and closed the gate behind them. They were going to avenge their murdered hero by a wholesale massacre. That was the roar and screaming I had heard. Nobody in the theatre knew that Caligula was dead or that any attempt had been made against his life. But it was quite clear what the Germans intended because they were going through their curious performance of patting and stroking their assegais and speaking to them as if they were human beings, which is their invariable custom before shedding blood with those terrible weapons. There was no escape. Suddenly from the stage the trumpet blew the Attention, followed by the six notes which mean Imperial Orders. Mnester entered and raised his hand. And at once the terrible din died down into mere sobs and smothered groans, for when Mnester appeared on the stage it was a rule that nobody should utter the least sound on pain of instant death. The Germans, too, stopped their patting and stroking and incantations. The Imperial Orders stiffened them into statues.

Mnester shouted: 'He's not dead, Citizens. Far from it. The

assassins set on him and beat him to his knees, so! But he presently rose again, so! Swords cannot prevail against our Divine Caesar. Wounded and bloody as he was, he rose, so! He lifted his august head and walked, so! with divine stride through the ranks of his cowardly and baffled assassins. His wounds healed, a miracle! He is now in the Market Place loudly and eloquently haranguing his subjects from the Oration Platform.'

A mighty cheer arose and the Germans sheathed their swords and marched out. Mnester's timely lie (prompted, as a matter of fact, by a message from Herod Agrippa, King of the Jews, the only man in Rome who kept his wits about him that fateful afternoon) had saved 60,000 lives or more.

But the real news had by now reached the Palace, where it caused the most utter confusion. A few old soldiers thought that the opportunity for looting was too good to be missed. They would pretend to be looking for the assassins. Every room in the Palace had a golden door-knob, each worth six months' pay, easy enough to hack off with a sharp sword. I heard the cries, 'Kill them, kill them! Avenge Caesar!' and hid behind a curtain. Two soldiers came in. They saw my feet under the curtain. 'Come out of there, assassin. No use hiding from us.'

I came out and fell on my face. 'Don't k-k-k-k-kill me, Lords,' I said. 'I had n-nothing to d-d-d-d-do with it.'

'Who's this old gentleman?' asked one of the soldiers who was new at the Palace. 'He doesn't look dangerous.'

'Why! Don't you know? He's Germanicus's invalid brother. A decent old stick. No harm in him at all. Get up, sir. We won't hurt you.' This soldier's name was Gratus.

They made me follow them downstairs again into the banqueting-hall where the sergeants and corporals were holding a council-of-war. A young sergeant stood on a table waving his arms and shouting, 'Republic be hanged! A new Emperor's our only hope. Any Emperor so long as we can persuade the Germans to accept him.'

'Incitatus,' someone suggested, guffawing.

'Yes, by God! Better the old nag than no Emperor at all. We want someone immediately, to keep the Germans quiet. Otherwise they'll run amok.'

My two captors pushed their way through the crowd dragging me behind them. Gratus called out, 'Hey, Sergeant! Look whom we have here! A bit of luck, I think. It's old Claudius. What's wrong with old Claudius for Emperor? The best man for the job in Rome, though he do limp and stammer a bit.'

Loud cheers, laughter, and cries of 'Long live the Emperor Claudius!' The Sergeant apologized. 'Why, sir, we all thought you were dead. But you're our man, all right. Push him up, lads, where we can all see him!' Two burly corporals caught me by the legs and hoisted me on their shoulders. 'Long live the Emperor Claudius!'

'Put me down,' I cried furiously. 'Put me down! I don't want to be Emperor. I refuse to be Emperor. Long live the Republic!'

But they only laughed. 'That's a good one. He doesn't want to be Emperor, he says. Modest, eh?'

'Give me a sword,' I shouted. 'I'll kill myself sooner.'

Messalina came hurrying towards us. 'For my sake, Claudius, do what they ask of you. For our child's sake. We'll all be murdered if you refuse. They've killed Caesonia already. And they took her little girl by the feet and bashed out her brains against a wall.'

'You'll be all right, sir, once you get accustomed to it,' Gratus said, grinning. 'It's not such a bad life, an Emperor's isn't.'

I made no more protests. What was the use of struggling against Fate? They hurried me out into the Great Court, singing the foolish hymn of hope composed at Caligula's accession, *Germanicus is come Again, To Free the City from her Pain.* For I had the surname Germanicus too. They forced me to put on Caligula's golden oak-leaf chaplet, recovered from one of the looters. To steady myself I had to cling tightly to the corporals' shoulders. The chaplet kept slipping over one ear. How foolish I felt. They say that I looked like a criminal being hauled away to execution. Massed trumpeters blew the Imperial Salute.

The Germans came screaming towards us. They had just heard for certain of Caligula's death, from a senator who came to meet them in deep mourning. They were furious at having been tricked and wanted to go back to the theatre, but the theatre was empty now, so they were at a loss what to do next. There was nobody about to take vengeance on except the Guards, and the Guards were armed. The Imperial Salute decided them. They rushed forward shouting: 'Hoch! Hoch! Long live the Emperor Claudius!' and began frantically dedicating their assegais to my service and struggling to break through the crowd of Guardsmen to kiss my feet. I called to them to keep back, and they obeyed, prostrating themselves before me. I was carried round and round the Court.

And what thoughts or memories, would you guess, were passing through my mind on this extraordinary occasion? Was I thinking of the Sibyl's prophecy, of the omen of the wolf-cub, of Pollio's advice, or of Briseis's dream? Of my grandfather and liberty? Of my father and liberty? Of my three Imperial predecessors, Augustus, Tiberius, Caligula, their lives and deaths? Of the great danger I was still in from the conspirators, and from the Senate, and from the Guards battalions at the Camp? Of Messalina and our unborn child? Of my grandmother Livia and my promise to deify her if ever I became Emperor? Of Postumus and Germanicus? Of Agrippina and Nero? Of Camilla? No, you would never guess what was passing through my mind. But I shall be frank and tell you what it was, though the confession is a shameful one. I was thinking, 'So, I'm Emperor, am I? What nonsense! But at least I'll be able to make people read my books now. Public recitals to large audiences. And good books too, thirty-five years' hard work in them. It won't be unfair. Pollio used to get attentive audiences by giving expensive dinners. He was a very sound historian, and the last of the Romans. My *History of Carthage* is full of amusing anecdotes. I'm sure they'll enjoy it.'

That was what I was thinking. I was thinking, too, what opportunities I should have, as Emperor, for consulting the secret archives and finding out just what happened on this occasion or on that. How many twisted stories still remained to be straightened out! What a miraculous fate for an historian! And as you will have seen, I took full advantage of my opportunities. Even the mature historian's privilege of setting forth conversations of which he knows only the gist is one that I have availed myself of hardly at all.

TREE OF THE
IMPERIAL FAMILY AND CONNEXIONS
TO THE YEAR A.D. 41

GIVING NAMES AS ABBREVIATED
IN THIS BOOK

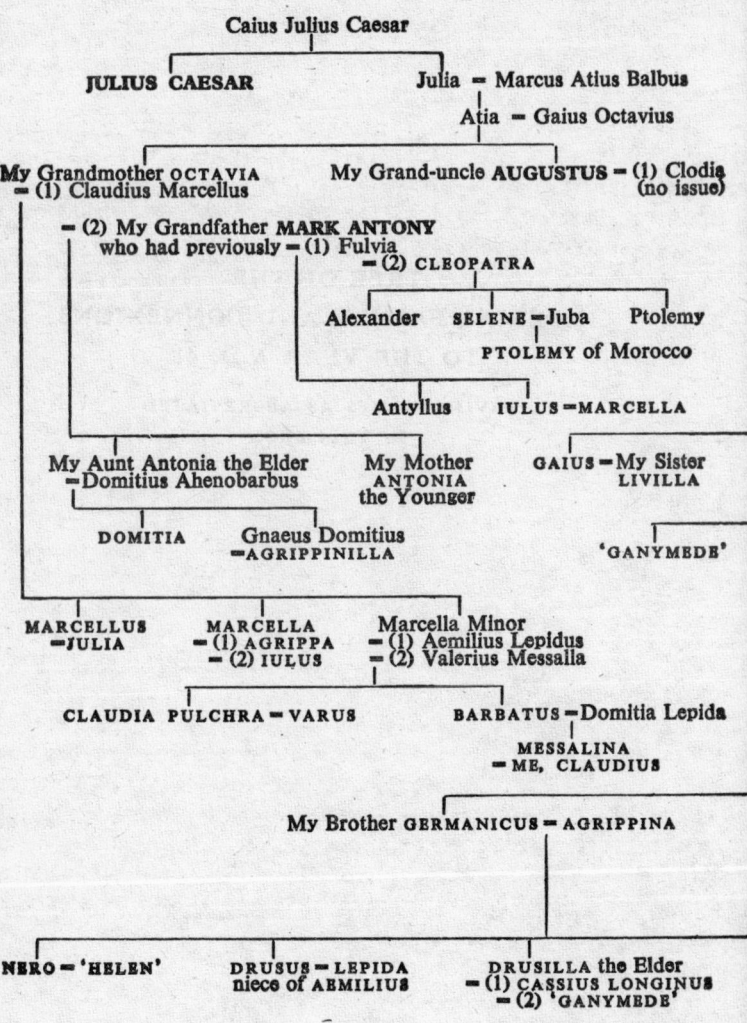

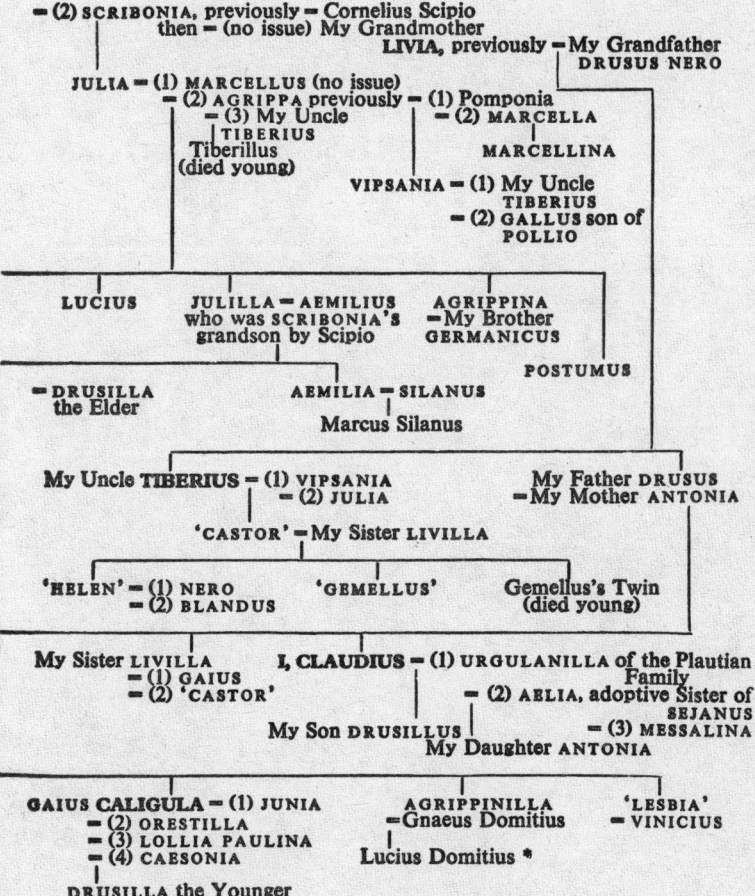

```
─ (2) SCRIBONIA, previously ─ Cornelius Scipio
           then ─ (no issue) My Grandmother
                        LIVIA, previously ─My Grandfather
                                            DRUSUS NERO
    JULIA ─ (1) MARCELLUS (no issue)
          ─ (2) AGRIPPA previously ─ (1) Pomponia
          ─ (3) My Uncle           ─ (2) MARCELLA
            │ TIBERIUS
           Tiberillus                  MARCELLINA
           (died young)
                       VIPSANIA ─ (1) My Uncle
                                      TIBERIUS
                                ─ (2) GALLUS son of
                                      POLLIO

  LUCIUS      JULILLA ─ AEMILIUS      AGRIPPINA
              who was SCRIBONIA'S    ─My Brother
              grandson by Scipio      GERMANICUS
                                                 POSTUMUS
 ─DRUSILLA           AEMILIA ─ SILANUS
  the Elder           Marcus Silanus

My Uncle TIBERIUS ─ (1) VIPSANIA        My Father DRUSUS
                  ─ (2) JULIA          ─My Mother ANTONIA
            'CASTOR' ─My Sister LIVILLA

 'HELEN' ─ (1) NERO      'GEMELLUS'    Gemellus's Twin
         ─ (2) BLANDUS                 (died young)

My Sister LIVILLA      I, CLAUDIUS ─ (1) URGULANILLA of the Plautian
        ─ (1) GAIUS                                    Family
        ─ (2) 'CASTOR'                ─ (2) AELIA, adoptive Sister of
                                              SEJANUS
          My Son DRUSILLUS │          ─ (3) MESSALINA
                      My Daughter ANTONIA

GAIUS CALIGULA ─ (1) JUNIA       AGRIPPINILLA        'LESBIA'
             ─ (2) ORESTILLA    ─Gnaeus Domitius    ─ VINICIUS
             ─ (3) LOLLIA PAULINA
             ─ (4) CAESONIA       Lucius Domitius *
  DRUSILLA the Younger
```

*Afterwards the Emperor NERO. – R.G.

CLAUDIUS THE GOD

AND HIS WIFE MESSALINA

THE TROUBLESOME REIGN OF TIBERIUS CLAUDIUS
CAESAR, EMPEROR OF THE ROMANS
(BORN 10 B.C., DIED A.D. 54),
AS DESCRIBED BY HIMSELF;
ALSO HIS MURDER AT THE HANDS OF THE
NOTORIOUS AGRIPPINA
(MOTHER OF THE EMPEROR NERO)
AND HIS SUBSEQUENT DEIFICATION,
AS DESCRIBED BY
OTHERS

Author's Note

THE 'gold piece', here used as the regular monetary standard, is the Latin *aureus*, a coin worth 100 *sestertii*, or twenty-five silver *denarii* ('silver pieces'): it may be thought of as worth one pound sterling, or five (pre-war) American dollars. The 'mile' is the Roman mile, some thirty paces shorter than the English mile. The marginal dates have for convenience been given according to Christian reckoning: the Greek reckoning, used by Claudius, counted the years from the First Olympiad, which took place in776 B.C. For convenience also, the most familiar geographical names have been used: thus 'France', not 'Transalpine Gaul', because France covers roughly the same territorial area and it would be inconsistent to call towns like Nîmes and Boulogne and Lyons by their modern names – their classical ones would not be popularly recognized – while placing them in *Gallia Transalpina* or, as the Greeks called it, *Galatia*. (Greek geographical terms are most confusing: Germany was called 'the country of the Celts'.) Similarly the most familiar forms of proper names have been used – 'Livy' for Titus Livius, 'Cymbeline' for Cunobelinus, 'Mark Antony' for Marcus Antonius. Claudius is writing in Greek, the scholarly language of his day, which accounts for his careful explanation of Latin jokes and for his translation of a passage from Ennius quoted by him in the original.

Some reviewers of *I, Claudius*, the prefatory volume to *Claudius the God*, suggested that in writing it I had merely consulted Tacitus's *Annals* and Suetonius's *Twelve Caesars*, run them together, and expanded the result with my own 'vigorous fancy'. This was not so; nor is it the case here. Among the Classical writers who have been borrowed from in the composition of *Claudius the God* are Tacitus, Dio Cassius, Suetonius, Pliny, Varro, Valerius Maximus, Orosius, Frontinus, Strabo, Caesar, Columella, Plutarch, Josephus, Diodorus Siculus, Photius, Xiphilinus, Zonaras, Seneca, Petronius, Juvenal, Philo, Celsus, the authors of the *Acts of the Apostles* and of the pseudo-gospels of Nicodemus and St James, and Claudius himself in his surviving letters and speeches. Few incidents here given are wholly unsupported by historical authority of some sort or other and I hope none are historically incredible. No character is invented. The most difficult part to write, because of the meagreness of contemporary references to it, has been Claudius's defeat of Caractacus. For a plausible view of British Druidism, too, I have had to help out the few Classical notices of it with borrowings from archaeological works, from ancient Celtic literature, and from accounts of modern megalithic culture in the New Hebrides, where the dolmen and menhir are still ceremonially used. I have been particularly careful in my account of early Christianity to invent no new libels; but some old ones are quoted, for Claudius himself was not well-disposed to the Church and derived most of his information about near-Eastern religious matters from his old school-friend Herod Agrippa, the Jewish king who executed St James and imprisoned St Peter.

I again thank Miss Laura Riding for her careful reading of the manuscript and her many suggestions on points of literary congruity; and Aircraftman T. E. Shaw for reading the proofs. Miss Jocelyn Toynbee, Lecturer in Classical History at Newnham College, Cambridge, has also given me help for which I am most grateful; and I must acknowledge my indebtedness to Signor Arnaldo Momigliano's monograph on Claudius recently published in translation by the Oxford University Press.

Chapter 1

Two years have gone by since I finished writing the long story of how I, Tiberius Claudius Drusus Nero Germanicus, the cripple, the stammerer, the fool of the family, whom none of his ambitious and bloody-minded relatives considered worth the trouble of executing, poisoning, forcing to suicide, banishing to a desert island or starving to death – which was how they one by one got rid of each other – how I survived them all, even my insane nephew Gaius Caligula, and was one day unexpectedly acclaimed Emperor by the corporals and sergeants of the Palace Guard. I ended the story at this dramatic point; which A.D. 41 was a most injudicious thing for a professional historian like myself to do. A historian has no business to break off at a moment of suspense. I should by rights have carried the story at least one stage farther. I should have told what the rest of the Army thought of the Palace Guard's most unconstitutional act, and what the Senate thought, and how they felt about accepting so unpromising a sovereign as myself, and whether bloodshed ensued, and what were the fates of Cassius Chaerea, Aquila, The Tiger – all officers of the Guard – and Vinicius, who was my niece's husband, and Caligula's other assassins. But, no, the last thing I wrote about was the very irrelevant train of thought that passed through my mind as I was being cheered round and round the Palace Court, seated uncomfortably on the shoulders of two Guards corporals, with Caligula's golden oak-chaplet set crooked on my head.

The reason that I did not take the story any farther was that I wrote it less as ordinary history than as a piece of special pleading – an apology for having ever allowed myself to become the monarch of the Roman world. You may recall, if you have read the story, that both my grandfather and my father were convinced Republicans and that I took after them; the reigns of my uncle Tiberius and of my nephew Caligula merely confirming my anti-monarchical prejudices. I was fifty years old when I was acclaimed Emperor and at that age one does not lightly change one's political colour. So I wrote, in fact, to show how innocent I was of any desire to reign, and how strong was the immediate necessity for yielding to the caprice of the soldiers: to have refused would have meant not only my own death but that of my wife Messalina, with whom I was deeply in love, and of our unborn child. (I wonder why it is that one feels so strongly about an unborn child?) I particularly did not want to be branded by posterity as a clever opportunist who pretended to be a fool, lying low and biding his time until he got wind of a Palace intrigue against his Emperor, and then came boldly forward as a candidate for the succession. This continuation of my story should serve as an apology for the crooked course that I have taken in my thirteen years of Empire. I hope, that is to say, to justify my seemingly inconsistent acts at different stages of my reign by showing their relation to the professed principles from which I have, I swear, never intentionally departed. If I cannot justify them, then I hope at least to show the extraordinarily difficult position in which I was placed, and leave my readers to decide what alternative course, or courses, remained for me to take.

So to pick up the thread just where I dropped it. First let me repeat that things might have turned out considerably worse for Rome if Herod Agrippa, the Jewish king, had not happened to be here on a visit. He was the only man who really kept his head in the crisis of Caligula's assassination and saved the entire audience of the Palatine Hill theatre from massacre by the German Household Battalion. It is a strange thing, but until almost the last page of my story my readers will not have come across a single direct reference to Herod Agrippa's surprising history, though it intertwined closely with mine at several points. The fact was that to have done justice to his adventures, as worth reading about on their own account, would have meant making him too important a figure in the story I had to tell: its chief centre of emphasis lay elsewhere. As it was, my story was constantly in danger of becoming burdened with matter of doubtful relevance. It was as well that I took this decision, because he does figure most importantly in what follows and I can now, without any fear of digressive irrelevance, tell the story of his life up to the point of Caligula's murder, and then continue it concurrently with my own until I reach his death. In this way there will be no such weakening of dramatic unity as would have occurred if I had spread the story over two books. I do not mean that I am a dramatic historian: as you have seen, I am rather wary of literary formalism. But as a matter of fact one could not possibly write about Herod without presenting the story in somewhat of a theatrical style. For this was how Herod himself lived – like the principal actor in a drama – and his fellow actors played up to him well throughout. His was not a drama in the purest classical tradition, although his life was finally cut off in classical tragic style by the conventional divine vengeance for the conventional Greek sin of arrogance – no, there were too many un-Greek elements in it. For instance, the God who inflicted the vengeance on him was not one of the urbane Olympian community: he was perhaps the oddest deity that you could find anywhere in my extensive dominions, or out of them, for that matter, a God of whom no image is in existence, whose name his devout worshippers are forbidden to pronounce (though in his honour they clip their foreskins and practise many other curious and barbarous rites), and who is said to live alone, at Jerusalem, in an ancient cedar chest lined with badger-skins dyed blue and to refuse to have anything to do with any other deities in the world or even to acknowledge the existence of such. And then there was too much farce mixed up with the tragedy to have made it a fit subject for any Greek dramatist of the Golden Age to handle. Imagine the impeccable Sophocles faced with the problem of dealing in a serious poetical vein with Herod's debts! But, as I was saying, I must now tell you at some length what I did not tell you before; and the best plan would be to finish off the old history here and now before getting into my stride with the new.

So here finally begins:

THE STORY OF HEROD AGRIPPA

Herod Agrippa was, you must understand, no blood-relation or connexion by marriage of the great Marcus Vipsanius Agrippa, Augustus's general, who married his only daughter Julia and became by her the grandfather of my nephew Gaius Caligula and my niece Agrippinilla. Nor was he a freedman of Agrippa's: though you might have guessed that too, for in Rome it is the custom of slaves when liberated to assume their former master's surname by way of compliment. No, it was like this: he was named in memory of this same Agrippa, recently dead, by his grandfather, Herod the Great, King of the Jews. For this remarkable and terrible old man owed his throne as much to his interest with Agrippa as to Augustus's patronage of him as a useful ally in the Near East.

The Herod family originally came from Edom, the hilly country lying between Arabia and Southern Judaea: it was not a Jewish family. Herod the Great, whose mother was an Arabian, was given the governorship of Galilee by Julius Caesar at the same time as his father was given that of Judaea. His age was then only fifteen. He got into trouble almost at once for putting Jewish citizens to death without trial, while repressing banditry in his district, and was brought up before the Sanhedrin, the Jewish supreme court. He showed great arrogance on this occasion, appearing before the judges in a purple gown and surrounded by armed soldiers, but forestalled the verdict by secretly leaving Jerusalem. The Roman Governor of Syria to whom he then went for protection gave him a new appointment in that province, the governorship of a district near Lebanon. To cut a long story short, this Herod the Great, whose father had meanwhile died of poison, was made King of the Jews by the joint order of my grandfather Antony and my granduncle Augustus (or Octavian, as he was then called), and ruled for thirty years, with severity and glory, over dominions that were constantly being enlarged by Augustus's bounty. He married no less than ten wives in succession, among them being two of his own nieces, and finally died, after several ineffectual attempts at suicide, of perhaps the most painful and disgusting disease known to medical science. I never heard that it had any name but *Herod's Evil* or that anyone else had ever suffered from it before him, but the symptoms were a ravenous hunger followed by vomiting, a putrescent stomach, a corpse-like breath, maggots breeding in the privy member, and a constant watery flow from the bowels. The disease caused him intolerable anguish and inflamed to madness an already savage nature. The Jews said that it was their God's punishment for Herod's two incestuous marriages. His first wife had been Mariamne, of the famous Maccabee family of Jews, and Herod had been passionately in love with her. But once, when he left Jerusalem to meet my grandfather Antony at Laodicea in Syria, he gave his Chamberlain secret orders that if he should fall a victim to the intrigues of his enemies, Mariamne should be put to death, to keep her from falling into Antony's hands; and he did the same on a later occasion when he went to meet Augustus at Rhodes. (Both Antony and Augustus had bad reputations as sensualists.) When Mariamne found out about these secret orders she naturally became resentful and said things in the presence of Herod's mother and sister which she would have been wiser to have left unsaid. For they were jealous of Mariamne's power over Herod and repeated her words to him as soon as he returned, at the same time accusing her of having committed adultery in his absence as an act of spite and defiance – they named the Chamberlain as her lover. Herod had them both executed. But afterwards he was overtaken by such extreme grief and remorse that he fell into a fever which nearly killed him; and when he recovered, his temper was so gloomy and ferocious that the slightest suspicion would lead him to execute even his best friends and nearest relatives. Mariamne's eldest son was one of the many victims of Herod's rage: he and his brother were put to death on a charge instigated by a half-brother, whom Herod afterwards also put to death, of plotting against their father's life. Augustus commented wittily on these executions: 'I would rather be Herod's pig than Herod's son.' For Herod, by religion a Jew, was not permitted to eat pork, and his pigs could therefore be expected to live to a comfortable old age. This unfortunate prince, Mariamne's eldest son, was the father of my friend Herod Agrippa, whom Herod the Great sent to Rome as soon as he had orphaned him, at the age of four, to be brought up at Augustus's court.

Herod Agrippa and I were exact contemporaries and had a good deal to do with each other through my dear friend Postumus, Agrippa's son, to whom Herod Agrippa naturally attached himself. Herod was a very handsome boy and was one of Augustus's favourites when he came to the cloisters of the Boys' College to play at taws and leap-frog and ducking stones. But what a little rogue he was! Augustus had a favourite dog, one of the big bushytailed temple watch-dogs from Adranos near Etna, who would obey nobody in the world but Augustus, unless Augustus definitely told him: 'Obey Such-and-Such until I call you again.' The brute would then do as he was told but with unhappy yearning looks towards Augustus as he walked away. Somehow little Herod managed to entice this dog when it was thirsty into drinking a basin of very strong wine, and made him as tipsy as any old soldier of the Line on the day of his discharge. Then he hung a goat-bell on his neck, painted his tail saffron-yellow and his legs and muzzle purple-red, tied pigs' bladders to his feet and the wings of a goose to his shoulders, and set him loose in the Palace Court. When Augustus missed his pet and called 'Typhon, Typhon, where are you?' and this extraordinary-looking animal wobbled through the gate towards him, it was one of the most ludicrous moments in the so-called Golden Age of Roman history.

But it happened on the All Fools' Festival in honour of the God Saturn, so Augustus had to take it in good part. Then Herod had a tame snake which he taught to catch mice and which he used to keep under his gown in school-hours to amuse his friends when the master's back was turned. He was such a distracting influence that in the end he was sent to study with me under Athenodorus, my old white-bearded tutor from Tarsus. He tried his schoolboy tricks on Athenodorus, of course, but Athenodorus took them in such good part and I sympathized so little with them, because I loved Athenodorus, that he soon stopped. Herod was a brilliant boy with a marvellous memory and a peculiar gift for languages. Athenodorus once told him: 'Herod, some day, I foresee, you will be called upon to occupy a position of the highest dignity in your native land. You must live every hour of your youth in preparation for that call. With your talents you may in the end become as powerful a ruler as your grandfather Herod.'

Herod replied: 'That is all very well, Athenodorus, but I have a large, bad family. You cannot possibly conceive what a cut-throat crew they are, the greatest rogues that you could meet in a year of travel; and since my grandfather died eight years ago they have not improved in the least, I am told. I can't expect to live six months if I am forced to return to my country. (That's what my poor father said when he was being educated here at Rome in the household of Asinius Pollio. And my uncle Alexander, who was with him, said the same. And they were right.) My uncle the King of Judaea is old Herod reborn, but mean instead of magnificent in his vices; and my uncles Philip and Antipas are a brace of foxes.'

'Single virtue is proof against manifold vice, my princeling,' said Athenodorus. 'Remember that the Jewish nation is more fanatically addicted to virtue than any other nation in the world: if you show yourself virtuous they will be behind you as one man.'

Herod answered: 'Jewish virtue does not agree any too well with Graeco-Roman virtue, such as you teach it, Athenodorus. But many thanks for your prophetic words. You can count on me once I am king to be a really good king; but until I am on the throne I cannot afford to be any more virtuous than the rest of my family.'

As for Herod's character, what shall I say? Most men – it is my experience – are neither virtuous nor scoundrels, good-hearted nor bad-hearted. They are a little of one thing and a little of the other and nothing for any length of time: ignoble mediocrities. But a few men remain always true to a single extreme character: these are the men who leave the strongest mark on history, and I should divide them into four classes. First there are the scoundrels with stony hearts, of whom Macro, the Guards Commander under Tiberius and Caligula, was an outstanding example. Next come the virtuous men with equally stony hearts, of whom Cato the Censor, my bugbear, was an outstanding example. The third class are the virtuous men with golden hearts, such as old Athenodorus and my poor murdered brother Germanicus. And last and most rarely found are the scoundrels with golden hearts, and of these Herod Agrippa was the most perfect instance imaginable. It is the scoundrels with the golden hearts, these anti-Catos, who make the most valuable friends in time of need. You expect nothing from them. They are entirely without principle, as they themselves acknowledge, and only consider their own advantage. But go to them when in desperate trouble and say, 'For God's sake do so-and-so for me,' and they will almost certainly do it – not as a friendly favour but, they will say, because it fits in with their own crooked plans; and you are forbidden to thank them. These anti-Catos are gamblers and spendthrifts; but that is at least better than being misers. They also associate constantly with drunkards, assassins, crooked business men, and procurers; yet you seldom see them greatly the worse for liquor themselves, and if they arrange an assassination you may be sure that the victim will not be greatly mourned, and they defraud the rich defaulters rather than the innocent and needy, and they consort with no woman against her will. Herod himself always insisted that he was congenitally a rogue. To which I would reply, 'No, you are a fundamentally virtuous man wearing the mask of roguery.' This would make him angry. A month or two before Caligula's death we had a conversation of this sort. At the end of it he said, 'Shall I tell you about yourself?' 'There's no need,' I answered, 'I'm the Official Fool of the Palace.' 'Well,' he said, 'there are fools who pretend to be wise men and wise men who pretend to be fools, but you are the first case I have encountered of a fool pretending to be a fool. And one day you'll see, my friend, what sort of a virtuous Jew you are dealing with.'

When Postumus had been banished Herod attached himself to Castor, my uncle Tiberius's son, and the two became known as the rowdiest young blades in the City. They were always drinking and, if the stories told of them were true, spent the greater part of their nights climbing in and out of windows and having tussles with night-watchmen and jealous husbands and angry fathers of respectable households. Herod had inherited a good deal of money from his grandfather, who died when he was six years old, but ran through it quickly as soon as he had the handling of it. Presently he was forced to borrow. He borrowed first from his noble friends, myself among them, in a casual way that made it difficult for us to press him for repayment. When he had exhausted his credit in this way he borrowed from rich knights who were flattered to give him accommodation because of his intimacy with the Emperor's only son; and when they became anxious about the repayment he made up to Tiberius's freedmen who handled Imperial accounts and bribed them to give him loans from the Treasury. He always had a story ready about his golden prospects – he had been promised this or that Eastern kingdom or was to inherit so many hundred thousands of gold pieces from an old senator now at the point of death. But at last, at the age of thirty-three or so, he began to approach the end of his inventive resources; and then Castor died (poisoned by his wife, my sister Livilla, as we learned some years later) and he was obliged to give his creditors leg-bail. He would have appealed personally to Tiberius for assistance, but Tiberius had made a public statement to the effect that he did not wish ever again to see any of his dead son's friends, 'for fear of his grief reviving'. That only meant, of course, that he suspected them of participation in the plot against his life which Sejanus, his chief minister, had persuaded him that Castor was contriving.

Herod fled to Edom, the home of his ancestors, and took refuge in a ruined desert fortress there. It was, I think, his first visit to the Near East since his childhood. At this time his uncle Antipas was Governor (or Tetrarch as the title was) of Galilee with Gilead. For the dominions of Herod the Great had been divided up between his three surviving sons: namely, this Antipas, his brother Archelaus, who became King of Judaea with Samaria; and his younger brother Philip, who became Tetrarch of Bashan, the country lying east of Galilee across the Jordan. Herod now pressed his devoted wife Cypros, who had joined him in the desert, to appeal on his behalf to Antipas. Antipas was not only Herod's uncle but also his brother-in-law, having married his beautiful sister Herodias, the divorced wife of another of his uncles. Cypros would not consent to this at first, because the letter would have to be addressed to Herodias, who had Antipas completely under her thumb, and she had recently quarrelled with Herodias, during the latter's visit to Rome, and sworn never to speak to her again. Cypros protested that she would far rather stay in the desert among their barbarous but hospitable kinsfolk than humiliate herself before Herodias. Herod threatened to commit suicide by leaping from the battlements of the fortress, and actually persuaded Cypros that he was sincere, though I am sure that no man ever lived who was less suicidally inclined than Herod. So she wrote the letter to Herodias after all.

Herodias was much flattered by Cypros's acknowledgement that she had been in the wrong throughout the quarrel and persuaded Antipas to invite Herod and her to Galilee. Herod was made a local magistrate (with a small yearly pension) at Tiberias, the capital town which Antipas had built in honour of the Emperor. But he soon quarrelled with Antipas, an indolent, miserly fellow, who made him feel too keenly the obligations under which he was now laid. 'Why, nephew, you owe your daily food and drink to me,' said Antipas one evening at a banquet to which he had invited Herod and Cypros at Tyre, where they had all gone for a holiday together, 'and I wonder that you presume to argue with me.' Herod had been contradicting him on a point of Roman Law.

Herod replied, 'Uncle Antipas, that is exactly the sort of remark I should have expected you to make.'

'What do you mean, sirrah?' asked Antipas angrily.

'I mean that you are no more than a provincial boor,' replied Herod, 'as lacking in manners as you are ignorant of the principles of law which govern the Empire, and as ignorant of these principles of law as you are stingy with your money.'

'You must be drunk, Agrippa, to talk to me like this,' stuttered Antipas, very red in the face.

'Not on the sort of wine that *you* serve out, Uncle Antipas. I have more regard for my kidneys than that. Where in the world do you manage to lay hands on such filthy brew as this? It must take a lot of ingenuity to find it. Perhaps it's salvage from that long-sunken vessel that they were raising in the harbour yesterday? Or do you scald out the lees from empty wine-jars with boiling camel-stale and then run the mixture into that beautiful golden mixing-bowl of yours?'

After that, of course, he and Cypros and the children had to hurry down to the docks and jump aboard the first out-going ship. It happened to take them north to Antioch, the capital city of Syria, and here Herod presented himself before the Governor of the province, by name Flaccus, who treated him very kindly for my mother Antonia's sake. For you will be surprised to hear that my mother, that virtuous woman, who set her face resolutely against extravagance and disorderliness in her own household, had taken a great liking to this scapegrace. She felt a perverse admiration for his dashing ways, and he used often to come to her for advice and with an air of sincere repentance give her a full account of his follies. She always professed herself shocked by his revelations but certainly derived a deal of pleasure from them and was much flattered by his attentiveness. He never asked her for any loans of money, or not in so many words, but she used voluntarily to lend him quite large sums from time to time on promise of good behaviour. Some of it he paid back. It was really my money, and Herod knew it, and used afterwards to come and thank me profusely as if I were the actual giver. I once suggested to my mother that she was perhaps a little over-liberal to Herod; but she flew into a rage and said that if money had to be wasted she would rather see it wasted in decent style by Herod than diced away by me in low pot-houses with my disreputable friends. (I had had to conceal the dispatch of a large sum of money to help my brother Germanicus pacify the mutineers on the Rhine; so I had pretended that I had lost it by gambling.) I remember once asking Herod whether he did not sometimes grow impatient with my mother's long discourses to him about Roman virtue. He said, 'I greatly admire your mother, Claudius, and you must remember that I am still an uncivilized Edomite at heart, and that it is therefore a great privilege to be instructed by a Roman matron of the highest blood and of such unblemished character. Besides, she talks the purest Latin of anyone in Rome. I learn more from your mother, in a single one of her lectures, about the proper placing of subordinate phrases and the accurate choice of adjectives, than I would from attending a whole course of expensive lectures by a professional grammarian.'

This Governor of Syria, Flaccus, had served under my father and so had come to have a great admiration for my mother, who always accompanied him on his campaigns. After my father's death he made my mother an offer of marriage, but she refused him, saying that, though she loved him as a very dear friend and would continue to do so, she owed it to her glorious husband's memory never to marry again. Besides, Flaccus was many years her junior and there would have been unpleasant talk if they had married. The two carried on a warm correspondence for a great many years until Flaccus died, four years before my mother. Herod knew about this correspondence and gained Flaccus's goodwill by frequent references to my mother's nobility of soul and beauty and kindliness. Flaccus himself was no moral paragon: he was famous at Rome as the man who once, challenged by Tiberius at a banquet, matched him cup for cup throughout one day and two whole nights of uninterrupted drinking. As a courtesy to his Emperor he let Tiberius drain the last cup at dawn of the second day and so come off victorious; but Tiberius was plainly exhausted and Flaccus, according to witnesses, could have continued at least an hour or two longer. So Flaccus and Herod got on very well together. Unfortunately Herod's younger brother Aristobulus was also in Syria and the two were not friends; Herod had obtained some money from him once, promising to invest it for him in a trading venture to India, and had afterwards told him that the ships had gone to the bottom. But it turned out that not only had the ships not gone to the bottom, but they had never sailed. Aristobulus complained to Flaccus about this swindle, but Flaccus said that he was sure that Aristobulus was mistaken about his brother's dishonesty and that he did not wish to take sides in the matter or even to act as adjudicator. However, Aristobulus kept a close watch on Herod, aware that he needed money badly and suspecting that he would get it by some sort of sleight of hand: he would then blackmail him into paying the trading debt.

A year or so later there was a boundary dispute between Sidon and Damascus; and the Damascenes, knowing how much Flaccus had come to depend on Herod for advice in arbitrating on matters of this sort – because of Herod's remarkable command of languages and his capacity, inherited no doubt from his grandfather Herod, for sifting the contradictory evidence given by Orientals – sent a secret deputation to Herod offering him a large sum of money, I forget how much, if he would persuade Flaccus to give a verdict in their favour. Aristobulus found out about this, and when the case was over, settled in favour of Damascus by the persuasive pleading of Herod, he went to Herod and told him what he knew, adding that he now expected payment of the shipping debt. Herod was so angry that Aristobulus was lucky to escape with his life. It was quite clear that he could not be frightened into paying back a single penny, so Aristobulus went to Flaccus and told him about the bags of gold that would shortly be arriving for Herod from Damascus. Flaccus intercepted them at the City gate and then sent for Herod, who, in the circumstances, could not deny that they were sent in payment for services rendered in the matter of the boundary dispute. But he put a bold face on it and begged Flaccus not to regard the money as a bribe, for he had, while giving evidence in the case, kept strictly to the truth: Damascus had justice on its side. He told Flaccus, too, that the Sidonians had also sent him a deputation whom he had dismissed, telling them that he could do nothing to help them, for they were in the wrong.

'I suppose Sidon didn't offer you so much money as Damascus,' sneered Flaccus.

'Please do not insult me,' Herod virtuously replied.

'I refuse to have justice in a Roman court bought and sold like merchandise.' Flaccus was thoroughly vexed.

'You judged the case yourself, my Lord Flaccus,' said Herod.

'And you made a fool of me in my own court,' Flaccus raged. 'I have done with you. You can go to Hell for all I care, and by the shortest road.'

'I am afraid that it will be the Taenaran road,' said Herod, 'for if I die now I won't have a farthing in my purse to pay the Ferryman.' (Taenarum is the southermost promontory of the Peloponnese, where there is a short cut to Hell which avoids the River Styx. It was by this way that Hercules dragged the Dog Cerberus to the Upper World. The thrifty natives of Taenarum bury their dead without the customary coin in the mouth, knowing that they will not need it to pay Charon their ferryfare.) Then Herod said, 'But, Flaccus, you must not lose your temper with me. You know how it is. I didn't think that I was doing wrong. It is difficult for an Oriental like myself, even after nearly thirty years of City education, to understand your noble Roman scruples in a case of this sort. I see the matter in this light: the Damascenes were employing me as a sort of lawyer in their defence, and lawyers at Rome are paid enormous fees and never keep nearly so close to the truth, when presenting their cases, as I did. And certainly I did the Damascenes a good service in presenting their case so lucidly to you. So what harm could there have been in taking the money, which they quite voluntarily sent me? It's not as though I publicly advertised myself as having influence with you. They flattered and surprised me by suggesting that it might be so. Besides, as the Lady Antonia, that most extraordinarily wise and beautiful woman, has frequently pointed out to me – –'

But it was no use appealing even to Flaccus's regard for my mother. He gave Herod twenty-four hours' law and said that if at the end of that time he was not well on his way out of Syria he would find himself up before the tribunal on a criminal charge.

Chapter 2

HEROD asked Cypros, 'Where in the world are we to go now?'

Cypros answered miserably: 'So long as you don't ask me to humble myself again by writing begging letters that I would almost rather die than write, I don't care where we go. Is India far enough away from our creditors?'

Herod said, 'Cypros, my queen, we'll survive this adventure as we have survived many others and live to a prosperous and wealthy old age together. And I give you my solemn word that you'll have the laugh against my sister Herodias before I have finished with her and her husband.'

'That ugly harlot,' Cypros cried with truly Jewish indignation. For, as I told you, Herodias had not only committed incest by marrying an uncle but had divorced him in order to marry her richer and more powerful uncle Antipas. The Jews could make certain allowances for the incest, because marriage between uncle and niece was a common practice among Eastern royal families – the Armenian and Parthian royal families especially – and the family of Herod was not of Jewish origin. But divorce was regarded with the greatest disgust by every honest Jew (as, formerly, by every honest Roman) as being shameful both to the husband and to the wife; and nobody who had been under the disagreeable necessity of getting divorced would consider it the first step towards remarriage. Herodias had, however, lived long enough at Rome to be able to laugh at these scruples. Everyone at Rome who is anyone gets divorced sooner or later. (Nobody, for instance, could call *me* a profligate, and yet I have divorced three wives already and may come to divorcing my fourth.) So Herodias was most unpopular in Galilee.

Aristobulus went to Flaccus and said, 'In recognition of my services, Flaccus, would you perhaps be generous enough to give me that confiscated money from Damascus? It would almost cover the debt that Herod owes me – the shipping-fraud that I told you about some months ago.'

Flaccus said: 'Aristobulus, you have done me no service at all. You have been the cause of a breach between me and my ablest adviser, whom I miss more than I can tell you. As a matter of governmental discipline I had to dismiss him, and as a matter of honour I cannot recall him; but if you had not brought that bribe to light nobody would have been any the wiser and I would still have had Herod to consult on complicated local questions which absolutely baffle a simple-minded Westerner like myself. It's in his blood, you see. I have, in point of fact, lived far longer in the East than he has, but he instinctively knows in cases where I can only clumsily guess.'

'What about myself?' asked Aristobulus. 'Perhaps I can fill Herod's place?'

'*You*, little man?' Flaccus cried contemptuously. 'You haven't the Herod touch. And, what's more, you'll never acquire it. You know that, as well as I do.'

'But the money?' asked Aristobulus.

'If it's not for Herod, still less is it for you. But to avoid all ill-feeling between you and me I am going to send it back to Damascus.' He actually did this. The Damascenes thought that he must have gone mad.

After a month or so Aristobulus, being out of favour at Antioch, decided to settle in Galilee, where he had an estate. It was only a two-days' journey from here to Jerusalem, a city which he liked to visit on all the important Jewish festivals, being more religiously inclined than the rest of his family. But he did not wish to take all his money with him to Galilee, because if he happened to quarrel with his uncle Antipas he might be forced to go away in a hurry, and Antipas would be just so much the richer. He therefore decided to transfer most of his credit from a banking firm at Antioch to one at Rome and wrote to me as a trustworthy family friend, giving me authority to invest it in landed property for him as opportunity should present itself.

Herod could not return to Galilee: and he had also quarrelled with his uncle Philip, the Tetrarch of Bashan, over a question of some property of his father which Philip had misappropriated;

and the Governor of Judaea with Samaria – for Herod's eldest uncle, the King, had been removed for misgovernment some years previously and his kingdom proclaimed a Roman province – was Pontius Pilate, one of his creditors. Herod did not wish to retire permanently to Edom – he was no lover of deserts – and his chances of a welcome in Egypt by the great Jewish colony at Alexandria were inconsiderable. The Alexandrian Jews are very strict in their religious observances, almost stricter than their kinsmen at Jerusalem, if that were possible, and Herod from living so long at Rome had fallen into slack habits, especially in the matter of diet. The Jews are forbidden by their ancient law-giver Moses, on hygienic grounds, I understand, to eat a variety of ordinary meat foods: not merely pork – one could make a case against pork, perhaps – but hare and rabbit, and other perfectly wholesome meats. And what they do eat must be killed in a certain way. Wild duck that has been brought down by a sling-stone, or a fowl that has had its neck wrung, or venison got by bow and arrow, are forbidden them. Every animal that they eat must have had its throat cut and have been allowed to bleed to death. Then, too, they must make every seventh day a day of absolute rest: their very household servants are forbidden to do a stroke of work, even cooking or stoking the furnace. And they have days of national mourning in commemoration of ancient misfortunes, which often clash with Roman festivities. It had been impossible for Herod while he was living at Rome to be at the same time both a strict Jew and a popular member of high society; and so he had preferred the contempt of the Jews to that of the Romans. He decided not to try Alexandria or waste any more of his time in the Near East, where every door seemed closed to him. He would either take refuge in Parthia, where the king would welcome him as a useful agent in his designs against the Roman province of Syria, or he would return to Rome and throw himself upon my mother's protection: it might be just possible to explain away the misunderstanding with Flaccus. He rejected the idea of Parthia, because to go there would mean a complete breach with his old life, and he had greater confidence in the power of Rome than in that of Parthia; and besides it would be rash to try to cross the Euphrates – the boundary between Syria and Parthia – without money to bribe the frontier guards, who were under orders to allow no political refugee to pass. So he finally chose Rome.

And did he get there safely? You shall hear. He had not even enough ready money with him to pay for his sea-passage – he had been living on credit at Antioch and in great style; and though Aristobulus offered to lend him enough to take him as far as Rhodes, he refused to humble himself by accepting it. Besides, he could not risk booking his passage on a vessel sailing down the Orontes, for fear of being arrested at the docks by his creditors. He suddenly thought of someone from whom he could perhaps raise a trifle, namely, a former slave of his mother's whom she had bequeathed in her will to my mother Antonia and whom my mother had liberated and set up as a corn-factor at Acre, a coastal city somewhat south of Tyre: he paid her a percentage of his earnings and was doing quite well. But the territory of the Sidonians lay between and Herod had, as a matter of fact, accepted a gift from the Sidonians as well as from the Damascenes; so he could not afford to fall into their hands. He sent a trustworthy freedman of his to borrow from this man at Acre and himself escaped from Antioch in disguise, travelling east, which was the one direction that nobody expected him to take, and so eluding pursuit. Once in the Syrian desert he made a wide circuit towards the south, on a stolen camel, avoiding Bashan, his uncle Philip's tetrarchy, and Petraea (or, as some call it, Gilead, the fertile Transjordanian territory over which his uncle Antipas ruled as well as over Galilee), and skirting the farther end of the Dead Sea. He came safely to Edom, where he was greeted warmly by his wild kinsmen, and waited in the same desert fortress as before for his freedman to come with the money. The freedman succeeded in borrowing the money – 20,000 Attic drachmae: as the Attic drachma is worth rather more than the Roman silver piece, this came to something over 900 gold pieces. At least, he had given Herod's note of hand to that amount, in exchange; and would have arrived with the 20,000 drachmae complete if the corn-factor at Acre had not deducted 2,500, of which he accused Herod of having defrauded him some years previously. The honest freedman was afraid that his master would be angry with him for not bringing the whole amount, but Herod only laughed and said: 'I counted on that twenty-five hundred to secure me the balance of the twenty thousand. If the stingy fellow had not thought that he was doing a smart trick in making my note of hand cover the old debt he would never have dreamed of lending me any money at all; for he must know by now what straits I am in.' So Herod gave a great feast for the tribesmen and then made cautiously for the port of

Anthedon, near the Philistine town of Gaza, where the coast begins curving west towards Egypt. Here Cypros and her children were waiting in disguise on board the small trading-vessel in which they had sailed from Antioch and which had been chartered to take them on to Italy by way of Egypt and Sicily. Affectionate greetings between all members of the family thus happily reunited were just being exchanged when a Roman sergeant and three soldiers appeared alongside in a rowing-boat with a warrant for Herod's arrest. The local military governor had signed this warrant, the reason for which was the non-payment to the Privy Purse of a debt of 12,000 gold pieces.

Herod read the document and remarked to Cypros: 'I take this as a very cheerful omen. The Treasurer has scaled down my debts from forty thousand to a mere twelve. We must give him a really splendid banquet when we get back to Rome. Of course, I've done a lot for him since I have been out in the East, but twenty-eight thousand is a generous return.'

The sergeant interposed, 'Excuse me, Prince, but really you can't think about banquets at Rome until you have seen the Governor here about this debt. He has orders not to let you sail until it's paid in full.'

Herod said: 'Of course I shall pay it. It had quite escaped my memory. A mere trifle. You go off now in the rowing-boat, and tell His Excellency the Governor that I am entirely at his service, but that his kind reminder of my debt to the Treasury has come a little inconveniently. I have just been joined by my devoted wife, the Princess Cypros, from whom I have been parted for over six weeks. Are you a family man, Sergeant? Then you will understand how earnestly we two desire to be alone together. You can leave your two soldiers on board as a guard if you don't trust us. Come again in the boat in three or four hours' time and we'll be quite ready to disembark. And here's an earnest of my gratitude.' He gave the sergeant 100 drachmae; upon which the sergeant, leaving the guard behind, rowed ashore without further demur. An hour or two later it was dusk and Herod cut the cables of the vessel and stood out to sea. He made as if to sail north towards Asia Minor but soon changed his course and turned south-west. He was making for Alexandria, where he thought he might as well try his luck with the Jews.

The two soldiers had been suddenly seized, trussed up, and gagged by the crew, who had engaged them in a game of dice; but

Herod released them as soon as he was sure that he was not being pursued and said that he would put them safe ashore at Alexandria if they behaved sensibly. He only stipulated that on his arrival there they should pretend to be his military bodyguard for a day or two; and promised in return to pay their passage back to Anthedon. They agreed hastily, terrified of being thrown overboard if they displeased him.

I should have mentioned that Cypros and the children had been helped out of Antioch by a middle-aged Samaritan called Silas, Herod's most faithful friend. He was a gloomy-looking, solidly-built fellow with an enormous square-cut black beard, and had once served in the native cavalry as a troop commander. He had been awarded two military decorations for his services against the Parthians. Herod had on several occasions offered to have him made a Roman citizen, but Silas had always refused the honour on the ground that if he became a Roman he would be obliged to shave his chin in Roman fashion, and that he would never consent to do that. Silas was always giving Herod good advice, which he never took, and whenever Herod got into difficulties used to say: 'What did I tell you? You should have listened to what I said.' He prided himself upon his bluntness of speech, and was sadly wanting in tact. But Herod bore with Silas because he could be trusted to stand by him through thick and thin. Silas had been his only companion during the first flight to Edom, and again but for Silas the family would never have escaped from Tyre the day that Herod insulted Antipas. And at Antioch it had been Silas who had provided Herod with his disguise for escaping from his creditors, besides protecting Cypros and the children and finding the vessel for them. When things were really bad Silas was at his best and cheerfullest, for then he knew that Herod would need his services and would give him an opportunity for saying, 'I am entirely at your disposal, Herod Agrippa, my dear friend, if I may call you so. But if you had taken my advice this would never have occurred.' In times of prosperity he always grew more and more gloomy, seeming to look back with a sort of regret to the bad old days of poverty and disgrace; and even encouraging them to return by his warnings to Herod that if he continued in his present course (whatever it might be) he would end as a ruined man. However, things were bad enough now to make Silas the brightest of companions. He cracked jokes with the crew and told the children long complicated stories of his military adventures. Cypros, who usually resented Silas's tediousness, now felt ashamed of her rudeness to this golden-hearted friend.

'I was brought up with a Jewish prejudice against Samaritans,' she told Silas, 'and you must forgive me if it has taken all these years for me to overcome it.'

'I must ask your forgiveness too, Princess,' Silas replied '– forgiveness, I mean, for my bluntness of speech. But such is my nature. I must take the liberty of saying that if your Jewish friends and relatives were in general a little less upright and a little more charitable I should like them better. A cousin of mine was once riding on business from Jerusalem to Jericho. He came upon a poor Jew lying wounded and naked in the hot sun by the roadside. He had been set on by bandits. My cousin cleansed his wounds and bound them up as best he could and then took him on his beast to the nearest inn, where he paid in advance for his room and his food for a few days – the inn-keeper insisted on payment in advance – and then visited him on his way back from Jericho and helped him to get home. Well, that was nothing: we Samaritans are made that way. It was all in a day's work for my cousin. But the joke was that three or four well-to-do Jews – a priest among them – whom my cousin had met riding towards him just before he came on the wounded man, must have actually seen him lying by the roadside; but because he was no relation of theirs they had left him there to die and ridden on, though he was groaning and calling out for help most pitifully. The innkeeper was a Jew too. He told my cousin that he quite understood the reluctance of these travellers to attend to the wounded man: if he had died on their hands they would have become ritually unclean from touching a corpse, which would have been a great inconvenience to themselves and their families. The priest, the innkeeper explained, was probably on his way to Jerusalem to worship at the Temple: he, least of all, could risk pollution. Well, thank God, I am a Samaritan, and a man with a blunt tongue. I say what I think. I – –'

Herod interrupted, 'My dear Cypros, isn't that a most instructive story? And if the poor fellow had been a Samaritan he wouldn't have had enough money to make it worth the bandits' while to rob him.'

At Alexandria Herod, accompanied by Cypros, the children, and the two soldiers, went to the chief magistrate of the Jewish colony there – or Alabarch, as he was called. The Alabarch was answerable to the Governor of Egypt for the good behaviour of his co-religionists. He had to see that they paid their taxes regularly and refrained from street riots with the Greeks and from other breaches of the peace. Herod greeted the Alabarch suavely and presently asked him for a loan of 8,000 gold pieces, offering in exchange to use his influence at the Imperial Court on behalf of the Alexandrian Jews. He said that the Emperor Tiberius had written asking him to come to Rome immediately to advise him on Eastern affairs and that in consequence he had left Edom, where he was visiting his cousins, in a great hurry and with very little money in his purse for travelling expenses. The Roman bodyguard seemed to the Alabarch to furnish impressive proof of the truth of Herod's story, and he considered that it would indeed be very useful to have an influential friend at Rome. There had been riots lately in which the Jews had been the aggressors and had done serious damage to Greek property. Tiberius might feel inclined to curtail their privileges, which were considerable.

Alexander the Alabarch was an old friend of my family's. He had acted as steward of a large property at Alexandria which had been left to my mother in my grandfather Mark Antony's will and which Augustus, for my grandmother Octavia's sake, had allowed her to inherit, though he cancelled most of the other bequests. My mother brought this property as a dowry to my father when she married him, and it then went to my sister Livilla, who brought it as a dowry to Castor, Tiberius's son, when she married him; but Livilla soon sold it, because she led an extravagant life and needed the money, and the Alabarch lost the management of it. After this, correspondence between him and my family gradually ceased; and though my mother had used her interest with Tiberius to raise him to his present dignity and might be supposed to be well-disposed towards him still, the Alabarch was not sure how far he could count on her support if he became involved in any political trouble. Well, he knew that Herod had once been an intimate friend of the family, and so would have lent him money very readily had he been sure that Herod was still on good terms with us; but he could not be sure. He questioned Herod about my mother; and Herod, who had foreseen the situation very clearly and had been clever enough not to be the first to mention her name, answered that she was in the best of health and spirits when she last wrote. He had brought with him, as if accidentally, a cordial letter from her, written to him just before he left Antioch, in which she included a budget of detailed family news. He handed it to the Alabarch to read and the Alabarch was even more impressed by it than by the bodyguard. But the letter concluded with the hope that Herod was now at last settled down to a useful political life on the staff of her esteemed friend Flaccus, and the Alabarch had just heard from friends at Antioch that Flaccus and Herod had quarrelled, and besides he could not be sure that Tiberius had really written the letter of invitation – which Herod had not offered to show him. He could not make up his mind whether to lend the money or not. However, he had just decided to do so, when one of the kidnapped soldiers, who understood a little Hebrew, said, 'Give me only eight gold pieces, Alabarch, and I'll save you eight thousand.'

'What do you mean, soldier?' asked the Alabarch.

'I mean that this man's a swindler and a fugitive from justice. We are not his bodyguard, but two men whom he has kidnapped. There's an Imperial warrant out for his arrest because of a big debt at Rome.'

Cypros saved the situation by falling at the Alabarch's feet and sobbing, 'For the sake of your old friendship with my father Phasael have mercy on me and my poor children. Do not condemn us to beggary and utter destruction. My dear husband has committed no fraud. The substance of what he has told you is perfectly true, though perhaps he has slightly coloured the details. We are indeed on our way to Rome, and owing to recent political changes we have the most golden expectations there; and if you lend us just enough money to help us out of our present difficulties, the God of our fathers will reward you a thousandfold. The debt on account of which my dear Herod was so nearly arrested is a legacy of his improvident youth. Once arrived at Rome he will soon find honourable means of repaying it. But to fall into the hands of his enemies in the Syrian Government would be his ruin and the ruin of my children and myself.'

The Alabarch turned towards Cypros, whose fidelity to Herod in his misfortunes almost brought tears to his eyes, and asked, kindly but cautiously, 'Does your husband observe the Law?'

Herod saw her hesitate a little and spoke for himself. 'You must remember, sir, that I am an Edomite by blood. You cannot reasonably expect as much from an Edomite as from a Jew. Edom and Jewry are blood-brothers through our common ancestor, the patriarch Isaac; but before any Jew congratulates himself on God's peculiar favour to his nation let him remember how Esau, the ancestor of Edom, was tricked of his birthright and of his father's blessing by Jacob, the ancestor of Jewry. Drive no hard bargains with me, Alabarch. Show more compassion to a distressed and improvident Edomite than old Jacob did, or, as the Lord my God lives, the next spoonful of *red lentil porridge* that you put into your mouth will surely choke you. We have lost our birthright to you and with it God's peculiar favour, and in return we demand from you such generosity of heart as we ourselves have never failed to show. Remember Esau's magnanimity when, meeting Jacob by chance at Peniel, he did not kill him.'

'But do you observe the Law?' asked the Alabarch, impressed by Herod's vehemence and unable to contradict his historical references.

'I am circumcised, and so are my children, and I and my whole household have always kept the Law revealed to your ancestor Moses as strictly as our difficult position as Roman citizens and our imperfect consciences as Edomites have allowed us.'

'There are no two ways of righteousness,' said the Alabarch stiffly. 'Either the Law is kept, or it is broken.'

'Yet I have read that the Lord once permitted Naaman, the Syrian proselyte, to worship in the Temple of Rimmon by the side of the King, his master,' said Herod. 'And Naaman proved a very good friend to the Jews, did he not?'

At last the Alabarch said to Herod: 'If I lend you this money will you swear in the name of the Lord – to whom be Glory Everlasting – to keep His Law as far as in you lies, and cherish His People, and never by sins of commission or omission offend against His Majesty?'

'I swear by His most Holy Name,' said Herod, 'and let my wife Cypros and my children be my witnesses, that I will henceforth honour Him with all my soul and with all my strength and that I will constantly love and protect His People. If ever wittingly I blaspheme, from hardness of heart, may the maggots that fed upon my grandfather Herod's living flesh so feed upon mine and consume me utterly!'

So he got the loan. As he told me afterwards, 'I would have sworn anything in the world only to lay my hands on that money, I was so hard pressed.'

But the Alabarch made two further conditions. The first was that Herod should now be paid only the equivalent, in silver, of 4,000 gold pieces and receive the rest of the money on his arrival in Italy. For he did not yet trust Herod entirely. He might have thoughts of going off to Morocco or Arabia with the money. The second condition was that Cypros should take the children to Jerusalem to be educated as good Jews there under the guardianship of the Alabarch's brother-in-law, the High Priest. To this Herod and Cypros agreed, the more cheerfully as they knew that no good-looking boy or girl in high Roman society was safe from Tiberius's unnatural lusts. (My friend Vitellius, for example, had had one of his sons taken away from him to Capri, under the pretence that he would be given a liberal education there, and put among the filthy Spintrians, so that the boy's whole nature became warped. The name 'Spintrian' has stuck to him all his life, and a worse man I do not know.) Well, they decided that Cypros would rejoin him at Rome as soon as she had settled the children safely at Jerusalem.

What had made Herod come to Alexandria to borrow money from the Alabarch was the rumour that his freedman had brought with him from Acre of the fall of Sejanus. At Alexandria it had been fully confirmed. Sejanus had been my uncle Tiberius's most trusted minister but had conspired with my sister Livilla to kill him and usurp the monarchy. It was my mother who discovered the plot and warned Tiberius; and Tiberius, with the help of my nephew Caligula and the stony-hearted villain Macro, soon managed to bring Sejanus to book. It was then discovered that Livilla had poisoned her husband Castor seven years previously and that Castor had, after all, never been the traitor to his father that Sejanus had represented him as being. So naturally Tiberius's strict rule against the reappearance in his presence of any of Castor's former friends must now be considered cancelled; and my mother's patronage was more valuable than ever before. Had it not been for this news Herod would not have wasted his time and dignity by trying to borrow from the Alabarch. Jews are generous but very careful. They lend to their own needy fellow-Jews if they have fallen into misfortune through no fault or sin of their own, and they lend without charging any interest, because that is forbidden in their Law: their only reward is a feeling of virtue. But they will lend nothing to any non-Jew, even if he is dying of starvation, still less to any Jew who has put himself 'outside the congregation', as they call it, by following un-Jewish customs in foreign lands – unless they are quite sure that they will get some substantial return for their generosity.

Chapter 3

My mother and I were unaware of Herod's return to Italy until one day a hurried note came from him, saying that he was coming to see us and adding darkly that he counted on our help to tide him over a great crisis of his fortunes. 'If it's money that he wants,' I said to my mother, 'the answer is that we have none.' And indeed we did not have any money to throw away at this time, as I have explained in my previous book. But my mother said: 'It is very base to talk in that strain, Claudius. You were always a boor. If Herod needs money because he is in difficulties we must certainly raise money in some way or other: I owe it to the memory of his dead mother Berenice. In spite of her outlandish religious habits Berenice was one of my best friends. And such a splendid household manager, too!'

My mother had not seen Herod for some seven years and had missed him greatly. But he had been a most dutiful correspondent, writing to her about each of his troubles in turn and in such an amusing way that they seemed the most delightful adventures that you would find anywhere in Greek story-books, instead of genuine troubles. Perhaps the gayest letter of all was the one that he wrote from Edom shortly after leaving Rome, telling how his sweet, dear, silly wife Cypros had discouraged him from his leap from the fortress battlements. 'She was quite right,' he concluded. 'It was an excessively high tower.' A recent letter, also written from Edom, was in the same strain; it was while he was waiting for the money from Acre. He told of his shame at having sunk so low morally as to steal a Persian merchant's riding-camel. However, he wrote, shame had soon turned to a feeling of virtue for having done the owner so signal a service: the beast being apparently the permanent home of seven evil spirits, each worse than the last. The merchant must have been incomparably relieved to have awakened one morning and found his treasured possession really gone, saddle, bridle, and all. It had been a most terrifying journey through the Syrian desert, the camel doing its best to kill him at every dry water-course or narrow pass that they came to and even sneaking up at night to trample on his sleeping body. He wrote again from Alexandria to tell us that he had turned the beast loose in Edom, but that it had stalked him with a wicked look in its eye all the way down to the coast. 'I swear to you, most noble and learned Lady Antonia, my earliest friend and my most generous benefactress, that it was terror of that horrible camel rather than fear of my creditors that made me give the Governor the slip at Anthedon. It would certainly have insisted on sharing my prison cell with me if I had yielded to arrest.' There was a postscript: 'My cousins of Edom were extraordinarily hospitable, but I must not allow you to carry away the impression that they were *extravagant*. They carry economy so far that they only put on clean linen on three occasions – when they marry, when they die, and when they raid a caravan which supplies them with clean linen free of charge. There is not a single fuller in the whole of Edom.' Herod naturally put the most favourable construction possible on his quarrel, or misunderstanding as he called it, with Flaccus. He blamed himself for his thoughtlessness and praised Flaccus as a man with almost too high a sense of honour, if that were possible – certainly it was much too high for the people whom he governed to appreciate: they regarded him as an eccentric.

Herod now told us the parts of his story that he had omitted from his letters, concealing nothing, or practically nothing, for he knew that this was the best way to behave with my mother; and he especially delighted her – though of course she pretended to be dreadfully shocked – with his story of the kidnapping of the soldiers and his attempt to bluff the Alabarch. He also described his voyage from Alexandria in a dangerous storm when everyone but himself and the captain had, so he said, been prostrated by seasickness for five days and nights. The captain had spent all his time weeping and praying, leaving Herod to navigate the vessel single-handed.

Then he went on: 'When at last, standing in the forecastle of our gallant ship, which had now stopped its rolling and pitching, and heedless of the thanks and praises of the now convalescent crew, I saw the Bay of Naples stretched shining before me, its shores gleaming with beautiful temples and villas, and mighty Vesuvius towering above, and reeking with wisps of cloud, like a domestic hearth – I confess I wept. I realized that I was coming home to my first and dearest homeland. I thought of all my beloved Roman friends from whom I had been so long parted, and especially of you, most learned and beautiful and noble Antonia – of you too, Claudius, naturally – how happy we would be to greet one another again. But first, it was clear, I had to establish myself decently. It would have been most unsuitable for me to have presented myself at your door like a beggar or poor client, asking for relief. As soon as we had landed and I had cashed the Alabarch's draft, which was on a Naples bank, I wrote at once to the Emperor, at Capri, begging to be allowed the privilege of an audience. He granted it most graciously, saying that he was pleased to hear of my safe return, and we had a most encouraging talk together the next day. I am sorry to say that I felt bound to divert him – for he was in a rather morose humour at first – with some Asiatic stories that I certainly would not injure your modesty by repeating here. But you know how it is with the Emperor: he has an ingenious mind and is very catholic in his tastes. Well, when I had told him a particularly characteristic story in that style he said, "Herod, you're a man after my own heart. I wish you to undertake an appointment of great responsibility – the tutoring of my only grandchild, Tiberius Gemellus, whom I have here with me. As an intimate friend of his dead father you will surely not refuse it, and I trust that the lad will take to you. He is, I am sorry to say, a sullen, melancholy little fellow and needs an open-hearted lively elder companion on whom to model himself."

'I stopped the night at Capri, and by morning the Emperor and I were better friends than ever – he had disregarded his doctors' advice and drunk with me all night. I thought that my fortunes were restored at last, when suddenly the single horse-hair, by which the sword of Damocles had so long been suspended over my unlucky head, contrived to snap. A letter arrived for the Emperor from that idiot of a Governor at Anthedon reporting that he had served a warrant on me for non-payment of a twelve-thousand debt to the Privy Purse and that I had "eluded arrest by an artifice" and had escaped, kidnapping two of his garrison, who had not yet returned and had probably been murdered. I assured the Emperor that the soldiers were alive and that they had stowed away in my vessel without my knowledge and that no warrant had been served on me. Perhaps they had been sent to serve it, I said, but had decided to go for a holiday to Egypt. At all events we found them hiding in the cargo when we were half-way to Alexandria. I assured the Emperor that at Alexandria I had returned them at once to Anthedon for punishment.'

'Herod Agrippa,' said my mother severely, 'that was a deliberate lie and I am most ashamed of you.'

'Not so ashamed as I have been of myself since, dear Lady

Antonia,' said Herod. 'How often have you told me that honesty is the best policy? But in the East everyone tells lies and one naturally discounts nine-tenths of what one hears, and expects one's hearers to do the same. For the moment I had forgotten that I was back in a country where it is considered dishonourable to deviate a hair's breadth from the strict truth.'

'Did the Emperor believe you?' I asked.

'I hope so, with all my heart,' said Herod. 'He asked me, "But what about the debt?" I told him that it was a loan granted me in proper form and on good security by the Privy Purse, and that if a warrant had been issued for my arrest on that account it must have been that traitor Sejanus's doing: I would speak to the Treasurer at once and settle the matter with him. But the Emperor said: "Herod, unless that debt is paid in full within a week you shall not be tutor to my grandson." You know how strict he is about debts to the Privy Purse. I said in as casual a tone as I could command, that I would certainly pay it within three days. But my heart was like lead. And so I immediately wrote to you, my dear benefactress, thinking that perhaps ...'

My mother said again, 'It was very, very wrong of you, Herod, to tell the Emperor such lies.'

'I know it, I know it,' said Herod, feigning deep repentance. 'If you had been in my position you would undoubtedly have told the truth: but I lacked the courage. And, as I say, these seven years in the East away from you have greatly blunted my moral sensibilities.'

'Claudius,' said my mother with sudden resolution, 'how can we raise twelve thousand in a hurry? What about the letter you had from Aristobulus this morning?'

By a pretty coincidence I had had a letter from Aristobulus only that morning asking me to invest some money for him in landed property, which was going cheap at that time, because of the scarcity of coin. He had enclosed a banker's draft for 10,000. My mother told Herod about it.

'Aristobulus!' cried Herod. 'How in the world did *he* rake ten thousand together? The unprincipled fellow must have been making use of his influence with Flaccus to take bribes from the natives.'

'I consider, in that case,' said my mother, 'that he behaved very shabbily towards you in reporting to my old friend Flaccus that the Damascenes were sending you a present for having pleaded their cause so well. I should have thought better of Aristobulus than that. And now perhaps it would only be justice if that ten thousand were used as a temporary – *temporary*, mind you, Herod – loan to help you on your feet again. There will be no difficulty about the remaining two thousand – will there, Claudius?'

'You forget that Herod still has eight thousand from the Alabarch, Mother. Unless he has already spent it. He'll be better off than we are if we entrust Aristobulus's money to him.'

Herod was warned that he must repay the debt within three months without fail or I would be guilty of a breach of fiduciary trust. I did not like the business in the least, but I preferred it to mortgaging our house on the Palatine Hill to raise the money, which would have been the only other course. However, everything turned out unexpectedly well. Not only was Herod's appointment as tutor to Gemellus confirmed, as soon as he had paid the Privy Purse the 12,000, but he also repaid me the whole amount of the Aristobulus loan two days before it was due and, besides that, a former debt of 5,000 which we had never expected to see again. For Herod, as Gemellus's tutor, was thrown a great deal into the company of Caligula, whom Tiberius, now seventy-five years old, had adopted as his son and who was his heir-presumptive. Tiberius kept Caligula very short of money, and Herod, after gaining Caligula's confidence by some fine banquets, handsome presents and the like, became his accredited agent for borrowing large sums, in the greatest secrecy, from rich men who wanted to stand in well with the new Emperor. For Tiberius was not expected to live much longer. When Caligula's confidence in Herod was thus proved and a matter of common knowledge in financial circles, he found it easy to borrow money in his own name as well as in Caligula's. His unpaid debts of seven years before had mostly settled themselves by the death of the creditors: for the ranks of the rich had been greatly thinned by Tiberius's treason trials under Sejanus, and under Macro, Sejanus's successor, the same destructive process continued. About the rest of his debts Herod was easy enough in his mind: nobody would dare to sue a man who stood so high in Court favour as himself. He paid me back with part of a loan of 40,000 gold pieces which he had negotiated with a freedman of Tiberius's, a fellow who, as a slave, had been one of the warders of Caligula's elder brother Drusus, when he was starved to death in the Palace cellars. Since his liberation he had become immensely rich by traffic in high-class slaves –

he would buy sick slaves cheap and doctor them back to health in a hospital which he managed himself – and was afraid that Caligula when he became Emperor would take vengeance on him for his ill-treatment of Drusus; but Herod undertook to soften Caligula's heart towards him.

So Herod's star grew daily brighter, and he settled several matters in the East to his entire satisfaction. For instance, he wrote to friends in Edom and Judaea – and anyone to whom he now wrote as a friend was greatly flattered – and asked them whether they could provide him with any detailed evidence of maladministration against the Governor who had tried to arrest him at Anthedon. He collected quite an imposing amount of evidence in this way and had it embodied in a letter purporting to come from leading citizens of Anthedon; which he then sent to Capri. The Governor lost his appointment. Herod paid back his debt in Attic drachmae to the corn-factor at Acre, less twice the amount which had been unwarrantably deducted from the money sent to him in Edom; explaining that these 5,000 drachmae which he was retaining represented a sum which the corn-factor had borrowed from the Princess Cypros some years back and had never returned. As for Flaccus, Herod made no attempt to be revenged on him, for my mother's sake; and Flaccus died shortly afterwards. Aristobulus he decided to forgive magnanimously, knowing that he must be feeling not only ashamed of himself but most vexed at his lack of foresight in antagonizing a brother now grown so powerful. Aristobulus could be made very useful, once he was properly chastened in spirit. Herod also revenged himself on Pontius Pilate, from whom the order for his arrest at Anthedon had originated, by encouraging some friends of his in Samaria to protest to the new Governor of Syria, my friend Vitellius, about Pilate's rough handling of civil disturbances there and to charge him with bribe-taking. Pilate was ordered to Rome to answer these charges before Tiberius.

One fine spring day as Caligula and Herod were out riding together in an open coach in the country near Rome, Herod remarked gaily, 'It is high time, surely, for the old warrior to be given his wooden foil.' By the old warrior he meant Tiberius, and by the wooden foil he meant the honourable token of discharge that worn-out sword-fighters are given in the arena. He added, 'And if you will pardon what may sound suspiciously like flattery, my dear fellow, but is my honest opinion, you will make a far finer showing at the game of games than *he* ever made.'

Caligula was delighted, but unfortunately Herod's coachman overheard the remark, understood it, and stored it in his memory. The knowledge that he had power to ruin his master encouraged this turnip-witted fellow to attempt a number of impertinences towards him, which for a time, as it happened, passed unnoticed. But at last he took it into his head to steal some very fine embroidered carriage-rugs and sell them to another coachman whose master lived at some distance from Rome. He reported that they had been accidentally ruined by the leakings of a tar-barrel through the planks of the stable-loft, and Herod was content to believe him; but one day, happening to go for a pleasure-drive with the knight to whose coachman they had been sold, he found them tucked about his knees. And so the theft came out. But the knight's coachman gave the thief timely warning and he ran away at once to avoid punishment. His original intention had been to face Herod, if he were found out, with the threat to reveal to the Emperor what he had overheard. But he lost courage when the appropriate moment came, suddenly realizing that Herod was quite capable of killing him if he tried blackmail and of producing witnesses that the blow had been struck in self-defence. The coachman was one of those people whose muddled minds get everyone into trouble, themselves most of all.

Herod knew the fellow's probable haunts in Rome and, not realizing what was at stake, asked the City officers to arrest him. He was found and brought up in court on a charge of theft, but claimed the privilege as a freedman of appealing to the Emperor instead of being summarily sentenced. He added: 'I have something to tell the Emperor which concerns his personal security. It is what I once heard when driving a coach on the road to Capua.' The magistrate had no alternative but to send him under armed escort to Capri.

From what I have already told you about the character of my uncle Tiberius you will perhaps be able to guess what course he took when he read the magistrate's report. Though he realized that the coachman must have overheard some treasonable remark of Herod's, he did not yet wish to know precisely what it was: Herod obviously was not the sort of man to make any very dangerous statement in a coachman's hearing. So he kept the coachman in prison, unexamined, and instructed young Gemellus, now about ten years old, to keep a sharp watch on his tutor and to report any word or action of his that seemed to have any treasonable significance. Herod meanwhile grew anxious at Tiberius's delay in examining the coachman and talked the matter over with Caligula. They decided that nothing had been said by Herod, on the occasion to which the coachman was apparently referring, that could not be explained away. If Herod himself pressed for an investigation Tiberius would be the more likely to take his word that the 'wooden foil' was intended literally. For Herod would say that they had been discussing Yellow Legs, a famous sword-fighter who had since retired, and that he had merely been congratulating Caligula on his fencing abilities.

Herod then noticed that Gemellus was behaving in a most suspicious manner – eavesdropping and turning up at his apartments at curious times. It was clear that Tiberius had set him to work. So he went once more to my mother and explained the whole case, begging her to press for a trial of the coachman, on his behalf. The excuse was to be that he wished to see the man well punished for his theft and for his ingratitude, Herod having voluntarily given him his freedom from slavery only the year before. Nothing was to be said about the man's intended revelations. My mother did as Herod asked. She wrote to Tiberius and, after the usual long delay, back came a letter. It is now in my possession, so that I can quote the very words. For once Tiberius went straight to the point.

'If this coachman means to accuse Herod Agrippa falsely of some treasonable utterance or other in order to cover his own misdoings, he has suffered enough for that folly by his long confinement in my not very hospitable cells at Misenum. I was thinking of letting him go with a caution against appealing to me in future, when about to be sentenced in the lower courts for a trivial offence like theft. I am too old and too busy to be bothered with such frivolous appeals. But if you force me to investigate the case and it turns out that a treasonable utterance was in fact made, Herod will regret having brought the matter up; for his desire to see his coachman severely punished will have brought a very severe punishment upon himself.'

This letter made Herod all the more anxious to have the man tried, and in his own presence. Silas, who had come to Rome, dissuaded him from this, quoting the proverb: 'Don't tamper with Camarina'. (Near Camarina, in Sicily, was a pestilent marsh which the inhabitants drained for hygienic reasons. This exposed the city to attack: it was captured and destroyed.) But Herod would not listen to Silas; the old fellow had been growing very tiresome after five years of unbroken prosperity. Soon he heard that Tiberius, who was at Capri, had given orders for the big villa at Misenum, the one where he afterwards died, to be made ready to receive him. He immediately arranged to go down to that neighbourhood himself, with Gemellus, as a guest of Caligula, who had a villa close by at Bauli; and in the company of my mother, who was, you will recall, grandmother both to Caligula and to Gemellus. Bauli is quite close to Misenum on the north coast of the Bay of Naples, so nothing was more natural than for the whole party to go together to pay their respects to Tiberius on his arrival. Tiberius invited them all to dine on the following day. The prison where the coachman was languishing lay close by, so Herod persuaded my mother to ask Tiberius in everyone's presence to settle the case that very afternoon. I had been invited to Bauli myself, but had declined, for neither my uncle Tiberius nor my mother was very patient of my company. But I have heard the whole story from several people who were present. It was a fine dinner and only spoilt by the great scarcity of wine. Tiberius was now following his doctors' advice and abstaining altogether from drink, so as a matter of fact and caution nobody asked for his cup to be refilled after he had emptied it; and the waiters did not offer to do so, either. Going without wine always put Tiberius in a bad humour, but, nevertheless, my mother boldly brought up the subject of the coachman again. Tiberius interrupted her, as if unintentionally, by starting a new topic of conversation, and she made no further attempt until after dinner, when the whole party went out for a stroll under the trees surrounding the local racecourse. Tiberius did not walk: he was carried in a sedan, and my mother, who had become quite brisk in her old age, walked alongside. She said: 'Tiberius, may I speak to you about that coachman? It is high time, surely, that his case was settled, and we should all feel much easier, I think, if you were good enough to settle it to-day, once and for all. The prison is just over there and it could be all got over in a very few minutes.'

'Antonia,' Tiberius said, 'I have already given you the hint to leave well alone, but if you insist I shall do as you ask.' Then he called up Herod, who was walking behind with Caligula and Gemellus, and said: 'I am now about to examine your coachman,

Herod Agrippa, at the insistence of my sister-in-law, the Lady Antonia, but I call the Gods to witness that what I am doing is not done by my own inclination but because I am forced to it.'

Herod thanked him profusely for his condescension. Then Tiberius called for Macro, who was also present, and ordered him to bring the coachman up for trial before him immediately.

It seems that Tiberius had enjoyed a few words in private with Gemellus on the previous evening. (Caligula, a year or two afterwards, forced Gemellus to give him an account of this interview.) Tiberius had asked Gemellus whether he had anything to report against his tutor, and Gemellus answered that he had overheard no disloyal words and witnessed no disloyal action; but that he saw very little of Herod these days – he was now always about with Caligula and left Gemellus to study books by himself instead of coaching him personally. Tiberius then questioned the boy about loans, whether Herod and Caligula had ever discussed loans in his presence. Gemellus considered for awhile and then answered that on one occasion Caligula had asked Herod about a P.O.T. loan and Herod had answered, 'I'll tell you about it afterwards: for little pitchers have long ears.' Tiberius immediately guessed what P.O.T. meant. It surely meant a loan negotiated by Herod on Caligula's behalf which would be repayable *post obitum Tiberii* – that is, after the death of Tiberius. So Tiberius dismissed Gemellus and told him that a P.O.T. loan was a matter of no significance and that he now had the fullest confidence in Herod. But he immediately sent a confidential freedman to the prison, who ordered the coachman, in the Emperor's name, to disclose what remark of Herod's he had overheard. The coachman repeated Herod's exact words and the freedman took them back to Tiberius. Tiberius considered awhile and then sent the freedman back to the prison with instructions as to what the coachman must say when brought up for trial. The freedman made him memorize the exact words and repeat them after him, and then gave him to understand that if he spoke them properly he would be set at liberty and given a money reward.

So there on the race-track itself the trial took place. The coachman was asked by Tiberius whether he pleaded guilty to stealing the carriage rugs. He answered that he was not guilty, since Herod had given them to him as a present but afterwards repented of his generosity. At this point Herod tried to interrupt the evidence by exclamations of disgust at his ingratitude and mendacity, but

Tiberius begged him to be silent and asked the coachman: 'What else have you to say in your defence?'

The coachman replied: 'And even if I had stolen those rugs, as I did not, it would have been an excusable act. For my master is a traitor. One afternoon shortly before my arrest I was driving a coach in the direction of Capua with your grandson, the Prince, and my master, Herod Agrippa, seated behind me. My master said: "If only the day would come when the old warrior finally dies and you find yourself named as his successor in the monarchy! For then young Gemellus won't be any hindrance to you. It will be easy enough to get rid of him, and soon everyone will be happy, myself most of all." '

Herod was so taken aback by this evidence that for the moment he could not think what to say, except that it was perfectly untrue. Tiberius questioned Caligula, and Caligula, who was a great coward, looked anxiously at Herod for guidance, but got none, so said in a great hurry that if Herod had made any such remark he had not heard it. He remembered the ride in the coach and it had been a very windy day. If he had heard any such treasonable words he certainly would not have let them pass but would have reported them immediately to his Emperor. Caligula was most treacherous towards his friends, if his own life was in danger, and always hung on the lightest word of Tiberius: so much so that it was said of him that never was a better slave to a worse master. But Herod spoke up boldly: 'If your son, who was sitting next to me, didn't hear the treasons that I am alleged to have uttered – and nobody has quicker ears than he for hearing treasons against you – then surely the coachman could not have heard them, sitting as he was with his back to me.'

But Tiberius had already made up his mind. He said shortly to Macro, 'Put that man in handcuffs,' and then to his sedan-men, 'Proceed.' They stepped off, leaving Herod, Antonia, Macro, Caligula, Gemellus, and the rest staring at each other in doubt and astonishment. Macro could not make out who it was whom he was supposed to handcuff, so when Tiberius, having been carried all the way round the race-track, returned to the scene of the trial, where the whole company was still standing just as he had left them, Macro asked him, 'Pardon me, Caesar, but which of these men am I to arrest?' Tiberius pointed to Herod and said, 'That's the man I mean.' But Macro, who had great respect for Herod and hoped perhaps to break down Tiberius's resolution by pretending to misunderstand him, once more asked, 'You surely cannot mean Herod Agrippa, Caesar?' 'I mean no one else,' growled Tiberius. Herod ran forward and all but prostrated himself before Tiberius. He did not dare to do it quite, because he knew Tiberius's dislike of being treated like an Oriental monarch. But he stretched out his arms in a pitiful way and protested himself Tiberius's most loyal servant and absolutely incapable of so much as admitting the least treasonable thought to cross his mind, let alone uttering it. He began to talk eloquently of his friendship with Tiberius's dead son (a victim, like himself, of unfounded charges of treason), whose irreparable loss he had never ceased to mourn, and of the extraordinary honour that Tiberius had done him in appointing him tutor to his grandchild. But Tiberius looked at him in that cold, crooked way of his and sneered, 'You can make that speech in your defence, my noble Socrates, when I fix the date of your trial.' Then he told Macro, 'Take him away to the prison yonder. He can use the chain discarded by this honest coachman-fellow.'

Herod did not utter another word except to thank my mother for her generous but unavailing efforts on his behalf. He was marched off to the prison, with his wrists handcuffed behind him. It was a place where misguided Roman citizens who had appealed to Tiberius from sentences in lower courts were confined – in cramped and unhealthy quarters, with poor food and no bedding – until Tiberius should have time to settle their cases. Some of them had been there many years.

Chapter 4

HEROD, as he was being led towards the prison gates, saw a Greek slave of Caligula's waiting there. The slave seemed out of breath, as if he had been running, and held a water pitcher in his hand. Herod hoped that Caligula had sent him there as a sign that he was still a friend, but that he could not openly declare his friendship, for fear of offending Tiberius. He called to the boy, 'Thaumastus, for God's sake give me a drink of water.' It was very hot weather for September and, as I told you, there had been hardly any wine to drink for dinner. The boy came forward readily, as if he had been warned for this service; Herod, greatly reassured, put his lips to the pitcher and drank it nearly dry. For it contained wine, not water. He said to the slave: 'You have earned a prisoner's gratitude for this drink and I promise you that when I am free again I shall pay you well for it. I shall see that your master, who certainly is not a man to desert his friends, gives you your liberty as soon as he has secured mine, and I shall then employ you in a position of trust in my household.' Herod was able to keep his promise and Thaumastus eventually became his chief steward. He is still alive at the time I write this, in the service of Herod's son, though Herod himself is dead.

When Herod was led into the prison compound it happened to be the hour for exercise, but there was a strict rule that prisoners should not converse with each other without express permission from the warders. Each group of five prisoners had a warder assigned to it who watched every movement they made. Herod's arrival caused a great commotion among these bored and listless men, for the sight of an Eastern prince wearing a cloak of real Tyrian purple was something that had never been seen there before. He did not greet them, however, but stood gazing at the distant roof of Tiberius's villa, as if he could read on it some message as to what his fate was to be.

Among the prisoners was an elderly German chieftain whose history, it seems, was as follows. He had been an officer of German auxiliaries under Varus when Rome still held the province across the Rhine, and had been given Roman citizenship in recognition of his services in battle. When Varus was treacherously ambushed and his army massacred by the famous Hermann, this chieftain, although he had not (or so he said) served in Hermann's army or given him any assistance in his plans, took no steps to prove his continued loyalty to Rome but became the head-man of his ancestral village. During the wars carried on by my brother Germanicus he left this village with his family and retired inland, returning only when Germanicus was recalled to Rome and the danger seemed past. He was then unlucky enough to be captured by the Romans in one of the cross-river raids that were made from time to time to keep our men in good fighting condition and to remind the Germans that one day the province would be ours again. The Roman general would have had him flogged to death as a deserter, but he protested that he had never shown any disloyalty to Rome, and now exercised his right as a Roman citizen to appeal to the Emperor. (In the interval, however, he had forgotten all his camp-Latin.) This man asked his warder, who understood a little German, to tell him about that melancholy, handsome young man standing under the tree. Who was he? The warder answered that he was a Jew and a man of great importance in his own country. The German begged for permission to speak to Herod, saying that he had never in all his life met a man of the Jewish race, but that he understood the Jews to be by no means inferior in intelligence or courage even to the Germans: one might learn a lot from a Jew. He added that he too was a man of great importance in his own country. 'This place is getting to be quite a university,' said the warder, grinning. 'If you two foreign gentlemen care to swap philosophy, I'll do my best to act as interpreter. But don't expect too much of my German.'

Now, while Herod had been standing under the tree, with his head muffled in his cloak because he did not wish the inquisitive prisoners and warders to see his tears, a curious thing had happened. An owl had perched on the branches above his head and dropped dirt on him. It is very rare for an owl to appear in broad daylight, but only the German had noticed the bird's performance; for everyone else was so busy looking at Herod himself.

The German, speaking through the warder, greeted Herod courteously and began saying that he had something of importance to tell him. Herod uncovered his face when the warder began speaking and replied with interest that he was all attention. For the moment he expected a message from Caligula, and did not realize that the warder was merely an interpreter for one of the prisoners.

The warder said, 'Excuse me, sir, but this German gentleman wants to know whether you are aware that an owl has just dropped dirt on your cloak? I am acting as this German gentleman's interpreter. He is a Roman citizen but his Latin's got a bit rusty in that damp climate of theirs.'

This made Herod smile in spite of his disappointment. He knew that prisoners with nothing to do spend a great deal of their time in playing tricks on each other, and that sometimes the warders, equally bored with their duties, assist them. So he did not look up into the tree or examine his cloak to see whether the man was not perhaps making fun of him. He replied in a bantering tone: 'Stranger things than that have happened to me, friend. A flamingo recently flew in at my bedroom window, laid an egg in one of my shoes, and then flew out again. My wife felt quite upset. If it had been a sparrow or a thrush or even an owl she would not have given the incident a second thought. But a flamingo, now ...'

The German did not know what a flamingo was, so he disregarded this sally, and went on: 'Do you know what it signifies when a bird drops dirt on your head or shoulder? In my country it is always taken for a very lucky sign indeed. And that so holy a bird as an owl has done this and has abstained from uttering any ill-omened cries should be a sign to cause you the profoundest joy and hope. We Chaucians know all that is to be known about owls. The owl is our totem and gives our nation its name. If you were a Chaucian I should say that the God Mannus had sent this bird as a sign to you that as a result of this imprisonment, which will only be a short one, you will be promoted to a position of the greatest dignity in your own country. But I am told that you are a Jew. May I ask, sir, the name of the God of your country?'

Herod, who was still not sure whether the German's earnestness was real or assumed, answered, quite truthfully, 'The Name of our God is too holy to be pronounced. We Jews are obliged to refer to it by periphrases, and even by periphrases of periphrases.'

The German decided that Herod must be making fun of him and said: 'Do not think, please, that I am saying this in the hope of any reward from you; but seeing the bird do what it did I felt impelled to congratulate you on the omen. Now I have one more thing to tell you, because I am a well-known augur in my country: when next you see this bird, though it may be in the time of your highest prosperity, and it settles near you and begins to utter cries, then you will know that your days of happiness are over and that the number of those days which still remain for you to live will be no greater than the number of cries that the owl has given. But may that day be long in coming!'

Herod had quite recovered his spirits by this time and said to the German: 'I think, old man, that you talk the most charming nonsense that I have heard since my return to Italy. You have my sincere thanks for trying to cheer me and if ever I get out of this place a free man, I shall see what I can do to have you freed too. If you are as good company out of chains as in chains we shall have some enjoyable evenings together, drinking and laughing and telling funny stories.'

The German went off in a huff.

Meanwhile Tiberius had given sudden orders to his servants to pack up his things and sailed back to Capri that very afternoon. He was afraid, I suppose, that my mother would try to persuade him to release Herod, and it would be difficult for him to refuse, being so much in her debt over the matter of Sejanus and Livilla. My mother, realizing that she could do nothing for Herod now, except perhaps to arrange that prison life should be made as easy as possible for him, asked Macro to oblige her in this as far as was possible. Macro replied that if he gave Herod more considerate treatment than the other prisoners he would certainly get into trouble with Tiberius. My mother replied, 'Short of allowing him any facilities for escape, do all that you can for him, I beg you, and if Tiberius happens to hear of it and to be displeased I promise to bear the full weight of his displeasure myself.' She much disliked being in the position of asking favours from Macro, whose father had been one of our family slaves. But she felt great personal concern for Herod and would have done almost anything for him then. Macro was flattered by her pleas and promised to choose a warder for Herod who would show him every consideration, and also to appoint as governor of the prison a captain whom she knew personally. More than this, he arranged that Herod should take his meals with the governor and should be allowed to visit the local baths daily under escort. He said that if Herod's freedmen cared to bring him extra food and warm bedding – for winter was now drawing on – he would see that no difficulties were made, but that the freedmen must tell the porter at the gate that these comforts were for the governor's own use. So Herod's experience of prison was not too painful, though he was chained to the wall by a heavy iron chain whenever his warder was not in actual attendance; but he worried greatly as to what was happening to Cypros and the children, for he was allowed no news from the outside world. Silas, though he had not had the satisfaction of telling Herod that he should have listened to his advice (about not tampering with the marsh of Camarina), saw to it that the freedmen brought the prisoner his food and other necessities punctually and discreetly; and did as much for him as lay in his power to do. In the end he was himself arrested for trying to smuggle a letter into the prison, but was released with a caution.

Early in the following year Tiberius decided to leave Capri for Rome and told Macro to send all the prisoners there, because he intended to settle their cases on his arrival. Herod and the rest were therefore taken from Misenum and marched, by stages, to the detention barracks in the Guards Camp outside the City. You will recall that Tiberius turned back when within sight of the City walls because of an unlucky omen, the death of his pet wingless dragon; he hurried back to Capri, but caught a chill and got no farther than Misenum. You will recall, too, that when he was believed to be dead and Caligula was already strutting about the hall of the villa, flashing his signet ring among a crowd of admiring courtiers, the old man started up from his coma and called loudly for food. But the news of his death and Caligula's succession had already reached Rome by courier. Herod's freedman, the one who brought him the money from Acre, happened to meet the courier on the outskirts of the City, who shouted out the news as he galloped past. The freedman ran to the camp, entered the detention barracks, and running excitedly towards Herod cried out in Hebrew, 'The Lion is dead.' Herod questioned him rapidly in the same language and appeared so extraordinarily pleased that the governor came up and demanded to be told what news the freedman had brought. This was a breach of prison rules, he said, and must not occur again. Herod explained that it was nothing, only the birth of a male heir to one of his relatives in Edom; but the governor made it plain that he insisted on knowing the truth, so Herod finally said, 'The Emperor is dead.'

The governor, who was on very good terms with Herod by this time, asked the freedman whether he was sure that the news was true. The freedman replied that he had heard it directly from an Imperial courier. The governor knocked off Herod's chain with his own hands and said, 'We must celebrate this, Herod Agrippa, my friend, with the best wine in the camp.' They were just eating a most cheerful meal together, Herod being in his best form and telling the governor what a good fellow he was, and how considerately he had behaved, and how happy they would all be now that Caligula was Emperor, when news came that Tiberius was not dead after all. This put the governor into a great state of alarm. He decided that Herod had arranged for this false message to be brought just to get him into trouble. 'Back to your chain this instant,' he shouted angrily, 'and never expect me to trust you again.' So Herod had to get up from the table and go gloomily back to his cell. But, as you will again recall, Macro had not allowed Tiberius to enjoy his new lease of life for very long but had gone into the Imperial bed-chamber and smothered him with a pillow. So again the news came that Tiberius was dead, this time really dead. But the governor kept Herod chained up all night. He was not taking any risks.

Caligula wished to release Herod at once, but curiously enough it was my mother who prevented him from doing so. She was at Baiae, close to Misenum. She told him that until Tiberius's funeral was over it would be indecent to release anyone who had been imprisoned by him on a charge of treason. It would look much better if Herod, though allowed to return to his house at Rome, were to remain for a time under open arrest. So this was done. Herod went home but still had his warder with him and was expected to wear prison dress. When the official mourning for Tiberius was at an end, Caligula sent Herod a message telling him to shave and put on clean clothes and come to dine with him the next day at the Palace. Herod's troubles seemed over at last.

I do not think that I mentioned the death, three years before this, of Herod's uncle Philip: he left a widow – Salome, Herodias's daughter, reputed the most beautiful woman in the Near East. When the news of Philip's death reached Rome, Herod had immediately spoken to the freedman who was most in Tiberius's confidence where Eastern questions were concerned, and persuaded him to do something for him. The freedman was to remind Tiberius that Philip had left no children, and was to suggest that his tetrarchy of Bashan should be given to no other member of the Herod family but be temporarily attached, for administrative purposes, to the province of Syria. The freedman was on no account to remind Tiberius of the royal revenues of the tetrarchy, which amounted to 160,000 gold pieces a year. Should Tiberius take his advice and instruct him to write a letter informing the Governor of Syria that the tetrarchy would now pass under his jurisdiction, he was to smuggle in a postscript to the effect that the royal revenues must be allowed to accumulate until a successor to Philip should be appointed. Herod was reserving Bashan and its revenues for his own use. So it happened that when, at the dinner to which he had invited Herod, Caligula gratefully rewarded him for his sufferings by granting him the tetrarchy complete with revenues, with the title of king thrown in too, Herod found himself very well off indeed. Caligula also called for the chain which Herod had worn in prison and gave him an exact replica of it, link for link, in the purest gold. A few days later Herod, who had not forgotten to secure the old German's release and to get the coachman condemned for perjury, deprived of his freedom, and whipped nearly to death, sailed joyfully to the East to take over his new kingdom. Cypros went with him, more joyful even than he. During Herod's imprisonment she had been looking thoroughly ill and miserable, for she was the most faithful wife in the world and even refused to eat or drink anything better than the prison rations that her husband was drawing. She stayed at the house of Herod's younger brother, Herod Pollio.

This happy pair, then, Herod and Cypros, reunited once more, and accompanied as usual by Silas, sailed to Egypt on their way to Bashan. At Alexandria they disembarked, to pay their respects to the Alabarch. Herod intended to enter the city with as little ostentation as possible, not wishing to be the cause of any disturbances between the Jews and Greeks; but the Jews were overjoyed at the visit of a Jewish king, and one so high in the Emperor's favour. They met him at the docks, many thousands strong, in holiday dress, crying 'Hosanna, hosanna!' and singing songs of rejoicing, and so escorted him to their quarter of the city, which is called 'The Delta'. Herod did his best to calm popular enthusiasm, but Cypros found the contrast between this arrival in Alexandria and their former one so delightful that for her sake he let many extravagances go by. The Alexandrian Greeks were angry and jealous. They dressed up in mock-royal state a well-known idiot of the city, or pretended idiot rather, Baba by name, who used to go begging around the principal squares and raising laughs and coppers by his clowning. They provided this Baba with a grotesque guard of soldiers armed with sausage swords, pork shields, and pig's-head helmets and paraded him through 'The Delta'. The crowd shouted *Marin! Marin!* which means 'King! King!' They made a demonstration outside the Alabarch's house and another outside the house of his brother Philo. Herod visited two of the leading Greeks and lodged a protest. He said no more than, 'I shall not forget to-day's performance and I think that one day you'll regret it.'

From Alexandria Herod and Cypros continued their voyage to the port of Jaffa. From Jaffa they went to Jerusalem to visit their children there and to stay in the Temple precincts as guests of the High Priest, with whom it was important for Herod to arrive at an understanding. He created an excellent impression by dedicating his iron prison-chain to the Jewish God, hanging it up on the wall of the Temple Treasury. Then they passed through Samaria and the borders of Galilee – without, however, sending any complimentary message to Antipas and Herodias – and so came to their new home at Caesarea Philippi, the lovely city built by Philip as his capital on the southern slopes of Mount Hermon. There they collected the accumulated revenues laid up for them since Philip's death. Salome, Philip's widow, made a set at Herod and tried all her most captivating arts on him, but it was no use. He told her: 'You are certainly very good looking and very gracious and very witty; but you must remember the proverb: "Move into a new house, but take the old earth with you." The only possible queen for Bashan is my dear Cypros.'

You can imagine that when Herodias heard of Herod's good fortune she was wild with jealousy. Cypros was now a Queen, while she herself was the wife of a mere Tetrarch. She tried to rouse Antipas into feeling the same as she did; but Antipas, an indolent old man, was perfectly satisfied with his position; though he was only a Tetrarch, he was a very rich one and it was a matter of very little importance to him by what title or titles he was known. Herodias called him a pitiful fellow – how could he expect her to have any further respect for him? 'To think,' she said, 'that my brother, Herod Agrippa, who came here not so long ago as a penniless refugee, dependent on your charity for the very bread that he ate, and then grossly insulted us and fled to Syria, and was hounded out of Syria for corruption, and was nearly arrested at Anthedon for debt, and then went to Rome and was imprisoned for treason to the Emperor – to think that a man with such a record, a spendthrift who has left a trail of unpaid bills behind him wherever he has gone, should now be a King and in a position to insult us! It is unbearable. I insist that you go to Rome at once and force the new Emperor to give you at least equal honours with Herod.'

Antipas answered: 'My dear Herodias, you are not talking wisely. We are very well off here, you know, and if we tried to improve our position it might bring us bad luck. Rome has never been a safe place to visit since Augustus died.'

'I won't speak to you or sleep with you again,' said Herodias, 'until you give me your word that you will go.'

Herod heard of this scene from one of his agents at Antipas's court; and when, shortly after, Antipas started out for Rome he sent a letter to Caligula by a fast vessel, offering the captain a very large reward if he reached Rome before Antipas did. The captain cracked on as much sail as he dared and just managed to win the money. When Antipas presented himself before Caligula, Caligula already had Herod's letter in his hand. It was to the effect that Herod while staying in Jerusalem had heard grave charges against his uncle Herod Antipas, which he had not at first credited, but which had on investigation proved true. Not only had his uncle been engaged in treasonable correspondence with Sejanus at the time that Sejanus and Livilla were plotting to usurp the monarchy – that was an old story – but he had lately been exchanging letters with the King of Parthia, planning with his help to organize a widespread revolt against Rome in the Near East. The King of Parthia had undertaken to give him Samaria, Judaea, and Herod's own kingdom of Bashan as a reward for his disloyalty. As a proof of this accusation Herod mentioned that Antipas had 70,000 complete suits of armour in his palace armoury. What, otherwise, was the meaning of these secret preparations for war? His uncle's standing army numbered only a few hundred men, a mere guard of honour. The armour was certainly not intended for arming *Roman* troops.

Herod was very sly. He knew perfectly well that Antipas had no war-like intentions whatsoever and that it was merely his fondness for display that had led him to stock his armoury in this lavish style. The revenues from Galilee and Gilead were rich, and Antipas, though stingy in his hospitality, liked to spend money on costly objects: he collected suits of armour as rich men at Rome collect statues, pictures, and inlaid furniture. But Herod knew that this explanation would not occur to Caligula, whom he had often told about Antipas's miserliness. So when Antipas came to the Palace and saluted Caligula, congratulating him on his accession, Caligula greeted him coldly and asked him at once: 'Is it true, Tetrarch, that you have seventy thousand suits of armour in your palace armoury?' Antipas was startled and could not deny it: for Herod had been careful not to exaggerate. He muttered something about the armour being intended for his own personal pleasure.

Caligula said: 'This audience is already over. Don't make feeble excuses. I shall consider what to do with you to-morrow.' Antipas had to retire, abashed and anxious.

That evening Caligula asked me at dinner: 'Where was it that you were born, Uncle Claudius?'

'Lyons,' I answered.

'An unhealthy sort of place, isn't it?' asked Caligula, twiddling a gold wine-cup in his fingers.

'Yes,' I answered. 'It has the reputation of being one of the most unhealthy places in your dominions. I blame the climate of Lyons for having condemned me, while still an infant, to my present useless and inactive life.'

'Yes, I thought I had once heard you say that,' said Caligula. 'We'll send Antipas there. The change of climate may do him good. There's too much sun in Galilee for a man of his fiery character.'

Next day Caligula told Antipas that he must consider himself degraded from his rank of Tetrarch, and that a vessel was waiting at Ostia to carry him away to exile at Lyons. Antipas took the matter philosophically – exile was better than death – and I will say this much to his credit, that so far as I know he never gave Herodias, who had accompanied him from Galilee, a word of reproach. Caligula wrote to Herod thanking him for his timely warning and awarding him Antipas's tetrarchy and revenues in recognition of his loyalty. But knowing that Herodias was Herod's sister, he told her that for her brother's sake he would allow her to keep any property of her own that she might possess and return to Galilee, if she wished, to live under his protection. Herodias was too proud to accept this and told Caligula that Antipas had always treated her very well and that she would not desert him in the hour of his need. She began a long speech intended to soften Caligula's heart, but he cut it short. Herodias and Antipas sailed together for Lyons the next morning. They never returned to Palestine.

Herod replied in terms of the most boundless gratitude for Caligula's gift. Caligula showed me the letter. 'But what a man!' Herod had written. 'Seventy thousand suits of armour, and all for his own personal pleasure! Two a day for nearly a hundred years! But it seems almost a pity to condemn a man like that to rot away at Lyons. You ought to send him out to invade Germany single-handed. Your father always said that the only way to deal with the Germans was to exterminate them, and here you have the perfect exterminator at your service – such a glutton for combat that he lays in a stock of seventy thousand suits of armour, all made to measure.' We had a good laugh over that. Herod ended by saying that he must come back at once to Rome to thank Caligula by word of mouth: pen and paper were not sufficient to express what he felt. He would make his brother Aristobulus temporary regent in Galilee and Gilead, with Silas to keep a careful eye on him, and his youngest brother, Herod Pollio, temporary regent of Bashan.

He came back to Rome, with Cypros, and paid his creditors every penny of his debts: and went about saying that he never intended to borrow again. For the first year of Caligula's reign he had no difficulties worth mentioning. Even when Caligula quarrelled with my mother over his murder of Gemellus – from which, you may be sure, Herod had not actively dissuaded him – so that, as I described in my previous story, she was forced to commit suicide, Herod was so sure of Caligula's continued trust in his loyalty that almost alone of her friends he wore mourning for her sake and attended her funeral. He felt her death pretty keenly, I believe, but the way he put it to Caligula was: 'I should be a thankless wretch if I failed to pay my respects to the ghost of my benefactress. That you showed your displeasure at her grandmotherly interference in a matter which did not concern her must have affected the Lady Antonia with the profoundest grief and shame. If I felt that I earned your displeasure by any similar behaviour – but of course the case is absurd – I should certainly do as she has done. My mourning is a tribute to her courage in leaving a modern world which has superannuated women of her antique sort.'

Caligula took this well enough and said: 'No, Herod, you have done rightly. The injury she did was to me, not to you.' But when his brain turned altogether as a result of his illness and he declared his divinity and began cutting off the heads of statues of Gods and substituting his own, Herod began to grow anxious. As ruler of many thousands of Jews he foresaw trouble. The first certain signs of this trouble came from Alexandria, where his enemies, the Greeks, pressed the Governor of Egypt to insist on the erection of the Emperor's statues in Jewish synagogues as well as in Greek temples, and on the use, by Jews as well as by Greeks, of Caligula's divine name in the taking of legal oaths. The Governor of Egypt had been an enemy of Agrippina's and also a partisan of Tiberius Gemellus's, and decided that the best way to prove his loyalty to Caligula was to enforce the Imperial edict which had, as a matter of fact, been intended only for the Greeks of the city. When the Jews refused to swear by Caligula's godhead or admit his statues within the synagogues the Governor published a decree declaring all Jews in the city aliens and intruders. The Alexandrians were jubilant and began a pogrom against the Jews, driving the richer ones from other parts of the city, where they lived in style side by side with Greeks and Romans, into the crowded narrow streets of 'The Delta'. Over 400 merchants' houses were sacked, and the owners murdered or maimed. Countless insults were heaped on the survivors. The loss in lives and the damage to property were so heavy that the Greeks decided to justify their action by sending an embassy to Caligula at Rome, explaining that the refusal of the Jews to worship his majesty had so outraged the younger and less disciplined Greek citizens that they had taken vengeance into their own hands. The Jews sent a counter-embassy, led by the Alabarch's brother, one Philo, a distinguished Jew with a reputation as the best philosopher in Egypt. When Philo reached Rome he naturally called upon Herod, to whom he was now related by marriage; for Herod, after paying back the Alabarch those 8,000 gold pieces, together with interest at ten per cent for two years – greatly to the Alabarch's embarrassment, for as a Jew he could not lawfully accept interest on a loan from a fellow-Jew – had further shown his gratitude by betrothing Berenice, his eldest surviving daughter, to the Alabarch's eldest son. Philo asked Herod to intervene on his behalf with Caligula, but Herod said that he preferred to have nothing to do with the embassy: if events took a serious turn he would do what he could to mitigate the Emperor's displeasure, which he expected to be severe – and that was all that he could say at present.

Caligula listened affably to the Greek embassy, but dismissed the Jews with angry threats, as Herod had foreseen, telling them that he did not wish to hear any more talk about Augustus's promises to them of religious toleration: Augustus, he shouted, had been dead a long time now and his edicts were out of date and absurd. 'I am your God, and you shall have no other Gods but me.'

Philo turned to the other ambassadors and said in Aramaic: 'I am glad that we came; for these words are a deliberate challenge to the Living God and now we can be sure that this fool will perish miserably.' Luckily none of the courtiers understood Aramaic.

Caligula sent a letter to the Governor of Egypt informing him that the Greeks had done their duty in forcibly protesting against the Jews' disloyalty, and that if the Jews persisted in their present disobedience he would himself come with an army and exterminate them. Meanwhile, he ordered the Alabarch and all other officials of the Jewish colony to be imprisoned. He explained that but for the Alabarch's kinship with his friend Herod Agrippa he would have put him and his brother Philo to death. The only satisfaction that Herod was at present able to give the Jews in Alexandria was to have the Governor of Egypt removed. He persuaded Caligula to arrest him on the grounds of his former enmity to Agrippina (who was, of course, Caligula's mother) and banish him to one of the smaller Greek islands.

Then Herod told Caligula, who now found himself short of funds: 'I must see what I can do in Palestine to raise some money for your Privy Purse. My brother Aristobulus informs me that my fire-eating old uncle Antipas was even richer than we supposed. Now that you are off on your British and German conquests – and, by the way, if you happen to pass through Lyons, please remember me very kindly to Antipas and Herodias – Rome will seem very dismal to us left-behinds. It will be a good opportunity for me to absent myself and visit my kingdom again; but as soon as I hear that you are on the way back I shall hurry home too, and I hope that you will be satisfied with my efforts on your behalf.' The fact was that most disquieting news had just arrived for Herod from Palestine. He sailed east on the day after Caligula had fixed for his absurd military expedition; though as a matter of fact it was nearly a year before Caligula set out.

Caligula had given orders for his statue to be placed in the Holy of Holies in the Temple at Jerusalem, a secret inner chamber where the God of the Jews is supposed to dwell in his cedar chest and which is only visited once a year by the High Priest. His further orders were that the statue should be taken out from the Holy of Holies on days of public festival and worshipped in the outer court by the assembled congregation, Jews and non-Jews alike. He either did not know or did not care about the intense religious awe in which the Jews hold their God. When the proclamation was read at Jerusalem by the new Governor of Judaea sent to succeed Pontius Pilate (who by the way had committed suicide on his arrival at Rome) there were such extraordinary scenes of riot that the Governor was forced to take refuge in his camp outside the city, where he sustained something very like a siege. The news reached Caligula at Lyons. He was utterly enraged and sent a letter to the new Governor of Syria who had succeeded my friend Vitellius, ordering him to raise a strong force of Syrian auxiliaries and with these and the two Roman regiments under his command to march into Judaea and enforce the edict at the point of the sword. This Governor's name was Publius Petronius, a Roman soldier of the old school. He lost no time in obeying Caligula's orders, so far as his preparations for the expedition were concerned, and marched down to Acre. Here he wrote a letter to the High Priest and chief notables of the Jews informing them of his instructions and of his readiness to carry them out. Herod meanwhile had taken a hand in the game, though he kept as much in the background as possible. He secretly advised the High Priest as to the best course to follow. At his suggestion the Governor of Judaea and his garrison were sent under safe conduct to Petronius at Acre. They were followed by a delegation of some 10,000 leading Jews, who came to appeal against the intended defilement of the Temple. They had come with no warlike intentions, they declared, but nevertheless would rather die than permit this terrible injury to be done to their ancestral land, which would immediately be struck by a curse and never recover. They said that they owed political allegiance to Rome and that there could be no complaints against them for disloyalty or failure to pay their taxes; but that their principal allegiance was to the God of their Fathers, who had always preserved them in the past (so long as they obeyed his laws) and had strictly forbidden the worship of any other Gods in his domain.

Petronius answered: 'I am not qualified to speak on matters of religion. It may be as you say, or it may not be so. My own allegiance to the Emperor is not divided into political and religious halves. It is an unquestioning allegiance. I am his servant and shall obey his orders, come what may.'

They replied: 'We are the faithful servants of our Lord God and shall obey his orders, come what may.'

So there was a deadlock. Petronius then moved down into Galilee. On Herod's advice no hostile act was committed against him, but although it was time for the autumn sowing the fields were left unploughed and everyone went about in mourning dress with ashes sprinkled on his head. Trade and industry were at a standstill. A new delegation met Petronius at Caesarea (the Samarian Caesarea), headed by Herod's brother Aristobulus, and he was told again that the Jews had no warlike intentions, but that if he persisted in carrying out the Imperial edict, no God-fearing Jew would have any further interest in life and the land would go to ruin. This put Petronius in a quandary. He wanted to ask Herod for help or advice, but Herod, realizing the insecurity of his own position, had already sailed for Rome. What could a soldier like Petronius do, a man who had always shown himself ready to face the fiercest enemy drawn up in line of battle or charging down on him from ambush with shouts, when these venerable old men came forward and stretched out their necks to him, saying: 'We offer no resistance. We are loyal tributaries of Rome, but our religious duty is to the God of our Fathers, by whose laws we have lived from infancy; kill us, if it so please you, for we cannot see our God blasphemed and live'?

He made them a very honest speech. He told them that it was his duty as a Roman to keep the oath of allegiance that he had sworn the Emperor and to obey him in every particular; and they could see that with the armed forces at his disposal he was perfectly capable of fulfilling the orders that he had received. Nevertheless he praised them for their firmness and for their abstention from any act of violence. He confessed that though, in his official capacity as Governor of Syria, he knew where his duty lay, yet as a humane and reasonable man he found it next to impossible to do what he had been charged to do. It was not a Roman act to kill unarmed old men merely because they persisted in worshipping their ancestral God. He said that he would write again to Caligula and present their case in as favourable a light as possible. It was more than likely that Caligula would reward him with death, but if, by sacrificing his own life, he could save the lives of so many thousands of industrious, inoffensive provincials, he was willing to do so. He urged them to pluck up their spirits and hope for the best. The first thing to be done, once he had written the letter, which would be that very morning, was for them to renew the cultivation of their land. If they neglected this, famine would ensue, followed by banditry and pestilence, and matters would become far worse than they already were. It happened that as he was speaking storm-clouds suddenly blew up from the west and a heavy downpour began. The ordinary autumn rains had not fallen that year and it was now almost past the season for them; so this was taken as an omen of extraordinary good fortune, and the crowds of mourning Jews dispersed, singing songs of praise and joy. The rain continued to fall and soon the whole land came alive again.

Petronius kept his word. He wrote to Caligula informing him of the obstinacy of the Jews and asking him to reconsider his decision. He said that the Jews had shown themselves perfectly respectful to their Emperor, but they insisted that a terrible curse would fall on their land if any statue whatsoever were erected in the Temple – even that of their glorious Emperor. He enlarged on their despairing refusal to cultivate the land and suggested that only two alternatives now presented themselves: the first, to erect the statue and sentence the land to ruin, which would mean an immense loss of revenue; the second, to reverse the Imperial decision and earn the undying gratitude of a noble people. He begged the Emperor at the very least to postpone the dedication of the statue until after harvest.

But before this letter arrived at Rome Herod Agrippa had already set himself to work on the Jewish God's behalf. Caligula and he greeted each other with great affection after their long absence from each other and Herod brought with him great chests full of gold and jewels and other precious objects. Some came from his own treasury, some from that of Antipas, and the rest had, I believe, been part of an offering made to him by the Jews of Alexandria. Herod invited Caligula to the most expensive banquet that had ever been given in the City: unheard-of delicacies were served, including five great pasties entirely filled with the tongues of tit-larks, marvellously delicate fish brought in tanks all the way from India, and for the roast an animal like a young elephant, but hairy and of no known species – it had been found embedded in the ice of some frozen lake of the Caucasus, and brought here packed in snow by way of Armenia, Antioch, and Rhodes. Caligula was astonished by the magnificence of the table and admitted that he would never have had sufficient ingenuity to provide such a display even if he had been able to afford it. The drink was as remarkable as the food, and Caligula became so lively as the meal went on that, deprecating his own generosity to Herod in the past as something hardly worth mentioning, he now promised to give him whatever it lay in his power to grant.

'Ask me anything, my dearest Herod,' he said, 'and it shall be yours.' He repeated: 'Absolutely anything. I swear by my own Divinity that I will grant it.'

Herod protested that he had not provided this banquet in the hope of winning any favour from Caligula. He said that Caligula had done as much for him already as any prince in the world had done for any subject or ally of his in the whole panorama of history or tradition. He said that he was far more than content: he wanted absolutely nothing at all but to be allowed in some measure to show his gratitude. However, Caligula, continuing to help himself from the crystal wine-decanter, kept on pressing him: wasn't there something very special that he wanted? Some new Eastern kingdom? Chalcis, perhaps, or Iturea? Then it was his for the asking.

Herod said: 'Most gracious and magnanimous and divine Caesar, I repeat that I want nothing for myself at all. All that I can hope for is the privilege of serving you. But you have already read my mind. Nothing escapes your astonishingly quick and searching eyes. There is indeed something that I do really desire to ask, but it is a gift that will directly benefit only yourself. My reward will be an indirect one – the glory of having been your adviser.'

Caligula's curiosity was excited. 'Don't be afraid to ask, Herod,' he said. 'Haven't I sworn that I will grant it, and am I not a God of my word?'

'In that case, my one wish,' said Herod, 'is that you will no longer think of dedicating that statue of yourself in the Temple of Jerusalem.'

A very long silence followed. I was present at this historic banquet myself and never remember having felt so uncomfortable or so excited in my life as then, waiting to see the result of Herod's boldness. What in the world would Caligula do? He had sworn by his own Divinity to grant the boon, in the presence of many witnesses; yet how could he go back on his resolution to humble this God of the Jews, who alone of all Gods in the world continued to oppose him?

At last Caligula spoke. He said, mildly, almost beseechingly, as though he counted on Herod to help him out of his dilemma: 'I don't understand, dearest Herod. How do you suppose that the granting of this boon will benefit me?'

Herod had worked the whole thing out in detail before ever he sat down to table. He replied with seeming earnestness: 'Because, Caesar, to place your sacred statue in the Temple at Jerusalem would not redound to your own glory at all. Oh, quite to the contrary! Are you aware of the nature of the statue that is now kept in the innermost shrine of the Temple, and the rites which are performed about it on holy days? No? Then listen and you will at once understand that what you have regarded as wicked obstinacy among my co-religionists is no more than a loyal desire not to injure your Majesty. The God of the Jews, Caesar, is an extraordinary fellow. He has been described as an anti-God. He has a rooted aversion to statues, particularly to statues of majestic bearing and dignified workmanship like those of the Greek Gods. In order to symbolize his hatred for other divinities he has ordered the erection, in this inner shrine, of a large, crude, and ludicrous statue of an Ass. It has long ears, huge teeth, and enormous genitals, and on every holy day the priests abuse this statue with the vilest incantations and bespatter it with the most loathsome excrement and offal and then wheel it on a carriage around the Inner Court for the whole congregation to abuse similarly; so that the whole Temple stinks like the Great Sewer. It is a secret ceremony. No non-Jews are admitted to it and the Jews themselves are not allowed to speak about it under penalty of a curse. Besides, they are ashamed. You understand everything now, don't you? The leading Jews are afraid that if your statue were erected in the Temple it would cause profound misunderstandings; that in their religious fanaticism the common people would subject it to the gravest indignities, while thinking to honour you by their zeal. But, as I say, natural delicacy and the holy silence imposed on them have prevented them from explaining to our friend Petronius why they would rather die than allow him to put your orders into execution. It is lucky that I am here to tell you what they are unable to tell. I am only a Jew on my mother's side, so that perhaps frees me from the curse. In any case I am risking it, for your sake.'

Caligula drank all this in with perfect credulity and even I was half-convinced by Herod's gravity. All that Caligula said was: 'If the fools had been as frank with me as you have been, my dearest Herod, it would have saved us all a lot of trouble. You don't think that Petronius has yet carried out my orders?'

'I hope for your sake that he has not,' Herod replied.

So Caligula wrote Petronius a short letter: 'If you have already put my Statue in the Temple, as I ordered, let it stand; but see that the rites are closely supervised by armed Roman soldiers. If not, disband your army and forget about the matter. On the advice of King Herod Agrippa, I have come to the conclusion that the Temple in question is an extremely unsuitable place for my Sacred Statue to be erected.'

This letter crossed with the one Petronius had written. Caligula was furious that Petronius should dare to write as he did, attempting to make him change his mind on mere grounds of humanity.

He replied: 'Since you appear to value the bribes of the Jews more highly than my Imperial Will, my advice to you is to kill yourself quickly and painlessly before I make such an example of you as will horrify all future ages.'

As it happened, Caligula's second letter arrived late – the ship lost its mainmast between Rhodes and Cyprus and lay disabled for several days – so that the news of Caligula's death arrived at Caesarea first. Petronius almost embraced Judaism, he was so relieved.

This ends the first part of the story of Herod Agrippa, but you shall hear the rest as I continue to tell my own.

Chapter 5

So here we are back again at the point where I was being carried round the great court of the Palace on the shoulders of two corporals of the Guard, with the Household Battalion of Germans crowding about me and dedicating their assegais to my service. Eventually I prevailed on the corporals to put me down and on four Germans to fetch my sedan. They brought it and I climbed into it. I was told that they had decided to take me to the Guards' Camp at the other side of the City, where I would be protected from possible attempts at assassination. I was beginning to protest again when I saw a glint of colour at the back of the crowd. A purple-sleeved arm was waving at me in a peculiar circular motion which brought back memories of my schooldays. I said to the soldiers: 'I think I see King Herod Agrippa. If he wishes to speak to me, let him come through at once.'

When Caligula was murdered Herod had not been far off. He had followed us out of the theatre but had been led aside by one of the conspirators, who pretended that he wished him to speak to Caligula about some favour. So Herod did not witness the actual murder. If I knew him as well as I think I did, he would certainly have saved Caligula's life by some trick or other; and now when he came upon the dead body he showed his gratitude for past favours in no uncertain terms. He embraced it, all bloody as it was, and carried it tenderly in his own arms into the Palace, where he laid it on the Imperial bed. He even sent out for surgeons, as though Caligula was not really dead and had a chance of recovery.

He then left the Palace by another door and hurried round to the theatre again, where he prompted Mnester, the actor, to make his famous speech, the one which reassured the excited Germans and prevented them from massacring the audience in vengeance for their master's death. Then back he darted to the Palace. When he heard there what had happened to me he came boldly into the court to see whether he could be of any service. I must admit that the sight of Herod's crooked smile – one corner of the mouth turned up, the other down – heartened me considerably.

His first words were: 'Congratulations, Caesar, on your election: may you long enjoy the great honours that these brave soldiers have bestowed on you, and may I have the glory of being your first ally!' The soldiers cheered lustily. Then, coming close to me and clasping my hand tightly in his, he began talking earnestly in Phoenician, a language with which he knew I was acquainted because of my researches into the history of Carthage, but which none of the soldiers would understand. He gave me no opportunity of interrupting him. 'Listen to me, Claudius. I know what you are feeling. I know that you don't really want to be Emperor, but for all our sakes, as well as your own, don't be a fool. Don't let slip what the Gods have given you of their own accord. I can guess what you are thinking. You have some crazy idea of yielding up your power to the Senate as soon as the soldiers let you go. That would be madness; it would be the signal for civil war. The Senate are a flock of sheep, but there are three or four wolves among them who are ready, the moment you lay down your power, to fight for it among themselves. There's Asiaticus for a start, not to mention Vinicius. They were both in the conspiracy, so they are likely to do something desperate for fear of being executed. Vinicius thinks himself a Caesar already because of his marriage with your niece Lesbia. He'll recall her from banishment and they'll make a very strong combination. If it's not Asiaticus or Vinicius it will be someone else, probably Vinicianus. You are the only obvious Emperor for Rome and you'll have the armies solidly behind you. If you won't take on the responsibility because of some absurd prejudice it will be the ruin of everything. That's all I'll say. Think it over and keep up your spirits!' Then he turned and shouted to the soldiers, 'Romans, I congratulate you too. You could not have made a wiser choice. Your new Emperor is courageous, generous, learned, and just. You can trust him as completely as you trusted his glorious brother Germanicus. Don't let yourselves be fooled with the Senate or by any of your Colonels. Stick by the Emperor Claudius and he'll stick by you. The safest place for him is in your camp. I have just been advising him to pay you well for your loyalty.' With these words he disappeared.

They carried me in my sedan towards their camp, going at a jog trot. As soon as one chairman showed any signs of flagging his place was taken by another. The Germans ran shouting ahead. I sat quite numb; self-possessed but never so blankly miserable in all my life before. With Herod gone the outlook seemed hopeless again. We had just reached the Sacred Way at the foot of the Palatine Hill when messengers came hurrying along it to intercept us and protest against my usurpation of the monarchy. The messengers were two 'Protectors of the People'. (This office was a survival from the middle days of the Republic, when the Protectors maintained the rights of the common people against the tyrannous encroachments of the nobility: their persons were inviolate and, though they claimed no legislative power, they had forced from the nobles the right to veto any act of the Senate which displeased them. But Augustus and his two Imperial successors had also adopted the title of 'Protector of the People', with its prerogatives; so that the real ones, though they continued to be elected and to perform certain functions under Imperial direction, had lost their original importance.) It seemed clear that the Senate had chosen these messengers not only as an indication that all Rome was behind them in their protest, but also because their inviolateness of person would protect them from any hostility on the part of my men.

These Protectors, who were unknown to me personally, did not behave with conspicuous courage when we stopped to parley with them, or even dare to utter the stern message with which I afterwards learned that they had been entrusted. They called me 'Caesar', a title to which I then had no claim, not being a member of the Julian house; and said very humbly: 'You will pardon us, Caesar, but the Senate would be much obliged by your immediate attendance at the House: they are anxious to learn your intentions.'

I was willing enough to go, but the Guards would not allow it. They felt only contempt for the Senate and, now that they had chosen an Emperor of their own, were resolved not to let him out of their sight, and to resist every attempt on the part of the Senate either to restore the Republic or to appoint a rival Emperor.

Angry shouts arose, 'Clear off, d'ye hear?' 'Tell the Senate to mind their own business and we'll mind ours!' 'We won't allow our new Emperor to be murdered too.' I leaned through the window of my sedan and said: 'Pray give my respectful compliments to the Senate and inform them that for the present I am unable to comply with their gracious invitation. I have a prior one. I am being carried off by the sergeants, corporals, and private soldiers of the Palace Guard to enjoy their hospitality at the Guards' Camp. It is as much as my life is worth to insult this devoted soldiery.'

So away we went again. 'What a wag our new Emperor is!' they roared. When we reached the Camp I was greeted with greater enthusiasm than ever. The Guards Division consisted of some 12,000 infantrymen besides the attached cavalry. It was not only the corporals and sergeants who now acclaimed me Emperor, but the captains and the colonels too. I discouraged them as much as I could while thanking them for their goodwill. I said that I could not consent to be their Emperor until I had been so appointed by the Senate, in whose hands the election rested. I was conveyed to Headquarters, where I was treated with a deference to which I was wholly unaccustomed, but found myself virtually a prisoner.

As for the assassins, as soon as they had made sure of Caligula and escaped from the pursuing Germans; and from Caligula's chairmen and yeomen who also came hurrying up with cries of vengeance, they had run down to Vinicius's house, which was not far from the Market Place. Here were waiting the colonels of the three City Battalions, who were the only regular troops stationed in Rome besides the Watchmen and the Imperial Guards. These colonels had not taken any active part in the conspiracy but had promised to put their forces at the disposal of the Senate as soon as Caligula was dead and the Republic restored. Cassius now insisted that someone must go at once and kill Caesonia and myself: we were too closely related to Caligula to be allowed to survive him. A colonel called Lupus volunteered for the task; he was a brother-in-law of the Guards' Commander. He came up to the Palace and, striding sword in hand through many deserted rooms, finally reached the Imperial bedchamber where Caligula's body was lying, bloody and frightful, just as Herod had left it. But Caesonia was now sitting on the bed with the head on her lap, and little Drusilla, Caligula's only child, was at her knees. As Lupus entered, Caesonia was wailing to the corpse, 'Husband, husband, you should have listened to my advice.' When she saw Lupus's sword she looked up anxiously into his face and knew that she was doomed. She stretched out her neck. 'Strike clean,' she said. 'Don't bungle it like the other assassins did.' Caesonia was no coward. He struck and the head fell. He then caught up the little brat, who came rushing at him, biting and scratching. He held her by the feet, swung her head against a marble pillar, and so dashed out her brains. It is always unpleasant to hear of the murder of a child: but the reader must take my word for it that if he too had known little Drusilla, her father's pet, he would have longed to do what Lupus did.

There has been a great deal of argument since about the meaning of Caesonia's address to the corpse, which certainly was ambiguous. Some say that what she meant was that Caligula should have listened to some advice that she had given him about killing Cassius, whose intentions she suspected, before he had time to put them into effect. The people who explain it in this way are those who blame Caesonia for Caligula's madness, saying that it was she who first disordered his wits by giving him the love-philtre which bound him to her so entirely. Others hold, and I must say that I agree with them, that she meant that she had advised Caligula to mitigate what he was pleased to call his 'immovable rigour' and behave more like a humane and sensible mortal.

Lupus then came in search of me, to complete his task. But by this time the shouts 'Long live the Emperor Claudius' were just beginning. He stood in the doorway of the hall where the meeting was being held, but when he saw how popular I had become he lost courage and stole quietly away.

In the Market Place the excited crowds could not decide whether to cheer themselves hoarse in honour of the assassins or howl themselves hoarse in demands for their blood. A rumour ran about that Caligula had not been murdered at all, that the whole business was an elaborate hoax stage-managed by himself, and that he was only waiting for them to express joy at his death before beginning a general massacre. That was what he had meant, it was said, by his promise to exhibit an entirely new spectacle that night, to be called *Death, Destruction, and the Mysteries of Hell*. Caution prevailed and they had begun to bawl loyally, 'Search out the murderers! Avenge our glorious Caesar's death!' when Asiaticus, an ex-Consul, who was a man of imposing figure and one who had been in Caligula's close confidence, climbed up on the Oration Platform and exclaimed: 'You are looking for the assassins? So am I. I want to congratulate them. I only wish I had struck a blow myself. Caligula was a vile creature and they acted nobly in killing him. Don't be idiots, men of Rome! You all hated Caligula, and now that he is dead you will be able to breathe freely again. Go back to your homes and celebrate his death with wine and song!'

Three or four companies of City troops were drawn up close by, and Asiaticus said to them: 'We are counting on you soldiers to keep the peace. The Senate is supreme once more. Once more we are a Republic. Obey the Senate's orders and I give you my word that every man of you will be considerably richer by the time things have settled down again. There must be no plundering or rioting. Any offence against life or property will be punished by death.' So the people changed their tune at once and began cheering the assassins and the Senate and Asiaticus himself.

From Vinicius's house those of the conspirators who were senators were proceeding to the Senate House, where the Consuls had hastily called a meeting; when Lupus came running down from the Palatine Hill with the news that the Guards had acclaimed me Emperor and were hurrying me off to their camp. So they sent me a threatening message by two Protectors of the People, whom they mounted on cavalry horses and told to overtake me. They were to deliver the message as if from the Senate in session: I have already related how, when it came to the point, the threat lost most of its force. The other conspirators, the Guards officers, headed by Cassius, then seized the Citadel on the Capitoline Hill, manning it with one of the City Battalions.

I should like to have been an eye-witness of that historic meeting of the Senate, to which crowded not only all the senators but also a large number of knights and others who had no business to be there. As soon as news came of the successful seizure of the Citadel they all left the Senate House and moved up to the Temple of Jove, near by, thinking it a safer place. But the excuse they gave themselves was that the official designation of the Senate House was 'The Julian Building' and that free men should not meet in a place dedicated to the dynasty from whose tyranny they had now at last so happily escaped. When they were comfortably settled in their new quarters everyone began speaking at once. Some senators cried out that the memory of the Caesars should be utterly abolished, their statues broken, and their temples destroyed. But the Consuls rose and pleaded for order. 'One thing at a time, my

Lords,' they said. 'One thing at a time.' They called on a senator named Sentius to make a speech – because he always had one ready in his head and was a loud and persuasive orator. They hoped that once somebody began speaking in proper form instead of exchanging random shouts and congratulations and arguments with neighbours, the House would soon settle down to business.

Sentius spoke. 'My Lords,' he said, 'this is well-nigh incredible! Do you realize that we are free at last, no longer slaves to the madness of a tyrant? Oh, I trust that your hearts are all beating as strongly and proudly as mine, though how long this blessed condition will last, who will dare to prophesy? At all events let us enjoy it while we can, and let us be happy. It is nearly a hundred years now since it was possible to announce in this ancient and glorious city, "We are free"; so of course neither you nor I can recall what it felt like in the old days to utter those splendid words, but certainly at the present moment my soul is as buoyant as a cork. How happy are the decrepit old men who at the end of a long life of slavery can breathe their last breath to-day with that sweet phrase on their lips – "We are free"! How instructive, too, for the young men, to whom freedom is but a name, to know what it means when they hear the glad universal cry go up: "We are free"! But, my Lords and gentlemen, we must remember that virtue alone can preserve liberty. The mischief of tyranny is that it discourages virtue. Tyranny teaches flattery and base fear. Under a tyranny we are straws upon the wind of caprice. The first of our tyrants was Julius Caesar. Since his reign there has been no sort of misery which we have not experienced. For there has been a steady decline since Julius in the quality of the Emperors who have been chosen to rule over us. Each has named as successor a man a little worse than himself. These Emperors have hated virtue with a malignant hatred. The worst of them all was this Gaius Caligula – may his ghost suffer torment! – the enemy of both men and Gods. Once a tyrant does an injury to a man, that man is suspected of harbouring resentment even if he gives no sign of it. A criminal charge is trumped up against him and he is condemned without hope of reprieve. That happened to my own brother-in-law, a very worthy, honest knight. But now, I repeat, we are free. Now we are only accountable each to the other. Once more this is a House of frank speech and frank discussion. Let us confess it, we have been cowards, we have lived like slaves, we have heard of intolerable calamities striking at our neighbours, but so long as they have not struck us we have kept mute. My Lords, let us decree the greatest honours in our power to the tyrannicides, especially to Cassius Chaerea, who has been prime mover in the whole heroic affair. His name should be made more glorious even than that of Brutus, who killed Julius Caesar, or Cassius's namesake, who stood by this Brutus and also struck a blow; for Brutus and Cassius by their action began a civil war which plunged the country into deepest degradation and misery. Whereas Cassius Chaerea's action can lead to no such calamity. He has placed himself like a true Roman at the disposal of the Senate and has made us a gift of the precious freedom that has been so long, ah, so long, denied us.'

This puerile speech was applauded vociferously. Somehow nobody considered that Sentius had been one of Caligula's most notorious flatterers and had even earned the nickname of 'The Lap-dog'. But the senator sitting next to him suddenly noticed that he was wearing on his finger a gold ring with an enormous cameo portrait of Caligula in coloured glass on it. This senator was another former lap-dog of Caligula's, but, anxious to excel in republican virtuousness, he snatched the ring off Sentius's finger and dashed it to the floor. Everyone joined in stamping it to bits. This energetic scene was interrupted by the entry of Cassius Chaerea. He was accompanied by Aquila, 'The Tiger', two other Guards officers who had been among the assassins, and Lupus. On entering the Senate Cassius did not waste a single glance on the crowded benches of cheering senators and knights, but marched straight up to the two Consuls and saluted. 'What is the watchword to-day?' he asked. The jubilant Senate felt this as the greatest moment of their lives. Under the Republic the Consuls had been joint commanders-in-chief of the forces, unless there happened to be a dictator appointed who took precedence over them; but it had now been over eighty years since they had given out the watchword of the day. The Senior Consul, another of the lap-dog breed, puffed himself up and replied: 'The watchword, Colonel, is *Liberty*.'

It was ten minutes before the cheers had died down sufficiently for the voice of the Consul to be heard again. He then rose, in some agitation, to announce that the messengers had returned that had been sent to me in the Senate's name: they reported that I had expressed myself unable to obey their summons, and had explained that I was being forcibly taken away to the Guards'

Camp. This news caused consternation and confusion among the benches, and a ragged debate followed, the conclusion of which was that my friend Vitellius suggested sending for King Herod Agrippa: Herod, being an outsider, but in close touch with political currents in Rome, and a man of great reputation both in the West and the East, might be able to give them seasonable advice. Someone seconded Vitellius, pointing out that Herod was known to have a strong influence over me, that he was respected by the Imperial Guards, and that at the same time he had always been well-disposed towards the Senate, among whom he had numerous personal friends. So a messenger was sent to beg Herod to attend as soon as possible. I believe that Herod had arranged for this invitation, but I cannot be sure. At all events he did not show himself either too ready to go or too slack in going. He sent a servant downstairs from his bedroom to tell the messenger that he would be ready in a few minutes, but that at the moment he must be excused, as he was in a state of dishabille. Presently he came down smelling very strongly of a peculiar Oriental scent called patchouli, which was a standing joke at the Palace: it was supposed to have an irresistible effect on Cypros. Caligula, whenever he smelt it on Herod, used to sniff loudly and say: 'Herod, you uxorious old man! How well you advertise your marital secrets!' Herod, you understand, did not wish it to be known that he had spent so long on the Palatine Hill, or they might suspect that he had been taking sides. He had, in fact, left the Palace disguised as a servant, mixed with the crowd in the Market Place, and only just reached home when the message came for him. He used the scent as an alibi, and it seems to have been accepted. When he arrived at the Temple the Consuls explained the position to him and he pretended to be surprised to hear that I had been acclaimed Emperor, and made a lengthy protestation as to his absolute neutrality in City politics. He was merely an allied king and the trusted friend of Rome, and so he would remain, by their leave, whatever her government. 'Nevertheless,' he said, 'since you appear to be in need of my advice I am prepared to speak frankly. The republican form of government appears to me in certain circumstances a most estimable thing. I would say the same of a benignant monarchy. Nobody can, in my opinion, make a hard-and-fast pronouncement that one form of government is essentially better than another. The suitability of each form depends on the temper of the people, the capacity of the ruler or rulers, the geographical extent of the

State, and so on. Only one general rule can be made, and it is this: No sensible man would give *that*' (here he gave a contemptuous snap of his fingers) 'for any government, whether democratic, plutocratic, aristocratic, or autocratic, that cannot count on the loyal support of the armed forces of the State over which it pretends to rule. And so, my lords, before I begin to offer you any practical advice I must ask you a question. My question is: *Have you the Army behind you?*'

It was Vinicius who jumped up to answer him. 'King Herod,' he cried, 'the City Battalions are loyal to a man. You see their three colonels here among us to-night. We have great stores of weapons too and vast supplies of money with which to pay any further forces that we may require to raise. There are many of us here who could enlist a double company of troops from our own household slaves, and would gladly give them their liberty on their undertaking to fight for the Republic.'

Herod ostentatiously covered his mouth so that they should see that he was trying not to laugh. 'My friend Lord Vinicius,' he said, 'my advice is *don't you try it!* What sort of a show do you think that your porters and bakers and bath-attendants would make against the Guards, the best troops in the Empire? I mention the Guards because if they had been on your side you would certainly have told me about it. If you think that you can make a slave into a soldier by tying a breastplate on him, putting a spear in his hand, hanging a sword round his middle and saying: "Now, fight, my boy!" – well, I repeat, *don't you try it!*' Then he addressed the Senate again as a whole. 'My Lords,' he said, 'you tell me that the Guards have acclaimed as Emperor my friend Tiberius Claudius Drusus Nero Germanicus, the ex-Consul, but without first asking your consent. And I gather that the Guards have shown some hesitation in allowing him to obey your summons to attend this House. But I also gather that the message that was sent him did not emanate from you as a body but from an unofficial caucus of some two or three senators; and that only a small party of excited soldiers – no officers among them – were in attendance on Tiberius Claudius when it was delivered. Perhaps if another delegation were now sent to him, with proper authority, the officers at the Guards' Camp would advise him to treat it with the respect that it deserves and would check the holiday spirit of the men under their command. I suggest that the same two Protectors of the People should be sent again, and I am ready, if you desire, to go with them and add my voice to theirs – in a quite disinterested way, of course. I believe that I have sufficient influence with my friend Tiberius Claudius, whom I have known from boyhood – we studied under the same venerable tutor – and sufficient interest with the officers at the Camp – I am a frequent guest at their mess-table – and certainly, let me assure you, my Lords, I have sufficient eagerness for your good opinion, to be able to settle matters to the satisfaction of all parties concerned.'

So at about four o'clock that afternoon, as I was eating my long-delayed luncheon in the Colonels' Mess at the Guards' Camp, with every movement that I made silently, closely, though respectfully watched by my companions, a captain came in with the news that a delegation had arrived from the Senate and that King Herod Agrippa, who was here too, wished to speak to me privately beforehand.

'Bring King Herod in here,' said the Senior Colonel. 'He's our friend.'

Presently Herod entered. He greeted each of the Colonels by name and slapped one or two of them on the back and then came over to me and made me a most formal obeisance.

'May I speak to you in private, Caesar?' he asked, grinning.

I was disconcerted at being addressed as Caesar and asked him to call me by my proper name.

'Well, if *you're* not Caesar, I don't know who else is,' Herod answered, and the whole room laughed with him. He turned round. 'My gallant friends,' he said, 'I thank you. But if you had been present at the meeting of the Senate this afternoon you really would have had something worth laughing at. I have never seen such a mob of infatuated enthusiasts in my life. Do you know what they think? They actually think that they are going to start a civil war and challenge you Guards to a pitched battle, with no one to help them but the City Battalions, and perhaps a Watchman or two, and their own household slaves masquerading as soldiers, under the command of sword-fighters from the amphitheatre! That's rich, eh? As a matter of fact, what I have come to tell the Emperor I can say in front of you all. They have now sent him a delegation of Protectors of the People, because, you see, there is not a single one of their own number who dares come himself: the Emperor is going to be asked to submit himself to the Senate's authority, and if he doesn't, why then they'll make him. What do you think of *that*? I came along with them after promising the Senate that I'd give the Emperor a few words of disinterested advice. I am now going to keep my promise.' He turned sharply round again and addressed me. 'Caesar, my advice is, be rough with them! Stamp on the worms and watch them wriggle.'

I said stiffly: 'My friend King Herod, you seem to forget that I am a Roman and that the powers even of an Emperor depend constitutionally on the will of the Senate. If the Senate sends me a message which I am able to answer politely and submissively I shall not fail to do so.'

'Have it your own way,' Herod answered with a shrug, 'but they won't treat you any the better for it. Constitutionally, eh? I must bow of course to your superior authority as an antiquarian, but has the word "constitution" any practical meaning to-day?'

Then the two Protectors were admitted. They repeated what the Senate had asked them to say, in a mechanical and unpersuasive duet. I was desired to do nothing by violence, but to yield without further hesitation to the power of the Senate. I was reminded of the dangers that they and I had escaped under the late Emperor and begged to commit no act that could be a cause of fresh public disasters.

The sentence about the dangers that they and I had escaped under Caligula was repeated three times in all, because first one of them made a mistake, and then the other went to his rescue, and then the first one said it all over again. I said, rather testily: 'Yes, that verse occurred once before, I think,' and quoted the Homeric tag that is found so often in the *Odyssey*:

> Glad from death's peril to have won scot-free –
> Our comrades not so fortunate as we.

Herod was delighted with this. He recited comically: 'Our comrades not so fortunate as we,' and then whispered to the Colonels: 'That's the point. All that they really care about is their own dirty hides.'

The Protectors of the People grew flustered and went on gabbling their message like a brace of ducks. If I resigned the supreme power that had been unconstitutionally awarded me, they said, the Senate promised to vote me the greatest honours that a free people could bestow. But I must place myself unreservedly in their hands. If, on the contrary, I acted foolishly and persisted in my refusal to attend the House, I would have the armed forces of the

City sent against me, and once I was captured I need expect no mercy.

The Colonels crowded round the two Protectors with such threatening looks and mutterings that they hastily explained that they were only repeating what had been put into their mouths by the Senate, and that personally they wished to assure me that I was the only proper person, in their opinion, to rule the Empire. They begged us to remember that in their quality both as ambassadors of the Senate and as Protectors of the People their persons were inviolate, and not to do them any indignity. Then they said: 'And the Consuls privately gave us a second message that we were to give you in case our first doesn't please you.'

I wondered what this second message could be.

'Caesar,' they answered, 'we were ordered to tell you that if you *do* want the monarchy you must accept it as the Senate's gift and not as the gift of the Guards.'

That made me laugh outright: it was the first time that I had so much as smiled since Caligula's assassination. I asked, 'Is that all, or is there a third message in case I don't like the second?'

'No, there is nothing more, Caesar,' they answered humbly.

'Well,' I said, still much amused, 'tell the Senate that I don't blame them for not wanting another Emperor. The last one somehow lacked the gift of endearing himself to his people. But, on the other hand, the Imperial Guards insist on making me Emperor, and the officers have already sworn their allegiance to me and forced me to accept it – so what can I do? You may carry the Senate my respectful compliments and tell them that I shall do nothing unconstitutional' – here I looked defiantly at Herod – 'and that they can trust me not to deceive them. I acknowledge their authority, but at the same time I must remind them that I am in no position to oppose the wishes of my military advisers.'

So the Protectors were dismissed, and very glad they were to get away alive. Herod said: 'That was all right, but you would have done much better to have spoken firmly, as I suggested. You are only delaying matters.'

When Herod had gone the Colonels told me that they expected me to pay every Guardsman 150 gold pieces as a bounty on my accession, and 500 gold pieces each to the Captains. As to what I should pay the Colonels, I could please myself. 'Would you be satisfied with ten thousand apiece?' I joked. We agreed on 2,000, and then they asked me to appoint one of themselves in the place of Caligula's Commander, who had taken part in the conspiracy and was now apparently attending the meeting of the Senate.

'Choose whomever you like,' I said, indifferently.

So they chose the Senior Colonel, who was called Rufrius Pollius. Then I had to go out and make an announcement about the bounty from the tribunal platform and receive the oaths of allegiance from each company of soldiers in turn. I was also asked to announce that the same bounty would be paid to the regiments stationed on the Rhine, in the Balkans, in Syria, in Africa, and in all other parts of the Empire. I was the more willing to do this because I knew that there were arrears of pay owing everywhere, except among the Rhine troops, whom Caligula had paid with the money stolen from the French. The swearing of allegiance took hours, for every man had to repeat the oath, and there were 12,000 of them; and then the City Watchmen came into the camp and insisted on doing the same, and then sailors of the Imperial Navy came crowding up from Ostia. It seemed endless.

When the Senate received my message they adjourned until midnight. The motion for adjournment was made by Sentius and seconded by the senator who had pulled the ring off his finger. As soon as it was voted they hurried out and back to their houses, where they packed up a few belongings and drove out of the City to their country estates: they realized the insecurity of their position. Midnight came and the Senate met, but what a thin House it was! Hardly a hundred members were present, and even these were in a panic. The officers of the City Battalions were present, however, and as soon as proceedings opened, bluntly asked the Senate to give them an Emperor. It was the only hope for the City, they said.

Herod was quite right: the man who first offered himself as Emperor was Vinicius. He seemed to have a few supporters, including his rat-like cousin Vinicianus, but not many, and he was snubbed by the Consuls. They did not even put the motion to the House that the monarchy should be offered to him. As Herod had also foreseen, Asiaticus then came forward as a candidate. But Vinicius rose and asked whether anyone present took the suggestion seriously. A wrangle followed and blows were exchanged. Vinicianus came off with a bloody nose and had to lie down until the flow ceased. The Consuls had difficulty in restoring order. Then news was brought that the Watchmen and Sailors had joined the

Guards at the Camp, and the sword-fighters too (I forgot just now to mention the sword-fighters); so Vinicius and Asiaticus both withdrew their candidatures. Nobody else came forward. The meeting broke up into small groups talking anxiously together in whispers. At dawn Cassius Chaerea, Aquila, Lupus, and The Tiger entered. Cassius attempted to speak. He began by referring to the splendid restoration of the Republic. At this there were angry shouts from the officers of the City Battalions.

'Forget about the Republic, Cassius. We've decided now to have an Emperor, and if the Consuls don't give us one pretty soon, and a good one too, that's the last they'll see of us. We'll go to the Camp and join Claudius.'

One of the Consuls said nervously, looking at Cassius for support: 'No, we're not quite agreed yet about appointing an Emperor. Our last resolution – carried unanimously – was that the Republic was now restored. Cassius didn't kill Caligula merely for the sake of a change of Emperors – did you, Cassius? – but because he wished to give us back our ancient liberties.'

Cassius sprang to his feet, white with passion, and cried: 'Romans, I for one refuse to tolerate another Emperor. If another Emperor were appointed I should not hesitate to do to him as I did to Gaius Caligula.'

'Don't talk nonsense,' the City officers told him. 'There's no harm in an Emperor, if he's a good one. We were all very well off under Augustus.'

Cassius said, '*I'll* give you a good Emperor, then, if you promise to bring me the watchword from him – I'll give you Eutychus.' You may remember that Eutychus was one of Caligula's 'Scouts'. He was the best charioteer in Rome and drove for the Leek Green faction in the Circus. Cassius was reminding them of the fatigues that Caligula had forced the City troops to do for him, such as building stables for his race-horses and cleaning them out when they were in use, under Eutychus's fussy and arrogant supervision. 'I suppose you enjoy going down on your knees and scrubbing the muck from a stable floor at the orders of an Emperor's favourite charioteer?'

One of the Colonels sneered: 'You talk very big, Cassius, but you're afraid of Claudius, none the less. Admit it.'

'*I* afraid of Claudius?' Cassius shouted. 'If the Senate told me to go to the Camp and bring his head back, I'd cheerfully do so. I can't understand you people. It amazes me that after having been ruled for four years by a madman you should be ready to commit the government to an idiot.'

But Cassius could not convince the officers. They left the Senate without another word, assembled their men in the Market Place under the company banners and marched out to the Camp to swear allegiance to me. The Senate, or what remained of the Senate, was now left alone and unprotected. Everyone, I am told, began reproaching his neighbours, and all pretence of devotion to the failing Republican cause vanished. If a single man of them had shown himself courageous it would have been something: I should have felt less ashamed of my country. I had long suspected the veracity of certain of the heroic legends of ancient Rome related by the historian Livy, and on hearing of this scene in the Senate I even began to have doubts about my favourite passage, the one describing the fortitude of the senators of old after the disaster of the River Allia, when the Celts were advancing on the City and all hope of defending the walls was gone. Livy tells how the young men of military age, with their wives and children, withdrew into the Citadel after getting in a store of arms and provisions, resolved to hold out to the last. But the old men, who could be only an encumbrance to the besieged, remained behind and awaited death, wearing senatorial robes and seated in chairs of office in the porticoes of their houses, their ivory rods of office grasped firmly in their hands. When I was a boy, old Athenodorus made me memorize all this and I have never forgotten it:

The halls of the patricians stood open and the invaders gazed with feelings of true awe upon the seated figures in the porticoes, impressed not only by the superhuman magnificence of their apparel and trappings but also by their majestic bearing and the serene expression that their countenances wore: they seemed very Gods. So they stood marvelling, as at so many divine statues, until, as the legend tells, one of them began gently to stroke the beard of a patrician, by name Marcus Papirius – beards in those days were universally worn long – who rose and smote him on the head with his ivory staff. Admiration yielded to passion and Marcus Papirius was the first patrician to meet his death. The rest were butchered, still seated in their chairs.

Certainly Livy was a fine writer. He wrote to persuade men to virtue by his inspiring, though unhistorical, tales of Rome's greatness in times past. But no, he had not been particularly successful in his persuasions, I reflected.

Even Cassius, Lupus, and The Tiger were quarrelling now. The

Tiger swore that he would rather kill himself than consent to salute me as Emperor and see slavery return.

Cassius said, 'You don't mean what you say; and it's not yet time to talk like that.'

The Tiger shouted angrily: 'You too, Cassius Chaerea? Are you going to fail us now? You love your life too well, I think. You claim that you planned the whole assassination, but who struck the first blow – you or I?'

'I did,' said Cassius promptly, 'and I struck him from in front, not from behind. As for loving my life, who but a fool doesn't? I am certainly not going to lay it down unnecessarily. If I had followed Varus's example that day in the Teutoburger forest, more than thirty years ago – if I had killed myself because all hope seemed gone, who would have brought the eighty survivors back and held the Germans in play until Tiberius arrived with his army of relief? No, I loved life that day. And now it is quite possible that Claudius will decide, after all, to resign the monarchy. His answer was quite consistent with such an intention: he's idiot enough for anything, and as nervous as a cat. Until I know definitely that he is not going to do so I shall continue to live.'

By this time the Senate had dissolved, and Cassius, Lupus, and The Tiger were left arguing in the deserted vestibule. When Cassius looked round and saw that they were alone he burst into a cackle of laughter.

'It's absurd for us, of all people, to quarrel,' he said. 'Tiger, let's have some breakfast. You too, Lupus! Come on, you Lupus!'

I was having breakfast too, after only an hour or so of uninterrupted sleep, when I was informed that the Consuls and the diehard Republican senators who had attended the midnight meeting had now arrived in Camp to pay their homage to me and offer their congratulations. The Colonels showed their satisfaction with an ironical 'They have come too early: let them wait.' Sleeplessness had made me very irritable. I said that, for my part, I was in no mood to receive them: I liked men who clung courageously to their opinions. I tried to dismiss the senators from my mind and went on eating my breakfast. But Herod, who seemed to be everywhere at once throughout those two eventful days, saved their lives. The Germans, who were drunk and quarrelsome, had caught up their assegais and were on the point of killing them, and they were down on their knees yelling for mercy. The Guards made no attempt to interfere; Herod had to use my name to bring the Germans to their senses. He came into the breakfast-room as soon as he had put the rescued senators into a place of safety and said in a bantering voice: 'Excuse me, Caesar, but I didn't expect you to take my advice about stamping on the Senate quite so seriously. You must treat the poor fellows with more gentleness. If any mischief happens to them, where are you going to rake up such a marvellously subservient crew again?'

It was becoming increasingly difficult for me now to sustain my Republican convictions. What a farcical situation – myself, the only true anti-monarchist, forced to act as monarch! On Herod's advice I summoned the Senate to meet me at the Palace. The officers made no difficulty about my leaving Camp. The whole Guards Division came with me as escort, nine battalions marching ahead of me and three marching in the rear, followed by the rest of my troops, the Palace Guard being in the van. Then a most embarrassing incident occurred. Cassius and The Tiger, having had their breakfast, joined the parade and put themselves at the head of the Palace Guard with Lupus between them. I knew nothing about this myself because the vanguard was far out of sight of my sedan. The Palace Guard, accustomed to obey Cassius and The Tiger, concluded that they were acting under the orders of Rufrius, the new Guards Commander, though as a matter of fact Rufrius had sent these two a message informing them that they were deprived of their command. The spectators were mystified, and when they understood that the two were acting in deliberate disobedience of orders they made a scandal of it. One of the Protectors of the People came running down the column to inform me what was happening. I did not in the least know what to say or do. But I could not let this act of bravado pass unnoticed: they were defying Rufrius's order and my authority too.

When we reached the Palace I asked Herod and Vitellius and Rufrius and Messalina (who greeted me with the greatest delight) to consult with me at once as to what action I should take. The troops were drawn up outside the Palace – Cassius, Lupus, and The Tiger still with them, speaking together in loud, confident tones, but shunned by all the other officers. I opened the consultation by remarking that although Caligula had been my nephew and although I had promised his father, my dear brother Germanicus, to care for and protect him, I could not find it in me to blame Cassius for the murder. Caligula had invited assassination in a thousand ways. I said, too, that Cassius had a military record unequalled by that of any other officer in the Army, and that if I could be sure that he had struck the blow from such lofty motives as had, for example, animated the second Brutus, I would be very ready to pardon him. But what really had been his motives?

Rufrius spoke first. 'Cassius says now that he struck the blow in the name of Liberty, but the fact is that what encouraged him to strike the blow was an injury to his own dignity – Caligula's constant teasing of him by giving him comic and indecent watchwords.'

Vitellius said: 'And if it had been a sudden strong resentment that overcame him some excuse could be made, but the conspiracy was planned days and even months beforehand. The murder was done in cold blood.'

Messalina said: 'And are you forgetting that it was not an ordinary murder that he committed, but a breach of his most solemn oath of unquestioning loyalty to his Emperor? For this he has no right to be allowed to live. If he were an honest man he would now already have fallen on his own sword.'

Herod said: 'And are you forgetting that Cassius sent Lupus to murder you, and the Lady Messalina too? If you let him go free the City will conclude that you are afraid of him.'

I sent for Cassius and said to him: 'Cassius Chaerea, you are a man accustomed to obey orders. I am now your Commander-in-Chief, whether I like it or not; and you must obey my orders, whether you like them or not. My decision is as follows: If you had done as Brutus did, killing a tyrant for the common good although you loved him personally, I should have applauded you; though I should have expected you, since you had broken your solemn oath of fidelity by that act, to die by your own hand. But you planned the murder (and carried it out boldly where others hung back) because of feelings of personal resentment; and such motives cannot earn my praise. Moreover, I understand that on no authority but your own you sent Lupus to murder the Lady Caesonia and my wife the Lady Messalina and myself too, if he could find me; and for that reason I shall not grant you the privilege of suicide. I shall have you executed like a common criminal. It grieves me to do this, believe me. You have called me an idiot before the Senate and have told your friends that I deserve no mercy from their swords. It may be that you are right. But fool or no fool, I wish now to pay a tribute to your great services to Rome in the past. It was you who saved the Rhine bridges after the defeat of Varus, and my dear brother once commended you to me in a letter as the finest soldier serving under his command. I only wish that this story could have had a happier ending. I have no more to say. Good-bye.'

Cassius saluted without a word and was marched out to his death. I also gave orders for Lupus's execution. It was a very cold day and Lupus, who had put off his military cloak so as not to get it blood-stained, began to shiver and complain of the cold. Cassius was ashamed for Lupus and said reprovingly, 'A wolf should never complain of the cold.' (Lupus is the Latin for wolf.) But Lupus was weeping and seemed not to hear him. Cassius asked the soldier who was to act as executioner whether he had had any previous practice in that trade.

'No,' replied the soldier, 'but I was a butcher in civil life.'

Cassius laughed and said: 'That is very well. And now will you do me the favour of using my own sword on me? It is the one with which I killed Caligula.'

He was dispatched at a single stroke. Lupus was not so fortunate: when he was ordered to stretch out his neck he did so timorously and then flinched at the blow, which caught him on the forehead. The executioner had to strike several times before he could finish him.

As for The Tiger, Aquila, Vinicius, and the rest of the assassins, I took no vengeance on them. They benefited from the amnesty which, on the arrival of the Senate at the Palace, I immediately proclaimed for all words spoken and deeds done on that day and on the day preceding. I undertook to restore Aquila and The Tiger to their commands, provided that they took the oath of allegiance to me; but I gave the former Commander of the Guards another appointment, for Rufrius was too good a man to lose in that capacity. Here I must pay a tribute to The Tiger, as a man of his word. He had sworn to Cassius and Lupus that he would rather die than salute me Emperor, and now that they were executed he felt a debt of honour to their ghosts. He bravely killed himself just before their funeral pyre was lighted, and his body was burned with theirs.

Chapter 6

THERE were so many things to be done in the process of cleaning up the mess that Caligula had left behind him – nearly four years of misrule – that it makes my head swim even now to think of it. Indeed, the chief argument by which I justified to myself my failure to do what I had intended, namely, to resign the monarchy as soon as the excitement aroused by Caligula's assassination had died down, was that the mess was such a complete mess: I knew of nobody in Rome, besides myself, who would have the patience, even if he had the authority, to undertake the hard and thankless work that the cleaning-up process demanded. I could not with a clear conscience hand the responsibility over to the Consuls. Consuls, even the best of them, are incapable of planning a gradual reconstructive programme to be carried out over a course of five or ten years. They cannot think beyond their single twelve months of office. They always either aim at immediate splendid results, forcing things too quickly, or else do nothing at all. This was a task for a dictator appointed for a term of years. But even if a dictator with the proper qualities could be found, could he be trusted not to consolidate his position by adopting the name of Caesar and turning despot?

I remembered with dull resentment the beautifully clean start that Caligula had been given: well-filled Treasury and Privy Purse, capable and trustworthy advisers, the goodwill of the entire nation. Well, the best choice of many evils was to remain in power myself, for a time at least, hoping to be relieved as soon as possible. I could trust myself better than I could trust others. I would concentrate on the work before me and shake things into some sort of order before proving that my Republican principles were real principles and not just talk as they were with Sentius and men of his kind. Meanwhile I would remain as unEmperor-like as possible. But the problem of what titles I should temporarily allow myself to be voted arose at once. Without titles that carry with them the necessary authority to act, nobody can go very far. I would accept what was necessary. And I would find assistants somewhere, probably more among Greek clerks and enterprising City business men than among members of the Senate. There is a neat Latin proverb,

'Olera olla legit', which means 'The pot finds its own herbs'. I would manage somehow.

The Senate wanted to vote me every title of honour that had ever been held by my predecessors, just to show me how thoroughly they regretted their Republican fervour. I refused as many as I could. I did accept the name of Caesar to which I had a right in a way, because I was of the blood of the Caesars through my grandmother Octavia, Augustus's sister, and no true Caesars were left. I accepted it because of the prestige that the name carried with foreign peoples like the Armenians, Parthians, Germans, and Moroccans. If they had thought that I was a usurper founding a new dynasty they would have been encouraged to make trouble on the frontier. I also accepted the title of Protector of the People, which made my person inviolate and gave me the right to veto decrees of the Senate. This inviolacy of person was important to me because I proposed to annul all laws and edicts imposing penalties for treason against the Emperor, and without it I would not be even reasonably safe from assassination. However, I refused the title of Father of the Country, I refused the title of Augustus, I ridiculed attempts to vote me divine honours, and I even told the Senate that I did not wish to be styled 'Emperor'. This, I pointed out, had from ancient times been a title of distinction won by successful service in the field: it did not signify merely the supreme command of the armies. Augustus had been acclaimed Emperor on account of his victories at Actium and elsewhere. My uncle Tiberius had been one of the most successful Roman generals in the whole of our history. My predecessor Caligula had allowed himself to be styled Emperor from youthful ambition, but even he had felt it incumbent on him to earn the title in the field; hence his expedition across the Rhine and his attack upon the waters of the English Channel. His military operations, bloodless though they were, were symbolic of his understanding of the responsibilities that the title of Emperor carried with it. 'One day, my Lords,' I wrote to them, 'I may feel it necessary to take the field at the head of my armies, and if the Gods prosper me I shall earn the title, which I shall be very proud to bear, but until that day I must ask you not to address me by it, out of respect for those capable generals of the past who have really earned it.'

They were so pleased by this letter of mine that they voted me a golden statue – no, it was three golden statues – but I vetoed the motion on two grounds. One was that I had done nothing to earn this honour; and the other, that it was an extravagance. I did allow them, though, to vote me three statues which were to be put up in prominent places in the City; but the most expensive one was to be of silver, and not solid silver at that, but a hollow statue filled with plaster. The other two were of bronze and marble respectively. I accepted these three statues because Rome was so full of statues that two or three more would not make much difference, and I was interested to sit for my sculptured portrait to a really good sculptor, now that the best sculptors in the world were at my service.

The Senate also decided to dishonour Caligula by every means in their power. They voted that the day of his assassination should be made a festival of national thanksgiving. Again I interposed my veto and, apart from annulling Caligula's edicts about the religious worship that was to be paid to himself and to the Goddess Panthea, which was the name he gave my poor niece Drusilla whom he murdered, I took no further action against his memory. Silence about him was the best policy. Herod reminded me that Caligula had not done any dishonour to the memory of Tiberius, though he had good cause to hate him; he had merely abstained from deifying him and left the arch of honour which had been voted to him uncompleted.

'But what shall I do with all Caligula's statues?' I asked.

'That's simple enough,' he said. 'Set the City Watchmen to collect them all at two o'clock to-morrow morning when everyone is asleep and bring them here to the Palace. When Rome wakes up it will find the niches and pedestals unoccupied, or perhaps filled again with the statues originally moved to make room for them.'

I took Herod's advice. The statues were of two sorts – the statues of foreign Gods whose heads he had removed and replaced with his own; and the ones that he had made of himself, all in precious metals. The first sort I restored as nearly as possible to their original condition, the others I broke up, melted down and minted into my new coinage. The great gold statue that he had placed in his temple melted down into nearly 1,000,000 gold pieces. I do not think I mentioned about this statue, that every day his priests – of whom I, to my shame, had been one – clothed it with a costume similar to the one he himself was wearing. Not only did we have to dress it in ordinary civil or military costume with his especial badges of Imperial rank, but on days when he happened to believe himself to be Venus or Minerva or Jupiter or the Good

Goddess, we had to rig it out appropriately with the different divine insignia.

It pleased my vanity to have my head on the coins, but this was a pleasure which prominent citizens had enjoyed under the Republic too, so I must not be blamed for that. Portraits on coins, however, are always disappointing because they are executed in profile. Nobody is familiar with his own profile, and it comes as a shock, when one sees it in a portrait, that one really looks like that to people standing beside one. For one's full face, because of the familiarity that mirrors give it, a certain toleration and even affection is felt; but I must say that when I first saw the model of the gold piece that the mint-masters were striking for me I grew angry and asked whether it was intended to be a caricature. My little head with its worried face perched on my long neck, and the Adam's apple standing out almost like a second chin, shocked me. But Messalina said: 'No, my dear, that's really what you look like. In fact, it is rather flattering than otherwise.'

'Can you really love a man like that?' I asked.

She swore that there was no face so dear to her in the world. So I tried to get accustomed to the coin.

Besides Caligula's statues a good deal of his wasteful expenditure was represented by gold and silver objects in the Palace and elsewhere which could also be removed and converted into bullion. For instance, the golden door-knobs and window-panes and the gold and silver furniture in his temple. I removed it all. I gave the Palace a great clearing-out. In Caligula's bed-chamber I found the poison chest which had belonged to Livia and of which Caligula had made good use, sending presents of poisoned sweetmeats to men who had drawn their wills in his favour and sometimes pouring poison into the plates of dinner-guests, after first distracting their attention by some prearranged diversion. (He experienced most pleasure, he confessed, in watching them die from arsenic.) I took the whole chest down to Ostia with me the first calm day of spring and, rowing down the estuary in one of Caligula's pleasure-barges, dumped it overboard about a mile from the coast. A minute or two later thousands of dead fish came floating up. I had not told the sailors what the chest contained and some of them grabbed at the fish floating near, meaning to take them home to eat; but I stopped that, forbidding them to do so on pain of death.

Under Caligula's pillow I found his two famous books, on one of which was painted a bloody sword and on the other a bloody dagger. Caligula was always followed by a freedman carrying these two books, and if he heard something about a man which happened to displease him he used to say to the freedman, 'Protogenes, write that fellow's name down under the dagger' or 'write his name down under the sword.' The sword was for those destined to execution, the dagger for those who were to be invited to commit suicide. The last names in the dagger-book were Vinicius, Asiaticus, Cassius Chaerea, and Tiberius Claudius – myself. These books I burned in a brazier with my own hands. And Protogenes I put to death. It was not only that I loathed the sight of this grim-faced, bloody-minded fellow who had always treated me with insufferable impudence, but that I was now given evidence that he had threatened senators and knights to write their names down in the book unless they paid him large sums of money. Caligula's memory was so bad at this time that Protogenes could easily have persuaded him that the entries were his own.

When I tried Protogenes he insisted that he had never uttered any such threats and never put any name down in the book except at Caligula's orders. This raised the question of the authority sufficient for a man's execution. It would be easy for one of my colonels to report to me dishonestly one morning: 'So-and-so was executed at dawn in accordance with your instructions of yesterday.' If I knew nothing of the matter it would merely be his word against mine that I had issued these instructions; and, as I am always ready to admit, my memory is none of the best. So I reintroduced the practice, started by Augustus and Livia, of immediately committing all decisions and directions to writing. Unless a paper could be produced by my subordinates giving signed orders from me for any strong disciplinary action that they had taken or any important financial commitment or startling innovation in procedure that they had made, such action must not be regarded as authorized by me, and if I disapproved of it they must bear the blame themselves. In the end this practice, which was also adopted by my chief ministers in dealing with their own subordinates, became such a matter of course that one hardly ever heard a word spoken in government offices, during working hours, except for consultations between heads of departments or visits from City officials. Every Palace servant carried a wax-tablet about with him in case it should be needed for special orders to be written upon.

All casual applicants for posts, grants, favours, indulgences, or what-not were warned to present a document on entering the Palace, stating exactly what they wanted, and why; and except in rare instances were not permitted to press their case by pleas and arguments delivered by word of mouth. This saved time but won my ministers an undeserved reputation for arrogance.

I shall tell you about my ministers. During the reigns of Tiberius and Caligula the real direction of affairs had fallen more and more into the hands of Imperial freedmen, originally trained in secretarial duties by my grandmother Livia. The Consuls and City magistrates, though independent authorities answerable only to the Senate for carrying out their duties properly, had come to depend on the advice issued to them, in the Emperor's name, by these secretaries, especially in the case of complicated documents connected with legal and financial matters. They were shown where to affix their seals, or sign their names, the documents being already prepared for them, and seldom troubled to acquaint themselves with the contents. Their signature was in most cases a mere formality and they knew nothing at all about administrative detail compared with what the secretaries knew. Besides, the secretaries had developed a new sort of handwriting, full of abbreviations and hieroglyphs and hastily formed letters, that nobody but themselves could read. I knew that it was impossible to expect any sudden change in this relation between the secretariat and the rest of the world, so for the present I strengthened rather than weakened the powers of the secretariat, confirming the appointments of those of Caligula's freedmen who were capable. For instance, I kept Callistus, who had been Secretary both to the Privy Purse and to the Public Treasury, which Caligula treated as a sort of Privy Purse. He had been aware of the plot against Caligula but had taken no active part in it. He told me a long story about having been recently instructed by Caligula to poison my food, but having nobly refused to do so. I did not believe it. In the first place, Caligula would never have given him those orders, but would have administered the poison with his own hands as usual; and in the second place, if he had, Callistus would never have dared to disobey. However, I let that go because he seemed anxious to continue with his Treasury duties and was the only man who really understood the ins and outs of the present financial situation. I encouraged him by saying that I thought he had done remarkably well in keeping Caligula supplied with money so long and that I counted on him henceforth to use his gold-divining powers for the salvation of Rome instead of for its destruction. His responsibilities extended to the direction of judicial inquiries into all public financial questions. I retained Myron as my legal secretary and Posides as my military Treasurer and put Harpocras in charge of all matters relating to Games and Entertainments; and Amphaeus kept the Roll of Citizens. Myron also had the task of accompanying me whenever I went out in public, examining the messages and petitions handed to me, and sorting out the important, immediate ones from the customary shower of irrelevancies and importunities. My other chief ministers were Pallas whom I put in charge of my Privy Purse, his brother Felix whom I made my secretary for Foreign Affairs, Callon whom I made Superintendent of Stores, and his son Narcissus whom I made chief secretary for Home Affairs and private correspondence. Polybius was my religious secretary – for I was High Pontiff – and would also assist me in my historical work if ever I should get time for it. The last-named five were my own freedmen. During my days of bankruptcy I had been forced to dismiss them from my service and they had readily found clerical work to do at the Palace; so they were initiates in the Secretarial Mysteries and had even learned to write illegibly. I gave them all quarters in the New Palace, removing the rabble of sword-fighters, charioteers, grooms, actors, jugglers, and other hangers-on that Caligula had installed there. I made the Palace above all things a place for governmental work. I lived privately at the Old Palace, and in very modest style too, following the example of Augustus. For important banquets and visits of foreign princes I used Caligula's suite at the New Palace, where Messalina also had a wing for her own use.

When I gave my ministers their appointments I explained that I wanted them to act as much as possible on their own initiative; I could not be expected to direct them all in everything, even if I had been more experienced. I was not in the position of Augustus who, when he assumed control of affairs, was not only young and active but had a corps of capable advisers at his command, men of public distinction – Maecenas, Agrippa, Pollio, to name only three. I told them that they must do the best they could and that whenever they were faced by any difficulty they should consult *The Roman Transactions of the God Augustus*, the great memorial work published by Livia in the reign of Tiberius, and should keep closely to the forms and precedents that they found in it. If cases occurred where no precedent could be found in this invaluable record, they were, of course, to consult me; but I trusted them to save me as much unnecessary labour as possible. 'Be bold,' I said, 'but not too bold.'

I confessed to Messalina, who had helped me with these ministerial appointments, that the sharp edge of my Republican fervour was getting a little blunted: every day I felt more and more sympathy with, and respect for, Augustus. And respect for my grandmother Livia too, in spite of my personal dislike for her. She had surely had a wonderfully methodical mind, and if, before restoring the Republic, I could get the governmental system working again even half as well as it had worked under her and Augustus I would be most satisfied with myself. Messalina smilingly offered to play the part of Livia for the occasion if I undertook that of Augustus. '*Absit omen*,' I exclaimed, spitting in my bosom for luck. She answered that, joking aside, she had something of Livia's gift for summing up people's characters and deciding just what appointments they were fit to hold. If I cared to give her a free hand she would act on my behalf in all social questions, relieving me of all the cares connected with my office as Director of Public Morals. I was deeply in love with Messalina, you must know, and in the matter of choosing my ministers had found her judgement very shrewd, but I hesitated to allow her to take on as much responsibility as this. She begged me to let her give me some stronger proof of her capacity. She suggested that we should together go through the nominal roll of the Senatorial Order: she would tell me which names in her opinion were fit to remain on it. I called for the roll and we began to go through the list. I must confess that I was astonished at the detailed knowledge of the capacities and characters and private and public histories of the first twenty or so senators named in it. Wherever I could check her facts she was so accurate that I readily granted her request. I only consulted my own inclinations in a few doubtful cases, where she did not care very much whether the name was kept on the roll or struck off. After making inquiries through Callistus as to the financial qualifications of certain members, as well as deciding about their mental and moral qualifications, we removed about one-third of the names and filled up the vacancies with the best knights available, and with former senators struck off the roll by Caligula for frivolous reasons. One of my own choices for removal was Sentius. I felt the need of getting rid of him, not merely because of his foolish speech to the Senate and his subsequent cowardice, but because he was one of the two senators who had accompanied me to the Palace at the time of Caligula's assassination and had then deserted me. The other, by the way, was Vitellius, but he now assured me that he had hurried off only to find Messalina and put her into a place of safety, expecting Sentius to stay and look after me; so I quite forgave him. I made Vitellius my understudy in case I should happen to fall ill or anything worse should happen to me. At all events, I got rid of Sentius. The reason that I gave for his degradation was that he had not appeared at the meeting of the Senate that I summoned to the Palace, having fled from Rome to his country estate without informing the Consuls that he would be absent; he had not returned for several days, and thus failed to benefit by the amnesty. Another leading senator that I degraded was Caligula's horse Incitatus who was to have become Consul three years later. I wrote to the Senate that I had no complaints to make against the private morals of this senator or his capacity for the tasks that had hitherto been assigned to him, but that he no longer had the necessary financial qualifications. For I had cut the pension awarded him by Caligula to the daily rations of a cavalry horse, dismissed his grooms and put him into an ordinary stable where the manger was of wood, not ivory, and the walls were whitewashed, not covered with frescoes. I did not, however, separate him from his wife, the mare Penelope: that would have been unjust.

Herod warned me to be constantly on my guard against assassination, saying that our revisions of the Roll of Senators and the further revisions that we had made in the Roll of Knights had won me many enemies. An amnesty was all very well, he said, but the generosity must not be too one-sided. Vinicius and Asiaticus, according to him, were already saying cynically that new brooms sweep clean, that Caligula and Tiberius had also started their reigns with a pretence of benevolence and rectitude, and that I would probably end by becoming as mad a despot as either of them. Herod advised me not to enter the Senate House for some time and even then to take every safeguard against assassination. This alarmed me. It was difficult to decide what safeguards were sufficient, and so I did not enter the Senate House for a whole month. By that time I had decided on the appropriate safeguard: I asked for and was granted permission to enter the House with an armed escort consisting of four Guards Colonels and Rufrius, the Guards Commander. I even put Rufrius on the Roll of Senators, though he did not have the proper financial qualifications, and the Senate at my request gave him permission to speak and vote whenever he entered in my company. On Messalina's advice, too, everyone who came into my presence at the Palace or elsewhere was first searched for concealed weapons: even women and boys. I did not like the notion of women being searched, but Messalina insisted, and I consented on condition that the searching was done by her freedwomen and not by my soldiers. Messalina also insisted on my having armed soldiers in attendance during banquets. In Augustus's day this would have been considered a most despotic practice and I was ashamed to see them lined up along the walls; but I could take no risks.

I worked hard to restore the Senate's self-respect. In choosing new members Messalina and I were as careful in our inquiries about their family histories as we were about their personal capacities. As if at the request of the senior members of the Senatorial Order, though it was really my own idea, I promised not to choose anyone who could not reckon four descents in the male line from a Roman citizen. I kept this promise. The only apparent exception I made was in the case of Felix, my foreign secretary, whom some years later I had occasion to invest with senatorial dignity. He was a younger brother of my freedman Pallas, and born after their father had been given his freedom: so he was never a slave, as Pallas had been. But even here I did not break my promise to the Senate: I asked a member of the Claudian house – not a true Claudian, but a member of a family of Claudian retainers, originally immigrants to the City from Campania, who had been given the citizenship and allowed to take the Claudian name – to adopt Felix as his son. So now Felix, in theory at least, has the necessary four lines of descent. But there were jealous murmurs from the House when I introduced him to them. Someone said: 'Caesar, these things were not done in the days of our ancestors.'

I replied angrily: 'I do not think, my Lord, that you have any right to talk in this way. Your own family is not as noble as all that: I've heard that they were selling faggots in the streets in my great-great-grandfather's time, and I've heard that they gave short weight, too.'

'It's a lie,' shouted the Senator. 'They were honest innkeepers.'

The House laughed the man down. But I felt obliged to say a little more. 'When he was appointed Censor more than three hundred years ago, my ancestor Claudius the Blind, victor of the Etruscans and Samnites and the first Roman author of distinction, admitted the sons of freedmen to the Senate just as I have done. Numerous members of this House owe their presence here to-day to this innovation of my ancestor. Would they care to resign?' The House then welcomed Felix warmly.

There were many rich idlers among the knights – as there had been, indeed, even in Augustus's day. But I did not follow Augustus's example in permitting them to remain idle. I gave out that any man who shirked public office when asked to undertake it would be expelled from the Order. In three or four cases I was as good as my word.

Among the papers that I found at the Palace in Caligula's private safe were those referring to the trials and deaths, under Tiberius, of my nephews Drusus and Nero, and their mother Agrippina. Caligula had pretended to burn the whole lot at the beginning of his reign, as a magnanimous gesture, but had not really done so, and the witnesses against my nephews and sister-in-law and the senators who had voted for their deaths had been in constant terror of his vengeance. I went carefully through the papers and called up before me as many as survived of the men mentioned in them as having been implicated in these judicial murders. The document which concerned each man was read over to him in my presence and then given into his own hands to burn in the fire before him. I may here mention the cipher dossiers of the private lives of prominent citizens which Tiberius had taken from Livia after Augustus's death but had been unable to read. Later I managed to decipher them, but they referred to events by this time so out of date that my interest in reading them was more a historical than a political one.

The two most important tasks that now presented themselves were the gradual reorganization of State finances and the abolition of the most offensive of Caligula's decrees. Neither could, however, be undertaken in a hurry. I had a long conference with Callistus and Pallas about finances immediately after their appointment. Herod was present too; because he probably knew more than any other man living about the raising of loans and the management of debts. The first question that presented itself was how to get hold of ready money for immediate expenses. We agreed to settle this, as I have already explained, by the melting down of gold statues and gold plate and ornaments in the Palace and the gold furniture in Caligula's temple. Herod suggested that I should add to the money thus realized by borrowing in the name of Capitoline Jove from other Gods whose temple treasuries had become cluttered in the course of the last hundred years or so by useless and showy votive offerings in precious metal. These were mostly the gift of people who wished to call attention to themselves as successful public men, not made in any real spirit of piety. For instance, a merchant, after a successful trading venture to the East, would present the God Mercury with a golden horn of plenty, or a successful soldier would present Mars with a golden shield, or a successful lawyer would present Apollo with a golden tripod. Clearly, Apollo could have no use for 200 or 300 gold and silver tripods; and if his father Jove was in need he surely would be only too pleased to lend him a few. So I melted down and minted into coin as many of these votive offerings as I could remove without offending the families of the donors or destroying works of historic or artistic value. For a loan to Jove was the same as a loan to the Treasury. We agreed at this conference that loans must also be raised from the bankers. We would promise them an attractive rate of interest. But Herod said that the most important thing was to restore public confidence and so force back into circulation the money that had been hoarded by nervous businessmen. He declared that although a policy of great economy was necessary, economy could be carried too far. It must not be interpreted as meanness. 'Whenever I ran short of money,' he said, 'in my needy days, I always made a point of spending all the money I had left on personal adornment – rings and cloaks and beautiful new shoes. This sent my credit up and enabled me to borrow again. I would advise you to do much the same. A little bit of gold leaf, for example, goes a long way. Suppose you were to send along a couple of goldsmiths to gild the goals in the Circus, it would make everyone feel very prosperous and wouldn't cost you more than fifty or a hundred gold pieces. And another idea occurred to me this morning as I was watching those great slabs of marble from Sicily being carried up the hill for facing the inside of Caligula's temple. You're not going to do any more work on the temple, are you? Well, then, why not use them to face the sandstone barrier of the Circus? It's beautiful marble and ought to cause a tremendous sensation.'

Herod was always a man of ideas. I wished that I could keep him always with me, but he told me that he could not possibly stay;

he had a kingdom to govern. I told him that if he would stay at Rome for only a few months longer I would make his kingdom as big as his grandfather Herod's had been.

But about this conference. We agreed to raise these Treasury loans and we agreed to abolish, at first, only the most extraordinary of the taxes imposed by Caligula: such as taxes on the takings of brothels, on the sales of hawkers and on the contents of the public urinals – the big pots standing at the street corners which the fullers used to carry away, when the liquid reached a certain level, to use for cleaning clothes. In my decree abolishing these taxes I promised that as soon as sufficient money came in I would abolish others too.

Chapter 7

I SOON found myself popular. Among the edicts of Caligula that I annulled were those concerned with his own religious cult, and his treason edicts, and those removing certain privileges of the Senate and the People. I decreed that the word 'treason' was henceforth meaningless. Not only would written treason not be held as a criminal offence, but neither would overt acts; in this I was more liberal even than Augustus. My decree opened the prison gates for hundreds of citizens of all degrees. But on Messalina's advice I kept everybody under open arrest until I had satisfied myself that the charge of treason did not include other crimes of a more felonious nature. For the charge of treason was often only a formality of arrest: the crime might be murder, forgery, or any other offence. These cases were not ones that I could leave for settlement to the ordinary magistrates. I felt bound to investigate them myself. I went every day to the Market Place and there, in front of the temple of Hercules, tried cases all morning long with a bench of senator colleagues. No Emperor had admitted colleagues to his tribunal for a number of years – not since Tiberius went to Capri. I also paid surprise visits to other courts and always took my place there on the bench of advisers to the presiding judge. My knowledge of legal precedents was very faulty. I had never taken the ordinary course of honours which every Roman nobleman went through, gradually rising in rank from third-class magistrate to Consul, with intervals of military service abroad;

and except for the last three years I had lived out of Rome a great deal and very rarely visited the law-courts. So I had to rely on my native wit rather than on legal precedent and to struggle hard the whole time against the tricks of lawyers who, trading on my ignorance, tried to entangle me in their legal webs.

Every day as I came into the Market Place from the Palace I used to pass a stuccoed building across the face of which was tarred in enormous letters:

Founded and Directed by the most Learned and Eloquent Orator and Jurist Telegonius Macarius of This City and of the City of Athens.

Underneath this on a huge square tablet appeared the following advertisement:

Telegonius gives instruction and advice to all who have become involved in financial or personal difficulties necessitating their appearance in Civil or Criminal courts; and has a positively encyclopaedic knowledge of all Roman edicts, statutes, decrees, proclamations, judicial decisions, etcetera, past and present, operative, dormant, or inoperative. At half an hour's notice the most learned and eloquent Telegonius can supply his clients with precise and legally incontrovertible opinions on any judicial matter under the sun that they care to present to him and his staff of highly trained clerks. Not only Roman Law, but Greek Law, Egyptian Law, Jewish Law, Armenian, Moroccan, or Parthian Law – Telegonius has it all at his fingers' ends. The incomparable Telegonius, not content with dispensing the raw material of Law, dispenses also the finished product: namely, beautifully contrived forensic presentations of the same complete with appropriate tones and gestures. Personal appeals to the jury a speciality. Handbook of brilliant rhetorical figures and tropes, suitable for any case, to be had on request. No client of Telegonius has ever been known to suffer an adverse verdict in any court – unless his opponent has by chance also drunk from the same fountain of oratorical wisdom and eloquence. Reasonable fees and courteous attention. A few vacancies for pupils.
'The tongue is mightier than the blade':
EURIPIDES.

I gradually came to memorize this tablet by seeing it so often, and now when the counsel for the defence or prosecution used to appeal to me with expressions like, 'Surely, Caesar, you are aware of the fifteenth subsection of the fourth article of Marcus Porcius Cato's Sumptuary Law published in the year that So-and-So and So-and-So were Consuls?' or, 'You will agree with me, Caesar, that in the island of Andros, of which my client is a native, great latitude is shown to forgers if it can be proved that they were influenced by regard for the well-being of their aged parents rather than by hope of personal gain,' or similar foolish talk, I would just smile back and reply: 'You are mistaken, sir: I am quite unaware of this. I am not the most learned and eloquent Telegonius, who can supply precise and legally incontrovertible opinions on any judicial matter under the sun. I am merely the Judge of this Court. Proceed, and don't waste my time.' If they tried to badger me further I would say: 'It's no use. In the first place, if I don't want to answer, I won't answer. You can't make me. I'm a free man, aren't I – in fact one of the freest in Rome? In the second place, if I do answer now, by Heaven you'll wish that I hadn't.'

Telegonius, by the way, seemed to be doing quite a thriving business and I came to resent his activities greatly. I detest forensic oratory. If a man cannot state his case in a brief and lucid way, bringing the necessary witnesses and abstaining from irrelevant talk about the nobility of his ancestry, the number of impoverished relatives dependent on him, the clemency and wisdom of the judge, the harsh tricks that Fate plays, the mutability of human fortune and all that stale, silly bag of tricks, he deserves the extreme penalty of the law for his dishonesty, pretension, and his waste of public time. I sent Polybius to buy Telegonius's handbook as advertised; and studied it. A few days later I was visiting a lower court when a defendant launched out on one of the brilliant rhetorical figures recommended by Telegonius. I asked the judge to allow me to intervene. He granted me this, and I said to the orator: 'Stop, sir, this will never do. You have made a mistake in your recitation-lesson. Telegonius's figure was as follows – let me see – "*If accused of theft*" – yes, here we are.' I produced the handbook:

Hearing of my neighbour's loss, and filled with pity for him, through what woods and vales, over what windy and inhospitable mountains, in what damp and gloomy caverns did I not search for that lost sheep (or lost cow – lost horse – lost mule) until at last, extraordinary to relate, returning home, weary, footsore, and disappointed, I found it (*here shade eyes with hand and look startled*): and where but in my own sheepcote (or cowshed – stable – barn) where it had perversely strayed during my absence!

'Sir,' I said, 'you put groves where the vales should have been and you left out "footsore" and the telling adverb "perversely".

You didn't look startled, either, at the word "found", only stupid. The judgement goes against you. Blame yourself, not Telegonius.'

Because I devoted myself to my judicial duties for so many hours every day, religious holidays not excepted; and even ran the summer and winter law-terms together, so that the dispensation of justice should be continuous and no accused person be forced to spend longer than a few days in prison – because of all this, I expected more considerate treatment from lawyers, court officials, and witnesses than I got. I made it quite plain that the non-appearance or late appearance in court of one of the principal parties in any suit would prejudice me in favour of his opponent. I tried to get through cases as quickly as possible and won (most unfairly) a reputation for sentencing prisoners without giving them a proper opportunity for defence. If a man was accused of a crime and I asked him straight out, 'Is this accusation substantially true?' and he shuffled and said: 'Let me explain, Caesar. I am not exactly guilty, but ...', I would cut him short. I would pronounce, 'Fined a thousand gold pieces' or 'Banished to the Island of Sardinia' or just 'Death', and then turn to the beadle: 'Next case, please.' The man and his lawyer were naturally vexed that they had not been able to charm me with their extenuating-circumstance pleas. There was one case in which the defendant claimed to be a Roman citizen and so appeared in a gown, but the plaintiff's lawyer objected and said that he was really a foreigner and should be wearing a cloak. It made no difference to this particular case whether or not he was a Roman citizen, so I silenced the lawyers by ordering the man to wear a cloak during all speeches for the prosecution and a gown during all speeches for the defence. The lawyers did not like me for that and told each other that I was ridiculing justice. Perhaps I was. On the whole they treated me very badly. Some mornings if I had been unable to settle as many cases as I had hoped and it was long past the time for my dinner they would make quite a disturbance when I adjourned proceedings until next day. They would call to me quite rudely to come back and not keep honest citizens waiting for justice, and would even catch me by the gown or foot as if forcibly to prevent me from leaving the court.

I did not discourage familiarity, provided that it was not offensive, and found that an easy atmosphere in court encouraged witnesses to give proper evidence. If anyone answered me back with spirit when I had expressed an ill-advised opinion I never took it ill. On one occasion the counsel for the defence explained that his client, a man of sixty-five, had recently married. His wife was a witness in the case, and was quite a young woman. I remarked that the marriage was illegal. According to the Poppaean–Papian Law (with which I happened to be familiar) a man over sixty was not allowed to marry a woman under fifty: the legal assumption was that a man over sixty is unfit for parentage. I quoted the Greek epigram:

> The old man weds, for Nature's rule he scorns –
> 'Father a weakly stock, or else wear horns'.

The lawyer considered for a few moments and then extemporized:

> And that old man, yourself, is a plain fool
> To foist on Nature this unnatural rule.
> A sturdy old man fathers sturdy sons;
> A weakly young man fathers weakly ones.

This was so just a point and so neatly made that I forgave the poet-lawyer for calling me a plain fool, and at the next meeting of the Senate amended the Poppaean–Papian Law accordingly. The severest anger to which I ever remember having given way in court was roused by a court official whose duty it was to summon witnesses and see that they arrived punctually. I had given a fraud case a hearing but had been forced to adjourn it for lack of evidence, the principal witness having fled to Africa to avoid being charged with complicity in the fraud. When the case came on again I called for this witness; but he was not in court. I asked the court official whether this man had been duly subpoenaed to attend.

'Oh, yes, indeed, Caesar.'

'Then why is he not here?'

'He is unfortunately prevented from attending.'

'There is *no* excuse for non-attendance, except illness so serious that he cannot be carried into court without danger to his life.'

'I quite agree, Caesar. No, the witness is not ill now. He has been very ill, I understand. But that is all over.'

'What was wrong with him?'

'He was mauled by a lion, I am informed, and afterwards gangrene set in.'

'It's a wonder he recovered,' I said.

'He didn't,' sniggered the fellow. 'He's dead. I think that death can stand as an excuse for non-attendance.' Everyone laughed.

I was so furious that I flung my writing-tablet at him, took away his citizenship, and banished him to Africa. 'Go and hunt lions,' I shouted, 'and I hope they maul you properly, and I hope gangrene sets in.' However, six months later I pardoned him and reinstated him in his position. He made no more jokes at my expense.

It is only fair at this point to mention the severest anger that was ever directed in court against myself. A young nobleman was charged with unnatural acts against women. The real complainants were the Guild of Prostitutes, an unofficial but well-managed organization which protected its members pretty effectively from abuse by cheats or ruffians. The prostitutes could not very well bring a charge against the nobleman themselves, so they went to a man who had been done a bad turn by him and wanted revenge – prostitutes know everything – and offered to give evidence if he brought the charge: a prostitute was a capable witness in a law-court. Before the case came on, I sent a message to my friend Calpurnia, the pretty young prostitute who had lived with me before I married Messalina and had been so tender and faithful to me in my misfortunes: I asked her to interview the women who were to give evidence and privately find out whether the nobleman had really abused them in the manner alleged, or whether they had been bribed by the person who was bringing the charge. Calpurnia sent me word a day or two later that the nobleman had really behaved in a very brutal and disgusting way, and that the women who had complained to the Guild were decent girls, one of whom was a personal friend of hers.

I tried the case, took sworn evidence (overruling the objection of the defending lawyer that prostitutes' oaths were both proverbially and actually worth nothing) and had this put in writing by the court recorder. When one girl repeated some very filthy and vulgar remark that the accused had made to her, the recorder asked, 'Shall I put that down, Caesar?' and I answered, 'Why not?' The young nobleman was so angry that he did just what I had done to the court official who teased me – he threw his writing-tablet at my head. But whereas I had missed my aim, his aim was true. The sharp edge of the tablet gashed my cheek and drew blood. But all I said was, 'I am glad to see, my Lord, that you still have some shame left.' I found him guilty and put a black mark against his name in the Roll, which disqualified him from becoming a candidate for public office. But he was a relative by marriage of Asiaticus, who asked me some months later to scratch out the black mark, because his young relative had lately reformed his ways. 'I'll scratch it out, to please you,' I answered, 'but it will still show.' Asiaticus later repeated this remark of mine to his friends as a proof of my stupidity. He could not understand, I suppose, that a reputation was, as my mother used to say, like an earthenware plate. 'The plate is cracked; the reputation is damaged by a criminal sentence. The plate is then mended with rivets and becomes "as good as new"; the reputation is mended by an official pardon. A mended plate or a mended reputation is better than a cracked plate or a damaged reputation. But a plate that has never been cracked and a reputation that has never been damaged are better still.'

A schoolmaster always appears a very queer fellow to his pupils. He has certain stock-phrases which they come to notice and giggle at whenever he uses them. Everyone in the world has stock-phrases or tricks of speech, but unless he is in a position of authority – as a schoolmaster, or an army captain or a judge – nobody notices them particularly. Nobody noticed them in my case until I became Emperor, but then of course they became world-famous. I had only to remark in court, 'No malice or favour whatsoever' (turning to my legal secretary after summing-up a case), 'That's right, isn't it?' or 'When once my mind is made up, the thing is fixed with a nail,' or quote the old tag:

> As the rascal did he must
> Himself be done by. And that's just,

or utter the family oath, 'Ten thousand furies and serpents!' – and a great roar of laughter would go up about me as though I had let fall either the most absurd solecism imaginable or the most exquisitely witty epigram.

In the course of my first year in the courts I must have made hundreds of ridiculous mistakes, but I did get the cases settled and sometimes surprised myself by my brilliance. There was one case, I remember, where one of the witnesses for the defence, a woman, denied any relationship with the accused man, who was alleged by the prosecution to be really her son. When I told her that I would take her word for it and that in my quality as High Pontiff I would immediately join her and him in marriage she was so frightened by the prospect of having incest forced upon her that she pleaded guilty to perjury. She said that she had concealed her relationship in order to seem an impartial witness. That gave me a great reputation, which I lost almost at once in a case where the treason charge covered one of forgery. The prisoner was a freedman of one of Caligula's freedmen, and there were no extenuating circumstances to his crime. He had forged his master's will just before his death – whether he was responsible for the death could not be proved – and had left his mistress and her children completely destitute. I grew very angry with this man as I heard his story unfolded and determined to inflict the maximum penalty. The defence was very weak – no denial of the charge, only a stream of Telegonian irrelevancies. It was long past my dinner-time and I had been sitting in judgement solidly for six hours. A delicious whiff of cooking came floating into my nostrils from the dining-chamber of the Priests of Mars near by. They eat better than any other priestly fraternity: Mars never lacks for sacrificial victims. I felt faint with hunger. I said to the senior of the magistrates who were sitting with me, 'Please take over this case from me and impose the maximum penalty, unless the defence has any better evidence to offer than has yet been produced.'

'Do you really mean the maximum penalty?' he asked.

'Yes, indeed, whatever it may be. The man deserves no mercy.'

'Your orders shall be obeyed, Caesar,' he replied.

So my chair was brought and I joined the priests at their dinner. When I returned that afternoon I found that the accused man's hands had been chopped off and hung around his neck. That was a punishment ordained for forgery by Caligula and had not yet been removed from the penal code. Everyone considered that I had acted most cruelly, for the judge had told the Court that it was my sentence, not his own. It was hardly my fault, though.

I recalled all the exiles who had been banished on treason charges; but only after asking the Senate's permission. Among these were my nieces Agrippinilla and Lesbia who had been sent to an island off the coast of Africa. For my own part, though I would certainly not have allowed them to remain there, neither would I have invited them to return to Rome. They had both behaved very insolently to me and had both committed incest with their brother Caligula, whether willingly or unwillingly I do not know, and their other adulteries had been a matter of public scandal. It was Messalina who interceded with me for them. I realize now that it gave her a delightful sense of power to do this. Agrippinilla and Lesbia had always treated her with great haughtiness, and now that they were told that they were being recalled to Rome as a result of her generosity they would feel obliged to humble themselves before her. But at the time I thought it was plain goodness of heart in Messalina. So my nieces returned and I found that exile had by no means broken their spirits, though their delicate skins had become sadly tanned by the African sun. By Caligula's orders they had been forced to earn their living on the island by diving for sponges. However, the only comment that Agrippinilla made on her experiences was that she had not altogether wasted her time. 'I have become a first-class swimmer. If anyone ever wants to kill me, he had better not try drowning.' They decided to brazen out the disgracefully slave-girlish colour of their faces, necks, and arms, by inducing some of their noble friends to adopt sunburn as a fashion. Walnut-juice became a favourite toilet-water. Messalina's intimates, however, kept their natural pink-and-white complexions and referred contemptuously to the sunburn party as 'The Sponge Divers'. Lesbia's thanks to Messalina were most perfunctory and I was hardly thanked at all. She was positively unpleasant. 'You kept us waiting ten days longer than was necessary,' she complained, 'and the ship that was sent to fetch us was full of rats.' Agrippinilla was wiser: she made both of us very graceful speeches of gratitude.

I confirmed Herod's kingship of Bashan, Galilee, and Gilead, and added to it Judaea, Samaria, and Edom, so that his dominions were now as large as those of his grandfather. I rounded off the northern part with Abilene, which had formed part of Syria. He and I entered upon a solemn league, confirmed by oaths in the open Market Place in the presence of an immense crowd, and by the ritual sacrifice of a pig, an ancient ceremony revived for the occasion. I also conferred on him the honorary dignity of Roman Consul: this had never before been given to a man of his race. It signalized that in the recent crisis the Senate had come for advice to him, not finding a native Roman capable of clear and impartial thought. At Herod's request I also conferred the little kingdom of Chalcis on his younger brother, Herod Pollio: Chalcis lay to the east of the Orontes, near Antioch. He asked nothing for Aristobulus, so Aristobulus got nothing. I also gladly freed Alexander the Alabarch and his brother Philo, who were still in prison at Alexandria. While on the subject, I may mention that when the Alabarch's son, to whom Herod had married his daughter Berenice, died, Berenice then married her uncle Herod Pollio. I confirmed Petronius in his governorship of Syria and sent him a personal letter of congratulation on his sensible behaviour in the matter of the statue.

I took Herod's advice about the marble slabs that had been intended for facing the interior of Caligula's temple: they made a fine showing around the Circus. Then I had to decide what to do with the building itself, which was handsome enough even when stripped of its precious ornaments. It occurred to me that it would be only justice to the Twin Gods, Castor and Pollux – a decent apology for the insult that Caligula had offered them by turning their temple into a mere portico of his own – to give it to them as an annexe of theirs. Caligula had made a breach in the wall behind their two statues, to form the main entrance to his temple, so that they became as it were his doorkeepers. There was nothing for it but to reconsecrate the premises. I fixed a propitious day for the ceremony and won the Gods' approval of it by augury; for we make this distinction between augury and consecration, that the consecration is effected by the will of man, but first the augury must denote the willing consent of the deity concerned. I had chosen the fifteenth day of July, the day that Roman knights go out crowned with olive wreaths to honour the Twins in a magnificent horseback procession: from the Temple of Mars they ride through the main streets of the City, circling back to the Temple of the Twins, where they offer sacrifices. The ceremony is a commemoration of the battle of Lake Regillus which was fought on that day over 300 years ago. Castor and Pollux came riding in person to the help of a Roman army that was making a desperate stand on the lake-shore against a superior force of Latins; and ever since then they have been adopted as the particular patrons of the Knights.

I took the auspices in the little tabernacle dedicated to that purpose on the summit of the Capitoline Hill. I invoked the Gods and, after calculation, marked out the appropriate quarter of the Heavens in which to make my observations, namely, the part where the constellation of the Heavenly Twins then lay. I had hardly done so, when I heard a faint creaking sound in the sky and the looked-for sign appeared. It was a pair of swans flying from the direction that I had marked out, the noise of their wings growing stronger and stronger as they approached. I knew that these must be Castor and Pollux themselves in disguise, because, you know, they and their sister Helen were hatched out of the same treble-yolked egg that Leda laid after she had been courted by Jove in the form of a swan. The birds passed directly over their Temple and were soon lost in the distance.

I shall get a little ahead of the order of events by describing the festival. It began with a lustration. We priests and our assistants made a solemn procession around the premises, carrying laurel branches which we dipped in pots of consecrated water and waved, sprinkling drops as we went. I had been to the trouble of sending for water from Lake Regillus, where Castor and Pollux, by the way, had another temple: I mentioned the source of the water in the invocation. We also burned sulphur and aromatic herbs to keep off evil spirits, and flute-music was played to drown the sound of any ill-omened word that might be uttered. This lustration made everything holy within the bounds that we had walked, which included the new annexe as well as the Temple itself. We walled up the breach: I laid the first stone myself. I then sacrificed. I had chosen the combination of victims that I knew would please the Gods most – for each of them an ox, a sheep, and a pig, all unblemished and all twins. Castor and Pollux are not major deities: they are demigods who, because of their mixed parentage, spend alternate days in Heaven and the Underworld. In sacrificing to the ghosts of heroes one draws the head of the victim down, but in sacrificing to Gods one draws it up. So in sacrificing to the Twins I followed an old practice which had lapsed for many years, of alternately drawing one head down and one head up. I have seldom seen more propitious entrails.

The Senate had voted me triumphal dress for the occasion; the excuse was a small campaign that had recently been brought to a conclusion in Morocco, where disturbances had followed Caligula's murder of the King, my cousin Ptolemy. I had had no responsibility for the Moroccan expedition, and though it was now customary for the Commander-in-Chief to be voted triumphal dress at the close of a campaign, even though he had never left the City, I would not have accepted the honour but for one consideration. I decided that it would look strange for a Commander-in-Chief to dedicate a temple to the only two Greek demigods who had ever fought for Rome, in a dress which was a confession that he had never done any real army-commanding. But I only wore my triumphal wreath and cloak during the ceremony itself: for the rest of the five days' festival I wore an ordinary purple-bordered senator's gown.

The first three days were devoted to theatrical shows in the Theatre of Pompey, which I rededicated for the occasion. The stage and part of the auditorium had been burned down in Tiberius's reign, but rebuilt by him and dedicated to Pompey again. Caligula, however, had disliked seeing Pompey's title, 'The Great', in the inscription and had rededicated the Theatre to himself. I now gave it back to Pompey, though I put an inscription on the stage, giving Tiberius credit for its restoration after the fire and myself credit for this rededication to Pompey: it is the only public building on which I have ever let my name appear.

I had never liked the wholly un-Roman practice that had sprung up towards the end of Augustus's reign, of men and women of rank appearing on the stage to show off their histrionic and corybantic talents. I cannot think why Augustus did not discourage them more sternly than he did. I suppose it was because there was no law against the practice, and Augustus was tolerant of Greek innovations. His successor Tiberius disliked the theatre, whoever the actors might be, and called it a great waste of time and an encouragement to vice and folly. But Caligula not only recalled the professional actors whom Tiberius had banished from the City but strongly encouraged noble amateurs to perform and often appeared on the stage himself. The chief impropriety of the innovation lay for me in the sheer incapacity of the noble amateurs. Romans are not born actors. In Greece men and women of rank take their parts in theatrical shows as a matter of course, and never fail to acquit themselves honourably. But I have never seen a Roman amateur who was any good. Rome has only produced one great actor, Roscius, but he won his extraordinary perfection in the art by the extraordinary pains that he took over it. He never once made a single gesture or movement on the stage that he had not carefully rehearsed beforehand again and again – until it seemed a natural action. No other Roman has ever had the patience to forge himself into a Greek. So on this occasion I sent special messages to all noblemen and noblewomen who had ever appeared on the stage in Caligula's reign, ordering them under pain of my displeasure to act in two plays and an interlude which I had chosen for them. They were not to be helped out by any professional actor, I said. At the same time I called for Harpocras, my Games secretary, and told him that I wished him to get together the best cast of professional actors that he could find in Rome and see whether he could not, on the second day of the festival, show what acting really should be. It was to be the same programme; but I kept this a secret. My little object-lesson worked very well. The first day's performances were pitiable to witness. Such wooden gestures and awkward entrances and exits, such mumbling and mangling of parts, such lack of gravity in the tragedies and of humour in the comedies, that the audience soon grew impatient and coughed and shuffled and talked. But next day the professional company acted so brilliantly that since then no man or woman of rank has ever dared to appear upon the public stage.

On the third day the principal performance was the Pyrrhic sword-dance, the native dance of the Greek cities of Asia Minor. It was performed by the sons of the notables of those cities, whom Caligula had sent for on the pretence of wanting them to dance for him; in reality he intended them for hostages for their parents' good behaviour while he visited Asia Minor and raised money by his usual extortionate methods. Hearing of their arrival at the Palace, Caligula had gone to inspect them and was on the point of making them rehearse a song which they had learnt in his honour when Cassius Chaerea came up to ask for the watchword; and that was the signal for his assassination. So now the boys danced with the greater joy and skill for knowing what a fate they had escaped; and sang me a very grateful song when they had done. I rewarded them all with the Roman citizenship and sent them home a few days later, loaded with presents.

The fourth and fifth days' performances were in the Circus, which looked very fine with its gilt goals and marble barriers, and in the amphitheatres. We had twelve chariot-races and one camel-race, which was an amusing novelty. We also killed 300 bears and 300 lions in the amphitheatres, and had a big sword-fighting display. The bears and the lions had been ordered by Caligula from Africa just before his death and had only just arrived. I frankly told the people, 'This is the last big wild-beast show that you will see for some time: I am going to wait until the prices come down before I order any more. The African traders have run them up to an absurd height. If they can't bring them down again they can take their wares to another market – but I think that it will puzzle them to find one.' This appealed to the crowd's commercial sense and they cheered me gratefully. So that was the end of the festival, except for a big banquet which I gave afterwards at the Palace to the nobility and their wives, also to certain representatives of the

People. More than 2,000 people were served. There were no far-fetched delicacies, but it was a well-thought-out meal, with good wine and excellent roasts, and I heard no complaints about the absence of tit-lark-tongue pastries or antelope fawns in aspic or ostrich-egg omelettes.

Chapter 8

I soon came to a decision about the sword-fighting and wild-beast hunts. First about the wild beasts. I had heard of a sport practised in Thessaly which had the double advantage of being exciting to watch and cheap to provide. So I introduced it at Rome as an alternative to the usual leopard and lion hunts. It was played with half-grown wild bulls. The Thessalians used to rouse the bull by sticking small darts into its hide as it emerged from the pen where it was imprisoned – not enough to injure it, only enough to vex it. It used to come charging out and then they used to jump nimbly out of its way. They were quite unarmed. Sometimes they used to deceive it by holding coloured cloths before their bodies: when it charged the cloths they moved them away at the last moment without shifting their own ground. The bull would always charge the moving cloth. Or, as it charged, they would leap forward and either clear it in a single bound, or step on its rump for a moment before coming to ground again. The bull would gradually weary, and they would do still more daring tricks. There was one man who could actually stand with his back to the bull, bending down with his head between his legs, and then, as it charged, turn a back-somersault in the air and land standing on the bull's shoulders. It was a common sight to see a man ride around the ring balanced on a bull's back. If a bull would not tire quickly, they would make it gallop around the arena by sitting it as if it were a horse, holding a horn in the left hand and twisting its tail with the right. When it was sufficiently out of breath the chief performer would wrestle with it, holding it by both horns and slowly forcing it to the ground. Sometimes he would catch the bull's ear between his teeth to help him in his task. It was a very interesting sport to watch, and the bull often caught and killed a man who took too great liberties with it. The cheapness of the sport lay in the very reasonable demands for payment made by the Thessalians, who were simple countrymen, and in the survival of the bull for another performance. Clever bulls who learned how to avoid being tricked and dominated soon became great popular favourites. There was one called Rusty, who was almost as famous in its way as the horse Incitatus. He killed ten of his tormentors in as many festivals. The crowd came to prefer these bull-baitings to all other shows except sword-fighting.

About the sword-fighters: I decided now to recruit them principally from the slaves who in the reigns of Caligula and Tiberius had testified against their masters at treason trials and so brought about their deaths. The two crimes that I abominate most are parricide and treachery. For parricide, indeed, I have reintroduced the ancient penalty: the criminal is whipped until he bleeds and then sewed up in a sack together with a cock, a dog, and a viper, representing lust, shamelessness, and ingratitude, and finally thrown into the sea. I regard treachery of slaves towards their masters as a sort of parricide too, so I would always make them fight until one combatant was dead or severely wounded; and I never granted any man remission, but made him fight again at the next Games, and so on until he was killed or wholly disabled. Once or twice it happened that one of them pretended to be mortally injured when he had only received a slight cut, and would writhe on the sand as if unable to continue. If I found that he was shamming I always gave orders for his throat to be cut.

I believe the populace enjoyed the entertainments that I gave them far more than Caligula's, because they saw them much more rarely. Caligula had such a passion for chariot-racing and wild-beast hunts that almost every other day was made the excuse for a holiday. This was a great waste of public time and the audience got bored long before he did. I removed 150 of Caligula's new holidays from the calendar. Another decision that I took was to make a regulation about repetitions. It was the custom that if a mistake had been made in the ceremony of a festival, even if it was only a small one on the last day of all, the whole business had to be gone through again. In Caligula's reign repetitions had become quite a farce. The nobles whom he had forced to celebrate games in his honour at their own cost knew that they would never escape with only a single performance: he would be sure to find some flaw in the ceremony when it was all over and force them to repeat it two, three, four, five, and even as many as ten times. So they learned to appease him as a matter of course by making an obviously intentional mistake on the last day, and so winning the favour of only repeating the show once. My edict was that if any festival had to be repeated, the repetition should not occupy more than a single day, and if a mistake were then made, that would be an end of the matter. As a result no mistakes at all were made: it was seen that I did not encourage them. I also ordered that there should be no official celebrations of my birthday and no sword-fighting displays given for my preservation. It was wrong, I said, for men's lives to be sacrificed, even the lives of sword-fighters, in an attempt to purchase the favour of the Infernal Gods towards a living man.

Yet, so that I should not be accused of stinting the City's pleasures, I sometimes used to proclaim suddenly one morning that there would be games held that afternoon in the Enclosure in Mars Field. I explained that there was no particular reason for the games, except that it was a good day for them, and that since I had made no particular preparations it would be a case of taking pot-luck. I called them *Sportula* or Pot-luck Games. They lasted only for the single afternoon.

I mentioned just now my hatred of slaves who betrayed their masters. But I realized that unless masters had a properly paternal attitude to their slaves, slaves could not be expected to have a sense of filial duty to their masters. Slaves, after all, are human. I protected them by legislation, of which I may give an example. The rich freedman from whom Herod had once borrowed money to pay back my mother and myself had greatly enlarged his hospital for sick slaves, which was now situated on the Island of Aesculapius, in the Tiber. He advertised himself as ready to buy slaves in any condition with a view to curing them, but promised first option of repurchase to the former owner at a price not to exceed three times the original. His doctoring methods were very rigorous, not to say inhumane. He treated the sick slaves exactly like cattle. But he did a very large and profitable business because most masters could not be bothered to have sick slaves in their house, distracting the other slaves from their ordinary duties and, if they were in pain, keeping everyone awake at nights by their groans. They preferred to sell them as soon as it was clear that the illness would be a long and tedious one. In this they were, of course, following the base economical precepts of Cato the Censor. But I put a stop to the practice. I made an edict that any sick slave who had been sold to a hospital-keeper should, on recovery, be granted his liberty and not return to his master's service, and that the master should refund the purchase money to the hospital-keeper. If a slave fell sick the master must henceforth either cure him at home or pay for his cure in the hospital. In the latter case he would become free on recovery, like the slaves already sold to the hospital-keeper, and would be expected, like them, to pay a thank-offering to the hospital, to the extent of one-half his money-earnings for the next three years. If any master chose to kill the slave rather than cure him at home or send him to the hospital, he would be guilty of murder. I then personally inspected the island hospital and gave instructions to the manager for obvious improvements in accommodation, diet, and hygiene.

Though, as I say, I removed 150 of Caligula's holidays from the calendar, I did, I admit, create three new festivals, each lasting three days. Two were in honour of my parents. I made these fall on their birthdays, postponing to vacant dates two minor festivals which happened to coincide with them. I ordered dirges to be sung in my parents' memories and provided funeral banquets at my own expense. My father's victories in Germany had already been honoured with an Arch on the Appian Way and with the hereditary title Germanicus, which was the surname of which I was proudest; but I felt that his memory deserved to be refreshed in this way as well. My mother had been granted important honours by Caligula, including the title of 'Augusta', but when he quarrelled with her and forced her to commit suicide, he meanly took them all away again: he wrote letters to the Senate accusing her of treason to himself, impiety to the other Gods, a life of malice and avarice, and the entertainment in her house of fortune-tellers and astrologers in defiant disobedience to the laws. Before I could decently make my mother 'Augusta' once more I had to plead before the Senate that she was entirely guiltless of these charges: that though strong-minded she was extremely pious, and though thrifty, extremely generous, and that she never bore malice against anyone and never once consulted a fortune-teller or astrologer in all her life. I introduced the necessary witnesses. Among them was Briseis, my mother's wardrobe-maid, who had been my property as a slave until she was given her freedom in old age. In fulfilment of a promise made a year or two before to Briseis, I presented her to the House as follows: 'My Lords, this old woman was once a faithful slave of mine, and for her life of industry and devotion in the service of the Claudian family – as maid first of all to my grandmother Livia, and then to my mother Antonia, whose hair she used to dress – I recently rewarded her with freedom. Some persons, even members of my own household, have suggested that she was really my mother's slave: I take this opportunity of branding any such suggestion as a mischievous lie! She was born as my father's slave when my father was a mere child; on his death my brother inherited her: and then she came to me. She has had no other masters or mistresses. You can place the fullest reliance on her testimony.' The senators were astonished at the warmth of my words, but cheered them, hoping to please me; and I was indeed pleased, because to old Briseis this was the most glorious moment of her life and the applause seemed intended as much for herself as for me. She began to weep, and her rambling tributes to my mother's character were hardly audible. She died a few days later in a splendid room in the Palace and I gave her a most luxurious funeral.

My mother's stolen titles were restored to her and in the great Circensian Games her coach was included in the sacred procession, like the coach of my poor sister-in-law Agrippina. The third festival that I created was in honour of my grandfather Mark Antony. He had been one of our most brilliant Roman generals and won many remarkable victories in the East. His sole mistake had been to fall out with Augustus after a long partnership with him and to lose the battle of Actium. I did not see why my grand-uncle Augustus's victory should continue to be celebrated at my grandfather's expense. I did not go so far as to deify my grandfather, whose many failings disqualified him for Olympus, but the festival was a tribute to his qualities as a soldier and gratified the descendants of those Roman soldiers who had been unlucky enough to choose the losing side at Actium.

Nor did I forget my brother Germanicus. I instituted no festival in his honour, for I felt somehow that his ghost would not approve. He was the most modest and self-effacing man of his rank and ability that I have ever known. But I did something that I felt sure would please him. There was a festival held at Naples, which is a Greek colony, and at the competition held there every five years for the best Greek comedy I submitted one that Germanicus had written, which I found among his papers after his death. It was called *The Ambassadors* and was written with considerable grace and wit somewhat in the style of Aristophanes. The plot was that two Greek brothers, one of whom was commander of his city's forces in the war against Persia, and the other a mercenary in the Persian service, happened to arrive at the same time as ambassadors to the court of a neutral kingdom, each asking the king for his military co-operation. I recognized comic reminiscences of the recriminations that had once passed between the two Cheruscan chieftains, Flavius and Hermann, brothers who fought on opposite sides in the German war which followed Augustus's death. The comic ending to the play was that the foolish king was convinced by both brothers. He sent his infantry to help the Persians and his cavalry to help the Greeks. This comedy won the prize, by the unanimous vote of the judges. It may be suggested that a certain favouritism was shown here, not only on account of Germanicus's extraordinary popularity during his lifetime among all who came in contact with him, but because it was known that it was I, the Emperor, who was submitting the entry. But there could be no doubt that it was incomparably the best work that was offered for the prize, and it was much applauded during its performance. Recalling that Germanicus on his visit to Athens, Alexandria, and other famous Greek cities had worn Greek dress, I did the same at the Naples festival. I wore a cloak and high boots at the musical and dramatic performances, and a purple mantle and golden crown at the gymnastic contests. Germanicus's prize was a bronze tripod: the judge wanted to vote him a golden one as a peculiar honour; but I refused that on the grounds of extravagance. Bronze was the customary metal for the prize tripod. I dedicated it in his name at the local temple of Apollo.

It only remained for me now to keep the promise I had made to my grandmother Livia. I was bound by my word of honour, which I had given her, to use all the influence that I could command to obtain the Senate's consent to her deification. I had not changed my opinion of the ruthlessness and unscrupulousness of the methods that she had used for gaining control over the Empire and keeping it in her hands for some sixty-five years; but, as I remarked a little way back, my admiration for her organizing abilities increased every day. There was no opposition in the Senate to my request except from Vinicianus, Vinicius's cousin, who played the same sort of part as Gallus had played twenty-seven years before when Tiberius proposed the deification of Augustus. Vinicianus rose to ask on precisely what grounds I made this unprecedented request and what sign had been given from Heaven to indicate that Livia Augusta would be welcomed by the Immortals as their permanent associate. I was ready with my answer. I told him that not long before her death my grandmother, prompted no doubt by divine inspiration, had called separately first on my nephew Caligula and then on myself and had secretly informed each of us in turn that we would one day become Emperor. In return for this assurance she made us swear that we would do all that lay in our power to deify her when we succeeded to the monarchy; pointing out that she had played as important a part as Augustus in the great work of reform that they had undertaken together after the Civil wars, and that it was most unjust that Augustus should enjoy perpetual bliss in the Heavenly mansions while she went below to the gloomy halls of Hell, to be judged by Aeacus and thereafter to be lost for ever among the countless hosts of insignificant and mouthless shades. Caligula, I told them, was only a lad at the time he made this promise, and had two elder brothers living, so it was remarkable that Livia knew that he and not they would become Emperor; for she extracted no such promise from them. Caligula, at all events, had made this promise, but had broken it when he became Emperor; and if Vinicianus needed a sure sign of the feelings of the Gods in this matter, he was at liberty to find it in the bloody circumstances of Caligula's death.

I then turned to address the House as a whole. 'My Lords,' I said, 'it is not for me to decide whether my grandmother Livia Augusta is worthy of national deification by your votes or whether she is not. I can only repeat that I swore to her by my own head that if ever I became Emperor – an event which, I admit, seemed both improbable and absurd, though she herself was positive that it would come to pass – I would do my best to persuade you to raise her to Heaven, where she might stand once more at the side of her faithful husband, who is now, next to Capitoline Jove, the most venerated of all our deities. If you refuse my request to-day I shall renew it every year at this same season, until you grant it: so long as my life is spared and so long as I am still privileged to address you from this chair.'

That was the end of the little speech that I had prepared but I found myself launched on a further, extempore, appeal, 'And I really think, my Lords, that you should consider Augustus's feelings in this matter. For more than fifty years he and Livia worked hand in hand together, all day and every day. There were few things that he did without her knowledge and advice, and if ever he did act on his own initiative, it cannot be said that he always acted wisely or that he met with any great success in these undertakings. Yes, whenever he was faced by a problem which taxed his own powers of judgement, he would always call for Livia. I would not go so far as to say that my grandmother was without the faults that are complementary to the extraordinary qualities with which she was endowed: I am probably more cognizant of them than anybody here. To begin with, she was entirely heartless. Heartlessness is a grave human fault and is unforgivable when combined with profligacy, greed, sloth, and disorderliness; but when combined with boundless energy and a rigid sense of order and public decency, heartlessness takes on a different character altogether. It becomes a divine attribute. Many Gods do not indeed possess it in nearly so full a measure as my grandmother did. Then again, she had a will that was positively Olympian in its inflexibility, and though she never spared any member of her own household who failed to show the devotion to duty that she expected of him, or who created a public scandal by his loose living, neither, we must remember, did she spare herself. How she worked! By going at it night and day she enlarged those sixty-five years of rule to one hundred and thirty. She soon came to identify her own will with that of Rome, and anyone who withstood it was a traitor in her eyes, even Augustus. And Augustus, with occasional lapses into self-will, saw the justice of this identification; and though, in an official way of speaking, she was merely his unofficial adviser, yet in his private letters to her he made a thousand acknowledgements of his entire dependence on her divine wisdom. Yes, he used the word "divine", Vinicianus: I call that conclusive. And you are old enough to remember that whenever he happened to be temporarily parted from her, Augustus was not at all the man that he was in her company; and it may be argued that his present task in Heaven of watching over the fortunes of the Roman people has been made very difficult by the absence of his former helpmeet. Certainly Rome has not flourished since his death nearly so prosperously as during his lifetime, except for the years that my grandmother Livia ruled through her son, the Emperor Tiberius. And has it occurred to you, my Lords, that Augustus is almost the only male deity in Heaven without a consort? When Hercules was raised to heaven, he was given a bride at once, the Goddess Hebe.'

'What about Apollo?' interrupted Vinicianus. 'I never heard that Apollo was married. That seems to me a very *lame* argument.'

The Consul called Vinicianus to order. It was clear that the word 'lame' was intended offensively. But I was accustomed to insults and answered quietly: 'I have always understood that the God Apollo remains a bachelor either because he is unable to choose between the Nine Muses, or because he cannot afford to offend eight of them by choosing the other as his bride. And he is immortally young, and so are they, and it is quite safe for him to postpone his choice indefinitely; for they are all in love with him, as the poet What's-his-name says. But perhaps Augustus will eventually persuade him to do his duty by Olympus, by taking one of the Nine in honourable wedlock, and raising a large family – "as quick as boiled asparagus".'

Vinicianus was silenced in the burst of laughter that followed, for 'as quick as boiled asparagus' was one of Augustus's favourite expressions. He had several others: 'As easily as a dog squats' and 'There are more ways than one of killing a cat' and 'You mind your own business, I'll mind mine' and 'I'll see that it gets done on the Greek Kalends' (which, of course, means never) and 'The knee is nearer than the shin' (which means that one's first concern is with matters that affect one personally). And if anyone tried to contradict him on a point of literary scholarship, he used to say: 'A radish may know no Greek, but I do'. And whenever he was encouraging anyone to bear an unpleasant condition patiently he always used to say: 'Let us content ourselves with this Cato'. From what I have told you about Cato, that virtuous man, you will easily understand what he meant. I now found myself often using these phrases of Augustus's: I suppose that this was because I had consented to adopt his name and position. The handiest was the one he used when he was making a speech and had lost his way in a sentence – a thing that constantly happens to me, because I am inclined, when I make an extempore speech, and in historical writing too when I am not watching myself, to get involved in long, ambitious sentences – and now I am doing it again, you notice. However, the point is that Augustus, whenever he got into a tangle, used to cut the Gordian knot, like Alexander, saying: 'Words fail me, my Lords. Nothing that I might utter could possibly match the depth of my feelings in this matter.' And I learned this phrase off by heart and constantly made it my salvation. I used to throw up my hands, shut my eyes, and declaim:

'Words fail me, my Lords. Nothing that I might utter could possibly match the depth of my feelings in this matter.' Then I would pause for a few seconds and recover the thread of my argument.

We deified Livia without further delay and voted her a statue to be placed alongside that of Augustus in his Temple. At the deification ceremony cadets of noble families gave a performance of the sham-fight on horseback which we call the Troy Game. We also voted her a chariot to be drawn by elephants in the procession during the Circensian Games, an honour which she shared only with Augustus. The Vestal Virgins were instructed to offer sacrifices to her in the Temple; and just as in taking legal oaths all Romans now used the name of Augustus, so henceforth all Roman women were to use my grandmother's name. Well, I had kept my promise.

All was fairly quiet in Rome now. Money was coming in plentifully and I was able to abolish more taxes. My secretaries were managing their departments to my satisfaction; Messalina was busy reviewing the roll of Roman citizens. She found that a number of freedmen were describing themselves as Roman citizens and claiming privileges to which they were not entitled. We decided to punish all such pretenders with the greatest rigour, confiscating their property and making them slaves again, to work as City scavengers or road-menders. I trusted Messalina so completely that I allowed her to use a duplicate seal for all letters and decisions made by her on my behalf in these matters. To make Rome still more quiet I disbanded the Clubs. The night-watchmen had been unable to cope with the numerous bands of young rowdies that had recently been formed on the model of Caligula's 'Scouts' and which used to keep honest citizens awake at night by their scandalous goings-on. There had, as a matter of fact, been such clubs in Rome for the last 100 years or more – an introduction from Greece. At Athens, Corinth, and other Greek cities the club-men had all been young men of family, and it was the same in Rome until Caligula's reign, when he set the fashion of admitting actors, professional sword-fighters, chariot-drivers, musicians, and such-like to membership. The result was increased rowdiness and shamelessness, great damage to property – the fellows sometimes even set fire to houses – and many injuries to inoffensive people who happened to be out late at night, perhaps in search of a doctor or midwife, or on some such emergency errand. I published an order disbanding the Clubs, but knowing that this by itself would

not be enough to put an end to the nuisance, I took the only effec
tive step possible: I prohibited the use of any building as a club
house, under penalty of a ruinous fine, and made illegal the sale
of cooked meat and other ready-dressed food for consumption on
the premises where it was prepared. I extended this order to the
sale of drink. After sundown no drink must be consumed in the
bar-room of any tavern. For it was principally the fact of meeting
in a clubroom to eat and drink that encouraged the young fellows,
when they began feeling merry, to go out in the cool night air to
sing ribald songs, molest passers-by, and challenge the watchmen
to tussles and running fights. If they were forced to dine at home,
this sort of thing would be unlikely to occur.

My prohibition proved effective and pleased the great mass of
the people; whenever I went out now I was always greeted enthusiastically. The citizens had never greeted Tiberius so cordially as
this, nor Caligula, except in the first few months of his reign when
he was all generosity and affability. But I did not realize how beloved I was and how seemingly important to Rome the preservation of my life had become until one day a rumour ran through the
City that I had been ambushed on my way to Ostia by a party of
senators and their slaves and murdered. The whole City began
lamenting in the most dismal fashion, wringing their hands and
mopping their eyes and sitting groaning on their doorsteps; but
those whose indignation prevailed over their grief ran to the Market Place, crying out that the Guards were traitors and the Senate
a parcel of parricides. There were loud threats of vengeance and
even talk of burning down the Senate House. The rumour had not
the slightest foundation except that I was indeed on my way to the
Ostia docks that afternoon to inspect the facilities for unloading
corn. (I had been informed that in bad weather a great deal of
corn was always lost between ship and land, and wanted to see
whether this could be avoided. Few great cities were cursed with
so awkward a harbour as Rome with Ostia: when the wind blew
strongly from the west and heavy tides swept up the estuary the
corn-ships had to ride at anchor for weeks on end, unable to discharge their cargoes.) The rumour had been put about, I suspect,
by the bankers, though I could get no proof of this: it was a trick
to create a sudden demand for cash. It was common talk that if I
happened to die civil commotions would immediately ensue, with
bloody combats in the streets between the partisans of rival candidates for the monarchy. The bankers, aware of this nervousness,

foresaw that property-holders who did not wish to be involved in such disorders would naturally hurry out of Rome as soon as a report of my death was started: and there would be a rush to the banks to offer land and house property in exchange for immediate gold at a price far below its real value. This is what actually happened. But once more Herod saved the situation. He went to Messalina and insisted on her publishing an immediate order in my name for the closing of the banks until further notice. This was done. But the panic was not checked until I had received news at Ostia of what was happening in the City and had sent four or five of my staff – honest men, whose word the citizens would trust – at full speed back to the Market Place, to appear on the Oration Platform as witnesses that the whole story was a fabrication, put about by some enemy of the State for his own crooked ends.

The facilities for discharging corn at Ostia I found most inadequate. Indeed, the whole corn supply question was a very difficult one. Caligula had left the public granaries as empty as the Public Treasury. It was only by persuading the corn-factors to endanger the vessels that they owned by running cargoes even in bad weather, that I succeeded in tiding over the season. I had, of course, to compensate them heavily for their losses in vessels, crews, and corn. I determined to solve the matter once and for all by making Ostia a safe port even in the worst weather and sent for engineers to survey the place and draw up a scheme.

My first real trouble abroad started in Egypt. Caligula had given the Alexandrian Greeks tacit permission to chastise the Alexandrian Jews, as they thought fit, for their refusal to worship his Divine Person. The Greeks were not allowed to bear arms in the streets – that was a Roman prerogative – but they performed countless acts of physical violence nevertheless. The Jews, many of whom were tax-farmers and therefore unpopular with the poorer and more improvident sort of Greek citizens, were exposed to daily humiliations and dangers. Being less numerous than the Greeks, they could not offer adequate resistance, and their leaders were in prison. But they sent word to their kinsmen in Palestine, Syria, and even Parthia, acquainting them of their plight, and begging them to send secret help in men, money, and munitions of war. An armed uprising was their only hope. Help came in abundance, and the Jewish revolt was planned for the day of Caligula's arrival in Egypt, when the Greek population would be crowding in holiday dress to greet him at the docks, and the whole Roman garrison would be there as a guard of honour, leaving the city unprotected. The news of Caligula's death had the effect of setting the rebellion off before its proper time in an ineffectual and half-hearted manner. But the Governor of Egypt was alarmed and sent me an immediate appeal for reinforcements: there were few troops in Alexandria itself. However, the next day he received a letter that I had written him a fortnight before in which I announced my elevation to the monarchy and ordered the release of the Alabarch, with the other Jewish elders, as also the suspension of Caligula's religious decrees and his order penalizing the Jews, until such time as I should be able to inform the Governor of their complete abrogation. The Jews were jubilant, and even those who had hitherto taken no part in the rising now felt that they enjoyed my Imperial favour and could get their own back on the Greeks with impunity. They killed quite a large number of the most persistent Jew-baiters. Meanwhile I replied to the Governor of Egypt, ordering him to put an end to the disturbances, by armed force if necessary; but saying that in view of the letter which by now he must have received from me, and the sedative effects that I hoped from it, I did not consider it necessary to send reinforcements. I told him that it was possible that the Jews had acted under great provocation, and hoped that, being men of sense, they would not continue hostilities, now that they knew that their wrongs were in process of being redressed.

This had the effect of ending the disturbances; and a few days later, after consulting the Senate, I definitely cancelled Caligula's decrees and restored to the Jews all the privileges that they had held under Augustus. But many of the younger Jews were still smarting under the sense of injustice and went marching through the streets of Alexandria carrying banners which read: 'Now Our Persecutors Must Lose Their Civic Rights', which was absurd, and 'Equal Rights For All Jews Throughout The Empire', which was not so absurd. I published an edict which ran as follows:

Tiberius Claudius Caesar Augustus Germanicus, High Pontiff, Protector of the People, Consul-Elect for the second time, issues the following decree:

I hereby very willingly comply with the petitions of King Agrippa, and his brother King Herod, personages whom I hold in the highest esteem, that I should grant to the Jews throughout the Roman Empire the same rights and privileges as I have granted, or rather restored, to the Jews of Alexandria. I do these other Jews this favour not only for the gratification of the aforesaid royal petitioners, but because I consider them worthy of these rights and privileges: they have always shown themselves faithful friends of the Roman people. I should not consider it just, however, that any Greek city should (as has been suggested) be deprived of any rights and privileges which were granted it by the Emperor Augustus (now the God Augustus), any more than that the Jewish colony in Alexandria should have been deprived of its rights and privileges by my predecessor. What is justice for Jews is justice for Greeks; and contrariwise. I have therefore decided to permit all Jews throughout my Empire to keep their ancient customs – in so far as these do not conflict with the conduct of Imperial business – without hindrance from anyone. At the same time I charge them not to presume upon the favour that I am hereby granting them, by showing contempt for the religious beliefs or practices of other races: let them content themselves with keeping their own Law. It is my pleasure that this decision of mine shall forthwith be engraved on stone tablets at the instance of the governors of all kingdoms, cities, colonies, and municipalities, both in Italy and abroad, whether Roman officials or Allied Potentates, and that these tablets shall be posted for public reading, during a full month, in some prominent public place and at a height from which the words will be plainly legible from the ground.

Talking privately to Herod one night I said: 'The fact is that the Greek mind and the Jewish mind work in quite different ways and are bound to come in conflict. The Jews are too serious and proud, the Greeks too vain and laughter-loving; the Jews hold too fast to the old, the Greeks are too restless in always seeking for something new; the Jews are too self-sufficient, the Greeks too accommodating. But though I might claim that we Romans understand the Greeks – we know their limitations and potentialities and can make them very useful servants – I should never claim that we understand the Jews. We have conquered them by our superior military strength but we have never felt ourselves their masters. We recognize that they retain the ancient virtues of their race, which goes back much farther in history than ours, and that we have lost our own ancient virtues; and the result is that we feel rather ashamed before them.'

Herod asked: 'Do you know the Jewish version of Deucalion's Flood? The Jewish Deucalion was called Noah, and he had three married sons who, when the Flood subsided, repeopled the earth. The eldest was Shem, the middle one was Ham, and the youngest was Japhet. Ham was punished for laughing at his father when he accidentally got drunk and threw off all his clothes, by being fated to serve the other two, who behaved with greater decency. Ham is the ancestor of all the African peoples. Japhet is the ancestor of the Greeks and Italians, and Shem the ancestor of the Jews, Syrians, Phoenicians, Arabians, Edomites, Chaldeans, Assyrians, and the like. There is an ancient prophetic saying that if Shem and Japhet ever live under the same roof there will be endless bickering at the fireside, at the table, and in the bed-chamber. That has always proved true. Alexandria is a neat example. And if the whole of Palestine were cleared of Greeks, who don't belong there, it would be far easier to govern. The same with Syria.'

'Not for a Roman governor,' I smiled. 'The Romans are not of the family of Shem and they count on Greek support. You'd have to get rid of us Romans too. But I agree with you so far as to wish that Rome had never conquered the East at all. She would have been much wiser if she had limited herself to ruling a federation of the descendants of Japhet. Alexander and Pompey have much to answer for. Both won the title "The Great" for their Eastern conquests, but I cannot see that either of them conferred a real benefit on his country.'

'It will all settle itself one day, Caesar,' said Herod thoughtfully, 'if we have patience.'

Then I began telling Herod that I was about to betroth my daughter Antonia, who was now nearly old enough to marry, to young Pompey, a descendant of Pompey the Great. Caligula had taken away young Pompey's title, saying that it was too magnificent a one for a boy of his age to bear, and that in any case there was only one 'Great' in the world now. I had just restored the title, and all the other titles that Caligula had taken from noble Roman houses, together with such commemorative badges as the Torquatan Torque and the Cincinnatan Lock. Herod did not volunteer any more of his views on the subject. I did not realize that the future political relations of Shem and Japhet was the problem that had recently come to occupy his mind to the exclusion of all others.

Chapter 9

WHEN Herod had established me in the monarchy and set me a proper course to follow – this, I am sure, is how he put the situation to himself – and in return won a number of favours from me, he said that he must take his leave at last unless there was some work of real importance that I wished him to do, such as nobody but himself was capable of undertaking. I could not think of any excuse for detaining him, and I would have felt obliged to pay him with more territory for every extra month he remained, so after a farewell banquet, which was appropriately magnificent, I let him go. We were both rather drunk that evening, I must confess, and I shed tears at the thought of his departure. We recalled our schooldays together, and when nobody seemed to be listening I leant across and called him by his old nickname.

'Brigand,' I said quietly, 'I always expected you to be a king, but if anyone had ever told me that I'd be your Emperor I'd have called him a madman.'

'Little Marmoset,' he replied in the same low tones. 'You're a fool, as I've always told you. But you have fool's luck. And fool's luck holds. You'll be an Olympian God when I'm only a dead hero; yes, don't blush, for that's how it will be, though there's no question which of us two is the better man.'

It did me good to hear Herod speak in his old style again. For the last three months he had been addressing me in the most formal and distant way, never failing to call me Caesar Augustus and to express only the most profound admiration for my opinions, even if he was often regretfully forced to disagree with them. 'Little Marmoset' (Cercopithecion) was the playful nickname Athenodorus had given me. I now begged him that when he wrote to me from Palestine he would always enclose with his official letter, signed with all his new titles, an unofficial letter signed 'The Brigand' and giving me his private news. He agreed to this on condition that I replied in the same vein, signing myself 'Cercopithecion'. As we shook hands on the bargain he looked me steadily in the eyes and said: 'Marmoset, do you want a little more of my excellent knavish advice? I'll give it you absolutely free this time.'

'Please, dear Brigand, let me have it.'

'My advice to you, old fellow, is this: *never trust anyone!* Never trust your most grateful freedman, your most intimate friend, your dearest child, the wife of your bosom, or the ally joined to you by the most sacred oath. Trust yourself only. Or at least trust your fool's luck, if you can't honestly trust yourself.'

The earnestness of his tones penetrated the cheerful fumes of wine that were clouding my brain and roused my attention. 'Why do you say that, Herod?' I asked sharply. 'Don't you trust your wife Cypros? Don't you trust your friend Silas? Don't you trust young Agrippa, your son? Don't you trust Thaumastus and your freedman Marsyas, who got you the money at Acre, and brought you food in prison? Don't you trust *me*, your ally? Why did you say that? Against whom are you putting me on my guard?'

Herod laughed stupidly. 'Don't pay any attention to me, Marmoset. I'm drunk, hopelessly drunk. I say the most extraordinary things when I'm drunk. The man who made the proverb "There's truth in wine" must have been pretty well soaked when he made it. Do you know, the other day at a banquet I said to my steward: "Now look here, Thaumastus, I never want roasted sucking-pig stuffed with truffles and chestnuts served at my table ever again. Do you hear?" "Very good, your Majesty," he replied. Yet if there is one dish in the world which I really love beyond all others it is roasted sucking-pig stuffed with truffles and chestnuts. What was it I told you just now? Never to trust your allies? That was funny, eh? I forgot for the moment that you and I were allies.' So I let the remark go, but it came back to me the next day, as I stood at a window watching Herod's coach roll away in the direction of Brindisi: I wondered what he had meant, and felt uncomfortable.

Herod was not the only king at that farewell banquet. His brother Herod Pollio, of Chalcis, was there; and Antiochus, to whom I had restored the kingdom of Commagene, on the north-eastern border of Syria, which Caligula had taken away from him; and Mithridates, whom I had now made King of the Crimea; and, besides these, the King of Lesser Armenia and the King of Osröene, both of whom had been hanging about Caligula's court, thinking it safer to be at Rome than in their own kingdoms, where Caligula might suspect them of plotting against him. I sent them all back together.

It would be just as well to follow Herod's story a little farther and to bring the account of what happened at Alexandria to a more conclusive point before returning to write of events at Rome and giving an indication of what was happening on the Rhine, in Morocco, and on other frontiers. Herod returned to Palestine, with more pomp and glory even than on the last occasion. On arrival at Jerusalem he took down from the Temple Treasury the iron chain which he had hung up there as a thank-offering and put in its place the golden one that Caligula had given him: now that Caligula was dead he could do this without offence. The High Priest greeted him most respectfully, but after the usual compliments had passed took it upon himself to reprove Herod for having given his eldest daughter in marriage to his brother: no good, he said, would come of it. Herod was not the man to allow himself to be dictated to by any ecclesiastic, however important or holy. He asked the High Priest, whose name was Jonathan, whether or not he considered that he, King Agrippa, had done a good service to the God of the Jews by dissuading Caligula from defiling the Temple and by persuading me to confirm the religious privileges of the Jews at Alexandria, and to grant similar privileges to Jews throughout the world. Jonathan replied that all this was well done. So Herod told him a little parable. A rich man one day saw a beggar by the roadside, who cried out to him for alms and claimed to be a cousin. The rich man said: 'I am sorry for you, beggar-man, and will do what I can for you, since you are my cousin. To-morrow if you go to my bank you will find ten bags of gold waiting for you there, each containing two thousand gold pieces in coin of the realm.' 'If you are speaking the truth,' the beggar said, 'may God reward you!' The beggar went to the bank and, sure enough, the bags of gold were handed to him. How pleased he was and how grateful! But one of the beggar's own brothers, a priest, who had himself done nothing for him when he was in distress, came to call on the rich man the next day. 'Do you call this a joke?' he asked indignantly. 'You swore to give your poor cousin twenty thousand gold pieces in coin of the realm, and deceived him into thinking that you had actually done so. Well, I came to help him count them, and do you know, in the very first bag I found a Parthian gold-piece masquerading as a real one! Can you pretend to believe that Parthian money passes current here? Is this an honest trick to play on a beggar?'

Jonathan was not abashed by the parable. He told Herod that the rich man had been foolish to spoil his gift by the inclusion of the Parthian coin, if, indeed, he had deliberately done so. And he said, too, that Herod must not forget that the greatest kings were only instruments in the hands of God and were rewarded by Him in proportion to their devotion to His service.

'And His High Priests?' asked Herod.

'His High Priests are sufficiently rewarded for their faithfulness to Him, which includes the rebuking of all Jews who fail in their religious duty, by being allowed to put on the sacred vestments and once a year enter that marvellously holy chamber where He dwells apart in immeasurable Power and Glory.'

'Very well,' said Herod. 'If I am an instrument in His hands, as you say, I hereby depose you. Someone else will wear the sacred vestments at the Passover Festival this year. It will be someone who knows the right times and seasons for uttering rebukes.'

So Jonathan was deposed and Herod appointed a successor, who also after a time offended Herod by protesting that it was not proper for the Master of Horse to be a Samaritan: a Jewish king should have only Jewish officers on his staff. The Samaritans were not of the seed of Father Abraham, but interlopers. This Master of Horse was none other than Silas; and for Silas's sake Herod deposed the High Priest and offered the office to Jonathan again. Jonathan refused it, though with seeming gratitude, saying that he was content to have once put on the sacred vestments and that a second consecration to the High Priesthood could not be so holy a ceremony as the first. If God had empowered Herod to depose him, it must have been a punishment for his pride; and if now God was in a forgiving mood, he rejoiced, but would not risk a second offence. Might he therefore suggest that the High Priesthood be given to his brother Matthias, as holy and God-fearing a man as was to be found in all Jerusalem? Herod consented.

Herod took up his residence in Jerusalem, in the part called Bezetha, or the New City, which surprised me very much, for he now had several fine cities luxuriously built in the Graeco-Roman style, any one of which he could have made his capital. He visited all these cities from time to time in ceremonial style and treated the inhabitants with courtesy, but Jerusalem, he said, was the only city for a Jewish king to live and reign in. He made himself extremely popular with the inhabitants of Jerusalem not only by his gifts to the Temple and his beautification of the city but by his abolition of the house-tax, which diminished his revenues by 100,000 gold pieces annually. His total annual income, however, amounted even without this to some 500,000 gold pieces. What surprised me still more was that he now worshipped daily in the Temple and kept the Law with great strictness: for I remembered the contempt that I had often heard him express for 'that holy psalm-singer' his devout brother Aristobulus, and in the private letters that he now always enclosed in his official dispatches there was no sign of any moral change of heart.

One letter that he sent me was almost all about Silas. It ran as follows:

Marmoset, my old friend, I have the saddest and most comical story to tell you: it concerns Silas, the 'faithful Achates' of your brigand friend Herod Agrippa. Most learned Marmoset, from your rich store of out-of-the-way historical learning can you inform me whether your ancestor, the pious Aeneas, was ever as bored by the faithful Achates as I have lately been by Silas? Have Virgilian commentators anything to tell us on that head? The fact is that I was foolish enough to appoint Silas my Master of Horse, as I think I wrote to you at the time. The High Priest didn't approve of the appointment, because he was a Samaritan – the Samaritans once vexed the Jews at Jerusalem, the ones who had returned there from their Babylonian captivity, by knocking down every night the walls they built by day; and the Jews have never forgiven them this. So I went to the trouble of deposing the High Priest on Silas's account. Silas had already begun to be very self-important and was daily giving fresh proof of his famous frankness and bluntness of speech. My removal of the High Priest encouraged him to put on greater airs than ever. Upon my word, sometimes visitors at Court could not make out which of us was the King and which was only the Master of Horse. Yet if I hinted to Silas that he was presuming on his friendship he used to sulk, and dear Cypros used to reproach me for my unkindness to him, and remind me of all that he had done for us. I had to be pleasant to him again and as good as apologize to him for my ingratitude.

His worst habit was constantly harping on my former troubles – in mixed company too – and giving most embarrassingly circumstantial details of how he had saved me from this danger and that, and how faithful he had shown himself, and how much excellent advice of his I had neglected, and how he had never looked for any reward but my friendship, in fine weather or rain or tempest – for that was the Samaritan character. Well, he opened his mouth once too often. I was at Tiberias, on the Lake of Galilee, where I was once magistrate under Antipas, and the leading men of Sidon were banqueting with me. You may remember the difference of opinion that I once had with the Sidonians when I was Flaccus's adviser at Antioch? Trust Silas to be on his worst behaviour at a banquet of such unusual political importance. Almost the first thing that he said to Hasdrubal, the harbour-master of Sidon, a man of the greatest influence in Phoenicia, was: 'I know your face, don't I? Isn't your name Hasdrubal? Of course, yes, you were one of the delegation that came to King Herod Agrippa, about nine years ago, asking him to use his influence with Flaccus on behalf of Sidon in that boundary dispute with Damascus. I well remember advising Herod to refuse your presents, pointing out that it was dangerous to take bribes from both parties in a dispute: he would be sure to get into trouble. But he only laughed at me. That's his way.'

Hasdrubal was a man of delicacy and said that he had no recollection of the incident at all: he was sure that Silas must be mistaken. But you can't stop Silas. 'Surely your memory isn't as bad as that?' he persisted. 'Why, it was because of that case that Herod had to clear out of Antioch in the disguise of a camel-driver – I provided him with it – leaving his wife and children behind – I had to smuggle them aboard a ship to take them away – and make a long detour by way of the Syrian desert to Edom. He went on a stolen camel. No, in case you ask me about that camel, it wasn't I who stole it, but King Herod Agrippa himself.'

This made me pretty hot, and it was no use denying the main facts of the story. But I did my best to gloze it over with a light-hearted romance of how one day my desert blood stirred in me and I grew weary of Roman life at Antioch and felt an overpowering impulse to ride out into the vast desert spaces and visit my kinsmen in Edom; but knowing that Flaccus would detain me – he was dependent on me for political advice – I was forced to take my leave secretly, and so arranged with Silas for my family to meet me at the port of Anthedon at the conclusion of my adventure. And a very enjoyable holiday it had proved to be. At Anthedon, I said, I had been met by an Imperial courier, who had failed to find me at Antioch, with a letter from the Emperor Tiberius: inviting me to Rome to act as his adviser, because my brains were wasted in the provinces.

Hasdrubal listened with polite interest, admiring my lies, for he knew the story almost as well as Silas did. He asked, 'May I inquire of your Majesty whether this was your first visit to Edom? I understand that the Edomites are a very noble, hospitable, and courageous race, and despise luxury and frivolity with a primitive severity which I find it easier, myself, to admire than to imitate.'

That fool Silas must needs put his oar in again. 'Oh, no, Hasdrubal, that wasn't his first visit to Edom. I was his only companion – except for the Lady Cypros, as she was then, and the two elder children – on his first visit. That was the year that Tiberius's son was murdered. King Herod had been obliged because of this to escape from his creditors at Rome, and Edom was the only safe place of refuge. He had run up the most enormous debts in spite of my repeated warnings that a day of reckoning would come at last. He loathed Edom, to tell the honest truth, and was contemplating suicide; but the Lady Cypros saved him by swallowing her pride and writing a very humble letter to her sister-in-law Herodias, with whom she had quarrelled. King Herod was invited here to Galilee and King Antipas made him a judge of the Lower Courts in this very town. His annual income was only seven hundred gold pieces.'

Hasdrubal was opening his mouth to express surprise and incredulity when Cypros suddenly came to my help. She had not minded Silas's telling tales about me, but when he brought up that old memory of the letter to Herodias, it was quite another matter. 'Silas,' she said, 'you talk far too much and most of what you say is inaccurate and nonsensical. You will oblige me by holding your tongue.'

Silas grew very red and once more addressed Hasdrubal: 'It is my Samaritan nature to tell the truth frankly, however disagreeable. Yes, King Herod passed through many vicissitudes before he won his present kingdom. Of some of these he does not appear to be ashamed – for instance, he has actually hung up in the Temple Treasury at Jerusalem the iron chain with which he was once fettered by order of the Emperor Tiberius. He was put in gaol for treason, you know. I had warned him repeatedly not to have private conversations with Gaius Caligula in the hearing of his coachman, but as usual he disregarded my warning. Afterwards Gaius Caligula gave him a gold chain, a replica of the iron one, and the other day King Herod hung this gold chain up in the Treasury and took down the iron one, which did not shine brightly enough, I suppose.' I caught Cypros's eye and we exchanged understanding looks. So I told Thaumastus to go to my bedroom where the chain was hanging on the wall facing my bed and bring it down. He did so, and I passed it round the table as a curiosity; the Sidonians examining it with ill-concealed embarrassment. Then I called Silas to me. 'Silas,' I said, 'I am about to do you a signal honour. In recognition of all your services to me and mine, and the fine frankness that you have never failed to show me even in the presence of distinguished guests, I hereby invest you with the Order of the Iron Chain; and may you live long to wear it. You and I are the only two companions of this very select Order and I gladly surrender the regalia to you complete. Thaumastus, chain this man and take him away to prison.'

Silas was too astonished to say a word and was led away like a lamb to the slaughter. The joke was that if he hadn't been so obstinate at Rome about refusing the citizenship that I had offered to get for him, I should never have been able to play that trick on him. He would have appealed to you and you would no doubt have pardoned him, you softhearted fellow. Well, I had to do it, or the Sidonians would never have respected me again. As it was, they seemed gratifyingly impressed and the rest of the banquet proved a great success. That was some months ago, and I kept him there in gaol – unpleaded for by Cypros – to learn his lesson; intending, however, to release him in time to attend my birthday feast, which took place yesterday. I sent Thaumastus to Tiberias to to visit Silas in his cell. He was to say: 'I was once a messenger of hope and comfort to our Lord and Master King Herod Agrippa when he was entering the prison gates at Misenum: I am now here, Silas, as a messenger of hope and comfort to you. This pitcher of wine is the token.

524

Our gracious sovereign invites you to banquet with him at Jerusalem in three days' time and will allow you to present yourself, if you prefer it, without the insignia of the Order that he has conferred on you. Here, take this and drink it. And my own advice to you, my friend Silas, is never remind people of services that you have done them in times past. If they are grateful and honourable men they will not need any reminder and if they are ungrateful and dishonourable the reminder will be wasted on them.'

Silas had been brooding over his wrongs all these months and was bursting to tell someone about them – besides his warder. He said to Thaumastus: 'So that is King Herod's message, is it? And I am supposed to be grateful, am I? What new honour does he intend to confer on me? The Order of the Whip, perhaps? When was an honest man ever so badly treated at a friend's hands as I have been at King Herod's? Does he expect that the awful miseries I have suffered here in solitary confinement will have taught me to hold my tongue when I feel impelled to speak the truth and shame his lying counsellors and flattering courtiers? Tell the King that he has not broken my spirit and that if he releases me I shall celebrate the occasion by franker and blunter speech than ever: I shall tell the whole nation through how many dangers and misfortunes he and I passed together and how I always saved the situation in the end after he had nearly ruined us both by his refusal to listen to my warnings in time, and how generously he rewarded me for all this with a heavy chain and a dark dungeon. No, I shall never forget this treatment. My very soul when I die will remember it, and remember too all the glorious deeds I did for his sake.' 'Drink,' said Thaumastus. But Silas would not drink. Thaumastus tried to reason with the madman, but he insisted on sending the message and refusing the wine. So Silas is still in gaol and it is quite impossible for me to release him; as Cypros agrees.

I was amused by that affair at Doris. You remember what I said to you at that farewell banquet when we were both so drunk and so Samaritanly frank: you'll be a God, my Marmoset, in spite of everything you do to prevent it. You can't stop that sort of thing. And as for what I said then about sucking-pigs stuffed with truffles and chesnuts I think I know what I must have meant. I am such a good Jew now that I never, never on any occasion let a morsel of unclean food pass my lips – or at least if I do, nobody but I and my Arabian cook and the watching Moon knows about it. I abstain even when I visit my Phoenician neighbours or dine with my Greek subjects. When you write give me news of cunning old Vitellius and those scheming scoundrels Asiaticus, Vinicius, and Vinicianus. I have sent my highflown compliments to your lovely Messalina in my official letter. So good-bye for the present and continue to think well (better than he deserves) of your knavish old playmate,

THE BRIGAND

I shall explain about the 'Doris affair'. In spite of my edict some young Greeks at a place in Syria called Doris had got hold of a statue of mine and broken into a Jewish synagogue, where they set it up at the south end, as if for worship. The Jews of Doris at once appealed to Herod, as their natural protector, and Herod went in person to Petronius at Antioch to make a protest. Petronius wrote the magistrates of Doris a very severe letter, ordering them to arrest the guilty persons and send them to him for punishment without delay. Petronius wrote that the offence was a double one – not only to the Jews whose desecrated synagogue could no longer be used for worship, but to myself whose edict on the subject of religious toleration had been shamelessly violated. There was one curious remark in his letter: that the proper place for my statue was not in a Jewish synagogue but in one of my own temples. He thought, I suppose, that by now I must surely have given in to the Senate's entreaties, and that therefore it would be politic to anticipate my deification. But I was most firm about refusing to become a God.

You can imagine that the Alexandrian Greeks did their utmost to win my favour now. They sent a deputation to congratulate me on my accession and to offer to build and dedicate a splendid temple to me, at the City's expense; or, if I refused this, at least to build and stock a Library of Italian Studies, and dedicate this to me as the most distinguished living historian. They also asked permission to give special public readings of my *History of Carthage* and my *History of Etruria* every year on my birthday. Each work was to be read out from end to end by relays of highly trained elocutionists, the former in the old library, the latter in the new. They knew that this could not fail to flatter me. In accepting the honour I felt very much as the parents of still-born twins might be expected to feel if, some time after the delivery, the little cold corpses awaiting their funeral in a basket set somewhere in a corner were suddenly to glow with unexpected warmth and sneeze and cry in unison. After all, I had spent more than twenty of the best years of my life on these books and taken infinite trouble to learn the various languages necessary for collecting and checking my facts; and not a single person hitherto had to my knowledge been to the trouble of reading them. When I say 'not a single person' I must make two exceptions. Herod had read the *History of Carthage* – he was not interesteb in the subject of Etruria – and said that he had learned a lot from it about the Phoenician character; but that he did not think that many people would have the same interest in it as he had. 'There's too much meat in that sausage,' he said, 'and not enough spices and garlic.' He meant that there was too much information in it and not enough elegant writing. He told me this while I was still a private citizen, so there could be no question of flattery. The only person except my secretaries and research assistants who had read both books was Calpurnia. She preferred a good book to a bad play, she said, my histories to many quite good plays she had seen, and the Etruscan book to the Carthaginian one because it was about places that she knew. When I became Emperor, I should record here, I bought Calpurnia a charming villa near Ostia and gave her a comfortable annual income and a staff of well-trained slaves. But she never came to visit me at the Palace and I never visited her, for fear of making Messalina jealous. She lived with a close friend, Cleopatra, an Alexandrian, who had also been a prostitute; but now that Calpurnia had enough money, and to spare, neither of them continued in the profession. They were quiet girls.

But, as I was saying, I was very proud indeed of the Alexandrian offer, for after all Alexandria is the cultural capital of the world, and had I not been addressed by its leading citizens as the most distinguished living historian? I regretted that I could not spare the time for a visit to Alexandria to be present at one of the readings. The day that the embassy came I sent for a professional reader and asked him to read over to me in private a few passages from each of the histories. He did so with so much expression and such beautiful articulation that, forgetting for the moment that I was the author, I began clapping loudly.

Chapter 10

MY immediate preoccupation abroad was with the Rhine frontier. Towards the end of Tiberius's reign the Northern Germans had been encouraged by reports of his general inactivity to make raids across the river, into what we call the Lower Province. Small parties used to swim across at unguarded spots by night to attack lonely houses or hamlets, murder the occupants, and loot what gold and jewels they could find; and then swim back at dawn. It would have been difficult to stop them doing this, even if our men had been constantly on the alert – as in the North at least they certainly were not – because the Rhine is an immensely long river and most difficult to patrol. The only effective measure against the raiders would have been retaliation; but Tiberius had refused permission for any large-scale punitive expedition. He wrote: 'If hornets plague you, burn their nest; but if it is only mosquitoes, pay no attention.' As for the Upper Province, it may be recalled that Caligula during his expedition to France sent for Gaetulicus, the commander of the four regiments on the Upper Rhine, and executed him on the unfounded charge of conspiracy; that he crossed the river with an enormous army and advanced a few miles, the Germans offering no resistance; that he then grew suddenly alarmed and rushed back. The man whom he had appointed as Gaetulicus's successor was commander of the French auxiliary forces at Lyons. His name was Galba,* and he was one of Livia's men. She had marked him out for preferment when he was still a youngster, and he had amply justified the trust she had placed in him. He was a courageous soldier and a discerning magistrate, worked hard, and bore an exemplary private character. He had attained his Consulship six years before this. Livia, when she died, had left him a special legacy of 500,000 gold pieces; Tiberius, however, as Livia's executor, pronounced that this must be a mistake. The sum had been written in figures, not in words, and he ruled that 50,000 was all the testatrix had intended. As Tiberius never paid a single one of Livia's legacies, this did not make much difference at the time, but when Caligula became Emperor and paid Livia's legacies in full, it was bad luck for Galba that Caligula was unaware of Tiberius's fraud. Galba did not press for the whole 500,000, and perhaps it was as well for him that he did not, for if he had done so Caligula would have remembered the incident when he ran short of funds and, so far from giving him this important command on the Rhine, would probably have accused him of taking part in Gaetulicus's conspiracy.

How Caligula chose Galba makes a curious story. He had ordered a big parade at Lyons one day, and when it was over he called before him all the officers who had taken part in it and gave them a lecture on the necessity for keeping in good physical condition. 'A Roman soldier,' he said, 'should be as tough as leather and as hard as iron, and all officers should set a good example to their men in this. I shall be interested to see how many of you will

* Afterwards Emperor (A.D. 69). – R.G

survive a simple test which I am about to set you. Come, friends, let us go for a little run in the direction of Autun.' He was sitting in his chariot with a couple of fine French cobs in the shafts. His driver cracked his whip and off they went. The already sweating officers dashed after him with their heavy weapons and armour. He kept just far enough ahead of them not to let them drop behind out of sight, but never let his horses fall into a walk, for fear that the officers would follow their example. On and on he went. The line strung out. Many of the runners fainted and one dropped dead. At the twentieth milestone he finally pulled up. Only one man had survived the test – Galba. Caligula said: 'Would you prefer to run back, General, or would you prefer a seat beside me?' Galba had sufficient breath left to reply that as a soldier he had no preferences: he was accustomed to obey orders. So Caligula let him walk back, but the next day gave him his appointment. Agrippinilla became greatly interested in Galba when she met him at Lyons: she wanted to marry him, though he was married already to a lady of the Lepidan house. Galba was perfectly satisfied with his wife and behaved as coldly towards Agrippinilla as his loyalty to Caligula permitted. Agrippinilla persisted in her attentions and there was a great scandal one day at a reception given by Galba's mother-in-law to which Agrippinilla came without an invitation. Galba's mother-in-law called her out in front of all the noblemen and noblewomen assembled, abused her roundly as a shameless and lascivious hussy and actually struck her in the face with her fists. It would have gone badly for Galba if Caligula had not decided the next day that Agrippinilla was implicated in the plot against his life and banished her as I have described.

When Caligula had fled back to Rome in terror of a reported German raid across the Rhine (a lie humorously put about by the soldiers) his forces were all concentrated at one point. Great stretches of the river were left unguarded. The Germans heard of this at once, and also of Caligula's cowardice. They took the opportunity of crossing the Rhine in force and establishing themselves in our territory, where they did a great deal of damage. Those who crossed were the tribesmen called the Chattians, which means the Mountain Cats. The Cat was their tribal ensign. They had fortresses in the hill country between the Rhine and the Upper Weser. My brother Germanicus always used to give them credit for being the best fighting men in Germany. They kept their ranks in battle, obeyed their leaders almost like Romans and at night used to dig entrenchments and put outposts out – a precaution seldom taken by any other German tribe. It cost Galba several months and considerable losses in men to dislodge them and drive them back across the river.

Galba was a strict disciplinarian. Gaetulicus had been a capable soldier but rather too lenient. The day that Galba arrived at Mainz to take over his command the soldiers were watching some games that were being held in Caligula's honour. A huntsman had shown great skill in dispatching a leopard and the men all started clapping. The first words that Galba spoke on entering the General's box were, 'Keep your hands under your cloaks, men! I am in command now and I don't permit any slovenliness.' He kept this up, and for so severe a commander was extremely popular. His enemies called him mean, but that was unjust: he was merely most abstemious, discouraged extravagance in his staff, and exacted a strict account of expenditure from his subordinates. When news came of Caligula's assassination his friends urged him to march on Rome at the head of his corps, saying that he was now the only fit person to take control of the Empire. Galba replied, 'March on Rome and leave the Rhine unguarded? What sort of a Roman do you take me to be?' And he continued: 'Besides, from all accounts, this Claudius is a hard-working and modest man; and though some of you seem to think him a fool, I should hesitate to call any member of the Imperial family a fool who has successfully survived the reigns of Augustus, Tiberius, and Caligula. I think that in the circumstances the choice is a good one and I shall be pleased to take the oath of allegiance to Claudius. He is not a soldier, you say. So much the better. Campaigning experience is sometimes not altogether a blessing in a Commander-in-Chief. The God Augustus – I speak with all respect – was inclined, as an old man, to hamper his generals by giving them over-detailed instructions and advice: that last Balkan campaign would never have dragged on as it did, if he had not been so anxious to re-fight from far in the rear the battles that he had fought at the head of his troops some forty years previously. Claudius will not, I think, either take the field himself, at his age, or be tempted to override the decisions of his generals in matters of which he is ignorant. But at the same time he is a learned historian and has, I am told, a grasp of general strategical principles that many Commanders-in-Chief with actual fighting experience might envy him.'

These remarks of Galba's were later reported to me by one of his staff, and I sent him a personal letter of thanks for his good opinion of me. I told him that he could count on me to give my generals a free hand in such campaigns as I ordered or authorized them to undertake. I would merely decide whether the expedition was to be one of conquest or whether it would have merely a punitive character. In the former case vigour was to be tempered with humanity – as little damage as possible was to be done to captured villages and towns and to standing crops, the local Gods were not to be humiliated, and no butchery must be allowed once the enemy was broken in battle. In the case, however, of a punitive expedition no mercy whatsoever need be shown: as much damage as possible must be done to crops, villages, towns, and temples, and such of the inhabitants as were not worth taking home as slaves were to be massacred. I would also indicate the maximum number of reserves that could be called upon and the maximum number of Roman casualties that would be permitted. I would decide beforehand, in consultation with the general himself, the precise objectives of attack and ask him to state how many days or months he would need for taking them. I would leave all strategical and tactical dispositions to him, and only exercise my right of taking personal command of the campaign, bringing with me such further reinforcements as I thought necessary, should the objectives not be reached within the agreed time, or should the Roman casualties rise beyond the stipulated figure.

For I had a campaign in mind for Galba to make against the Chattians. It was to be a punitive expedition. I did not propose to enlarge the Empire beyond the natural and obvious frontier of the Rhine, but when the Chattians and the Northern tribesmen, the Istaevonians, failed to respect that frontier, a vigorous assertion of Roman dignity had to be made. My brother Germanicus always used to say that the only way to win the respect of Germans was to treat them with brutality; and that they were the only nation in the world of whom he would say this. The Spaniards, for example, could be impressed by the courtesy of a conqueror, the French by his riches, the Greeks by his respect for the arts, the Jews by his moral integrity, the Africans by his calm authoritative bearing. But the German, who is impressed by none of these things, must always be struck to the dust, and struck down again as he rises, and struck again as he lies groaning. 'While his wounds still pain him he will respect the hand that dealt them.'

At the same time as Galba was advancing, another punitive expedition was to be made against the Istaevonian raiders, by Gabinius, the General commanding the four regiments on the Lower Rhine. Gabinius's expedition interested me far more than Galba's, for its object was not merely punitive. Before ordering it I sacrificed in Augustus's Temple and privately informed the God that I was bent on completing a task that my brother Germanicus had been prevented from completing, and which was, I knew, one in which He was Himself much interested: it was the rescue of the third and last of the lost Eagles of Varus, still in German hands after more than thirty years. My brother Germanicus, I reminded Him, had recaptured one Eagle in the year following His Deification and another in the campaigning season after that; but Tiberius had recalled him before he could avenge Varus in a last crushing battle and win back the Eagle that was still missing. I therefore begged the God to favour my arms and restore the honour of Rome. As the smoke of the sacrifice rose, the hands of Augustus's statue seemed to move in a blessing and his head to nod. It may only have been a trick of the smoke, but I took it for a favourable omen.

The fact was, I was now confident that I knew exactly where in Germany the Eagle was hidden, and proud of myself for the way I had discovered this secret. My predecessors could have done what I did if they had only thought of it; but they never did. It was always a pleasure to prove to myself that I was by no means the fool that they had all thought me, and that indeed I could manage some things better than they. It occurred to me that in my Household Battalion, composed of captured tribesmen from almost every district in Germany, there must be a half a dozen men at least who knew where the Eagle was hidden; yet when the question had once been put to them on parade by Caligula, with an offer of freedom and a large sum of money in return for the information, every face had immediately gone blank: it seemed that nobody knew. I tried a very different method of persuasion. I ordered them all out on parade one day and addressed them very kindly. I told them that as a reward for their faithful services I was going to do them an unprecedented kindness: I was going to send back to Germany – the dear, dear Fatherland about which they nightly sang such melancholy and tuneful songs – all members of the battalion who had completed twenty-five years' service with it. I said that I should have liked to send them home with gifts of gold, weapons, horses, and the like, but unfortunately I was unable to do this or even to allow them to take back across the Rhine any possessions that they had acquired during their captivity. The obstacle was the still missing Eagle. Until this sacred emblem was returned, Roman honour was still in pawn, and it would create a bad impression in the City if I were to reward with anything beyond their bare freedom men who had in their youth taken part in the massacre of Varus's army. However, to true patriots liberty was better than gold and they would, I felt sure, accept the gift in the spirit that it was made in. I did not ask them, I said, to reveal to me the whereabouts of the Eagle, because no doubt this was a secret which they had been bound by oaths to their Gods not to reveal: and I would not ask any man to perjure himself for the sake of a bribe, as my predecessor had done. In two days' time, I promised, all the twenty-five-year veterans would be sent back across the Rhine under safe conduct.

I then dismissed the parade. The sequel was as I had foreseen. These veterans were even less anxious to return to Germany than the Romans captured by the Parthians at Carrhae were to return to Rome when, thirty years later, Marcus Vipsanius Agrippa bargained with the King for their exchange. Those Romans in Parthia had settled down, married, raised families, grown rich, and quite forgotten their past. And these Germans at Rome, though technically slaves, lived a most easy and enjoyable life, and their regret for home was not at all a sincere emotion, merely an excuse for tears when they were maudlin-drunk. They came to me in a body and begged for permission to remain in my service. Many of them were fathers, and even grandfathers, by slave-women attached to the Palace, and they were all comfortably off: Caligula had given them handsome presents from time to time. I pretended to be angry, called them ungrateful and base to refuse so priceless a gift as liberty and said that I had no further use for their services. They asked pardon and permission at least to take their families with them. I refused this plea, mentioning the Eagle again. One of them, a Cheruscan, cried out: 'It's all the fault of those cursed Chaucians that we have to go like this. Because they have sworn to keep the secret, we other innocent Germans are made to suffer.'

This was what I wanted. I dismissed from my presence all but the representatives of the Greater and Lesser Chaucian tribes. (The Chaucians lived on the North German coast between the

Dutch Lakes and the Elbe; they had been confederates of Hermann's.) Then I said to these: 'I have no intention of asking you Chaucians where the Eagle is, but if any of you have *not* sworn an oath about it, please tell me so at once.' The Greater Chaucians, the western half of the nation, all declared that they had not sworn any such oath. I believed them, because the second Eagle that my brother Germanicus won back had been found in a temple of theirs. It was unlikely that one tribe would have been awarded two Eagles in the distribution of spoils that followed Hermann's victory.

I then addressed the chief man of the Lesser Chaucians: 'I do not ask you to tell me where the Eagle is, or to what God you swore the oath. But perhaps you will tell me in what town or village you took that oath. If you tell me this I shall suspend my order for your repatriation.'

'Even to say as much as that would be a violation of my oath, Caesar.'

But I used an old trick on him that I had read about in my historical studies: once, when a certain Phoenician judge visiting a village on his assizes wished to find out where a man had hidden a gold cup that he had stolen, he told the man that he did not believe him capable of theft and would discharge him. 'Come, sir, let us go for a friendly walk instead and you will perhaps show me your interesting village.' The man guided him down every street but one. The judge found by inquiry that one of the houses in this street was occupied by the man's sweetheart; and the cup was discovered hidden in the thatch of her roof. So in the same way I said: 'Very well, I shall not press you further.' I then turned to another member of the tribe who also seemed, by his sullen, uncomfortable looks, to be in the secret, and asked conversationally: 'Tell me: in what towns or villages in your territory are these temples raised to your German Hercules?' It was probable that the Eagles had been dedicated to this God. He gave me a list of seven names, which I noted down. 'Is that all?' I asked.

'I cannot recall any more,' he answered.

I appealed to the Great Chaucians. 'Surely there must be more than seven temples in so important a territory as Lesser Chaucia – between the great rivers of Weser and Elbe?'

'Oh, yes, Caesar,' they replied. 'He has not mentioned the famous temple at Bremen on the eastern bank of the Weser.'

That is how I was able to write to Gabinius: 'You will, I think, find the Eagle somewhere hidden in the temple of the German Hercules at Bremen on the eastern bank of the Weser. Don't spend too much time at first in punishing the Istaevonians: march in close formation straight through their territory and that of the Ansibarians, rescue the Eagle and do the burning, killing, and pillaging on your return.'

Before I forget it, there is another story that I want to tell about a stolen gold cup, and it may as well go in here as anywhere. Once I invited a number of provincial knights to supper – and would you believe it, one of the rogues, a Marseilles man, went off with the gold wine-cup that had been put before him. I didn't say a word to him, but invited him to supper again the next day, and this time gave him only a stone cup. This apparently frightened him, for the next morning the gold cup was returned with a fulsomely apologetic note explaining that he had taken the liberty of borrowing the cup for two days in order to get the engravings on it, which he much admired, copied by a goldsmith: he wished to perpetuate the memory of the enormous honour that I had done him, by drinking from a similarly chased gold cup every day for the rest of his life. In answer I sent him the stone cup, asking, in exchange, for the reproduction of the gold one as a memento of the charming incident.

I arranged a date in May for both Galba's and Gabinius's expeditions to start, increased their forces by levies in France and Italy to six regiments apiece – leaving two regiments to hold the Upper Rhine, and two to hold the Lower – allowed them each a maximum of 2,000 casualties, and gave them until July the First to conclude their operations and be on the way home. Galba's objective was a line of three Chattian towns originally built when the country was under Roman rule – Nuaesium, Gravionarium, and Melocavus – which lie parallel with the Rhine about 100 miles inland from Mainz.

I shall content myself by recording that both campaigns were a complete success. Galba burned 150 stockaded villages, destroyed thousands of acres of crops, killed great numbers of Germans, armed and unarmed, and had sacked the three towns indicated by the middle of June. He took about 2,000 prisoners of both sexes, including men and women of rank to hold as hostages for the Chattians' good behaviour. He lost 1,200 men, killed or disabled, of whom 400 were Romans. Gabinius had the harder task and accomplished it with the loss of only 800 men. He took a last-minute suggestion of mine, which was not to make straight for Bremen but to invade the territory of the Angrivarians, who live to the south of the Lesser Chaucians; and from there to send a flying column of cavalry against Bremen, in the hope of capturing the town before the Chaucians thought it worth while to remove the Eagle to some safer repository. It all worked out exactly to plan. Gabinius's cavalry, which he commanded personally, found the Eagle just where I had expected, and he was so pleased with himself that he called up the rest of his force and drove right through Lesser Chaucia from end to end, burning the timber shrines of the German Hercules one after the other, until none was left standing. His destruction of crops and villages was not so methodical as Galba's, but on the way back he gave the Istaevonians plenty to remember him by. He took 2,000 prisoners.

The news of the rescue of the Eagle came to Rome simultaneously with that of Galba's successful sacking of the Chattian towns, and the Senate immediately voted me the title of Emperor, which this time I did not refuse. I considered that I had earned it by my location of the Eagle and by suggesting the long-distance cavalry raid, and by the care that I had taken to make both campaigns a surprise. Nobody knew anything about them until I signed the order instructing the French and Italian levies to be under arms and on their way to the Rhine within three days.

Galba and Gabinius were given triumphal ornaments. I should have had them granted triumphs if the campaigns had been more than mere punitive expeditions. But I persuaded the Senate to honour Gabinius with the hereditary surname 'Chaucius' in commemoration of his feat. The Eagle was carried in solemn procession to the Temple of Augustus, where I sacrificed and gave thanks for his divine aid: and dedicated to him the wooden gates of the temple where the Eagle had been found – Gabinius had sent them to me as a gift. I could not dedicate the Eagle itself to Augustus, because there was a socket long ago prepared for its reception in the temple of Avenging Mars, alongside the other two rescued Eagles. I took it there later and dedicated it, my heart swelling with pride.

The soldiers composed ballad verses about the rescue of the Eagle. But this time, instead of building them on to their original ballad, 'The Three Griefs of Lord Augustus', they made them into a new one called 'Claudius and the Eagle'. It was by no means flattering to me, but I enjoyed some of the verses. The theme was that I was an absolute fool in some respects and did the most ridiculous things – I stirred my porridge with my foot, and shaved myself with a comb, and when I went to the Baths used to drink the oil handed me to rub myself with and rub myself with the wine handed me to drink. Yet I had amazing learning, for all that: I knew the names of every one of the stars in Heaven and could recite all the poems that had ever been written, and had read all the books in all the libraries of the world. And the fruit of this wisdom was that I alone was able to tell the Romans where the Eagle was that had been lost so many years and had resisted all efforts to recapture it. The first part of the ballad contained a dramatic account of my acclamation as Emperor by the Palace Guard; and I shall quote three verses to show the sort of ballad it was:

> Claudius hid behind a curtain,
>> Gratus twitched the thing away.
> 'Be our Leader,' said bold Gratus.
>> 'All your orders we'll obey.'

> 'Be our Leader,' said bold Gratus,
>> 'Learned Claudius, courage take!
> There's an Eagle to be rescued
>> For the God Augustus' sake.'

> Learned Claudius, feeling thirsty,
>> Drank a mighty pot of ink.
> '*Owl* was it you said, or *Eagle*?
>> I could rescue both, I think.'

Early in August, twenty days after I had been voted the title of Emperor, Messalina bore me her child. It was a boy, and for the first time I experienced all the pride of fatherhood. For my son Drusillus, whom I had lost some twenty years before at the age of eleven, I had felt no warm paternal feelings at all, and very few for my daughter Antonia, though she was a good-hearted child. This was because my marriages with Urgulanilla, Drusillus's mother, and with Aelia, Antonia's mother (both of whom I divorced as soon as the political situation enabled me to do so), had been forced on me: I had no love for either of these women. Whereas I was passionately in love with Messalina; and seldom, I suppose, had our Roman Goddess Lucina, who presides over childbirth, been so persistently courted with prayers and sacrifices as she was by me in the last two months of Messalina's pregnancy. He was a fine healthy baby, and being my only son he took all my names, as the custom was. But I gave it out that he was to be known as Drusus Germanicus. I knew that this would have a good effect on the Germans. The first Drusus Germanicus to make that name terrible across the Rhine – more than fifty years before this – had been my father, and the next had been my brother, twenty-five years later; and I was also a Drusus Germanicus, and had I not just won back the last of the captured Eagles? In another quarter of a century, no doubt, my little Germanicus would repeat history and slaughter a few score thousands more of them. Germans are like briars on the edge of a field: they grow quickly and have to be constantly checked with steel and fire to prevent them from encroachment. As soon as my boy was a few months old and I could pick him up without risk of injuring him, I used to carry him about with me in my arms in the Palace grounds and show him to the soldiers; they all loved him almost as much as I did. I reminded them that he was the first of the Caesars since the great Julius who had been born a Caesar, not merely adopted into the family, as Augustus, Marcellus, Gaius, Lucius, Postumus, Tiberius, Castor, Nero, Drusus, Caligula had each in turn been. But here, as a matter of fact, my pride tempted me into inaccuracy. Caligula, unlike his brothers Nero and Drusus, was born two or three years after his father, my brother Germanicus, had been adopted by Augustus (a Caesar in virtue of his adoption by Julius) as his son; so he was really born a Caesar. What misled me was the fact that Caligula was not adopted by Tiberius (a Caesar in virtue of his adoption by Augustus) as *his* son until he was about twenty-three years old.

Messalina did not keep our little Germanicus at her own breast, as I wished her to do, but found him a foster-mother. She was too busy to nurse a child, she said. But nursing a child is an almost certain insurance against renewed pregnancy, and pregnancy interferes with a woman's health and freedom of action even more than nursing does. So it was bad luck for Messalina when she became pregnant again, so soon afterwards that only eleven months elapsed between Germanicus's birth and that of our daughter Octavia.

There was a poor harvest that summer and so meagre a supply of corn in the public granaries that I grew alarmed and cut down the free ration of corn, which the poor citizens had come to regard as their right, to a very small daily measure. I only maintained it even at that measure by commandeering or buying corn from every possible source. The heart of the populace lies in its belly. In the middle of winter, before supplies began to come through from Egypt and Africa (where, fortunately, the new harvest was a particularly good one), there were frequent disorders in the poorest quarters of the City, and much loose revolutionary talk.

Chapter 11

By this time my engineers had finished the report which I had told them to make on the possibility of converting Ostia into a safe winter harbour. The report was at first sight a most discouraging one. Ten years and 10,000,000 gold pieces seemed to be needed. But I reminded myself that the work once carried out would last for ever and that the danger of a corn famine would never arise again, or at least not so long as we held Egypt and Africa. It seemed to me an undertaking worthy of the dignity and greatness of Rome. In the first place, a considerable tract of land would have to be excavated and strong retaining walls of concrete built on every side of the excavation, before the sea could be let into it to form the inner harbour. This harbour in turn must be protected by two huge moles built out into deep water, on either side of the harbour entrance, with an island between their extremities to act as a breakwater when the wind blew from the west and big seas came rushing up the mouth of the Tiber. On this island it was proposed to build a lighthouse like the famous one at Alexandria, to guide shipping safely in, however dark and stormy the night. The island and the moles would form the outer harbour.

When the engineers brought me their plans they said: 'We have done as you told us, Caesar, but of course the cost will be prohibitive.'

I answered rather sharply: 'I asked for a plan and an estimate and you have been good enough to provide both, for which many thanks; but I do not employ you as my financial advisers and I shall thank you not to take that upon yourselves.'

'But Callistus, your Public Treasurer – –' one of them began.

I cut him short: 'Yes, of course, Callistus has been speaking to you. He is very careful with public money, and it is right that he should be. But economy can be carried too far. This is a matter of the utmost importance. Besides, I should not be surprised to learn that it is the corn-factors who have persuaded you to send in this discouraging report. The scarcer corn becomes, the richer they grow. They pray for bad weather and thrive on the miseries of the poor.'

'Oh, Caesar,' they chorused virtuously, 'can you believe that we would take bribes from corn-factors?'

But I could see that my shot had gone home. '*Persuaded*, not *bribed*, was my word. Don't accuse yourselves unnecessarily. Now listen to me. I am determined to carry this plan out whatever it is going to cost: get that into your heads. And I'll tell you another thing: it is not going to take nearly so long a time or cost nearly so much money as you seem to think. Three days from now you and I are going to go into the question thoroughly.'

On a hint given me by my secretary Polybius I consulted the Palace archives, and there, sure enough, I found a detailed scheme that had been prepared by Julius Caesar's engineers some ninety years before for the very same work. The scheme was almost identical with the one that had just been made, but the estimated time and cost were, I was delighted to find, only four years and 4,000,000 of gold. Allowing for a slight increase in the cost of materials and labour it should be possible to carry the task out for only half what my own engineers had estimated, and in four years instead of ten. In certain respects the old plan (abandoned as too costly!) was an improvement on the new, though it left out the island. I studied both plans closely, comparing their points of difference; and then visited Ostia myself, in company with Vitellius, who knew a great deal about engineering, to make sure that no important physical changes had occurred on the site of the proposed harbour since Julius's day. When the conference met I was so primed with information that the engineers found it impossible to deceive me – by under-estimating, for instance, the amount of earth that 100 men could shift from this point to that in a single day, or by suggesting that the excavations would entail the cutting away of many thousands of square feet of living rock. I now knew almost as much about the business as they did. I did not tell them how I came to know: I let it appear that I had taught myself engineering in the course of my historical studies, and that a couple of visits to Ostia had sufficed me for mastering the whole problem and drawing my own conclusions. I profited from the great impression that I thus made on them by saying that if there was any attempt to slow down the work once it started, or any lack of enthusiasm, I would send them all down to the Underworld to build Charon a new jetty on the River Styx. Work on the harbour must begin at once. They should have as many workmen as they needed, up to the number of 30,000, and 1,000 military foremen, with the necessary materials, tools, and transport; but begin they must.

Then I called Callistus and told him what I had decided. When he threw up his hands and turned up his eyes in a despairing gesture I told him to stop play-acting.

'But, Caesar, where's the money to come from?' he bleated like a sheep.

'From the corn-factors, fool,' I answered. 'Give me the names of principal members of the Corn Ring and I'll see that we get as much as we need.'

Within an hour I had the six richest corn-factors in the City before me. I frightened them.

'My engineers report that you gentlemen have been bribing them to send in an unfavourable report on the Ostia scheme. I take a very serious view of the matter. It amounts to conspiracy against the lives of your fellow-citizens. You deserve to be thrown to the wild beasts.'

They denied the charge with tears and oaths and begged me to let them know in what way they could prove their loyalty.

That was easy: I wanted an immediate loan of 1,000,000 gold pieces for the Ostia scheme, which I would pay back as soon as the financial situation justified it.

They pretended that their combined fortunes did not amount to half that sum. I knew better. I gave them a month to raise the money and I warned them that if they did not do so they would all be banished to the Black Sea. Or farther. 'And remember,' I said, 'that when this harbour is built it will be *my* harbour – if you want to use it you will have to come to me for permission. I advise you to keep on the right side of me.'

The money was paid over within five days, and the work at Ostia began at once with the erection of shelters for the workmen and the pegging out of tasks. On occasions of this sort it was, I must admit, very pleasurable to be a monarch: to be able to get important things done by smothering stupid opposition with a single authoritative word. But I had to be constantly reminding myself of the danger of exercising my Imperial prerogatives in such a way as to retard the eventual restoration of a Republic.

I did my best to encourage free speech and public-spiritedness, and to avoid transforming personal caprices of my own into laws which all Rome must obey. It was very difficult. The joke was that free speech, public-spiritedness, and Republican idealism itself seemed to come under the heading of personal caprices of my own. And though at first I made a point of being accessible to everyone, in order to avoid the appearance of monarchical haughtiness, and of speaking in a friendly familiar way with all my fellow-citizens, I soon had to behave more distantly. It was not so much that I had not the time to spare for continuous friendly chat with everyone who came calling at the Palace: it was rather that my fellow-citizens, with few exceptions, shamefully abused my good feelings towards them. They did this either by answering my familiarity with an ironically polite haughtiness, as if to say, 'You can't fool us into loyalty,' or by a giggling impudence as if to say, 'Why don't you behave like a real Emperor?' or by thoroughly false good-comradeship, as if to say, 'If it pleases your Majesty to unbend, and to expect us to unbend in conformity with your humour, then look how obligingly we do so! But if you please to frown, down we'll go on our faces at once.'

Speaking of the harbour, Vitellius said to me one day: 'A republic can never hope to carry through public works on so grand a scale as a monarchy. All the grandest constructions in the world are the work of Kings or Queens. The walls and hanging gardens of Babylon. The Mausoleum at Halicarnassus. The Pyramids. You have never been to Egypt, have you? I was stationed there as a young soldier and, ye Gods, those Pyramids! It is impossible to convey in words the crushing sense of awe with which they overwhelm everyone who sees them. One first hears about them at home, as a child, and asks: "What are the Pyramids?" and the answer is, "Huge stone tombs in Egypt, triangular in shape, without any ornaments on them: just faced with white stucco." That doesn't sound very interesting or impressive. The mind makes "huge" no huger than some very big building with which one happens to be familiar – say the Temple of Augustus yonder or the Julian Basilica. And then again, visiting Egypt, one sees them at a great distance across the desert, little white marks like tents, and says: "Why, surely *that's* nothing to make a fuss about!" But, Heavens, to stand beneath them a few hours later and look up! Caesar, I tell you, they are incredibly and impossibly huge. It makes one feel physically sick to think of them as having been built by human hands. One's first sight of the Alps was nothing by comparison. So white, smooth, pitilessly immortal. Such a terrific monument of human aspiration – –'

'And stupidity and tyranny and cruelty,' I broke in. 'King Cheops, who built the Great Pyramid, ruined his rich country, bled it white and left it gasping; and all to gratify his own absurd vanity and perhaps impress the Gods with his superhuman power. And what practical use did this Pyramid serve? Was it intended as a tomb to house Cheops's corpse for all eternity? Yet I have read that this absurdly impressive sepulchre has long been empty. The invading Shepherd Kings discovered the secret entrance, rifled the inner chamber, and made a bonfire of proud Cheops's mummy.'

Vitellius smiled. 'You haven't seen the Great Pyramid or you wouldn't talk like that. Its emptiness makes it all the more majestic. And as for use, why, it has a most important use. Its pinnacle serves as a mark of orientation for the Egyptian peasants when the yearly Nile flood subsides and they must mark out their fields again in the sea of fertile mud.'

'A tall pillar would have served just as well,' I said, 'and two tall pillars, one on each bank of the Nile, would have been still better; and the cost would have been negligible. Cheops was mad, like Caligula; though apparently he had a more settled madness than Caligula, who always did things by fits and starts. The great city that Caligula planned, to command the Great St Bernard Pass on the Alps, would never have got very far towards completion, though he had lived to be centenarian.'

Vitellius agreed. 'He was a jackdaw. The nearest he ever came to raising a Pyramid was when he built that out-size ship and stole the great red obelisk from Alexandria. A jackdaw and a monkey.'

'Yet I seem to remember that you once adored that jackdaw-monkey as a God.'

'And I gratefully remember that the advice and example came from you.'

'Heaven forgive us both,' I said. We were standing talking outside the Temple of Capitoline Jove, which we had just been ritually purifying, because of the recent appearance, on the roof, of a bird of evil omen. (It was an owl of the sort we call 'incendiaries' because they foretell the destruction by fire of any building on which they perch.) I pointed across the valley with my finger. 'Do you see that? That's part of the greatest monument ever built, and though monarchs like Augustus and Tiberius have added to it and kept it in repair, it was first built by a free people. And I have no doubt that it will last as long as the Pyramids, besides having proved of infinitely more service to mankind.'

'I don't see what you mean. You seem to be pointing at the Palace.'

'I am pointing at the Appian Way,' I replied solemnly. 'It was begun in the Censorship of my great ancestor, Appius Claudius the Blind. The Roman Road is the greatest monument ever raised to human liberty by a noble and generous people. It runs across mountain, marsh, and river. It is built broad, straight, and firm. It joins city with city and nation with nation. It is tens of thousands of miles long, and always thronged with grateful travellers. And while the Great Pyramid, a few hundred feet high and wide, awes sight-seers to silence – though it is only the rifled tomb of an ignoble corpse and a monument of oppression and misery, so that no doubt in viewing it you may still seem to hear the crack of the taskmaster's whip and the squeals and groans of the poor workmen struggling to set a huge block of stone into position – –' But in this unpremeditated gush of eloquence I had forgotten the beginning of my sentence. I broke off, feeling foolish, and Vitellius had to come to the rescue. He threw up his hands, shut his eyes, and declaimed: 'Words fail me, my Lords. Nothing that I might utter could possibly match the depth of my feelings in this matter.' We both laughed uproariously at this. Vitellius was one of the few friends I had who treated me with the right sort of familiarity. I never knew whether it was genuine or artificial; but if artificial, it was so good an imitation of the real thing that I accepted it at its face value. I should never perhaps have called it in question if his former adoration of Caligula had not been so well acted, and if it had not been for the matter of Messalina's slipper. I shall tell you about this.

Vitellius was going up a staircase at the Palace, one day in summer, in company with Messalina and myself, when Messalina said: 'Stop a moment, please: I've lost my slipper.' Vitellius quickly turned and retrieved it for her, handing it back with a deep obeisance. Messalina was charmed. She said, smiling: 'Claudius, you won't be jealous, will you, if I confer the Order of the Jewelled Slipper on this brave soldier, our dear friend Vitellius? He really is most gallant and obliging.'

'But don't you need the slipper, my dear?'

'No, it's cooler to go barefoot on a day like this. And I have scores of other pretty pairs.'

So Vitellius took the slipper and kissed it and put it in the pocket-fold of his robe, where he kept it continually; bringing it out to kiss once more when enlarging, in sentimental private talk with me, on Messalina's beauty, brains, bounty, and on my extraordinarily good fortune in being her husband. It always brought a great sense of warmth to my heart and sometimes even tears to my eyes to hear Messalina praised. It was a constant wonder to me that she could care as much for a lame, pedantic, stuttering old fellow like myself as she swore she did; yet nobody, I argued, could pretend that she had married me for mercenary reasons. I was a bankrupt at the time, and as for the possibility of my ever becoming Emperor, it could surely never have occurred to her.

The harbour at Ostia was by no means my only great public work. The verse that the Sibyl of Cumae recited when I visited her once, in disguise, ten years before I became Emperor, prophesied that I should 'give Rome water and winter bread'. The winter bread was a reference to Ostia, but the water meant the two great aqueducts I built. It is very curious about prophecies. A prophecy is made, perhaps, when one is a boy, and one pays great attention to it at the time, but then a mist descends: one forgets about it altogether until suddenly the mist clears and the prophecy is fulfilled. It was not until my aqueducts were completed and consecrated, and the harbour completed too, that I recalled the Sibyl's verse. Yet I suppose that it had been at the back of my mind all the time, as it were the God's whisper to me to undertake these great projects.

My aqueducts were most necessary: the existing water supply was by no means sufficient for the City's needs, though greater than that of any other city in the world. We Romans love fresh water. Rome is a town of baths and fish-pools and fountains. The fact was that, though Rome was now served by no less than seven aqueducts, the rich men had managed to draw away most of the public water for their own use, getting permission to connect private reservoirs with the mains – their swimming-baths had to have fresh water every day, and their great gardens had to be watered – so that many of the poorer citizens were reduced in the summer to drinking and cooking with Tiber water, which was most unhealthy. Cocceius Nerva, that virtuous old man, whom my Uncle Tiberius kept by him as his good genius, and who eventually committed suicide – this Nerva, then, whom Tiberius had made his Inspector of Aqueducts, advised him to show his magnanimity by giving the City a water-supply worthy of its greatness; and reminded him that his ancestor Appius Claudius the Blind had won eternal fame for bringing the Appian Water into Rome, from eight miles away, by the City's first aqueduct. Tiberius undertook to do as Nerva advised, but put the project off, and put it off again and again, as his way was, until Nerva's death. Then he felt remorse and sent his engineers out to discover suitable springs, according to the rules laid down by the famous Vitruvius. Such springs must run strongly all the year round, and run clean and sweet, and not fur the pipes, and must have such an elevation that, allowing for the fall necessary to give the channel of the aqueduct its proper inclination, the water will enter the final reservoir at a height sufficient to allow of its distribution, by pipes, to the highest houses in Rome. The engineers had to go far afield before they came on water that answered their purpose: they found it eventually in the hills to the south-east of the City. Two copious and excellent springs called the Blue Spring and the Curtian Spring broke out near the thirty-eighth milestone on the Sublacentian Road: they could be run together as one. Then there was the New Anio stream which could be drawn upon at the forty-second milestone on the same road, but on the other side: that would have to be carried by a second aqueduct and would pick up another stream, the Herculanean, opposite the Blue Spring. They reported that the water from these sources fulfilled all the necessary conditions, and that there was no nearer supply that did so. Tiberius had plans for two aqueducts drawn out and called for estimates; but decided at once that he could not afford the work, and shortly afterwards died.

Caligula, immediately on his accession, to show that he was of a more generous and public-spirited nature than Tiberius, began work on Tiberius's plans, which were very detailed and good ones. He started well, but as his Treasury grew empty he could not keep it up and, taking his workmen from the most difficult parts (the great arched bridges, arch over arch in tiers, which carried the water across valleys and low ground), he put them to work on the easier levels where the channel ran round the slopes of hills or directly across the plain. He still could boast of rapid progress in terms of miles, and the expense was negligible. Some of the arches which he thus shirked building needed to be over 100 feet high.

The first aqueduct, afterwards called the Claudian Water, was to be over forty-six miles long, of which ten miles were to run on arches. The second, called the New Anio, was to be nearly fifty-nine miles long, and fifteen miles or so were to run on arches. When Caligula quarrelled with the people of Rome, the time they made the disturbance in the amphitheatre and sent him running in fright out of the City, he made his quarrel an excuse for abandoning all work on the aqueducts. He took the workmen away and put them on other tasks, such as building his temple and clearing sites at Antium (his birthplace) for the erection of a new capital city there.

So it fell to me to take up the work, which seemed to me one of first importance, where Caligula had abandoned it, though it meant having to concentrate on the more difficult stretches. If you wonder why the New Anio, though picking up the Herculanean stream close to the beginning of the Claudian Water, had to make a great circuit, instead of being run along the same arches, the answer is that the New Anio started at a much higher level and would have had too swift a flow if it had been brought down immediately to the Claudian Water. Vitruvius recommends an inclination of half a foot in 100 yards and the height of the New Anio did not allow it to join the Claudian Water, even on a higher tier of arches, until quite near the City, having travelled thirteen miles farther. In order to keep the water clean, there was a covered top to the channel with vent-holes at intervals to prevent bursts. There were also frequent large reservoirs through which the water passed, leaving its sediment behind. These reservoirs were also useful for purposes of irrigation, and amply paid for themselves by making it possible for the neighbouring landowners to put land under cultivation which otherwise would have been waste.

The work took nine years to complete, but there were no setbacks; and when it was finished it was among the chief wonders of Rome. The two waters entered the City by the Praenestine Gate, the New Anio above, the Claudian below, where a huge double arch had to be built to cross two main roads. The terminus was a great tower from which the water was distributed to ninety-two smaller towers. There were already some 160 of these small water-towers in existence at Rome, but my two aqueducts doubled the actual supply of water. My Inspector of Aqueducts now calculated the flow of water into Rome as equal to a stream thirty feet broad and six feet deep, flowing at the rate of twenty miles an hour. Experts and ordinary people agreed that mine was the best quality of water of any, except that brought by the Marcian Water, the most important of the existing aqueducts, which accounted for fifty-four of the towers and had been in existence for about 170 years.

I was very strict about the thieving of water by irresponsible persons. The chief thieving in the old days before Agrippa undertook the work of overhauling the whole water-system – he built two new aqueducts himself, one chiefly underground on the left bank of the Tiber – was done by deliberately punching holes in the main, or bribing the persons in charge of the aqueducts to do so, and making the damage look accidental; for there was a law giving people the right to casual water from leaks. This practice had lately started again. I reorganized the corps of aqueduct-workers and gave orders that all leakages were to be immediately repaired. But there was another kind of thieving going on too. There were pipes leading from the main to private water-towers built by the common subscriptions of wealthy families or clans. These pipes were made of lead and of a regulation size, so that no more water should be taken from the main than could flow through the pipe in its normal horizontal position; but by enlarging the pipe by pushing a stake through, lead being a very ductile metal, and furthermore inclining it from the horizontal, a much greater flow of water was obtained. Sometimes more impudent or powerful families substituted pipes of their own. I was determined to stop this. I had the pipes cast of bronze and officially stamped and so fixed to the main that they could not be declined without breaking them, and ordered my inspectors to visit the water-towers regularly to see that nothing was tampered with.

I might as well mention here the last of my three great engineering undertakings, the draining of the Fucine Lake. This lake, which lies some sixty miles due east of Rome under the Alban Hills, surrounded by marshes, is about twenty miles long and ten wide, though of no great depth. The project for draining it had long been discussed. The inhabitants of that part of the country, who are called Marsians, once petitioned Augustus about it, but, after due consideration, he turned down their request on the ground that the task was too laborious and that the possible results could not justify it. Now the question was raised again and a group of rich landowners came to me and volunteered to pay two-thirds of the expense of the drainage if I undertook to carry it out. They asked in return grants of the land that would be reclaimed from the marshes and from the lake itself when the water was drained off. I refused their offer, because it occurred to me that if they were willing to pay so much for the reclaimed land it was probably worth far more. The problem seemed a simple one. One had only to cut a channel three miles long through a hill at the south-west extremity of the lake, thus allowing the water to escape into the River Liris which ran on the opposite side of the hill. I decided to start at once.

The work began in the first year of my monarchy, but it was soon evident that Augustus had been right in not attempting it. The labour and expense of cutting through that hill was infinitely greater than my engineers had reckoned it would be. They came on huge masses of solid rock that had to be hacked away piece by piece, and the debris dragged off along the channel; and there were troubles with springs in the hill which kept bursting out and interfering with the work. In order to finish it at all I soon had to set 30,000 men working constantly at it. But I refused to be beaten: I hate throwing up a task. The channel was completed only the other day, after thirteen years' labour. Soon I shall give the signal for opening the sluice-gates and letting out the lake-water.

Chapter 12

ONE day, just before Herod left Rome, he suggested that I should see a really good Greek doctor about my health; pointing out how important it was for Rome that I should take myself in hand physically. I had been showing signs of great fatigue lately, he said, as a result of the extraordinary long hours that I worked. If I did not either shorten these hours or put myself into a condition which would enable me to stand the strain better I could not expect to live much longer. I grew vexed and said that no Greek doctor had been able to cure me as a young man, though I had consulted many; and assured him that it was not only too late to do anything about my infirmities but that I had grown quite attached to them as an integral part of myself, and that I had no use for Greek doctors in any case.

Herod grinned. 'This is the first time in my life that I have heard you agree with old Cato. I remember that *Commentary on Medicine* which he wrote for his son, forbidding him ever to consult a

Greek doctor. Instead he recommended prayers, common sense, and cabbage leaves. They were good enough for every common physical ailment, he said. Well, there are enough prayers going up for your health in Rome to-day to make you a positive athlete, if prayers were enough. And common sense is the birthright of every Roman. Perhaps, Caesar, you have forgotten the cabbage leaves?'

I stirred irritably on my couch. 'Well, what doctor do you recommend? I'll see just one, to please you, but no more. What about Largus? He's the Palace Physician now. Messalina says that he's quite clever.'

'If Largus had known of a cure for your ailments he would have volunteered it quick enough. No use going to him. If you will only consent to consult a single one, consult Xenophon of Cos.'

'What, my father's old field-surgeon?'

'No, his son. He was with your brother Germanicus on his last campaign, you may remember; then he went to practise at Antioch. He was extraordinary successful there and recently he's come to Rome. He uses the motto of the great Asclepiades, *Cure quickly, safely, pleasantly*. No violent purges and emetics. Diet, exercise, massage, and a few simple botanical remedies. He cured me of a violent fever with a distillation of the leaves of a purple flowered weed called monk's-hood and then set me right generally with advice about diet, and so forth: told me not to drink so much, and what spices to avoid. A marvellous surgeon too, when it comes to that. He knows exactly where every nerve, bone, muscle, and sinew in the body lies. He told me that he learned his anatomy from your brother.'

'Germanicus wasn't an anatomist.'

'No, but he was a German-killer. Xenophon picked up his knowledge on the battle-field: Germanicus provided the subjects. No surgeon can learn anatomy in Italy or Greece. He has either to go to Alexandria, where they don't mind cutting up corpses, or follow in the wake of a conquering army.'

'I suppose he'll come if I send for him?'

'What doctor wouldn't? Do you forget who you are? But of course, if he cures you you'll have to pay him handsomely. He likes money. What Greek doesn't?'

'*If* he cures me.'

I sent for Xenophon. I took an immediate liking to him because his professional interest in me as a case made him forget that I was Emperor and had the power of life and death over him. He was a man of about fifty. After his first formal obeisances and compliments he talked curtly and dryly and kept strictly to the point.

'Your pulse. Thanks. Your tongue. Thanks. Excuse me' (he turned up my eyelids). 'Eyes somewhat inflamed. Can cure that. I'll give you a lotion to bathe them with. Slight retraction of eyelids. Stand up, please. Yes, infantile paralysis. Can't cure that, naturally. Too late. Could have done so before you stopped growing.'

'You were only a child yourself at the time, Xenophon,' I smiled.

He appeared not to hear me. 'Were you a premature birth? Yes? I suspected it. Malaria too?'

'Malaria, measles, colitis, scrofula, erysipelas. The whole battalion answers "present", Xenophon, except epilepsy, venereal disease, and megalomania.'

He consented to smile briefly. 'Strip!' he said. I stripped. 'You eat too much and drink too much. You must stop that. Make it a rule never to rise from the table without an unsatisfied longing for just one little thing more. Yes, left leg much shrunk. No good prescribing exercise. Massage will have to do instead. You may dress again.' He asked me a few more intimate questions, and always in a way that showed he knew the answer and was merely confirming it from my mouth as a matter of routine. 'You dribble on your pillow at night, of course?' I owned with shame that this was so. 'Fits of sudden anger? Involuntary twitching of the facial muscles? Stuttering when in a state of embarrassment? Occasional weakness of bladder? Fits of aphasia? Rigidity of muscles, so that you often wake up cold and stiff even on warm nights?' He even told me the sort of things I dreamed about.

I asked, astonished: 'Can you interpret them, too, Xenophon? That ought to be easy.'

'Yes,' he answered in a matter-of-fact way, 'but there's a law against it. Now, Caesar, I'll tell you about yourself. You have a good many more years to live if you care to live them. You work too hard, but I cannot prevent you from doing that, I suppose. I recommend reading as little as possible. The fatigue of which you complain is largely due to eye-strain. Make your secretaries read everything possible out to you. Do as little writing as you can. Rest for an hour after your principal meal: don't rush off to the law-courts as soon as you have gobbled your dessert. You must find time for twenty minutes' massage twice a day. You will need a properly trained masseur. The only properly trained masseurs in Rome are slaves of mine. The best is Charmes: I shall give him special instructions in your case. If you break my rules you must not expect a complete cure, though the medicine that I shall prescribe will do you appreciable good. For instance, the violent cramp in the stomach of which you complain, the cardiac passion as we call it: if you neglect your massage and eat a heavy meal in a hurry, when in a state of nervous excitement about something or other, that cramp will come on you again, as sure as fate, in spite of my medicine. But follow my directions and you'll be a sound man.'

'What's the medicine? Is it difficult to come by? Will I have to send to Egypt or India for it?'

Xenophon permitted himself a little creaking laugh. 'No, nor any farther than the nearest bit of waste land. I belong to the Cos school of medicine: I am a native of Cos, in fact, a descendant of Aesculapius himself. At Cos we classify diseases by their remedies, which are for the most part the herbs that if eaten in great quantities produce the very symptoms that when eaten in moderate quantities they cure. Thus if a child wets his bed after the age of three or four and shows certain other cretinous symptoms associated with bed-wetting we say: "That child has the Dandelion disease." Dandelion eaten in large quantities produces these symptoms, and a decoction of dandelion cures them. When I first came into the room and noticed the twitch of your head and the tremor of your hand and the slight stutter of your greeting, together with the rather harsh quality of your voice, I summed you up at once. "A typical bryony case," I said to myself. "Bryony, massage, diet." '

'What, Common Bryony?'

'The same. I'll write out a prescription for its preparation.'

'And the prayers?'

'What prayers?'

'Don't you prescribe special prayers to be used when taking the medicine? All the other doctors who have tried to cure me have always given me special prayers to repeat while mixing and taking the medicine.'

He answered, rather stiffly: 'I suggest, Caesar, that as High Pontiff and the author of a history of religious origins at Rome, you are better equipped than myself for undertaking the theurgical side of the cure.'

I could see that he was an unbeliever, like so many Greeks, so I did not press the matter, and that ended the interview: he begged to be excused because he had patients waiting in his consulting-room.

Well, bryony cured me. For the first time in my life I knew what it was to be perfectly well. I followed Xenophon's advice to the letter and have hardly had a day's illness since. Of course, I remain lame and occasionally I stammer and twitch my head from old habit if I get excited. But my aphasia has disappeared, my hand hardly trembles at all, and I can still at the age of sixty-four do a good fourteen hours' work a day, if necessary, and not feel utterly exhausted at the end of it. The cardiac passion has recurred occasionally, but only in the circumstances against which Xenophon warned me.

You may be sure that I paid Xenophon well for my bryony. I persuaded him to come and live at the Palace as Largus's colleague: Largus was a good physician in his way and had written several books on medical subjects. Xenophon would not come at first. He had built up a large private practice during the few months he had been at Rome: he assessed it as now worth 3,000 gold pieces a year. I offered him 6,000 – Largus's salary was only 3,000 – and when he hesitated even then I said: 'Xenophon, you must come: I insist. And when you have kept me alive and well for fifteen years, the Governors of Cos will be sent an official letter informing them that the island where you learned medicine will henceforth be excused from furnishing its military contingent and from paying tribute to the Imperial Government.'

So he consented. If you wish to know to whom my freedman addressed prayers when mixing my medicine and to whom I addressed mine when taking it, it was the Goddess Carna, an old Sabine Goddess whom we Claudians have always cultivated since the time of Appius Claudius, of Regillus. Medicine mixed and taken without prayers would have seemed to me as unlucky and useless as a wedding celebrated without guests, sacrifice, or music.

Before I forget it, I must record two valuable health hints that I learned from Xenophon. He used to say: 'The man is a fool who puts good manners before health. If you are troubled with wind, never hold it in. It does great injury to the stomach. I knew a man who once nearly killed himself by holding in his wind. If for some reason or other you cannot conveniently leave the room –

say, you are sacrificing or addressing the Senate – don't be afraid to belch or break wind downwards where you stand. Better that the company should suffer some slight inconvenience than that you should permanently injure yourself. And again, when you suffer from a cold, don't constantly blow your nose. That only increases the flow of rheum and inflames the delicate membranes of your nose. Let it run. Wipe, don't blow.' I have always taken Xenophon's advice, at least about nose-blowing: my colds don't last nearly so long now as they did. Of course, caricaturists and satirists soon made fun of me as having a permanently dripping nose, but what did I care for that? Messalina told me that she thought I was extremely sensible to take such care of myself: if I were suddenly to die or fall seriously ill, what would become of the City and Empire, not to mention herself and our little boy?

Messalina said to me one day: 'I am beginning to repent of my kind heart.'

'Do you mean that my niece Lesbia should after all have been left in exile?'

She nodded. 'How did you guess that I meant that? Now tell me, my dear, why does Lesbia go to your rooms in the Palace so often when I'm not about? What does she talk of? And why don't you let me know when she comes? You see, it's no good trying to keep secrets from me.'

I smiled reassuringly but felt a little awkward. 'There's nothing secret about it, nothing at all. You remember that about a month ago I gave her back the remainder of the estates which Caligula had taken from her? The Calabrian ones that you and I decided not to give back until we saw how she and Vinicius would behave? Well, as I told you, when I gave them back she burst into tears and said how ungrateful she had been and swore that she was now going to change her way of living altogether and conquer her stupid pride.'

'Very touching, I am sure. But this is the first word I have heard of any such dramatic scene.'

'But I distinctly remember telling you the whole story, one morning at breakfast.'

'You must have dreamed it. Well, what *was* the whole story? Better late than never. When you gave her back the estates I certainly thought it rather queer that you should reward her insolence to me. But I said nothing. It was your business, not mine.'

'I cannot understand this. I could have sworn I told you. My memory has the most extraordinary lapses sometimes. I am very sorry indeed, my dearest. Well, I gave her back the estates, simply because she said that she had just gone to you and made a whole-hearted apology and that you had said: "I forgive you freely, Lesbia. Go and tell Claudius that I forgive you." '

'Oh, what a bare-faced lie! She never came to me at all. Are you sure she said that? Or is your memory at fault again?'

'No, I'm positive about it. Otherwise I should never have given her back the estates.'

'You know the legal formula about evidence? "False in one thing, false in all." That fits Lesbia. But you haven't yet told me why she visits you. What is she trying to get out of you?'

'Nothing, so far as I know. She just comes occasionally for a friendly visit to repeat how grateful she is and to ask whether she can be of any use to me. She never stays long enough to be a nuisance and always asks how you are. When I say that you're working she says that she wouldn't dream of disturbing you and apologizes for disturbing me. Yesterday she said that she thought you were still a little suspicious of her. I said that I thought not. She chatters a little about things in general for a few minutes, kisses me like a good niece, and off she goes. I quite enjoy her visits. But I was convinced that I'd mentioned them to you.'

'Never. That woman's a snake. I think I know her plan. She'll worm her way into your confidence – like a good niece, of course – and then begin slandering me. In a quiet, hinting sort of way at first and then more directly as she gets bolder. She'll probably make up a wonderful story about the double life I lead. She'll say that behind your back I live a regular life of debauchery – sword-fighters and actors and young gallants and the rest. And you'll believe her, of course, like a good uncle. O God, what cats women are! I believe she's begun already. Has she?'

'Certainly not. I wouldn't let her. I wouldn't believe anyone who told me that you were unfaithful to me in deed or word. I wouldn't believe it even if you told me so yourself with your own lips. There, does that satisfy you?'

'Forgive me, dear, for being so jealous. It's my nature. I hate you to have friendships with other women behind my back, even relations. I don't trust any woman alone with you. You're so simple-minded. And I'm going to make it my business to find what poisonous trick Lesbia has at the back of her mind. But I don't want her to know that I suspect her. Promise me that you won't let her know that you have caught her out in a falsehood, until I have some more serious charge against her.'

I promised. I told Messalina that I didn't believe in Lesbia's change of heart now and that I would report all conversational remarks that she made to me. This satisfied Messalina, who said that now she could continue her work with an easier mind.

I faithfully repeated to Messalina all Lesbia's remarks. They seemed to me of little importance, but Messalina found significance in many of them and caught especially at one – to me – perfectly inoffensive remark that Lesbia had made about a senator called Seneca. Seneca was a magistrate of the second rank, and had once incurred the jealous dislike of Caligula by the eloquence with which he had conducted a case in the Senate. He would certainly have lost his head then but for me. I had done him the service of depreciating his oratorical abilities, saying to Caligula: 'Eloquent? Seneca's not eloquent. He's just very well educated and has a prodigious memory. His father compiled those *Controversies* and *Persuasories*, school-exercises in oratory on imaginary cases. Childish stuff. He wrote a lot more which have remained unpublished. Seneca seems to have got the whole lot off by heart. He has a rhetorical key now to fit any lock. It's not eloquence. There's nothing behind it, not even strong personal character. I'll tell you what it is – it's like sand without lime. You can't build up a reputation for true eloquence out of that.' Caligula repeated my own words as his own judgement on Seneca. 'School-exercises only. Puerile declamations, borrowings from his father's unpublished papers. Sand without lime.' So Seneca was permitted to live.

Now Messalina asked me: 'You are sure that she went out of her way to commend Seneca as an honest and unambitious man? You didn't bring up his name yourself first?'

'No.'

'Then you may depend on it, Seneca's her lover. I have known for some time that she was keeping a secret lover, but she hides her tracks so well that I couldn't be sure whether it was Seneca or her husband's cousin Vinicianus, or that fellow Asinius Gallus, Pollio's grandson. They all live in the same street.'

Ten days later she told me that she now had complete proof of adultery between Lesbia and Seneca during the recent absence from Rome of Vinicius, Lesbia's husband. She brought witnesses who swore that they had seen Seneca leave his house late at night, in disguise; had followed him to Lesbia's house, which he had entered by a side door; had seen a light suddenly appear at Lesbia's bedroom window and presently go out again; and three or four hours later had seen Seneca emerge and return home, still in disguise.

It was clear that Lesbia could not be allowed to stay at Rome any longer. She was my niece, and therefore an important public figure. She had already been banished once on a charge of adultery and recalled by me only on an understanding that she would behave more discreetly in future. I expected all members of my family to set a high moral standard for the City. Seneca would have to be banished too. He was a married man and a senator, and though Lesbia was a beautiful woman I suspected that with a man of Seneca's character ambition was a stronger motive for the adultery than sexual passion. She was a direct descendant of Augustus, of Livia, and of Mark Antony, a daughter of Germanicus, a sister of the late Emperor, a niece of the present one: while he was merely the son of a well-to-do provincial grammarian and had been born in Spain.

Somehow I did not wish to interview Lesbia myself, so I asked Messalina to do so. I felt that Messalina had more cause for resentment in the matter than I had, and wished to stand well with her again and show how sorry I was that I had given her occasion for the slightest twinge of jealousy. She gladly undertook the task of lecturing Lesbia for her ingratitude and acquainting her with her sentence; which was banishment to Reggio in the South of Italy, the town where her grandmother Julia had died in banishment for the same offence. Messalina afterwards reported that Lesbia had spoken most insolently, but had finally admitted adultery with Seneca, saying that her body was her own to do with as she liked. On being informed that she would be banished, she had flown into a passion and threatened us both: she said: 'One morning the Palace servants will enter the Imperial bed-chamber and find you both lying with your throats cut,' and 'How do you think my husband and his family will take this insult?'

'Only words, my dear,' I said. 'I don't take them seriously, though perhaps we had better keep a careful watch on Vinicius and his party.'

On the very night that Lesbia started out for Reggio, towards dawn, Messalina and I were awakened by a sudden cry and scuffle in the corridor outside our door, some violent sneezing and shouts of, 'Seize him! Murder! Assassins! Seize him!' I jumped out of bed, my heart pounding because of the sudden shock, and snatched up a stool as a weapon of defence, shouting to Messalina to get behind me. But my courage was not called in question. It was only one man and he had already been disarmed.

I ordered the guards to stand to arms for the rest of the night and went back to bed, though it took me some time to fall asleep again. Messalina needed a deal of comforting. She seemed scared almost out of her wits, laughing and crying in turns. 'It's Lesbia's doing,' she sobbed; 'I'm sure it is.'

When morning came I had the would-be assassin brought before me. He confessed to being a freedman of Lesbia's. But he had come disguised in Palace livery. He was a Syrian Greek and his story was a grotesque one. He said that he had not intended to murder me. It was all his own fault for repeating the wrong words at the close of the Mystery. 'What Mystery?' I asked.

'I am forbidden to tell, Caesar. I'll only reveal as much as I dare. It is the most sacred of all sacred Mysteries. I was initiated into it last night. It happened underground. A certain bird was sacrificed and I drank its blood. Two tall spirits appeared, with shining faces, and gave me a dagger and a pepper-pot, explaining what these instruments symbolized. They blindfolded me, dressed me in a new dress, and told me to keep perfect silence. They repeated magic words and told me to follow them to Hell. They led me here and there, up steps and down steps, along streets and through gardens, describing many strange sights as we went. We entered a boat and paid the ferryman. It was Charon himself. We were then put ashore in Hell. They showed me the whole of Hell. The ghosts of my ancestors talked to me. I heard Cerberus bark. Finally they took off the bandage from my eyes and whispered to me: "You are now in the Halls of the God of Death. Hide this dagger in your gown. Follow this corridor round to the right, mount the stairs at the end, and then turn to the left down a second corridor. If any sentry challenges you, give him the pass-word. The pass-word is 'Fate'. The God of Death and his Goddess lie asleep in the end room. At their door two more sentries are on watch. They are not like the other sentries. We do not know their pass-word. But creep up close to them in the shadows and suddenly throw this holy pepper-powder in their eyes. Then boldly burst open the door and slay the God and Goddess. If you succeed in this enterprise you shall live for ever in regions of perpetual bliss and be accounted greater than Hercules, greater than Prometheus, greater than Jove himself. There will be no more Death. But, as you go, you must say over and over to yourself the words of the same charm that we have used to bring you so far in safety. If you do not do so, all our guidance will have been wasted. The spell will break and you will find yourself in quite a different place." I was frightened. I suppose that I must have made a mistake in the spell, because as I drew back my hand to fling the pepper I suddenly found myself back here in Rome, in your Imperial Palace, struggling with the guards at your bedroom door. I had failed. Death still reigns. Some other bolder, more collected soul than I must one day strike that blow.'

'Lesbia's confederates are very clever,' Messalina whispered. 'What a perfect plot!'

'Who initiated you?' I asked the man.

He would not answer, even under torture, and I could not get much information from the Guard at the main gate, who happened to be newly-joined men. They said that they had admitted him because he was wearing Palace livery and had the correct pass-word. I could not blame them. He had arrived at the Gate in the company of two other men in Palace livery, who had said good-night to him and strolled off.

I was inclined to believe the man's story; but he persisted in his refusal to say who it was who had sponsored his initiation into these so-called mysteries. When I assured him in quite a pleasant way that they could not have been real mysteries but an elaborate hoax, and that therefore his oath was not binding he flared up and spoke to me most rudely. So he had to be executed. And after long debate with myself I agreed with Messalina that for the sake of public safety it was now necessary to have Lesbia executed too. I sent a detachment of Guards Cavalry after her, and on the following day they brought me back her head in token of her death. It was very painful for me to have had to execute a daughter of my dear brother Germanicus after swearing at his death to love and protect all his children as if they were my own. But I comforted myself by the thought that he would have acted as I had done if he had been in my place. He always put public duty before private feeling.

As for Seneca, I told the Senate that unless they knew some good reason to the contrary I desired them to vote for his banishment to Corsica. So they banished him, allowing him thirty hours in which to leave Rome and thirty days in which to leave Italy. Seneca was not popular with the House. While in Corsica he had plenty of opportunity for practising the philosophy of the Stoics – to which he announced himself converted by a chance word of mine once spoken in their commendation. The flattery of which that fellow was capable was really nauseating. When a year or two later my secretary Polybius lost a brother, of whom he was fond, Seneca, who knew Polybius only slightly and his brother not at all, sent him, from Corsica, a long carefully-phrased letter, which at the same time he arranged to have published in the City under the title *Consolation for Polybius*. The consolation took the form of gently reproving Polybius for giving way to private grief for his brother while I, Caesar, lived and enjoyed good health, and continued to show him my princely favour.

While Caesar needs Polybius (Seneca wrote), Polybius has no more right to give way than has the giant Atlas, who is said to carry the world on his shoulders in obedience to the will of the Gods.

To Caesar himself, to whom all is permitted, many things are for that very reason denied. His vigilance defends every home; his labours establish general leisure; his industry procures civic happiness; his hard work spells a public holiday. From the very moment that Caesar first dedicated himself to humanity he robbed himself of himself, and, like the stars which perpetually run their tireless courses, he has never since allowed himself to rest or attend to any business of his own. And in some way, Polybius, your fate is linked with his august fate, and you too cannot now attend to your own personal interests, pursue your own private studies. While Caesar owns the world you cannot honourably partake of pleasure, of grief, or of any other human emotion. You are wholly Caesar's. And is it not always on your lips that Caesar is dearer to you than your life? How, then, is it right for you to complain of this stroke of fortune, while Caesar still lives and thrives?

There was a lot more about my wonderful loving-kindness and mercy and a passage putting into my mouth the most extravagant sentiments about the noblest way of bearing the loss of a brother. I was supposed to cite my grandfather Mark Antony's grief for his brother Gaius, my uncle Tiberius's grief for my father, Gaius Caesar's grief for young Lucius, my own grief for my brother Germanicus, and then relate how valiantly we had each in turn borne these calamities. The only effect that this slime and honey had on me was to make me quite satisfied in my mind that I had not wronged anyone by his banishment – except perhaps the island of Corsica.

Chapter 13

THE Alexandrian Greeks sent instructions to their envoys, who were still in Rome, to congratulate me on my victories in Germany, to complain of the insolent behaviour of the Jews towards them (there had been a recrudescence of trouble in the city), to ask my permission for the re-establishment of the Alexandrian Senate, and once more to offer me temples endowed and furnished with priests. They intended several other lesser honours for me besides this supreme one, among them being two golden statues, one representing the 'Peace of Claudius Augustus', the other 'Germanicus the Victor'. The latter statue I accepted because it was principally an honour to my father and brother, whose victories had been far more important than mine, and personally won, and because the statue's features were theirs, not mine. (My brother had been the living image of my father, everyone agreed.) As usual, the Jews sent a counter-embassy, congratulating me on my victories, thanking me for my generosity to them in the matter of the circular letter I had written about religious toleration for all Jews, and accusing the Alexandrians of having provoked these new disturbances by interrupting their religious worship with ribald songs and dances outside the synagogues on holy days. I shall here attach my exact answer to the Alexandrians, to show how I now handled questions of this sort:

Tiberius Claudius Caesar Augustus Germanicus, Emperor, High Pontiff, Protector of the People, Consul Elect, to the City of Alexandria, greetings.

Tiberius Claudius Barbillus, Apollonius son of Artemidorus, Chaeremon son of Leonides, Marcus Julius Asclepiades, Gaius Julius Dionysius, Tiberius Claudius Phanias, Pasion son of Potamon, Dionysius son of Sabbion, Tiberius Claudius Apollonius son of Ariston, Gaius Julius Apollonius, and Hermaiscus son of Apollonius, your envoys, have delivered me your decree and spoken to me at length about the City of Alexandria, recalling the goodwill which for many years past, as you know, I have always felt towards you; for you are naturally loyal to the House of Augustus, as many things go to prove. Especially there has been an exchange of amity between your city and my immediate family: I need only mention in this context my brother Germanicus Caesar whose goodwill towards you was shown more plainly than by any of us:

he came to Alexandria and addressed you with his own lips. For this reason I gladly accepted the recent honours you offered me, though I am usually not partial to honours.

In the first place I permit you to keep my birthday as a 'Day of Augustus' in the way mentioned in your own proclamation. Next, I agree to your erecting, in the places stated, the statues to myself and other members of my family, for I see that you have been zealous to establish memorials of your loyalty to my House on all sides. Of the two golden statues, that representing the Peace of Claudius Augustus, made at the suggestion and plea of my friend Barbillus, I have refused as appearing somewhat offensive to my fellow-men, and it is now to be dedicated to the Goddess Roma; the other shall be carried in your processions in whatever way you think best, on the appropriate birthdays; and you may provide it with a throne too, suitably decorated. It would perhaps be foolish, while accepting these great honours at your hands, to refuse to introduce a Claudian tribe and sanction sacred precincts for each Egyptian district; so I permit you to do both these things and, if you wish, to set up, too, the equestrian statue of my Governor, Vitrasius Pollio. Also, I give my consent to the erection of the four-horse chariots which you wish to establish in my honour at the frontiers: one at Taposiris in Libya, one at the Pharos in Alexandria, the third at Pelusium in Lower Egypt. But I must ask you not to appoint a High Priest for my worship or to build temples in my honour, for I do not wish to be offensive to my fellow men and it is quite clear to my mind that shrines and temples have, throughout history, been built in honour of the Gods, as their peculiar due.

As for the requests which you are so anxious for me to grant, these are my decisions: all Alexandrians who had officially come of age before I entered on the monarchy I confirm in their citizenship with all the privileges and amenities that this carries with it; the only exceptions being such pretenders, born of slave mothers, as may have contrived to intrude themselves among the free-born. And it is also my pleasure that all those favours which were granted you by my predecessors shall be confirmed, and those favours too which were granted by your former kings and City Prefects and confirmed by the God Augustus. It is my pleasure that the ministers of the Temple of the God Augustus of Alexandria shall be chosen by lot, like the ministers of his Temple at Canopus. I commend your plan for making the municipal magistracies triennial as a very sensible one; for the magistrates will behave with the greater prudence during their terms of office for knowing that when it ends they will be called upon to account for any maladministration of which they may have been guilty. As for the question about re-establishing the Senate, I am unable to say offhand what your custom was under the Ptolemies, but you know as well as I do that you have not had a Senate under any one of my predecessors of the House of Augustus. So since this is an entirely novel proposal and I am not sure whether it will prove either to your advantage or mine to adopt it, I have written to your City Prefect, Aemilius Rectus, to hold an inquiry and report whether a Senatorial Order should be formed, and, if so, in what way it should be formed.

As for the question as to who must bear responsibility for the recent riots and the feud or – to speak frankly – the war that has been waged between you and the Jews, I have been unwilling to commit myself to a decision on this matter, though your envoys, especially Dionysius, son of Theon, pleaded your cause with great spirit in the presence of their Jewish opponents. But I must reserve for myself a stern indignation against whichever party it was that started this new disturbance; and I wish you to understand that if both parties do not desist from this destructive and obstinate hostility I shall be compelled to show you what a benevolent ruler can do when roused to righteous anger. I therefore once more beg you Alexandrians to show a friendly tolerance to the Jews who have been your neighbours in Alexandria for so many years, and offer no outrage to their feelings whilst they are engaged in worshipping their God according to their ancestral rites. Let them practise all their national customs as in the days of the God Augustus, for I have confirmed their right to do so after an impartial hearing of both sides in the dispute. On the other hand, I desire the Jews to press for no privileges in excess of those that they already hold, and never again to send me a separate embassy as if you and they lived in different cities – a quite unheard of procedure! – nor to enter competitors for athletic and other contests at Public Games. They must content themselves with what they have, enjoying the abundance supplied by a great city of which they are *not* the original inhabitants; and they must not introduce any more Jews from Syria or from other parts of Egypt into the city, or they will fall more deeply under my suspicion than at present. If they fail to take this warning I shall certainly take vengeance on them as deliberately fomenting a world-wide plague. So long therefore as both sides abstain from this antagonism and live in mutual forbearance and goodwill, I undertake to show the same friendly solicitude for the interests of Alexandria as my family has always shown in the past.

I must testify here to the constant zeal for your interests which my friend Barbillus has now once again shown in his exertions on your behalf and also to a similar zeal on the part of my friend Tiberius Claudius Archibus.

Farewell.

This Barbillus was an astrologer of Ephesus, in whose powers Messalina had complete faith, and I must admit that he was a very clever fellow, second only in the accuracy of his prognostications to the great Thrasyllus. He had studied in India and among the Chaldees. His zeal for Alexandria was due to the hospitality he had been shown by the principal men of the city when forced, many years before, to leave Rome because Tiberius had banished from Italy all astrologers and soothsayers except his favourite Thrasyllus.

I received a letter from Herod a month or two later formally congratulating me on my victories, on the birth of my son, and on having won the title of Emperor by my victories in Germany. He enclosed his usual private letter:

What a great warrior you are, Marmoset, to be sure! You just have to put pen to paper and order a campaign, and presto! banners wave, swords fly from their scabbards, heads roll on the grass, towns and temples go up in flames! What fearful destruction you would cause if one day you were to mount on an elephant and take the field *in person*! I remember your dear mother once speaking of you, not very hopefully, as a future conqueror of the Island of Britain. Why not? For myself, I contemplate no military triumphs. Peace and security are all that I ask. I am busy putting my dominion in a state of defence against a possible Parthian invasion. Cypros and I are very happy and well, and so are the children. They are learning to be good Jews. They learn faster than I do, because they are younger. By the way, I don't like Vibius Marsus, your new Governor of Syria. I am afraid that he and I will fall out one day soon if he doesn't mind his own business. I was sorry when Petronius's term came to an end: a fine fellow. Poor Silas is still in confinement. I have given him the pleasantest possible prison quarters, however, and allowed him writing materials as a vent for his sense of my ingratitude. Not parchment or paper, of course, only a wax-tablet, so that when he comes to the end of one complaint he must scrape it off before starting on another.

You are extremely popular here with the Jews and the severe phrases in your letter to the Alexandrians were not taken amiss: Jews are quick at reading between the lines. I have heard from my old friend Alexander the Alabarch that copies were circulated to the various city-wards of Alexandria to be posted up, with the following endorsement by the City Prefect:

Proclamation by Lucius Aemilius Rectus
Since the whole populace was unable owing to its numbers to assist at the reading of that most sacred and gracious letter to the City, I have found it necessary to post it up publicly so that individual readers may admire the Majesty of our God Caesar Augustus and show their gratitude for His goodwill towards the City.

Fourteenth day of August, in the second year of the reign of Tiberius Claudius Caesar Augustus Germanicus, Emperor.

They'll make you a God in spite of yourself; but keep your health and spirits, eat well, sleep sound, and trust nobody.

THE BRIGAND

Herod's schoolboy taunt about the ease with which I had won my title of Emperor touched me in a sensitive spot. His reminder of my mother's remark influenced me too: it touched me in a superstitious spot. She had once – many years before – declared in a fit of annoyance when I was telling her of my proposal for adding three new letters to the Latin alphabet: 'There are three notably impossible things in this world: the first that shops should stretch across the Bay of Naples yonder, the second that you should conquer the island of Britain, the third that a single one of your ridiculous new letters should ever be put into general circulation.' Yet the first impossible thing had already come to pass – on the day that Caligula built his famous bridge from Bauli to Puteoli and lined it with shops. The third impossible thing could be accomplished any day that I pleased, merely by asking the Senate's permission – and why not the second?

A letter came from Marsus a few days later marked 'urgent and confidential'. Marsus was a capable governor, and an upright man though a most uncongenial companion – reserved, cold in his manner, perpetually sarcastic, and without either follies or vices. I had given him his appointment in gratitude for the prominent part he had taken more than twenty years before, while commanding a regiment in the East, in bringing Piso to trial for the murder of my brother Germanicus. He wrote:

... My neighbour, your friend King Herod Agrippa, is, I am informed, fortifying Jerusalem. You are probably aware of this, but I write to make it plain to you that the fortifications when completed will make the city impregnable. I wish to make no accusations of disloyalty against your friend King Herod, but as Governor of Syria I view the matter with alarm. Jerusalem commands the route to Egypt, and if it were to fall into irresponsible hands Rome would be in grave danger. Herod is said to fear a Parthian invasion: he has, however, already amply protected himself against this most improbable occurrence by a secret alliance with his royal neighbours on the Parthian frontier. No doubt you approve of his friendly advances to the Phoenicians: he has made enormous gifts to the city of Beirut and is building an amphitheatre there, also porticoes and public baths. It is difficult for me to understand his motives for courting the Phoenicians. However, for the present the chief men of Tyre and Sidon appear to have little trust in him. Perhaps they have good reason: it is not for me to say. At the risk of your displeasure I shall continue to report on political events to the south and east of my command as they come to my attention.

This made most uncomfortable reading, and my first feeling was one of anger against Marsus for disturbing my confidence in Herod; but when I thought things over the feeling changed to one of gratitude. I did not know what to think about Herod. On the one hand, I was confident that he would keep his oath of friendship, publicly sworn in the Market Place, with me; on the other hand, he was obviously engaged in some private scheme of his own which in the case of any other man I would call thoroughly treasonable. I was glad that Marsus was keeping his eyes open. I said nothing about the business to anyone, not even to Messalina, and wrote to Marsus merely: 'I have your letter. Be discreet. Report further events.' To Herod I wrote a sly letter:

I shall probably take your kind advice about Britain, my dear Brigand, and if I do invade that unfortunate isle I shall certainly ride on the back of an elephant. It will be the first elephant ever seen in Britain and no doubt cause widespread admiration. I am glad to hear good news of your family; don't worry about that Parthian invasion on their account. If I hear news of trouble in that quarter I shall send at once to Lyons for your Uncle Antipas to go out and quell it in his seventy-thousand-and-first suit of armour; so Cypros can sleep sound at night in that confidence and you can stop work on your fortifications at Jerusalem. We don't want Jerusalem made too strong, do we? Suppose that there was a sudden raid made by your brigand cousins from Edom, and they managed to get into Jerusalem just before you'd built the final bastion – why, we'd never get them out again, not even with siege-engines and tortoises and rams – and then what about the trade-route to Egypt? I am sorry that you dislike Vibius Marsus. How is your amphitheatre at Beirut progressing? I shall take your advice about trusting absolutely *nobody*, with the possible exceptions of my dear Messalina, Vitellius, Rufrius, and my old schoolfellow the Brigand, in whose self-accusations of roguery I have never and shall never believe, and to whom I shall always affectionately sign myself his

MARMOSET

Herod replied in his usual bantering style, as if he did not care one way or the other about the fortifications: but he must have known that my playful letter was not as playful as it pretended to be; and he must have known, too, that Marsus had been writing to me about him. Marsus replied shortly to my short note, reporting that work on the fortifications had now been discontinued.

I took my second Consulship in March, which is the New Year, but resigned the office two months later in favour of the next senator due for it: I was too busy to be bothered with the routine duties it involved. This was the year that my A.D. 42 daughter Octavia was born, that the Vinicianus–Scribonianus rising took place, and that I added Morocco to the Empire as a province. I shall first tell briefly what happened in Morocco. The Moors had risen again under a capable general named Salabus, who had led them in the previous campaign. Paulinus, who was commanding the Roman forces, overran the country as far as the Atlas range, but was unable to come to grips with Salabus himself and suffered heavy losses from ambushes and night attacks. His term of command presently expired and he had to return to Rome. He was succeeded by one Hosidius Geta whom I instructed, before he set out, not on any account to allow Salabus to become another Tacfarinas. (Tacfarinas was the Numidian who, under Tiberius, had earned three Roman generals the laurel-crown by allowing himself to be defeated by them in apparently decisive engagements, but who always reappeared at the head of his reconstituted army as soon as the Roman forces were withdrawn; however, a fourth general ended the business by catching and killing Tacfarinas himself.) I said to Geta: 'Don't be satisfied with partial successes. Search out Salabus's main force, crush it and kill or capture Salabus. Chase him all round Africa if necessary. If he runs off inland to the country where they say that men's heads sprout from under their armpits, why, follow him there. You'll easily recognize him by his having his head in a different place.' I also said to Geta: 'I won't attempt to direct your campaign: but one word of advice – don't be bound by hard-and-fast campaigning rules like Augustus's general Aelius Gallus who marched to the conquest of Arabia as if Arabia were a second Italy, or Germany. He loaded up his men with the usual entrenching tools and heavy armour instead of water-skins and extra corn-rations, and even brought a train of siege-engines. When colic attacked the men and they began boiling the bad water that they found in the wells, to make it safer to drink, Aelius came along and cried: "What! boiling your water! No disciplined Roman soldier boils his water! And using dried dung for fuel! Unheard of! Roman soldiers collect brushwood or else go without a fire." He lost the greater part of his force. The interior of Morocco is a dangerous quarter too. Suit your tactics and equipment to the country.'

Geta took my advice in the most literal way. He chased Salabus from end to end of Morocco, defeating him twice, and on the second occasion only just failing to capture him. Salabus then fled to the Atlas mountains and crossed them into the unexplored desert beyond, instructing his men to hold the pass while he collected reinforcements from his allies, the desert nomads. Geta left a detachment near the pass and with the hardiest of his men struggled across another, more difficult, pass a few miles away and went in faithful search of Salabus. He had taken as much water with him as his men and mules could possibly carry, cutting down his equipment to the least possible weight. He reckoned on finding some water at least, but followed Salabus's criss-cross track in the desert sands for more than 200 miles before he saw so much as a thorn-bush growing. The water began to give out and the men to weaken. Geta concealed his anxiety, but realized that even if he retreated at once, and gave up all hope of capturing Salabus, he had not enough water to see him safely back. The Atlas was 100 miles off, and only a divine miracle could save him.

Now, at Rome when there is a drought we know how to persuade the Gods to send rain. There is a black stone called the Dripping Stone, captured originally from the Etruscans and stored in a temple of Mars outside the City. We go in solemn procession and fetch it within the walls, where we pour water on it, singing incantations and sacrificing. Rain always follows – unless there has been some slight mistake in the ritual, as is frequently the case. But Geta had no Dripping Stone with him, so he was completely at a loss. The nomads were accustomed to going without water for days at a time and knew the country perfectly besides. They began to close in on the Roman force; they cut off, killed, stripped, and mutilated a few stragglers whom the heat had driven out of their wits.

Geta had a black orderly who had been born in this very desert but had been sold as a slave to the Moors. He could not remember where the nearest water was, because he had been sold when only a child. But he said to Geta, 'General, why don't you pray to Father Gwa-Gwa!' Geta inquired who this person might be. The man replied that he was the God of the Deserts who gave rain in time of drought. Geta said, 'The Emperor told me to suit my tactics to the country. Tell me how to invoke Father Gwa-Gwa and I shall do so at once.' The orderly told him to take a little pot, bury it up to the neck in the sand and fill it with beer, saying as he did so: 'Father Gwa-Gwa, we offer you beer.' Then the men were to fill their drinking vessels with all the water that they had with them in their water-skins except enough to dip their fingers in and sprinkle on the ground. Then everyone must drink and dance and adore Father Gwa-Gwa, sprinkling the water and drinking every drop in the skins. Geta himself must chant: 'As this water is sprinkled, so let rain fall! We have drunk our last drop, Father. None remains. What would you have us do? Drink beer, Father Gwa-Gwa, and make water for us, your children, or we die!' For beer is a powerful diuretic and these nomads had the same theological notions as the early Greeks who considered that Jove made water when it rained; so that the same word (with a mere difference in gender) is still used in Greek for Heaven and for chamberpot. The nomads considered that their God would be encouraged to make water, in the form of rain, by offering him a drink of beer. The sprinkling of water, like our own lustrations, was to remind him how rain fell, in case he had forgotten.

Geta in desperation called his tottering force together and inquired whether anyone happened to have a little beer with him. And by good luck a party of German auxiliaries had a pint or two hoarded in a water-skin; they had brought it with them in preference to water. Geta made them give it up to him. He then equally distributed all the water that was left, but the beer he reserved for Father Gwa-Gwa. The troops danced and drank the water and sprinkled the necessary drops on the sand, while Geta uttered the prescribed formula of invocation. Father Gwa-Gwa (his name apparently means 'Water') was so pleased and impressed by the honour paid him by this imposing force of perfect strangers that the sky was immediately darkened with rain-clouds and a downpour began which lasted for three days and turned every sandy hollow into a brimming pool of water. The army was saved. The nomads, taking the abundant rain as an undeniable token of Father Gwa-Gwa's favour towards the Romans, came humbly forward with offers of alliance. Geta refused this unless they first delivered up Salabus to him. Salabus was presently brought to the camp in bonds. Presents were exchanged between Geta and the nomads and a treaty made; then Geta marched back without further loss to the mountains, where he caught Salabus's men, who were still holding the pass, in the rear, killing or capturing the whole detachment. The other Moorish forces, seeing their leader brought back to Tangier as a prisoner, surrendered without further fighting. So two or three pints of beer had saved the lives of more than 2,000 Romans and gained Rome a new province. I ordered the dedication of a shrine to Father Gwa-Gwa in the desert beyond the mountains, where he ruled; and Morocco, which I now divided up into two provinces – Western Morocco with its capital at Tangier and Eastern Morocco with its capital at Caesarea – had to furnish it with a yearly tribute of 100 goat-skins of the best beer. I awarded Geta triumphal ornaments and would have asked the Senate to confer on him the hereditary title of Maurus ('of Morocco') had he not exceeded his powers by putting Salabus to death at Tangier without first consulting me. There was no military necessity for this act; he only did it for vainglory.

I mentioned just now the birth of my daughter Octavia. Messalina had come to be much courted by the Senate and People, because it was well known that I had delegated to her most of the duties which fell to me in my capacity as Director of Public Morals. She acted, in theory, only as my adviser, but had, as I have explained, a duplicate seal of mine to ratify documents with; and within certain limits I let her decide what knights or senators to degrade for social offences and whom to appoint to the resulting vacancies. She had now also undertaken the laborious task of deciding on the fitness of all candidates for the Roman Citizenship. The Senate wished to vote her the title of Augusta and made the birth of Octavia the pretext. Much as I loved Messalina, I did not think that she had yet earned this honour: it was something for her to look forward to in middle life. She was as yet only seventeen, whereas my grandmother Livia had earned the title only after her death and my mother in extreme old age. So I refused it to her. But the Alexandrians, without asking my permission – and once the thing was done I could not undo it – struck a coin with my head on the obverse and on the reverse a full-length portrait of Messalina in the dress of the Goddess Demeter, holding in the palm of one hand two figurines representing her little boy and girl, and in the other a sheaf of corn representing fertility. This was a flattering play on the name Messalina – the Latin word *messis* meaning the corn-harvest. She was delighted.

She came to me shyly one evening, peeped up at my face without saying anything, and at last asked, plainly embarrassed, and after one or two false starts: 'Do you love me, dearest husband?'

I assured her that I loved her beyond anyone else in the world.

'And what did you tell me, the other day, were the Three Main Pillars of the Temple of Love?'

'I said that the Temple of True Love was pillared on kindness, frankness, and understanding. Or rather I quoted the philosopher Mnasalcus as having said so.'

'Then will you show me the greatest kindness and understanding that your love for me is capable of showing? *My* love will have to provide only the frankness. I'll come straight to the point. If it's not too hard for you, would you – could you possibly – allow me to sleep in a bedroom apart from you for a little while? It isn't that I don't love you every bit as much as you love me, but now that we have had two children in less than two years of marriage, oughtn't we to wait a little before we risk having a third? It is a very disagreeable thing to be pregnant: I have morning-sickness and heartburn and my digestion goes wrong, and I don't feel I could go through that again just yet. And, to be honest, quite apart from this dread, I somehow feel less passionately towards you than I did. I swear that I love you as much as ever, but now it's rather as my dearest friend and as the father of my children than as my lover. Having children uses up a lot of a woman's emotions, I suppose. I'm not hiding anything from you. You do believe me, don't you?'

'I believe you, and I love you.'

She stroked my face. 'And I'm not like any ordinary woman, am I, whose business is merely to have children and children and children until she wears out? I am your wife – the Emperor's wife – and I help him in his Imperial work, and that should take precedence over everything, shouldn't it? Pregnancy interferes with work terribly.'

I said rather ruefully: 'Of course, my dearest, if you really feel like that, I am not the sort of husband to insist on forcing anything on you. But is it really necessary for us to sleep apart? Couldn't we at least occupy the same bed, for company's sake?'

'O Claudius,' she said, nearly crying, 'it has been difficult enough for me to make up my mind to ask you about this, because I love you so much and don't want to hurt you in the least. Don't make it more difficult. And now that I have frankly told you how I feel, wouldn't it be dreadfully difficult for you if you had violently passionate feelings for me while we were sleeping together and I could not honestly return them? If I repulsed you, that would be as destructive of our love as if I yielded against my will; and I am sure you would feel very remorseful afterwards if anything happened to destroy my love for you. No, can't you see now how much better it would be for us to sleep apart until I feel about you again as I used to do? Suppose, just to distance myself from temptation, I were to move across to my suite in the New Palace? It's more convenient for my work to be over there. I can get up in the morning and go straight to my papers. This lying-in has put me greatly behind-hand with my Citizens' Roll.'

I pleaded: 'How long do you think you will want to be away?'

'We'll see how it works out,' she said, kissing the back of my neck tenderly. 'Oh, how relieved I am that you aren't angry. How long? Oh, I don't know. Does it matter so much? After all, sex is not essential to love if there is any other strong bond between lovers such as common idealistic pursuit of Beauty or Perfection. I do agree with Plato about that. He thought sex positively an obstruction to love.'

'He was talking of homosexual love,' I reminded her, trying not to sound depressed.

'Well, my dear,' she said lightly, 'I do a man's work, the same as you, and so it comes to much the same thing, doesn't it? And as for a common idealism, we have to be very idealistic indeed to get through all this drudgery in the name of attempted political perfection, don't we? Well, is that really settled? Will you really be a dear, dear Claudius, and not insist on my sharing your bed – in a literal sense, I mean? In all other senses I am still your devoted little Messalina, and do remember that it has been very, very painful for me to ask you this.'

I told her that I respected and loved her all the more for her frankness, and of course she must have her way. But that naturally I should be impatient for the time when she felt again for me as she once had done.

'Oh, please don't be impatient,' she cried. 'It makes it so difficult for me. If you were impatient I should feel that I was being unkind to you, and should probably pretend feelings that I didn't have. I may be an exception, but somehow sex doesn't mean much to me. I suspect, though, that many women get bored with it – without ceasing to love their husbands or to want their husbands to love them. But I'll always continue to be suspicious of other women. If you were to have affairs with other women I think I should go mad with jealousy. It isn't that I mind the thought of your sleeping with someone other than me; it's the fear that you might come to love her better than me, not merely regarding her as a pleasant sexual convenience, and then want to divorce me. I mean, if you were to sleep with a pretty housemaid occasionally, or some nice clean woman too low in rank for me to be jealous of, I should be very glad, really delighted, to think that you were having a nice time with her; and if you and I ever slept together afterwards we wouldn't consider it as anything that had come between us. We'd merely think of it as a measure that you had taken for the sake of your health – like a purge or an emetic. I shouldn't expect you even to tell me the woman's name, in fact I'd prefer you not to, so long as you first promised not to have doings with anyone about whom I would have a right to feel jealous. Wasn't that how Livia is said to have felt about Augustus?'

'Yes, in a way. But she never really loved him. She told me so. That made it easier for her to be attentive to him. She used to pick out young women from the slave-market and bring them secretly into his bedroom at night. Syrians, mostly, I believe.'

'Well, you're not asking me to do *that*, are you? I'm human, after all.'

This was how Messalina played, very cleverly and very cruelly, on my blind love for her. She moved over to the New Palace that very evening. And for a long time I said nothing further, hoping that she would come back to me. But she said nothing, only indicating by her tender behaviour that a very fine understanding existed between us. As a great concession she did sometimes consent to sleep with me. It was seven years before I heard so much as a whisper of what went on in her suite at the New Palace, when the old cuckold-husband was away at his work or safely snoring in his bed at the Old Palace.

And this brings me to the story of the fate of Appius Silanus, an ex-Consul who had been Governor of Spain since Caligula's reign. It may be recalled that it was marriage with this Silanus that Livia had made the bribe for Aemilia's betrayal of Postumus: Aemilia was Augustus's great-granddaughter, whom as a boy I had nearly married. Through Aemilia, Silanus had become the father of three boys and two girls, now all grown up. Except for Agrippinilla and her little son, they were the only surviving descendants of Augustus. Tiberius had regarded Silanus as a danger because of his illustrious connexions and had arranged to have him accused of treason in company with several other senators, including Vinicianus. However, the evidence against them broke down and they escaped with nothing worse than a bad fright. At the age of sixteen Silanus had been the handsomest youth in Rome; at the age of fifty-six he was still remarkably fine-looking, his hair only slightly grizzled, his eyes bright, and his step and carriage like those of a man in the prime of life. He was now a widower, Aemilia having died of a cancer. One of his daughters, Calvina, had married a son of Vitellius's.

One day, shortly before little Octavia's birth, Messalina had said to me: 'The man whom we really need at Rome is Appius Silanus. I wish you could recall him and keep him permanently at the Palace as an adviser. He's remarkably intelligent and quite wasted in Spain.'

I said: 'Yes, that isn't a bad plan: I admire Silanus, and he's a man of great influence in the Senate. But how can we persuade him to come and live with us? We can't very well plant him in the Palace as we might plant a new secretary or accountant. There must be some sort of honourable pretext for his presence.'

'I've thought of that, and I've got a brilliant idea. Why not connect him with the family by marrying him to my mother? She'd like to marry again: she's only thirty-three. And she's your mother-in-law, so it would be a great honour for Silanus. Do say that you think it a good idea.'

'Well, if you can make it right with your mother. ...'

'I have already asked her about it. She says that she'd be charmed.'

So Silanus came to Rome and I married him to Domitia Lepida, Messalina's mother, and assigned them a suite in the New Palace, next to Messalina's. I soon noticed that Silanus was very ill at ease with me. He readily did any services that I asked him to do, such as paying surprise visits to the lower courts on my behalf to see that justice was being properly done, or inspecting and reporting upon housing conditions in the poorer quarters of the City, or attending the public auction of property confiscated by the State, to see that the auctioneers did not play any tricks; but he seemed unable to look me in the face and always avoided any intimacy with me. I was rather offended. But after all I could not have been expected to guess the truth: which was that Messalina had only asked me to send for Silanus from Spain because she had been in love with him as a girl, and that she had married him to her mother merely as a means of having easy access to him, and that ever since his arrival she had been pressing him to sleep with her. To think of it! Her own step-father and a man five years my senior, with a granddaughter not much younger than Messalina herself! Naturally, his manner to me was queer, since Messalina had told him that she had moved over to the New Palace at my orders, and that I had myself suggested that she should become his mistress! She explained that I wanted to keep her amused while I had a silly affair with that Julia, once the wife of my nephew Nero, whom we used to call Helen, to distinguish her from the other Julias, but now called Heluo because she was such a glutton. Apparently Silanus believed this story, but he firmly refused to sleep with his daughter-in-law, in spite of her beauty, even at the Emperor's suggestion: he said that he was of an amorous but not an impious nature.

'I'll give you ten days to make up your mind about it,' Messalina threatened. 'If you refuse me at the end of that time I shall tell Claudius. You know how vain he has become since they made him Emperor. He wouldn't like to hear that you'd scorned his wife. He'd certainly kill you, wouldn't he, Mother?'

Domitia Lepida was entirely under Messalina's thumb, and bore her out. Silanus believed them. His experiences under Tiberius and Caligula had made him a secret anti-monarchist, though he was not a man who mixed much in politics. He fully believed that nobody could now find himself at the head of the State without giving way very soon to tyranny, cruelty, and lust. By the ninth day he had not yet yielded to Messalina, but had worked himself up into such a state of nervous desperation that he had, it appears, fully resolved to kill me.

My secretary Narcissus was a witness of Silanus's distracted state that evening; he overtook him in a corridor of the Palace muttering unintelligibly to himself, 'Cassius Chaerea – Old Cassius. Do so – but not alone.' Narcissus was busy at the moment working out something in his head, and heard the words but did not consider them fully. They stuck in his mind and, as often happens in cases of this sort, when he went to bed that night without having thought about them again, they came into his dream and enlarged themselves into a terrifying picture of Cassius Chaerea handing Silanus his bloody sword and shouting 'Do so! Strike! Strike again. Old Cassius is with you! Death to the tyrant!' and of Silanus then rushing at me and hacking me to pieces. The dream was so vivid and so violent that Narcissus leaped out of bed and came hurrying to my bedroom to tell me about it.

The shock of being suddenly awakened just before dawn and told in a terrified voice about this nightmare – I was sleeping alone and not sleeping very well either – put me into a cold sweat of horror. I called for lights – hundreds of lights – and sent at once for Messalina. She was terrified too at this hasty summons; afraid that I had found her out, I suppose. It must have been a great relief to her when I merely told her of Narcissus's dream. She shuddered. 'No! Did he really dream that? O Heavens! That's the same terrible nightmare that I've been trying to remember every morning for the last seven days! I always wake up screaming, but I can't ever remember what I was screaming about. It must be true. Of course it must. It's a divine warning. Send for Silanus at once and make him confess.'

She ran from the room to give the message to one of her freedmen. I know now that she told him to say: 'The ten days are over. The Emperor now orders you to his presence immediately and asks for an explanation.' The freedman did not understand what ten days were meant, but delivered the message, arousing Silanus from his sleep. Silanus cried: 'Come? Indeed I will!' He dressed hurriedly, thrusting something into the fold of his robe and rushed stumbling and wild-eyed ahead of the messenger to my rooms. The freedman was alert. He stopped a slave-boy. 'Run like lightning to the Council Chamber and tell the guards there to search Appius Silanus when he arrives.' The Guards found the hidden dagger and arrested him. I tried him then and there. It was, of course, impossible for him to explain the dagger, but I asked him whether he had anything to say in his defence. His only defence was to rage and splutter inarticulately, cursing me for a monster and Messalina for a she-wolf. When I asked him why he had wished to kill me he would only answer: 'Give me back my dagger, tyrant. Let me use it on my own breast!' I sentenced him to execution. He died, poor fellow, because he did not have the sense to speak out.

Chapter 14

IT was the execution of Silanus that encouraged Vinicianus to make his insurrection. When I reported in the Senate, the same day, that Silanus had intended to kill me but that my guards had frustrated his designs and that I had already executed him, a groan of astonishment rose, followed by a dismayed whisper, instantly smothered. This was the first execution of a senator since I had assumed the monarchy, and nobody believed Silanus capable of trying to murder me. It was felt that at last I was showing myself in my true colours and that a new reign of terror was about to start. I had recalled Silanus from Spain under the pretext of doing him a great honour but had really intended all the time to murder him. Just like Caligula! Naturally, I was quite unaware of all this feeling and even ventured on a little joke, saying how grateful I was to Narcissus for being so vigilant for my safety even in his sleep. 'But for that dream I should not have sent for Silanus and consequently he would not have been frightened into giving himself away: he would have made his attempt on my life in a more considered manner. He had many opportunities for assassinating me, having lately been taken so deeply into my confidence that I spared him the indignity of being searched for weapons.' The applause was hollow.

Vinicianus told his friends afterwards: 'So the noble Appius Silanus is executed just because the Emperor's Greek freedman has a bad dream. Are we to allow a creature as weak-minded as this pumpkin-headed Clau-Clau-Claudius to rule over us? What do you say?'

They agreed that a strong, experienced Emperor was needed, not a makeshift like myself, who knew nothing, learned nothing, and acted in a perfectly crazy way half the time. They began reminding each other of my most remarkable errors or eccentricities. Apart from those that I have already mentioned, they brought up, for instance, a decision that I had made a few days before when reviewing the jury-lists. It must here be explained that there were about 4,000 qualified jurymen at Rome and that these were obliged to attend trials when called upon, under penalty of a heavy fine: jury-service was extremely laborious and extremely unpopular. The jury-lists were first prepared by a first-rank magistrate, and this year more than half the men named in them came forward as usual to excuse themselves on one account or another; but in nineteen cases out of twenty their appeals were dismissed. The magistrate handed me the final lists for my scrutiny with a mark against the names of those whose appeal for exemption had been dismissed. I happened to notice that among the men who had *willingly* presented themselves for jury-service was one whom I knew to be the father of seven children. Under a law of Augustus's he was exempt for the rest of his life; yet he had not pleaded for exemption or mentioned the size of his family. I told the magistrate: 'Strike this man's name off. He's a father of seven.' He protested: 'But, Caesar, he has made no attempt to excuse himself.' 'Exactly,' I said, 'he wants to be a juryman. Strike him off.' I meant, of course, that the fellow was concealing his immunity from what every honest man considered a very thankless and disagreeable duty and that he therefore was almost certain to have crooked intentions. Crooked jurymen could pick up a lot of money by bribes, for it was a commonplace that one interested juryman could sway the opinions of a whole bunch of uninterested ones; and the majority verdict decided a case. But the magistrate was a fool and simply reported my words, 'He wants to be a juryman; strike him off,' as a characteristic example of my fatuity.

Vinicianus and the other malcontents spoke, too, of my extraordinary decision in insisting that every man who appeared before me in court should give the usual preliminary account of his parentage, connexions, marriage, career, financial condition, present occupation, and so on – with his own mouth, as best he could, instead of calling upon some patron or lawyer to do it for him. My reasons for this decision should have been obvious: one learns more about a man from ten words which he speaks himself on his own behalf than from a ten-hour eulogy by a friend. It does not matter so much what he says in those ten words: what really counts is the way in which he says them. I had found that to have some knowledge before a case starts as to whether a man is slow-witted or glib, boastful or modest, self-possessed or timorous, capable or muddle-headed, is a great help to my understanding of what follows. But to Vinicianus and his friends I seemed to be doing the accused a great injustice by robbing him of the patronage or eloquence on which he counted.

Strangely enough, what shocked them most of all my Imperial misdemeanours was my action in the case of the silver chariot.

This is the story. As I happened to pass through the Goldsmiths' Street one day I saw about 500 citizens gathered around a shop. I wondered what the attraction could be and told my yeomen to move the crowd on, because it was blocking the traffic. They did so, and I found that the shop was exhibiting a chariot entirely plated with silver, except for the rim of the body, which was gold. The axle was silver-plated too, ending in golden dog-heads with amethyst eyes; the spokes were ebony carved in the form of negroes with silver girdles, and even the lynchpins were of gold. The silver sides of the body were embossed with scenes illustrating a chariot-race in the Circus and the felloes of the wheels were decorated with a golden inlay of vine-leaves. The extremities of the yoke and pole – silver-plated too – were golden cupids' faces with turquoise eyes. This wonderful vehicle was for sale at 100,000 gold pieces. Someone whispered to me that it had been commissioned by a rich senator and already paid for, but that he had asked the goldsmiths to expose it for sale for a few days (at a far higher price than he had actually paid) because he wished publicly to advertise its costliness before taking possession of it. This seemed likely: the goldsmiths themselves would not have built so expensive a thing on the mere chance of its finding a millionaire buyer. In my capacity as Director of Public Morals I had a perfect right to do what I then did. I made the goldsmiths, in my presence, strip off the gold and silver with a hammer and chisel and sell it by weight to the competent Treasury official, whom I sent for, to be melted down into coin. There were loud cries of protest, but I silenced them by saying: 'A car of this weight will damage the public pavements: we must lighten it a bit.' I had a pretty shrewd notion who the owner was: it was Asiaticus, who now felt it safe to make no secret of his immense riches, though he had successfully concealed them from Caligula's greedy eyes by parcelling them out into hundreds of small deposits which he left with scores of different bankers in the names of his freedmen or friends. His present ostentation was a direct incitement to popular disorder. The extraordinary additions he had made to the Gardens of Lucullus, which he had now bought! They had been considered only second in beauty to the Gardens of Sallust; but Asiaticus boasted, 'When I have finished with the Gardens of Lucullus, the Gardens of Sallust will seem by contrast to be little better than a few acres of waste land.' He put in such fruits, flowers, fountains, and fishpools as Rome had never seen before. It occurred to me that when food was scarce in the City nobody would like to see a jolly senator with a big belly driving about in a silver car with golden axle-ends and lynchpins. A man wouldn't be human if he didn't at least feel a desire to pull out the lynchpins. I still think that I did right in this instance. But the destruction by me of a work of art – the goldsmith was a famous craftsman, the same who had been entrusted by Caligula with the modelling and casting of his golden statue – was regarded as a wanton act of barbarism and caused far more resentment among these friends of Vinicianus than if I had hauled a dozen common citizens out of the crowd and had them knocked to pieces with hammer and chisel and sold as meat to the butchers. Asiaticus himself did not express any irritation, and was indeed careful not to acknowledge ownership of the chariot, but Vinicianus made the most of my crime. He said: 'He'll be pulling our gowns off our backs next and unravelling the wool to sell to the weavers again. The man's insane. We must get rid of him.'

Vinicius was not in the party of malcontents either. He guessed that he was under my suspicion for having proposed himself as Emperor in opposition to me, and was now very careful not to offend me in the slightest particular. Besides, he must have known that it was no use trying to get rid of me yet. I was still extremely popular with the Guards, and took so many precautions against assassination – a constant escort of soldiers, careful searchings for weapons, a taster against poison at every meal – and my household was so faithful and alert, besides, that a man would have had to be extremely lucky as well as ingenious to take my life and escape with his own. There had been two unsuccessful attempts by individuals recently, both made by knights whom I had threatened to degrade from the order for sexual offences. One waited at the gate of Pompey's Theatre to murder me as I came out. That was not a bad idea, but one of my soldiers saw him snatch the hollow top off a stick that he was carrying, showing it to be really a short javelin; he rushed at him and struck him on the head just as he was about to hurl the thing at me. The other attempt was made in the Temple of Mars where I was sacrificing. The weapon on this occasion was a hunting-knife, but the man was immediately disarmed by the bystanders.

The only way to get rid of me, in fact, was by force of arms, and where were troops to be found to oppose me? Vinicianus thought that he knew the answer to the question. He would get help from Scribonianus. This Scribonianus was a first cousin of little Camilla, whom my grandmother Livia had poisoned long ago on the day that she and I were to have been betrothed. When I was in Carthage, the year before my brother died, Scribonianus had been very insulting to me because he had just distinguished himself in a battle against Tacfarinas, in which I had been unable to take part; and his father, Furius Camillus, who was Governor of the province of Africa, had thereupon made him beg my pardon in public. He had been forced to obey, because in Rome a father's word is law, but he had never forgiven me and on two or three occasions since then had behaved very unpleasantly to me. Under Caligula he had been foremost among my tormentors at the Palace: nearly all the booby-traps and similar practical jokes that I had been plagued with were of his contrivance. So you may imagine that when Scribonianus, whom Caligula had recently sent to command the Roman forces in Dalmatia, heard of my election as Emperor he was not only jealous and disgusted but alarmed for his own safety. He began to wonder whether, when his term of command expired and he had to return to Rome, I was the sort of man to forgive him his insults; and if so, whether my forgiveness might not be less easy to bear even than my anger. He decided to pay me the usual respects due to a Commander-in-Chief but to do everything possible to win the personal loyalty of the forces under his command: when the time came to recall him he would write to me what Gaetulicus had once written to the Emperor Tiberius from the Rhine: 'You can count on my loyalty *so long as I retain my command.*'

Vinicianus was a personal friend of Scribonianus's and kept him informed by letter of what was happening at Rome. When Silanus was executed Vinicianus wrote:

I have bad news for you, my dear Scribonianus. Claudius, after disgracing the dignity of Rome by his stupidity, ignorance, and clowning, and by his complete dependence on the advice of a pack of Greek freedmen, a spendthrift rogue of a Jew, Vitellius his fellow boozer, and Messalina his lustful and ambitious girl-wife, has committed his first important murder. Poor Appius Silanus was recalled from his command in Spain, kept hanging about the Palace in suspense for a month or two and then suddenly hauled out of bed early one morning and summarily executed. Claudius came into the House yesterday and actually joked about it. All the right-minded men in the City agree that Silanus must be avenged, and consider that if a suitable leader appeared the whole nation would welcome him with open arms. Claudius has turned things completely upside-down and one almost wishes Caligula back again. Unfortunately he has the Guards to rely upon at present, and without troops we can do nothing. Assassination has been unsuccessfully tried: he is such a coward that one can't bring so much as a bodkin into the Palace without having it removed by searchers in the vestibule. We look to you to come to our rescue. If you were to march on Rome with the Seventh and Eleventh Regiments and whatever local forces you are able to muster, all our troubles would be over. Promise the Guards a bounty as big as the one that Claudius gave them and they will desert to you at once. They despise him as a meddling civilian and he hasn't given them more than a single gold piece a man, to drink his health with on his birthday, since his original act of enforced generosity. As soon as you land in Italy – the transport difficulty can easily be got over – we shall join you with a volunteer force and provide you with all the money you may need. Don't hesitate. Now is the time before matters get any worse. You can reach Rome before Claudius is able to send for reinforcements from the Rhine; and anyhow I don't think that he would get any if he did send for them. The Germans are said to be planning their revenge, and Galba isn't the man to leave his post on the Rhine when the Chattians are on the move. And Gabinius won't go if Galba stays: they always work in partnership. So the revolution promises to be bloodless. I do not wish to appeal to you by warnings as to your own personal safety, for I know that you put the honour of Rome before self-interest. But it is as well for you to know that Claudius a few nights ago told my cousin Vinicius: 'I don't forget old scores. When a certain Governor returns to Rome from his command in the Balkans, mark my words, he's going to pay with his blood for the tricks he once played me.' One thing more. Don't have any compunction about leaving the province undefended. The regiments need not be away long, and why not take a large number of hostages with you to discourage the provincials from rising in your absence? It's not as though Dalmatia were a frontier province, either. Let me know at once if you are with us, and ready to earn as glorious a name as your great ancestor Camillus, becoming the second saviour of Rome.

Scribonianus decided to take the risk. He wrote to Vinicianus that he would need 150 transports from Italy besides what vessels he could commandeer in Dalmatian ports. He would also need 1,000,000 gold pieces in bounty money to persuade the two regular regiments – each 5,000 strong – and the 20,000 Dalmatian levies whom he would call to the colours, to break their allegiance to me. So Vinicianus and his fellow conspirators – six senators and seven knights, and ten knights and six senators whom I had degraded from their Orders – now left Rome unobtrusively under the pretence of visiting their country estates. The first news that I had of the rebellion was a letter which reached me from Scribonianus, addressed in the most insolent terms: calling me an impostor and an imbecile and ordering me to lay down all my offices immediately and retire to civil life. He told me that I had proved my lamentable incapacity for the task that had been entrusted to me by the Senate in a moment of confusion and aberration, and that he, Scribonianus, now repudiated his allegiance and was on the point of sailing to Italy with a force of 30,000 men to restore order and decent government to Rome and the rest of the world. If I resigned my monarchy, on receipt of this notice, my life would be spared and the same amnesty granted me and mine as I had been wisely persuaded to grant my political opponents on my accession.

The first thing that I did on reading this letter was to burst out laughing. Good heavens, what a delightful experience that would be, to retire into private life again and live quietly and easily under an orderly government with Messalina and my books and my children! Certainly, of course, and by all means, I would resign if Scribonianus thought himself capable of governing better than I. And to be able to loll back in my chair, so to speak, and watch someone else struggling with the impossible task which I had never wished to undertake and which had proved more burdensome, anxious, and thankless than I can easily convey in words! It was as though King Agamemnon had leaped forward when Laocöon and his two children were struggling with the two great serpents sent by an angry God to destroy them and had shouted out: 'Here, leave those splendid creatures for me to deal with. You aren't worthy to fight with them. Leave them alone, I say, or it will be the worse for you.' But could I trust Scribonianus to keep his word about the amnesty and spare my life and that of my family? And would his government be as orderly and decent as he expected it to be? And what would the Guards have to say on the matter? And was Scribonianus as popular at Rome as he seemed to think? Would the serpents, in fact, consent to leave Laocöon and his children and coil, instead, about the body of this Agamemnon?

I hurriedly convened the Senate and addressed them: 'My Lords, before reading you this letter, I must tell you that I am most ready to agree to the demands contained in it and should welcome the rest and security that it somewhat severely promises me. The only reason, indeed, that would induce me to decline the propositions made by this Furius Camillus Scribonianus would be a strong feeling on your part that the country would be worse rather than better off if I did so. I admit that until last year I was shamefully ignorant of the arts of government and of legal and military procedure; and though I am daily learning, my education is still in arrears. There are no men of my age and rank who could not teach me plenty of technical commonplaces with which I am totally unfamiliar. But that is the fault of my original bad health and the poor opinion that my brilliant – and now in part deified – family had of my wits when I was a boy; it has not been due to any shirking of my duties to our fatherland. And even when I did not expect ever to be raised to responsible office I improved myself by private study with, I think you will grant, commendable application. I take the liberty of suggesting that my family were mistaken: that I never was an imbecile. I won a verbal testimony to that effect from the God Augustus shortly after his visit to Postumus Agrippa on his island, and from the noble Asinius Pollio in the Apollo Library three days before his death – who however advised me to assume a mask of stupidity, like the first Brutus, as a protection against certain persons who might wish to remove me if I showed too great intelligence. My wife Urgulanilla, too, whom I divorced for her sullen temper, unfaithfulness, and general brutality, took the trouble to record in her will – I can show it you if you wish – her conviction that I was no fool. The Goddess Livia Augusta's last words to me on her death-bed, or perhaps, I should say "shortly before her Apotheosis", were: "To think that I ever called you a fool". I admit that my sister Livilla, my mother Antonia Augusta, my nephew the late Emperor Gaius, and my uncle Tiberius, his predecessor, never revised their ill opinion of me; and that the two last-named recorded the same in official letters to this House. My uncle Tiberius refused me a seat among you, on the ground that no speech that I could make could be anything but a trial of your patience and a waste of your time. My nephew Gaius Caligula did allow me a seat, because I was his uncle and he wished to seem magnanimous. But he ruled that I should speak last of all in any debate, and said in a speech which, if you do not remember it, you will find recorded in the archives, that if any member wished to ease himself during any session would he please in future have the good manners to contain himself and not distract attention by running out in the middle of an important speech – his own, for example – but wait until the signal for a general lapse of attention was given by the Consul's calling on Tiberius Claudius Drusus Nero Germanicus (as I was then known) to give his opinion on the matter in hand. Well, you took his advice, I remember, not supposing that I had any feelings to wound, or thinking that they had been so often wounded before that I must by now be armoured all over like Tiberius's wingless dragon; or perhaps agreeing with my nephew that I was indeed an imbecile. However, the considered opinions to the contrary of the two Gods, Augustus and Livia – for which, however, you have to take my word because they are nowhere recorded in writing – surely outweigh those of any number of mere mortals? I should be inclined to hold it blasphemous for anyone here to contradict them. Not that blasphemy is a criminal offence nowadays – we have changed that; but it is at least bad manners and perhaps dangerous if the Gods happen to overhear. Besides, my nephew and uncle both met violent deaths and were not mourned, and their speeches and letters are no longer quoted with the respect with which the God Augustus's speeches and letters are quoted, and much of their legislation has lapsed. They were lions in their day, my Lords, but now they are dead and in the words of the Jewish proverb that the God Augustus was fond of quoting – he borrowed it from King Herod the Great of Judaea, for whose wit he had as much respect as I have for the wit of King Herod Agrippa, his grandson – *A live dog is worth more than a dead lion.* I am not a lion – you know that. But I consider that I have not made so bad a watch-dog; and to say that I have grossly mismanaged national affairs or that I am an imbecile is, I think, an insult to you rather than to me, because you pressed the monarchy on me and have on many occasions since congratulated me on my successes and rewarded me with many great honours, including that of Father of the Country. If the father is an imbecile, surely his children will have inherited the taint?'

I then read Scribonianus's letter and glanced around inquiringly. Everyone had been looking extremely uncomfortable during my speech, though nobody ventured to do other than applaud, protest, or show surprise at the points where this seemed to be expected. You, my readers, will no doubt be thinking what no doubt they all were thinking: 'What a curious speech to make on the eve of a rebellion! Why should Claudius have insisted on raking up a matter which we might be expected to have forgotten about altogether – his supposed imbecility? Why did he find it necessary to remind us that this family once regarded him as mentally incapable, and to read the passages of Scribonianus's letter referring to this, and why did he lower himself by arguing about it?' Yes, it looked very suspicious, as though I really knew that I was an imbecile and was trying to persuade myself that I wasn't. But I knew just what I was doing. I was, in fact, being rather clever. I had in the first place spoken extremely frankly, and unexpected frankness about oneself is never unacceptable. I was reminding the Senate what sort of a man I was – honest and devoted; not clever, but not self-seeking – and what sort of men they themselves were – clever but self-seeking, and neither honest nor devoted nor even courageous. Cassius Chaerea had warned them not to hand over the monarchy to an idiot and they had disregarded his advice for fear of the Guards – yet things on the whole had turned out very well, so far. Prosperity was returning to Rome, justice was being evenly dispensed, the people were contented, our armies were victorious abroad, I was not playing the tyrant in any extravagant way; and, as I told them in the discussion that followed, I had perhaps travelled farther, hobbling on my lame leg, than most men would have travelled on a sound pair; because, only too conscious of my disability, I allowed myself no halts or slackening of pace. On the other hand, I wished to show them by my speech that they were perfectly free to dismiss me if they pleased; and my undignified frankness about my own shortcomings should encourage them not to be harsh or revengeful when I was a private citizen once more.

Several loyal speeches were made, all in rather guarded terms, for fear of the vengeance of Scribonianus, should he force me to resign. Only Vinicius spoke out strongly:

'My Lords, I think that many of us must be feeling keenly the reproach that the Father of the Country has been, however gently, heaping on us. I confess that I am heartily ashamed that I misjudged him before his accession and that I thought him unfitted for the offices which he has since so nobly filled. It is incredible to me now that his mental powers were ever underrated by any of us, and the only explanation that I can offer is that he deceived us, first by his great modesty and next by his deliberate self-depreciation in the reign of the late Emperor. You know the proverb "No man cries 'Stinking Fish'." That proverb was discredited under Caligula, when no wise man with fish in his basket would cry it as anything but stinking, for fear Caligula should become greedy or jealous. Valerius Asiaticus concealed his wealth, Tiberius Claudius concealed his wit; I had nothing to conceal except my disgust of tyranny, but I concealed that until the time came for action. Yes, we all cried "Stinking fish". Caligula is dead now, and under Claudius frankness has come into its own. I shall be frank. My cousin Vinicianus spoke violently against Claudius lately in my presence and suggested his deposition. I reproached him angrily but did not report the matter to the House, because there is no treason-law now in force, and, after all, he is my cousin. Free speech must be indulged, especially in the case of kinsmen. Vinicianus is not here to-night. He has left the City. I fear that he has gone to join Scribonianus. Six of his intimate friends are also absent, I notice. They must have gone with him. Yet what are seven discontented men – seven against five hundred? A negligible minority. And is theirs a genuine discontent or is it personal ambition?

'I condemn my cousin's action on three counts: the first, that he is ungrateful; the second, that he is disloyal; the third, that he is foolish. His ingratitude: the Father of the Country freely forgave him for supporting me as a candidate for the monarchy and has shown great tolerance since of his impertinent and obstructive speeches in this House. His disloyalty: he engaged himself by an oath to obey Tiberius Claudius Caesar as the Head of the State. A breach of this oath could only be excused in the unlikely event of Caesar flagrantly breaking his oath to rule justly, with respect for the common good; Caesar has not broken his oath. Disloyalty to Caesar is therefore impiety to the Gods by whom Vinicianus swore, and enmity to the State, which is more content than ever before to be ruled by Caesar. His folly: though it is possible that Scribonianus may persuade a few thousand of his troops by lies and bribes to invade Italy and may even win a few military successes, does any member of this honourable House really believe that he is destined to be our Emperor? Does anyone believe that the Guards, our chief bulwark, will secede to him? The Guards are not fools: they know when they are well off. The Senate and People are not fools either: they know that under Claudius they are enjoying a liberty and prosperity consistently denied them by his immediate predecessors. Scribonianus cannot impose himself on the City except by promising to redress existing wrongs, and it will puzzle him to find any wrongs to redress. As I see the case, my Lords, this promised revolt is actuated by personal jealousy and personal ambition. We are now asked not merely to exchange an Emperor who has proved himself in every way worthy of our admiration and obedience for one of whose capacities we know little and whose intentions we suspect, but to run the risk of a bloody Civil War. For supposing that Caesar were persuaded to resign, would the armies necessarily acknowledge Scribonianus as their commander? There are several men of rank far more capable of undertaking the monarchy than Scribonianus. What is there to prevent some other corps-commander with four regular regiments at his back, instead of Scribonianus's two, from setting himself up as a rival Emperor and marching on Rome? And even if Scribonianus's attempt were to succeed, which I regard as most unlikely, what of Vinicianus? Would he be content to bow the knee to the haughty Scribonianus? Has he not perhaps offered his support only on the understanding that the Empire shall be shared between them? And if so, may we not expect another death-duel to be fought, as once between Pompey and the God Julius Caesar, and again between Mark Antony and the God Augustus? No, my Lords. This is a case where our loyalty, our gratitude, and our interest go hand in hand. We must loyally support Tiberius Claudius Caesar if we wish to earn the thanks of the country, the approval of the Gods, and our own self-congratulations later when Vinicianus and Scribonianus have met the traitors' deaths that they so richly deserve.'

Then Rufrius spoke. 'I regard it as unfortunate that the possibility of the Guards' disloyalty has been so much as mentioned in this House. As their Commander I repudiate the notion that even a single man will forget his duty to the Emperor. You must recall, my Lords, that it was the Guards who first called upon Tiberius Claudius Caesar, now the Father of the Country, to undertake the supreme command of the Army, and that this House was for a time unwilling to confirm their choice. It therefore ill befits a senator to suggest that the Guards will be disloyal. No, as they were the first to acclaim Tiberius Claudius Caesar Emperor, so they will be the last to desert his cause. And if news reaches the Camp that the Senate has decided to offer the supreme command to any other person – in that case, my Lords, I advise you immediately on reaching the decision either to fortify this edifice as best you can with barricades of benches and piles of cobble-stones, or to adjourn *sine die* and scatter in all directions.'

So I was given a unanimous vote of confidence and the Senate authorized me to write to Scribonianus, informing him that he was suspended from his command and must return to Rome forthwith to explain himself. But Scribonianus never received my letter. He was already dead.

I shall tell you what had happened. Having succeeded, as he thought, in making himself very popular with his troops by relaxation of discipline, plenty of free entertainments and a wine-ration increased at his own expense, he had paraded the Seventh and Eleventh Regiments together in the local amphitheatre and told them that his life was in danger. He read them Vinicianus's letter, or most of it, and asked them whether they would stand by him in his attempt to deliver Rome from a tyranny which seemed to be rapidly becoming as capricious and cruel as that of Caligula. 'The Republic must be restored,' he shouted. 'Only under the Republic has true liberty ever been enjoyed.' He sowed with the sack, as the saying is, and some of the seed seemed to sprout at once. The common soldiers smelt money in his tones: they liked money, and it seemed most unjust that so generous a commander should be sacrificed to my anger or jealousy. They cheered him loudly, and also cheered Vinicianus, who had once commanded the Eleventh Regiment; and swore to follow them both, if need be, to the ends of the earth. Scribonianus promised them ten gold pieces each, on the spot, a further forty each on arrival in Italy, and a further 100 each on the day that they marched victoriously into Rome. He paid out the ten gold pieces and sent them back to camp, ordering them to hold themselves in readiness for the coming campaign. The call would come as soon as the transports arrived from Italy and the native levies were under arms. But Scribonianus had made a great mistake in underrating the loyalty and intelligence of his men. True, they could be easily worked up into a state of temporary indignation on his behalf and were not above accepting gifts in coin while in that mood; but an overt breach of their soldiers' oath was a different matter. That wasn't so easily bought. They would follow him to the ends of the earth; but not to Rome, its centre. It would take more than ten gold pieces a man to persuade them to embark for Italy, with a promise of forty more on landing. To leave their province and invade Italy was to make rebellion, and the punishment for unsuccessful rebellion was death – death in battle, or death under the executioner's sword – perhaps even death by flogging or crucifixion if the Emperor felt like making an example of them.

A meeting of officers was called to decide whether to follow

Scribonianus or not. Some sympathy was expressed for him, but no great desire to resort to rebellion. In any case nobody wanted the Republic to be restored. Scribonianus had told them that he counted on their support, and hinted that he would give them over to the just fury of the common soldiers if they refused to join him in so glorious a cause as the restoration of ancient Roman liberties. They decided to play for time. They sent him a deputation informing him that they were not yet agreed among themselves, but would let him know of their common decision – if he would forgive them their conscientious hesitations – on the day that the expedition sailed. Scribonianus told them to please themselves – he had plenty of capable men to put in their places – but warned them that if they declined to join him they must be prepared to die for their obstinacy. More important than this meeting of officers, there was also held a secret meeting of standard-bearers, sergeants, and corporals, all men of over twelve years' service and most of them married to Dalmatian women, because all their service had been done here: a Roman legion was almost never shifted from one province to another. The Seventh and Eleventh, in fact, looked on Dalmatia as their permanent home and had no interests or ideas beyond making themselves as comfortable as possible there and defending their possessions.

The Eagle-bearer of the Seventh addressed the meeting: 'Lads, you don't really intend to follow the General to Italy, do you? It looks like a very foolish adventure to me, quite apart from the matter of regimental honour. We've sworn allegiance to Tiberius Claudius Caesar, haven't we? He's proved himself a decent man, hasn't he? He may have a down on old Scribonianus, but who knows on which side the right lies? Old Scribonianus can have *his* downs, we've all noticed. Why not leave the two of them to settle their own differences? I'm ready to fight Germans, Moors, Parthians, Jews, Britons, Arabians, Chinese – send me where you like – that's my job as an enlisted man. But I'm not going to do any fighting in Italy against the Guards Division. The Emperor's very popular with them, I'm told, and besides it's ridiculous in my opinion to think of us and them fighting each other. The General ought never to have asked us. Personally, I haven't spent that gift of his, and I don't intend to do so. My vote is that we call the whole business off.'

Everyone agreed. But the young soldiers and the hard cases – old soldiers with bad characters – had grown so excited now with the hope of easy money and plenty of loot that the question before the meeting was how to call the rebellion off without putting themselves into a false position. Someone had a sensible idea. A mutiny among these very regiments thirty years before had been quelled suddenly by an ominous sign from Heaven – an eclipse, followed by torrential rain: why not now provide another ominous sign to discourage the rebellion? So they decided on a suitable one.

Five days later the order came from Scribonianus for the regiments to march down to the port fully armed, rationed, and equipped, prepared to embark at once for Italy. The Eagle-bearers of the Seventh and Eleventh simultaneously reported to their commanders that they had been unable that morning to dress the Eagles in the customary way with laurel garlands. The garlands had fallen off as soon as they tied them on, and immediately withered away! Then the standard-bearers also came running in pretended consternation to report another miracle: the standards had refused to be pulled out from the earth into which they had been stuck! The officers were only too pleased to hear of these dreadful omens and reported them to Scribonianus. Scribonianus flew into a rage and came rushing into the camp of the Eleventh. 'You say that the standards refuse to be moved, you liars? It's because you're a pack of cowards and haven't the courage of dogs. Look! Who says that this standard can't be moved?' He went up to the nearest standard and heaved at it. He heaved and tugged and strained until the veins stood out on his forehead like cords: but he couldn't so much as budge the thing. As a matter of fact, it had been secretly planted in concrete on the night of the meeting, and so had all the other standards, with earth heaped above. The concrete had set like rock.

Scribonianus saw that all was lost. He shook his fist at Heaven and running down to the port jumped aboard his private yacht and told his crew to cast off and stand out to sea at once. He was making for Italy, intending, I suppose, to warn Vinicianus of his failure. But instead the crew put him ashore at the island of Lissa, near Corfu, suspecting that his plans had gone astray and not wishing to have anything more to do with him. One freedman alone remained with him and was present when he committed suicide. Vinicianus also killed himself when the news reached him a day or two later; so did most of his fellow-rebels. The revolt was over.

I shall not pretend that I did not spend an anxious ten days between addressing the Senate and hearing the happy news of Scribonianus's failure. I grew very excitable, and if it had not been for Xenophon's exertions I should probably have had a serious return of my old nervous trouble. But he dosed me with this and that and kept me well massaged and encouraged me, in his dry way, to have no fears for the future; and so steered me through without serious damage to my health. A verse of Homer's stuck in my head and I kept repeating it to everyone I met:

> Do thou resist that man with all thy might
> Who, unprovoked, provokes thee to a fight.

I even gave it to Rufrius one day as a watchword. Messalina teased me about it, but I had an answer ready: 'It stuck in Homer's mind too. He used it again and again. Once in the *Iliad* and two or three times in the *Odyssey*.' Messalina's devotion was a great comfort, and so were the loyal shouts of the citizens and the soldiers whenever I appeared in public, and the confidence that the Senate seemed to feel in me.

I rewarded the Seventh and Eleventh by asking the Senate to rename them 'The Loyal Claudian Regiments', and on Messalina's insistence (Vitellius agreed with her that it was no occasion for an amnesty) I put to death the principal rebels who survived. I did not, however, execute them summarily, as I had executed Silanus, but gave them each in turn a formal trial. The procedure that I adopted was to read the charge sitting on a chair of state with the Consuls standing one on either side of me. I would then retire to my ordinary seat and the Consuls would call for their own chairs of state and conduct the trial as judges. I happened to be suffering from a severe cold, which reduced my voice, never very strong, to a whisper; but I had Narcissus, Polybius, and the Guards colonels at my side, and if I wished to cross-examine a prisoner or witness I would hand one of them a list of questions to ask on my behalf, or whisper them to him. Narcissus made the best mouthpiece, so I employed him more often than the rest: this caused a misunderstanding. He was later represented by my enemies as having conducted the prosecution on his own initiative – a mere freedman prosecuting noble Romans, what a scandal! Narcissus certainly had a very assured, independent manner and I must admit that I joined in the general laugh against him, when Scribonianus's faithful freedman, whom he was cross-examining, proved his master in repartee.

NARCISSUS: You were a freedman of Furius Camillus Scribonianus's? You were present at his death?

FREEDMAN: I was.

NARCISSUS: You were in his confidence about this intended rebellion? You knew who his confederates were?

FREEDMAN: You wish to suggest that I was unworthy of his confidence? That if he had confederates, as you call them, in this alleged rebellion I should betray them?

NARCISSUS: I suggest nothing. I am asking you a plain question of fact.

FREEDMAN: Then I give you a plain answer. I do not remember.

NARCISSUS: Not remember?

FREEDMAN: His last words to me were: 'Whatever I have said to you in this matter, forget. Let my secrets die with me.'

NARCISSUS: Ah, then I may assume that you *were* in his confidence.

FREEDMAN: Assume whatever you like. It does not interest me. My master's dying injunctions were to forget. I have obeyed him implicitly.

NARCISSUS (*striding forward angrily into the middle of the floor, so that he actually obscured my view of the witness*): A very honest freedman, by Hercules. And tell me, fellow, what would you have done if Scribonianus had made himself Emperor?

FREEDMAN (*with sudden warmth*): I should have stood behind him, fellow, and kept my mouth shut.

Fifteen rebel noblemen or ex-noblemen were put to death, but only one of these was a senator, one Juncus, a magistrate of the first rank, and I made him resign his office before I condemned him. The other senators had committed suicide before arrest. Contrary to the usual custom, I did not confiscate the estates of the executed rebels, but let their heirs inherit as if they had decently killed themselves. In three or four cases, indeed, where their estates were found to be greatly encumbered by debt – the reason probably for their participation in the rebellion – I actually made the heirs a present of money. It has been said that Narcissus took bribes to cover up evidence of guilt against certain rebels: this is certainly an invention. I conducted the preliminary inquiries myself with Polybius's help and took down depositions. Narcissus did not have the opportunity of suppressing any evidence. Messalina, however, had access to the papers and may have destroyed some of them; I cannot say whether she did or not. But neither Narcissus nor Polybius handled them except in my presence. It has also been said that freedmen and citizens were put to the torture in an attempt to extract evidence from them. This is also untrue. A few slaves were racked, but not to force them to give evidence against their masters, only to make them give evidence against certain freedmen whom I suspected of perjury. The origin of the report that I tortured freedmen and citizens must probably be found in the case of certain of Vinicianus's slaves to whom he gave their freedom, when he saw that the rebellion had failed, to prevent them giving evidence against him under torture; he pre-dated their freedom, in the deed of manumission, by twelve months. This was an illegal procedure, or at any rate the men were still liable to be examined under torture, by a law passed under Tiberius to prevent this sort of evasion. One so-called citizen was put to torture when it was discovered that he had no claims to be regarded as such. Juncus indeed protested at his trial that he had been grossly maltreated in prison. He appeared swathed in bandages, with severe cuts on his face, but Rufrius testified that it was a downright lie; the injuries were due to his having resisted arrest – leaping naked from a bedroom window at Brindisi and trying to break through a quickset hedge. Two Guards captains confirmed this.

However, Juncus had his revenge on Rufrius. 'If I must die, Rufrius,' he said, 'then I shall take you with me.' Then he turned to me: 'Caesar, your trusted Commander of the Guards hates and despises you as much as I do. Paetus and I interviewed him, on Vinicianus's behalf, asking him whether on the arrival of the forces from Dalmatia he would bring over the Guards to our side. He undertook to do so, but only on condition that he, Scribonianus, and Vinicianus should share the Empire between them. Deny this, Rufrius, if you dare.'

I arrested Rufrius on the spot. At first he tried to laugh off the charge, but Paetus, one of the rebel knights awaiting trial, supported Juncus's evidence, and finally he broke down and pleaded for mercy. I gave him the mercy of being his own executioner.

A few women were also executed. I did not see why a woman's sex should protect her from punishment if she had been guilty of fomenting rebellion, particularly a woman who had not married a man in the strict form of marriage but had kept her independence and her own property, and so could not plead coercion. They were brought to the scaffold in chains, just like their husbands, and on the whole showed much greater courage in facing death. One woman, Arria, Paetus's wife but a close friend of Messalina's, married in the strict form, could no doubt have won a pardon if she had dared to sue for one. But no, she preferred to die with Paetus. Paetus, as a reward for his evidence in the case of Rufrius, was allowed to commit suicide before any charge was formally brought against him. He was a coward and could not nerve himself to fall on his sword. Arria snatched it from him and drove it home under her own ribs. 'Look, Paetus,' she said as she died, 'it doesn't hurt.'

The most distinguished person to die because of complicity in this rebellion was my niece Julia (Helen the Glutton). I was glad to have a good excuse for getting rid of her. It was she who had betrayed her husband, my poor nephew Nero, to Sejanus and had got him banished to the island where he died. Tiberius afterwards showed his contempt for her by giving her in marriage to Blandus, a vulgar knight of no family. Helen was jealous of Messalina's beauty as well as of her power: she had lost her own great beauty because of her passion for food and her indolence, and become excessively stout; however, Vinicianus was one of those little rat-like men who have the same love for women of abundant charms as rats have for large pumpkins; and if he had become Emperor, as he intended, knowing himself more than a match for Rufrius and Scribonianus combined, Helen the Glutton would have become his Empress. It was Vinicianus who betrayed her to Messalina, as a token of his loyalty to us.

Chapter 15

So I was still Emperor and my hopes of a safe and speedy return to private life were dashed. I began to tell myself that Augustus had been sincere in the speeches which he made from time to time about soon restoring the Republic, and that even my uncle Tiberius had not been so false as I suspected when he talked of resignation. Yes, it was easy enough for a private citizen to be a staunch Republican and grumble: 'Why, what could there be simpler than to choose a moment of general tranquillity, resign and hand the government over to the Senate?' The difficulty could only be understood if that private citizen were to become Emperor himself. It lay in the phrase 'moment of tranquillity': there were no moments of tranquillity. There were always disturbing factors in the situation. One said, sincerely enough, 'Perhaps in six months' time, perhaps in a year's time.' But the six months passed and the year passed; and even if some disturbing factors in the situation had been successfully disposed of, new ones were sure to have sprung up to take their places. I was determined to hand the government over as soon as the confusion left behind by Tiberius and Caligula had been cleared up and I had encouraged the Senate to recover its self-respect – one cannot have liberty without self-respect – by treating it as a responsible legislative body. Yet I could not be more respectful to the Senatorial Order than it deserved. I put the best available men into it, but the tradition of subservience to the Imperial pleasure was hard to break down. They suspected my good-nature, and whispered ill-manneredly to each other behind their hands if I behaved with natural affability towards them; and then if I suddenly lost my temper with them, as sometimes happened, they would suddenly fall silent and tremble like a lot of naughty schoolboys who have trespassed on the forbearance of an easy-going master. No, I could not give up yet. I was thoroughly ashamed of myself, in theory, as having been forced to put to death the leaders of an abortive anti-monarchical revolt; but in practice what else could I have done?

I brooded over the problem. Wasn't it Plato who wrote that the only sound excuse that anyone can offer for ruling is that by doing so he avoids being ruled by people inferior in talents to himself? There's something in that. But I was afraid, on the contrary, that, if I resigned, my place would be taken by someone superior in talents (though, I flattered myself, not in industry) – for example, Galba or Gabinius, from the Rhine, so that the monarchy would become stronger than ever and the Republic never be restored. In any case, the moment of tranquillity had not come. I must get to work again.

The rebellion and its aftermath had interrupted public business and put me back a couple of months in my schedule. To gain time I abolished several more unnecessary public holidays. When the New Year came I took on my third consulship, with Vitellius as my colleague, but resigned after two months in favour of Asiaticus. This was one of the most important years in my life – the year of my expedition to Britain. But before

A.D. 43

596

I come to that I must write about a few domestic matters. It was time now for my daughter Antonia to marry young Pompey, a capable young man and apparently well-disposed to me. I did not, however, allow the ceremony to be made the subject of any great public rejoicing – I celebrated it quietly at home. I did not wish it to be thought that I regarded my son-in-law as a member of the Imperial House. In fact, I did not care to think of my family as the Imperial House: we were not an Eastern dynasty – we were Julio-Claudians and no better or worse than the Cornelians, Camillans, Servians, Junians, or any other leading family. Nor did I wish my little son to be honoured above all other children of noble birth. The Senate asked permission to celebrate his birthday with Games at the public expense, but I refused this. However, the first-rank magistrates on their own initiative did observe his first birthday with a magnificent spectacle and banquet for which they paid themselves: and this practice was followed by their successors. It would have been discourteous not to have thanked them for their goodwill towards me, and the Games pleased Messalina greatly. All that I did for young Pompey was to allow him to stand for his first magistracy five years before the usual time and to make him City Warden during the Latin holidays. Pompey was descended from Pompey the Great through his maternal grandmother, the Pompey heiress: through her he inherited the family masks and statues and was able to adopt the name. I was proud to be able to link the name of Caesar with that of Pompey after so many generations. My grandmother Octavia had been offered in marriage by Julius Caesar to Pompey the Great nearly 100 years before this, but he had refused her and quarrelled with Julius. Later she married Mark Antony and became the great-grandmother of my daughter Antonia, whom I was now marrying to a great-great-grandson of Pompey.

The State finances were still in rather a difficult way, in spite of retrenchment. The world harvests continued to be poor and I had to devote a great deal of money to buying corn at high prices in distant markets. Among other economies I asked for the return of public revenues which had been granted by Caligula to certain of his favourites – charioteers, actors, and so on – as permanent pensions. I had been unaware that these were still being paid, for Callistus never mentioned them to me. He was probably bribed by the pensioners to keep quiet about them.

I arrived at one important decision. Since the time of Augustus the charge of the Public Treasury had been taken from the usual Treasury officials, who formed the lowest of magistrates, and given to the first-rank magistrates. In practice, however, these first-rank magistrates, though acting as paymasters and receivers of revenue, did not do much more than take in or pay out the sums indicated to them by the Emperor, whose freedmen kept all Treasury accounts. I decided to return the charge of the Treasury to the original Treasury officials, who were now employed in other ways – the government of Lombardy, the collection of harbour-dues at Ostia, and so on – and give them a chance to understand State finances thoroughly; so that when the change-over came from monarchical to republican government there would be no confusion. At present the Treasury accounts, which were never audited except by myself, were wholly managed by Callistus and his clerks. But I did not wish any of these officials to take advantage of their position to rob the Treasury – it was, unfortunately, easier to trust freedmen than men of rank. So I only made those men eligible for the post who would undertake to present Public Games at their own expense during their term of office: rich men, I argued, are less likely to rob the State than poor ones. The young men I chose were obliged, for one whole year before their appointment, to attend every day at the New Palace and study Treasury routine. Each, on appointment, was then given a Treasury department under myself – still, of course, represented by Callistus – with a freedman, the head-clerk of that department, as his adviser and secretary. The plan worked well. Freedmen and officials kept check on each other. I instructed Callistus that the cipher-like communications between departments must cease and correct Latin or Greek longhand be substituted: the new officials must be allowed to understand what was going on.

In the same spirit I did my best to inculcate a high sense of duty in all magistrates and governors. For instance, I insisted that senators who had been chosen by lot in the New Year to administer provinces (the home provinces I mean, as opposed to frontier provinces whose military governors I nominated myself in my capacity as Commander-in-Chief) should not hang about in Rome, as they usually did, until June or July when the weather made sailing pleasant, but be on their way by the middle of April.

Messalina and I were making a thorough revision of the Roll of Citizens, into which a great number of quite unworthy persons had inserted themselves. I left most of this business to her and thousands of names were removed and tens of thousands added. I had no objection to the enlargement of the Roll. The Roman citizenship gave all who held it an immense advantage over freedmen, provincials, and foreigners, and so long as it was not made either too inclusive or too exclusive a guild, but kept at the right proportion to the great mass of the population in the Roman dominion – say, about one citizen to every six or seven others – it was a great steadying factor in world politics. I only insisted that the new citizens should be men of substance, honest parentage, and good reputation, that they should be able to speak Latin, that they should have a sufficient education in Roman law, religion, and ethics, and that they should dress and comport themselves in a manner worthy of the honour. Any applicant with the necessary qualifications who was sponsored by a senator of good standing I put on the list. I expected him, however, to make a gift proportionate to his means to the Public Treasury, from which he would now benefit in a variety of ways. Persons who could find no sponsor applied to me indirectly through my secretaries, and Messalina then inquired into their antecedents. Those whom she recommended I put on the list without further question. I did not realize at the time that she was charging applicants a heavy fee for her interest with me and that the freedmen, notably Amphaeus, and Polybius whom I had temporarily transferred to this duty, were making enormous sums of money too. Many senators who sponsored candidates for citizenship got wind of this and began to take money under the table (as the saying is) and some even advertised in a cautious way through their agents that they made a more reasonable charge for their patronage than any other senator in the business. I knew nothing about this at the time, though. I suppose that they thought I was getting money from the business myself, using Messalina as my agent, and so would wink at their own practices.

I was aware, I own, that many of my secretaries received money-presents from suitors. I discussed this point with them one day. I said: 'I permit you to take presents but I forbid you to solicit them. I shall not wrong you by suggesting that you could be bribed to commit any falsification or other irregularity, and I don't see why you should not be rewarded for doing favours for people which take your time and energy, and for, *ceteris paribus*, giving priority to their business. If a hundred applications for the same favour are sent in simultaneously and there is nothing to choose between the candidates, yet only ten can have their applications granted – well, I should think you foolish not to choose the ten who are capable of showing the most gratitude. My loyal friend and ally, King Herod Agrippa, is fond of quoting a Jewish proverb – or rather a Jewish law which has won proverbial force – "Thou shalt not muzzle the ox that treadeth out the corn". That is appropriate and just. But I don't want any indecent haggling or auctioning of favours and priorities; and if I find that any of my oxen devote more of their attention to snatching mouthfuls of corn than to treading it out, I shall take them straight from the threshing-floor to the slaughter-house.'

My new Commander of the Guards was called Justus; I had called up the other Guards colonels to suggest one of their number for the appointment, and though I would have preferred someone other than Justus I accepted their choice. Justus took too meddling an interest in politics for a mere soldier: for instance, he came to me one day and informed me that some of the new citizens I had created were not adopting my name, as they should do in loyalty, or altering their wills in my favour, as they should do in gratitude. He had a list already prepared of these ungrateful and disloyal men and asked whether I wished to have charges framed against them; I silenced him by asking him whether his recruits made a practice of adopting his name and altering their wills in his favour. Justus took the trouble to tell me this, but neither he nor anyone else let me know that not only was Messalina selling the citizenship and encouraging others to sell it; but, more shameful still, was being paid huge sums of money in return for her influence with me in the choice of magistrates, governors, and military commanders. In some cases she not only exacted the money but – I might as well tell you at once – insisted on the man sleeping with her as a seal to the bargain. The most shameful thing of all was that she brought me into it without my knowledge: telling them that I had cast her off in scorn of her beauty, but allowed her to choose what bed-fellows she liked on condition that she persuaded them to pay a good price for the appointments which I gave her to sell on my behalf! However, I knew nothing about any of this at the time, and flattered myself that I was doing well enough and acting in an upright way that should command the affection and gratitude of the whole nation.

In my self-confident ignorance I did one particularly stupid thing: I listened to Messalina's advice on the subject of monopolies. You must remember how clever she was and how slow-witted I was, and how much I relied on her: she could persuade me to almost anything. She said to me one day: 'Claudius, I have been thinking about something; and that is, that the nation would be much more prosperous if competition between rival merchants were to be suppressed by law.'

'What do you mean, my dear?' I asked.

'Let me explain by analogy. Suppose that in our governmental system we had no departments. Suppose that every secretary in this place were free to move from job to job just as he thought fit. Suppose that Callistus were to come rushing into your study one morning and say: "I got here first and I want to do Narcissus's secretarial work this morning," and then Narcissus, arriving a moment later and finding his stool occupied by Callistus, were to dash into Felix's room, just in time to anticipate Felix, and begin work on some foreign-affairs document that Felix had not quite finished drawing up the night before. That would be ridiculous, wouldn't it?'

'Very ridiculous. But I don't see what this has to do with merchants.'

'I'll show you. The trouble with merchants is that they won't stick to a single task or let their rivals stick to one. None of them is interested in serving the community, but merely in finding the easiest way of making money. A merchant may start with an inherited business as a wine-importer, and manage that soberly for a while, and then suddenly break into the oil-business, underselling some old-established firm in his neighbourhood; perhaps he will force this firm out of business or buy it up, and then perhaps dabble in the fig-trade or slave-trade and either crush competitors or get crushed himself. Trade is constant fighting, and the mass of the population suffers from it, just like non-combatants in a war.'

'Do you really think so? Often they get things surprisingly cheap when one merchant is underselling another merchant or when he goes bankrupt.'

'You might as well say that sometimes non-combatants can get quite good pickings from a battle-field – scrap-metal, the hides and shoes of dead horses, enough sound parts of broken chariots to build one good one with. Those windfalls aren't to be reckoned against the burning of their farms and the trampling down of their crops.'

'Are merchants as bad as all that? They never struck me as being anything but useful servants of the State.'

'They could be and ought to be useful. But they do great harm by their lack of co-operation and their insane jealous competition. The word goes round, for example, that there's to be a demand for coloured marble from Phrygia, or Syrian silk, or ivory from Africa, or Indian pepper; and for fear of missing a chance they scramble for the market like mad dogs. Instead of persisting with their ordinary lines of commerce, they rush their ships to the new centre of excitement, with orders to their captains to bring as much marble, pepper, silk, or ivory as possible at whatever cost, and then of course the foreigners raise the prices. Two hundred ship-loads of pepper or silk are brought home at great expense when there is really only a demand for twenty, and the hundred and eighty ships could have been far better employed in importing other things for which there would have been a demand and for which a fair price could have been got. Obviously trade ought to be centrally controlled in the same way as armies and law-courts and religion and everything else is controlled.'

I asked her how she would control trade if I gave her the chance.

'Why, that's simple enough,' she answered. 'I should grant monopolies.'

'Caligula granted monopolies,' I said, 'and sent prices up with a rush.'

'He *sold* monopolies to the highest bidder, and of course prices went up. I shouldn't do that. And my monopolies wouldn't be so huge as Caligula's. He sold one man the world's trading-rights in figs! I'd simply calculate a normal year's demand for any given commodity and then freely allocate that trade for the next two years to one firm or more of traders. I should, for instance, grant the sole right to import and sell Cyprian wines to such-and-such a firm, and the sole right to import and sell Egyptian glass to such-and-such a firm; and Baltic amber and Tyrian purple and British enamel would go to other firms. Control trade like this and there is no competition, so the foreign manufacturer or dealer in raw materials can't put up the price; "take it or leave it", says the trader, as he fixes the price himself. The traders who have not sufficient standing to be granted monopolies must either come to terms with monopoly-holders, if the latter think that they have more trade than they can manage themselves, or must discover new industries or trades. If I had my way everything would be thoroughly orderly and we should be well supplied, and the State would get bigger harbour-dues than ever.'

I agreed that it sounded a very sensible plan; and one good effect would be to release a large number of ships and merchants for the corn trade. I immediately empowered her to grant a large number of monopolies, never suspecting that the clever woman had talked me over to her scheme merely with an eye to enormous bribes that she would get from the merchants. Six months later the removal of competition in the monopoly trades, which included necessaries as well as luxuries, had sent prices up to a most ridiculous height – the merchants were recovering from the consumers what they had paid in bribes to Messalina – and the City became more restless than at any time since the famine-winter. I was continually shouted at in the streets by the crowd, and there was nothing for me to do but to set up a big platform on Mars Field, from which, with the help of a big-voiced Guards captain, I fixed the prices, for the ensuing twelve months, of the commodities affected. I based the prices on those of the previous twelve months, as far as I was able to get accurate figures; and then of course all the monopolists came to the Palace afterwards to beg me to modify my decision in their own particular cases, because they were poor men and beggary was facing their starving families, and nonsense of that sort. I told them that if they could not make their monopolies pay at the prices now fixed they could retire in favour of other traders with better business methods; and then warned them to go away at once before I charged them with 'waging war against the State' and threw them from the Capitoline cliff. They made no further protests but tried to beat me by withdrawing their goods from the market altogether. However, as soon as any complaints reached me that a certain class of goods – say pickled fish from Macedonia or medicinal drugs from Crete – was not reaching the City in sufficient quantities I added another firm to those already sharing the monopoly.

I was always most attentive to the City food-supply. I instructed the steward of my Italian estates to devote as much land as possible in the neighbourhood of the City to the growing of vegetables for the City Market, especially cabbage, onion, lettuce, endive, leek, skirret, and other winter vegetables. My physician Xenophon told me that the frequent outbreaks of disease in the poorer quarters of Rome in the winter months were largely due to the scarcity of green vegetables. I wanted an abundant supply raised, brought in every day before dawn and sold at the lowest possible prices. I also encouraged pig, poultry, and cattle-breeding; and a year or two later won special privileges from the Senate for City butchers and wine-sellers. There was some opposition in the Senate to these grants. The Senators themselves were supplied from their own country estates and were not interested in the people's food. Asiaticus said: 'Cold water, bread, beans, pulse-porridge, and cabbage are good enough for working-men. Why pamper them with wine and butchers' meat?' I protested against Asiaticus's inhumanity and asked him whether he preferred cold water to Chian wine, or cabbage to roast venison. He answered that he had been brought up on a rich diet and would find it quite impossible to change to the simpler sort, but that no doubt he would be a hardier man if he could, and that it was wrong to encourage poor men to a diet above their station.

'I appeal to you, my Lords,' I protested, trembling with vexation, 'what man is able to live a self-respecting life without a little bit of meat now and then?' The House seemed to think this funny. I didn't. And the same thing happened at the end of the same debate when I was on the subject of the wine-sellers. 'They want encouragement,' I said. 'There has been a great falling off in the number of wine-shops even in the last five years: I mean honest jug-and-bottle houses, not those dirty places that I have had shut up now where they sold cooked meat as well as wine – and what wine too! Awful stuff, for the most part, doctored with salts of lead – and a brothel full of diseased women attached, with pornographic pictures smudged on the wall. Why, five years ago, within a quarter of a mile of my house on the Palatine, there were at least fifteen – no, what am I saying? at least twenty-five jug-and-bottle houses, and now there aren't more than three or four. And they served good wine too. There was "The Flask", and "The Bacchus", and "The Veteran", and "The Two Brothers", and "The Glory of Agrippa", and "The Swan" ("The Swan's" still in business, but the others are gone – the best wine came from "The Two Brothers"), and the "Baucis and Philemon" – that's disappeared too, a very pleasant place. And so has "The Yew Tree" – I liked the old "Yew Tree". ...'

How they laughed at me! They were all men who kept their own cellars and had probably never been into a wine-shop to buy drink in their life. I silenced them with an angry look. I said: 'You may recall that five years ago, owing to the caprices of my nephew, the late Emperor, I went bankrupt and was forced to live on the charity of my friends – not a man of you among them, by the way – real friends, such as a few grateful freedmen, a girl prostitute, and an old slave or two. I visited those taverns to buy wine because my cellar was up for public auction along with my house, of which I could only afford to occupy a few rooms. So I know what I'm talking about. And I hope that if any of you happen to fall a victim to the caprices of an Emperor and find yourself in poverty you will remember this debate, and regret that you have not voted for the maintenance of a proper supply of butcher's meat in the City and for the preservation of such honest wine-shops as the old "Swan", "The Coronet", and "The Black Dog", which are still in business but won't survive long if you don't do something for them. To Hell with cold water and pulse-porridge! And if I see so much as a smile cross your faces, my Lords, before I have finished this speech – or after – I shall take it as a personal affront.'

I was really angry, shaking with anger, and I saw the fear of death gradually stealing over them. They passed my motion without a single contrary vote.

My success gave me momentary pleasure, but afterwards I felt deeply ashamed and made things worse by apologizing to them for my ill-temper. They thought that I was showing weakness and timidity by doing so. Now, I wish to make it clear that I had not been using my Imperial power, contrary to all my most cherished principles of equality and justice and human self-respect, to bully and browbeat the Senate. I had just felt outraged by Asiaticus and the rest of those rich heartless men who treated their fellow-citizens like dirt. I was not threatening, I was merely expostulating. But those words of mine were used against me afterwards by my enemies, in spite of my apology for them and in spite of the following letter that I composed and circulated in the City:

Tiberius Claudius Caesar Augustus Germanicus, Emperor, High Pontiff, Protector of the People, Consul for the third time, to the Senate and People of Rome, greetings.

I am aware of a certain failing in myself, which distresses me perhaps more than it distresses you, because one grieves more for a trouble of one's own making than for trouble that comes upon one from another source, particularly from some powerful source over which one has little or no control, such as lightning, disease, hail, or the severity of a judge: I refer to the sudden bursts of anger to which I have been increasingly subject since I first assumed the burden of government that, against my inclinations, you laid on me. For example, the other day I sent word to the citizens of Ostia that I was coming to view the progress of the excavations at their new port, sailing down the Tiber, and that they might expect me about noon, and that if they had any complaints to make about the behaviour of my army of workmen there or any petitions to offer I should be pleased to attend to them; but when I reached Ostia no boat put out to meet me and no group of city officials was waiting at the quay. I was incensed and sent for the leading men of the city, including the chief magistrate and the harbour-master, and addressed them in the most violent terms, asking why it was that I had become so contemptible and worthless in their eyes that there was not even a sailor there ready to tie my yacht up to the quay when I landed, and I supposed that they would charge me a fee for entering their port at all, and what sort of ingrates were the men of Ostia to growl and snap at the hand that fed them, or at the best, to turn away from it with indifference? However, a simple explanation was offered: my message had never reached them. They apologized, and I apologized, and we became the best of friends again, no ill-will remaining on either side. But I suffered more from my anger than they did, because they were not conscious of any wrong-doings when I shouted at them, whereas I was most ashamed, afterwards, to have insulted them.

So let me confess that I am subject to these fits of anger but beg you to bear with me in them. They never last long and are quite harmless: my physician Xenophon says that they are due to over-work, like my insomnia. Recently I have been unable to sleep after midnight; the distant rumble of country wagons coming into the City with market-stuff keeps me awake until dawn, when I sometimes am lucky enough to snatch an hour's sleep. That's why I am often so sleepy at the law-courts after luncheon.

Another fault to which I must confess is my tendency to bear malice: I cannot lay the blame for this on over-work or ill-health, but I can and do say that any malice to which I may from time to time give way is never wholly unjustified or due to an irrational dislike of a man's features or bearing or to jealousy of his property or parts. It is always based on some unprovoked personal injury once done to me for which apology has never been offered or other satisfaction made. For example, on my first visit to the law-courts – shortly after my accession – to settle the cases of men charged with treason I noticed the same audacious court-official who had once done his best to curry favour with my nephew, the late Emperor, at my expense, on the occasion that I was unjustly charged with forgery. He had then exclaimed, pointing at me: 'One can read guilt written all over his face. Why prolong proceedings? Condemn him at once, Caesar.' Was it not natural for me to remember this? I cried to the fellow as he cringed towards me at my entry: 'I can read guilt in your face. Leave this court and never appear in any court of law in Rome again!'

You all know the old patrician saying: *Aquila non captat muscas.* The eagle is the noble soul and he does not hawk for flies, which means that he does not pursue petty ends, or go out of his way to revenge himself on mean little men that have provoked him. But let me quote an enlargement made many years ago by my noble brother, Germanicus Caesar:

> 'Captat non muscas aquila; at quaeque advolat ultro
> Faucibus augustis, musca proterva perit.'

Bear all this mind and we shall have no misunderstandings but remain bound in the mutual affection which we have so often protested to each other. Farewell.

(The couplet, translated, means: 'The eagle does not hawk for flies, but if any impudent fly comes buzzing of its own free will into his august throat, that's the end of the creature.')

My execution of Appius Silanus had been the pretext for the revolt; so to show that I entertained no enmity against his family I arranged for his eldest son, Marcus Silanus, Augustus's great-great-grandson and born in the year that he died, to be Consul in four years' time: and I also promised Appius's youngest son, Lucius Silanus, who had come with his father from Spain to live with us at the Palace, to betroth my daughter Octavia to him as soon as she was able to understand the betrothal ceremony.

Chapter 16

BRITAIN lies in a northerly position, but the climate, though very damp, is not nearly so cold as one would expect; if properly drained the country could be made extremely fruitful. The aboriginal inhabitants, a small, dark-haired people, were dispossessed about the time that Rome was founded, by an invasion of Celts from the south-east. Some still maintain themselves independently in small settlements in inaccessible mountains or marshes; the rest became serfs and mixed their blood with that of their conquerors. I use the word 'Celts' in the most general sense to cover the many nations which have appeared in Europe in the course of the last few centuries, travelling westward from some remote region lying to the north of the Indian mountains. They have, some authorities hold, been driven from this region, not by any love of wandering or by the pressure of stronger tribes on their borders, but by a slow natural catastrophe on an enormous scale, the gradual drying-up of immense tracts of fertile land which hitherto maintained them. Among these Celts, if the word is to have any true significance, I should reckon not only most of the inhabitants of France – but the Aquitanians are Iberian aborigines – and the many nations of Germany and the Balkans, but even the Achaean Greeks, who had established themselves for some time in the Upper Danube valley before pushing southward into Greece. Yes, the Greeks are comparatively new-comers to Greece. They displaced the native Pelasgians, who derived their culture from Crete, and brought new Gods with them, the chief of these being Apollo. This happened not long before the Trojan War; the Dorian Greeks came still later – eighty years after the Trojan War. Other Celts of the same race invaded France and Italy at about the same time, and the Latin language is derived from their speech. It was then, too, that the first Celtic invasion of Britain took place. These Celts, whose language is akin to primitive Latin, were called Goidels – a tall, sandy-haired, big-limbed, boastful, excitable but noble race, gifted in all the arts, including fine weaving and metal-work, music and poetry; they still survive, in Northern Britain, in the same state of civilization as has been immortalized for the Greeks, now so greatly changed, in the verses of Homer.

Four or five hundred years later another Celtic nation appeared in Northern Europe, namely, those tribes that we call Galates. They invaded Macedonia, after the death of Alexander, and crossed into Asia Minor, occupying the region which is now called Galatia, after them. They also entered Northern Italy, where they broke the power of the Etruscans, penetrating as far as Rome, where they defeated us at the Allia and burned our City. This same nation occupied most of France, though their predecessors remained in the centre, the north-west, and the south-east. These Galates are also a gifted people; though inferior to the earlier Celts in arts, they are more united in spirit and finer fighting men. They are of middle stature with brown or black hair, round chins, and straight noses. About the time of the Allia disaster some tribes of this nation invaded Britain by way of Kent, the south-eastern district of the island, and compelled the Goidels to spread out fanwise before them, so that these are now only found, except as serfs, in the North of Britain and in the neighbouring island of Ireland. The Galates who went to Britain became known as the Brythons, or painted men, because they used caste-marks of blue dye on their faces and bodies, and have given their name to the whole island. However, 200 years later still came a third race of Celts moving up the Rhine from Central Europe. These were the people whom we call the Belgians, the same that are now settled along the Channel Coast and are known as the best fighting men in France. They are a mixed race, akin to the Galates but with German blood in them; they have light hair, big chins, and aquiline noses. They invaded Britain by way of Kent and established themselves in the whole southern part of the island with the exception of the south-west corner, which was still occupied by the Brythons and their Goidel serfs. These Belgians kept in close touch with their kinsmen across the Channel (one of their kings ruled on both sides of the water), trading with them constantly and even sending armed help to them in their wars with Julius Caesar; as in the south-west Brythons traded with and sent help to their kinsmen, the Galates of the Loire.

So much for the races of Britain; now for the story of their contact with the power of Rome. The first invasion of Britain was made 108 years ago by Julius Caesar. He had found numerous Britons fighting in the ranks of his enemies, the Belgians and the Galates of the Loire, and he thought that the island should now be taught to respect the power of Rome. He could not hope to keep France pacified so long as Britain remained a safe place of refuge for the more stubborn of his enemies and a starting-point for new attempts to recover the independence of their country. Next he wished, for political reasons, to gain some remarkable military glory to balance his colleague Pompey's victories. His victories in Spain and France had been an answer to Pompey's in Syria and Palestine, and a campaign in distant Britain could be set off against Pompey's feats among the remote nations of the Caucasus. Lastly, he needed money. The Loire traders and the Channel traders seemed to do very well out of Britain, and Julius wanted to have the market for himself, first exacting a heavy tribute from the islanders. He knew that there was gold in Britain, for gold pieces from there were circulating freely in France. (It was, by the way, an interesting coinage: the original model was the gold stater of Philip of Macedon, which had come to Britain by way of the Danube and Rhine, but the design had become so debased in course of time that of the two horses of the chariot only one remained, the charioteer and chariot having become a mere pattern; of Apollo's laurelled head only the laurel was left.) Britain is not, as a matter of fact, particularly rich in gold, and though the tin mines of the south-west were once of importance – the Carthaginians traded there – and are still worked, the chief supply of tin for Rome now comes from the tin islands off the coast of Galicia. There is some silver in Britain, and copper and lead, and there are important iron-workings on the south-east coast, and fresh-water pearls of a good quality, though small and not to be compared with the Oriental variety. There is no amber, except for tide-washed pieces – it comes from the Baltic – but very fine jet, and other valuable exports, including slaves, skins, wool, flax, domestic animals, enamelled bronze, blue dye, wickerwork baskets, and corn. Julius was most interested in gold and slaves; although he knew that the slaves that he would get from the island would not be of particularly high quality – the women are by no means seductive and have fierce tempers, and the men, except those of the upper classes who make excellent coachmen, only fitted for the roughest sort of farm-labour. He could not expect to find among them cooks, goldsmiths, musicians, barbers, secretaries, or accomplished courtesans. The average price they would fetch at Rome would not exceed forty gold pieces.

He twice invaded Britain by way of the south-east, as the Goidels, Brythons, and Belgians had all done in their turn. On the first occasion the Britons hotly disputed his landing and gave a good account of themselves: so that apart from some hostages which he took from the men of Kent he accomplished little, only advancing ten miles inland. On the second occasion, however, profiting from his experiences, he landed with a strong force – 20,000 men; before, only 10,000. He marched from Sandwich, a point close to the French coast, along the southern bank of the Thames estuary, forcing first the passage of the River Stour and then that of the Thames near London. He was making for the territory of the Catuvellaunians, a Belgic tribe whose king had become the overlord of several petty kings in the south and east of the island: his capital city was Wheathampstead, some twenty-five miles north-east of London. By 'city' I do not of course mean a city in the Graeco-Roman sense, but a big settlement of wattle-and-daub huts and a few huts of undressed stone. It was this king Cassivellaunus, who organized the resistance against Julius; but he found that while his cavalry and chariotry were superior to the French cavalry that Julius had brought with him, his infantry could not compete with the Roman infantry. He decided that his best tactics were to dispense with infantry altogether and with his cavalry and chariots prevent the Roman army from deploying. Julius found that he could not safely send foraging parties out except in compact bodies with cavalry supports; the British chariot-fighters had perfected the technique of surprising and cutting off stragglers and small groups. So long as the Roman army remained in column of march the damage that it could inflict by the burning of cornfields and hamlets was of no great importance; and the Britons always had plenty of time to get their women and children and cattle to a safe place. Once across the Thames, however, Julius had the support of some tribesmen who had recently been defeated by their enemies, the Catuvellaunians. These were the Trinovants who lived north-west of London, with Colchester as their capital. An exiled prince of the Trinovants, whose father had been killed by Cassivellaunus, had fled to Julius in France just before the expedition started and undertaken, if Julius invaded the territory of the Catuvellaunians, to raise the whole east coast in his support. He fulfilled his undertaking, and Julius now had a secure base in Trinovant country. After revictualling there he resumed his march on Wheathampstead.

Cassivellaunus knew that he had little hope of victory now, unless Julius could be forced by some diversion to retrace his steps. He sent an urgent message to his subject allies, the men of Kent, begging them to rise in force and attack Julius's base-camp. Julius had already once been checked, shortly after landing, by the news that a storm had wrecked some of his transports, which he had neglected to draw up on the beach and had left riding at anchor. He had been forced to return all the way from the Stour and it had taken him ten days to repair the damage; which gave the Britons the opportunity of reoccupying and strengthening the positions that he had already with some difficulty captured. If the men of Kent consented to attack the base-camp, which was manned by only 2,000 men and 300 cavalry, and contrived to capture it and to seize the fleet, then Julius would be trapped and the whole island would rise against the Romans – even the Trinovants would desert their new allies. The men of Kent did make a mass attack on the base-camp but were repulsed with heavy loss. On hearing the news of this defeat all the allies of Cassivellaunus who had not already done so sent peace embassies to Julius. But he was now marching on Wheathampstead, which he stormed by a simultaneous attack on two of its fronts. This fortress was a great earthwork ring protected by woods and deep ditches and stockades and was considered impregnable. It served as a place of refuge for all members of the tribe who were too old or too young to fight. In it were captured immense quantities of cattle and hundreds of prisoners. Cassivellaunus, though his army had not yet been beaten, was forced to sue for peace. Julius gave him easy terms, because not much of the summer remained and he was anxious to get back to France; a rebellion threatened there. The Catuvellaunians were merely asked to hand over certain principal men and women as hostages, to pay an annual tribute in gold to the Roman people, and to promise not to molest the Trinovants. So Cassivellaunus paid Julius an instalment of tribute and handed over his hostages, as did the kings of all the other tribes except the Trinovants and their east-coast allies, who had voluntarily offered Julius assistance. Julius went back to France with his prisoners and as many of the cattle as he had not sold cheap to the Trinovants to save himself the trouble of getting them safely across the Channel.

The rebellion broke out in France two years later and Julius was so busy crushing it that he could not spare men for a third expedition to Britain; though Cassivellaunus had stopped paying tribute as soon as the news of the rebellion reached him and had sent help to the insurgents in France. Soon after this the Civil Wars started and though, when these had ended, the question of an invasion of Britain was from time to time raised, there was always a good reason for postponing it, usually trouble on the Rhine frontier. Sufficient troops could never be spared. Augustus eventually decided against extending the bounds of the Empire beyond the Channel. He concentrated instead on civilizing France and the Rhine provinces and those parts of Germany across the Rhine captured by my father. When he lost Germany after Hermann's revolt he was still less prepared to add Britain to his anxieties. He had recorded his opinion in a letter to my grandmother Livia, dated the year of my birth, that not until the French were ripe for the Roman citizenship and could be trusted not to rebel in the absence of part of the Roman army of defence, could an invasion of Britain be politically justified:

But it is none the less my opinion, my dearest Livia, that Britain must eventually be converted into a frontier province. It is unsafe to allow an island, so near to France and manned by so fierce and so numerous a population, to remain independent. Looking into the future, I can see Britain becoming as civilized as southern France is now; and I think that the islanders, who are racially akin to us, will become far better Romans than we shall ever succeed in making of the Germans, who in spite of their apparent docility and willingness to learn our arts, I find more alien-minded even than the Moors or the Jews. I cannot explain my feeling except by saying they have been much too quick in learning: you know the proverb, 'Quick to learn, quick to forget'. You may think me rather foolish in writing of the British as if they were already Romans, but it is interesting to speculate on the future. I don't mean twenty years hence, or even fifty years hence, but allowing the French fifty years to be ready for the citizenship and allowing twenty years or so for the complete subjugation of Britain, perhaps in 100 years from now Italy will be knit closely with the whole British archipelago and (do not smile) British noblemen may well take their seats in the Roman Senate. Meanwhile we must continue our policy of commercial penetration. This King Cymbeline, who has now made himself overlord of the greater part of the island, gives a generous welcome to Roman-French traders and even to Greek doctors, especially oculists, for the British seem to suffer pretty severely from ophthalmia, owing to the marshiness of the country; and his Roman moneyers strike him a beautiful silver coinage – the gold coins remain barbarous – and he is in friendly touch with our governors in France. British trade has increased greatly in the past few years. I am told that at Cymbeline's court at Colchester as much Latin as British is spoken.

In this context I might quote the historian Strabo who, writing early in the reign of Tiberius, remarks:

In our own days certain of the princes of Britain have secured the friendship of Caesar Augustus by their embassies and attentive courtesies: they have even sent votive-offerings to the temple of Capitoline Jove and made the whole island almost, as it were, native soil to the Romans. They pay very moderate customs-dues both on their exports to France and on their imports, the latter being for the most part ivory bracelets, necklaces, amber, glassware, and the like.

Strabo then lists the exports as gold, silver, iron, skins, slaves, hunting-dogs, corn, and cattle. His conclusions – inspired, I think, by Livia herself – are these:

So the Romans have no need to garrison the island. It would take at least one infantry regiment, supported by cavalry, to force them to pay tribute; but the cost of keeping the garrison there would be at least as much as the tribute received, and the imposition of the tribute would necessitate the lowering of the customs-dues, and besides this there would be considerable military risks attendant on the policy of forcible subjection.

This estimate 'at least one infantry regiment' was far too modest. 'At least four regiments' would have been nearer to the mark. Augustus never raised the question of the interrupted repayment of tribute as a Catuvellaunian breach of faith nor protested against Cymbeline's subjugation of the Trinovants. This Cymbeline was a grandson of Cassivellaunus and reigned for forty years; the later years being clouded, as seems to be the fate of elderly rulers, by family troubles. His eldest son tried to seize the throne and was expelled from the kingdom, but fled to Caligula in France and asked for his help in an invasion of Britain, undertaking if he were put on his father's throne to acknowledge the suzerainty of Rome. Caligula sent off dispatches at once to the Senate, informing them of the surrender of the island, then marched to Boulogne at the head of a huge army as if to begin the invasion without a moment's delay. However, he was a nervous man and was afraid of being drowned in the Channel, where the tides run high, or of being killed in battle, or captured and burned in a wicker votive-image; so he announced that since Britain had yielded in the person of this prince the expedition was superfluous. Instead, he launched his attack on Neptune, ordering his troops to shoot arrows and hurl javelins and sling stones into the water, as I have described, and to gather sea-shells for spoils. He brought the prince back to Rome in chains and, after celebrating his triple triumph over Neptune, Britain, and Germany, put him to death as a punishment for the unpaid tribute and for his father's cowardly attack on the Trinovants and for the help sent by certain British tribes to the Autun rebels in the eighth year of Tiberius's reign.

Cymbeline's death occurred in the same month as that of Caligula and was followed by civil war. The eldest surviving prince, by name Bericus, was proclaimed king, but he was a man for whom neither his own tribesmen nor his subject allies had any respect. His two younger brothers Caractacus and Togodumnus rebelled against him a year later and forced him to fly across the Channel. He came to me at Rome and asked for my help in the same way as his brother had asked help from Caligula. I made no promises, but allowed him to live in Rome with his family and a few noblemen who had come with him.

Togodumnus, who now reigned jointly with Caractacus, had been told by merchants that I was no soldier but a cowardly old fool who wrote books. He sent me an insolent letter demanding the instant return of Bericus and the other exiles, together with the sacred regalia – thirteen magical objects – a crown, a cup, a sword, and so on – which Bericus had brought to Rome with him. If Togodumnus had written in a courteous tone I should certainly have replied courteously and at least returned the regalia, which it appears were necessary for the proper crowning of a Catuvellaunian king. As it was, I answered shortly that I was not accustomed to being addressed in this disrespectful manner, and did not, in consequence, feel obliged to do him any service. He replied, still more insolently, that I was not telling the truth: for until quite recently everyone, including my own family, had treated me with disrespect; and that since I had refused to obey him he had detained all the Roman-owned trading ships in his ports and would hold these as hostages until I gave him what he had demanded. There was nothing for it but to make war. The French would have lost all respect for me if I had hesitated. I took my decision quite independently of Herod, though his teasing letter happened to coincide with it.

I had other reasons for making war, too. One was that the time had come which Augustus had foreseen: I was about to extend the Roman citizenship to large numbers of our more civilized French allies, but the one element in Northern France that was checking the orderly progress of civilization there was the Druidical cult, a magical religion which was still kept alive, in spite of all that we could do to discourage or suppress it, by Druidical training-colleges in Britain from where it had originally been imported. Young Frenchmen went to Britain for their magical education as naturally as young Spaniards go to Rome to study law, or young Romans to Athens to study philosophy, or young Greeks to Alexandria to study surgery. Druidism could not readily be reconciled with Greek or Roman religious worship, involving as it did human sacrifices and necromancy, and the Druids therefore, though they were not warriors themselves but only priests, were always fomenting rebellion against us. Another reason for war was that the golden reign of Cymbeline was over. Togodumnus and Caractacus were, I learned, about to be involved in a struggle with their north-eastern neighbours, the Icenians, and with two subject tribes on the south coast; so that regular trade with Britain would be interrupted for some time if I did not intervene. I could now count on the help of the Icenians and the other tribes, not to mention the cross-Channel merchants, so the opportunity seemed too good to miss.

It would be as well to give here in brief an account of the main features of Druidism, a religion which seems to be a fusion of Celtic and aboriginal beliefs. I cannot guarantee that the details are true, for reports are conflicting. No Druidical lore is allowed to be consigned to writing and a terrible fate is threatened to those who reveal even the less important mysteries. My account is based on the statements of prominent apostates from the religion, but these include no Druidical priests. No consecrated Druid has ever been persuaded to reveal the inner mysteries even under torture. The word 'Druid' means 'Oak-man', because that is their sacred tree. Their sacred year begins with the budding of the oak and ends with the falling of its leaves. There is a god called Tanarus whose symbol is the oak. It is he who with a flash of lightning generates the mistletoe on the oak-tree branch, which is the sovereign remedy against witchcraft and all diseases. There is also a sun-god called Mabon whose symbol is a white bull. And then there is Lug, a god of medicine, poetry, and the arts, whose symbol is the snake. These are all, however, the same person, a God of Life-in-Death, worshipped in different aspects, like Osiris in Egypt. As Osiris is yearly drowned by a god of waste waters, so this triple deity is yearly killed by the God of Darkness and Water, his uncle Nodons, and restored to life by the power of his sister Sulis, the Goddess of Healing who corresponds to Isis. Nodons manifests himself by a monstrous wave of water, twelve feet high, that at regular intervals comes running up the mouth of the Severn, chief of the western rivers, causing great destruction to crops and huts as far as thirty miles inland. The Druidical religion is not practised by the tribes as such, for they are fighting units commanded by kings and noblemen, but by thirteen secret societies, named after various sacred animals, the members of any one of which belong to a variety of tribes; because it is the month in which one is born – they have a thirteen-month year – which decides the society to which one is to belong. There are the Beavers, and the Mice, and the Wolves, and the Rabbits, and the Wild Cats, and the Owls, and so on, and each society has a particular lore of its own and is presided over by a Druid. The Arch-Druid rules over the whole cult. The Druids take no part in fighting, and members of the same society who meet in tribal battles on opposite sides are pledged to run to each other's rescue.

The mysteries of the Druidical religion are concerned with a belief in the immortality of the human soul, in support of which many natural analogies are offered. One of these is the daily death and daily rebirth of the sun, another is the yearly death and yearly rebirth of the leaves of the oak, another is the yearly cutting of the corn and the yearly springing up of the seed. They say that man when he dies goes westward, like the setting sun, to live in certain sacred islands in the Atlantic ocean, until the time shall come for him to be born again. All over the island there are sacred altars known as 'dolmens', one flat stone laid on two or more uprights. These are used in the initiation ceremonies of the societies. The initiation is at once a death and a rebirth. The candidate lies on the lintel stone and a mock-sacrifice is then performed. By some magical means the Druid who performs it seems to cut off the man's head, which is exhibited bleeding to the crowd. The head is then joined to the trunk again and the supposed corpse is placed underneath the dolmen, as in a grave, with mistletoe between its lips; from which, after many prayers and charms, the new man comes forth as if he were a child emerging from the womb and is instructed in his new life by god-parents. Besides these dolmens there are upright stone altars, devoted to phallic rites; for the Celtic Osiris resembles the Egyptian one in this respect too.

Rank in the societies is decided by the number of sacrifices a man makes to the Gods, standing on the lintel stone of his ancestral dolmen, by the number of enemies he kills in battle and by the honours he wins in the annual religious games as charioteer, juggler, wrestler, poet, or harper. Rank is shown by the masks and head-dresses which are worn during the ceremonies and by the blue designs executed in woad (a marsh plant) with which their whole bodies are painted. The Druid priesthood is recruited from young men who have attained high rank in their secret societies and to whom certain marks of divine favour have been given. But twenty years of hard study at the Druidical college are first called for and it is by no means every candidate who succeeds in passing through the necessary thirty-two degrees. The first twelve years are spent in being initiated in turn into all the other secret societies, in learning by heart enormous sagas of mythological poetry and in the study of law, music, and astronomy. The next three years are spent in the study of medicine. The next three are spent in the study of omens and magic. The tests put upon candidates for the priesthood are immensely severe. For example, there is a test of poetical composition. The candidates must lie naked all night in a coffin-like box, only his nostrils protruding above the icy water with which it is filled, and with heavy stones laid on his chest. In this position he must compose a poem of considerable length in the most difficult of the many difficult bardic metres, on a subject which is given him as he is placed in the box. On his emergence next morning he must be able to chant this poem to a melody which he has been simultaneously composing, and accompany himself on the harp. Another test is to stand before the whole body of Druids and be asked verse-questions in riddling form which must be answered in further riddles, also in verse. These riddles all refer to obscure incidents in the sacred poems with which the candidate is supposed to be familiar. Besides all this he must be able to raise magic mists and winds and perform all sorts of conjuring tricks.

I shall tell you here of my only experience of Druidical magic. I once asked a Druid to show me his skill. He called for three dried peas and put them in a row across the palm of my outstretched hand. He said: 'Without moving your arm, can you blow away the middle pea and not blow away the outer ones?' I tried, but of course I could not. my breath blew all three peas away. He picked them up and laid them in a row across his own palm. Then he held down the outer ones with the forefinger and little finger of the same hand and blew the centre one away easily. I was angry at being fooled. 'Anyone could do that,' I said. 'That's not magic.'

He handed me the peas again. 'Try it,' he ordered.

I began to do what he had done, but to my chagrin I found that not only could I not command enough breath to blow away the pea – my lungs seemed suddenly tightened – but that when I wanted to straighten out my bent fingers again I could not. They were tightly cramped against my palm and the nails were gradually driving into my flesh so that it was with difficulty that I refrained from crying out. The sweat was pouring down my face.

He asked, 'Is it so easy to do?'

I answered ruefully: 'Not when a Druid is present.' He touched my wrist and my fingers recovered from their cramp.

The candidate's last test but one is to spend the longest night of the year seated on a rocking-stone called the 'Perilous Seat' which is balanced over a deep chasm in a mountain somewhere in the west of the island. Evil spirits come and talk to him all night and try by various means to make him lose his balance. He must not answer a word, but address prayers and hymns of praise to the Gods. If he escapes from this ordeal he is permitted to take the final test, which is to drink a poisoned cup and go into a death trance, and visit the Island of the Dead, and bring back from there such proofs of his visit as will convince the examining Druids that he has been accepted by the God of Life-in-Death as his priest.

There are three ranks of Druid priests. There are those who have passed all the tests, the true Druids; then come the Bards, those who have passed in the bardic tests but have not yet satisfied the examiners in soothsaying, medicine, and magic; then come those who have satisfied the examiners in these latter tests, but have not yet taken their bardic degree – they are known as the Ovates or Listeners. It needs a bold heart to enter for the final tests, which result in the death of three candidates out of every five, I am informed, so most men are content enough with the degree of Bard or Ovate.

The Druids, then, are the law-givers and judges and the controllers of public and private religion, and the greatest punishment that they can inflict is to interdict men from the holy rites. Since this excommunication is equivalent to sentencing men to perpetual extinction – for only by taking part in these rites can they hope to be reborn when they come to die – the Druids are all-powerful, and it is only a fool who will dare to oppose them. Every five years there is a great religious cleansing – like our five-yearly census – and in expiation of national sins human victims are burned alive in great wicker cages built to resemble men. The victims are bandits, criminals, men who have revealed religious secrets or have been guilty of any similar crime, and men whom the Druids accuse of having unlawfully practised magic to suit their private ends and of having blighted crops or caused a pestilence by doing so. The Druids at that time outlawed any man who had embraced the Roman religion or allied himself by marriage with a family that had done so. That, I suppose, they were entitled to do; but when it came to burning such people alive, then they had to be taught a lesson.

They have two peculiarly holy places. The first is the island of Anglesey on the west coast, where their winter quarters are, among great groves of sacred oaks, and the sacred oak-log fire is kept burning. This fire, kindled originally by lightning, is distributed for the cremation of corpses, to ensure their reincarnation. The other sacred place is a great stone temple in the middle of Britain, consisting of concentric rings of enormous trilithic and monolithic altars. It is dedicated to the God of Life-in-Death, and from the New Year, which they reckon from the spring equinox, until midsummer, they hold their annual religious Games there. A red-haired young man is chosen to represent the God and is dressed in marvellous robes. While the Games last he is free to do exactly as he pleases. Everything is at his disposal, and if he takes a fancy to any jewel or weapon, the owner counts himself honoured and gives it up gladly. All the most beautiful girls are his playmates, and the competing athletes and musicians do everything they can to win his favour. Shortly before midsummer, however, he goes with the Arch-Druid, who is the representative of the God of Death, to an oak on which mistletoe grows. The Arch-Druid climbs the oak and cuts the mistletoe with a golden sickle, taking care that it does not touch the ground. This mistletoe is the soul of the oak, which then mysteriously withers away. A white bull is sacrificed. The young man is wrapped in leafy oak branches and taken to the Temple, which is so oriented that at dawn on Midsummer Day the sun strikes down an avenue of stones and lights up the principal altar where the young man is laid, fast bound, and where the Arch-Druid sacrifices him with the sharpened stem of the mistletoe. I cannot discover what eventually happens to the body, which for the present remains laid out on the stone of sacrifice, showing no sign of decay. But the priestess of Sulis, from a western town called the 'Waters of Sulis', where there are medicinal springs, comes to claim it at the autumn festival of farewell and the Goddess is then supposed to restore it to life. The God is said to go by boat to the western island where Nodons lives and to conquer him after a fierce fight. The winter storms are the noise of that fight. He reappears next year in the person of the new victim. The withered oak tree provides new logs for the sacred fire. At the autumn festival of farewell each society sacrifices its tribal animal, burning a wicker cage full of them, and all ritual masks and head-dresses are burned too. It is at this stone temple that the complicated initiation ceremony for new Druids takes place. It is said to involve the sacrifice of newly-born children. The temple stands in the centre of a great necropolis, for all Druids and men of high religious rank are buried here with ceremonies that ensure reincarnation.

There are British battle-gods and goddesses too, but they have little connexion with the Druid religion and sufficiently resemble our own Mars and Bellona to make no description necessary.

In France the centre of Druidism was at Dreux, a town lying to the west of Paris, some eighty miles from the Channel coast. Human sacrifices continued to be performed there just as if Roman civilization did not exist. Imagine, the Druids used to cut open the bodies of victims whom they had sacrificed to the God Tanarus and examine their entrails for auspices with as little compunction as you or I would feel in the case of a ram or sacred chicken! Augustus had not attempted to put down Druidism; he had merely forbidden Roman citizens to belong to secret societies or to attend Druidical sacrifices. Tiberius had ventured to publish an edict dissolving the Druidical order in France; but this edict was not intended to be literally obeyed, only to withhold Roman official sanction from any decisions arrived at or penalties imposed by a Druidical council.

The Druids continued to cause us trouble in France, though many tribes now abandoned the cult altogether, and adopted our Roman religion. I was determined, as soon as I had conquered Britain, to strike a bargain with the Arch-Druid: in return for permission to conduct his religion in Britain in the customary way (though abstaining from any unfriendly preaching against Rome) he must refuse to admit French candidates for initiation into the Druidical order and must allow no British Druids to cross the Channel. Without priests, the religion would soon die out in France, where I should make illegal any Druidical ceremony or festival involving human sacrifice, and charge with murder all who were found to have taken part in one. Eventually, of course, Druidism would have to be stamped out in Britain too; but that need not be thought about yet.

Chapter 17

MY study of Julius Caesar's commentaries on his two British campaigns made it clear to me that unless conditions had changed considerably since his day it was possible to beat the Britons in any engagement by only a slight modification of our fighting tactics. Considerable forces, however, would have to be employed.

It is a great mistake to start a campaign with only a couple of regiments, get them badly knocked about in attempting the work of four, and then send home for reinforcements, thereby giving the enemy a breathing space. It is best to start with as imposing a force as can be commanded and to strike as hard as possible.

The British infantry are armed with broadswords and small leather bucklers. Man for man, they are the equals and even the superiors of the Romans, but their fighting value decreases with their numbers, as ours increases. In the clash of a battle a company of British warriors has no chance against an equal force of disciplined Romans. The Roman javelin, short stabbing sword, and long shield with its flanges for interlocking with neighbour shields, make an ideal equipment at close quarters. British arms are designed for single combat, but need plenty of space for manoeuvre. If the press of battle is too close to allow one to swing the broadsword handily and if the locking of enemy shields prevents one from dealing lateral strokes with it, it is of little use; and the small buckler is insufficient protection against javelin-thrusts.

British noblemen fight from chariots like the Greek heroes at Troy, and like the early Latin chieftains. The chariot has now, of course, disappeared from civilized warfare and only remains as an emblem of high military rank or of victory. This is because cavalry has taken the place of chariotry, the breed of horses having greatly improved. In Britain there are few horses suitable for mounting cavalry. British chariots are drawn by small strong ponies, highly trained. They can be pulled up sharp even when travelling downhill at a good speed and turned right-about in a flash. Each chariot is a fighting-unit in itself. The driver and commander is the nobleman, who has two fighters with him in the chariot, and two or more runners, armed with knives, who keep up with the ponies. The fighters often run along the pole and stand balanced on the cross-piece. The runners try to hamstring the ponies of opposing chariots. A column of chariots driven at full speed will usually break an infantry line by dashing straight at it. But if the line seems disposed to stand its ground, the chariot column will wheel right past it, the fighting men raining down spears as they go by, and then turn in behind and launch another volley from the rear. When this manoeuvre has been repeated several times the charioteers withdraw to a safe place, and the fighting men, dismounting and now joined by infantry supports, lead these to a final attack.

Should this attack fail, the chariots are once more manned and are ready to fight a rearguard action. The British chariot combines indeed, as Julius remarked, the celerity of cavalry with the stability of infantry. Naturally, enveloping tactics are much favoured by chariot squadrons. Naturally, too, the British suffer from the common fault of undisciplined fighting men – they will always go for plunder before destroying the main body of the enemy. I had to evolve some new tactical plan for dealing with the British chariotry: Julius's French cavalry had been unable to hold them in check – perhaps he should have borrowed an idea from the enemy and used them in conjunction with light-armed infantry. But I could count on winning every infantry engagement.

I decided that the largest force that the Empire could spare for the expedition would be four regular infantry regiments and four regiments of auxiliaries, together with 1,000 cavalry. After consultation with my army commanders I withdrew three regiments from the Rhine – namely, the Second, Twentieth, and Fourteenth – and one from the Danube, the Ninth. I entrusted the command of the expedition to Galba, with Geta as his Master of Horse, and planned it for the middle of April. But there was considerable delay in getting the transports built, and when these were ready Galba fell ill and I decided to wait for his recovery; by the middle of June he was still very feeble and I had regretfully to decide against waiting any longer. I gave his command to a veteran who had the reputation of being the cleverest tactician and one of the bravest men in the army, Aulus Plautius, a distant connexion of my first wife, Urgulanilla. He was a man in the late fifties and had been Consul fourteen years previously: old soldiers remembered him as a popular commander of the Fourteenth under my brother. He went to Mainz to take command of the regiments detailed for the expedition. The delay caused by Galba's illness was the more unwelcome because news of the coming invasion, which had been kept a close secret until April, had now been carried over the Channel, and Caractacus and Togodumnus were busily preparing defensive positions. The Ninth Regiment had reached Lyons from the Danube some time before and two regiments of French auxiliaries and one of Swiss had long been under arms there too. I sent Aulus the order to march the Rhine regiments up to Boulogne, picking up a regiment of Batavian auxiliaries on his way – the Batavians are a German tribe living on an island at the mouth of the Rhine – and cross the Channel in the transports which he would find waiting there. The Lyons forces would arrive at Boulogne simultaneously. An unexpected difficulty arose. The Rhine regiments could not be persuaded to start. They said quite openly that they were very well off where they were and regarded the expedition to Britain as a dangerous and useless undertaking. They said that the Rhine defences would be seriously weakened by their removal – though I had brought the garrison there up to strength by brigading large forces of French auxiliaries with the remaining regiments, and by forming an entirely new regiment, the Twenty-second – and that the invasion of Britain was against the wishes of the God Augustus, who had permanently fixed the strategic boundaries of the Empire at the Rhine and Channel.

I was at Lyons myself by this time – the middle of July – and would have gone to the Rhine in person to persuade the men to do their duty, but signs of unrest were showing themselves in the Ninth regiment too, and among the French, so I sent Narcissus, who was with me, there as my representative. It was really a foolish thing to do, but my fool's luck gave it a happy ending. I had not quite realized how unpopular Narcissus was. It was commonly believed that I took his advice on every point and that he led me by the nose. Narcissus on his arrival at the Mainz camp greeted Aulus in rather an offhand way and asked him to parade the men before the Tribunal platform. When this was done he mounted it, puffed out his chest, and began the following speech: 'In the name of our Emperor, Tiberius Claudius Caesar Augustus Germanicus. Men, you have been ordered to march to Boulogne, there to embark for an invasion of Britain. You have grumbled and made difficulties. This is very wrong. It is a breach of your oath to the Emperor. If the Emperor orders an expedition you are expected to obey and not to argue. I have come here to recall you to your senses. ...'

Narcissus was not speaking like a messenger but as though he were Emperor himself. Naturally this had an irritating effect on the men. There were shouts of 'Get down from that Tribunal, you Greek valet', and 'We don't want to hear what *you* have to say.'

But Narcissus had a very good opinion of himself and embarked upon floods of reproachful oratory. 'Yes,' he said, 'I am only a Greek, and only a freedman, but it seems that I know my duty better than you Roman citizens.'

Suddenly someone shouted out, '*Io Saturnalia*' and all the irritation vanished in a great roar of laughter. '*Io Saturnalia*' is the cry that goes up on our All Fools' Festival, which is celebrated annually in honour of the God Saturn. During the festival everything is topsy-turvy. Everyone has licence to say and do just as he likes. Slaves wear their masters' clothes and order them about as though they were slaves. The noble is abased and the base is ennobled. Everyone now took up the cry '*Io Saturnalia, Io Saturnalia!* The Freedman is Emperor to-day.' Ranks were broken and an absurd riot of jokes and horseplay started, in which first the captains, then one or two senior officers, and finally Aulus Plautius himself strategically joined. Aulus dressed up as a woman of the camp and bustled round with a kitchen cleaver. Four or five sergeants climbed up on the Tribunal and pretended to be rivals for Narcissus's love. Narcissus was bewildered and burst into tears. Aulus rushed to his rescue, swinging his cleaver. 'You vile men,' he screamed in falsetto, 'leave my poor husband alone! He's a worthy, respectable man!' He drove them off the platform and embraced Narcissus, whispering in his ear as he did so: 'Leave this to me, Narcissus. They're like a lot of children. Humour them now and afterwards you can do anything you like with them!' He dragged Narcissus forward by the hand and said: 'My poor husband isn't quite himself, you see – he's not accustomed to Camp wine and your rough ways. But he'll be all right after a night in bed with me, won't you, my poppet?' He took Narcissus by the ear. 'Now listen to me, husband! This Mainz is a tough place. It's where mice nibble iron, and cocks blow the reveillez with little silver trumpets, and wasps carry javelins slung round their waists.'

Narcissus pretended to be frightened – and he was frightened. But they soon forgot all about him. There were other games to play. When the fun was beginning to slacken, Aulus resumed his general's cloak and called for a trumpeter and told him to blow the Attention. In a minute or two order was restored and he held up his hand for silence and made a speech:

'Men, we've had our All Fools' Day fun and we've enjoyed it, and now the trumpet has ended it. So let's get back to work and discipline again. To-morrow I shall take the auspices, and if they are favourable you must be prepared to strike camp. We have to go to Boulogne, whether we like it or not. It's our duty. And from Boulogne we have to go to Britain, whether we like it or not. It's our duty. And when we get there we are going to fight a big battle, whether we like it or not. It's our duty. And the Britons are going to get the worst beating of their lives, whether they like it or not.

It's their bad luck. Long live the Emperor!' That speech saved the situation and there was no further trouble. Narcissus was able to leave the camp without further loss of dignity.

Ten days later, on August the first, my birthday, the expeditionary force sailed. Aulus had agreed with me that it would be best to send over the troops in three divisions, at intervals of two or three hours, because the landing of one division would concentrate all the British forces at that point, and the others could sail up the coast to some undefended spot and land unopposed. But as it happened not even the first division met with any resistance on landing, because the news had reached Britain that the Rhine troops had refused to march, and besides it was thought to be too late in the season now for us to attempt anything that year. The only event worthy of note in the crossing was the sudden wind that sprang up and drove the first division back on to the second; but a lucky portent then occurred, a flash of light travelling from the east across to the west, which was the direction in which they were sailing; so everyone who was not incapacitated by sea-sickness took heart again, and the landing was made in a victorious mood. Aulus's task was to occupy the whole southern part of their land, drawing his strategical frontier from the River Severn on the west to the great bay, the Wash, on the east: thus including the whole of the former dominions of Cymbeline in a new Roman province. He was, however, to permit any tribes who voluntarily offered their submission to Rome the usual privileges of subject allies. Since it was a war of conquest and not a mere punitive expedition, the greatest magnanimity must be shown the conquered – consistent only with their not mistaking it for weakness. Property must not be needlessly destroyed, nor women ravished, nor children and old people killed. He was to tell his men: 'The Emperor wants prisoners, not corpses. And since you are to be permanently stationed in this country his advice is to do as little damage to it in the process as possible. Wise birds do not foul their own nests; not even nests captured from other birds.'

His main objective was Colchester, the Catuvellaunian capital city. When it was captured, the Icenians of the east coast would no doubt come to him there to offer him their alliance, and he could build a strong base for the conquest of the centre and southwest of the island. I told him that should his losses amount to more than a couple of thousand killed or disabled before the enemy's main resistance was crushed, or should there appear to be any doubt as to the issue of the campaign before winter set in, he was to send me a message at once, and I would come to his help with my reserves. The message would be relayed across France and Italy by bonfire signal, and if the bonfire-men kept their eyes open I ought to receive the news at Rome a few hours after the message left Boulogne. The reserves that I would bring up would include eight battalions of Guards, the entire Guards cavalry, four companies of Nubian spearmen, and three companies of Balearic slingers. They would be quartered at Lyons in readiness.

I had intended to remain at Lyons with these reserves, but was forced to return to Rome. Vitellius, who was acting as my understudy, wrote that he found the work incredibly difficult, that he was already two months behindhand in his judicial work, and that he had reason to suspect that my legal secretary, Myron, was not as honest as we had both supposed. There was another most unwelcome letter that reached me from Marsus at the same time and made me feel that I ought not to be away from Rome a day longer than I could help. Marsus's letter ran as follows:

The Governor of Syria, Vibius Marsus, has the honour to greet the Emperor on the occasion of his approaching birthday and report that the province is prosperous, contented, orderly, and loyal. At the same time he confesses himself somewhat disquieted by a recent incident at the town of Tiberias, on the Lake of Galilee, and begs the Emperor to approve the measures that he has taken in dealing with it.

An unofficial report reached headquarters at Antioch that King Herod Agrippa had invited to a secret meeting the following neighbouring potentates – Antiochus, King of Commagene, Sampsigeramus, King of Osroëne, Cotys, King of Lesser Armenia, Polemo, King of Pontus and Cilicia, Sohemus, King of Iturea, Herod Pollio, King of Chalcis. If the news of this meeting leaked out, the explanation was to be that it was a commemoration of King Herod Agrippa's marriage to his Queen Cypros exactly twenty years before. No invitation to any such banquet was sent me as your representative, though the decencies clearly required it: let me repeat that the only information that reached me about this extraordinary assemblage of potentates came from unofficial, not to say underground, sources. Sohemus of Iturea was ill, but sent his chamberlain to represent him. The other kings all obeyed King Herod's summons. Those whose route would naturally have led them by way of Antioch (namely, all those mentioned above except King Herod Pollio and King Sohemus) and who, on a visit to Galilee, should certainly have turned aside to pay their compliments to me as your representative, chose to follow a roundabout route, travelling incognito and for the most part at night. It was only through the vigilance of certain of my agents in the Syrian desert east of Chalcis that I learned that they were already on their way.

I immediately proceeded to Tiberias myself, at all speed, accompanied by my two daughters and my chief staff-officers, hoping to take the gathering by surprise. King Herod Agrippa, however, must have been informed of my approach. He came driving out from Tiberias in his royal carriage to welcome me. We met at a point seven furlongs from the city. He had not come alone, but was escorted by his five royal visitors, the last of whom, the King of Pontus, had only that moment arrived. King Herod did not appear in the least abashed, but climbed out of his coach and came hurrying to greet me in the warmest manner imaginable. He exclaimed how delighted he was that I had managed to come after all, after making no reply to his two letters of invitation, and remarked that this was indeed an extraordinary event – seven Eastern rulers meeting at the seventh furlong-stone. He would have the stone replaced by a marble pillar of commemoration with our names and titles engraved on it in letters of gold. I was bound to reply politely and accept his story that he had sent me two invitations, and even swear that as soon as I discovered the enemy who had intercepted the letters – which had not reached me – I would punish him with the utmost rigour of the law. The other kings had also dismounted, and an exchange of civilities began between us. The King of Commagene, whom I used to know at Rome, suggested that perhaps King Herod's invitation had been, somewhat officiously, withheld from me by one of my servants out of consideration for my feelings. I asked him what he meant and he replied that the recent death of my wife might be too fresh in my memory to make an invitation to someone's else's wedding anniversary altogether a pleasing one. I replied that my wife had been dead these four years, and he said, sighing: 'As long ago as all that? It seems like yesterday that I last saw her. A very lovely woman.' I then asked the King of Pontus point-blank why he had not stopped at Antioch to greet me. He told me without a blush that he had counted on seeing me at the banquet and that he had taken a more easterly route because of the advice of a soothsayer.

It was impossible to shake the self-possession of any of the six of them, so we all drove into Tiberias together through a cheering mob. The wedding banquet, the most lavish that I have ever attended, was served a few hours later. Meanwhile I sent one of my staff-officers to each of the kings to tell him privately that if he wished to keep the friendship of Rome he would be advised to return to his own country as soon as politeness to our host permitted, and meanwhile not to take part in any secret conference with his royal neighbours. To be brief, the banquet ended at a late hour and the guests made their excuses and left on the following day: no conference took place. I was the last to leave, and the King and I parted with the usual compliments. However, on my return to Antioch I found an unsigned letter awaiting me. It ran: 'You have insulted my guests and you must accept the consequences: I am now your enemy.' I assume it to be a message from King Herod Agrippa.

My compliments to the most virtuous and beautiful Lady Valeria Messalina, your wife.

The more I studied this report, the less I liked it. It looked as though Herod, taking advantage of my preoccupation with Britain, and the presence there of so large an army – which might easily need further reinforcements – was planning a general rising in the East, for which his fortification of Jerusalem had been the prelude. I grew extremely anxious, but there was nothing that I could do except pray for a speedy victory in Britain and let Herod know that Marcus was keeping me in touch with Near Eastern affairs. I wrote to him at once, giving exaggeratedly cheerful news of the British expedition – for at the time of writing Aulus had not yet been able to get into touch with any considerable force of the enemy, who were adopting the same tactics that their forefathers had employed against Julius in his march through Kent – and saying, quite untruly, that since the expedition was only intended as a punitive one I expected the regiments back across the Channel in a couple of months.

This was the first lie that I had ever told Herod, and since I merely committed it to paper without the embarrassment of telling it verbally, I managed to make him believe it. I wrote:

... And are you able to tell me anything definite, Brigand, about this prophesied Eastern Ruler who is destined after his death to become the greatest God that has ever appeared on earth? I am continually coming across references to him. There was one in court the other day. A Jew was accused of creating a disturbance in the City. He was alleged to have shaken his fist at a priest of Mars and exclaimed: 'When the Ruler manifests himself, that will be the end of men like you. Your temples will be razed to the ground and you'll be buried in the ruins, you dog! And the time is not far off now.' Under cross-examination he denied having said anything of the sort, and as the evidence was conflicting I did no more than banish him – if you can call it banishment to send a Jew back to Judaea. Well, Caligula believed himself to be this prophesied Ruler and in certain respects the prophecy, as it was reported to me, did indeed seem to point to him. My grandmother Livia had also been misled, by something that the astrologer Thrasyllus said about the year of her death corresponding with that of this prophesied person, into believing that it was she who was meant. She did not realize that it was a God and not a Goddess who was prophesied, nor that his first manifestation should be at Jerusalem – Caligula was there as a child – though later he should reign at Rome. Is there anything written about him in the Jewish sacred writings? If so, precisely what? I understand that your learned relative Philo is an expert in such matters. I was talking the matter over with Messalina the other day and she asked me whether anyone had inherited this peculiar obsession from my now deified grandmother Livia Augusta and from my crazy nephew Caligula. I told her, 'I haven't, I swear, in spite of the divinity that Herod Agrippa is always trying to curse me with'. But what about you yourself, my old Brigand? Perhaps you are really the person meant? No, on second thoughts you certainly are not, in spite of your connexion with Jerusalem. The prophesied Ruler is specified as a man of extreme holiness. Besides, Thrasyllus was quite positive as to the year of his death, the fifteenth year of Tiberius's reign, which was the year Livia was to die – and did actually die. Thrasyllus never to my knowledge made a mistake in dates. So you have lost your chance. But, on the other hand, if Thrasyllus was right, why have we not yet heard about this dead King? Caligula knew a part of the prophecy, which was that this King was to die forsaken by his friends and that afterwards they would drink his blood. Curiously enough, that was fulfilled in his case: Bubo, one of the assassins, you remember, had sworn to kill him and drink his blood in revenge, and did dabble his fingers in the wound he had made and then lick them dry, the madman. But Caligula died nine years too late to agree with the prophecy. I should be very grateful if you would tell me what you know about all this. Perhaps there are two or three prophecies that have got mixed up together? Or perhaps Caligula was misinformed as to the particulars? He was told of the prophecy by the poisoner Martina, the one who was concerned in my poor brother Germanicus's murder at Antioch. But I hear that it has long been current in Egypt, as a pronouncement of the oracle of Jupiter Ammon.

Why I wrote in this way was that I now knew that Herod did really fancy himself to be this prophesied Ruler. I had been told all about it by Herodias and Antipas, whom I had visited in their place of banishment during my stay in France. I could not allow them to return to Judaea, though I knew now that they had not been guilty of plotting against Caligula, but I allowed them to leave Lyons and gave them a fair-sized estate at Cadiz in Spain, where the climate was more like the one to which they were accustomed. They showed me an indiscreet letter from Herodias's daughter Salome, now married to her first cousin, Herod Pollio's son.

Herod Agrippa is growing more and more religious every day. He tells his old friends that he is only playing at being a strict Jew for political reasons, and that he still secretly worships the Roman Gods. But I know now that this is only pretence. He is extraordinarily conscientious in his observances. The Alabarch's son, Tiberius Alexander, who has abandoned the Jewish faith, much to the shame and grief of his excellent family, tells me that while he was staying at Jerusalem the other day he took Herod aside and whispered: 'I hear you have an Arabian cook who really understands how to stuff and roast a midnight sucking-pig. Would you be good enough to invite me in some night? It is impossible to get really eatable food in Jerusalem.' Herod went scarlet and stammered that his cook was ill! The truth is that he dismissed this cook long ago. Tiberius Alexander has another queer story about Herod. You have heard of that farcical occasion when he visited Alexandria with a bodyguard of two soldiers whom he had kidnapped to prevent them from serving a warrant on him, and borrowed money from the Alabarch? It appears that the Alabarch afterwards went to Philo, that learned brother of his who tries to reconcile Greek philosophy with Jewish scripture, and said, 'I have probably been a fool, brother Philo, but I have lent Herod Agrippa a large sum of money on rather doubtful security. In return he has promised to protect our interests at Rome, and has sworn before Almighty God to cherish and protect His people, so far as in him lies, and to obey His Law.' Philo asked: 'From where did this Herod Agrippa suddenly appear? I thought that he was at Antioch.' The Alabarch said: 'From Edom: wearing a purple cloak – Bozrah purple – and stepping like a king. I cannot help believing that in spite of his former follies and vicissitudes he is destined to play a great part in our national history. He is a man of outstanding talent. And now that he has definitely pledged himself ...' Philo suddenly grew very serious and began to quote the prophet Isaiah: 'Who is this that cometh from Edom, with dyed garments from Bozrah? This that is glorious in his apparel, travelling in the greatness of his strength? ... I have trodden the wine-press alone; and of the people there was none with me. But the day of vengeance is in mine heart, and the year of my Redeemed is come.' Philo has long been convinced that the Messiah is at hand. He has written several volumes on that head. He builds his argument on the text in *Numbers* about the Star out of Jacob, and reconciles it with a number of others in the Prophets. He's quite crazy, poor man. And now that Herod has become so powerful and has kept his promise about observing the Law so faithfully and done the Alexandrian Jews so many services, Philo is really convinced that Herod is the Messiah. What finally decided him was the discovery that Herod's family, though an Edomite one, is descended from a son of Zedekiah, the last king of Judah before the Captivity. (This Zedekiah managed to smuggle his newly-born son out of the city and get him safe to friends in Edom before Nebuchadnezzar captured the place.) Herod seems to have been persuaded by Philo that he really is the Messiah and that he is destined not to redeem the Jews from the yoke of the foreigner, but to combine all the Children of Shem together in a great spiritual Empire under the rule of the Lord of Hosts: this is the only possible explanation for his recent political activities which, I must confess, make me feel extremely nervous for the future. Indeed, there seems to be altogether too much religion in the air. It's a bad sign. It reminds me of what you said when we had that mystical idiot John the Baptist beheaded – 'Religious fanaticism is the most dangerous form of insanity.'

I have said too much, I think, but I can trust you, my dear mother, not to let the story go any farther. Burn this when you have read it.

There was no more news from Marsus and I did not get an answer from Herod himself before I sailed for Britain – for, a fortnight after landing, Aulus was indeed obliged to send for me. But I reckoned that Herod would read between the lines of my letter that I suspected him, though I was careful not to mention Marsus in it, or the wedding celebrations at Tiberias; and that he would be very careful about his next step. I also strengthened the garrison at Alexandria and told Marsus to call up all Greek levies in Syria and give them an intensive drilling: letting the rumour go about that a Parthian invasion was expected. He was to do this as if on his own initiative, and not to tell anyone that the orders came from me.

Chapter 18

AULUS, as I have already related, landed in Britain without meeting any opposition. He built a strong base camp at Richborough, which he garrisoned with veterans from each regiment, pulled up his transport on the shore, well out of the reach of storms, and began a cautious advance through Kent, taking the route followed by Julius on his second expedition – the route indeed that all the invaders of the island have naturally taken. At first he met with less resistance than Julius, because the passage of the Stour did not need to be forced. The King of East Kent, a vassal of Caractacus and Togodumnus, decided not to man the prepared positions there. His overlords had withdrawn their main army to Colchester when they heard that our invasion could not possibly take place that year, and his own forces were insufficient to defend the river successfully. He came to meet Aulus with tokens of peace and after an exchange of presents swore alliance and friendship with Rome. The King of East Sussex, which lies to the west of Kent, came into camp on the same errand a few days later. Between the Stour and the River Medway, the next natural barrier, Aulus encountered little serious resistance. But small parties of chariot-fighters disputed the frequent barriers of felled trees and thorn bushes that had been thrown across the track. Aulus's advance-guard commander was now instructed not to force these barriers, but as soon as they were sighted to envelop them with cavalry detachments and capture the defenders. This slowed down progress, but no lives were wasted. Most of the Kentish men seemed to have retired into the Weald – thick forest-land from which it would be most difficult to dislodge them. But increasingly large forces of chariotry began to appear on the flanks of the advancing column, charging down on foraging parties and forcing them to fall back on the main body. Aulus was aware that the mood in which the Kentish men would finally emerge from the Weald, whether meekly to offer their submission or valiantly to cut off his retreat, depended on his success against the Catuvellaunians. However, his base camp was well defended.

When he came to the tidal reaches of the Medway, which Julius, in his second campaign, had forded without loss, he found the enemy assembled in great force behind positions that had been prepared some months before. Caractacus and Togodumnus were both present with all their tributary princes and an army of some 60,000 men. Aulus had no more than 35,000 effectives with him. The narrow ford across the river had been made practically impassable by a succession of deep wide channels cut across it parallel with the banks. The Britons were bivouacked in a careless fashion on the other side. The nearest ford upstream was a day's march away and was reported by prisoners to be similarly fortified. Downstream there was no ford: the river, after debouching into the Thames estuary not far from this spot, spread out across impassable mud-flats. Aulus set his men to work at making the ford passable, filling in the channels with basketfuls of rubble. But it was clear that at this rate two or three days would pass before he could attempt to cross. The enemy bank was defended by two strong stockades, and the Britons, who now harassed the workers with arrows and insults, were building a third one behind that. Twice a day a huge tide welled up into the river mouth – a commonplace in this part of the world, though never seen in the Mediterranean, except during storms – and hindered Aulus's work greatly. But he was counting on the tide as his ally. At high tide, just before dawn on the third day, he sent the Batavian auxiliaries swimming across the motionless water. All Germans swim well, and the Batavians better than any. They swam across, 3,000 strong, with their weapons tied on their backs, and caught the Britons completely by surprise. However, instead of attacking the startled men at their camp-fires, they rushed to the horse-lines and began disabling the chariot-ponies, putting 2,000 or 3,000 of these out of action before their owners realized what was happening. They then established themselves at the enemy end of the ford behind the middle barricade, which had been designed to face the other way, and held it against strong British attacks while two battalions of the Ninth Regiment struggled across the river to their assistance, on blown-up wine-skins and improvised rafts and in captured British coracles. The struggle was a fierce one, and the British detachments posted higher up the stream, to prevent our men from crossing at any point there, came charging down to take part in the fight. Aulus saw what was happening, and detailed the Second under a certain Vespasian * to go upstream under cover of a forest and cross over at some now unguarded bend. Vespasian found the right place four or five miles upstream where the river narrowed somewhat and sent a man swimming over with a line. The line served to pull a rope across, which was made fast to a tree on either bank and then tautened. The Second were trained to this manoeuvre and were all across the river in an hour or two. Numerous ropes had to be used, because the distance was so great that to keep any one rope taut enough to hold the weight of more than twenty or thirty heavily armed men at a time was to risk it snapping. Once over, they hurried downstream, meeting none of the enemy as they went, and an hour later suddenly appeared on the enemy's unprotected right flank. They locked shields, shouted, and burst right through to the stockade, killing hundreds of British tribesmen in a single charge. The Batavians and the men of the Ninth joined forces with the Second; and

* Afterwards Emperor (A.D. 69–79). – R.G.

although greatly outnumbered, the combined forces drove the confused and disordered but still courageous enemy slowly backwards until they broke in undeniable rout. The river bank was clear of the British, and Aulus spent the rest of the day in hastily constructing a narrow brushwood causeway across the ford: at low tide this was anchored down firmly and the channels filled in. It was late that night, however, before the work was finished, and the whole army was not safely over – the rising tide interrupted their crossing – until next morning.

The Britons had rallied on the rising ground behind, and in the afternoon a pitched battle took place. The French infantry, who had taken no part in the previous day's fighting, led the attack; but the defence was stubborn and a great column of chariotry suddenly broke across the centre from the left flank, cutting in just behind the leading French regiment, which was advancing in line and causing it heavy casualties with a quick volley of spears. When this column, which was led by Caractacus in person, reached the right flank it daringly wheeled round and cut in behind the second French regiment, which was moving up in support, and played the same game with them, driving away without loss. The French were unable to take the ridge, and Aulus, seeing that the British chariotry and cavalry were concentrated on his right flank, about to make a strong attack on the now disordered French, galloped a third of his own cavalry up to the threatened position with instructions to hold it at all costs. Off went the cavalry and Aulus threw the whole of his regular infantry after them, with the exception of the Second Regiment. Leaving the Second to support the French, should the British make a counter-attack, and moving Geta with some Batavian infantry and the remainder of the cavalry forward to the left flank, Aulus pushed home the attack on the right. The British chariotry could not check this advance, though our cavalry lost heavily before the leading regiment, the Fourteenth, came up to relieve them. Caractacus then wheeled his column round behind the ridge for an attack on our left flank.

Geta was the hero of the battle. He and his 700 cavalrymen stood up against a desperate charge of nearly 2,000 chariots; 500 of the same Batavians who had maimed the ponies during the dawn raid were mixed in with the cavalry and used their knives to good purpose again. But for them Geta would have been overwhelmed. Geta himself was unhorsed and nearly captured, but Caractacus finally withdrew, leaving 100 wrecked chariots behind him. By this time the pressure of the regular infantry on the right flank was being felt by the British. The French, too, were more than holding their own, and suddenly the cry went up that Togodumnus had been carried off the field, mortally wounded. The British were disheartened. Their lines wavered and broke, streaming towards our left flank, where they ran unexpectedly into Geta's men advancing through a little wood. Geta charged, and when the battle was over 1,500 British corpses were found on that part of the field alone. The total British casualties in killed amounted to 4,000. Ours amounted to 900, of whom 700 were French; with about the same amount of seriously wounded. Among those who died of wounds was Bericus, the cause of the war, who had been fighting by Geta's side and saved his life when he was unhorsed.

Aulus's next important obstacle was the Thames, which Caractacus now held in much the same way as he had held the Medway. The defeated Britons retired behind it by taking a secret path across the mud-flats at its mouth when the tide was out. Our advance-guard tried to follow them, but got bogged and had to retire. The ensuing battle was almost a repetition of the previous one, the conditions being very similar. This time it was Crassus Frugi, the father of young Pompey, my son-in-law, who made the upstream crossing. He forced his way across the bridge at London, which was held by a company of young British noblemen sworn to fight to the last man. The Batavians again swam across the lower reaches of the river at high tide. The British defence was weaker on this occasion and their losses were again heavy. Ours were inconsiderable – 300 – and 2,000 prisoners were taken. London was captured, with rich booty. The victory was spoilt, however, by the loss of nearly 1,000 French and Batavians who incautiously pursued the beaten enemy into marshland and were swallowed up in a quaking bog.

Aulus was now across the Thames, but the enemy resistance suddenly stiffened with the arrival of reinforcements from the south, west, and centre of the island. Strong new chariot-contingents appeared. The death of Togodumnus proved a positive advantage to the Britons: the supreme command of the Catuvellaunian army was no longer divided, and Caractacus, who was an able leader and in great favour with the Druids, could make an impassioned plea to his allies and vassals to avenge his noble brother's death. As the Roman losses had exceeded the stipulated maximum and the enemy's resistance could not be claimed to have been broken, Aulus now wisely sent the agreed message back to me. It went to Boulogne by one of the ships which, as arranged, had now reached London from Richborough with a cargo of wine, blankets, and military stores. At Boulogne the first beacon was lighted and within a very short time the message had crossed the Alps and was hurrying on to Rome.

It was the day that I had finally found convincing proof of Myron's fraud and forgeries. I had just had him flogged in the presence of all my other chief secretaries and then executed. I was tired out by a difficult and unpleasant day and had just settled down before supper to a friendly game of dice with Vitellius, when the eunuch Posides, my military secretary, came running in excitedly with the news: 'Caesar, the beacon! You're wanted in Britain.'

'Britain?' I exclaimed. I had the dice-cup in my hand, and mechanically shook it once more and threw down the dice before hurrying to the window of the room that faced north. 'Show me!' I said. It was a clear evening and in the direction that Posides pointed I could make out, even with my weak eyes, the little red point of light on the summit of Mount Soracte, thirty miles away. I returned to the table, where I found Vitellius beaming at me. 'What do you think of that for an omen?' he asked. 'Here you have been making the lowest possible scores for the last half-hour and now suddenly you call out "Britain!" and throw Venus.'

Sure enough, the three dice were lying in a neat equilateral triangle and each showed a six! The odds against Venus are 216 to one, so I can be pardoned for feeling great elation. There is nothing like a really good omen for starting a campaign with, and you must understand that Venus was not only the patroness of the dice-cup but was the mother of Aeneas, and so my own ancestress through my grandmother Octavia, Augustus's sister, and guardian of the fortunes of the Julian House, of which I was now the acknowledged head. I saw significance in the triangle too, for that is the shape of Britain on the maps.

Now that I come to think of it, I wonder whether it was Vitelius, not the Goddess, after all, who when my back was turned arranged those dice so nicely for me? I am one of the easiest people in the world to deceive: or at least that is the common verdict against me. If he did, he did well, for Venus sent me off on my conquests in the most exalted mood possible. I offered prayers to her that night (as also to Augustus and Mars) and promised her that if she helped me to victory I would do her whatever service she required of me. 'One hand washes the other,' I reminded her, 'and I really expect you to do your best.' It is a custom with us Claudians to address Venus with joking familiarity. She is supposed to enjoy it, as great-grandmothers, especially great-grandmothers with a reputation for having been very gay in their youth, sometimes encourage favourite great-grandchildren to address them with as little courtesy as if they belonged to the same generation.

The next day I sailed from Ostia for Marseilles with my staff and 500 volunteers for the war. The wind was blowing pleasantly from the south and I preferred sea-travelling to the jolting of a carriage. I would be able to get some well-needed sleep. The whole City came down to the port to see us off, and everyone tried to outdo everyone else in his expressions of loyalty and in the warmth of his good wishes. Messalina threw her arms about my neck and wept. Little Germanicus wanted to come too. Vitellius promised the God Augustus to plate his temple doors with gold if I returned victorious.

We were a fleet of five fast-sailing, two-masted, square-rigged men-of-war, each with three banks of oars, and with the hulls well frapped around with strong ropes in case of stormy weather. We raised anchor an hour after dawn and stood out to sea. There was no time to waste, so I told the captain to put on all possible sail, which he did, both sails on each mast, and the sea being calm, we were soon driving along at a good ten knots. Late that afternoon we sighted the island of Planasia, near Elba, where my poor friend Postumus had been exiled, and I could make out the now deserted buildings where his guards had been quartered. We had come 120 miles, or about a third of the way. The breeze still held. My stomach was unaffected by the pitching of the vessel and I retired to the cabin for a good sleep. That night we rounded Corsica, but the breeze dropped about midnight, and we had to rely entirely on oars. I slept well. To shorten the story, the following day we ran into rough weather and made slow progress, the wind veering gradually round to the west-north-west.

The French coast was only sighted at dawn on the third day. The sea was now extraordinarily rough and the oars were often either buried in water up to the rowlocks or beating the empty air. Only two of our four sister-vessels were still in sight. We made for the protection of the shore and coasted along it, very slowly. We were now fifty miles west of Fréjus, a station of the fleet, and threading through the Hyères islands. By midday we should have reached Marseilles. As we passed Porquerolles, the largest and most westerly of the islands, separated at one point by only a mile of sea from the peninsula of Giens which juts out to meet it, the wind struck us with terrific force; and though the crew rowed like madmen we could make no headway at all and found ourselves slowly drifting on the rocks. We were within 100 yards of destruction when the gale momentarily slackened and we managed to pull clear. But a few minutes later we were in trouble again, and this time the danger was greater still. The last headland that we had to struggle past ended in a great black rock which the action of wind and waves had carved into a grinning Satyr-head. The water boiled and hissed at its chin, giving it as it were a white beard. The wind, blowing dead amidships, was rapidly forcing us into this monster's jaws. 'If he catches us, he'll crack our bones and mangle our flesh,' the captain assured me grimly. 'Many a good ship has broken up on that black rock.' I offered prayers for succour to every God in the Pantheon. I was told afterwards that the sailors who had overheard me swore that it was the most beautiful praying that they had ever heard in their lives and that it gave them new hope. Especially I prayed to Venus and begged her to persuade her Uncle Neptune to behave with more consideration, for the fate of Rome depended very largely on the survival of this vessel: she must please remind Neptune that I did not associate myself with my predecessor's impious quarrel with him, and that on the contrary I had always held the God in the profoundest respect. The exhausted rowers strained and groaned and the rowing-master ran along the platforms with a rope-end in his hand, cursing and flogging fresh vigour into them. We scraped through somehow – I don't know how – and when a gasp of joy went up that we were out of danger I promised the rowers twenty gold pièces each as soon as we landed.

I was glad that I had kept my head. It was the first time that I had experienced a storm at sea, and I had heard it said that some of the bravest men in the world break down when faced with the prospect of death by drowning. It had even been whispered that the God Augustus was a dreadful coward in a storm, and that only his sense of the dignity of his office kept him from screaming and tearing his hair. He certainly used often to quote the tag about how 'Impious was the man who first spread sail, And braved the dangers of the frantic deep.' He was most unlucky at sea, except in his sea-battles, and – speaking of impiety – once showed his deep resentment at the loss of a fleet in a sudden storm by forbidding the statue of Neptune to be carried as usual in a sacred procession around the Circus. After this he seldom put to sea without raising a storm and was all but shipwrecked on three or four occasions.

Our vessel was the first to reach Marseilles, and fortunately not a single one of the five was lost, though two were forced to turn back and run into Fréjus. The earth felt splendidly firm under my feet at Marseilles: I determined never again to travel by sea when I could possibly travel by land, and have not once departed from this resolution since.

As soon as I had heard that a successful landing had been made in Britain I had moved up my reserves to Boulogne and ordered Posides to have transports assembled there ready, together with whatever extra military stores might suggest themselves as likely to be needed for the campaign. At Marseilles twenty fast gigs were waiting for me and my staff – Posides had arranged this – and carried us, with constant relays of horses, up the Rhône valley from Avignon to Lyons, where we spent the second night, and then on north along the Saône, travelling eighty or ninety miles a day – which was the most that I could manage because of the continuous jolting, which racked my nerves and upset my digestion and gave me violent headaches. The third night, at Châlons, my physician Xenophon insisted on my resting the whole of the next day. I told him that I could not afford to waste a whole day; he answered that if I did not rest I could not expect to be of any use to the army in Britain when I did arrive. I raged at him and tried to override his opinion, but Xenophon insisted on reading this behaviour as a further sign of nervous exhaustion and told me that either he was my doctor or I was my own. In the latter case he would resign and resume his interrupted practice at Rome: in the former, he must ask me to do as he advised me, relax completely and submit to a thorough massage. So I apologized and pleaded that to be suddenly halted in my journey would cause me such nervous anxiety that my physical condition would not be improved by any amount of compensatory massage; and that to say 'relax' was no more practical advice in the circumstances than to tell a man whose clothes have caught fire that he must keep cool. In the end we arrived at a compromise: I would not continue my journey in a gig, but neither would I remain at Châlons. I would be carried in a light sedan on the shoulders of six well-trained chairmen and thus knock off at least thirty miles or so of the 500 that still lay before me. I would submit to as much massage as he pleased both before I started and after the day's journey was over.

From Lyons it took me eight days to reach Boulogne by way of Troyes, Rheims, Soissons, and Amiens, for in the stage out of Rheims Xenophon forced me to use a sedan again. All this time I was not exactly idle. I was turning over in my mind my historical memories of great battles of the past – Julius's battles, Hannibal's battles, Alexander's, and especially those of my father and brother in Germany – and wondering whether, when it came to the point, I should be able to apply all this detailed and extensive knowledge to any practical purpose. I congratulated myself that whenever it had been possible to draw a plan of any battle from the accounts handed down by eye-witnesses I had always done so; and had thoroughly mastered the general tactical principles involved in the use of a small force of disciplined fighters against a great army of semi-civilized tribesmen, and also the strategical principles involved in the successful occupation of their country when the battle had been won.

At Amiens, lying sleepless in the early morning, I began picturing the battle-field. The British infantry would probably be occupying a wooded ridge, with their cavalry and chariotry manoeuvring in the low ground in front. I would draw up my regular infantry in ordinary battle formation, on a two-regiment front, with the auxiliaries on either flank and the Guards in reserve. The elephants, which would be a complete novelty to the Britons, no such animal having ever been seen on that island – but here a most uncomfortable thought came to me. 'Posides,' I called, in an anxious voice.

'Yes, Caesar,' Posides answered, springing up from his pallet, half-asleep still.

'The elephants *are* at Boulogne, aren't they?'

'Yes, Caesar.'

'How long ago did I give you the order to move them up there from Lyons?'

'When we heard news of the landing, Caesar; that would be on the seventh of August.'

'And to-day is the twenty-seventh.'

'Yes, Caesar.'

'Then how in the world are we going to get those elephants over? We should have had special elephant transports built.'

'The ship that brought the obelisk from Alexandria is at Boulogne.'

'But I thought that it was still at Ostia.'

'No, Caesar, at Boulogne.'

'But if you sent it up there on the seventh it can't possibly have arrived there yet. It can't possibly be any nearer than the Bay of Biscay. It took three weeks to get to Rome from Egypt, you remember; in perfect sailing weather, too.'

But Posides was a really able minister. It appears that as soon as I had decided to put elephants among my reinforcements and sent them up to Lyons – in May, I think it was – he had considered the question of transport across the Channel and without saying a word to me had fitted up the obelisk-ship as an elephant-transport – it was the only ship big and strong enough for the purpose – and sent it up to Boulogne, where it had arrived six weeks later. If he had waited for my orders the elephants would have had to be left behind. The obelisk-ship deserves more than a passing mention. It was the largest vessel ever launched. It was no less than 200 feet long and broad in proportion, and its main timbers were of cedar. Caligula had built it in the first few months of his monarchy to bring from Egypt an eighty-foot red granite obelisk, together with four enormous stones which formed the pediment. The obelisk was originally from Heliopolis, but had been set up in Augustus's temple at Alexandria a few years before. Caligula now wanted it set up in his own honour in the new Circus that he was building on the Vatican Hill. To understand what a monstrous sort of ship it was you must be told that its seventy-foot main mast was a silver fir eight feet in diameter at its base; and that among the ballast used to keep it steady when the obelisk and pediment were secured on deck were 120,000 pecks of Egyptian lentils – a gift for the people of Rome.

When I reached Boulogne I was delighted to find the troops in good spirits, the transports ready, and the sea calm. We embarked without delay, and our passage across the Channel was so pleasant and uneventful that on landing at Richborough I sacrificed to Venus and Neptune, thanking the latter for his unexpected favours and the former for her kindly intercession. The elephants gave no trouble. They were Indian elephants, not African. Indian elephants are about three times the size of African, and these were particularly fine ones which Caligula had bought for ceremonial use in his own religion: they had since been employed at the docks at Ostia moving timbers and stones under the direction of their Indian drivers. I found to my surprise that twelve camels had been added to the elephants. That was an idea of Posides's.

Chapter 19

At Richborough we were anxious to hear the latest news from Aulus, and I found a dispatch from him just arrived. It reported that the Britons had made two attacks, one by day and the other by night, on the camp which he had fortified just north of London, but had been beaten off with some loss. However, new enemy reinforcements seemed to be arriving every day, from as far west as South Wales; and the men of Kent who had retired into the Weald were reported to have sent a message through to Caractacus that as soon as Aulus was forced to retreat they would leave their woods and cut him off from his base. He begged me therefore to join forces with him as soon as possible. I talked to a few seriously wounded men whom Aulus had evacuated to the Base, and they all agreed that the British infantry was nothing to be afraid of, but that their chariotry seemed to be everywhere at once and was now so numerous as to prevent any force of less than 200 or 300 regular infantry from leaving the main body.

My column was now preparing for its advance. The elephants carried great bundles of spare javelins and other munitions of war; but certain curious machines slung across the back of the camels puzzled me.

'An invention of your Imperial Predecessor, Caesar,' Posides explained. 'I took the liberty of having a set of six made at Lyons when we were there in July and sent up to Boulogne on camelback. They're a sort of siege-engine for use against uncivilized tribes.'

'I didn't know that the late Emperor had been responsible for any military inventions.'

'I think, Caesar, that you will find this type of machine extremely effective, especially in conjunction with light rope. I have taken the liberty of bringing up several hundred yards of light rope in coils.'

Posides was grinning broadly, and I could see that he had some clever scheme at the back of his mind which he was keeping a secret from me. So I said to him: 'Xerxes the Great had a war-minister called Hermotimus, a eunuch like you, and whenever Hermotimus was allowed to solve a tactical problem by himself, such as the reduction of an impregnable town without siege-engines or the crossing of an unfordable river without boats, that problem was always solved. But if Xerxes or anyone else tried to interfere with advice or suggestions Hermotimus used to say that the problem had now become too complicated for him and beg to be excused. You're a second Hermotimus, and for good luck I am going to leave you to your own devices. Your forethought in the matter of the obelisk-ship has earned you my confidence. Understand that I expect great things from your camels and their loads. If you disappoint me I shall be greatly displeased with you and shall probably throw you to the panthers in the amphitheatre on our return.'

He answered, still grinning: 'And if I help to win the victory for you, what then?'

'Then I'll decorate you with the highest honour that it is in my power to bestow and one not inappropriate to your condition: you shall be awarded the Untipped Spear. Have you any other novelties smuggled away in the baggage? These camels and elephants and black spearmen from Africa already suggest a spectacle on Mars Field rather than a serious expedition.'

'No, Caesar, nothing else much. But I think that the Britons will have an eyeful before we have done, and we can collect the entrance money after the performance is over.'

We marched up from Richborough and met with no opposition: the river-crossings were held for us by detachments of the Fourteenth sent back by Aulus for this purpose. When we had passed they fell in behind us. I did not see a single enemy Briton between Richborough and London, where Aulus and I joined forces on the fifth of September. I think that he was as pleased to see me as I was to see him. The first thing I asked him was whether the troops were in good spirits. He answered that they were and that he had only promised them half the forces that I had brought, and had not mentioned the elephants, so that our real strength was a surprise to them. I asked him where the enemy were expected to give battle, and he showed me a contour map he had made in clay of the country between London and Colchester. He pointed out a place about twenty miles along the London–Colchester road – not a road in the Roman sense, of course – which Caractacus had been busily fortifying and which would almost certainly be the site of the coming battle. This was a wooded ridge called Brentwood Hill, which curved round the road in a great horseshoe, at each tip of which was a great stockaded fort, with another in the centre. The road ran north-east. The enemy's left flank beyond the ridge was protected by marshland, and a deep brook, called the Weald Brook, formed a defendable barrier in front. On the right flank the ridge bent round to the north and continued for three or four miles, but the trees and thorn bushes and brambles grew so densely along it that to try to turn that flank by sending a force of men to hack their way through would, Aulus assured me, be useless. Since the only feasible approach to Colchester was by this road, and since I wished to engage the main forces of the enemy as soon as possible, I studied the tactical problem involved very carefully. Prisoners and deserters volunteered precise information about the defences in the wood and these seemed to be extremely well planned. I did not welcome the notion of making a frontal attack. If we marched against the central fort without first reducing the other two we would be exposed to heavy attacks from both flanks. But to attack the other two first would not help us much either; for if we succeeded in taking them, at great cost to ourselves, it would mean fighting our way through a series of further stockades inside the wood, each of which would have to be taken in a separate operation.

At a council of war to which Aulus and I summoned all general staff-officers and regimental commanders, everyone agreed that a frontal attack on the central fort was inevitable, and that we must be prepared to suffer heavy losses. It was unfortunate that the forward slopes of the ridge between the wood and the stream were admirably suited to chariot-manoeuvre. Aulus recommended a mass attack in diamond formation. The head of the diamond would consist of a single regiment in two waves, each wave eight men deep. Then would follow two regiments marching abreast, in the same formation as the leading one; then three regiments marching abreast. This would be the broadest part of the diamond and here the elephants would be disposed as a covering for each flank. Then would come two regiments, again, and then one. The cavalry and the rest of the infantry would be kept in reserve. Aulus explained that this diamond afforded a protection against charges from the flank: no attack could be made on the flank of the leading regiment without engaging the javelin-fire of the overlapping second line, nor on the second line without engaging the fire of the overlapping third. The third line was protected by the elephants. If a heavy chariot charge was made from a rear flank the regiments there could be turned about and the same mutual protection given.

My comments on this diamond were that it was a pretty formation and that it had been used successfully in such and such battles – I listed them – in republican times; but that the Britons outnumbered us so greatly that once we had advanced into the centre of the horse-shoe they could attack us from all sides at once with forces that we could not drive off without disorganization: the front of the diamond would almost certainly become separated from the rear. I said too, very forcibly, that I was not prepared to suffer one-tenth of the number of casualties that it had been estimated the frontal attack would cost. Vespasian came out with the old proverb about not being able to make an omelette without breaking eggs, and asked somewhat impatiently whether I proposed to cut my losses and return to France immediately, and how long, if so, I expected to keep the respect of the armies.

I countered with: 'There are more ways of killing a cat than beating it to death with a horn porridge-spoon; and breaking the spoon into the bargain.'

They argued with me in the superior way of old campaigners, trying to impress me with technical military terms, as though I were an entire ignoramus. I burst out angrily: 'Gentlemen, as the God Augustus used to say, "A radish may know no Greek, but I do". I have been studying tactics for forty years and you can't teach me a thing: I know all the conventional and unconventional moves and openings in the game of human draughts. But you must understand that I am not free to play the game in the way you wish me to play it. As Father of the Country I now owe a duty to my sons: I refuse to throw away three or four thousand of their lives in an attack of this sort. Neither my father Drusus nor my brother Germanicus would ever have dreamed of making a frontal attack against a position as strong as this.'

Geta asked, perhaps ironically: 'What would your noble relatives have done, Caesar, in a case of this sort, do you think?'

'They'd have found a way round.'

'But there *is* no way round here, Caesar. That has been established.'

'They'd have found a way round, I say.'

Crassus Frugi said: 'The enemy's left flank is guarded by the Heron King and their right by the Hawthorn Queen. That's their boast, according to prisoners.'

'Who's this Heron King?' I asked.

'The Lord of the Marshes. He's a cousin, in their mythology, of the Goddess of Battle. She appears in the disguise of a raven and perches on the spear-heads. Then she drives the conquered into the marshes, and her cousin the Heron King eats them up. The Hawthorn Queen is a virgin who dresses in white in the spring and helps soldiers in battle by defending their stockades with her thorns: you see, they fell thorn-trees and pile them in a row with the thorns outwards, making the trunks fast together. That's a fearful obstacle to get through. But the Hawthorn Queen holds that right flank of theirs without any artificial felling of trees. Our scouts are positive that the whole wood is in such a fearful tangle that it's no use trying to get through at any point there.'

Aulus said: 'Yes, Caesar, I am afraid that we must make up our minds to that frontal attack.'

'Posides,' I suddenly called, 'were you ever a soldier?'

'Never, Caesar.'

'That makes two of us, thank God. Now suppose I undertake to do the impossible and get our cavalry through on the enemy's right flank, past this impenetrable tangle of thorns, can you undertake to get the Guards round on their left through that impassable bog?'

Posides answered: 'You have given me the easier flank, Caesar. There is, as it happens, a track through the marshes. One would have to go along it in single file, but there is a track. I met a man in London yesterday, a travelling Spanish oculist, who goes about the country curing the people of marsh-ophthalmia. He's in the Camp now, and he says he knows that marsh well, and the track – which he always uses to avoid the tollgate on the hill. Since Cymbeline's death they have been levying no fixed toll, but a traveller must pay according to the amount of money he has in his saddlebags, and this oculist got tired of being skinned. In the early mornings there's nearly always a mist on the marsh and he takes the path and slips round unobserved. He says that it's easy to follow once you are on it. It comes out half a mile beyond the ridge, at the edge of a pine copse. The Britons are likely to have a guard posted at that end – Caractacus is a careful general – but I think now that I can undertake to dislodge them and get as many men across the marsh as care to follow me.'

He explained his ruse, which I approved, though many of the generals raised their eyebrows at it; and then I explained my plan for forcing the other flank, which was really very simple. An important fact had been overlooked in the general concentration of interest on the diamond formation; the fact that Indian elephants are capable of bursting through the densest undergrowth imaginable and are daunted by no briars or thorns. However, in order not to tell the story twice, I shall say no more about the council of war and what was decided at it. I shall proceed to the battle, which took place at Brentwood on the seventh of September, a date that had long been memorable to me as the day on which my brother Germanicus had defeated Hermann at the Weser: if he had lived he would still have been only fifty-eight years old, which was no older than Aulus.

We marched out from London along the Colchester road. Our vanguard was kept busy by British skirmishers, but no serious resistance was offered until we reached Romford, a village about seven miles from Brentwood, where we found the ford across the River Rom strongly defended. The enemy held us up there for a whole morning, at the cost to themselves of 200 killed and 100 prisoners. We lost only fifty, but two of these were captains and one a battalion commander, so in a sense the Britons got the best of the exchange. That afternoon we sighted Brentwood Ridge and encamped for the night this side of the brook, which we used as a defensive barrier.

I took the auspices. Auspices are always taken before battle by giving the sacred chickens lumps of pulse-cake and watching how they eat it. If they have no appetite the battle is already as good as lost. The best possible omen is when the chickens, as soon as the cage-door is opened by the chicken-priest, rush out without any cry or beating of wings and eat so greedily that big bits drop from their mouths. If the sound of these striking the ground can be distinctly heard it prophesies the total defeat of the enemy. And, sure enough, this best possible omen was granted. The chicken-priest did not show himself to the birds, but standing with me behind the cage suddenly slid the door back at the very moment that I threw the cake before them. Out they rushed, without so much as a cackle, and fairly tore at the cake, throwing lumps about in a way which absolutely delighted us all, it was so reckless.

I had prepared what I considered a very suitable speech. It was somewhat reminiscent of Livy, but I felt that the historic importance of the occasion called for something in that style. It ran:

Romans, let no tongue among you wag and no voice bellow vainly, praising the days of old as days of true gold, and belittling the present age, of whose glories we should be the doughty champions, as a graceless age of gilded plaster. The Greek heroes before Troy, of whom the august Homer sang, bore, if we are to believe his record, this verse perpetually upon their lips:

> We pride ourselves as better men by far
> Than all our forebears who e'er marched to war.

Be not over-modest, Romans. Hold your heads high. Puff out your chests. Ranged in battle before you to-day are men who as closely resemble your ancestors, as eagle, eagle, or wolf, wolf – a fierce, proud, nervous, unrefined race, wielding weapons that are long centuries out of date, driving chariot-ponies of an antique breed, employing pitiable battle tactics only worthy of the pages of epic poets, not organized in regiments but grouped in clans and households – as certain of defeat at your disciplined hands as the wild boar who lowers his head and charges the skilled huntsman armed with hunting-spear and net. To-morrow when the dead are counted and the long ranks of sullen prisoners march beneath the yoke, it will be a matter for laughter to you if you ever for a moment lost faith in the present, if your minds were ever dazzled by the historied glories of a remote past. No, comrades, the bodies of these primitive heroes will be tumbled by your swords upon the field of battle as roughly and indiscriminately as, just now, when I, your general, took the auspices, the holy fowl flung upon the soil from their avid bills the fragments of sanctified cake.

Some of you, I have heard, no doubt slothful rather than fearful or undutiful, hesitated when called upon to set out upon this expedition, alleging as your excuse that the God Augustus had fixed the bounds of the Roman Empire for ever at the waters of the Rhine and the channel. If this were true, as I undertake to prove to you that it is not, then the God Augustus would be unworthy of our worship. The mission of Rome is to civilize the world – and where in the world would you find a race worthier of the benefits which we propose to confer upon it than the British race? The strange and pious task is laid upon us of converting these fierce compeers of our ancestors into dutiful sons of Rome, our illustrious City and Mother. What were the words that the God Augustus wrote to my grandmother, the Goddess Augusta? 'Looking into the future I can see Britain becoming as civilized as Southern France is now. And I think that the islanders, who are racially akin to us, will become far better Romans than we shall ever succeed in making of the Germans. ... And, one day (do not smile), British noblemen may well take their seats in the Roman Senate.'

You have already quitted yourselves bravely in this war. Twice you have inflicted a resounding defeat on the enemy. You have slain King Togodumnus, my enemy, and avenged his insults. This third time you cannot fail. Your forces are more powerful than ever, your courage higher, your ranks more united. You, no less than the enemy, are defending your hearths and the sacred temples of your Gods. The Roman soldier, whether his battlefield be the icy rocks of Caucasus, the burning sands of the desert beyond Atlas, the dank forests of Germany, or the grassy fields of Britain, is never unmindful of the lovely City which gives him his name, his valour, and his sense of duty.

I had composed several more paragraphs in this same lofty strains, but strangely enough not one word of the speech was delivered. When I mounted the tribunal platform, and the captains shouted in unison: 'Greetings, Caesar Augustus, Father of our Country, our Emperor!' and the soldiers took up the shout with roaring applause, I fairly broke down. My fine speech went altogether out of my head and I could only stretch out my hands to them, my eyes swimming with tears, and blurt out: 'It's all right, lads: the chickens say that it's going to be all right, and we have prepared a grand surprise for them, and we're going to give them such a beating as they'll never forget so long as they live – I don't mean the chickens, I mean the British.' [Tremendous laughter, in which I thought it best to join, as if the joke had been intentional.]

'Stop laughing at me, lads,' I cried. 'Don't you remember what happened to the little black boy in the Egyptian story who laughed at his father when he said the evening prayer by mistake for the morning one? The crocodile ate him; so you be careful. Well, I am getting to be an old man now, but this is the proudest moment of my life, and I wish my poor brother Germanicus were here to share it with me. Do any of you remember my great brother? Not very many, perhaps, for he died twenty-four years ago. But you've all heard of him as the greatest general Rome has ever had. To-morrow is the anniversary of his magnificent defeat of Hermann, the German chieftain, and I want you to celebrate it suitably. The pass-word to-night is *Germanicus!* and the battle-cry to-morrow will be *Germanicus!* and I think that if you shout his name loud enough he'll hear it down in the Underworld and know that he's remembered by the regiments that he loved and led so well. It will make him forget the wretched fate that overtook him – he died poisoned in bed, as you know. The Twentieth Regiment will have the honour of leading the assault: Germanicus always said that though, in barracks, you Twentieth were the most insubordinate, most drunken, and most quarrelsome troops in the entire regular army, you were absolute lions on the field. Second and Fourteenth, Germanicus called you the Backbone of the Army. It will be your duty to-morrow to stiffen the French allies, who will act as the army's ribs. The Ninth will come up last, because Germanicus always used to say that you Ninth were the slowest regiment in the Army but also the surest. You Guards are detailed for special duty. You have the easiest time and the best pay when you're not on active service, so it's only fair to the rest of the troops to give you the most dangerous and disagreeable task when you are. That's all I have to say now. Be good lads, sleep well, and earn your father's gratitude to-morrow!'

They cheered me till they were hoarse, and I knew then that Pollio was right and Livy wrong. A good general couldn't possibly deliver a studied oration on the eve of battle, even if he had one already prepared; for his lips would inevitably speak as his heart prompted. One effect of this speech – which, you will agree, reads very poorly by comparison with the other one – was that ever since I made it the Ninth have been familiarly known not as the 'Ninth Spanish' (their full title) but as the 'Ninth Snails'. The Twentieth, too, whose full title is 'The Conquering Valerian Twentieth' are known to other regiments as the 'Drunken Lions'; and when a man of the Fourteenth meets a man of the Second they are now expected to salute each other as 'Comrade Backbone'. The French auxiliaries are always known as 'The Ribs'.

A light mist settled over the camp, but there was a moon soon after midnight, which was of the greatest service; if the weather had been cloudy we would not have been able to manage the marshes. I slept until midnight and then Posides woke me as arranged and handed me a candle and a blazing pine branch from the camp-fire. I lighted the candle with it and prayed to the nymph Egeria. She is a Goddess of Prophecy, and good King Numa in the days of old used to consult her on every occasion. It was the first time that I had performed this family ceremony, but my brother Germanicus and my uncle Tiberius and my father and grandfather and great-grandfather and their ancestors before them had always performed it at midnight on the day before a battle; and if they were to be victorious the same favourable sign was invariably given by the nymph. It might be the stillest night imaginable, and yet, as soon as the last words of the prayer were uttered, the light would suddenly go out of itself as if snuffed between two fingers.

I had never been sure whether to believe in this mystery or not: I thought that it might perhaps be due to natural causes – a draught, or a bad patch in the wick, or even an involuntary sigh on the part of the watcher. The nymph Egeria could hardly be expected to leave her native grove by Lake Nemi and fly at a moment's notice to the middle of Germany or Northern Spain or the Tyrol – in each of which countries she is said to have obliged at one time or other with the customary sign – at the prayer of a Claudian. So I had set the lighted candle at the farthest end of my tent, screened from any draught that might come in by the flap, and then, walking ten paces away, addressed Egeria in solemn tones. It was a short prayer, in the Sabine dialect. The text had become grossly mutilated by oral tradition, for Sabine, which was the original patrician language, had long fallen into disuse at Rome; but I had studied Sabine in the course of my historical studies and was able to recite the prayer in something like its original form. And sure enough, I had hardly spoken the last word when the candle, as I watched it, suddenly went out. I immediately relighted it, to see whether there was perhaps a fault in the wick, or whether Posides had doctored the wax; but no, it burned brightly again and continued to burn until finally the wick fell over in a little pool of wax no bigger than a farthing. This is one of the very few genuine mystical experiences that have happened to me in a long life. I have no great gift that way. My brother Germanicus, on the other hand, was constantly plagued by visions and apparitions. At one time or another he had met most of the demi-gods, nymphs, and monsters celebrated by the poets, and on his visit to Troy, when he was Governor of Asia, was granted a splendid vision of the Goddess Cybele, whom our Trojan ancestors worshipped.

Chapter 20

AULUS came hurrying eagerly in. 'Our outposts report that the enemy are withdrawing from the Weald Brook, Caesar. What action shall we take? I suggest putting a regiment over at once. I don't know what the enemy's plan is, but we have to cross the brook to-morrow in any case, and if they have chosen to abandon it to us without fight, that will save us time and men.'

'Send the Ninth across, Aulus. Supply them with bridging material. They'll not have as much fighting to do to-morrow as the rest, I hope, so they'll not need so long a sleep. That's splendid news. Scouts must be pushed ahead to get in touch with the enemy and report as soon as they're located.'

The Ninth were hurriedly roused and sent across the Weald Brook. A message came back from them that the enemy had withdrawn half-way up the ridge, that twenty plank-bridges were now fixed àcross the brook and that they were standing by for further orders.

'It's time the Guards were on their way,' said Posides.

'Is the oculist trustworthy, do you think?' I asked.

'I'm going ahead with him myself, Caesar,' said Posides. 'It's my plan, and, by your leave, if it fails I don't intend to survive.'

'Very well. Give them the order to start in five minutes.'

So he kissed my hand and I gave him a clap on the back and out he went. A few minutes later I saw the first company of Guards march silently out of the eastern gate of the camp. They were told to break step so that their measured tread should not be heard by the enemy's outposts, and their arms were muffled with rags so that they should not knock together. Each man had his shield slung across his back and a big chalk circle smudged on it. This was to enable them to keep touch in the dark without shouting to each other. The white circles showed up well: Aulus had observed that deer follow each other through dark forests guided by the gleam of white fur patches on each other's rumps. The oculist led them over three or four miles of rough, boggy country, until they reached the marsh proper. It stank, and the will-o'-the-wisp darted about it, and to reach the beginning of the secret track the Guards had to wade thigh-deep after their guide through a slimy pool full of leeches. But the oculist made no mistakes. He found the track and kept to it.

A British outpost was stationed in the pine copse at the further end, and as the moon rose these watchful men saw a sight and heard a sound which filled their hearts with the utmost dismay. A great bird with a long shining bill, a huge grey body, and legs fifteen feet long suddenly rose through the mist a javelin's throw away and came stalking towards them, stopping every now and then to boom hoarsely, flap his wings, preen his feathers with his dreadful bill and boom again. The Heron King! They crouched in their bivouacs, terrified, hoping that this apparition would disappear, but it came slowly on and on. At last it seemed to notice their camp-fire. It jerked its head angrily and hurried towards them, with outspread wings, booming louder and louder. They sprang up and ran for their lives. The Heron King pursued them through the copse with a fearful chuckling laughter, then turned and slowly promenaded along the edge of the marsh, booming dully at intervals.

In case you imagine that it was indeed the Heron King who had come to frighten them – for if Egeria could appear so strangely, why not a Heron King? – I must explain the ruse. The Heron King was a French soldier from the great marshes which lie to the west of Marseilles, where the shepherds are accustomed to walk on long stilts as a means of striding across soft patches too wide to jump. Posides had rigged this man up in a wicker-work basket constructed in the shape of a bird's body, and stitched over with blanket stuff. Wicker wings covered with cloth were attached to his arms. The head and bill were improvised of stuff-covered laths and fastened to his head: he could move them by moving his neck. The beak was treated with phosphorus. The boom was made by an ingenious water-pipe he carried in his mouth. The soldier knew the habits of herons and imitated the walk with his stilts, which were strapped firmly to his legs. The oculist led him and Posides along the track until the dark outline of the copse could just be made out. The Guards were following 200 yards behind, and Posides sent back a message halting them. He waited until he saw the bird striding around the copse again and knew that the ruse had been successful. He ran back and told them that the coast was clear. They hurried forward and occupied the copse. Eight thousand men in single file take a long time to pass a given spot, and it was more than five hours before they were all across, by which time dawn had appeared, but the mist had not cleared, so they were not seen from the hill.

An hour before dawn I sacrificed to Mars and then breakfasted with my staff, and we made a few further arrangements about what to do if everything did not go according to plan. But now we knew that most of the Guards must already be in position – for there had evidently been no interruption of their progress across the marsh – and we were confident of victory. Geta was absent: he had taken an odd battalion of the Eighth Regiment (I had forgotten to mention this battalion as part of our reinforcements) with the cavalry, the Batavians, and the elephants, to a position about two miles away on our left flank. My son-in-law, young Pompey, was also absent. I had entrusted him with the command of the Nubians and the Balearic slingers, and he had taken them across the Weald Brook. The Balearics carried coils of tent-rope, tent-pegs, and camp mallets; the Nubians, native drums and their long white spears.

It was a fine breakfast and we all drank just the right amount of wine – enough to make us feel very pleased with ourselves and yet not enough to induce recklessness – and in the intervals of serious discussion we did a great deal of joking. They were mostly witticisms about camels, which were much on our minds at the time. My contribution was a quotation from a letter of Herod Agrippa's to my mother: 'The camel is one of the seven wonders of nature. He shares this honour with the Rainbow, the Echo, the Cuckoo, the Negro, the Volcano, and the Sirocco. But he is the first and greatest of the seven.'

I gave the order for the army to move forward into its positions beyond the Weald Brook. Massed trumpeters blew a call that could be heard miles away. It was answered by a great din of war-horns and shouting from the hill. That gave me a sudden shock. Although, naturally, I had been aware that battles cannot be fought without an enemy, I had been thinking of this battle all night as a diagram on the map, a silent affair of squares and oblongs gently pushing each other this way and that; the Roman squares and oblongs inked in black, the British left white. When the trumpets and horns blew I had to translate the diagram into terms of man, horse, chariot, and elephant. I had not slept since midnight, and I suppose my face and gestures betrayed the strain I was under: for Xenophon actually suggested that I should rest a few minutes after my breakfast and go forward only when all the regiments were in position. As though it was not essential for me to be waiting at the brook dressed in my Imperial armour and purple cloak to greet each regiment as it arrived and watch it cross over! If Xenophon had so much as whispered the word 'massage' I believe I should have killed him.

I rode forward to the brook on a steady old mare, none other than Penelope, the widow of ex-citizen and might-have-been Consul Incitatus, who had recently broken a leg on the race-track and had to be destroyed. The mist was pretty thick here. One could only see ten to fifteen paces ahead, and what a terrible stink of camel! You have perhaps, at some time or other, passed in the mist through a field where an old he-goat was loose: at ordinary times wind and sun carry off most of the smell, but mist seems to suck it up and hold it, so that you will have been astonished by the rankness of the air. These were he-camels which I had imported for circus-shows – female camels are too expensive – and they smelt pretty bad. If there is one thing that horses hate it is the smell of camel, but as all our cavalry were far away on the flank this did not affect us, and Penelope was inured to circus-smells. There was no confusion in the crossing of the brook, and in spite of the mist the regiments formed up beyond in perfect order. A disciplined regiment can perform quite complicated drill movements in the pitch dark: the Guards often practise at night on Mars Field.

Now I want to make you see the battle as it was seen by the Britons, because that way you will be better able to appreciate my plan of attack. The best British infantry are manning the three forts, each of which has a sally-port for sorties and an avenue running back through the wood into the open country behind. The forts are linked together by a strong stockade facing the entire semicircle of wood, and the wood is so full of Britons that no advantage would be won by attacking the stockade at a point between two forts. Just before dawn the sally-port of the central fort opens and out drives a division of chariotry. It is commanded by Cattigern, Caractacus's brother-in-law, King of the Trinovants. Another division drives out from the fort on the British right flank. It is led by Caractacus himself. The two divisions draw up on either side of the central fort. Caractacus is angry and reproaches Cattigern, because he has just been told that the Trinovantian infantry posted at the Weald Brook have fallen back during the night. Cattigern is angry at being spoken to in this way in front of his whole tribe. He asks Caractacus haughtily whether he accuses the Trinovants of cowardice. Caractacus wishes to know what other excuse they have for deserting their posts. Cattigern explains that they retired for religious reasons. Their commander had been coughing violently because of the mist and suddenly began to cough blood. They regarded this as a most unlucky sign, and respect for the nymph of the brook did not allow them to stay. They therefore offered a propitiatory sacrifice – the chief's two ponies – and withdrew. Caractacus has to accept this explanation, but does not conceal his displeasure. He does not yet know of the retirement of the other outpost from the copse by the marsh, but he has heard alarming rumours of the appearance of the Heron King in person in that quarter: the Heron King has not been seen since legendary times. Our trumpets are then heard and the British reply with horns and shouts. British scouts come rushing up to report that the enemy are crossing the brook in force.

Dawn has broken, and the whole semicircle of wood stands out clearly, with open ground shelving down towards the brook, but after 300 or 400 yards the field of vision is obscured by a sea of mist. Caractacus cannot tell yet in which direction the Roman attack will develop. He sends more scouts forward to report. They hurry back twenty minutes later to report that the enemy are on the move at last. They are coming up the road towards the centre in mass formation. Caractacus wheels his chariot division across to the right flank again and anxiously waits for the first Roman companies to appear through the mist. A Briton comes up to report that before the chariots emerged from the wood a muffled sound of hammering was heard from the mist, as if the Roman soldiers were driving tent-pegs; and that a party sent out to investigate the noise did not return. Caractacus replies, 'Tent-pegs can't hurt us.'

At last the tramp and clank of our approaching regiments can be clearly heard, and the encouraging shouts of the officers. The leading company of the Twentieth appears dimly through the mist. The Britons roar defiance. Cattigern swings his division across to the left. The Romans suddenly halt. A curious sight is seen. A company of immensely tall, long-necked beasts with humps on their backs are being trotted up and down, in and out of the mist, on the flank which Cattigern has been told to attack. The Britons are alarmed at the sight and mutter charms against magic. Cattigern should now be attacking, but he cannot yet be sure whether the Roman advance is only a feint; for only 500 men are as yet visible. The main attack may be taking place elsewhere. He waits. Caractacus sends a mounted messenger, ordering him to attack without delay. Cattigern signals the advance. And then a strange thing happens. As soon as the column of chariots sweeps down into the mist where the beasts have been seen, the ponies go quite mad. They squeal, buck, snort, baulk, and cannot be forced to go a step farther. It is clearly a magic mist. It has a peculiar and frightening odour.

While Cattigern's division is in confusion, the ponies plunging and kicking and the charioteers shouting, cursing, and trying to get them under control, trumpets sound and two battalions of the Twentieth, followed by two battalions of the Second, suddenly charge out of the mist at them. 'Germanicus! Germanicus!' they shout. Shower after shower of javelins flies from their hands. Caractacus then launches his own attack. His division is unaffected by the spell and sweeps down, 3,000 strong, on the flank of the halted Roman mass, which seems unprovided with a flank-guard. But a more powerful charm than a stinking mist protects this flank. The column is going at full speed and is just out of javelin range when suddenly there come six terrific claps of thunder and six simultaneous flashes of lightning. Balls of burning pitch hurtle through the air. The terrified column swings away to the right, and as they go a shower of lead bolts comes whizzing at them from the Balearic slingers posted behind the thunder and lightning. Charioteers fall right and left; as they have the reins tightly wound about their waists, this involves the wreck of a number of chariots. The column is almost out of control, but Caractacus manages to swing it back again on its course. He is aiming at the Roman rear, which can now be clearly seen, for a light breeze is rolling the mist away to the other flank. But a catastrophe follows. As the column, which has lost its formation and is now pressed together in a disorderly mass, rushes forward, chariot after chariot comes crashing to the ground as if halted by an invisible power. The chariots behind are bunched so close and the impetus of the downhill rush is so great that nobody can pull up or turn without colliding with a neighbour. The mass charges blindly on and the wreckage in front piles higher and higher. Above the crash of splintered chariots, the screams and groans, rises a dreadful noise of drums and up springs a horde of tall, naked black men brandishing white spears. They fling themselves on the wreckage, and their long spears dart here and there among the fallen men. They laugh and crow and shout and no Briton dares defend himself against them, mistaking them for evil spirits. Caractacus escapes from the slaughter. His own car has been among the first to overturn, but he has been thrown clear. He runs off to the right, stumbling as he goes over the tightly-stretched tent-rope pegged knee-high in the long grass. The last section of the column, Belgic chariot-men from the West Country, have realized in time what is happening in front. Five hundred of their chariots manage to avoid disaster by swerving away to the right. There Caractacus hails them and is rescued. The rest of the division is lost, for the Fourteenth has pushed two battalions round in their rear and two battalions of the Ninth rush obliquely forward to assist the Nubians.

Caractacus leads his chariots back up the hill and instructs the Belgic commander to go to Cattigern's aid on the other flank. He himself drives up to the central fort, for he notices that the sallyport is open and wants to know why. He enters and finds the garrison gone. Meanwhile Cattigern is fighting bravely at the head of a force of dismounted chariot-men, supported by infantrymen who have streamed out of the wood to his assistance. He is wounded. His chariotry has disappeared. His brother has headed the flight back to the central fort, down the avenue through the wood, and so away. The garrison of the fort has gone after him. Our Twentieth and Second are gradually forcing Cattigern's men back, keeping unbroken formation as they advance. Caractacus, returning to the sally-port, hears the noise of chariots racing towards him: it is the Belgic section of chariotry, now also in flight. He tries to halt them, but they refuse to listen to him; and realizing that the battle is lost he turns his own chariot and blows two long blasts on his ivory horn as signal for a general retreat. He hopes to overtake the fugitives and rally them a few miles farther along the Colchester road. He hears a sound of Roman trumpets, and as his chariot drives clear of the wood on the other side he sees eight battalions of Roman regulars advancing towards it on his right. It is the Guards. And away on his left he sees elephants and Roman cavalry emerging from the wood and charging towards him. He shouts to his driver to whip on the horses. He escapes.

With Caractacus gone, the battle was over. The Guards cut off the British retreat from the wood and the infantry remaining in it put up little fight. Cavalry were sent down the avenue to capture the fort on the British right, but half-way along it they came across a party of British spearmen: these had the presence of mind to cut the cords, releasing a sort of portcullis which fell squarely across the avenue, barring progress. The three avenues were all provided with a series of these portcullises, each connected with stockades on either side, but this was the only one of which use had been made. By the time that the cavalry had demolished this obstacle the retreating British party had released another portcullis and hurried on to warn the garrison of the fort that all was lost. The garrison escaped safely in a westerly direction. The other fort surrendered an hour later; by which time Cattigern had been severely wounded and the resistance of his men broken.

We took 8,000 prisoners, and counted 4,700 corpses on the battle-field. Our own losses were insignificant: 380 killed, 600 wounded, of whom only 150 were disabled from further fighting. Our cavalry and elephants were sent ahead in the direction of Colchester, to prevent fugitives from rallying on the road. They overtook Caractacus at Chelmsford, where he was trying to organize the defence of the River Chelmer. The sight of the elephants was enough to send the British scurrying in all directions. Caractacus escaped again. This time he gave up all hope of saving Colchester. With a force of 200 chariots of his own tribe he turned west and disappeared from the scene. He had gone to throw himself on the protection of his allies, the men of South Wales.

We piled a great trophy on the battle-field, of broken chariots and weapons, and burned it as a thank-offering to Mars. That night we camped on the farther side of the wood. The men had been roaming about in search of plunder. Gold chains and enamelled breastplates and helmets were found in abundance. I had issued strict orders against the violation of captured women – for hundreds of women had been fighting in the wood beside their husbands – and three men of the Fourteenth were duly executed that evening for disobeying me. When night fell I felt the reaction after victory and at supper with my staff was suddenly seized by the most painful attack of stomachic cramp, 'the cardiac passion' as they call it, that I have ever experienced. It was like 100 swords stuck into my vitals at once, and I let out a fearful bellow which made everyone present think that I had been poisoned. Xenophon rushed to my aid and hastily cutting the straps of my corselet with a carving-knife and throwing it aside, he knelt over me and began kneading at my stomach with both hands, while I continued to roar and bellow, unable to stop. He mastered the cramp at last, and had me wrapped in hot blankets and carried away to bed, where I spent one of the wretchedest nights of my life. However, the extraordinary completeness of my victory was the medicine that really cured me. By the time that we reached Colchester, three days later, I was myself again. I travelled on elephant-back like an Indian prince.

Near Colchester the advance-guard of a friendly army met us. It was the Icenians, who had risen in our support on the day that they heard of my arrival at London. Together we invested and stormed the city, which was defended bravely by a few old·men and a number of women. I swore honourable alliance there in the name of Rome with the King of the Icenians, the King of East Kent, and the King of East Sussex, in recognition of their assistance in the campaign. The remainder of Caractacus's empire I formally declared a Roman province, under the governorship of Aulus, and presently received the homage of all its petty kings and chiefs, including those Kentish chiefs who had been hiding in the Weald. After this I decided that I had done all that I had come to Britain to do. I said farewell to Aulus and his army and returned to Richborough with the Guards, the elephants, and the 500 volunteers who had sailed with me from Ostia but arrived too late for the battle. We embarked in our transports and crossed without further incident to France. I had been a mere sixteen days in Britain.

My only regret was perhaps rather an ungrateful one. I was with the Ninth throughout the battle and, feeling very courageous at the moment that their two battalions went forward to help the Nubians, I had galloped excitedly ahead of them to join in the fighting. However, I changed my mind: I did not wish to get mixed up with the Nubians, who often in battle mistake friends for foes. I turned Penelope round behind them and pulled up on the flank. There I saw a British chief doubling back between me and the tangle of broken chariots and kicking horses. I drew my sword and spurred after him. I was nearly on him when a big body of chariots swept into view and I had to turn and gallop back. I know now that the chief was Caractacus. To think that I was cheated by a few seconds from a single combat with him! Since I had a horse and a sword and he had neither, I might easily have had the luck to kill him. And if I had done so, what immortal glory I would have won! Only two Roman generals in history have ever killed an enemy commander in single combat, and stripped him of his arms.

Chapter 21

A ROMAN general, in order to be granted a full triumph as a reward for victory over his country's enemies, must have fulfilled certain conditions required by ancient custom. In the first place, he must have attained consular rank or the rank of first-class magistrate, and be the official Commander-in-Chief of the victorious forces, not an acting-commander or lieutenant: and as Commander-in-Chief he must have personally taken the auspices before battle. Next, he must have been engaged against a foreign enemy, not against rebel citizens; and the war must have been fought not for the recovery of territory that once belonged to Rome, but for the extension of Roman rule over entirely new territory. Next, he must have decisively beaten the enemy in a pitched battle which has ended the campaign; he must have killed at least 5,000 of the enemy; and the Roman losses must have been comparatively light. Finally, the victory must have been so complete that he is able to withdraw his victorious troops without prejudice to his conquests and bring them back to Rome to take part in the triumph.

Permission to celebrate a triumph is granted by the Senate, but always after jealous and prolonged deliberation. They usually meet in the Temple of Bellona outside the City to scrutinize the laurel-wreathed dispatch sent in by the general, and if they have reason to suppose that his claims are unfounded or exaggerated they will send for him to substantiate them. If, however, they decide that he has really won a notable victory they proclaim a day of public thanksgiving and ask formal permission from the people of Rome for the victorious army to be led inside the walls for the day of the triumph. The Senate has the discretionary power of relaxing certain of the conditions necessary for a triumph if the victory seems to them of sufficient general merit. That is only just, but I am sorry to record it as my opinion that at least sixty or seventy of the 315 triumphs that have been celebrated since the time of Romulus did not deserve celebration; while, on the other hand, a good many generals have been robbed of well-earned triumphs by the spiteful influence of rivals in the Senate. If, however, a general has been cheated of the honour by enemies or by a mere technicality, he usually celebrates a triumph unofficially on the Alban Mount, outside the City, which the whole City attends, so that it is almost as good as a real triumph; only, it cannot be recorded as such in the City annals nor can his funeral-mask, after his death, be worn with triumphal dress. Perhaps the two most disgraceful triumphs that have been witnessed at Rome were Julius Caesar's triumph over the sons of Pompey the Great, his relatives, and one celebrated by an ancestor of mine, one Appius Claudius, in spite of the refusal of both the Senate and People to allow him the honour – he induced his sister, a Vestal Virgin, to sit in his triumphal car so that the City officials did not venture to pull him out of it for fear of offending her sanctity.

When I sent in my dispatch and applied for a triumph, it was a foregone conclusion that it would be granted, because nobody would dare oppose my claims, even if they were utterly groundless – as groundless as Caligula's had been when he celebrated his triple triumph over Germany, Britain, and Neptune. He had marched a few miles into Germany, met no resistance, fallen a prey to terrors of his imagination and fled in a panic; he had never even crossed the Channel into Britain, nor sent any of his troops there; and as for Neptune, well, the kindest thing to be said about that is that triumphs cannot be awarded for victories, real or supposed, over national Gods. But I was anxious to observe the decencies, and so I stated in my dispatch that the number of Britons killed during my personal conduct of the campaign had been 300 short of the required figure of 5,000, but that the prisoners were sufficiently numerous, perhaps, to compensate for this shortage, and that the gratifying brevity of our own casualty-list might also weigh with the House, should they consider waiving this condition for once. I undertook, if the triumph were granted, to let 600 prisoners fight to the death in the Circus, thus bringing the enemy dead up to the 5,000 mark. I wrote that I could not return to Rome before March, because Aulus would need the entire expeditionary force with him that winter to accustom the British to our permanent presence in their island; and that even then I could not leave the new province undefended, because hitherto unconquered tribes on the border would probably overrun it. But I could bring back the troops who had been actively engaged in the final battle – namely, the Twentieth Regiment, four battalions of the Fourteenth, two of the Ninth, two of the Second, one of the Eighth, and some allied troops – if that was enough to satisfy them. Meanwhile, in accordance with old custom I would not return to the City (which Vitellius would continue to govern, with their co-operation, as my representative); I would remain in France, with my headquarters at Lyons, hearing appeal cases, settling disputes between tribes or cities, reviewing troops, inspecting defences, auditing departmental accounts, and seeing that my order for the total suppression of the Druidical Order was strictly obeyed.

This dispatch was well received and the Senate kindly waived the 5,000-dead clause and asked the People to vote permission for me to march my army into the City, which the People gladly did. The Senate voted me 500,000 gold pieces of public money for the celebrations of my triumph, and the date was fixed for New Year's Day, the first of March.

My tour of France was not marked by any event of interest, though I took certain important decisions about the extension of the Roman citizenship. I shall not waste time over recording my impressions of the country. Dispatches came from Aulus at regular intervals, reporting the occupation of various Catuvellaunian strongholds, detailing the distribution of his troops, and sending me for my approval a plan of campaign for the following spring, after the return of the troops from the triumph. I received a great many letters of congratulation from provincial governors, allied kings and cities, and personal friends. Marsus wrote from Antioch that my victory had been most timely. It had caused a great impression in the East, where rumours of the internal decay of Rome and the impending collapse of her empire were being constantly put about by hidden enemies and produced a most disquieting effect on the Syrian provincials. But this was by no means all that Marsus had to tell me. He reported the recent death of the old King of Parthia – the one whom Vitellius had surprised during Caligula's reign, when he was on the point of invading Syria, and forced to give important hostages for future good behaviour – and the accession of his son Gotarzes, an indolent and debauched prince with many enemies among the nobility. He wrote:

But this Gotarzes has a brother, Bardanes, a most gifted and ambitious prince. I am informed that Bardanes is now on the way to Parthia to dispute the throne with his brother. He has been visiting Alexandria lately, on the pretext of consulting a famous physician there who undertakes to cure deafness – Bardanes is slightly deaf in one ear. But his journey has led him through Jerusalem, and my agents assure me that he went away from King Herod's dominions far richer than he came.

With the help of this Jewish gold I expect to see him oust Gotarzes: Parthian nobles can always be bribed. He can count, too, on the unbought assistance of the King of Adiabene – the Assyrian kingdom which, I need hardly remind you, lies across the Tigris River just south of Nineveh – and on the King of Osroëne, in Western Mesopotamia. You will recall that this King of Adiabene recently restored the late King of Parthia to his throne after he had been removed by a conspiracy of nobles, and was rewarded for this service with the Golden Bed and the Upright Tiara. But it will probably be news to you that this important personage is a secret convert to Judaism and that his mother, who was the first of his household to change her religion, is now resident at Jerusalem. She has brought with her five young princes of Adiabene, her grandsons, to be educated in the Jewish language, literature, and religion. They have all been circumcised.

King Herod has now therefore close dealings with the following kings:

> The King of Chalcis,
> The King of Iturea,
> The King of Adiabene,
> The King of Osroëne,
> The King of Lesser Armenia,
> The King of Pontus and Cilicia,
> The King of Commagene, and
> The prospective King of Parthia.

The Crown of Parthia commands, of course, an alliance of a great many other kings of the Middle East – as far as Bactria and the Indian border. King Herod also enjoys the support of Jews throughout the world, not forgetting the Jews of Alexandria, and of the Edomites and Nabateans, and is now angling for the support of the King of Arabia. The Phoenicians, too, are slowly being won over by his blandishments: only Tyre and Sidon continue cold. He has broken off diplomatic relations with these cities and forbidden his subjects to trade with them under penalty of death. Tyre and Sidon will be forced to come to terms. Their economic prosperity depends on trade with the interior; and, except for the corn which they import from Egypt, and fish, which is often scarce in bad weather, King Herod controls their entire food supply.

It would be difficult to exaggerate the dangers of the situation and we can all be most thankful that your British victory has been so complete, though I could have wished that the regiments now stationed in Britain were available for hurried transference to the East, where I am pretty sure that they will before long be needed.

If you are willing to consider, with your usual graciousness and perspicacity, the advice that I have to offer you in these difficult circumstances, it is this: I suggest that you immediately restore to his throne

Mithridates, the ex-King of Armenia, who is at present living at Rome. It was, if I may say so without offence, a lamentable mistake on the part of your uncle, the Emperor Tiberius Caesar, to allow the late King of Parthia to unite the Armenian crown with his own, and not immediately to avenge with force of arms that most insulting letter the King wrote to him. If, therefore, you send Mithridates to me at Antioch at once, I undertake to put him back on the throne of Armenia while Bardanes and Gotarzes are disputing the throne of Parthia. The present Governor of Armenia can be bribed not to oppose us too strongly and Mithridates is a by no means incapable prince and a great admirer of Roman institutions. His brother, too, is King of Georgia and commands quite a strong army of Caucasian mountaineers. I can get in touch with him and arrange for an invasion of Armenia from the north while we march up from the south-west. If we succeed in restoring Mithridates we can have nothing to fear from the Kings of Pontus and Lesser Armenia, whose kingdoms will be cut off from Parthia by Armenia; nor from the King of Commagene (whose son has now been betrothed to King Herod's daughter Drusilla), because his kingdom lies directly between Armenia and my own command. We shall, in fact, hold the north, and when Bardanes has fought his civil war and ousted King Gotarzes (as I think he is bound to do) his next expedition will have to be against Mithridates in Armenia. The recovery of Armenia will be no easy matter if we give Mithridates adequate support, and Bardanes's southern and eastern allies will not easily be persuaded to help him in so distant and hazardous an expedition. And, until he recovers Armenia, Bardanes will be in no position to further any of the imperialistic schemes that I confidently believe King Herod Agrippa to be planning. This is the first definite accusation I have made against the loyalty of your supposed friend and ally, and I know the great danger I am running of incurring your displeasure by making it. But I put the safety of Rome before my own safety and I should consider myself a traitor if I suppressed any of the political information that comes to me, merely because it makes unsavoury reading in an official dispatch. Having said so much, I shall further make so bold as to suggest that King Herod's son, Herod Agrippa the Younger, be invited back to Rome to attend your triumph. He can then, if necessary, be detained indefinitely on some pretext, and may prove a useful hostage for his father's good behaviour.

I had two courses before me. The first was to summon Herod to Lyons at once to answer Marsus's charges, in which, in spite of my bias in Herod's favour, I could not help believing. If guilty, he would refuse to come and that would mean an immediate war, for which I was unprepared. The second course was to play for time and give no indication of my mistrust; but the danger of that was that Herod might benefit from the delay more than I would. If I decided on this course I would certainly take Marsus's advice about Armenia; but was Marsus right in reckoning on a friendly Armenia as sufficient protection against the enormously powerful Eastern confederation that Herod seemed to have built up?

Letters came from Herod. In the first he answered my questions about the prophesied king. In the second he congratulated me most warmly on my victories and, curiously enough, asked permission to send his son to Rome to witness my triumph; he hoped that I would not mind the lad enjoying a few months' holiday in Rome before returning to Palestine in the summer to assist him at the great feast in honour of my birthday, which he hoped to celebrate at Caesarea. The letter about the prophesied king ran as follows:

Yes, my dear Marmoset, as a child I used to hear plenty of mystical talk about this Anointed One, or Messiah as they call him in our language, and it still goes on in theological circles at Jerusalem; but I never paid much attention to it, until now, when your request for a report on the prophecy has led me to investigate the matter seriously. At your suggestion I consulted our worthy friend Philo, who was in Jerusalem paying some vow or other which he had sworn to our God – he is always either vowing or paying vows. Philo, you know, has made a daring and I should say a most absurd identification of the Deity ideally conceived by Plato and his philosophical crew – Unchanging and Unyielding and Eternal and Uncompounded Intellectual Perfection, exalted above all predicates – with our passionate tribal God at Jerusalem. I suppose that he found the Platonic Deity too cold and abstract, and wanted to infuse some life into him, at the same time glorifying his own God by extending his rule over the universe. At all events, I asked Philo what the sacred Scriptures had to say about this enigmatic Person. Philo grew very serious at once and assured me that the whole hope of our race is centred on the coming of the Messiah. He gave me the following particulars:

This Messiah is a king who shall come to redeem Israel from its sins, and as the human representative of our Jewish God. He is not necessarily a great conqueror, though he must release the Jews from any foreign yoke which interferes with their freedom of worship. This prophecy was first made, according to Philo, shortly after the Jews had been led out of Egypt by their law-giver Moses in the days of Rameses II. In a book which we call the Book of Numbers, ascribed to Moses, he is spoken of as a 'Star and Sceptre out of Jacob'. In later sacred writings, dating from about the time that Rome was founded, he is spoken of as a man who shall gather the lost sheep of Israel from many quarters and restore them to their native fold in Palestine – for already by that time the Jews had become scattered in colonies all over the Near and Middle East. Some had left Palestine voluntarily as traders and settlers, some had been carried away as captives. Philo says that Jewish theologians have never been able to decide whether this Messiah is a real or a symbolic figure. At the time of the heroic Maccabees (my mother's priestly ancestors) he was regarded as only a symbol. At other times he has not only been regarded as a real person, but has even been popularly identified with non-Jewish deliverers of the race, such as Cyrus the Persian, and even Pompey, who put an end to the Hasmonean oppression. Philo declares that both these views are wrong: the Messiah is yet to come and he must be a Jew, in direct line from our King David whose son Solomon built the Temple at Jerusalem, and must be born in a village called Bethlehem, and must gather Israel together and cleanse it from its sins by a most thorough-going ritual of confession, repentance, and placation of the offended Deity. Jerusalem is to be sanctified down to 'the very cooking-pots and the bells on the horses' necks'. Philo even knows the date of the Messiah's birth, namely, 5,500 years from that of the earliest ancestor of the Jewish race: but opinions differ as to when *he* lived, so that is not much help.

The scriptures are not entirely consistent in their various foreshadowings of this Messiah. He is sometimes represented as an angry powerful warrior dressed in royal purple and bathed in the blood of his country's foes, and sometimes as a meek, sorrowful outcast, a sort of poor prophet preaching repentance and brother love. Philo says, however, that the most trustworthy and clearest statement made about him occurs in a book called *The Psalter of Solomon*. It is in the form of a prayer:

'Behold, O Lord, and raise up their king, the Son of David, at the time thou hast appointed, to reign over Israel Thy servant; and gird him with strength to crush unjust rulers; to cleanse Jerusalem from the heathen that tread it under foot, to cast out sinners from Thy inheritance; to break the pride of sinners and all their strength as potter's vessels with a rod of iron; to destroy the lawless nations with the words of his mouth; to gather a holy nation and lead them in righteousness. The heathen nations shall serve under his yoke; he shall glorify the Lord before all the earth and cleanse Jerusalem in holiness, as in the beginning. From the ends of the earth all nations shall come to see his glory and bring the weary sons of Zion as gifts; to see the glory of the Lord with which God hath crowned him, for he is over them a righteous King taught by God. In his days there shall be no unrighteousness in their midst; for they are all holy and their king the Anointed of the Lord.'

This Messiah legend has naturally spread through the East in different fantastic forms, losing its Jewish setting in the process. The version you quote about the King's painful death, deserted by his friends, who afterwards drink his blood, is not Jewish, but I think Syrian. And in the Jewish version he is only a king of the Jews and head of a great religious confederation centred at Jerusalem, not the God himself. He could not usurp godhead, because the Jews are the most obstinate monotheists in the world.

You ask whether anyone now identifies himself with the Messiah. I have met nobody lately who does so. The last one that I remember was a man called Joshua bar Joseph, a native of Galilee. When I was magistrate of Tiberias (under my uncle Antipas) he had a considerable following among the uneducated and used to preach to large crowds at the lake-side. He was a man of striking appearance and, though his father was only an artisan, claimed descent from David. I have heard that there was a scandal connected with his birth: one Panthera, a Greek soldier in my grandfather's guard, was supposed to have seduced his mother, who was a tapestry worker for the Temple. This Joshua had been an infant prodigy (a common phenomenon among Jews) and knew the Scriptures better than most doctors of divinity. He used to brood about religion and perhaps there was foundation to the story of his Greek parentage, because he found Judaism a very irksome creed (as no true Jew does) and began to criticize it as inadequate for ordinary human needs. He attempted in a naïve manner to do what Philo has since done so elaborately – to reconcile Judaic revelational literature with Greek philosophy. It reminds me of what Horace wrote in his *Art of Poetry* about a painter making a lovely woman end in an ugly fishtail:

'Would you not laugh, my friends, to view the sight?'

If there is one thing that I hate more than an Orientalized Greek or Roman, it is a Graeco-Romanized Oriental, or any attempt at a fusion of cultures. This is written against myself, but I mean it. Your mother never succeeded in making a good Roman of me; she merely spoilt a good Oriental.

Well, Joshua ben Joseph (or, ben Panthera), had a taste for Greek philosophy. He was handicapped, however, by not being a Greek scholar. And he had to work hard at his trade – he was a joiner – to make his living. However, he made the acquaintance of a man called James, a fisherman with literary tastes who had attended lectures at the Epicurean University at Gadara which lies at the other side of the lake from Tiberias. Gadara was rather a rundown place by then, though in its prime it had produced four great men: Meleager the poet, Mnasalcus the philosopher, Theodorus the rhetorician, under whom your uncle Tiberius studied, and Philo the mathematician who worked out the proportion of the circumference of a circle to its diameter as far as the ten-thousandth decimal place. At any rate, Joshua used James's philosophical gleanings from Gadara and his own knowledge of the Jewish scriptures to compose a synthetic religion of his own. But a religion without authority is nothing, so secretly at first and then publicly he identified himself with the Messiah and spoke (as Moses had once spoken) as if from the mouth of God. He had a most ingenious mind and used to deliver his messages in the form of simple fables with moral endings. He also claimed to perform supernatural cures and miracles. He made himself very troublesome to the Jewish religious authorities, whom he accused of combining strict observance of the Law with rapaciousness and insolence towards the poor. There are many good stories told of him. One of his political opponents tried to catch him out once by asking whether it was right for a conscientious Jew to pay the Roman Imperial tax. If he had answered Yes, he would have lost his hold on the nationalists. If he had answered No, he would have made himself liable for arrest by the civil authorities. So he pretended to be quite innocent about the matter and asked to be shown the amount of money due before he would make any answer. They showed him a silver piece and said: 'Look, every householder has to pay this much.' He asked: 'Whose head is this on the coin? I can't read Latin.' They said: 'It's the head of Tiberius Caesar, of course.' He said: 'Why, if it's Caesar's coin, pay it to Caesar. But don't fail to pay God what is due to God.' They also tried to catch him out on points of Jewish law, but he always had chapter and verse ready to justify his teachings. Eventually, however, he compromised himself as a religious heretic, and the end of the story was that our old friend Pontius Pilate, then Governor of Judaea and Samaria, arrested him for creating popular disorders and handed him over for trial by the supreme Jewish religious court at Jerusalem, where he was condemned to death for blasphemy. When I come to think of it he did die the same year as the Goddess Livia, and his followers did desert him, so that much of the prophecy you quote was fulfilled in him. And there are now people who say that he was God and that they saw his soul ascend to Heaven after his death – just like Augustus's and Drusilla's – and claim that he was born at Bethlehem and that he fulfilled all the other Messianic prophecies in one way or another; but I propose to stop this nonsense once and for all. Only three days ago I arrested and executed James, who seems to be the chief intellect of the movement; I hope to recapture and execute another leading fanatic called Simon, arrested at the same time, who somehow escaped from prison. The trouble is that though sensible men may 'laugh to view the sight' of a brightly-painted fish-tailed woman, the mob are just as likely as not to gape at her, see her as a sea-goddess, and worship her.

This apparently ingenuous letter contained one detail which convinced me that Herod really thought himself the Messiah, or at least intended soon to use the tremendous power of that name to further his own ambitions. Once he had revealed himself, the Jews would be his to a man: they would flock back to Palestine at his summons from all over the world, and I foresaw that his prestige would soon be so great that the whole of the Semitic race would embrace the new faith and join with him in removing 'the stranger and the infidel' from their midst. The conversion of the King of Adiabene and his entire household was a straw showing which way the wind was blowing, and no small straw either, for this king was known as 'The King-maker', and was immensely respected in Parthia. In his next letter Marsus further reported the rumoured conversion to Judaism of the King of Commagene, who had been a favourite of Caligula's. (He was sometimes credited with having first persuaded Caligula to rule with Oriental absoluteness; Caligula certainly always used to appeal to him for approval after having perpetrated some particularly bloody and capricious crime.)

The detail which convinced me that Herod intended to proclaim himself Messiah was that in mentioning Bethlehem he had not mentioned the fact that this was his own birthplace, and not, as was usually supposed, Jerusalem. His mother Berenice once told my mother the story with graphic detail. She had been on her way from her husband's estates in Hebron to Jerusalem for her lying-in, when she had been suddenly overtaken by her pains and had an unforgettably unpleasant experience at a village on the road with an avaricious innkeeper and an unskilled midwife. It was only some hours after Herod had been born that it occurred to Berenice to ask the name of the village, which was a very dirty and dilapidated place; and the midwife answered: 'Bethlehem, the birthplace of the patriarch Benjamin, and the birthplace of King David, and the place of which the prophet spoke: "But thou, Bethlehem Ephrata, though thou be little among the thousands of Judah, yet out of thee shall he come forth unto Me that is to be Ruler in Israel." ' Berenice, infuriated by the treatment she had received, exclaimed in ironical tones: 'May God Almighty everlastingly bless Bethlehem!' To which the midwife replied approvingly: 'That's what visitors always say!' This story appealed very much to my mother, and for some years after that, when she wished to express her contempt for some very overrated place she used to exclaim in imitation of Berenice's voice: 'May God Almighty everlastingly bless Bethlehem!' That was how I remembered the name.

As for this Joshua, or Jesus as his Greek followers call him, he is now also claimed as a native of Bethlehem – I cannot say on what foundation, because Bethlehem is not in Galilee – and his cult has since spread to Rome and seems to flourish here quite strongly in an underground sort of way. The ceremonies include a love-feast which men and women attend in order to eat, symbolically, the flesh of the Anointed One and drink his blood. I am told that this ceremony is often the occasion for disorderly and hysterical scenes, as is only to be expected when most of its initiates are slaves and men and women of the lowest class. Before they are allowed to sit down they must first confess their sins in nauseating detail to the assembled gathering. This provides a deal of entertainment, a sort of competition in self-abasement. The chief priest of the cult (if I may dignify him with the title) is a Galilean fisherman, that Simon of whom Herod wrote, whose chief claim to the position seems to rest on the fact that he deserted this Joshua, or Jesus, on the day of his arrest, and repudiated his beliefs, but has since sincerely repented. For according to the ethics of this sorry sect the greater the original crime, the greater the forgiveness!

Not being a recognized religion (the better sort of Jews repudiate it strongly), the cult falls under the regulations against drinking-clubs and sodalities; and is of the dangerous sort that grows the stronger by prohibition. The chief article in the faith is the absolute equality of man with man in the sight of the Jewish God – with whom this Joshua is now practically identified – and of this God's granting everlasting bliss to sinners on the single condition of their repentance and acknowledgement of his supremacy over all other Gods. Anyone can be enrolled in the cult, irrespective of class, race, or character, so people join who cannot hope for admittance to the legitimate mysteries of Isis, Cybele, Apollo, and the rest, either because they have never had the necessary social standing, or because they have lost it by some disgrace or crime. At first an initiate had to submit to circumcision, but even this ritual preliminary has now been waived because the sect has broken away so completely from orthodox Judaism that a mere sprinkling of water and the naming of the Messiah is the only initiatory ceremony. The cult has occasionally been known to exercise a perverse fascination on quite well-educated persons. Among the converts is an ex-Governor of Cyprus, one Sergius Paullus; whose delight in the society of street-cleaners, slaves, and old-clothes hawkers shows the degrading effect of the cult on civilized manners. He wrote to me resigning his governorship on the ground that he could no longer conscientiously take an oath by the God Augustus, because his allegiance to this new God forbade it. I let him resign, but struck him off the roll. Later, when I questioned him about this new faith, he assured me that it was entirely non-political, that Jesus had been a man of deep wisdom and the most exemplary character, and loyal to Roman rule. He denied that Jesus's teaching was a confused medley of Greek and Jewish religious commonplaces. He said that it derived from and transcended a disciplined body of moderate Jewish opinion called Rabbinical, which contrasted strongly with the superstitious formalism of the party of scribes (on whose support Herod relied) by laying more emphasis on brotherly love, in the name of God, than on the divine vengeance which awaited those who disobeyed the Law; on the spirit rather than on the letter of the Law.

I paid my vow to Venus as soon as I returned to Italy. In answer to a dream in which she appeared to me and said smilingly, 'Claudius, my roof leaks: repair it, please', I rebuilt, on a grand scale too, her famous temple at Mount Eryx in Sicily, which had fallen into disrepair: I provided it with priests of ancient Sicilian family and endowed it with a large yearly income from the Treasury. I also built a handsome shrine to the nymph Egeria in her grove at Aricia, and dedicated in it a golden votive offering – a beautiful female hand snuffing a candle, with the following sentence inscribed on the candle-stick in the Sabine dialect:

To the swift-flying herald of victory, Egeria, from lame Claudius, in gratitude. Grant that his candle may burn to the socket, giving a clear light, and that the flame of his enemies' candles may suddenly fail and go out.

Chapter 22

I DULY celebrated my triumph at the New Year. The Senate had been good enough to vote me five further honours. First they had voted me a Civic Crown. This was a golden oak-leaf chaplet, originally only awarded to a soldier who, in battle, went to the rescue of a comrade who had been disarmed and was at A.D. 44 the mercy of an opponent, killed the opponent and maintained the ground. The honour was more rarely won than you would suppose; because a necessary witness was the man who had been rescued and whose duty it would be to present the crown to his saviour. It was very difficult to make a Roman soldier confess that he had been at the mercy of an enemy champion and only owed his life to the superior strength and courage of a comrade; he was more likely to complain that his foot had slipped and that he was just about to leap up again and finish off his opponent when this ambitious fellow had officiously broken in and robbed him of his victory. Later the honour was also granted to regimental or army commanders who by their heroism or good generalship saved the lives of troops under their command. I was given the Crown in this sense, and really I think that I deserved it for not listening to the advice given me by my staff. It was inscribed *For Saving the Lives of Fellow Citizens.* You will remember that when I was first proclaimed Emperor the Palace Guard had forced me to wear a similar chaplet, the one with which Caligula had been pleased to honour himself for his German victories. I had no right to it then and was much ashamed of wearing it (though really Caligula had had no right to it either), so it was a great pleasure to me now to wear one that was rightfully mine. The second honour was a Naval Crown. This crown, decorated with the beaks of ships, was awarded for gallantry at sea – for example, to a sailor for being the first to board an enemy ship or to an admiral for destroying an enemy fleet. It was voted me because I had risked my life by putting to sea in dangerous weather with the object of reaching Britain as soon as possible. I afterwards hung both these Crowns on the pinnacle over the main entrance to the Palace.

The third honour the Senate gave me was the hereditary title of Britannicus. My little son was now known as Drusus Britannicus, or merely as Britannicus, and I shall henceforward always refer to him by that name. The fourth honour was the erection of two triumphal arches in commemoration of my victory: one at Boulogne, because that had been my base for the expedition, the other at Rome itself, on the Flaminian Way. They were faced with marble, decorated on both sides with trophies and bas-reliefs illustrative of my victory and surmounted with triumphal chariots in bronze. The fifth honour was a decree making the day of my triumph an annual festival for all time. Besides these five honours there were two complimentary ones awarded Messalina, namely, the right to sit in a front seat in the Theatre with the Vestal Virgins, next to the Consuls, magistrates, and foreign ambassadors, and the right to use a covered carriage of state. Messalina had now been voted every one of the honours awarded my grandmother Livia in her lifetime, but I still opposed the granting to her of the title Augusta.

The sun consented to shine brightly for the day of triumph, after several days of unsettled weather, and the ward-masters and other officials had seen to it that Rome was looking as fresh and gay as so venerable and dignified a city could possibly look. The fronts of all the temples and houses had been scoured, the streets were swept as clean as the floor of the Senate House, flowers and bright objects decorated every window, and tables heaped with food were set outside every door. The temples were all thrown open, the shrines and statues were garlanded, incense burnt on every altar. The whole population, too, was dressed in its best clothes.

I had not yet entered the City, having spent the night at the Guards Camp. At dawn I ordered a general parade there of the troops who were to take part in the triumph and distributed the bounty money that I calculated was due to them from the sale of the spoil we had taken at London and Colchester and elsewhere, and from the sale of prisoners. This money amounted to thirty gold pieces for every private soldier and proportionately more for the higher ranks. I had already sent bounty money on the same scale to the soldiers in Britain who could not be spared to return for the triumph. At the same time I awarded decorations: neckchains for distinguished conduct on the field, to the number of 1,000; 400 frontlets (gold medallions in the shape of the foreheadamulets of horses) reserved for gallant cavalry-men or for infantry soldiers who had succeeded in killing an enemy cavalry-man or charioteer; forty massive gold bracelets given in recompense for outstanding valour – when awarding these I read out an account of each of the feats which had earned them; six olive garlands conferred on men who had contributed to the victory, though not actually present at it (the commander of the base camp and the admiral commanding the fleet were among those who won this honour); three Rampart Crowns, for being the first man over the stockade into an enemy's camp; and one Untipped Spear –

Posides's – which was granted, like the Civic Crown, for saving life, and which he had earned ten times over.

The Senate, on my recommendation, had voted triumphal ornaments to all men of senatorial rank who had taken part in the campaign – that is to say, to all regimental commanders and senior staff officers. It was a pity that Aulus could not be spared, or Vespasian, but all the others had come. Hosidius Geta and his brother Lusius Geta, who had commanded the eight Guards Battalions in Britain, were both honoured: I think that this was the first time in Roman history that two brothers have worn triumphal dress on the same day. Lusius Geta became my new Guards Commander, or rather he held the appointment jointly with a man named Crispinus whom Vitellius had appointed temporarily in my absence. For Justus, the former commander, was dead. Messalina had sent an urgent message which reached me on the eve of the battle of Brentwood to tell me that Justus had been sounding various Guards officers as to their willingness to stand by him in an armed revolt. Trusting Messalina completely and not daring to take any risks, I sent an immediate order for his execution. It was years before I learned the true facts: that Justus had got wind of what was going on in Messalina's wing at the Palace in my absence and asked one of his colonels what he had better do about it – whether he ought to write to me at once, or wait for my return. The colonel was one of Messalina's confidants, so he advised Justus to wait, for fear that the bad news might distract me from my military duties; and then went straight to Messalina. Justus's death, the cause of which was soon known throughout the City, was a general warning not to let me into a secret which finally everyone but myself knew – even my enemies in Britain and Parthia, if you can believe it! Messalina had been going from bad to worse. But I shall not record her behaviour in detail here because I was, so far, wholly ignorant of it. She had come to Genoa to meet me on my return from France and the warmth of her greeting was one of the things that was now making me feel so happy. In six months, too, little Britannicus and his baby sister had grown out of all recognition and were such beautiful children.

You must realize how much this day meant for me. There is nothing in this world, I suppose, so glorious as a Roman triumph. It is not like a triumph celebrated by some barbarous monarch over a rival king whom he has subdued: it is an honour conferred by a free people on one of their own number for a great service he has rendered them. I knew that I had earned it fairly and that I had finally disproved the ill opinion that my family had always had of me as a useless person, born under the wrath of Heaven, an imbecile, a weakling, a disgrace to my glorious ancestors. Asleep in the Guards Camp that night I had dreamed that my brother Germanicus came up to me and embraced me and said in that grave voice of his: 'Dear brother, you have done excellently well, better, I confess, than I ever thought you would do. You have restored the honour of Roman arms.' When I woke in the early morning I decided to abrogate the law that Augustus had made limiting triumphs to the Emperor himself and his sons or grandchildren. If Aulus continued the campaign in Britain and succeeded in the task I had given him of permanently subduing the whole southern part of the island I should persuade the Senate to give him a triumph of his own. In my opinion, it seemed that to be the only man who could legally be awarded a triumph rather detracted from the glory than added to it. Augustus's enactment had been designed to keep his generals from inciting border tribes to warfare in the hope of winning a triumph over them; but surely, I argued, there were other ways of restraining generals than making the triumph, which had once been open to everyone, a mere family rite of the Caesars?

The decoration ceremony over, I gave three audiences: the first to all governors of provinces, for whose temporary attendance at Rome I had asked the Senate's permission, the next to the ambassadors sent me from allied kings, and the last to the exiles. For I had won the Senate's permission for the return from their places of banishment of all exiles, but only for the duration of the triumphal festivities. This last audience was rather a sad one for me, because many of them looked very feeble and ill and they all begged piteously to have their sentences revised. I told them not to despair, for I would personally review every case, and if I decided that it was to the public interest for the sentence to be cancelled or mitigated I would intercede with the Senate on their behalf. This I afterwards did, and many of those whose recall I could not recommend were at least allowed a change of their place of banishment – in every case a change for the better. I offered Seneca a change, but he refused it, replying that while he lay under Caesar's displeasure he could not desire any amelioration of his lot; the perennial frost that (according to the fables of travellers) bound the land of the brutish Finns, the perpetual heat that scorched the sands of the deserts beyond Atlas (where Caesar's victorious armies had penetrated in defiance of Nature and in expansion of the map of the known world), the fever-ridden marshy estuaries of Britain now subjugated, no less than the fertile plains and valleys of that distant and famous island, by Caesar's outstanding military genius, nay, even the pestiferous climate of Corsica, where the unfortunate Seneca, author of this memorial, had now languished for two years – or was it two centuries? – this frost, this fire, this damp, this Corsican three-in-one medley of damp, fire, and frost, would pass as evils scarcely noticed by the exile, Stoic-minded, whose one thought was to bear in patience the crushing weight of the disgrace under which he laboured, and make himself worthy of Caesar's pardon, should this supreme gift ever, beyond expectation, be bestowed upon him. I was quite ready to send him to his native Spain, as his friend my secretary Polybius pleaded for him, but if he himself insisted on Corsica, why, Corsica it must be. Narcissus learned from the harbour officials at Ostia that among the mementoes of his visit to Rome this brave Stoic took back in his luggage gem-studded golden drinking-cups, down pillows, Indian spices, costly unguents, tables and couches of the fragrant sandarach-wood from Africa, inlaid with ivory, pictures of a sort that would have delighted Tiberius, quantities of vintage Falernian, and (though this falls into a somewhat different category from the rest) a complete set of my published works.

At ten o'clock it was time to be on our way. The procession entered the City from the north-east by the Triumphal Gate and passed along the Sacred Way. Its order was as follows. First came the Senate, on foot, in its best robes, headed by the magistrates. Next, a picked body of trumpeters trained to blow triumphant marching tunes like one man. The trumpets were to call attention to the spoils, which then followed on a train of decorated wagons drawn by mules and escorted by the Germans of the Household Battalion dressed in the Imperial livery. These spoils were heaps of gold and silver coin, weapons, armour, horse-furniture, jewels and gold ornaments, ingots of tin and lead, rich drinking-vessels, decorated bronze buckets, and other furniture from Cymbeline's palace at Colchester, numerous examples of exquisite North-British enamel work, carved and painted wooden totem-poles, necklaces of jet and amber and pearl, feather head-dresses, embroidered Druidical robes, carved coracle paddles, and countless other beautiful, valuable, or strange objects. Behind these wagons came twelve captured British chariots, the finest we could choose, drawn by well-matched ponies. To each of these was fixed a placard, on poles above the head of the driver, giving the name of one of the twelve conquered British tribes. Next came more wagons, drawn by horses, containing models in painted wood or clay of the towns and forts we had captured, and groups of living statuary representing the yielding of various river gods to our troops, each group being backed by a huge canvas-picture of the engagement. Last of this series was a model of the famous stone-temple of the Sun God of which I have already spoken.

After these came a body of flute-players playing soft music. They introduced the white bulls that came along behind, under charge of the priests of Jove, roaring angrily and causing a lot of trouble. Their horns were gilded and they wore red fillets and garlands to show that they were destined for sacrifice. The priests carried pole-axes and knives. The acolytes of Jove followed, with golden dishes and other holy instruments. Next came an interesting exhibit – a live walrus. This bull-like seal with great ivory tusks was captured asleep on a beach by the guard of our base camp. The walrus was followed by British wild cattle and deer, the skeleton of a stranded whale, and a transparent-sided tank full of beavers. After this, the arms and insignia of the captured chiefs, and then the chiefs themselves, with all members of their families that had fallen into our hands, followed by all the inferior captives marching in fetters. I was sorry not to have Caractacus in the procession, but Cattigern was there and his wife, and the wife and children of Togodumnus, and an infant son of Caractacus, and thirty chiefs of importance.

After these came a company of public slaves, marching two and two, carrying on cushions the complimentary golden crowns which had been sent me by allied kings and states in token of grateful respect. Next came twenty-four yeomen, dressed in purple, each with an axe tied in a bundle of rods, the axes crowned with laurel. Then came a four-horse chariot which had been built at the order of the Senate, of silver and ebony: except for its traditionally peculiar shape and for the embossed scenes on its sides, which represented two battles and a storm at sea, it was not unlike the chariot which I had broken up in the Goldsmiths' Street as being too luxurious. It was drawn by four white horses and in it rode the author of this history – not 'Clau-Clau-Claudius', or 'Claudius the Idiot', or 'That Claudius', or 'Claudius the Stammerer', or even 'Poor Uncle Claudius', but the victorious and triumphant Tiberius Claudius Drusus Nero Caesar Augustus Germanicus Britannicus, Emperor, Father of the Country, High Pontiff, Protector of the People for the fourth year in succession, three times Consul, who had been awarded the Civic and Naval Crowns, triumphal ornaments on three previous occasions and other lesser honours, civil and military, too numerous to mention. This exalted and happy personage was attired in a gold-embroidered robe and flowered tunic and bore in his right hand, which was trembling a little, a laurel bough, and in his left an ivory sceptre surmounted with a golden bird. A garland of Delphic laurel shaded his brows and, in revival of an ancient custom, his face, arms, neck, and legs (as much of his body as showed) were painted bright red. In the Victor's chariot rode his little son Britannicus, shouting and clapping his hands, his friend Vitellius, wearing the Olive Crown, who had ruled the State in the Victor's absence, his infant daughter Octavia, held in the arms of young Silanus, who had been chosen as her future husband and who in company with young Pompey, married to the Victor's daughter Antonia, had brought the Senate the laurel-wreathed dispatch. Silanus had been voted triumphal dress and so had young Pompey, who also rode in this chariot and held Britannicus on his knee. Beside the chariot rode young Pompey's father, Crassus Frugi, who had now worn triumphal dress twice, the first time having been after Galba's defeat of the Chattians. And we must not forget the public slave who stood in the chariot holding over the Victor's head a golden Etruscan crown ornamented with jewels, the gift of the Roman people. It was his duty to whisper in the Victor's ear every now and then the ancient formula, 'Look behind thee: remember thyself mortal!' – a warning that the Gods would be jealous of the Victor if he bore himself too divinely, and would not fail to humble him. And to avert the evil eye of spectators a phallic charm, a little bell, and a scourge were fastened to the dash-board of the chariot.

Next came Messalina, the Victor's wife, in her carriage of state. Next, walking on foot, the commanders who had been awarded triumphal dress. Then the winners of the Olive Crown. Then the colonels, captains, sergeants, and other ranks who had been decorated for valour. Then the elephants. Then the camels, yoked two and two and drawing carriages on which were mounted the six thunder-and-lightning machines of Caligula's invention, which had been put to such apt use by Posides. Then came the Heron King on his stilts, a golden bracelet twisted about his neck. I am told that, after myself, the Heron King earned more cheers than anyone. After him walked Posides with his Untipped Spear, and the Spanish oculist, wearing a gown, for he had been rewarded with the Roman citizenship. Then came the Roman cavalry, and then the infantry in marching order, their weapons adorned with laurel. The younger soldiers were shouting 'Io Triumphe!' and singing hymns of victory, but the veterans exercised the right of free speech which was theirs for the day, indulging in sarcastic ribaldry at the Victor's expense. The veterans of the Twentieth had composed a fine song for the occasion:

> Claudius was a famous scholar,
>> Claudius shed less blood than ink,
> When he came to fight the Britons
>> From the fray he did not shrink,
> But the weapons of his choice were
>> Rope and stilts and camel stink.
>>> O, O, Oh!

> Rope and stilts and stink of camel
> Made the British army shake.
> Off they ran with yells of horror
>> And their cries the dead would wake –
> Cries as loud as Claudius utters
>> When he's got the stomach-ache.
>>> O, O, Oh!

I am told that at the tail of this column there were bawdy songs sung about Messalina, but I did not hear them where I was; indeed, if they had been sung by the yeomen walking just ahead of me I should not have heard them, the crowd was raising such a tremendous din. After the infantry came detachments of auxiliaries, headed by the Balearics and Nubians.

That ended the procession proper, but it was followed by a laughing and cheering rabble giving a mock triumph to Baba, the clown of Alexandria, who had come to Rome to improve his fortunes. He rode in a public dung-cart, to which had been yoked in a row a goat, a sheep, a pig, and a fox. He was painted blue, with British woad, and dressed in a fantastic parody of triumphal dress. His cloak was a patchwork quilt and his tunic an old sack trimmed with dirty coloured ribbons. His sceptre was a cabbage-stick with a dead bat tied to the end of it with a string, and his laurel branch was a thistle. Our most famous native-born clown, Augurinus, had recently consented to share the government of the Society of Vagabonds with Baba. Baba was held to resemble me closely, and therefore always played the part of Caesar in the theatricals that the two of them were constantly giving in the back streets of the City. Augurinus played the part of Vitellius, or a Consul of the year, or a Colonel of the Guards, or one of my ministers, according to circumstances. He had a very lively gift for parody. On this particular occasion he represented the slave who held the crown over Baba (an inverted chamber-pot into which, every now and then, Baba's head disappeared) and kept tickling him with a cock's feather. Baba's sack-tunic was torn behind and disclosed Baba's rump, painted blue with bold red markings to make it look like a grinning human face. Baba's hands trembled madly the whole time and he jerked his head about in caricature of my nervous tic, rolling his eyes, and whenever Augurinus molested him struck back with the thistle or the dead bat. In another dung-cart behind, under a tattered hood, reclined an enormous naked negress with a brass ring in her nose, nursing a little pink pig. The spoils of this rival triumph were displayed on handcarts wheeled by ragged hawkers – kitchen refuse, broken bedsteads, filthy mattresses, rusty iron, cracked cooking-pots, and all sorts of mouldy lumber – and the prisoners were dwarfs, fat men, thin men, albinos, cripples, blind men, hydrocephalitics, and men suffering from dreadful diseases or chosen for their surprising ugliness. The rest of the procession was in keeping: I am told that the models and pictures illustrating Baba's victories were the funniest things, in a dirty way, ever seen at Rome.

When we came to the Capitoline Hill, I dismounted and went through a performance which custom demanded but which I found a great physical strain: I ascended the steps of the Temple of Jove humbly kneeling on my knees. Young Pompey and Silanus supported me on either side. At this point it was the custom to lead aside the captured enemy chiefs and execute them in the prison adjoining the temple. This custom was the survival of an ancient rite of human sacrifice in thanksgiving for victory. I dispensed with it on grounds of public policy: I decided to keep these chiefs alive at Rome in order to give others in Britain who were still holding out against us a demonstration of clemency. The Britons themselves sacrificed war prisoners, but it would be absurd to commemorate our intention of civilizing their island with an act of primitive barbarism. I would grant these chiefs and their families small pensions from the public funds and encourage them to become Romanized, so that later when regiments of British auxiliaries were formed there would be officers to command them capable of acting in friendly co-operation with our own forces.

Though I failed to sacrifice the chiefs to Jove I did not at any rate fail to sacrifice the white bulls, or to give the God an offering from the spoils (the pick of the golden ornaments from Cymbeline's palace), or to place in the lap of his sacred image the laurel-crown from my brow. Then I and my companions in triumph, and Messalina, were entertained by the college of the Priest of Jove to a public banquet while the troops dispersed and were entertained by the City. A house whose table was not honoured by the presence of at least one triumphant hero was an unlucky house indeed. I had heard unofficially, the night before, that the Twentieth were planning another drunken orgy like the one in which they had taken part during Caligula's triumph: they intended to launch an assault on the Goldsmiths' Street and if they found the doors of the shops barred they would use fire or battering-rams. I thought at first of defending the street with a corps of Watchmen, but that would only have meant bloodshed, so I had the better idea of filling the flasks of all the troops with a free wine-ration with which to drink my health. The flasks were filled just before the procession started and my orders were not to drink until the trumpets gave them the signal that the sacrifice had been duly made. It was all good wine, but what I gave the Twentieth was heavily doctored with poppy-seed. So they drank my health and that put them so soundly to sleep that by the time they woke up the triumph was over: one man, I regret to say, never woke up. But at least there was no serious disturbance of the peace that day.

In the evening I was guided home to the Palace by a long torch-light procession and the corps of flute-players, and followed by enormous crowds of cheering and singing citizens. I was tired out and after washing off my red paint went straight to bed, but the festivities continued all night and would not let me sleep. At midnight I rose and with only Narcissus and Pallas as my companions went out into the streets. I was disguised as an ordinary citizen in a plain white gown. I wanted to hear what people really thought of me. We mixed with the crowd. The steps of the Temple of Castor and Pollux were dotted with groups of people resting and talking, and here we found seats. Everyone addressed everyone else without ceremony. I was glad that free speech had returned to Rome at last, after its long suppression by Tiberius and Caligula, even though some of the things I heard did not altogether please me. The general opinion seemed to be that it had been a very fine triumph but that it would have been still finer if I had distributed money to the citizens as well as to the soldiers, and increased the corn ration. (Corn had been scarce that winter again, through no fault of mine.) I was anxious to hear what a battle-scarred captain of the Fourteenth sitting near us had to say: he was with a brother whom he had apparently not seen for sixteen years. At first he would not talk about the battle, though his brother pressed him to do so, and would only discuss Britain as a military station: he thought that with luck he could count on very pretty pickings. Soon he would be able to retire, he hoped, with the rank of knight: he had made quite a packet of money in the last ten years by selling exemptions from duty to the men of his company, and 'on the Rhine one doesn't get a chance of spending much money – it's not like at Rome'. But in the end he said: 'Frankly speaking, we officers of the Fourteenth didn't think much of the Brentwood fighting. The Emperor made it too easy for us. Wonderfully clever man, the Emperor. One of these strategists. Gets it all out of books. That trip-rope, now, that was a typical stratagem. And that great bird, flapping its wings and making weird sounds. And getting the camels forward on the flank to scare the enemy's ponies with their stink. A first-class strategist. But strategy isn't what I call soldiering. Old Aulus Plautius was going straight at that central stockade, and be damned to the consequences. Old Aulus is a soldier. He'd have given us a better bloody battle if it had been left to him. We officers of the Fourteenth like a good bloody battle better than a clever bit of strategy. It's what we live for, a bloody battle is, and if we lose heavily, why, that's a soldier's luck and it means promotion for the survivors. No promotion at all in the Fourteenth this time. A couple of corporals killed, that's all. No, he made it too easy. I had a better time than most, of course: I got in among the chariots with my leading platoon and killed a good few British, and I won this chain here, so I can't complain. But speaking for the Regiment as a whole, that battle wasn't up to the standard of the two others we fought before the Emperor came: the Medway fight was a good one, now, nobody will deny that.'

An old woman piped up: 'Well, Captain, you're very gallant,

and we're all very grateful and proud of you, I'm sure, but for my part I've got two boys serving in the Second, and though I'm disappointed that they didn't get home-leave for to-day, I'm thankful they're alive. Perhaps if your General Aulus had had his way, they'd be lying there on Brentwood Hill for the crows to pick at.'

An old Frenchman agreed: 'For my part, Captain, I shouldn't care how a battle was won, so long as it was well won. I heard two other officers like yourself discussing the battle to-night. And one of them said: "Yes, a clever bit of strategy, but too clever: smells of the lamp." What *I* say is, did the Emperor win a splendid victory or did he not? He did. Then long live the Emperor.'

But the Captain said: '*Smells of the lamp*, they said, did they? That was very well put. A strategical victory, but it smelled of the lamp. The Emperor's altogether too clever to rank as a good soldier. For my part, I thank the Gods that I never read a book in my life.'

I said shyly to Narcissus as we went home: 'You didn't agree with that captain, did you, Narcissus?'

'No, Caesar,' said Narcissus, 'did you? But I thought he spoke like a brave and honest man and as he's only a captain, perhaps you ought to be rather pleased than otherwise. You don't want captains in the army who know too much or think too much. And he certainly gave you full credit for the victory, didn't he?'

But I grumbled: 'Either I'm an utter imbecile or I'm altogether too clever.'

The triumph lasted for three days. On the second day we had spectacles in the Circus and in the amphitheatre simultaneously. At the first we had chariot-races, ten in all, and athletic contests, and fights between British captives and bears; and boys from Asia Minor performed the national sword-dance. At the other a pageant of the storming and sacking of Colchester and the yielding of the enemy chiefs was re-enacted, and we had a battle between 300 Catuvellaunians and 300 Trinovants, chariots as well as infantry. The Catuvellaunians won. On the morning of the third day we had more horse-racing and a battle between Catuvellaunian broad-swordsmen and a company of Numidian spearmen, captured by Geta the year before. The Catuvellaunians won easily. The last performance took place in the Theatre – plays, interludes, and acrobatic dancing. Mnester was splendid that day; and the audience made him perform his dance of triumph in *Orestes and Pylades* – he was Pylades – three times over. He refused to take a fourth call. He put his head around the curtain and called archly: 'I can't come, my Lords. Orestes and I are in bed together.'

Messalina said to me afterwards: 'I want you to talk to Mnester very sternly, my dearest husband. He's much too independent for a man of his profession and origin, though he *is* a marvellous actor. During your absence he was most rude to me on two or three occasions. When I asked him to make his company rehearse a favourite ballet of mine for a festival – you know that I have been supervising all the Games and Shows because Vitellius found it too much for him, and then I found that Harpocras, the secretary, had been behaving dishonestly, and we had to have him executed, and Pheronactus whom I chose in his place has been rather slow in learning his business – well, anyhow, it was all very difficult for me, and Mnester instead of making things easier was most dreadfully obstinate. Oh, no, he said, he couldn't put on *Ulysses and Circe* because he hadn't anyone capable of playing Circe to his Ulysses, and when I suggested *The Minotaur* he said that Theseus was a part he greatly disliked playing but that on the other hand it would be below his dignity to dance in the less important part of King Minos. That's the sort of obstruction he made all the time. He simply refused to grasp that I was your representative and that he simply *must* do what I told him: but I didn't punish him because I thought you might not wish it. I waited until now.'

I called Mnester. 'Listen, little Greek,' I said. 'This is my wife, the Lady Valeria Messalina. The Senate of Rome thinks as highly of her as I do: they have paid her exalted honours. In my absence she has been taking over some of my duties for me and performing them to my entire satisfaction. She now complains that you have been both un-co-operative and insolent. Understand this: if the Lady Messalina tells you to do anything, however much obedience in the matter may happen to hurt your professional vanity, you must obey her. *Anything*, mark you, little Greek, and no arguments either. Anything and everything.'

'I obey, Caesar,' Mnester answered, sinking to the floor with exaggerated docility, 'and I beg forgiveness for my stupidity. I did not understand that I was to obey the Lady Messalina in *everything*, only in certain things.'

'Well, you understand now.'

So that was the end of my triumph. The troops returned to duty in Britain, and I returned to civil dress and duty at Rome. It is probable that it will never happen to anyone again in this world, as it is certain that it had never happened to anyone before, to fight his first battle at the age of fifty-three, never having performed military service of any sort in his youth, win a crushing victory, and never take the field again for the rest of his life.

Chapter 23

I CONTINUED my reforms at Rome, especially doing all I could to create a sense of public responsibility in my subordinates. I appointed the Treasury officials whom I had been training and made their appointments run for three years. I dismissed from the Senatorial Order the Governor of Southern Spain because he could not clear himself of the charges brought against him by the troops serving in Morocco that he had cheated them of half their corn-rations. Other charges of fraud were brought against him too, and he had to pay 100,000 gold pieces. He went round to his friends trying to gain their sympathy by telling them that the charges were framed by Posides and Pallas whom he had offended by remembering their slavish birth. But he got little sympathy. One early morning this governor brought all his house-furniture, which made about 300 wagon-loads of exceptionally valuable pieces, to the public auction-place. This cause a lot of excitement because he had an unrivalled collection of Corinthian vessels. All the dealers and connoisseurs came crowding up, licking their lips and searching round for bargains. 'Poor Umbonius is finished,' they said. 'Now's our chance to pick up cheap the stuff which he refused to part with when we made him really handsome offers for it.' But they were disappointed. When the spear was stuck upright in the ground, to show that a public auction was in progress, all that Umbonius sold was his senator's gown. Then he had the spear pulled out again to show that the auction was over, and that night at midnight, when wagons were allowed in the streets again, he took all his stuff back home. He was merely showing everyone that he had plenty of money still and could live very comfortably as a private citizen. However, I was not going to let the insult pass. I put a heavy tax on Corinthian vessels that year, which he could not evade because he had publicly displayed his collection and even listed them on the auction board.

This was the time that I began going closely into the question of new religions and cults. Some new foreign god came to Rome every year to serve the needs of immigrants and in general I had no objection to this. For example, a colony of 400 Arabian merchants and their families from Yemen, which had settled at Ostia, built a temple there to their tribal gods: it was orderly worship, involving no human sacrifices or other scandals. But what I objected to was disorderly competition between religious cults, their priests and missioners going from house to house in search of converts and modelling their persuasive vocabulary on that of the auctioneer or the brothel-pimp or the vagabond Greek astrologer. The discovery that religion is a marketable commodity like oil, figs, or slaves was first made at Rome in late Republican times, and steps had been taken to check such marketing, but without great success. There had been a notable breakdown in religious belief after our conquest of Greece, when Greek philosophy spread to Rome. The philosophers, while not denying the divine, made such a remote abstraction of it that a practical people like the Romans began to argue: 'Very well, the Gods are infinitely powerful and wise but also infinitely remote. They deserve our respect and we will honour them most devotedly with temples and sacrifices, but it is clear that we were mistaken in thinking that they were immediate presences and that they would bother to strike individual sinners dead or punish the whole city for one man's crime, or appear in mortal disguise. We have been mistaking poetical fiction for prose reality. We must revise our views.'

This decision made an uncomfortable void, for the ordinary common citizen, between himself and those remote ideals of (for example) Power, Intelligence, Beauty, and Chastity into which the philosophers had converted Jove, Mercury, Venus, and Diana. Some intermediary beings were needed. Into the void came crowding new divine or semi-divine characters. These were mostly foreign gods with very definite personalities, who could not easily be philosophized about. They could be summoned by incantation and take on visible human shape. They could appear in the middle of a circle of devotees and talk familiarly to each member of the cult. Occasionally they even had sexual intercourse with women-worshippers. There was one famous scandal in the reign of my uncle Tiberius. A rich knight was in love with a respectable married noblewoman. He tried to bribe her to sleep with him and offered her as much as 2,500 gold pieces for a single tryst. She refused indignantly, and thereafter would not even acknowledge his greetings when they met in the street. He knew that she was a devotee of Isis, who had a temple at Rome, and bribed the priests of the Goddess, for 500 gold pieces, to tell her that the God Anubis was in love with her and wished her to visit him. She was greatly flattered by the message and went to the Temple on the night ordained by Anubis, and there in the holiest part, on the very couch of the God, the knight, disguised as the God, enjoyed her until morning. The silly woman could not contain herself for felicity. She told her husband and friends of the signal honour that she had been shown. Most of them believed her. Three days later she met the knight in the street and as usual tried to pass by without answering his greeting. He barred her way and taking her familiarly by the arm said: 'My dear, you have saved me two thousand gold pieces. A thrifty woman like you ought to be ashamed to throw good money away. Personally, I care nothing for names. You happen to dislike mine and adore Anubis's, and so the other night I had to be Anubis. But the pleasure was just as great as if I had used my own name. Now, good-bye. I've had what I wanted and I'm satisfied.' Never was a woman so thunderstruck and horrified. She ran home to her husband and told him how she had been deceived and abused, and swore that if she was not immediately avenged she would kill herself for shame. The husband, a senator, went to Tiberius; and Tiberius, who thought highly of him, had the Temple of Isis destroyed, her priests crucified, and her image thrown into the Tiber. But the knight himself boldly told Tiberius: 'You know the power of love. Nothing can withstand it. And what I have done should be a warning to all respectable women not to embrace fancy religions but to stick to the good old Roman Gods.' So he was only banished for a few years. Then the husband, having had his married happiness ruined by this affair, began a campaign against all religious charlatans. He brought charges against four Jewish missionaries, who had converted a noblewoman of the Fulvian family to their faith, that they had persuaded her to send votive offerings of gold and purple cloth to the Temple at Jerusalem, but had sold these gifts for their own profit. Tiberius found the men guilty and crucified them. As a warning against similar practices he banished all the Jews in Rome to Sardinia: there were 4,000 of them and half that number died of fever within a few months after arriving there. Caligula allowed the Jews to come back again.

Tiberius, you will recall, also expelled all the fortune-tellers and pretended astrologers from Italy. He was a curious compound of atheism and superstition, credulity and scepticism. He once said at a dinner that he regarded the worship of the Gods as useless in view of the stars: he believed in predestination. His expulsion of the astrologers was due perhaps to his wishing to enjoy the monopoly of prediction: for Thrasyllus remained with him always. What he did not realize was that though the stars may tell no lies, astrologers, even the best of them, cannot be counted upon either to read their messages with perfect correctness or to report with perfect frankness what they have read. I am neither a sceptic nor particularly superstitious. I love ancient forms and ceremonies and have an inherited belief in the old Roman Gods which I refuse to subject to any philosophical analysis. I think that every nation ought to worship its own gods in its own way (so long as it is a civilized way) and not idly adopt exotic deities. As high priest of Augustus I have had to accept him as a god; and after all the demi-god Romulus was only a poor Roman shepherd to begin with, and probably far less gifted and industrious than Augustus. If I had been a contemporary of Romulus I would probably have laughed at the notion of his ever being paid semi-divine rites. But godhead is, after all, a matter of fact, not a matter of opinion: if a man is generally worshipped as a god then he is a god. And if a god ceases to be worshipped he is nothing. While Caligula was worshipped and believed in as a god he was indeed a supernatural being. Cassius Chaerea found it almost impossible to kill him, because there was a certain divine awe about him, the result of the worship offered him from simple hearts, and the conspirators felt it themselves and hung back. Perhaps he would never have succeeded if Caligula had not cursed himself with a divine premonition of assassination.

Augustus is worshipped now with genuine devotion by millions. I myself pray to him with almost as much confidence as I pray to Mars or Venus. But I make a clear distinction between the historical Augustus, of whose weaknesses and misfortunes I am well informed, and the God Augustus, the object of public worship, who has attained power as a deity. What I mean to say is that I cannot deprecate too strongly the wilful assumption by a mortal of divine power; but if he can indeed persuade men to worship him and they worship him genuinely, and there are no portents or other signs of heavenly displeasure at his deification – well, then he is a god, and he must be accepted as such. But the worship of Augustus as a major deity at Rome would never have been possible if it had not been for this gulf which the philosophers had opened between the ordinary man and the traditional gods. For the ordinary Roman citizen, Augustus filled the gap well. He was remembered as a noble and gracious ruler who had given perhaps stronger proofs of his loving care for the City and Empire than the Olympian Gods themselves.

The Augustan cult, however, rather provided a political convenience than satisfied the emotional needs of religiously-minded persons, who preferred to go to Isis or Serapis or Imouthes for an assurance, in the mysteries of these gods, that 'God' was more than either a remote ideal of perfection, or the commemorated glory of a deceased hero. To offer an alternative to these Egyptian cults – they did not in my opinion play a wholesome part in our Graeco-Roman civilization – I prevailed on our standing commission on foreign religions at Rome, the Board of Fifteen, to allow me to popularize mysteries of a more suitable nature. For example, the cult of Cybele, the Goddess worshipped by our Trojan ancestors and therefore well suited to serve our own religious needs, had been introduced into Rome some 250 years before, in obedience to an oracle; but her mysteries were carried on in private by eunuch priests from Phrygia, for no Roman citizen was allowed to castrate himself in the Goddess's honour. I changed all this: the High Priest of Cybele was now to be a Roman knight, though no eunuch, and citizens of good standing might join in her worship. I also attempted to introduce the Eleusinian mysteries to Rome from Greece: the conduct of this famous Attic festival in honour of the Goddess Demeter and her daughter Persephone I need hardly describe, for while Greek survives as a language everyone will know about it. But the nature of the mysteries themselves, of which the festival is only the outer pomp, is by no means a matter of common knowledge and I should much like to tell about them; but because of an oath that I once swore I unfortunately cannot do so. I shall content myself by saying that they are concerned with a revelation of life in the world to come, where happiness will be earned by a virtuous life lived as a mortal. In introducing them at Rome, where I would limit participation in them to senators, knights, and substantial citizens, I hoped to supplement the formal worship of the ordinary gods with an obligation to virtue felt from within, not enforced by laws or edicts.

Unfortunately my attempt failed. Unfavourable oracles were uttered at all the principal Greek shrines, including Apollo's at Delphi, warning me of the terrible consequences of my 'transplanting Eleusis to Rome'. Would it be impious to suggest that the Greek Gods were combining to protect the pilgrim-trade, which was now a chief source of their country's income?

I published an edict forbidding the attendance of Roman citizens at Jewish synagogues and expelled from the City a number of the most energetic Jewish missioners. I wrote to tell Herod of my action. He replied that I had done very wisely, and that he would apply the same principle or, rather, its converse, in his own dominions: he would forbid Greek teachers of philosophy to hold classes in Jewish cities and debar all Jews who attended them elsewhere from worship in the Temple. Neither Herod nor I had made any comment, in our letters to each other, on events in Armenia or Parthia, but this is what had happened. I had sent King Mithridates to Antioch, where Marsus greeted him with honour and sent him to Armenia with two regular battalions, a siege-train, and six battalions of Syrian Greek auxiliaries. He arrived there in March. The Parthian Governor marched out against him and was defeated. This did not mean that Mithridates was immediately left in undisputed possession of his kingdom. Cotys, King of Lesser Armenia, sent armed help to the Parthian Governor and, though his expedition was defeated in its turn, the Parthian garrisons of a number of fortresses refused to surrender and the Roman siege-train had to reduce them one by one. However, Mithridates's brother, the King of Georgia, made his promised invasion from the north and by July the two had joined forces on the River Aras and captured Mufarghin, Ardesh, and Erzerum, the three chief towns of Armenia.

In Parthia Bardanes had soon raised an important army, to which the Kings of Osroëne and Adiabene contributed contingents, and marched against his brother Gotarzes, whose court was then at the city of Ecbatana in the country of the Medes. In a sudden surprise raid at the head of a corps of dromedaries – he covered nearly 300 miles in two days – Bardanes drove the panic-stricken Gotarzes from the throne and presently received the homage of all the subject kingdoms and cities of the Parthian Empire. The only exception was the city of Seleucia, on the River Tigris, which, revolting some seven years before, had obstinately maintained its independence ever since. It was extremely fortunate for us that Seleucia refused to acknowledge Bardanes's suzerainty, because Bardanes made it a matter of pride to besiege and capture it before turning his attention to more important matters, and Seleucia with its huge walls was no easy place to capture. Though Bardanes held Ctesiphon, the city on the opposite bank of the Tigris, he did not command the river itself, and the strong Seleucian fleet could introduce supplies into the city, bought from friendly Arabian tribes on the western shore of the Persian gulf. So he wasted precious time on the Tigris, and Gotarzes, who had escaped to Bokhara, raised a new army there. The siege of Seleucia continued from December until April, when Bardanes, hearing of Gotarzes's new enterprises, raised it and marched northeast for 1,000 miles, through Parthia proper, to the province of Bactria where he eventually encountered Gotarzes. Bardanes's forces were somewhat larger and better equipped than his brother's, but the issue of the impending battle was doubtful, and Bardanes saw that even if he were the victor it was likely to be a Pyrrhic victory – he would lose more men than he could afford. So when Gotarzes offered at the last moment to bargain with him, he consented. As a result of their conference Gotarzes made a formal cession of his rights to the throne and in return Bardanes granted him his life, estates on the southern shores of the Caspian Sea, and a yearly pension worthy of his rank. Meanwhile pressure was put on Seleucia by the King of Adiabene and other neighbouring rulers to surrender on terms; and by the middle of July Marsus at Antioch knew that Bardanes was now the undisputed sovereign of Parthia and was on his way west with an enormous army. He reported this to me at once, and another uncomfortable piece of news too, namely, that on the pretence of having been insulted and threatened by the Greek regiments stationed at Caesarea, Herod had disarmed them and put them to work on road-building and the repairing of the city defences. And this was not all – there had been secret drilling in the desert of large bodies of Jewish volunteers, under the command of members of Herod's bodyguard. Marsus wrote: 'In three months the fate of the Roman Empire in the East will be decided one way or the other.'

I did all that I could do in the circumstances. I dispatched an immediate order to Eastern governors mobilizing all available forces. I also sent one division of the fleet to Egypt, to smother the Jewish rising that I expected in Alexandria, and another to Marsus at Antioch. I mobilized forces in Italy and the Tyrol. But nobody but Marsus and myself and my foreign minister Felix, in whom I was forced to confide because he wrote my letters for me, knew what tremendous storm-clouds were blowing up from the East. And we were the only three who ever knew, because, by an extraordinary fate, the storm never burst at all.

I have no dramatic gift, like my brother Germanicus: I am merely an historian and no doubt most people would call me, in general, dull and prosy, but I have come to a point in my story where the record of bare facts unimproved by oratorical beauties should stir the wonder of my readers as greatly as they stirred me at the time. Let me first tell in what an exalted mood King Herod Agrippa came up from Jerusalem to Caesarea to the festival that had been prepared there in honour of my birthday. He was nursing a secret pride so great that it almost choked him. The foundations of the great edifice that he had so long dreamed of raising, the Empire of the East, were grandly and firmly laid at last. He now had only to speak the word and the walls would (these are the words he used to his Queen Cypros) 'shoot up white and splendid into the dark blue sky, the crystal roof would close over it, and lovely gardens and cool colonnades and lily-ponds would surround it, spreading out as far as the enraptured eye could reach'. Inside all would be beryl and opal and sapphire and sardonyx and pure gold and in the mighty Hall of Judgement would blaze a diamond throne, the throne of the Messiah, whom men had hitherto known as Herod Agrippa.

He had already revealed himself, in secret, to the High Priest and the Sanhedrin, and they had all with one accord bowed themselves to the ground and glorified God and acknowledged him as the prophesied Messiah. He could now publicly reveal himself to the Jewish nation, and to the whole world. His word would go out: 'The Day of Deliverance is at hand, saith the Anointed of the Lord. Let us break the yoke of the Ungodly.' The Jews would rise as one man and cleanse the borders of Israel of the stranger and the infidel. There were now 200,000 Jews trained in the use of weapons in Herod's dominions alone, and thousands more in Egypt, Syria, and the East; and the Jew fighting in the name of his God, as the history of the Maccabees had shown, is heroic to the point of madness. Never was there a better disciplined race. Nor were arms and armour wanting: Herod had added to the 70,000 suits of armour that he had found in Antipas's treasury 200,000 more, besides those that he had taken from the Greeks. The fortifications of Jerusalem were not complete, but in less than six months the city would be impregnable. Even after my order to cease work Herod had secretly continued hollowing out great store-chambers under the Temple and driving long tunnels under the walls to points more than a mile outside, so that if ever it came to a siege the garrison could make surprise sorties and attack an investing army from the rear.

He had concluded a secret alliance against Rome with all the neighbouring kingdoms and cities for hundreds of miles around. Only Phoenician Tyre and Sidon had rejected his advances, and that had troubled him because the Phoenicians were a seafaring people and their fleet was needed to protect his coasts; but now they too had joined him. A joint deputation from both cities had approached his chamberlain Blastus and humbly told him that, faced with the necessity of having either Rome or the Jewish nation as their enemies, they had chosen the lesser evil and were now here to sue for his royal master's friendship and forgiveness. Blastus had informed them of Herod's terms, which eventually they accepted. To-day their formal submission would be made. Herod's terms were that they should forswear Ashtaroth and their other deities, accept circumcision and swear perpetual obedience to the God of Israel, and to Herod the Anointed, his representative here on earth.

With that symbolic act would Herod initiate his reign of glory! He would mount on his throne, the rams' horns would blow, and he would command his soldiers to bring before him that statue of the God Augustus which had been set up in the market-place of the town, and my own statue which stood next to it (wearing a fresh garland to-day in honour of my birthday), and he would call out to the multitude: 'Thus saith the Anointed of the Lord, hew Me in pieces all graven images that are found in My coasts, grind them to powder; for I am a jealous God.' Then with a hammer he would batter at Augustus's statue and mine, would strike off our heads and lop off our limbs. The people would utter a great shout of joy and he would cry again: 'Thus saith the Anointed of the Lord, O my children, the children of Shem, first-born of my servant Noah, cleanse ye this land of the stranger and the infidel, and let the habitations of Japhet be a prey unto you, for the hour of your deliverance is at hand.' The news would sweep the country like a fire: 'The Anointed has manifested himself and has hewn the images of the Caesars asunder. Be joyful in the Lord. Let us

defile the temples of the heathen, and lead our enemies captive.'
The Jews would hear of it in Alexandria. They would rise 300,000
strong, and seize the city, massacring our small garrison there.
Bardanes would hear of it at Nineveh and march on Antioch; and
the kings of Commagene, Lesser Armenia, and Pontus would join
forces with him on the Armenian border. Marsus with his three
regular battalions and his two regiments of Syrian Greeks would
be overwhelmed. Moreover, Bardanes had pledged himself by an
oath sworn in the Temple before the High Priest that if by Herod's
aid he won the throne from his brother (as he had now done) he
would make a public acknowledgement of his debt to Herod by
sending him back all the Jews that could be found in the whole
Parthian Empire, together with their families, flocks, and possessions, and by swearing eternal friendship with the Jewish people.
The scattered sheep of Israel would return at last to the fold. They
would be as many in number as the sand on the seashore. They
would occupy the cities from which they had expelled the stranger
and the infidel, and they would be a united holy people as in the
days of Moses, but ruled by a greater one than Moses, a more
glorious one than Solomon, namely, by Herod, the Beloved, the
Anointed of the Lord.

The festival in pretended honour of my birthday was to take
place in the amphitheatre at Caesarea: and wild beasts and sword-
fighters and racing chariots were all ready for the performance
that Herod never really intended to take place. The audience was
composed partly of Syrian-Greeks, and partly of Jews. They occupied different parts of the amphitheatre. Herod's throne was
among his own subjects, and next to it were the seats reserved for
distinguished visitors. There were no Romans present: they were
all at Antioch celebrating my birthday under the presidency of
Marsus. But ambassadors from Arabia were there, and the King
of Iturea, and the delegation from Tyre and Sidon, and the mother
and sons of the King of Adiabene, and Herod Pollio with his
family. The spectators were protected against the fierce August
sun by great awnings of white canvas, but over Herod's throne,
which was made of silver studded with turquoise, the awnings
were purple silk.

The audience flocked in and took their seats, waiting for
Herod's entrance. Trumpets sounded and presently he appeared
at the southern entrance with all his train and made a stately progress across the arena. The whole audience rose. He had on a

royal robe of silver tissue worked over with polished silver roundels that flashed in the sun so brightly that it tried the eyes to look at him. On his head was a golden diadem twinkling with diamonds and in his hand a flashing silver sword. Beside him Cypros walked in royal purple, and behind her came his lovely little daughters dressed in white silk embroidered with arabesques and edged with purple and gold. Herod held his head high as he walked and smiled a kingly greeting to his subjects. He reached his throne and mounted on it. King Herod Pollio, the ambassadors from Arabia, and the King of Iturea left their seats and came to the steps of the throne to greet him. They spoke in Hebrew: 'O King, live for ever!' But to the men of Tyre and Sidon this was not enough: they felt constrained to make amends for their discourteous treatment of him in the past. They grovelled before him.

The leader of the Tyrians pleaded in tones of the profoundest humility: 'Be merciful to us, Great King, we repent of our ingratitude.'

And the leader of the Sidonians: 'Hitherto we have reverenced you as a man, but we must now acknowledge that you are superior to mortal nature.'

Herod answered: 'You are forgiven, Sidon.'

The Tyrian exclaimed: 'It is the voice of a God, not of a man.'

Herod answered: 'Tyre, you are forgiven.'

He raised his hand to give the signal for the rams' horns to blow, but suddenly let it drop again. For a bird had flown in from the gate by which he had himself entered and was fluttering here and there about the arena. The people watched it and shouts of surprise arose: 'Look, an owl! An owl blinded by daylight.'

The owl perched on a guy-rope above Herod's left shoulder. He turned and gazed up at it. And not until then did he remember the oath he had sworn at Alexandria thirteen years before in the presence of Alexander the Alabarch and Cypros and his children, the oath to honour the living God and keep His laws so far as in him lay, and the curse that he had called upon himself if he ever wittingly blasphemed from hardness of heart. The first and greatest commandment of God, as spoken through Moses, was: 'THOU SHALT HAVE NONE OTHER GODS BUT ME', but when the Tyrian had called him a God, had Herod torn his clothes and fallen on his face to avert Heaven's jealous anger? No, he had smiled at the blasphemer and said, 'Tyre, you are forgiven', and the people standing about him had taken up the cry, 'A God, not a man'. The owl was gazing down in his face. Herod turned pale. The owl hooted five times, then flapped its wings, flew up over the tiers of seats, and disappeared beyond.

Herod said to Cypros: 'The owl that visited me in the prison yard at Misenum – the same owl,' and then a fearful groan burst from his lips and he cried weakly to Helcias, his Master of Horse, successor to Silas: 'Carry me out. I am ill. Let my brother the King of Chalcis take over from me the Presidency of the Games.'

Cypros clasped Herod to her: 'Herod, my king and sweetheart, why do you groan? What ails you?'

Herod replied in a dreadful whisper: 'The maggots are already in my flesh.'

He was carried out. The rams' horns never blew. The statues were not brought in to be broken. The Jewish soldiers posted outside the theatre, prepared to enter at Herod's signal and begin the massacre of the Greeks, remained at their posts. The Games ended before they had begun. The Jewish multitude raised a great wailing and lamentation, tearing their clothes and throwing dust on their heads. The rumour went round that Herod was dying. He was in frightful pain, but he called his brother Herod, and Helcias, and Thaumastus, and the son of the High Priest, to his bedside at the Palace and said to them: 'My friends, all is over now. In five days I shall be dead. I am luckier in this than my grandfather Herod: he lived eighteen months after the pain first fastened on him. I have no complaints to make. It has been a good life. I blame only myself for what has come upon me. For six days I was saluted by the elders of Israel as the Lord's Anointed and on the seventh I foolishly allowed His name to be blasphemed without reproof. Though it was my will to enlarge His Kingdom to the ends of the world, and purify it and bring back the lost tribes, and worship Him all the days of my life, yet because of this one sin I am rejected as my ancestor David was rejected for his sin against Uriah the Hittite. Now Jewry must wait another age until a holier Redeemer comes to accomplish what I have been proved unworthy to accomplish. Tell the confederate kings that the key-stone has fallen from the arch, and that no help can come to them now from the Jewish nation. Tell them that I, Herod, am dying and that I charge them not to make war against Rome without me, because without me they are a rudderless boat, a headless spear, a broken arch. Helcias, see that no violence is done the Greeks. Call in the arms that have been distributed secretly to the Jews and lay them up in the Armoury at Caesarea Philippi, putting a strong guard over them. Give the Greeks back their arms and recall them to their ordinary duties. My servant Thaumastus, see that my debts are paid in full. My brother Herod, see that my dear wife Cypros and my daughters Drusilla and Mariamne come to no harm, and above all dissuade the nation from any folly. Greet the Jews of Alexandria in my name, and ask them to pardon me for having offered them such high hopes and then utterly disappointed them. Go now, and God be with you. I can speak no more.'

The Jews put on sackcloth and lay in their tens of thousands prostrate on the ground about the Palace, even in that terrible heat. Agrippa saw them from the window of the upper room where his bed was laid and began to weep for them. 'Poor Jews,' he said. 'You have waited a thousand years, and must now wait a thousand more, perhaps two thousand, before your day of glory breaks. This has been a false dawn. I deceived myself and I deceived you.' He called for pen and paper and wrote me a letter while he still had strength to hold the pen. I have the letter here before me with the others he wrote me and it is pitiful to compare the handwritings – the others boldly and decisively written, line under line as regular as a flight of steps, and this scrawled crookedly, each letter jagged and broken with pain, like confessions written by criminals after they have been put on the rack or flogged with the cat-o'-nine-tails. It is short:

My last letter: I am dying. My body is full of maggots. Forgive your old friend, the Brigand, who loved you dearly, yet secretly plotted to take the East away from you. Why did I do this? Because Japhet and Shem can live as brothers, but each must rule his own house. The West would have remained yours from Rhodes to Britain. You would have been able to rid Rome of all the Gods and customs of the East: then and only then could the ancient liberty that you prize so much have returned to you. I have failed. I played too dangerous a game. Marmoset, you are a fool, but I envy you your folly: it is a sane folly. Now I charge you with my dying breath not to revenge yourself on my family. My son Agrippa is innocent: he knows nothing of my ambitions, and neither do my daughters. Cypros did all that she could to dissuade me. The best course for you now is to appear to know nothing. Treat all your Eastern allies as faithful allies still. With Herod gone what are they? Adders, but their fangs are drawn. They trusted me, but they have no trust in the Parthian. As for my dominions, make them a Roman province again, as in the time of Tiberius. Do not injure my honour by returning them to my uncle Antipas. To appoint my son Agrippa as my successor would be dangerous, but honour him in some way or other for my sake. Do not put my dominions under the rule of Syria, under my enemy Marsus. Rule them yourself, Marmoset. Make Felix your governor. Felix is a nobody and will do nothing either wise or foolish. I can write little more. My fingers fail me. I am in torment. Do not weep for me: I have had a glorious life and regret nothing but my one single folly – that I underrated the pride and power and jealousy of the ever-living God of Israel, that I bore myself towards Him like any foolish philosophizing Gadarene Greek. Now farewell for the last time, Tiberius Claudius, my friend whom I love more truly than you ever supposed. Farewell, little Marmoset, my schoolfellow, and trust nobody, for nobody about you is worthy of your trust.

Your dying friend Herod Agrippa, surnamed

THE BRIGAND

Before he died Herod called Helcias and Thaumastus and his brother Herod Pollio to him again and said to them: 'One last charge I lay upon you. Go to Silas in prison and tell him that I am dying. Say that *Herod's Evil* is on me. Remind him of the oath that I rashly swore at Alexandria in the house of Alexander the Alabarch. Tell him of the agony in which you see me writhing. Ask him to forgive me, if I have wronged him. Tell him that he may visit me and clasp my hand in friendship once more. Then deal with him as you think best, according to his answer.'

They went to the prison, where they found Silas in his cell with his writing-tablet on his knee. At sight of them he flung it face downwards on the floor. Thaumastus said: 'Silas, if that tablet is filled with reproaches against your King and master, Herod Agrippa, you do well to throw it down. When we tell you of the condition in which the King is lying you will surely weep. You will wish that you had never spoken a word of reproach against him, or put him to public shame by your unmannerly tongue. He is dying in agony. His disease is *Herod's Evil*, with which in a rash moment he once cursed himself at Alexandria, should he ever offend the Majesty of the Most High.'

'I know,' said Silas. 'I was present when he swore that, and afterwards I warned him ...'

'Silence for the King's message. The King says: "Tell Silas of the agony in which you see me writhing, and ask him to forgive me if ever I have wronged him. He is at liberty now to leave his cell and come with you to the Palace. I should be pleased to clasp his hand in friendship once more before I die."'

Silas said sullenly: 'You are Jews and I am only a despised Samaritan, so I suppose that I ought to feel honoured by your visit. But I'll tell you this about us Samaritans: we prize free speech and honest dealing above all the opinions, good or bad, that our Jewish neighbours may care to entertain about us. As for my former friend and master King Herod, if he is in torment, then he has only himself to blame for not listening to my advice – –'

Helcias turned to King Herod Pollio: 'He dies?'

Silas continued calmly: 'Three times I as good as saved his life, but this time I can do nothing for him. His fate is in God's hands. And as for friendship, what sort of a friend do you call ...?'

Helcias seized a javelin from the hand of the soldier who was standing guard at the door and ran Silas through the belly. He made no movement to avoid the thrust.

Silas died at the very moment that, worn out by five days of incessant pain, King Herod Agrippa himself died, in Cypros's arms, to the indescribable grief and horror of the Jewish nation.

By now the whole story was known. Herod's curse seemed to rest on all Jews alike: they were utterly unmanned. The Greeks were elated beyond measure. The regiments re-armed by Helcias at Herod's orders behaved in the most shameless and revolting way. They attacked the Palace and seized Cypros and her daughters, intending to lead them in mockery through the streets of Caesarea. Cypros snatched a sword from a soldier and killed herself, but her daughters were forced to put on their embroidered dresses and accompany their captors, and even to join in the hymns of thanksgiving sung for their father's death. When the procession ended they were taken to the regimental brothels and subjected there, on the roof-tops, to the grossest outrages and indecencies. And not only in Caesarea but in the Greek city of Samaria too, public banquets were spread in the squares and the Greeks, with garlands on their heads, and sweet-smelling ointments, ate and drank to their hearts' content, toasting each other and pouring libations to the Ferryman. The Jews did not raise a hand or voice in protest. 'Whom God has cursed, is it lawful to succour?' For God's curse was held to descend to a man's children. These princesses were aged only six and ten years when they were so mistreated.

Chapter 24

HEROD's death took place ten years ago to-day and I shall tell as briefly as possible what has happened in the East since then; though the East will now have little interest for my readers, I feel conscientiously bound to leave no loose threads in this story. Marsus, as soon as he heard of Herod's death, came down to Caesarea and restored order there and in Samaria. He appointed an emergency governor of Herod's dominions: this was Fadus, a Roman knight who had big mercantile interests in Palestine and was married to a Jewish woman. I confirmed this appointment and Fadus acted with the necessary firmness. The arms that had been distributed to the Jews had not all been returned to Helcias: the men of Gilead kept theirs for use against eastern neighbours, the Arabs of Rabboth Ammon. There were also a great many arms not returned by Judaeans and Galileans, and robber bands were formed which did the country a great deal of damage. However, Fadus, with the help of Helcias and King Herod Pollio, who were anxious to show their loyalty, arrested the leading Gileadites, disarmed their followers, and then hunted down the robber bands one by one.

The confederate Kings of Pontus, Commagene, Lesser Armenia, and Iturea took the advice Herod had sent them by his brother and resumed their allegiance to Rome, excusing themselves to Bardanes for not marching to meet him on the borders of Armenia. Bardanes nevertheless continued his westward progress: he was determined to recover Armenia. Marsus sent him a stern warning from Antioch that war against Armenia would spell war with Rome. The King of Adiabene thereupon told Bardanes that he would not join in the expedition, because his children were at Jerusalem and would be seized as hostages by the Romans. Bardanes declared war on him and was about to invade his territory when he heard that Gotarzes had raised another army and had resumed his pretensions to the Empire. Back he marched again, and this time the battle between the brothers was fought out stubbornly on the banks of the River Charinda, near the southern shore of the Caspian Sea. Gotarzes was beaten and fled away to the land of the Dahians, which lies 400 miles away to the east. Bardanes pursued him; but, after defeating the Dahians, he could persuade his victorious army to march no farther, for he had passed the bounds of the Parthian Empire. He returned in the following year and was on the point of invading Adiabene when he was assassinated by his nobles; they decoyed him into an ambush when he was out hunting. I was relieved when he was out of the way, for he was a man of great gifts and unusual energy.

Meanwhile Marsus's term of office had come to an end and I was glad to have him back at Rome to advise me. I sent out Cassius Longinus to take his place. He was a celebrated jurist, whom I had often consulted on difficult legal points, and a former brother-in-law of my niece Drusilla. When the news of Bardanes's death reached Rome Marsus was not surprised: it seems that he had had a finger in the plot. He now advised me to send out, as a claimant to the Parthian throne, Meherdates, the son of a former King of Parthia, who had been kept as a hostage at Rome for many years now. He said that he could undertake that the nobles who had killed Bardanes would favour Meherdates. However, Gotarzes reappeared with a Dahian army and the assassins of Bardanes were forced to pay him homage, so Meherdates had to remain at Rome until a favourable opportunity presented itself for us to send him east. Marsus thought that this would be soon: Gotarzes was cruel, capricious, and cowardly, and could not keep the loyalty of his nobles for long. Marsus was right. A secret embassy came two years later from various notables of the Parthian Empire, including the King of Adiabene, asking me to send them Meherdates. I agreed to do so, giving Meherdates a good character. In the presence of the ambassadors I admonished him not to play the tyrant but to regard himself merely in the light of a chief magistrate and his people as his fellow-citizens: justice and clemency had never yet been practised by a Parthian king. I sent him to Antioch, and Cassius Longinus escorted him as far as the River Euphrates and there told him to push on to Parthia at once because the throne was his if he acted with speed and courage. However, the King of Osroëne, a pretended ally who secretly favoured Gotarzes, purposely detained Meherdates at his court with luxurious entertainments and hunting and then advised him to go round by way of Armenia instead of risking a march direct through Mesopotamia. Meherdates took this bad advice, which gave Gotarzes time to make preparations, and lost several months in taking his army through the snow-covered Armenian highlands. On emerging from Armenia he marched down the Tigris and

captured Nineveh and other important towns. The King of Adiabene welcomed him on his arrival at the frontier, but immediately
summed him up as a weakling and decided to abandon his cause
at the first opportunity. So when the armies of Gotarzes and
Meherdates met in battle, Meherdates was suddenly deserted by
the Kings of Osroëne and Adiabene. He fought bravely and nearly
won, for Gotarzes was such a cowardly commander that his generals had to chain him to a tree to stop him from running away.
In the end, Meherdates was captured and the gallant Gotarzes
sent him back to Cassius in mockery with his ears sliced off.
Shortly afterwards Gotarzes died. More recent events in Parthia
will certainly not interest my readers more than they have interested me, which is very little indeed.

Mithridates kept his Armenian throne for some years but was
finally killed by his nephew, the son of his brother the King of
Georgia. That was a curious story. The King of Georgia had been
ruling for forty years and his eldest son was tired of waiting for
him to die and leave him the kingdom. Knowing his son's character and fearing for his own life, the King advised him to seize
the throne of Armenia which was a bigger and richer kingdom
than Georgia. The son agreed. The King then made a pretence of
quarrelling with him, and he fled to Armenia, to Mithridates's
protection, and was kindly received by him and given his daughter
in marriage. He immediately busied himself with intrigues against
his benefactor. He returned to Georgia, pretending to be reconciled to his father, who then picked a quarrel with Mithridates
and gave command of an invading army to his son. The Roman
colonel who acted as Mithridates's political adviser proposed a
conference between Mithridates and his son-in-law, and Mithridates agreed to attend it: but he was treacherously seized by
Georgian troops as a blood-covenant was on the point of being
sealed, and smothered with blankets. The Governor of Syria,
when he heard of this horrid act, called a council of his staff to decide whether Mithridates should be avenged by a punitive expedition against his murderer, who now reigned in his stead; but the
general opinion seemed to be that the more treacherous and
bloody the behaviour of Eastern kings on our frontier, the better
for us – the security of the Roman Empire resting on the mutual
mistrust of our neighbours – and that nothing should be done.
However, the Governor, to show that he did not countenance the
murder, sent a formal letter to the King of Georgia ordering him

to withdraw his forces and recall his son. When the Parthians heard of this letter they thought it a good opportunity for winning back Armenia. And so they invaded Armenia, and the new king fled, and then they had to abandon the expedition because it was a very severe winter and they lost a lot of men from frost-bite and sickness, so the king returned – but why continue the story? All Eastern stories are the same purposeless on-and-on to-and-fro story, unless very seldom, so seldom as almost to be never, a leader arises to give purpose and direction to the flux. Herod Agrippa was such a one, but he died before he could give full proof of his genius.

As for the Jewish hope of the Messiah, it was kindled again by one Theudas, a magician of Gilead, who gathered a great following during Fadus's governorship and told them to follow him to the River Jordan, for he would part it as the prophet Elisha had once done and lead them dry-shod across to take possession of Jerusalem. Fadus sent a troop of cavalry across, charged the fanatical crowd, captured Theudas and cut off his head. (There have been no subsequent pretenders to the title, though indeed the sect about which Herod wrote to me, the followers of Joshua ben Joseph, or Jesus, seems to have made considerable headway recently, even at Rome. Aulus Plautius's wife was accused before me of having attended one of their love-feasts; but Aulus was in Britain and I hushed the affair up for his sake.) Fadus's task was made difficult by a failure of the Palestinian harvest: Herod's treasury was found to be nearly empty (and no wonder, the way he spent his money), so there was no means of relieving the distress by buying corn from Egypt. However, he organized a relief committee among the Jews and money was found to get them through the winter; but then the harvest failed again, and if it had not been for the Queen-Mother of Adiabene, who gave her entire wealth to the purchase of corn from Egypt, hundreds of thousands of Jews must have died. The Jews viewed the famine as God's vengeance on the whole nation for Herod's sin. The second failure of the harvest was indeed not so much the fault of the weather as the fault of the Jewish farmers: they were so low-spirited that instead of sowing the seed-corn with which they had been supplied by Fadus's successor (the son of Alexander the Alabarch, who had abandoned Judaism) they ate it or even left it to sprout in the sack. The Jews are an extraordinary race. Under the governorship of one Cumanus, who came next, there were great disturbances. Cumanus was not a good choice, I am afraid, and his term of office began with a great disaster. Following Roman precedent, he had stationed a battalion of regulars in the Temple cloisters to keep order at the great Jewish Passover feast, and one of the soldiers who had a grudge against the Jews let down his breeches during the holiest part of the festival and exposed his privy members derisively to the worshippers, calling out: 'Here, Jews, look this way! Here's something worth seeing.' That started a riot, and Cumanus was accused by the Jews of having ordered the soldier to make this provocative and very foolish display. He was naturally annoyed. He shouted to the crowd to be quiet and continue their festival in an orderly manner: but they grew more and more threatening. It seemed to Cumanus that a single battalion was not enough in the circumstances. To overawe the crowd he sent for the entire garrison: which in my opinion was a grave error of judgement. The streets of Jerusalem are very narrow and tortuous and were crowded with vast numbers of Jews who had come as usual from all over the world to celebrate the festival. The cry went up: 'The soldiers are coming. Run for your lives!' Everyone ran for his life. If anyone stumbled and fell he was trampled underfoot, and at street corners where two streams of fugitives met the pressure was so great from behind that thousands were crushed to death. The soldiers did not even draw their swords, but no less then 20,000 Jews were killed in the panic. The disaster was so overwhelming that the final day of the festival was not celebrated. Then as the crowd dispersed to its homes a party of Galileans happened to overtake one of my own Egyptian stewards, who was travelling from Alexandria to Acre to collect some money due to me. He was doing some business of his own on the side and the Galileans robbed him of a very valuable casket of jewels. When Cumanus heard of this he took reprisals on the villages nearest the scene of the robbery (on the borders of Samaria and Judaea), disregarding the fact that the robbers were plainly Galileans, by their accents, and only passing through. He sent a party of soldiers to plunder the villages and arrest the leading citizens. They did so and one of the soldiers in plundering the houses came across a copy of the Laws of Moses. He waved it over his head and then began reading out an obscene parody of the sacred writings. The Jews screamed in horror at the blasphemy and rushed to take the parchment from him. But he ran away laughing, tearing the thing in pieces as he went and scattering them behind him. Feeling ran so high that when Cumanus heard the facts he was forced to execute the soldier as a warning to his comrades and as a sign of goodwill to the Jews.

A month or two later Galileans came up to Jerusalem to another festival and the inhabitants of a Samaritan village refused to let them pass, because of the previous trouble. The Galileans insisted on passing and in the ensuing fight several were killed. The survivors went to Cumanus for satisfaction, but he gave them none, telling them that the Samaritans had a perfect right to forbid their passage through the village: why couldn't they have gone round by the fields? The foolish Galileans called a famous bandit to their aid and revenged themselves on the Samaritans by plundering their villages with his aid. Cumanus armed the Samaritans and with four battalions of the Samaria garrison made a drive against the Galilean raiders and killed and captured a great number of them. Later, a delegation of Samaritans went to the Governor of Syria and asked satisfaction from him against another party of Galileans whom they accused of setting fire to their villages. He came down to Samaria determined to end this business once and for all. He had the captured Galileans crucified and then went carefully into the origin of the disturbances. He found that the Galileans had a right of way through Samaria and that Cumanus should have punished the Samaritans for the disturbances instead of supporting them, and that his action in taking reprisals on Judaean and Samaritan villages for a robbery committed by Galileans was unjustified; and further, that the original breach of the peace, the indecent self-exposure of the soldier during the Passover Festival, had been countenanced by the colonel of the battalion, who had laughed loudly and said that if the Jews did not like the sight they were not compelled to look at it. By a careful sifting of evidence he also decided that the villages had been burned by the Samaritans themselves and that the compensation which they asked was many times more than the value of the property destroyed. Before the fire had been started all objects of value had been carefully removed from the houses. So he sent Cumanus, the colonel, the Samaritan plaintiffs, and a number of Jewish witnesses to me at Rome, where I tried them. The evidence was conflicting, but I eventually came to the same conclusion as the Governor. I exiled Cumanus to the Black Sea; ordered the Samaritan plaintiffs to be executed as liars and incendiaries; and had the colonel who laughed taken back to Jerusalem to be led through the streets of the city for public execration and then executed on the scene of his crime – for I regard it as a crime when an officer whose duty it is to keep order at a religious festival deliberately inflames popular feeling and causes the death of 20,000 innocent people.

After Cumanus's removal I remembered Herod's advice and sent Felix out as governor: that was three years ago and he is still there, having a difficult time, because the country is in a most disturbed state and overrun with bandits. He has married the youngest of Herod's daughters; she was previously married to the King of Homs, but left him. The other daughter married the son of Helcias. Herod Pollio is dead, and young Agrippa who governed Chalcis for four years after his uncle's death I have now made King of Bashan.

At Alexandria there were fresh disturbances three years ago and a number of deaths. I inquired into the case at Rome and found that the Greeks had provoked the Jews once more by interrupting their religious ceremonies. I punished them accordingly.

So much, then, for the East, and perhaps it would now be as well to wind up my account of events in other parts of the Empire, so as to be able to concentrate on my main story, which centres now in Rome.

At about the same time as the Parthians sent to Rome for a king, so did the great German confederation over which Hermann had ruled, the Cheruscans. Hermann had been assassinated by members of his own family for trying to reign over a free people in a despotic manner, and a feud had then started between the two principal assassins, his nephews, which led to a prolonged civil war and finally to the extinction of the whole Cheruscan royal house, with one single exception. This was Italicus, the son of Flavius, Hermann's brother. Flavius remained loyal to Rome at the time that Hermann treacherously ambushed and massacred Varus's three regiments, but had been killed by Hermann in battle some years after while serving under my brother Germanicus. Italicus was born at Rome and was enrolled in the Noble Order of Knights, as his father had been. He was a handsome and gifted young man and had been given a good Roman education, but foreseeing that he might one day occupy the Cheruscan throne I had insisted on his learning the use of German weapons as well as Roman ones, and on his studying his native language and laws with close attention: members of my bodyguard were his tutors. They also taught him to drink beer: a German prince who cannot drink pot for pot with his thegns is considered a weakling.

A Cheruscan delegation then came to Rome to ask for Italicus as their new king. They created a great stir in the Theatre on the first afternoon of their arrival. None of them had even been in Rome before. They called on me at the Palace and were told that I was at the Theatre, so they followed me there. A comedy of Plautus's, *The Truculent Man*, was being played, and everyone was listening with the greatest attention. They were shown into the public seats, and not very good ones either, high up, almost out of earshot of the stage. As soon as they had settled down they looked about them and began asking in loud tones: 'Are these honourable seats?'

The ushers whisperingly tried to assure them that they were.

'Where's Caesar sitting? Where are his chief thegns?' they asked.

The ushers pointed down to the orchestra. 'There's Caesar. But he only sits down there because he's slightly deaf. The seats you are in are really the most honourable seats. The higher, the more honourable, you know.'

'Who are those dark-skinned men with jewelled caps, sitting quite close to Caesar?'

'Those are Parthian ambassadors.'

'What's Parthia?'

'A great Empire in the East.'

'Why are they sitting down there? Aren't they honourable? Is it because of their colour?'

'Oh no, they are very honourable,' the ushers said. 'But please don't talk so loud.'

'Then why are they sitting in such humble seats?' the Germans persisted.

('Hush, hush!' 'Quiet there, Barbarians, we can't hear!' and similar protests from the crowd.)

'Out of compliment to Caesar,' the ushers lied. 'They swear that if Caesar's deafness forces him to occupy such a lowly seat, they won't presume to sit any higher.'

'And do you expect us to be outdone in courtesy by a miserable parcel of blackamoors?' the Germans shouted indignantly. 'Come on, brothers, down we go!' The play was held up for five minutes as they forced their way down through the packed seats and fetched up triumphantly among the Vestal Virgins. Well, they meant no harm, and I greeted them honourably as they deserved, and at dinner that night consented to let them have the king they wanted; I was, of course, very glad to be able to do so.

I sent Italicus across the Rhine with an admonition that contrasted strangely with the one I had given Meherdates before I sent him across the Euphrates; for the Parthians and the Cheruscans are the two most dissimilar races, I suppose, that you could find anywhere in the world. My words to Italicus were these: 'Italicus, remember that you have been called upon to rule over a free nation. You have been educated as a Roman and accustomed to Roman discipline. Be careful not to expect as much from your fellow tribesmen as a Roman magistrate or general would expect from his subordinates. Germans can be persuaded but not forced. If a Roman commander says to a military subordinate: "Colonel, take so many men to such-and-such a place and there raise an earthwork so-and-so many paces long, thick, and high," he replies, "Very good, General": off he goes without argument and the earthwork is raised within twenty-four hours. You can't speak to a Cheruscan in that style. He'll want to know precisely why you want the earthwork raised and against whom, and wouldn't it be better to send someone else of less importance to perform this dishonourable task – earthworks are a sign of cowardice, he'll argue – and what gifts will you bestow on him if he consents, of his own free will, to carry out your suggestion? The art of ruling your compatriots, my friend Italicus, is never to give them a downright order, but to express your wishes clearly, disguising them as mere advice of State policy. Let your thegns think that they are doing you a favour, and thus honouring themselves, by carrying out these wishes of their own free will. If there is an unpleasant or thankless task to be done, make it a matter of rivalry between your thegns who shall have the honour of undertaking it, and never fail to reward with gold bracelets and weapons services which at Rome would be regarded as routine duties. Above all, be patient and never lose your temper.'

So he went off in high hopes, as Meherdates had gone off, and was welcomed by a majority of the thegns, the ones who knew that they had no chance of succeeding to the vacant throne themselves, but were jealous of all native-born claimants. Italicus did not know the ins-and-outs of Cheruscan domestic politics and could be counted on to behave with reasonable impartiality. But there was a minority of men who thought themselves worthy of the throne themselves and these temporarily sank their differences to unite against Italicus. They expected that Italicus would soon make a mess of the government from ignorance, but he disappointed them by ruling remarkably well. They therefore went secretly round to the chiefs of allied tribes raising feeling against him as a Roman interloper. 'The ancient liberty of Germany has departed,' they lamented, 'and the power of Rome is triumphant. Is there no native Cheruscan worthy of the throne, that the son of Flavius, the spy and traitor, should be permitted to usurp it?' They raised a large patriotic army by this appeal. Italicus's supporters, however, declared that Italicus had not usurped the throne, but had been offered it with the consent of a majority of the tribe; and that he was the only royal prince left and though born in Italy had studiously acquainted himself with the German language, customs, and weapons, and was ruling very justly; and that his father Flavius, far from being a traitor, had on the contrary sworn an oath of friendship with the Romans approved by the whole nation, including his brother Hermann, and unlike Hermann had not violated it. As for the ancient liberty of the Germans, that was hypocritical talk: the men who used it would think nothing of destroying the nation by renewed civil wars.

In a great battle fought between Italicus and his rivals, Italicus came off victorious, and his victory was so complete that he soon forgot my advice and grew impatient of humouring German independence and vanity: he began ordering his thegns about. They drove him out at once. Afterwards he was restored by the armed assistance of a neighbouring tribe, and then ousted again. I made no attempt to intervene: in the West as in the East the security of the Roman Empire rests largely on the civil dissensions of our neighbours. At the time of writing Italicus is king once more but much hated although he has just fought a successful war against the Chattians.

There was trouble farther north about this time. The Governor of the Lower Rhine province died suddenly and the enemy began their cross-river raids again. They had a capable leader of the same type as the Numidian Tacfarinas who had given us so much trouble under Tiberius: like Tacfarinas he was a deserter from one of our auxiliary regiments and had picked up a considerable knowledge of tactics. Gannascus was his name, a Frisian, and he carried on his operations on an extensive scale. He captured a number of light river transports from us and turned pirate on the coasts of Flanders and Brabant. The new Governor I appointed was called Corbulo, a man for whom I had no great personal liking but whose talents I gratefully employed. Tiberius had once made Corbulo his Commissioner of Highways and he had soon sent in a severe report on the fraud of contractors and the negligence of provincial magistrates whose task it was to see that the roads were kept in good repair. Tiberius, acting on the report, had fined the accused men heavily; and out of all proportion to their culpability because the roads had been allowed to get into a bad condition by previous magistrates and these particular contractors had only been employed to patch up the worst places. When Caligula succeeded Tiberius and began to feel the need of money, amongst his other tricks and shifts he brought out the Corbulo report and fined all previous provincial magistrates and contractors on the same scale as the ones who had been fined by Tiberius; he gave Corbulo the task of collecting the money. When I succeeded Caligula I paid back these fines, only retaining as much as was needed to repair the roads – about one-fifth of the total amount. Caligula had not, of course, used any of the money for road-repairs, and neither had Tiberius, and the roads were in a worse condition than ever. I really did repair them and introduced special traffic-regulations limiting the use of heavy private coaches on country roads. These coaches did far more damage than country wagons bringing in merchandise to Rome, and I did not think it right that the provinces should pay for the luxury and pleasure of wealthy idlers. If rich Roman knights wished to visit their country estates, let them use sedan-chairs, or ride on horseback.

But I was speaking of Corbulo. I knew him for a man of great severity and precision, and the garrison of the Lower Province needed a martinet to restore discipline there: the Governor who had died was much too easy-going. Corbulo's arrival at his headquarters at Cologne recalled Galba's at Mainz. (Galba was now my Governor of Africa.) He ordered a soldier to be flogged whom he found improperly dressed on sentry-duty at the camp gate. The man was unshaved, his hair had not been cut for at least a month, and his military cloak was a fancy yellow colour instead of the regulation brownish-red. Not long after this Corbulo executed two soldiers for 'abandoning their arms in the face of the enemy': they were digging a trench and had left their swords behind in their tents. This scared the troops into efficiency, and when Corbulo took the field against Gannascus and showed that he was a capable general as well as a strict disciplinarian they did all that he could have expected of them. Soldiers, or at least old soldiers, always prefer a reliable general, however severe, to an incompetent one, however humane.

Corbulo fitted out war-vessels, chased and sank Gannascus's pirate fleet, and then marched up the coast and compelled the Frisians to give hostages and swear allegiance to Rome. He wrote out a constitution for them on the Roman model and built and garrisoned a fortress in their territory. This was all very well, but instead of stopping here Corbulo pushed on into the land of the Greater Chaucians, who had taken no part in the raids. He heard that Gannascus had taken refuge in a Chaucian shrine and sent a troop of cavalry to hunt him down and kill him there. This was an insult to the Chaucian Gods, and after Gannascus's assassination the same troop rode on to the Ems and there at Emsbuhren presented the Chaucian tribal council with Corbulo's demands for their instant submission with payment of a heavy yearly tribute.

Corbulo reported his actions to me and I was furiously angry with him; he had done well enough in getting rid of Gannascus, but to pick a quarrel with the Chaucians was another matter. We had not sufficient troops to spare for a war: if the Greater Chaucians called in the Lesser Chaucians to their assistance and the Frisians revolted again I would have to find strong reinforcements from somewhere, and they were not to be had, because of our commitments in Britain. I wrote ordering him to recross the Rhine at once.

Corbulo received my orders before the Chaucians had had time to reply to his ultimatum. He was angry with me, thinking that I was jealous of any general who dared to rival my military feats. He reminded his staff that Geta had not been awarded proper honours for his fine conquest of Morocco and the capture of Salabus; and said that, though I had now made it legal for generals who were not members of the Imperial Family to celebrate a triumph, in practice, it seemed, no one but myself would be allowed to conduct a campaign for which a triumph could legally be awarded. My anti-despotic pretensions were mere affectation: I was just as much of a tyrant as Caligula, but I concealed it better. He said too that I was lowering Roman prestige by going back on the threats that he had made in my name; and that our allies would laugh at him, and so would his own troops. But this was only an angry talk to his staff. All that he told the troops when he sounded the signal for a general retirement was: 'Men, Caesar Augustus orders us back across the Rhine. We do not yet know why he has reached this decision, and we cannot question it, though I confess that I, for one, am greatly disappointed. How fortunate were the Roman generals who led our armies in the days of old!' However, he was awarded triumphal ornaments and I also wrote him a private letter exculpating myself from the angry charges which, I told him, I had heard that he had made against me. I wrote that if he had been angry, why, so had I, on hearing of his provocation of the Chaucians; and that though he should have thought better of me than to accuse me of jealous motives, I blamed myself for sending him so curt a dispatch instead of explaining at length my reasons for ordering him to withdraw. I then explained these reasons. He wrote back in handsome apology, withdrawing the charges of despotism and jealousy, and I think now that we understood each other. To keep his troops occupied and allow them no leisure for laughing at him, he put them to work on a canal twenty-three miles long between the Meuse and the Rhine, to carry off occasional inundations of the sea in this flat region.

Since that time there have been no other events of importance to record in Germany except, four years ago, another raid by the Chattians. They crossed the Rhine in great force one night a few miles north of Mainz. The Commander of the Upper Province was Secundus, the Consul who had behaved with such indecision when I became Emperor. He was also supposed to be the best living Roman poet. Personally, I think very little of the moderns, or indeed of the Augustans: their poetry does not ring true to me. To my mind Catullus was the last of the true poets. It may be that poetry and liberty go together: that under a monarchy true poetry dies and the best that one can hope for then is gorgeous rhetoric and remarkable metrical artifice. For my part I would exchange all twelve books of Virgil's *Aeneid* for a single book of Ennius's *Annals*. Ennius, who lived in Rome's grandest Republican days and counted the great Scipio as his personal friend, was what I would call a true poet: Virgil was merely a remarkable verse-craftsman. Compare the two of them when they are both writing about a battle: Ennius writes like the soldier he was (he rose from the ranks to a captaincy), Virgil like a cultured spectator from a distant hill. Virgil borrowed much from Ennius. Some say he overshadowed Ennius's rude genius by his cultured felicity of phrase and rhythm. But that is nonsense. It is like Aesop's fable of the wren and the eagle. The birds all competed as to which could fly the highest. The eagle won, but when he tired and could go no higher, the wren, who had been nestling on his back, mounted up a few score feet and claimed the prize. Virgil was a mere wren by comparison with Ennius the eagle. And even if you concentrate on single beauties, where in Virgil will you find a passage to equal in simple grandeur such lines of Ennius's as these? –

> Fraxinu' frangitur atque abies consternitur alta.
> Pinus prōcēras pervortunt: omne sonabat
> Arbustum fremitu silvaï frondosaï.

> The ash was hewn, the high white fir laid low,
> Down toppled they the princely pines, and all
> That grove of countless leaves rang with the timber's fall.

But they are untranslatable, and in any case I am not writing a treatise on poetry. And though Secundus's poetry was, in my opinion, as disingenuous and unpraiseworthy as his behaviour in the Senate House that day, he was at least capable of dealing decisively with the Chattians on their return in two divisions from the plunder of our French allies. Victory disorganizes the Germans, especially if their plunder includes wine, which they swill as if it were beer, disregarding its greater potency. Secundus's forces surrounded and defeated both enemy divisions, killing 10,000 men and capturing as many prisoners. He was given triumphal ornaments, but the regulations controlling the award of triumphs did not permit me to grant him one.

I had recently granted a similar honour to Secundus's predecessor, one Curtius Rufus, who, though only the son of a swordfighter, had risen under Tiberius to the dignity of first-rank magistrate. (Tiberius had won him this appointment, in spite of the competition of several men of birth and distinction, by remarking: 'Yes, but Curtius Rufus is his own illustrious ancestor'.) Rufus had become ambitious for triumphal ornaments but was aware that I would not approve of his picking a quarrel with the enemy. He knew of a vein of silver that had been discovered a few miles across the river, in the reign of Augustus, just before Varus's defeat, and sent a regiment across to work it. He got a good deal of silver out before the vein ran too far underground to be manageable – sufficient silver indeed to pay the whole Rhine army for two years. This was naturally worth triumphal ornaments. The troops found the mining very arduous and wrote me an amusing letter, in the name of the entire army:

The loyal troops of Claudius Caesar send him their best wishes and sincerely hope that he and his family will continue to enjoy long life and perfect health. They also beg that, in future, he will award his generals triumphal ornaments *before* he sends them out to command armies, because then they will not feel obliged to earn them by making Caesar's loyal troops sweat and drudge at silver-mining, canal-digging, and such-like tasks which would be more suitably done by German prisoners. If Caesar would only permit his loyal troops to cross the Rhine and capture a few thousand Chattians, they would be very pleased to do so, to the best of their ability.

Chapter 25

THE year after Herod died I celebrated the first annual festival in honour of my British triumph; and, remembering the complaints that I had overheard that night on the steps of the Temple of Castor and Pollux, I made a distribution of money to A.D. 45 the needy populace – three gold pieces a head with half a gold piece extra for every child in the family who had not yet come of age. In one case I had to pay as much as twelve and a half gold pieces, but that was because there were several sets of twins to subsidize. Young Silanus and young Pompey assisted me in the distribution. When I record that I had now removed all Caligula's extraordinary taxes and paid back the men he had robbed, and that work continued on the Ostia harbour scheme and the aqueducts and the Fucine Lake drainage scheme, and that, without defrauding anyone, I was able to pay out this bounty and still keep a substantial balance in the Public Treasury, you will admit, I think, that I had done extremely well in these four years.

The astronomer Barbillus (to whom I referred in my letter to the Alexandrians) made some abstruse mathematical calculations and informed me that there was to be an eclipse of the sun on my birthday. This caused me some alarm, because an eclipse is one of the most unlucky omens that can happen at any time, and happening on my birthday, which was also a national festival in honour of Mars, it would greatly disturb people and give anyone who wished to assassinate me every confidence of success. But I thought that if I warned the people beforehand that the eclipse was to take place they would feel very differently about it: not despondent but actually pleased that they knew what was coming and understood the mechanics of the phenomenon.

I published a proclamation:

Tiberius Claudius Drusus Nero Caesar Augustus Germanicus Britannicus, Emperor, Father of the Country, High Pontiff, Protector of the People for the fifth year in succession, three times Consul, to the Senate, People, and Allies of Rome, greetings.

My good friend Tiberius Claudius Barbillus of the city of Ephesus made certain astronomical calculations last year, since confirmed by a body of his fellow astronomers in the city of Alexandria, where that science flourishes, and found that an eclipse of the sun, total in some parts of Italy, partial in others, will take place on the first day of August next. Now, I do not wish you to feel any alarm on this account, though superstitious terrors have always in the past been awakened by this natural phenomenon. In the old days it was a sudden and inexplicable event and considered as a warning by the Gods themselves that happiness was to be blotted out on earth for a while, just as the sun's life-giving rays were blotted out. But now we so well understand eclipses that we can actually prophesy, 'On such and such a day an eclipse will take place.' And I think everyone should feel both proud and relieved that the old terrors are laid at last by the force of intelligent human reasoning.

The following, then, is the explanation that my learned friends give. The Moon, which revolves in its orbit below the Sun, either immediately below it or perhaps with the planets Mercury and Venus intervening – this is a disputed point and does not affect the present argument – has a longitudinal motion, like the Sun, and a vertical motion, as the Sun probably has too; but it has also a latitudinal motion which the Sun never has in any circumstances. So when, because of this latitudinal motion, the Moon gets in a direct line with the Sun over our heads and passes invisibly under its blazing disk – invisibly, because the Sun is so bright that by day, as you know, the Moon becomes a mere nothing – then the rays which normally dart from the Sun to the earth are obscured by the Moon's intervention. For some of the earth's inhabitants this obscuration lasts for a longer time than for others, according to their geographical position, and some are not affected by it at all. The fact is that the Sun never really loses its light, as the ignorant suppose, and consequently it appears in its full splendour to all people between itself and whom the Moon does not pass.

This is the simple explanation, then, of an eclipse of the Sun – as simple a matter as if anyone of you were to shade the flame of an oil-lamp or candle with your hand and plunge a whole room into temporary darkness. (An eclipse of the Moon, by the way, is caused by the Moon running into the cone-shaped shadow thrown by the Earth when the Sun is underneath it; it only happens when the Moon passes through the mean point in its latitudinal motion.) But in the districts most affected by the eclipse, which are indicated on the adjoining map, I desire all magistrates and other responsible authorities to take every precaution against popular panic, or robbery under cover of darkness, and to discourage people from staring at the sun during its eclipse, unless through pieces of horn or glass darkened with candle smoke, because for those with weak eyes there is a danger of blindness.

I think that I must have been the first ruler since the Creation of the World to issue a proclamation of this sort; and it had a very good effect, though of course the country people did not understand words like 'longitudinal' and 'latitudinal'. The eclipse occurred exactly as foretold and the festival took place as usual, though special sacrifices were offered to Diana as Goddess of the Moon, and Apollo as God of the Sun.

I enjoyed perfect health throughout the following year, and nobody tried to assassinate me, and the one revolution that was attempted ended in a most ignominious way for its prime mover. This was Asinius Gallus, grandson of Asinius Pollio and son of Tiberius's first wife, Vipsania, by Gallus whom she afterwards married and whom Tiberius hated so and finally killed by slow starvation. It is curious how appropriate some people's names are. *Gallus* means cock, and *Asinus* means donkey, and Asinius Gallus was the most utter little donkey-cock for his boastfulness and stupidity that one could find in a month's tour of Italy. Imagine, he had not got any troops ready or collected any funds for his revolution, but believed that the strength of his personality supported by the nobility of his birth would win him immediate adherents!

He appeared one day on the Oration Platform in the Market Place and began to hold forth to a crowd which soon assembled, on the evils of tyranny, dwelling on my uncle Tiberius's murder of his father, and saying how necessary it was to root out the Caesar family from Rome and give the monarchy to someone really worthy of it. From his mysterious hints the crowd gathered that he meant himself and began to laugh and cheer. He was a wretched orator and the ugliest man in the Senate, not more than four foot six in height, with bottle-shoulders, a great long face, reddish hair, and a tiny little bright red nose (he suffered from indigestion); yet he thought himself Hercules and Adonis rolled into one. There was not, I believe, a single person in the Market Place who took him seriously, and all sorts of jokes went flying about such as: '*Asinus in tegulis*' and '*Asinus ad lyram*' and '*Ex Gallo lac et ova.*' (A donkey on the roof-tiles is a proverbial expression for any sudden grotesque apparition, and a donkey playing on a lyre stands for any absurdly incompetent performance, and cock's milk and cock's eggs stand for nonsensical hopes.) However, they went on cheering every sentence to see what absurdity would come next: and sure enough, when his speech ended he tried to lead the whole mob up to the Palace to depose me. They followed him in a long column, eight abreast, up to about twenty paces from the outer Palace Gate and then suddenly halted and let him go on by himself, which he did. The sentries at the gate let him through without question, because he was a senator, and he went marching on into the Palace grounds for some distance, shouting threats against me, before he realized that he was alone. (Crowds can be very witty and very cruel sometimes, as well as very stupid and very cowardly.) He was soon arrested, and although the whole affair was so ridiculous I could hardly overlook it: I banished him, but no farther than Sicily, where he had family estates. 'Go away and crow on your own dung-hill or bray in your own thistle-field, whichever you prefer, but don't let me hear you,' I told the ugly, excitable little man.

The harbour at Ostia was not nearly completed yet and had already cost 6,000,000 gold pieces. The greatest technical difficulty now lay in forming the island between the extremities of the two great moles; and you may not credit it, but I solved it myself. You remember Caligula's great obelisk-ship which had taken the elephants and camels to Britain, and brought them safely back too? She was at Ostia again and had been used twice since for voyages to Egypt to fetch coloured marble for Venus's temple in Sicily. But the captain told me that she was becoming unseaworthy and he would not care to risk another voyage in her. So one night, as I lay awake, it occurred to me that it would be a good idea to fill her with stones and sink her as a foundation for the island. But I rejected that, because we would only be able to fill her about a quarter full of stones before the water rose over the gunwale, and when she rotted they would just fall out in a loose heap. So I thought, 'If we only had a Gorgon's head handy to turn her into a big solid rock!' And that foolish fancy, the sort that often flies into my mind when I am over-tired, gave birth to a really brilliant idea: why not fill her as full as possible with cement powder, which is comparatively light, and then batten down her hatches, sink her, and let the cement set under the water?

It was about two o'clock in the morning when this idea came to me and I clapped my hands for a freedman and sent him off at once to bring my chief engineer to me. About an hour later the engineer turned up from the other side of the City in a great hurry and trembling violently; expecting to be executed, perhaps, for some negligence of other. I asked him excitedly whether my idea was practicable, and was greatly disappointed to hear that cement would not set satisfactorily in sea-water. However, I gave him ten days to find some means of making it set. 'Ten days,' I repeated solemnly, 'or else ...'

He thought that 'or else' was a threat, but if he had failed I should have explained my little joke, which was simply 'or else we shall have to abandon the idea'. Fear improved his wits, and after eight days' frantic experimenting he invented a cement powder that set like a rock when it came into contact with sea-water. It was a mixture of ordinary cement powder from the cement works at Cumae with a peculiar sort of dust from the hills in the neighbourhood of Puteoli, and the shape of that obelisk-ship is now eternized in the hardest stone imaginable at the mouth of Ostia harbour. We have built an island over it, using large stones and more of the same cement; and there is a tall lighthouse on the island, with a beacon fire fed with turpentine shining every night from its summit. There are polished steel reflectors in the beacon chamber which double the light of the fire and send it out in a steady stream down the estuary. The harbour took ten years to complete and cost 12,000,000 in gold; and there are still men at work improving the channel. But it is a great gift to the City, and so long as we command the seas we can never starve.

Everything seemed to be going very well for me and Rome. The country was contented and prosperous and our armies were victorious everywhere – Aulus was consolidating my conquest of Britain by a series of brilliant victories over the yet unsubdued Belgic tribes of the south and south-west; religious observances were being regularly and punctually performed; there was no distress even in the poorest quarters of the City. I had managed to get even with my law-court business and find means of keeping down the number of cases. My health was good. Messalina was lovelier in my eyes than ever. My children were growing up strong and healthy, and little Britannicus was showing the extraordinary precocity which (though, I own, it missed me out) has always run in the Claudian family. The only thing that grieved me now was an invisible barrier between myself and the Senate that I could not break down. All that I could do in the way of paying respect to the Senatorial Order, especially to the Consuls in office and to the first-class magistrates, I did, but I was always met with a mixture of obsequiousness and suspicion that I found it difficult to account for and impossible to deal with. I decided to revive the ancient office of Censor which had been swallowed up in the Imperial Directorship of Morals, and in that popular capacity reform the Senate once more and get rid of all useless and obstruction-making members. I posted a notice in the House requesting every member to consider his own circumstances and decide whether he was still qualified to serve Rome well as a senator: if he decided he was not so qualified, either because he could not afford it, or because he felt himself not sufficiently gifted, he should resign. I hinted that those who failed to resign would be dishonourably expelled. And I hurried things along by sending round private notifications to those whom I proposed to expel if they didn't resign. I thus lightened the Order of about a hundred names, and those who remained I then rewarded by conferring patrician rank on their families. This enlargement of the patrician circle had the advantage of providing more candidates for the higher orders of priesthood and of giving a wider choice of brides and bridegrooms to members of the surviving patrician families; for the four successive patrician creations of Romulus, Lucius Brutus, Julius Caesar, and Augustus had each in turn become practically extinct. One would have thought that the richer and more powerful the family, the more rapidly and vigorously it would breed, but this has never been the case at Rome.

However, even this cleansing of the Senate did not have any appreciable effect. Debates were a mere farce. Once, during my fourth Consulship, when I was introducing a measure about certain judicial reforms, the House was so listless that I was obliged to speak very plainly:

'If you honestly approve of these proposals, my Lords, do me the kindness of saying so at once and quite simply. Or, if you do not approve of them, then suggest amendments, but do so here and now. Or if you need time to think the matter over, take time, but don't forget that you must have your opinions ready to be delivered on the day fixed for the debate. It is not at all proper to the dignity of the Senate that the Consul-Elect should repeat the exact phrases of the Consuls as his own opinion, and that everyone else when his turn comes to speak should merely say, "I agree to that" and nothing else, and that then, when the House has adjourned, the minutes should read "A debate took place ..." '

Among other marks of respect to the Senate, I restored Greece and Macedonia to the list of Senatorial provinces: my uncle Tiberius had made Imperial provinces of them. And I gave the Senate back the right of minting copper coinage for circulation in the provinces, as in the time of Augustus. There is nothing that commands such respect for sovereignty as coins: the gold and silver currency had my head on it, because after all I was the Emperor and the man actually responsible for the greater part of the government; but the Senate's familiar 'S.C.' appeared again on the copper, and copper is at once the most ancient, the most useful, and quantitatively the most important coinage.

The immediate cause of my decision to purge the Senate was the alarming case of Asiaticus. One day Messalina came to me and said: 'Do you remember wondering last year whether A.D 46 there wasn't something else at the bottom of Asiaticus's resignation of the Consulship besides the reason he gave – that people were jealous and suspicious of him, because it was his second time as Consul?'

'Yes, it didn't look like the whole reason.'

'Well, I'll tell you something which I should have told you about long ago. Asiaticus has been violently in love for some time with Cornelius Scipio's wife; what do you think of that?'

'Oh, yes, Poppaea – very good-looking girl, with a straight nose and a bold way of staring at men? And what does she think of it? Asiaticus isn't a good-looking young fellow like Scipio: he's bald and rather fat, but of course the richest man in Rome, and what marvellous gardens he has too!'

'Poppaea, I'm afraid, has thoroughly compromised herself with Asiaticus. Well, I'll tell you. It's best to be frank. Poppaea came to me some time ago – you know what good friends we are, or, rather, we used to be – and said, "Messalina, dearest, I want to ask you a great favour. You promise not to tell anyone that I've asked you?" Naturally I promised. She said: "I'm in love with Valerius Asiaticus and I don't know what to do about it. My husband is fearfully jealous and if he knew I think he'd kill me. And the nuisance is that I'm married to him in the strict form and you know how difficult it is to get a divorce from a strict form of marriage if the husband chooses to be nasty. It means you lose your children, for a start. Do you think that you could possibly do something to help me? Could you ask the Emperor to speak to my husband and arrange a divorce, so that Asiaticus and I can marry?" '

'I hope you didn't say that there was any chance of my consenting. Really, these women ...'

'Oh, no, dearest, on the contrary. I said that if she never mentioned the subject to me again I would try, for friendship's sake, to forget what I'd heard, but that if so much as a whisper came to me of anything improper still going on between her and Asiaticus I'd come straight to you.'

'Good. I'm glad you said that.'

'It was soon afterwards that Asiaticus resigned, and do you remember, then, that he asked the Senate's permission to visit his estates in France?'

'Yes, and he was away a long time. Trying to forget Poppaea, I suppose. There are a lot of pretty women in the South of France.'

'Don't you believe it. I have been finding out things about Asiaticus. The first thing is that lately he's been giving large money presents to the Guards captains and sergeants and standard-bearers. He does it, he says, because of his gratitude to them for their loyalty to you. Does that sound right?'

'Well, he has more money than he knows what to do with.'

'Don't be ridiculous. Nobody has more money than they know what to do with. Then the second thing is that he and Poppaea still meet regularly, whenever poor Scipio's out of town, and spend the night together.'

'Where do they meet?'

'At the house of the Petra brothers. They're cousins of hers. The third thing is that Sosibius told me the other day, quite on his own, that he thought it most unwise of you to have allowed Asiaticus to pay so long a visit to his estates in France. When I asked him what he meant, he showed me a letter from a friend of his in Vienne: the friend wrote that Asiaticus had actually spent very little time on his estates. He had gone round visiting the most influential people in the province and had even been for a tour along the Rhine, where he showed great generosity to the officers of the garrison. Then, of course, you must remember that Asiaticus was born at Vienne; and Sosibius says – –'

'Call Sosibius at once.' Sosibius was the man I had chosen as Britannicus's tutor, so you can imagine that I had the greatest confidence in his judgement. He was an Alexandrian Greek, but had long interested himself in the study of early Latin authors and was the leading authority on the texts of Ennius: he was so much at home in the Republican period, which he knew far better than any Roman historian, including myself, that I considered that he would be a constant inspiration to my little boy. Sosibius came, and when I questioned him answered very frankly. Yes, he believed Asiaticus to be ambitious and capable of planning a revolution. Hadn't he once offered himself as a candidate for the monarchy in opposition to me?

'You forget, Sosibius,' I said, 'that those two days have been wiped off the City records by an amnesty.'

'But Asiaticus was in the plot against your nephew, the late Emperor, and even boasted about it in the Market Place. When a man like that resigns his Consulship for no valid reason and goes off to France, where he already has great influence, and there tries to enlarge that influence by scattering money about, and no doubt saying that he was forced to resign his Consulship because of your jealousy, or because he stood up against you for the rights of his fellow Frenchmen. ...'

Messalina said: 'It's perfectly plain. He has promised Poppaea to marry her, and the only way that he can do that is by getting rid of you and me. He'll get leave to go to France again, and start his revolt there with the native regiments, and then bring the Rhine regiments into it too. And the Guards will be as ready to acclaim him Emperor as they were ready to acclaim you: it will mean another two hundred gold pieces a man for them.'

'Who else do you think is in the plot?'

'Let's find out all about the Petra brothers. That lawyer Suilius has just been asked to undertake a case for them: and he is one of my best secret agents. If there's anything against them besides their having accommodated Poppaea and Asiaticus with a bedroom, Suilius will find it out, you can rely on that.'

'I don't like spying. I don't like Suilius, either.'

'We have got to defend ourselves, and Suilius is the handiest weapon we have.'

So Suilius was sent for, and a week later he made his report, which confirmed Messalina's suspicions. The Petra brothers were certainly in the plot. The elder of them had privately circulated an account of a vision which had appeared to him one early morning between sleeping and waking and which the astrologers had interpreted in an alarming fashion. The vision was of my head severed at the neck and crowned with a wreath of white vine-leaves: the interpretation was that I should die violently at the close of the autumn. The younger brother had been acting as Asiaticus's go-between with the Guards, of which he was a colonel. Apparently associated with Asiaticus and the Petra brothers were two old friends of mine, Pedo Pompey, who used often to play dice with me in the evenings, and Assario, maternal uncle of my son-in-law, young Pompey, who also had free access to the Palace. Suilius suggested that these would naturally have been given the task of murdering me over a friendly game of dice. Then there were Assario's two nieces, the Tristonia sisters, who had an adulterous association with the Petra brothers.

There was nothing for it, I decided, but to strike first. I sent my Guards Commander, Crispinus, with a company of Guards whose loyalty seemed beyond question, down to Assario's house at Baiae; and there Asiaticus was arrested. He was handcuffed and fettered and brought before me at the Palace. I should, properly, have had him impeached before the Senate, but I could not be sure how far the plot extended. There might be a demonstration in his favour, and I did not wish to encourage that. I tried him in my own study, in the presence of Messalina, Vitellius, Crispinus, young Pompey, and my chief secretaries.

Suilius acted as public prosecutor, and I thought, as Asiaticus faced him, that if ever guilt was written on a man's features it was written there. But I must admit that Crispinus had not warned him what were the charges against him – I had not even told Crispinus – and there are few men who if suddenly arrested would be able to face their judges with absolute serenity of conscience. I know how badly I once felt myself when I was arrested by Caligula's orders on the charge of witnessing a forged will. Suilius was indeed a terrible and pitiless accuser: he had a thin, frosty face, white hair, dark eyes, and a long forefinger which probed and darted like a sword. He began with a mild rain of compliments and banter which we all recognized as a prelude to a thunderstorm of rage and invective. First he asked Asiaticus in a mock-friendly conversational tone, exactly when he proposed visiting his French estates again – was it before the vintage? and what had he thought of agricultural conditions in the neighbourhood of Vienne and how had they compared with those of the Rhine valley? 'But don't trouble to answer my questions,' he said. 'I don't really wish to know how high the barley grows in Vienne or how loud the cocks crow there, any more than you really wished to know yourself.' Then about his presents to the Guards: how loyal Asiaticus had shown himself! but was there not perhaps a danger of the simple-witted military misunderstanding those gifts?

Asiaticus was growing anxious, and breathing heavily. Suilius came a few steps nearer him, like a wild-beast hunter in the arena, some of whose arrows, fired from a distance, have gone home: he comes nearer, because the beast is wounded, and brandishes his hunting-spear. 'To think that I ever called you friend, that I ever dined at your board, that I ever allowed myself to be deceived by your affable ways, your noble descent, the favour and confidence that you have falsely won from our gracious Emperor and all honest citizens. Beast that you are, filthy pathic, satyr of the stews! Bland corrupter of the loyal hearts and manly bodies of the very soldiers to whose trust the sacred person of our Caesar, the safety of the City, the welfare of the world is committed. Where were you on the night of the Emperor's birthday that you could not attend the banquet to which you were invited? Sick, were you? Mighty sick, I have no doubt. I shall soon confront the court with a selection of your fellow invalids, young soldiers of the Guards, who caught their infection from you, you filth.'

There was a great deal more of this. Asiaticus had turned dead white now, and great drops of sweat stood on his brow. The chain clanked as he wiped them away. He was forbidden by the rules of the court to answer a word until the time came for him to make his defence, but at last he burst out in a hoarse voice: 'Ask your own sons, Suilius! They will admit that I am a man.' He was called to order. Suilius went on to speak of Asiaticus's adultery with Poppaea, but put little emphasis on this, as if it was the weakest point of his case, though really it was the strongest; and so tricked Asiaticus into making a general denial of all the charges against him. If Asiaticus had been wise he would have admitted the adultery and denied the other charges. But he denied everything, so his guilt seemed proved. Suilius called his witnesses, mostly soldiers. The chief witness, a young recruit from South Italy, was asked to identify Asiaticus. I suppose that he had been coached to recognize Asiaticus by his bald head, for he picked on Pallas as the man who had so unnaturally abused him. A great burst of laughter went up: Pallas was known to share with me a real hatred of this sort of vice, and, besides, everyone knew that he had acted as guest-master throughout my birthday banquet.

I nearly dismissed the case then and there, but reflected that the witness might have a bad memory for faces – I have myself – and that the other charges were not disproved by his failure to identify Asiaticus. But it was in a milder voice that I asked Asiaticus to answer Suilius's charges, point by point. He did so, but failed to account satisfactorily for his movements in France, and certainly perjured himself over the Poppaea business. The charge of corrupting the Guards I regarded as unproved. The soldiers testified in a formal, stilted way which suggested that they had learned the testimony off by heart beforehand, and when I questioned them merely repeated the same evidence. But then I have never heard a Guardsman testify in any other tones, they make a drill of everything.

I ordered everyone out of the room but Vitellius, young Pompey, and Pallas – Messalina had burst into tears and hurried off some minutes before – and told them that I would not sentence Asiaticus without first securing their approval. Vitellius said that, frankly, there seemed no reasonable doubt of Asiaticus's guilt, and that he was as shocked and grieved as I was: Asiaticus was a very old friend and had been a favourite of my mother Antonia's, who had used her interest at court to advance them both. Then he had had a most distinguished career and had never hung back where patriotic duty called: he had been one of the volunteers who came to Britain with me, and though he had not arrived in time for the battle, that was the fault of the storm, not due to any cowardice on his part. So if he had now become mad and betrayed his own past it would not be showing too much clemency to allow him to be his own executioner: of course, strictly, he deserved to be hurled from the Tarpeian Rock, and to have his corpse dishonoured by being dragged off by a hook through the mouth and thrown into the Tiber. Vitellius told me, too, that Asiaticus had practically confessed his guilt by sending him a message, as soon as he was arrested, begging him for old friendship's sake to secure his acquittal or, if it came to the worst, permission to commit suicide. Vitellius added: 'He knew that you would give him a fair trial: you have never failed to give anyone a fair trial. So how could my intercession be expected to help him? If he was guilty, then he would be pronounced guilty; or if he was innocent, he would be acquitted.' Young Pompey protested that no mercy should be shown Asiaticus; but perhaps he was thinking of his own safety. Assario and the Tristonia sisters, his relations, had been mentioned as Asiaticus's accomplices, and he wished to prove his own loyalty.

I sent a message to Asiaticus to inform him that I was adjourning the trial for twenty-four hours, and that, meanwhile, he was released from his fetters. He would surely understand that message. Meanwhile Messalina had hurried to Poppaea to tell her that Asiaticus was on the point of being condemned, and advised her to forestall her own trial and execution by immediate suicide. I knew nothing about this.

Asiaticus died courageously enough. He spent his last day winding up his affairs, eating and drinking as usual, and taking a walk in the Gardens of Lucullus (as they were still called), giving instructions to the gardeners about the trees and flowers and fish-pools. When he found that they had built his funeral pyre close to a fine avenue of hornbeams he was most indignant and fined the freedman responsible for choosing the site a quarter's pay. 'Didn't you realize, idiot, that the breeze would carry the flames into the foliage of those lovely old trees and spoil the whole appearance of the Gardens?' His last words to his family before the surgeon severed an artery in his leg and let him bleed to death in a warm bath were, 'Good-bye, my dear friends. It would have been less ignominious to have died by the dark artifices of Tiberius or the fury of Caligula, than now to fall a sacrifice to the imbecilic credulity of Claudius, betrayed by the woman I loved and by the friend I trusted.' For he was now convinced that Poppaea and Vitellius had arranged for the prosecution.

Two days later I asked Scipio to dine with me, and inquired after his wife's health, as a tactful way of indicating that if he still loved Poppaea and was ready to forgive her, I would take no further action in the matter. 'She's dead, Caesar,' he answered, and began sobbing with his head in his hands.

Asiaticus's family, the Valerians, to show that they did not wish to associate themselves with his treasonable words, were then obliged to present Messalina with the Gardens of Lucullus as a peace-offering; though naturally I never suspected it at the time, they were the real cause of Asiaticus's death. I tried the Petra brothers and executed them, and the Tristonia sisters then committed suicide. As for Assario, it seems that I signed his death-warrant: but I have no recollection of this. When I told Pallas to warn him for trial I was told that he had already been executed, and was shown the warrant, which was certainly not forged. The only explanation that I can offer is that Messalina, or possibly Polybius, who was her tool, smuggled the death-warrant in among a number of other unimportant ones that I had to sign, and that I signed it without reading it. I know now that this sort of trick was constantly played on me: that they took advantage of the strain from which my eyes were again suffering (so much that I had to stop all reading by artificial light) to read out as official reports and letters for my signature improvisations that did not correspond at all with the written documents.

About this time Vinicius died, of poison. I heard, some years later, that he had refused to sleep with Messalina and that the poison was administered by her; certainly he died on the day after he had dined at the Palace. The story is quite likely to be true. So now Vinicius, Vinicianus, and Asiaticus, the three men who had offered themselves as Emperor instead of me, were all dead, and their deaths seemed to lie at my door. Yet I had a clean conscience about them. Vinicianus and Asiaticus were clearly traitors, and Vinicius, I thought, had died as the result of an accident. But the Senate and People knew Messalina better than I did, and hated me because of her. That was the invisible barrier between them and me, and nobody had the courage to break it down.

As the result of a strong speech that I made about Asiaticus, at a session in which Sosibius and Crispinus were voted cash presents for their services, the Senate voluntarily surrendered to me the power of granting its members permission to leave Italy on any pretext.

Chapter 26

MY daughter Antonia had been married for some years to young Pompey but they had no children yet. One evening I visited her at her house, in Pompey's absence, and it occurred to me how disconsolate and bored she now always looked. Yes, she agreed, she was bored, and very bored and more than bored. So I suggested that she would feel much happier if she had a child and told her that I thought it was her duty as a healthy young woman with servants and plenty of money to have not only one child but several. With a family of young children she need never complain of boredom. She flared up and said: 'Father, only a fool would expect a field of corn to spring up where no seed has been sown. Don't blame the soil, blame the farmer. He sows salt, not seed.' And to my astonishment she explained that the marriage had never been properly consummated; and not only that, but she had been used in the vilest possible way by my son-in-law. I asked her why she had not told me of this before, and she said that she didn't think that I would believe her, because I had never really loved her, not as I loved her half-brother and half-sister; and that young Pompey had boasted to her that he stood so well with me now that he could make me do anything he wanted and believe anything that he told me. So what chance had she? Besides, there would be the shame of having to testify in court to the horrible things that he had done to her, and she could not face that.

I grew angry, as any father would, and assured her that I loved her dearly, and that it was chiefly on her account that I treated Pompey with such respect and confidence. I swore on my honour that if only half of what she had told me was true I would take immediate vengeance on the scoundrel. And that her modesty would be spared: the matter would never go to court. What was the use of being an Emperor if I couldn't use the privileges of my position to good private purpose occasionally, as a slight counterbalance to the responsibility and labour and pain that went with it? And at what hour was Pompey expected back?

'He'll be home at about midnight,' said Antonia, miserably, 'and by one o'clock he'll be in his room. He'll have a few drinks first. It's nine chances in ten that he'll take that disgusting Lycidas to bed with him: he bought him at the Asiaticus sale for twenty thousand gold pieces and he's not had eyes for anyone else since. In a way it's been a great relief to me. So you know how bad things must be when I say that I infinitely prefer him to sleep with Lycidas than with me. Yes, I was in love with Pompey once. Love's a funny thing, isn't it?'

'Very well, then, my poor, poor Antonia. When Pompey's in his room and settled down for the night, light a pair of oil lamps and put them on the window-sill of this room for a signal. Then leave the rest to me.'

She put the oil lamps on the window-sill an hour before dawn; then she came down and made the janitor open the front door. I was there. I brought Geta and a couple of Guards sergeants into the house with me and sent them upstairs while I waited in the hall below with Antonia. She had sent all the servants away except the janitor, who had been a slave-boy of mine. She was crying a little and we clasped hands as we anxiously listened for the sound of screams and scuffling from the bedroom. Not a sound was heard, but presently Geta came down with the sergeants and reported that my orders had been obeyed. Pompey and the slave Lycidas had been killed with a single javelin thrust.

This was the first time that I had used my power as Emperor to avenge a private wrong; but if I had not been Emperor I should have felt just the same and done whatever lay in my power to destroy Pompey; and though the law dealing with unnatural offences has fallen into abeyance for many years now, because no jury seems willing to convict, Pompey legally deserved to die. My only fault was that I executed him summarily; but that was the cleanest way of dealing with him. When a gardener comes across a filthy insect eating the heart out of one of his best roses he does not bring it to court before a jury of the gardeners: he crushes it then and there between his finger-nails. A few months later I married Antonia to Faustus, a descendant of the dictator Sulla, a modest, capable, and hard-working fellow who has turned out an excellent son-in-law. Two years ago he was Consul. They had a child, a boy, but it was very weakly and died, and Antonia has not been able to have another, because of the injury done to her by a careless midwife at the time of her delivery.

Shortly after this I executed Polybius, who was now my Minister of Arts, on Messalina's giving me proof that he was selling citizenships for his own profit. It was a great shock when I found that Polybius had been playing me false. I had trained him up in my service from a child, and had trusted him implicitly. He had just helped me complete the official autobiography that the Senate had requested me to write for the national archives. I had treated him so familiarly, in fact, that one day when he and I were walking in the Palace grounds, discussing some antiquarian point or other, I did not dismiss him when the two Consuls came up to give me their customary morning greeting. This offended their dignity, but if I was not too proud to walk beside Polybius and listen to his opinions, why should they have been? I allowed him the greatest freedom, and I had never known him to abuse it, though once he was rather too free with his tongue in the Theatre. They were playing a comedy of Menander's, and an actor had just delivered the line:

A prosperous whipstock scarce can be endured.

Someone in the wings laughed pointedly at this. It must have been Mnester. At any rate everyone turned and stared at Polybius, who as my Minister of Arts had the task of keeping the actors in order: if an actor showed too much independence Polybius saw to it for me that he was severely whipped.

Polybius shouted back: 'Yes, and Menander says in his *Thessaly*:

Who once were goatherds now have royal power.'

That was a hit at Mnester, who started life as a goatherd in Thessaly and was now known to be Messalina's chief infatuation.

I did not know it then, but Messalina had been having sexual relations with Polybius too and he was stupid enough to be jealous of Mnester. So she got rid of him, as I have told you. My other freedmen took Polybius's death as an affront to themselves – they formed a very close guild, always shielded each other loyally and never competed for my favour or showed any jealousy among themselves. Polybius had said nothing in his own defence, not wishing, I suppose, to incriminate his guild-brothers, many of whom must have been implicated in the same discreditable traffic in citizenships.

As for Mnester, it now happened on several occasions that when billed to dance he would fail to put in an appearance. It used to cause an uproar in the theatre. I must have been very stupid; though his absence always coincided with a sick headache of Messalina's, which prevented her attendance too, it never occurred to me to draw the obvious conclusion. I had to apologize several times to the public and undertake that it would not occur again. On one occasion I said, in joke: 'My Lords, you can't accuse me of hiding him away at the Palace.' This remark caused inordinate laughter. Everyone but myself knew where Mnester was. When I got back to the Palace Messalina used to send for me, and I would find her in bed in a darkened room with a damp cloth over her eyes. She would say in a faint voice: 'What, my dear, do you mean to say Mnester didn't dance again? Then I didn't miss anything after all. I was lying here simply seething with envy. I got up once and started to dress, to come after all, but the pain was so frightful that I had to get back to bed. Was the play very dull without him?'

I would say: 'We really must insist on his keeping his engagements: the City can't be treated like this, time after time.'

Messalina would sigh: 'I don't know. He's very highly strung, poor fellow. Just like a woman. Great artists are always like that. He gets sick headaches at the least provocation, he says. And if he felt only one-tenth as ill to-day as I have felt, it would be the greatest cruelty to insist on his dancing. It's not shamming, either. He loves his work and he's greatly distressed when he fails his public. Leave me now, dearest; I want to sleep if I can.'

So I would tiptoe out and nothing more would be said about Mnester until the same thing happened again. I never thought as highly of Mnester, though, as most people did. He has been compared to the great actor Roscius, who under the Republic attained to such eminence in his profession that he became a byword for artistic excellence. People, rather absurdly, still call a clever architect, or a learned historian, or even a smart boxer 'a very Roscius'. Mnester was no Roscius except in that very loose sense. I admit that I never saw Roscius act. There is nobody now living who ever did. We must all depend on the verdict of our great-grandparents in discussing him, and they agree that Roscius's chief aim in acting was 'to keep in character': and that noble king, or cunning pimp, or boastful soldier, or simple clown – whatever Roscius chose to be, that he was, to the life, without affectation. Whereas Mnester was a mass of mannerisms, very charming and graceful mannerisms, I'm sure, but in the final sense he was not an actor, he was just a pretty fellow with a neat pair of legs and a gift for choreographical improvisation.

It was now that Aulus Plautius returned home after four years' command in Britain and I had the pleasure of persuading the Senate to grant him a triumph. It was not, however, a full triumph, as I should have liked, but a lesser triumph, or ovation. If a general's services are too great to be rewarded merely with triumphal ornaments and yet have not, for some technical reason, entitled him to a full triumph, he is given this lesser sort. For example, if the war has not yet been completely finished; or if there has been insufficient bloodshed; or if the enemy is not considered a worthy one – as, long ago, after the defeat of the revolted slaves under Spartacus, though, indeed, Spartacus gave our armies more trouble than many a great foreign nation. In the case of Aulus Plautius, the objection was that his conquests were not yet secure enough to allow him to withdraw his troops. So instead of a chariot with four horses, he rode into the City on horseback, and he wore a myrtle wreath, not one of laurel, and carried no sceptre. The Senate did not head the procession, and there was no corps of trumpeters, and when the procession was done Aulus sacrificed a ram, not a bull. But otherwise the proceedings were the same as in a full triumph, and to show that it was no jealousy of mine that prevented him from winning the same honour as I had done, I came to meet him as he rode down the Sacred Way and offered him my congratulations and let him ride on my right side (the more honourable position) and myself supported him as he went on his knees up the Capitol steps. I also acted as his host at the banquet, and when the banquet was over, again put him on my right side when we brought him home to his house by torchlight.

Aulus was very grateful to me for this, but even more grateful, he told me in private, for having hushed up the scandal of his wife and the Christian love-feast (followers of that Jewish sect were now called Christians) and for having left her to his jurisdiction. He said that when a woman is unavoidably parted from her husband – her health had not allowed her to go to Britain – she is apt to feel lonely and take strange fancies into her head and fall an easy prey to religious charlatans, especially the Jewish and Egyptian sort. But she was a good woman and a good wife and he trusted that she would soon be cured of this nonsense. He was right. Two years later I arrested all the leading Christians in Rome, together with all the orthodox Jewish missionaries, and sent them out of the country, and Aulus's wife was a great help to me in rounding them up.

The chief emotional appeal of Christianity was that this Joshua, or Jesus, was said to have risen from the dead, as no man had ever done before, except in legends: after being crucified he had visited his friends apparently none the worse for his experience, had eaten and drunk to prove that he was no vision and then gone up to Heaven in a blaze of glory. And there was no proof that these were all lies, because, as it happened, there had been an earthquake just after the crucifixion, which had dislodged a heavy stone from the mouth of the tomb where the corpse had been put. The guard had fled in panic, and when they came back the corpse was gone; evidently it had been stolen. Once a story like this begins to circulate in the East it is difficult to stop it, and it would have been undignified to argue against its absurdity in a public edict; but I did publish a strong order in Galilee, where the Christians were most numerous, making it a capital offence to violate graves. But I must waste no more time over these ridiculous Christians: I must continue with my own story.

I must tell about the three letters which I added to the Roman alphabet, and about the great Saecular Games I celebrated, and about the census I took of Roman citizens, and about my revival of the ancient religious art of soothsaying which had now fallen into neglect, and about various important edicts of mine and laws which I inspired the Senate to pass. But perhaps it would be better first to finish briefly my account of Britain; now that Aulus Plautius has been brought safely home what happened there subsequently will not interest my readers greatly. I sent out one Ostorius to take Aulus's place, and he had a most difficult time. Plautius had completed the conquest of the plain of South Britain, but, as I say, the mountain tribes of Wales and the warlike North-Midlanders persisted in raiding the frontiers of the new province; Caractacus had married the daughter of the King of South Wales and was leading the South Welsh army in person. As soon as he arrived Ostorius announced that he would disarm all British provincials whose loyalty he suspected; he would thus be free to send his main forces against the tribes beyond the frontier, leaving only small garrisons behind. This announcement was generally resented, and it was understood by the Icenians, who were free allies of ours, that the disarmament rule would be extended to them too. They made a sudden rising, and Ostorius at Colchester found himself threatened by a large army of north-eastern tribes, with not one regular regiment at hand: they were all away in the centre or far west of the island and he had nobody with him but French and Batavians. However, he chose to risk an immediate battle and came off victorious. The Icenian confederacy sued for peace and was granted easy terms, and Ostorius then pushed his regular regiments north, annexing the entire Midlands, and halting on the frontier of the Brigantians. The Brigantians are a savage and powerful federation of tribes who occupy the north of the island as far as its narrowest point; beyond them, the wild mountainous

735

land that spreads out again, unexplored and frightful, for another few hundred miles is inhabited by those red-headed terrors, the Goidels. Ostorius made an expedition to the River Dee in the west and was plundering the valley of that river, which flows north to the Irish Sea, when he heard that the Brigantians were on the move behind him. He turned back and defeated a considerable force of them, capturing several hundred men, including some leading noblemen and a son of the King. The King of the Brigantians pledged himself to ten years of honourable peace if the prisoners were returned; and Ostorius accepted this, but kept the prince and five noblemen as hostages under the title of guests. He was then free to conduct operations in the Welsh hills against Caractacus. He used three out of his four regular regiments, basing one at Caerleon on the Usk, and two at Shrewsbury on the Severn. The remainder of the island was garrisoned only by auxiliaries, except for the Ninth, at Lincoln, and a colony of time-expired veterans at Colchester, where they had been given lands, live stock, and captives to work for them. This colony was the first Roman municipality in Britain, and I sent a letter sanctioning the foundation there of a temple to the God Augustus.

It took Ostorius three years to subdue South and Mid Wales. Caractacus was a brave enemy, and when he was forced up into North Wales with the remnants of his army he managed to fire the tribes there with his own courage. But Ostorius eventually defeated him in a last battle, in which we too lost heavily, and captured his wife, his daughter, a brother-in-law, and two of his nephews in the British camp. Caractacus himself fought his way north-east in a desperate rear-guard action and appeared a few days later at the court of the Queen of the Brigantians (her father, the King, had died and she was the only member of the royal house surviving, apart from the hostage prince in Ostorius's hands, so they had made her Queen). He urged her to continue the war, but she was no fool. She had him put in chains and sent him to Ostorius as a proof of her loyalty to the oath her father had sworn. Ostorius in return sent her back the noble hostages, one of whom she married. Her brother, the prince, she put to death because he was known to have shown cowardice on the field of battle, unlike her new husband, who had only been captured after receiving seven wounds and accounting for five Roman soldiers. This Queen, whose name is Cartimandua, has proved a most loyal ally. She quarrelled with her husband because he said that he did not regard himself as bound by the old King's oath to maintain peace with us. He could not persuade the Brigantians to make war on us, so he went down to South Wales and started a fresh revolt there. Our garrison at Caerleron was suddenly attacked in great force. The enemy were beaten off, but our losses included a battalion commander and eight captains of the Second. Not long after this two battalions of French auxiliaries, out foraging, were surprised and annihilated. Ostorius, worn out by three years of incessant fighting, took these reverses too much to heart: he fell sick and died, poor fellow, though it must have been some comfort to him that he was awarded triumphal ornaments just before this. That was two years ago. I sent out a general called Didius to take over the command of the province, but while he was on his way the Fourteenth were beaten in a pitched battle and had to retreat to their camp, leaving prisoners in the hands of the enemy.

Cartimandua's husband then left South Wales and made an attack on Cartimandua herself, who had earned his anger by putting to death two of his brothers who were plotting against her. She appealed for help to Didius, and he sent her four battalions of the Ninth and two of Batavians. With these and her own forces she defeated her husband, captured him, and made him swear vassalage to herself and friendship to the Romans. She then pardoned him, and they are reigning together again with apparent friendliness: there have been no border raids reported since. Meanwhile Didius has restored order in South Wales.

So let me now take leave of my province of Britain, which has cost us heavily in men and money and has so far yielded small returns except in glory. But I regard the occupation as a good investment for Rome in the long run, and if we treat the natives with justice and good faith they will become valuable allies and, eventually, valuable citizens. The riches of a country do not only lie in corn, metals, and cattle. What the Empire needs most is men, and if she can add to her resources by the annexation of a country where an honest, warlike, and industrious race is bred, that is a better acquisition than any spice island of the Indies or gold-bearing territory of Central Asia. The faith that Queen Cartimandua and her nobles have shown, and the courage in adversity of King Caractacus, are the happiest possible auguries of the future.

Caractacus was brought to Rome, and I decreed a general holiday to celebrate his arrival. The whole City came out to look at him. The Guards Division was on parade, outside the Camp, and I was sitting on a tribunal platform erected for the occasion at the Camp gate. Trumpeters sounded and in the distance a small procession was moving across the turf towards me. First came a detachment of captured British soldiers; then Caractacus's household thegns; then wagons heaped with trappings and collars and weapons – not only Caractacus's own, but all that he had won in wars with his neighbours, captured in that camp at Cefn Carnedd; then Caractacus's wife, daughter, brother-in-law, and nephews, and lastly Caractacus himself, carrying his head high and looking neither to the right nor the left until he came to my platform. There he made a dignified obeisance, and asked permission to address me. I granted him permission and he spoke in a frank and noble way, in such remarkably fluent Latin, too, that I positively envied him: I am a wretched speaker and always get entangled in my sentences.

'Caesar, you see me here in chains before you, suing for my life, after having resisted your country's arms for seven long years. I might well have held out for seven years longer if I had not trusted Queen Cartimandua to respect the sacred guest-right of our island. In Britain when a man claims hospitality at any house, and is given salt and bread and wine, the host then holds himself answerable for his guest's life with his own. A man took refuge once at my father Cymbeline's court and, after having eaten his salt, revealed himself as the murderer of my grandfather. But my father said: "You are my guest. I cannot harm you." Queen Cartimandua by putting me in these chains and sending me here did more honour to you as her ally than to herself as the Queen of the Brigantians.

'I make a voluntary confession of my own faults. The letter that my brother Togodumnus wrote to you, and that I did not dissuade him from sending, was as foolish as it was discourteous. We were young and proud then and trusting to hearsay we underestimated the strength of your Roman armies, the loyalty of your generals, and your own great qualities as a commander. If I had matched the glory of my lineage and of my own feats with a becoming moderation in prosperity I should no doubt have entered this City as a friend, not as a captive; nor would you then have disdained to welcome me royally, as a son of my father Cymbeline whom your God Augustus honoured as an ally and overlord like him of many a conquered tribe.

'For my prolonged resistance to you, once I found that you were bent on annexing my kingdom and the kingdoms of my allies, I have no apologies to offer. I had men and arms, chariots, horses, and treasure: do you wonder that I was unwilling to part with them? You Romans aim at extending your sway over all mankind, but it does not follow that all mankind will immediately accept that sway. You must first prove your right to rule, and prove it with the sword. It has been a long war between us, Caesar, and your armies have pursued me from tribe to tribe, and from fort to fort, and I have taken heavy toll of them; but now I am caught and the victory is yours at last. If I had surrendered to your lieutenant Aulus Plautius at that first engagement on the Medway I should have been proved an unworthy foe and Aulus Plautius would not have sent for you, and so you would never have celebrated your deserved triumph. Therefore respect your enemy, now that he is humbled, grant him his life, and your noble clemency will never be forgotten either by your own country or by mine. Britain will reverence the clemency of the victor, if Rome approves the courage of the conquered.'

I called Aulus to me. 'For my part I am willing to let this brave king go free. To restore him to his throne in Britain would be everywhere regarded as weakness, so that I cannot do. But I am inclined to let him stay here in Rome as a guest of the City, with a pension suited to his needs; and also to release his family and household thegns. What do you say?'

Aulus answered: 'Caesar, Caractacus has shown himself a gallant enemy. He has tortured or executed no prisoners, poisoned no wells, fought fair, and kept faith. If you release him I shall be proud to take him by the hand and offer him my friendship.'

I freed Caractacus. He thanked me gravely: 'I wish for every Roman citizen a heart like yours.' That night he and his family dined at the Palace. Aulus was there too and we old campaigners fought the battle of Brentwood over again as the wine went round. I told Caractacus how nearly he and I had met in a hand-to-hand conflict. He laughed and said: 'If I had only known! But if you are still eager for the fight, I'm your man. To-morrow morning on Mars Field, you on your mare and me on foot? The disparity of our ages will make that fair.' Another remark of his has since become famous: 'I cannot understand, my Lords, how as rulers of a City as glorious as this is, with its houses like marble cliffs, its shops like royal treasuries, its temples like the dreams that our

Druids report when they return from magical visits to the Kingdom of the Dead, you can ever find it in your hearts to covet the possession of our poor island huts.'

Chapter 27

EXPIATORY games, called Tarentine or Saecular, are celebrated at Rome to mark the beginning of each new cycle, or age of men. They take the form of a festival of three days and nights in honour of Pluto and Proserpine, the Gods of the Underworld. Historians agree that these games were first formally established as a public ritual by Publicola, a Valerian, in the two hundred and fiftieth year after the foundation of Rome – which was also the year in which the Claudians came to Rome from Sabine country; but they had been celebrated 110 years previously as a family ritual of the Valerians, in accordance with an oracle of Delphic Apollo. Publicola made a vow that they should be performed at the beginning of every new cycle thereafter so long as the City stood. Since his time there have been five celebrations, but at irregular intervals because of differences of opinion as to when each new cycle started. Sometimes the cycle has been taken as the natural cycle of 110 years, which is the ancient Etruscan method of reckoning, and sometimes as the Roman civil cycle of 100 years, and sometimes the Games have been celebrated as soon as it was clear that nobody survived who had taken part on the previous occasion.

The most recent celebration under the Republic was in the six hundred and seventh year from the foundation of the City, and the only celebration that had taken place since then was Augustus's in the seven hundred and thirty-sixth year. The year of Augustus's celebration could not be justified as marking the hundredth or hundred-and-tenth year from the previous celebration, nor as marking the death of the last man who had taken part in it; nor could it be understood as a date arrived at by calculation from Publicola's time, reckoning in 100 or 110 year terms. Augustus, or rather the Board of Fifteen, his religious advisers, were reckoning from a supposed first celebration of the Games in the ninety-seventh year from the foundation of the City. I admit that in my history of his religious reforms I had accepted this date as the correct one, but only because to criticize him on this important point would have got me into serious trouble with my grandmother Livia. The fact was (not to go into the matter in detail) that his reckoning was incorrect even if the first celebration had taken place when he said it did, which was not so. I reckoned forward from Publicola's festival in natural cycles of 110 years (for this clearly was what a cycle meant to Publicola himself) until I reached the six hundred and ninetieth year from the foundation of the City. That was when the last celebration A.D. 46 should have really taken place, and then not again until the eight hundredth year, the date which we have just reached in this story, namely, the seventh year of my own monarchy.

Now, each cycle has a certain fatal character, which is given it by the events of the inaugurating year. The first year of the previous cycle had been marked by the birth of Augustus, the death of Mithridates the Great, Pompey's victory over the Phoenicians and his capture of Jerusalem, Catiline's unsuccessful attempt at a popular revolution, and Caesar's assumption of the office of High Pontiff. Is it necessary for me to point out the significance of each of these events? that for the next cycle our arms were destined to be successful abroad, and the Empire to be greatly extended, popular liberty to be suppressed, and the Caesars to be the mouthpieces of the Gods? Now it was my intention to expiate the sins and crimes of this old cycle, and inaugurate a new one with solemn sacrifices. For it was in this year that I counted on completing my work of reform. I would then hand the government of a now prosperous and well-organized nation back to the Senate and People, from whom it had so long been withheld.

I had thought the whole plan out in detail. It was clear that government by the Senate under Consuls elected annually had great disadvantages: the single-year term was not long enough. And the Army did not wish to have its Commander-in-Chief constantly changed. My plan, briefly, was to make a free gift to the nation of the Privy Purse, except so much of it as was needed to support me as a private citizen, and the Imperial lands, including Egypt, and to introduce a law providing for a change of government every fifth year. The ex-Consuls of the previous five-year period together with certain representatives of the People and of the Knights would form a cabinet to advise and assist one of their number, chosen by religious lot and known as the Consul-in-Chief, in the government of the country. Each member of the cabinet would be responsible to the Consul-in-Chief for a department corresponding with the departments that I had been building up under my freedmen, or for the government of one of the frontier provinces. The Consuls of the year would act as a link between the Consul-in-Chief and the Senate, and would perform their usual duties as appeal judges; the Protectors of the People would act as a link between the Consul-in-Chief and the People. The Consuls would be elected from the Senatorial order by popular election, and in national emergencies recourse would be had to a plebiscite. I had thought out a number of ingenious safeguards for this constitution and congratulated myself that it was a workable one: my freedmen would remain as permanent officials in charge of the clerical staff, and the new government would benefit by their advice. Thus the redeeming features of monarchical government would be retained without prejudice to republican liberty. And to keep the Army contented I would embody in the new constitution a measure providing for a bounty of money to be paid every five years, proportionate to the success of our arms abroad and to the increase of wealth at home. The governorships of home provinces would be distributed between knights who had risen to high command in the Army, and senators.

For the present I told nobody of my plans, but continued with a light heart at my work. I was convinced that as soon as I proved by a voluntary resignation of the monarchy that my intentions had never been tyrannical and that such summary executions as I had ordered had been forced on me, I would be forgiven all my lesser errors for the sake of the great work of reform that I had accomplished, and all suspicions would be put to rest. I told myself: 'Augustus always said that he would resign and restore the Republic: but somehow he never did, because of Livia. And Tiberius always said the same, but somehow he never did, because he was afraid of the hatred that he had earned by his cruelty and tyranny. But I really am going to resign: there's nothing to prevent me. My conscience is clear, and Messalina's no Livia.'

These Saecular Games were celebrated not in the summer, as on previous occasions, but on the twenty-first of April, the Shepherds' Festival, because that was the very day on which A.D. 47 Romulus and his shepherds had founded Rome 800 years before. I followed Augustus's example in not making the Gods of the Underworld the only deities addressed; though the Tarentum, a volcanic cleft in Mars Field, which was the traditional place for the celebration and was said to be one entrance to

Hell, was converted into a temporary theatre and illuminated with coloured lights and made the centre of the Festival. I had sent heralds out some months before to summon all citizens (in the old formula) 'to a spectacle which nobody now living has ever seen before, and which nobody now living shall ever see again'. This provoked a few sneers, because Augustus's celebration of sixty-four years previously was remembered by a number of old men and women, some of whom had actually taken part in it. But it was the old formula, and it was justified by Augustus's celebration not having been performed at the proper time.

On the morning of the first day the Board of Fifteen distributed to all free citizens, from the steps of Jove's temple on the Capitoline Hill and Apollo's on the Palatine, torches, sulphur, and bitumen, the instruments of purification; also wheat, barley, and beans, some to serve as an offering to the Fates and some to be given as pay to the actors taking part in the festival. Early morning sacrifices had been simultaneously offered in all the principal temples of Rome, to Jove, Juno, Neptune, Minerva, Venus, Apollo, Mercury, Ceres, Vulcan, Mars, Diana, Vesta, Hercules, Augustus, Latona, the Fates, and to Pluto and Proserpine. But the chief event of the day was the sacrifice of a white bull to Jove and a white cow to Juno, on the Capitol, and everyone was expected to attend this. Then we went in procession to the Tarentum theatre and sang choruses in honour of Apollo and Diana. The afternoon was taken up by chariot races and wild-beast hunts and sword-fighting in the Circus and amphitheatres and scenic games in honour of Apollo in the theatre of Pompey.

At nine o'clock that night, after a great burning of sulphur and sprinkling of holy water in consecration of the whole of Mars Field, I sacrificed three male lambs to the Fates on three underground altars built by the bank of the Tiber, while a crowd of citizens with me waved their lighted torches, offered their wheat, barley, and beans, and sang a hymn of repentance for past errors. The blood of the lambs was sprinkled on the altars and their carcasses burned. At the Tarentum theatre more hymns were then sung and the expiatory part of the festival gone through with appropriate solemnity. Then scenes from Roman legend were acted, including a ballet illustrative of the fight between the three brothers Horatius and the three brothers Curiatius which was said to have occurred close by on the day of the first celebration of the Games by the Valerian family.

The next day the noblest matrons in Rome, headed by Messalina, assembled on the Capitol and performed supplications to Juno. The Games continued as on the previous day: 300 lions and 100 bears were killed in the amphitheatre, not to mention bulls and numerous sword-fighters. That night I sacrificed a black hog and a black pig to Mother Earth. On the last day Greek and Latin hymns were sung in chorus in the sanctuary of Apollo by three times nine beautiful boys and maidens, and white oxen were sacrificed to him. Apollo was so honoured because his oracle had originally ordered the institution of the Festival. The hymns were to implore the protection of Apollo, his sister Diana, his mother Latona, and his father Jove, for all cities, towns, and magistrates in the whole Empire. One of them was Horace's famous ode composed in honour of Apollo and Diana, which did not have to be brought up to date, as you might have supposed: in fact, one verse of the hymn was more appropriate than when it was first composed:

> Moved by the solemn voice of prayer
> Both deities shall make great Rome their care,
> Benignly turn the direful woes
> Of famine and of weeping war
> From Rome and noble Caesar far,
> And pour them on our British foes.

Horace had written that at a time when Augustus contemplated a war against Britain, but it never came off, so the British were not officially our foes, as they now were.

More sacrifices to all the Gods, more chariot races, swordfights, wild-beast hunts, athletic contests. That night at the Tarentum I sacrificed a black ram, a black sheep, a black bull, a black cow, a black boar, and a black sow, to Pluto and Proserpine; and the Festival was over for another 110 years. It had gone through without a single error or evil omen of any sort being reported. When I asked Vitellius whether he had enjoyed the Festival, he said: 'It was excellent and I wish you many happy returns of the day.' I burst out laughing and he apologized for his absent-mindedness. He had unconsciously been identifying Rome's birthday with mine, he explained, but hoped that the phrase might prove an omen of life prolonged for me to a remarkable and vigorous old age. But Vitellius could be very disingenuous: I believe now that he had thought the joke out weeks beforehand.

To me the proudest moment of the whole festival was on the

afternoon of the third day, when the Troy Game was performed on Mars Field and my little Britannicus, then only just six years old, took part in the skirmish with boys twice his age and managed his pony and his weapons like a Hector or Caractacus. The people reserved their loudest cheers for him. They commented on his extraordinary likeness to my brother Germanicus, and prophesied splendid triumphs for him as soon as he was old enough to go to the wars. A grand-nephew of mine also took part in the Games, a boy of eleven, the son of my niece Agrippinilla. His name was Lucius Domitius,* and I have mentioned him before, but only in passing. The time has now come for a fuller account of him.

He was the son of that Domitius Ahenobarbus (or Brassbeard), my maternal cousin, who had the reputation of being the bloodiest-minded man in Rome. Bloody-mindedness ran in the family, like the red beard, and it was said that it was no wonder they had brass beards, to match their iron faces and leaden hearts. When a young man Domitius Ahenobarbus had served on Gaius Caesar's staff in the East and had killed one of his own freedmen by locking him up in a room with no water to drink and nothing but salt fish and dry bread to eat, because he had refused to get properly drunk at his birthday banquet. When Gaius heard of this he told Domitius that his services were no longer needed and that he no longer counted him among his friends. Domitius returned to Rome, and on the way back, in a freak of petulance, suddenly spurred his horse along a village street on the Appian Way and deliberately ran down a child who was playing in the road with its doll. Again, once in the open Market Place, he picked a quarrel with a knight to whom he owed money, and gouged out one of his eyes with his thumb. My uncle Tiberius made a friend of Domitius in the latter years of his reign: for he deliberately cultivated the society of the cruel and base, with the object, it is supposed, of feeling somewhat virtuous by comparison. He married Domitius to his adoptive granddaughter, my niece Agrippinilla, and there was one child of the marriage, this Lucius. Congratulated by his friend on the birth of an heir, Domitius scowled: 'Spare your congratulations, blockheads. If you had any real patriotism you'd go to the cradle and strangle the child at once. Don't you realize that Agrippinilla and I between us command all the known vices, human and inhuman, and that he's destined to grow up the most

* Afterwards the Emperor Nero. – R.G.

detestable imp that ever plagued our unfortunate country? That's not guesswork, either: have any of you seen his horoscope? It's enough to make you shudder.' Domitius was arrested on the double charge of treason and incest with his sister Domitia – of course, that meant nothing in Tiberius's time, it was a mere formality. Tiberius died opportunely and he was liberated by Caligula. Not long afterwards Domitius himself died, of the dropsy. He had named Caligula in his will as young Lucius's co-heir, leaving him two-thirds of the estate. When Agrippinilla was banished to her island, Caligula seized the rest of the estate too, so Lucius was now practically an orphan and quite unprovided for. However, his aunt Domitia took care of him. (She must not be confused with her sister, Domitia Lepida, Messalina's mother.) She was a woman who gave herself wholly to pleasure and only bothered about young Lucius because of a prophecy that he would one day become Emperor: she wanted to stand in well with him. It is a comment on Domitia's character that the three tutors to whom she entrusted his education were a Syrian ex-ballet-dancer, who shared Domitia's favours with a Tyrolese ex-sword-fighter, this same ex-sword-fighter, and her Greek hairdresser. They gave him a fine popular education.

When two years later Agrippinilla returned she felt so little maternal feeling for her son that she told Domitia that he might as well stay with her for another few years; she would pay well to have the responsibility taken off her hands. I intervened and made Agrippinilla take him home; she took the tutors too, because Lucius was unwilling to come without them, and Domitia had other lovers. Agrippinilla also took Domitia's husband, an ex-Consul, and married him, but they soon quarrelled and separated. The next event in Lucius's life was an attempt to assassinate him while he was taking his afternoon siesta: two men walked in at the front door unchallenged by the porter, who was also taking his siesta, went upstairs, found nobody about in the corridors, wandered along until they saw a slave sleeping in front of a bedroom door which they decided must be the one that they were looking for, went in, found Lucius asleep in his bed, drew their daggers, and tiptoed close. A moment later they came rushing out again screaming: 'The snake, the snake!' Though the household was alarmed by the noise no effort was made to stop them, and they escaped. What had frightened them was the sight of a cobra's skin on Lucius's pillow. He had been wearing it wound around his leg as a cure for scrofula, from which he suffered greatly as a child, and I suppose had been playing with it before he went to sleep. In the darkened room it looked like a live cobra. I have since supposed that the assassins were sent by Messalina, who hated Agrippinilla but did not, for some reason or other, dare to bring any charge against her. At any rate, the story went round that two cobras stood on guard at Lucius's bed, and Agrippinilla encouraged it. She enclosed the snakeskin in a gold snake-shaped bracelet for him to wear and told her friends that it had indeed been found on the pillow and must have been sloughed there by a cobra. Lucius told his friends that he certainly had a cobra guard, but that it was probably an exaggeration to say that it was a double-guard: he had never seen more than a single cobra. It used to drink from his water-jug. No more attempts were made to assassinate him.

Lucius, as well as Britannicus, resembled my dear brother Germanicus, who was his grandfather, but in this case it was a hateful resemblance. The features were almost identical, but the frank, noble, generous, modest character that beamed from Germanicus's face was supplanted here by slyness, baseness, meanness, vanity. And yet most people were blinded to this by the degenerate refinement he had made of his grandfather's handsome looks: he had an effeminate beauty that made men warm to him as they would to a woman; and he knew the power of his beauty only too well, and took as long every morning over his toilet, especially over his hair, which he wore quite long, as his mother or his aunt. His hairdresser tutor tended his beauty as jealously as the head gardener in the Gardens of Lucullus tended the fruit on the famous peach wall or the unique white-fleshed cherry-tree which Lucullus had brought from the Black Sea. It was strange to watch Lucius on Mars Field doing military exercises with sword, shield, and spear: he handled them correctly enough, as his Tyrolese sword-fighter tutor had taught him, yet it was less a drill than a ballet-dance. When, at the same age, Germanicus was doing his exercises, one could always in imagination hear the clash of battle, trumpets, groans, and shouts, and see the gush of German blood; with Lucius one only heard the rippling applause of a theatre audience and saw roses and gold coins showered on the stage.

But enough of Lucius for the moment. A more pleasant topic is my improvement of the Roman alphabet. In my previous book I explained about the three new letters that I had suggested as necessary for modern usage: consonantal *u*, the vowel between *i* and *u* corresponding with Greek *upsilon*, and the consonant which we have hitherto expressed by *bs* or *ps*. I had intended to introduce these after my triumph, but then postponed the matter until the new cycle should start. I announced my project in the Senate on the day following the Saecular Games, and it was favourably received. But I said that this was an innovation which personally affected everyone in the Empire and that I did not wish to force my own ideas on the Roman people against their will or in a hurry, so I proposed to put the matter to a plebiscite in a year's time.

Meanwhile I published a circular letter explaining and justifying my scheme. I pointed out that though one was brought up to regard the alphabet as a series no less sacred and unalterable than the year of months, or the order of the numerals, or the signs of the Zodiac, this was not really so: everything in this world was subject to change and improvement. Julius Caesar had reformed the Calendar: the convention for writing numerals had been altered and extended; the names of constellations had been changed: even the stars that composed them were not immortal – since the time of Homer, for example, the seven Pleiades had become six through the disappearance of the star Sterope, or, as she was sometimes called, Electra. So with the Latin alphabet. Not only had the linear forms of the letters changed, but so also had the significance of the letters as denoting certain spoken sounds. The Latin alphabet was borrowed from the Dorian Greeks in the time of the learned King Evander, and the Greeks had originally had it from Cadmus who brought it with him when he arrived with the Phoenician fleet, and the Phoenicians had it from the Egyptians. It was the same alphabet, but only in name. The fact was that Egyptian writing began in the form of pictures of animals and other natural objects, and that these gradually became formalized into hieroglyphic letters, and that the Phoenicians borrowed and altered them, and that the Greeks borrowed and altered these alterations, and finally the Latins borrowed and altered these alterations of alterations. The primitive Greek alphabet contained only sixteen letters, but it was added to until it numbered twenty-four and in some cities twenty-seven. The first Latin alphabet contained only twenty letters, because three Greek aspirated consonants and the letter Z were found unnecessary. However, about 500 years from the foundation of Rome, G was introduced to supplement C, and more recently still the Z had returned. And still in my opinion the alphabet was not perfect. It would perhaps be a little awkward at first, if the country voted in favour of the change, to remember to use these convenient new forms instead of the old ones, but the awkwardness would soon wear off and a new generation of boys taught to read and write in the new style would not feel it at all. The awkwardness and inconvenience of the change that was made in the Calendar, not quite 100 years ago, when one year had to be extended to fifteen months, and thereafter the number of days in each month altered, and the name of one of the months changed too – now, that really was something to complain about, but had it not passed off all right? Surely nobody would wish to go back to the old style?

Well, everyone discussed the matter learnedly, but perhaps nobody cared very much about it, one way or the other, at any rate not so much as I did. When eventually the vote was taken it was overwhelmingly in favour of the new letters; but rather as a personal compliment to me, I think, than from any real understanding of the issue. So the Senate voted for their immediate introduction and they appear now in all official documents and in every sort of literature from poems, scientific treatises, and legal commentaries, to advertisements of auctions, duns, love-letters, and pornographic scrawls in chalk on the walls of buildings.

And now I shall give a brief account of various public works, reforms, laws, and decrees of mine dating from the latter part of my monarchy; I shall thus, so to speak, have the table cleared for writing the painful last chapters of my life. For I have now reached a turning-point in my story, 'the discovery' as tragedians call it, after which, though I continued to carry out my duties as Emperor, it was in a very different spirit from hitherto.

I finished building the aqueducts. I also built many hundreds of miles of new roads and put broken ones into good repair. I prohibited money-lenders from making loans to needy young men in expectation of their fathers' deaths: it was a disgusting traffic – the interest was always extortionate and it happened more often than was natural that the father died soon afterwards. This measure was in protection of honest fathers against prodigal sons, but I also provided for honest sons with prodigal fathers: I exempted a son's lawful inheritance from the sequestration of a father's property on account of debt or felony. I also legislated on behalf of women, freeing them from the vexatious tutelage of their paternal relatives, and forbidding dowries to be pledged in surety for a husband's debts.

On Pallas's suggestion I brought a motion before the Senate which was adopted as a law, that any woman of free birth who married a slave without the knowledge and consent of his master became a slave herself; but that if she did so with his knowledge and consent she remained free, and only her children born of the marriage were slaves. There was an amusing sequel to my introduction of this motion. A senator, who happened to be Consul-Elect, had offended Pallas some years before, and foresaw difficulties when he came into office if he could not regain Pallas's goodwill; I do not say that he was justified in expecting Pallas to show rancour, because Pallas is less subject to this fault than I am, but at any rate he had an uneasy conscience. So he proposed that Pallas should be awarded an honorary first-class magistracy and the sum of 150,000 gold pieces, for having performed a great service to the country by originating this law and prevailing on the Senate to pass it. Scipio, Poppaea's widower, sprang up and spoke with an irony reminiscent of Gallus and Haterius in the reign of my uncle Tiberius: 'I second that. And I move that public thanks should also be given this extraordinary man. For some of us amateur genealogists have recently discovered that he is directly descended from the Arcadian King Pallas, ancestor of that literary King Evander, recently mentioned by our gracious Emperor, who gave his name to the Palatine Hill. Public thanks, I say, should be given him not only for his services in the drafting of this law but for his modest magnanimity in concealing his royal descent – for putting himself at the disposal of the Senate like a mere nobody, and for even deigning to be known as a freedman secretary of the Emperor's.' Nobody dared to oppose this motion, so I played the innocent and pretended to take it seriously and did not interpose my veto. It would have been unfair to Pallas if I had. But as soon as the House adjourned I sent for him and told him about the motion. He grew very red, not knowing whether to be angry at the insult or pleased that it was publicly recognized what an important part he played in public affairs. He asked me what he ought to answer, and I said to him: 'Do you need the money?'

'No, Caesar. I'm very well off.'

'How well off? Come on, let's hear how much you're worth. Tell me the truth and I won't be angry.'

'About three million pieces, when I last went over my accounts.'

'What! Silver pieces?'

'No, gold.'

'Good God! And all honestly come by?'

'Every farthing. People present petitions or ask favours and I always say, "I can't promise to do anything for you!" And then they say, "Oh, no, we never expected it. But please accept this small money-present as an acknowledgement of your kindness in receiving us." So I put the money in the bank and smile nicely. It's all yours, Caesar, if you want it. You know that.'

'I know it, Pallas. But I had no idea that you were so wealthy.'

'I never get time to spend anything, Caesar.'

And that was true. Pallas worked like a galley-slave. So I told him that I would see that the Senate did not have the laugh over him; and advised him to accept the honorary rank but refuse the money. He consented, and I then gravely assured the Senate that Pallas was quite satisfied with the honorary rank that they had kindly awarded him, and would continue to live in his former poverty.

Scipio was not to be beaten. He introduced a motion begging me to plead with Pallas to yield to the Senate's entreaties, and accept the gift. The motion was passed. But Pallas and I held out. On my advice he refused my entreaties and the Senate's and the farce was completed by still another motion, introduced by Scipio and passed by the House, congratulating Pallas on his primitive parsimony; these congratulations were even officially engraved on a brass tablet. I think you will agree that it was not Pallas and I who were made fools of, but Scipio and the Senate.

I limited barristers' fees to 100 gold pieces a case. This limitation was directed against men like Suilius, Asiaticus's prosecutor, who could sway a jury to convict or acquit as surely as a farmer drives his pigs to market. Suilius would accept any brief, however desperate, so long as he got his whole fee: which was 4,000 a case. And it was the impressiveness of the fee as much as the assurance and eloquence with which he addressed the court that influenced the jury. Occasionally, of course, even Suilius could not hope to pull a case off, because his client's guilt was too clear to be concealed; but so as not to lose his credit with the court, which he would need in future cases where there was at least a fighting chance, he as good as directed the jury to decide against his client. There was a scandal about this; a rich knight accused of robbing the widow of one of his freedmen had paid Suilius his usual fee and had then been betrayed by him in this way. He went to Suilius and asked for a return of his 4,000 gold pieces. Suilius said that he had done his best and regretted he could not pay back the money – that would be a dangerous precedent. The knight committed suicide on Suilius's doorstep.

By thus reducing the barristers' fees, which in Republican Rome had been pronounced illegal, I damaged their prestige with the juries, who were thereafter more inclined to give verdicts corresponding with the facts of the case. I waged a sort of war with the barristers. Often when I was about to judge a case I used to warn the court with a smile: 'I am an old man, and my patience is easily tried. My verdict will probably go to the side that presents its evidence in the briefest, frankest, and most lucid manner, even if it is somewhat incriminating, rather than to the side that spoils a good case by putting up an inappropriately brilliant performance.' And I would quote Homer:

> Yea, when men speak, that man I most detest
> Who locks the verity within his breast.

I encouraged the appearance of a new sort of advocate, men without either eloquence or great legal expertness, but with common sense, clear voices, and a talent for reducing cases to their simplest elements. The best of these was called Agatho. I always gave him the benefit of the doubt when he pleaded a case before me in his pleasant, quick, precise way; in order to encourage others to emulate him.

The Forensic and Legal Institute of Telegonius, 'that most learned and eloquent orator and jurist', was closed down about three years ago. It happened as follows. Telegonius, fat, bustling, and crop-haired, appeared one day in the Court of Appeal where I was presiding, and conducted a case of his own. He had been ordered by a magistrate to pay a heavy fine, on the ground that he had incited one of his slaves to kill a valuable slave of Vitellius's in a dispute. It appears that Telegonius's slave, in a barber's shop, had put on insufferable airs as a lawyer and orator. A dispute started between this fellow and Vitellius's slave, who was waiting his turn to be shaved and was known as the best cook (except mine) in all Rome, and worth at the very least 10,000 gold pieces. Telegonius's slave, with offensive eloquence, contrasted the artistic importance of oratory and cookery. Vitellius's cook was not quarrelsome but made a few dispassionate statements of fact, such as that no proper comparison could be drawn between domestic practitioners of splendid arts and splendid practitioners of domestic arts; that he expected, if not deference, at least politeness from slaves of less importance than himself; and that he was worth at least a hundred times more than his opponent. The orator, enraged by the sympathy the cook got from the other customers, snatched the razor from the barber's hand and cut the cook's throat with it, crying: 'I'll teach you to argue with one of Telegonius's men.' Telegonius had therefore been fined the full value of the murdered cook, on the ground that his slave's violence was due to an obsession of argumental infallibility inculcated by the Institute in all its employees. Telegonius now appealed on the ground that the slave had not been incited to murder by violence, for the very motto of the Institute was: '*The tongue is mightier than the blade*', which constituted a direct injunction to keep to that weapon in any dispute. He also pleaded that it had been a very hot day, that the slave had been subjected to a gross insult by the suggestion that he was not worth more than a miserable 100 gold pieces – the lowest value that could be put upon his services as a trained clerk would be fifty gold pieces annually – and that therefore the only fair view could be that the cook had invited death by provocative behaviour.

Vitellius appeared as a witness. 'Caesar,' he said, 'I see it this way. This Telegonius's slave has killed my head-cook, a gentle, dignified person, and a perfect artist in his way, as you will yourself agree, having often highly praised his sauces and cakes. It will cost me at least ten thousand gold pieces to replace him, and even then, you may be sure, I'll never get anyone half so good. His murderer used phrases, in praise of oratory and in dispraise of cookery, that have been proved to occur, word for word, in Telegonius's own handbooks; and it has been further proved that in the same handbooks, in the sections devoted to "Liberty", many violent passages occur which seek to justify a person in resorting to armed force when arguments and reason fail.'

Telegonius cross-examined Vitellius, and I must admit that he was scoring heavily when a chance visitor to the court sprang a surprise. It was Alexander the Alabarch, who happened to be in Rome and had strolled into court for amusement. He passed me up a note:

The person who calls himself Telegonius of Athens and Rome is a runaway slave of mine named Joannes, born at Alexandria in my own household, of a Syrian mother. I lost him twenty-five years ago. You will find the letter A, within a circle, pricked on his left hip, which is my household brand.

Signed: ALEXANDER, ALABARCH

I stopped the case while Telegonius was taken outside by my yeomen and identified as indeed the Alabarch's property. Imagine, he had been masquerading as a Roman citizen for nearly twenty years! His entire property should have gone to the State, except for the 10,000 gold pieces which had been awarded to Vitellius, but I let the Alabarch keep half of it. In return the Alabarch made me a present of Telegonius, whom I handed over to Narcissus for disposal: Narcissus set him to work at the useful, if humble, task of keeping court records.

This, then, was the sort of way I governed. And I widely extended the Roman citizenship, intending that no province whose inhabitants were loyal, orderly, and prosperous should long remain inferior in civic status to Rome and the rest of Italy. The first city of Northern France for which I secured the citizenship was Autun.

I then took the census of Roman citizens.

The total number of citizens, including women and children, now stood at 5,984,072, compared with the 4,937,000 given by the census of the year that Augustus died, and again with the A.D. 48 4,233,000 given by the census taken in the year after my father died. Written briefly on a page these numbers are not impressive, but think of them in human terms. If the whole Roman citizenry were to file past me at a brisk walk, toe to heel, it would be two whole years before the last one came in sight. And these were only the true citizens. If the entire population of the Empire went past, over 70,000,000 in number, now that Britain, Morocco, and Palestine had to be reckoned in, it would take twelve times as long, namely, twenty-four years, for them to pass, and in twenty-four years an entire new generation has time to be born, so that I might sit a lifetime and the stream would still glide on,

Would glide and slide with still perpetual flow,

and never the same face appear twice. Numbers are a nightmare. To think that Romulus's first Shepherds' Festival was celebrated by no more than 3,300 souls. Where will it all end?

What I wish to emphasize most of all in this account of my activities as Emperor is that up to this point at least I acted, so

754

far as I knew how, for the public good in the widest possible sense. I was no thoughtless revolutionary and no cruel tyrant and no obstinate reactionary: I tried to combine generosity with common sense wherever possible and nobody can accuse me of not having done my best.

Two Documents Illustrating Claudius's Legislative Practice, also his Epistolary and Oratorical Style

CLAUDIUS'S EDICT ABOUT CERTAIN TYROLESE TRIBES
A.D. 46

Published at the Residence at Baiae in the year of the Consulship of Marcus Junius Silanus and of Quintus Sulpicius Camerius, on the fifteenth day of March, by order of Tiberius Claudius Caesar Augustus Germanicus.

Tiberius Claudius Caesar Augustus Germanicus, High Pontiff, Protector of the People for the sixth time, Emperor, Father of the Country, Consul-Elect for the fourth time, issues the following official statement:

As regards certain ancient controversies, the settlement of which had already been left pending for some years when my uncle Tiberius was Emperor: my uncle had sent one Pinarius Apollinaris to inquire into such of these controversies as concerned the Comensians (so far as I recall) and the Bergalians, but no others; and this Pinarius had neglected his commission because of my uncle's obstinate absence from Rome; and then when my nephew Gaius became Emperor and did not call for any report from him either, he offered none – he was no fool in the circumstances – and after that I had a report from Camurius Statutus to the effect that much of the agricultural and forest land in those parts was really under my own jurisdiction – so then, to come down to the present day, I recently sent my good friend Planta Julius there and, when he called a meeting of my governors, both the local governors and those whose districts lay some distance away, he went thoroughly into all these questions and drew his conclusions. I now approve the wording of the following edict which – first justifying it with a lucid report – he has drawn up for my signature; though it embodies wider decisions than Pinarius was called upon to make:

'As regards the position of the Anaunians, the Tulliassians, and the Sindunians, I understand from authoritative sources that some of these have become incorporated in the government of the Southern Tyrol, though not all. Now although I observe that the claims of men of these tribes to Roman citizenship rest on none too secure a foundation, yet, since they may be said to have come into possession of it by squatter's right and to have mixed so closely with the Southern Tyrolese that they could not be separated from them now without serious injury being done to that distinguished body of citizens, I hereby voluntarily grant them permission to continue in the enjoyment of the rights which they have assumed. I do this all the more readily because a large number of the men whose legal status is affected are reported to be serving in the Guards Division – a few of them have risen to command companies – and some of their compatriots have been enrolled for jury-service at Rome and are carrying out their duties there.

'This favour carries with it retrospective legal sanction for whatever actions they have performed, and whatever contracts they have entered into under the impression that they were Roman citizens, either among themselves or among the Southern Tyrolese, or in any other circumstances; and such names as they have hitherto borne, as though they were Roman citizens, I hereby permit them to retain.'

SURVIVING FRAGMENTS OF CLAUDIUS'S SPEECH TO THE SENATE, PROPOSING THE EXTENSION OF THE ROMAN CITIZENSHIP TO THE FRENCH OF THE AUTUN DISTRICT

A.D. 48

I must beg you in advance, my Lords, to revise your first shocked impressions, on listening to the proposal I am about to make, that it is a most revolutionary one: such feelings, I foresee, will be the strongest obstacle which I shall encounter to-day. Perhaps the best way for me to negotiate this obstacle is to remind you how many changes have been made in our constitution in the course of Roman history, how extremely plastic, indeed, it has proved from the very beginning.

At one time Rome was ruled by kings, yet the monarchy never became hereditary. Strangers won the crown, and even foreigners: such as Romulus's successor, King Numa, who was a native of Sabinum (then still a foreign state though lying so close to Rome), and Tarquin the First, who succeeded Ancus Martius. Tarquin was of far from distinguished birth – his father was Demarathus, a Corinthian, and his mother was so poor that though she came of the noble Tarquin family she was forced to marry below her – so, being debarred from holding honourable office at Corinth, Tarquin came here and was elected king. He and his son, or perhaps his grandson – historians are unable to agree even on this point – were succeeded by Servius Tullius, who, according to Roman accounts, was the son of Ocresia, a captive woman. Etruscan records make him the faithful companion of the Etruscan Caele Vipinas and sharer in all his misfortunes: they say that when Caele had been defeated, Servius Tullius left Etruria with the remnants of Caele's army

756

and seized the Caelian hill yonder, which he named after their former commander. He then changed his Etruscan name – it was Macstrna – to Tullius, and won the Roman crown, and made a very good king too. Later, when Tarquin the Proud and his sons began to be loathed for their tyrannical behaviour, the Roman people, please observe, grew tired of monarchical government and we had Consuls, annually elected magistrates, instead.

Need I then remind you of the dictatorship, which our ancestors found a stronger form of government even than the consular power in difficult times of war or political discord? Or of the appointment of Protectors of the People to defend the rights of the commons against encroachment? Or of the Board of Ten which for a time took over the government from the Consuls? Or of the sharing of the consular power between several persons? Or of the irregular appointment of army colonels to the Consulship – it happened seven or eight times? Or of the granting to members of the commons not only the highest magistracies but admission to the priesthood too? However, I shall not dilate on the early struggles of our ancestors and what the outcome of it all has been; you might suspect that I was immodestly making this historical survey an excuse for boasting of our recent extension of the Empire beyond the northern seas. ...

It was the will of my uncle, the Emperor Tiberius, that all leading colonies and provincial towns in Italy should have representatives sitting in this House; and representatives were indeed found with the necessary qualifications of character and wealth. 'Yes,' you will say, 'but there is a great difference between an Italian senator and a senator from abroad.' Well, when I begin justifying to you this part of my action, as Censor, in extending the full Roman citizenship to the provinces, I shall show you just how I feel about the matter. But let me say briefly that I do not think that we ought to debar provincials from a seat in this House, if they can be a credit to it, merely because they are provincials. The renowned and splendid colony of Vienne, in France, has been sending us senators for a long time now, has it not? My dear friend Lucius Vestinus comes from Vienne: he is one of the most distinguished members of the Noble Order of Knights and I employ him here to assist me in my administrative duties. (I have, by the way, a favour to ask from you for Vestinus's children: I wish to have the highest honours of the priesthood conferred on them – I trust that later they will earn distinctions by their own merits to add to those granted them on their father's account.) There is, however, one Frenchman whose name I shall keep out of this speech, because he was a rascally robber and I hate the very mention of him. He was a sort of wrestling-school prodigy and carried a Consulship back to his colony before the place had even been granted the Roman citizenship. I have an equally low opinion of his brother – such a miserable and unworthy wretch that he could not possibly be of any use to you as a senator.

But it is now high time, Tiberius Claudius Germanicus, for you to reveal to the House the theme of your speech: you have already reached the frontiers of the South of France. ...

... This House should be no more ashamed of these noble gentlemen, now standing before me, were they raised to the quality of senators, than my distinguished friend Periscus is ashamed when he finds the French name Allobrogicus among the funeral masks of his ancestors. If you agree that all this is as I say, what more do you want of me? Do you want me to prove to you from the map, putting my finger on the very spot, that you are already getting senators from beyond the frontier of Southern France, that no shame, in fact, has been felt about introducing men into our order who were born at *Lyons*?* O my Lords, I protest that it is with the greatest timidity that I venture beyond the familiar home-boundaries of Southern France! However, the cause of the rest of that great country must now definitely be pleaded. I grant you that the French fought against Julius Caesar (now deified) for ten years, but in return you must grant me that for a whole century since then they have preserved a more devoted loyalty to us, in times of disorder too, than we could ever have believed possible. When my father Drusus was engaged in the conquest of Germany the entire land of France remained at peace in his rear; and that, too, at a time when he had been called away from the business of taking a census of property-holders – a new and disquieting experience for the French. Why, even to-day, as I have only too good reason to know by personal experience, this taking of the census is a most arduous task, though it now means no more than a public review of our material resources. ...

Chapter 28

ONE morning in August, the year of the census, Messalina came early into my bedroom and woke me up. It always takes me a long time to collect my wits when I first wake up, especially if I have been unable to sleep between midnight and dawn, as is A.D. 48 often the case. She bent over me and kissed me and stroked my hair and told me in tones of the greatest concern that she had terrible news for me. I asked drowsily and rather crossly what it was.

'Barbillus the astrologer – you know that he never makes a mis-

* A joking reference to himself. – R.G.

take, don't you? Well, I asked him to read my stars yesterday, because he'd not done it for two or three years, and he observed them last night, and do you know what he has just come and told me?'

'Of course I don't know. Out with it and let me go on sleeping. I've had a wretched night.'

'Darling, I wouldn't dare to disturb you like this if it wasn't terribly important. What he said was, "Lady Messalina, a frightful fate is in store for one very near to you. This is Saturn's baleful influence once more. He is in his most malignant aspect. The blow will fall within thirty days, not later than the Ides of September." I asked him whom he meant, but he wouldn't tell me. He just kept on hinting, and at last I dragged it out of him by threatening to have him flogged. And guess what he said!'

'I hate guessing when I'm half-asleep.'

'But I hate telling you directly, it's so frightening. He said: "Lady Messalina, your husband will die a violent death".'

'He really said that?'

She nodded solemnly.

I sat up, my heart pounding. Yes, Barbillus was always right in his forecasts. And that meant that I would not survive my attempted introduction of the new constitution by more than a few days. I had planned my speech for the seventh of September, the anniversary of my victory at Brentwood: but I had kept the whole business a complete secret from everyone, even Messalina, from whom otherwise I had no secrets. I said: 'Is there nothing to be done? Can't we cheat the prophecy somehow?'

'I can't think of anything. You're my husband, aren't you? Unless ... unless ... listen, I have an idea! Suppose that just for this next month you aren't my husband.'

'But I am. You can't pretend I'm not.'

'You can divorce me, can't you, just for a month? And marry me again when Barbillus reports that Saturn has moved away to a safe distance.'

'No, that's not possible. If I divorce you we can't legally remarry unless there has been a marriage in between.'

'I didn't think of that. But don't let us be beaten by a mere technicality. Suppose, then, that I do marry someone – anyone – just as a matter of form. A cook or a porter or one of the Palace Guards. Only the ceremonial part of the marriage, of course. We'd go into the nuptial-chamber by one door and then come right out again by another. That's not a bad idea, is it?'

I thought that there was something in it; but obviously she must marry someone of rank and importance, or it would create a bad impression. First I suggested Vitellius, and she said smiling that Vitellius already felt so sentimentally about her that it would be cruel to marry him and not allow him to spend the night with her. Besides, what about the prophecy? I didn't want to doom Vitellius to a violent death, did I?

So we discussed various husbands for her. The only one that we could agree on was Silius, the Consul-Elect, a son of that Silius, my brother Germanicus's general, whom Tiberius had accused of high treason and forced to suicide. I disliked him because he had led the opposition in the Senate to my measure for the extension of the franchise and had been very insolent to me. After my speech about the franchise, he had been asked to give his opinion. He said that he thought it strange that our ancient allies, the noble and illustrious Greek cities of Lycia, should remain deprived of their freedom (I had annexed Lycia five years previously because of continued political unrest there, and also the neighbouring island of Rhodes, where they had impaled some Roman citizens) while the Celtic barbarians of the north should be admitted to the fullest rights of Roman citizenship. When I came to answer this objection, which was almost the only one raised, I did so in the pleasantest possible way. I began, 'It is indeed a long way from famous Lycia, from

Xanthus' lucid stream,

where, in the poet Horace's words that we heard sung last year at the Saecular Games,

Apollo most delights to bathe his hair,

to France and the huge dark River Rhône, the huge dark River Rhône ... of which no mention whatsoever appears in Classical legend, apart from a doubtful visit by Hercules, in the course of his Tenth Labour, on his way to win the oxen of Geryones. But I do not think ...' I was interrupted by a tittering that soon swelled into a roar of laughter. It appears that when I repeated 'the huge dark River Rhône' and hesitated for a moment, in search of a phrase, Silius had remarked in an audible voice – but he was sitting on my deaf side, so I had not heard the interruption – 'Yes, the huge dark River Rhône, where, if historians do not lie,

Claudius most delights to bathe his hair.'

A reference to the occasion when I was flung over a bridge into that river at Caligula's orders and nearly drowned. You can imagine how angry I was when Narcissus explained what the laughter was about. It is all very well to make little personal jokes at a private supper table or at the baths, or more boisterous ones during Saturn's All Fools' Festival (to which, by the way, I had restored the fifth day removed by Caligula), but for my own part it would never occur to me to make any sort of personal joke in the Senate which could raise an unkind laugh against a fellow member; and that a Consul-Elect had done so at my expense, and in the presence too of a group of prominent Frenchmen whom I had brought into the House, I took very ill. I shouted out: 'My Lords, I invited you to give your opinions on my motion, but from the noise that you are making anyone would mistake this for the cheapest sort of knocking-shop. Please observe the rules of the House. Whatever will these French gentlemen think of us?' The noise stopped instantly. It always did when they saw I was angry.

Messalina said that she would like very much to marry Silius, not only because of his rudeness to me, which certainly merited astral vengeance, but because by the way he looked at her she felt sure that his rudeness was based on jealousy and that he was passionately in love with her. It would be a neat punishment for his presumption if she told him that she was being divorced and would marry him, and then only at the very last minute let him discover that it was to be a marriage in form only.

So we chose Silius, and that very day I signed a document repudiating Messalina as my wife and permitting her to return to her paternal roof. There were a lot of jokes about it between us. Messalina pretended to plead for permission to stay, falling on her knees before me and asking pardon for her errors. She also weepingly embraced the children, who did not know what to make of the business: 'Must these poor darlings suffer for a mother's faults, cruel man?'

I replied that her faults were unpardonable: she was too clever, too beautiful and too industrious to stay with me an hour longer. She set an impossible standard for other wives to live up to, and made me the object of universal jealousy.

She whispered in my ear: 'If I come into the Palace some night next week and commit adultery with you, will you banish me? I might be tempted, you know.'

'Yes, I'll banish you, all right. I'll banish myself too. Where shall we go? I'd like to visit Alexandria. They say it's an ideal place for banishment.'

'And take the children too? They'd love it.'

'I don't think the climate would suit them. They'd have to stay here with your mother, I'm afraid.'

'Mother knows nothing about the proper bringing-up of children: look at the way she brought me up! If you won't bring the children too, I won't come and commit adultery with you.'

'Then I'll marry Lollia Paulina, just to spite you.'

'Then I'll murder Lollia Paulina. I'll send her poisoned cakes, like the ones Caligula used to send people who had made him their heir.'

'Well, here's your divorce document all signed and sealed, you slut. Now you're restored to all the rights and privileges of an unmarried woman.'

'Let us kiss, Claudius, before we part.'

'It reminds me of the famous farewell between Hector and Andromache in the Sixth Book of the *Iliad*:

> His princess parts with a prophetic sigh,
> Unwilling parts, and oft reverts her eye
> That streamed at every look; then, moving slow,
> Sought her own palace and indulged her woe.

Here, don't be in such a hurry to run off stage with your divorce. You ought to take a few private lessons in acting from Mnester.'

'I'm my own mistress now. If you're not careful I'll marry Mnester.'

Silius was supposed to be the best-looking nobleman in Rome and Messalina had long been fascinated by him. But he was not by any means an easy victim of her passion. In the first place he was a virtuous man, or at least prided himself on his virtue, and then he was married to a noblewoman of the Silanus family, a sister of Caligula's first wife, and finally, though Messalina attracted him physically in the highest degree, he knew of the indiscriminate generosity with which she had been conferring her favours on nobleman, commoner, sword-fighter, actor, guardsman, even on one of the Parthian ambassadors, and did not consider himself particularly honoured by being asked to join their company. So she had to hook and play her fish with great cunning. The first difficulty lay in persuading him to visit her privately. She invited him several times, but he excused himself. She managed it in the end only by an arrangement with the Commander of the Watchmen, a former lover of hers, who invited Silius to supper and then had him shown into a room where she was waiting for him with supper laid for two. Once he was there he could not easily escape, and she was very clever: she did not talk love at all at first, she talked revolutionary politics! She reminded him of his murdered father and asked him whether he could bear to see the murderer's nephew, a bloodier tyrant still, clamping the yoke of slavery tighter and tighter on the neck of a once free people. (This was myself, in case you do not recognize me.) Then she told him that she was in danger of her life because she had been constantly reproaching me for not restoring the Republic and for my cruel murders of innocent men and women. She said, too, that I had despised her beauty and preferred housemaids and common prostitutes and that it was only in revenge for my disregard that she had ever been unfaithful to me; her promiscuity had been the result of extreme despair and loneliness. He, Silius, was the only man she knew who was virtuous and bold enough to help her in the task to which she had now dedicated her life – the restoration of the Republic. Would he forgive the innocent trick that she had played in decoying him there?

Frankly I cannot blame Silius for being deceived by her: she deceived me daily for nine years. Remember that she was very beautiful; and you can assume, too, that she had doctored his wine. Naturally he tried to comfort her, and before he realized what was happening, they were lying in each other's arms on the couch mixing the words 'love' and 'liberty' with kisses and sighs. She said that only now did she know what true love meant, and he swore that with her help he would restore the Republic at the earliest opportunity, and she swore to remain everlastingly faithful to his love if he divorced his wife, who, she knew, was secretly unfaithful to him, and was barren too – Silius ought not to let his family die out – and so on, and so on. She had hooked him, and now she played him for all her worth.

But Silius was cautious as well as virtuous, and did not feel himself strong enough to raise an armed revolt. He divorced his wife but told Messalina, on second thoughts, that it would be best if they waited for me to die before restoring the Republic. Then he would marry her and adopt Britannicus, and this would make the City and Army look to him as their natural leader. Messalina saw that she would have to take action herself. So she worked the

Barbillus trick on me as I have described, and Silius (if what he told me afterwards was the truth) knew nothing of the divorce until she went to him with the document, without explaining how she came by it, and told him joyfully that they could now get married and live happily ever afterwards, but that he must tell nobody about it until she gave him permission.

Everyone at Rome was astounded at the news of Messalina's divorce, particularly as it seemed to make no difference to me: I continued to show her as much respect as before, or even more, and she continued her political work at the Palace. But every day she visited Silius at his house, quite openly, with a full retinue of attendants. When I suggested that she was carrying the joke rather too far, she told me that she was finding some difficulty in consenting to make him marry her. 'I'm afraid that he suspects that there's some catch in it, and he's very polite and reserved, but underneath he's boiling with passion for me, the beast!' After a few days of this she gleefully reported that he had consented and would marry her on the tenth of September. She asked me to officiate as High Pontiff and see the fun. 'Won't it be lovely to watch his baffled face when he finds he's been cheated?' By this time I had begun to repent of the whole business, especially of this practical joke on Silius, although he had insulted me in the Senate again with another ill-mannered interruption. I decided that I should not have taken the prophecy seriously and that I had only done so because I was half-awake when Messalina told me of it. And if the prophecy was really true, how could it be evaded by a mock-marriage? It occurred to me that no marriage is recognized as such by law until it has been physically consummated. I tried to persuade Messalina to drop the whole business, but she told me that I was jealous of Silius and that she thought that I was losing my sense of humour and becoming a silly old spoil-sport and pedant. I said no more.

On the morning of the fifth of September I went down to Ostia to dedicate a big new granary there. I had told Messalina that I would not be back until the following morning. Messalina said that she wanted to come too, and it was arranged that we would drive down there together; but at the last moment she had one of her famous sick-headaches and had to stay behind. I was disappointed, but it was too late to change my plans, since a civic reception had been arranged for me at Ostia, and I had promised to sacrifice in the Temple of Augustus there: ever since the occasion on which I had lost my temper with the Ostians for not receiving me properly I had been particularly careful not to hurt their feelings.

Early that afternoon as I was going into the Temple to the sacrifice, Euodus, one of my freedmen, handed me a note. It was now Euodus's duty to protect me from inopportune petitions from the general public: all notes were handed to him, and if he considered them frivolous or insane or not worth my attention I was not bothered with them. It is surprising what reams of nonsense people write in petitions. Euodus said, 'Excuse me, Caesar, but I can't read this. A woman handed it to me. Perhaps you can be bothered just this once?' To my surprise it was written in Etruscan, an extinct language known to not more than four or five living people, and read: 'Great danger to Rome and yourself. Come to my house at once. Don't waste a moment.' It startled and puzzled me. Why Etruscan? Whose house? What danger? And it was a minute or two before I understood. It must be from Calpurnia, the girl, you remember, who had lived with me before I married Messalina: it had amused me to teach her Etruscan while I was compiling my history of Etruria. Calpurnia had probably sent me the note in Etruscan not only because it would be unintelligible to anyone but myself, but because I would know that it really came from her. I asked Euodus: 'Did you see the woman?' He said that she looked like an Egyptian and had a pock-marked forehead but was otherwise very good-looking. I recognized this as Cleopatra, Calpurnia's friend who shared the house with her.

I was due to go down to the docks immediately after the sacrifice and could not decently postpone the engagement: it would be thought that I was more interested in visiting a couple of prostitutes than in attending to Imperial business. Yet I knew that Calpurnia was not the sort of person to send me an idle message, and while I was sacrificing I decided that I must hear what she had to say at all costs. I would sham sick, perhaps. Fortunately the God Augustus came to my assistance: the entrails of the ram I now sacrificed to him were the most unpropitious ones I had ever seen. It had seemed a fine animal, too, but inside it was as rotten as an old cheese. It was plainly impossible for me to transact any public business on that day, particularly so serious a matter as the dedication of the largest granary in the world, as this was. So I excused myself and everyone agreed that my decision was a proper one. I went to my own villa and gave out that I would rest there for the remainder of the day, but would be glad to attend the banquet to which I had been invited that night, so long as it had no official character. I then sent my sedan-chair round to the back entrance of the villa and was soon being carried in it, with the curtains drawn, to Calpurnia's pretty house on a hill just outside the town.

Calpurnia greeted me with a look of such anxious sorrow that I knew at once that something very serious had happened. 'Tell me at once!' I said. 'What's the matter?'

She began to cry. I had never seen Calpurnia cry before, except once on the famous occasion when I was sent for at midnight to the Palace by Caligula's orders and she thought that I was going to my execution. She was a self-possessed girl with none of the tricks and manners of the ordinary prostitute and 'as true as a Roman sword', as the saying is. 'You promise to listen? But you'll not want to believe me. You'll want to have me tortured and flogged. I don't want to tell you, either. But nobody else dares tell you, so I must. I promised Narcissus and Pallas that I would. They were good friends to me in the old days when we were all poor together. They said that you'd not believe them, or anyone, but I said that I thought you'd believe me, because once I showed myself your true friend when you were in trouble. I gave you all my savings, didn't I? I was never greedy or jealous or dishonest, was I?'

'Calpurnia, in my life I have known only three really good women, and I'll tell you their names. One was Cypros, a Jewish princess; one was old Briseis, my mother's wardrobe-maid; and the third is you. Now tell me what you have to say.'

'You've left out Messalina.'

'Messalina goes without saying. Very well, then, four really good women. And I don't consider that I'm insulting Messalina by linking her with an Oriental princess, a Greek freedwoman, and a prostitute from Padua. The sort of goodness I mean isn't the prerogative - -'

'If you put Messalina in the list, leave me out,' she said, gasping.

'Modest, Calpurnia? You needn't be. I mean what I say.'

'No. Not modest.'

'Then I don't understand.'

Calpurnia said, very slowly and painfully: 'I hate to hurt you, Claudius. But I mean this. I mean that if Cypros had been a typical princess of the Herod family – if she had been blood-thirsty and ambitious and unscrupulous and without any moral restraint; and if Briseis had been a typical wardrobe-maid – if she had been thieving and base-minded and lazy and clever at covering up her tracks; and if your Calpurnia had been a typical prostitute – if I had been vain, lustful, promiscuous, and greedy, and used my beauty as a means for dominating and ruining men – and if you were now listing the three worst types of women you knew and happened to pick on us as convenient examples –'

'– Then what? What are you getting at? You talk so slowly.'

'– Then, Claudius, you'd be right to add Messalina to us and to tell me, "Messalina goes without saying".'

'Am I mad, or are you?'

'Not I.'

'Then what do you mean? What's my poor Messalina done to be suddenly attacked in this violent and extraordinary way? I don't think that you and I are going to remain friends much longer, Calpurnia.'

'You left town at seven o'clock this morning.'

'Yes. And what of it?'

'I left at ten. I had been up there with Cleopatra doing some shopping. I looked in at the wedding. A curious hour of the day for a wedding, wasn't it? They were having a grand time. Everyone drunk. Marvellous show. The whole house decorated with vine-leaves and ivy and enormous bunches of grapes, and wine-vats, and wine-presses. The vintage festival, that was what it was supposed to represent.'

'What wedding? Talk sense.'

'Messalina's wedding to Silius. Weren't you invited? She was there dancing and waving a thyrsus in the biggest wine-vat she could find, dressed in a short wine-stained white tunic with one breast exposed and her hair flying loose. She was almost decent, though, compared with the other women. They only wore leopard-skins, because they were Bacchantes. Silius was Bacchus. He was crowned with ivy and wore buskins. He was even drunker than Messalina. He kept tossing his head about in time to the music and grinning like Baba.'

'But ... but ...,' I said stupidly. 'The wedding isn't until the tenth. I'm to officiate.'

'They're managing nicely without you. So I went to Narcissus at the Palace, and when he saw me, he said: "Thank God you're here, Calpurnia. You're the only one he'll believe." And Pallas – –'

'I don't believe. I refuse to believe.'

Calpurnia clapped her hands. 'Cleopatra, Narcissus!' They came in and fell at my feet. 'It's true about the wedding, isn't it?'

They agreed that it was true.

'But I know all about it,' I said feebly. 'It's not a real wedding, my friends. It's a sort of joke that Messalina and I planned. She's not going to bed with him at the end of the ceremony. It's all quite innocent.'

Narcissus said: 'Silius caught at her and pulled up her tunic and began kissing her body in full view of the company, and she screamed and laughed and then he carried her off to the nuptial-chamber, and they stayed there nearly an hour before coming out again to do a little more drinking and dancing. That's not innocent, Caesar, surely?'

Calpurnia said: 'And unless you act at once, Silius will be master of Rome. Everyone I met told me that Messalina and Silius have sworn by their own heads to restore the Republic, and that they have the whole Senate behind them and most of the Guards.'

'I must hear more,' I said. 'I don't know whether to laugh or cry. I don't know whether to pour gold in your laps or flog you until the bones show.'

They told me more, but Narcissus would only speak on condition that I forgave him for hiding Messalina's crimes from me so long. He said that when he was first aware of them and I seemed happy in my innocence, he had resolved to spare me the pain of disillusionment so long as Messalina did nothing which endangered my life or the safety of the country. He had hoped that she might mend her ways or else that I would find out about her for myself. But as time went on and her behaviour grew more and more shameless, it became more and more difficult to tell me. In fact, he could not believe that I did not know by now what all Rome, and all the provinces for that matter, and our enemies over the frontier, knew. In the course of nine years it seemed impossible that I should not have heard of her debaucheries, which were astounding in their impudence.

Cleopatra told me the most horrible and ludicrous story. During my absence in Britain Messalina had issued a challenge to the Prostitutes' Guild asking them to provide a champion to contend with her at the Palace, and see which of the two would wear out most gallants in the course of a night. The Guild had sent a famous Sicilian named Scylla, after the whirlpool in the Straits of Messina. When dawn came Scylla had been forced to confess herself beaten at the twenty-fifth gallant but Messalina had continued, out of bravado, until the sun was quite high in the sky. And, what was worse, most of the nobility at Rome had been invited to attend the contest, and many of the men had taken part in it; and three or four of the women had been persuaded by Messalina to compete too.

I sat weeping with my head in my hands, just as Augustus had done some fifty years before, when his grandsons Gaius and Lucius told him the same sort of story about their mother Julia; and in Augustus's very words I said that I had never heard the slightest whisper or entertained the faintest suspicion that Messalina was not the chastest woman in Rome. And like Augustus I had the impulse to shut myself away in a room and see nobody for days. But they would not let me. Two lines out of a musical comedy that Mnester's company had played a few days before – I forget the name – kept hammering absurdly in my brain :

> I know no sound so laughable, so laughable and sad,
> As an old man weeping for his wife, a girl gone to the bad.

I said to Narcissus: 'At the first Games I ever saw (I was acting as joint-President with my brother Germanicus) – Games in honour of my father, you know – I saw a Spanish sword-fighter have his shield-arm lopped off at the shoulder. He was close to me and I saw his face clearly. Such a stupid look when he saw what had happened. And the whole amphitheatre roared with laughter at him. I thought it was funny too, God forgive me.'

Chapter 29

THEN Xenophon came in and forced a drink between my lips, because I was on the point of collapse, and took me in hand generally. I don't know exactly what decoction he gave me, but it had the effect of making me feel very clear-headed and self-possessed and utterly impersonal about everything. My feet seemed to be treading on clouds like a god. It also affected the focus of my eyes, so that I saw Narcissus and Calpurnia and Pallas as if they were standing twenty paces away instead of quite close.

'Send for Turranius and Lusius Geta.' Turranius was my Superintendent of Stores now that Callon was dead, and Geta, as I have told you, was the joint-Commander of the Guards with Crispinus.

I cross-examined them, after first assuring them that I would not punish them if they spoke the truth. They confirmed all that Narcissus and Calpurnia and Cleopatra had told me, and told me a lot more. When I asked Geta to explain frankly why he had failed to report all this to me before, he said: 'May I quote a proverb, Caesar, that is often on your own lips: *The knee is nearer than the shin?* What happened to Justus, my predecessor, when he tried to let you know what was happening in your wife's wing of the Palace?'

Turranius replied to the same question by reminding me that when recently he had summoned the courage to come to me with a complaint of the seizure of public stores at Messalina's orders – basalt blocks imported from Egypt for the repaving of the Ox Market – for use, it turned out, in a new colonnade that she was building in the Gardens of Lucullus, I had grown angry and told him never again to question any act or order of hers, saying that nothing that she did was done except at my particular instance or at least with my full sanction. I had told him that if he ever again had any complaint to make against the Lady Messalina's behaviour he was to make it to the Lady Messalina herself. Turranius was right. I had actually said that.

Calpurnia, who had been fidgeting impatiently in the background while I was questioning Geta and Turranius, now caught my eye pleadingly. I understood that she wanted a word with me alone. I cleared the room at once and then she said gently and earnestly: 'My dear, you won't get anywhere by asking the same question over and over again from different people. It's quite plain: they were all afraid to tell you, partly because they knew how much you loved and trusted Messalina, but mostly because you were Emperor. You have been very foolish and very unlucky and now you must do something to retrieve the position. If you don't act at once you will be sentencing us all to death. Every minute counts. You must go at once to the Guards Camp and get the protection of all the loyal troops there. I can't believe that they'll desert you for Messalina's and Silius's sake. There may be one or two colonels or captains who have been bought over, but the rank and file are devoted to you. Send mounted messengers to Rome at once to announce that you are on your way to take vengeance on

Silius and your wife. Send warrants for the arrest of everyone present at the wedding. That will probably be enough to smother the revolt. They'll all be too drunk to do anything dangerous. But hurry!'

'Oh, yes,' I said. 'I'll hurry!'

I called in Narcissus again. 'Do you trust Geta?'

'To be honest, Caesar, I don't altogether trust him.'

'And the two captains he has with him here?'

'I trust them, but they're stupid.'

'Crispinus is away on leave at Baiae, so whom shall we put in command of the Guards, if we can't trust Geta?'

'If Calpurnia was a man, I'd say, Calpurnia. But since she's not, the next best choice is myself. I'm a mere freedman, I know, but the Guards officers know me and like me, and it would only be for a single day.'

'Very well, General-of-the-Day Narcissus. Tell Geta that he's confined to bed by doctor's orders until to-morrow. Give me pen and parchment. Wait a moment. What's the date? September the fifth? Here's your commission, then. Show it to the captains and send them on to Rome at once with their men to arrest the whole wedding party. No violence, though, except in self-defence; tell them. Let the Guards know that I'm coming and that I expect them to remain loyal to me, and that their loyalty won't pass unrewarded.'

It is about eighteen miles from Ostia to Rome, but the soldiers covered the distance in an hour and a half, using fast gigs. As it happened, the wedding was just breaking up when they arrived. The cause was a knight called Vettius Valens, who had been one of Messalina's lovers before Silius came on the scene, and was still in her favour. The party had come to the stage that parties reach when the first excitement of drink has worn off and everyone begins to feel a little tired and at a loss. Interest now centred on Vettius Valens: he was hugging a fine evergreen oak-tree which grew outside the house, and talking to an imaginary Dryad inside it. The Dryad had apparently fallen in love with him and was inviting him in a whisper, audible only to himself, to a rendezvous at the top of the tree. He finally consented to join her there and made his friends form a human pyramid to enable him to climb up to the first big bough. The pyramid collapsed twice amid shrieks of laughter, but Vettius persevered and at the third try got astride of the bough. From there slowly and dangerously he climbed higher and higher until he disappeared into the thick foliage at the summit. Everyone stood gazing up to watch what would happen next. Expectation ran high because Vettius was a famous comedian. Soon he began imitating the Dryad's affectionate cries and making loud smacking kiss-noises and uttering little squeals of excitement. Then Vettius kept very quiet, until the crowd began calling up to him: 'Vettius, Vettius, what are you doing?'

'I'm just viewing the world. This is the best look-out anywhere in Rome. The Dryad's sitting on my lap and pointing out places of interest; so don't interrupt. Yes, that's the Senate House. Silly girl, I knew that! And that's Colchester! But surely you're mistaken? You can't see as far as Colchester from this tree, can you? You must mean the Guards Camp. No, it *is* Colchester, by God. I can see the name written up on a notice board and blue-faced Britons walking about. What's that? What are they doing? No, I don't believe it. What, worshipping Claudius as a God?' And then in an imitation of my voice: '*Why*, though, I want to know *why*? Nobody else to worship? Have the other Gods refused to cross the Channel? I don't blame them. I was dreadfully sea-sick myself, crossing the Channel.'

Vettius's audience was entranced. When he was silent again they called out: 'Vettius, Vettius! What are you doing now?'

He answered, imitating my voice again: 'In the first place, if I don't want to answer, I won't answer. You can't make me. I'm a free man, aren't I? In fact one of the freest men in Rome.'

'Oh, do tell us, Vettius.'

'Look there! Look there! A thousand Furies and Serpents! Let me go, Dryad, let me go at once. No, no, another time. Can't wait for that sort of thing now. Must get down. Hands off, Dryad!'

'What's happening, Vettius?'

'Run for your lives. I've just seen a fearful sight. No, stop! Trogus, Proculus, help me down first! But everyone else run for your lives!'

'What? What?'

'A terrific storm coming up from Ostia! Run for your lives!'

And the crowd actually did scatter. Laughing and screaming and headed by the bride and bridegroom they rushed out of the garden into the street a few seconds before my soldiers came galloping up. Messalina got safely away, and so did Silius, but the soldiers had no difficulty in arresting about 200 of the guests, and later picked up about fifty more who were stumbling drunkenly home. Messalina was accompanied by only three companions. There had been twenty or more with her at first, but as soon as the alarm was raised that the Guards were coming they deserted her. She went on foot through the City until she came to the Gardens of Lucullus, by which time she had sobered somewhat. She decided that she must go to Ostia at once and try the effect of her beauty on me again – it had never hitherto failed to cheat me – and bring the children with her too as a reinforcement. She was still barefooted and wearing her vintage costume, which had earned her hisses and jeers as she hurried through the streets. She sent a maid to the Palace to fetch her the children, sandals, some jewellery, and a clean gown. The quality of the love between her and Silius was shown by their immediate desertion of each other at the first sign of danger. Messalina prepared to sacrifice him to my rage, and Silius went to the Market Place to resume his judicial work there as if nothing had happened. He was drunk enough to think that he could pretend complete innocence, and when the captains came to arrest him he told them that he was busy, and what did they want? Their answer was to handcuff him and lead him off to the Camp.

Meanwhile I had been joined by Vitellius and Caecina (my colleague in my second Consulship) who had accompanied me down to Ostia and after the sacrifice had gone off to visit friends on the other side of the town. I told them briefly what had happened and said that I was returning to Rome immediately: I expected them to support me and witness the impartiality with which I would visit judgement on the guilty of whatever rank or station. The Olympian effect of the drug continued. I talked calmly, fluently, and, I think, sensibly. Vitellius and Caecina made no reply at first, expressing astonishment and concern only in their looks. When I asked them what they thought about the whole business, Vitellius would still only utter exclamations of astonishment and horror such as, 'They really told you that! Oh, how horrible! What vile treason!' and Caecina followed his example. The carriage of state was announced and Narcissus, whom I had directed to write out a charge-sheet against Messalina, and who had been busy questioning the staff so as to make the list of her adulteries as full as possible, then showed himself a brave man and a faithful servant. 'Caesar, please inform your noble friends who I am for to-day and give me a seat in this carriage with you. Until my Lords Vitellius and Caecina come out with an honest opinion, and refrain from making remarks that can be construed either as a condemnation of your wife or as condemnation of her accusers, it is my duty as your Guards Commander to remain by your side.'

I am glad that he came with me. As we drove towards the City I began telling Vitellius about Messalina's pretty ways and how much I had loved her and how vilely she had deceived me. He sighed deeply and said: 'A man would have to be stone, not to be melted by beauty like hers.' I spoke about the children, too, and Caecina and Vitellius sighed in unison: 'The poor, dear children! They must not be allowed to suffer.' But the nearest that either of them came to expressing a real opinion was when Vitellius exclaimed: 'It is almost impossible for anyone who has felt for Messalina the admiration and tenderness that I have felt, to believe these filthy accusations, though a thousand trustworthy witnesses were to swear that they were true.' And when Caecina agreed, 'Oh, what an evil and sorrowful world we live in!' An embarrassment was in store for them. Two vehicles were seen approaching through the dusk. One was another carriage, drawn by white horses, and in it sat Vibidia, the oldest and most honoured of the Vestal Virgins: eighty-five years old and one of my dearest friends. Behind this carriage followed a cart with a big yellow L painted on it, one of the carts belonging to the Gardens of Lucullus and used for carrying soil and rubbish. In it were Messalina and the children. Narcissus took in the situation at a glance: he had better eyes than I have and stopped the carriage. 'Here's the Vestal Vibidia come to meet you, Caesar,' he said. 'No doubt she'll ask you to forgive Messalina. Vibidia is a dear old soul, and I think the world of her, but for God's sake don't make her any rash promises. Remember how monstrously you've been treated and remember that Messalina and Silius are traitors to Rome. Be polite to Vibidia, by all means, but don't give away anything at all. Here's the charge-sheet. Look at it now, read the names. Look at the eleventh charge – Mnester. Are you going to forgive that? And Caesoninus, what about Caesoninus? What can you think of a woman who can play about with a creature like that?'

I took the parchment from him and as he stepped out of the carriage he whispered something in Vitellius's ear. I don't know what it was, but it decided Vitellius to keep his mouth shut in Narcissus's absence. While I was reading the charges by the light of a lantern Narcissus ran along the road and met Vibidia and

Messalina, who had also dismounted, coming towards him. Messalina was comparatively sober now: she called out gently to me from the distance: 'Hullo, Claudius! I've been such a silly girl! You'd never believe it of me!' For once my deafness was of service to me. I didn't recognize her voice or hear a word. Narcissus greeted Vibidia courteously, but refused to let Messalina come any farther. Messalina cursed and spat in his face and tried to dodge past, but he ordered the two sergeants whom we had with us to escort her to her cart and see that it drove back to the City. Messalina screamed as if she were being murdered or outraged, and I looked up from the parchment to ask what was the matter. Vitellius said: 'A woman in the crowd. Overcome by labour-pains, by the sound of it.'

Then Vibidia came slowly up to our carriage and Narcissus panted back after her. Narcissus did all the talking for me. He told Vibidia that Messalina's notorious and unexampled whoredoms and treacheries made it ludicrous for a pious and aged Vestal to come and plead with me for her life. 'You Vestals surely don't approve of having the Palace turned into a brothel again, as in Caligula's days, do you? You don't approve of ballet-dancers and sword-fighters performing between the sheets of the High Pontiff's bed, do you, with the active co-operation of the High Pontiff's wife?'

That gave Vibidia a shock: Messalina had only confessed to an 'indiscreet familiarity' with Silius. She said: 'I know nothing about that, but at least I must urge the High Pontiff to do nothing rashly, to shed no innocent blood, to condemn nobody unheard, to consider the honour of his house and his duty to the Gods.'

I broke in: 'Vibidia, Vibidia, my dear friend, I shall deal justly with Messalina, you can count on that.'

Narcissus said: 'Yes, indeed. The danger is that the High Pontiff may show his former wife an undeserved clemency. It is very difficult indeed for him to judge the case as impartially as it will be his official duty to do. I must therefore ask you on his behalf not to make things more painful for him than they already are. May I courteously suggest that you retire, my Lady Vibidia, and attend to the solemnities of the Goddess Vesta, which you understand so well?'

So she retired, and we drove on. As we came into the City, Messalina made another attempt to see me, I am told, but was restrained by the sergeants. She then tried to send Britannicus and little Octavia to plead with me for her, but Narcissus saw them running towards us and waved them back. I was sitting silent, brooding over the list of Messalina's lovers. Narcissus had headed it: 'Provisional and incomplete account of Valeria Messalina's notorious adulteries, from the first year of her marriage to Tiberius Claudius Caesar Augustus Germanicus Britannicus, Father of the Country, High Pontiff, etc., until the present day.' It contained forty-four names, later extended to 156.

Narcissus sent a message ordering the cart back to the Gardens: the traffic regulations forbade it to be in the streets at this hour. Messalina saw that she was beaten, so allowed herself to be carried back to the Gardens. The children had been sent to the Palace but her mother Domitia Lepida, though lately there had been a coolness between the two, bravely joined her in the cart; otherwise Messalina would have been quite alone but for the carter. Narcissus then told our coachman to drive on to Silius's house. When we reached it I said: 'This isn't the place, is it? Surely this is the family mansion of the Asinians?'

Narcissus explained: 'Messalina bought it privately when Asinius Gallus was banished, and gave it to Silius as a wedding present. Come inside and see for yourself what has been going on.'

I went in and saw the litter of the wedding – the vine-leaf decorations, the wine-vats and presses, tables covered with food and dirty plates, trampled rose-leaves and garlands on the floor, discarded leopard-skins, and wine spilt everywhere. The house was deserted except for an old porter and two dead-drunk lovers lying in each other's arms on the bed in the nuptial-chamber. I had them arrested. One was a staff-lieutenant called Montanus, the other was Narcissus's own niece, a young married woman with two children. What shocked and distressed me most was to find the whole house full of Palace furniture, not merely things that Messalina had brought me as part of her dowry when we were married, but ancient heirlooms of the Claudian and Julian families, including the very statues of my ancestors and the family masks, cupboard and all! There could be no plainer proof of her intentions than that. So we climbed into the carriage again and drove on to the Guards Camp. Narcissus was gloomy and subdued now, because he had been very fond of his niece; but Vitellius and Caecina had made up their minds that it would be safer for them to believe the evidence of their eyes, and simultaneously began urging me to vengeance. We reached the Camp, where I found the whole Division on parade, by Narcissus's orders, in front of the tribunal. It was dark now and the tribunal was lit by flaring torches. I climbed up on the platform and made a short speech. My voice was clear, but sounded very far away:

'Guards, my friend the late King Herod Agrippa, who first recommended me to you as your Emperor and then persuaded the Senate to accept your choice, told me on the last occasion that I saw him alive, and also wrote to me in the last letter that I ever had from him, never to trust anyone, for nobody about me was worthy of my trust. I did not take his words literally. I continued to repose the fullest confidence in my wife, Valeria Messalina, whom I now know to have been a whore, a liar, a thief, a murderess, and a traitor to Rome. I don't mean, Guards, that I don't trust you. You're the only people I do trust, you know. You're soldiers and do your duty without question. I expect you to stand by me now and crush the plot which my former wife Messalina and her adulterer, the Consul-Elect Gaius Silius, have formed against my life under a pretence of restoring popular liberty to the City again. The Senate is rotten with conspiracy, as rotten as the entrails of the ram that I sacrificed this afternoon to the God Augustus; you never saw such an unholy sight. I am ashamed to talk as I do, but that's right, isn't it? Help me bring my enemies – our enemies – to book and, once Messalina's dead, if I ever marry again I give you free and full leave to chop me to pieces with your swords, and use my head as a football at the Baths, like Sejanus's. Three times married, and three times unlucky. Well, what about it, lads? Tell me what you think. I can't get a straight answer from my other friends.'

'Kill them, Caesar!' – 'No mercy!' – 'Strangle the bitch!' – 'Death to them all!' – 'We'll stand by you!' – 'You've been too damned generous.' – 'Wipe them out, Caesar!' There was no doubt what the Guards thought of the matter.

So I had the arrested men and women brought up before me there and then, and ordered the arrest of 110 more men now named in the charge-sheet as Messalina's adulterers, and four women of rank who had prostituted themselves, at Messalina's suggestion, in the course of that notorious Palace orgy. I finished the trial in three hours. But this was because all but thirty-four of the 360 persons who answered their names pleaded guilty to the charges brought against them. Those whose only crime was their attendance at the wedding I banished. Twenty knights, six senators, and a Guards colonel, who all pleaded guilty to adultery or attempted revolution, or both, demanded to be executed at once. I granted them this favour. Vettius Valens tried to buy his life by offering to reveal the names of the ringleaders of the plot. I told him that I could find them out without his assistance and he was led off to execution. Montanus was mentioned in Narcissus's list, but pleaded that Messalina had forced him to spend the night with her by showing him an order to do so signed and sealed by me: and that after that single night she had tired of him. Messalina must have got my signature to the document by reading it out to me – 'just to save your precious eyes, my darling' – as something quite different. However, I pointed out that he had no order from me to attend the wedding or to commit adultery with my friend Narcissus's niece; so he was executed too. There were also fifteen suicides in the City that night by persons who had not been arrested but expected to be. Three intimate friends of mine, all knights, Trogus, Cotta, and Fabius, were among these. I suspect that Narcissus knew of their guilt but left them out of the charge-sheet for friendship's sake, contenting himself with sending them a warning.

Mnester would not plead guilty: he reminded me that he was under orders from me to obey my wife in everything, and said that he had obeyed her much against his will. He pulled off his clothes and showed the marks of a lash on his back. 'She gave me that because my natural modesty prevented me from carrying out your orders as energetically as she wished, Caesar.' I was sorry for Mnester. He had once saved that theatre-audience from massacre by the Germans. And what can you expect from an actor? But Narcissus said: 'Don't spare him, Caesar. Look carefully at the bruises. The flesh isn't cut open at all. It's clear to anyone with eyes in his head that the lash wasn't meant to hurt; it was just part of their vicious practices.' So Mnester made a very graceful bow to the parade, his last bow, and spoke his usual little speech: 'If I have ever pleased you, that is my reward. If I have offended you, I ask your forgiveness.' They received it in silence, and he was led off to his death.

The only two people whom I spared except the obviously innocent were one Lateranus, who was accused of conspiracy but pleaded not guilty, and Caesoninus. The evidence against Lateranus was conflicting, and he was a nephew of Aulus Plautius, so I gave him the benefit of the doubt. Caesoninus I spared because he was so foul a wretch, though of good family, that I did not wish to insult his fellow-adulterers by executing him alongside of them: in Caligula's reign he had prostituted himself as a woman. I don't know what happened to him: he never reappeared in Rome. I also dismissed the charge against Narcissus's niece: I owed him that.

The Bacchantes, still wearing nothing but their leopard skins, I ordered to be hanged, quoting Ulysses's speech in the *Odyssey*, when he took vengeance on Penelope's wicked maidservants:

> Then thus the prince: 'To these shall we afford
> A fate so pure as by the martial sword?
> To these, the nightly prostitutes to shame
> And base revilers of our house and name?'

I strung them all up in Homeric fashion, twelve in a row, on a huge ship's cable tautened between two trees with a winch. Their feet were just off the ground and as they died I quoted once more:

> They twitched their feet awhile, but not for long.

And Silius? And Messalina? Silius attempted no defence: but when I questioned him he made a plain statement of fact giving an account of his seduction by Messalina. I pressed him: 'But *why*, I want to know *why*? Were you really in love with her? Did you really think me a tyrant? Did you really intend to restore the Republic, or just to become Emperor in my place?' He answered: 'I can't explain, Caesar. Perhaps I was bewitched. She made me see you as a tyrant. My plans were vague. I talked liberty to many of my friends and, you know how it is, when one talks liberty everything seems beautifully simple. One expects all gates to open and all walls to fall flat and all voices to shout for joy.'

'Do you wish your life to be spared? Shall I put you into the custody of your family as an irresponsible imbecile?'

'I wish to die.'

Messalina had written me a letter from the Gardens. In it she told me that she loved me as much as ever and that she hoped I wouldn't take her prank seriously; she had just been leading Silius on, as she and I had arranged, and if she had rather over-done the joke by getting beastly drunk, I mustn't be stupid and feel cross or jealous. 'There is nothing that makes a man so hateful and ugly in a woman's eyes as jealousy.' The letter was handed to me on the tribunal, but Narcissus would not let me answer it until the trials were over, except by a formal 'Your communication has been received, and will be granted my Imperial attention in due course.' He said that until I was satisfied as to the extent of her guilt it was better not to compromise myself in writing: I must not hold out any hope that she would escape death and merely be exiled to some small prison island.

Messalina's reply to my formal acknowledgement of her letter was a long screed, blotted with tears, reproaching me for my cold answer to her loving words. She now made a full confession, as she called it, of her many indiscretions, but did not admit to actual adultery in a single instance; she begged me for the sake of the children to forgive her and grant her a chance of starting again as a faithful and dutiful wife; and she promised to set a perfect example of matronly deportment to Roman noble-women for all ages to come. She signed herself by her pet name. It reached me during Silius's trial.

Narcissus saw tears in my eyes and said: 'Caesar, don't give way. A born whore can never reform. She's not honest with you even in this letter.'

I said: 'No, I won't give way. A man can't die twice of the same disease.'

I wrote again: 'Your communication has been received and will be granted my attention in due course.'

Messalina's third letter arrived just as the last heads had fallen. It was angry and threatening. She wrote that she had now given me every chance to treat her fairly and decently, and that if I did not immediately beg her pardon for the insolent, heartless, and ungrateful behaviour I had shown her, I must take the consequences; for her patience was wearing out. She secretly commanded the loyalty of all my Guards officers, and of all my freedmen with the exception of Narcissus, and of most of the Senate; she had only to speak the word and I would immediately be arrested and surrendered to her vengeance. Narcissus threw back his head and laughed. 'Well, at least she acknowledges my loyalty to you, Caesar. Now, let's go to the Palace. You must be nearly fainting with hunger. You have had nothing since breakfast, have you?'

'But what shall I answer?'

'It deserves no answer.'

We returned to the Palace and there was a fine meal waiting for us. Vermouth (recommended by Xenophon as a sedative) and oysters, and roast goose with my favourite mushroom and onion sauce – made according to a recipe given my mother by Berenice, Herod's mother – and stewed veal with horse-radish, and a mixed dish of vegetables, and apple-pie flavoured with honey and cloves, and water-melon from Africa. I ate ravenously and when I had done I began to feel very sleepy. I said to Narcissus: 'My mind won't work any more to-night. I'm tired out. I put you in charge of affairs until to-morrow morning. I suppose that I ought to warn that miserable woman to attend here to-morrow morning and defend herself against those charges. I promised Vibidia that I'd give her a fair trial.' Narcissus said nothing. I went to sleep on my couch.

Narcissus beckoned to the Colonel of the Guard. 'The Emperor's orders. You are to proceed with six men to the pleasure-house in the Gardens of Lucullus and there execute the Lady Valeria Messalina, the Emperor's divorced wife.' Then he told Euodus to run ahead of the Guards and warn Messalina that they were coming, thus giving her an opportunity of committing suicide. If she took it, as she could hardly fail to do, I would not need to hear of the unauthorized order for her execution. Euodus found her lying on her face on the floor of the pleasure-house, sobbing. Her mother knelt beside her. Messalina said, without looking up: 'O beloved Claudius, I'm so miserable and ashamed.'

Euodus laughed: 'You're mistaken, Madam. The Emperor is asleep, at the Palace, with orders not to be disturbed. Before he went off he told the Colonel of the Guard to come here and cut off your pretty head. His very words, Madam. "Cut off her pretty head and stick it on the end of a spear." I ran ahead to let you know. If you've as much courage as you have beauty, Madam, my advice is to get it over before they come. I brought this dagger along in case you hadn't one handy.'

Domitia Lepida said: 'There's no hope, my poor child; you can't escape now. The only honourable thing left for you to do is to take his dagger and kill yourself.'

'It's not true,' Messalina wept. 'Claudius would never dare to get rid of me like this. It's an invention of Narcissus's. I ought to have killed Narcissus long ago. Vile, hateful Narcissus!'

The tramp of heavy feet was heard on the pavement outside. 'Guard, halt! Order arms!' The door flew open and the Colonel stood with folded arms in the entrance, outlined against the night sky. He did not say a word.

Messalina screamed at the sight of him and snatched the dagger from Euodus. She felt the edge and point timorously. Euodus sneered: 'Do you want the Guards to wait there while I fetch a grindstone and sharpen it up for you?'

Domitia Lepida said: 'Be brave, child. It won't hurt if you drive it home quick.'

The Colonel slowly unfolded his arms: his right hand reached for the pommel of his sword. Messalina put the point of the dagger first to her throat and then to her breast. 'Oh, I can't, Mother! I'm afraid!'

The Colonel's sword was out of its sheath. He took three long steps forward and ran her through.

Chapter 30

XENOPHON had given me another dose of the 'Olympian mixture' just before I went to sleep, and the exalted feeling, which had been wearing off slightly during supper, revived in me. I woke up with a start – a careless slave had dropped a pile of dishes – yawned loudly and apologized to the company for my bad table-manners. 'Granted, Caesar,' they all cried. I thought how frightened they looked. Bad lives and bad consciences.

'Has anyone been poisoning my drink while I was asleep?' I bantered.

'God forbid, Caesar,' they protested.

'Narcissus, what was the sense of that Colchester joke of Vettius Valens's? Something about the Britons worshipping me as a God.'

Narcissus said: 'It was not altogether a joke, Caesar. In fact, you may as well know that a temple at Colchester had been dedicated to the God Claudius Augustus. They have been worshipping you there since the early summer. But I've only just heard about it.'

'So that's why I feel so queer. I've been turning into a God! But how did it happen? I wrote to Ostorius, I remember, sanctioning the erection and dedication of a temple at Colchester to the God Augustus, in gratitude for the victory he had given Roman arms in the island of Britain.'

'Then I suppose, Caesar, that Ostorius made the natural mistake of understanding "Augustus" as meaning yourself, particularly as you specified a victory given by Augustus to Roman arms in Britain. The God Augustus fixed the frontier at the Channel and his name means nothing to the British, in comparison with your own. The natives speak of you there, I am informed, with the deepest religious awe. There are poems composed about your thunder and lightning and your magic mists and your black spirits and your humped monsters and your monsters with snakes for noses. Politically speaking, Ostorius was perfectly correct in dedicating the temple to you. But I must regret that it was done without your consent, and, I suppose, against your wishes.'

'So I'm a God, now, am I?' I repeated. 'Herod Agrippa always said that I'd end as a God, and I told him that he was talking nonsense. I suppose that I can't cancel the mistake, can I, Narcissus, do you think?'

'It would create a very bad effect on the provincials, I should say,' Narcissus answered.

'Well, I don't care, the way I feel now,' I said. 'I don't care about anything. Suppose that I have that miserable woman brought here for trial at once. I feel completely free from petty mortal passions. I might even forgive her.'

'She's dead,' Narcissus said in a low voice. 'Dead, at your own orders.'

'Fill my glass,' I said. 'I don't remember giving the order, but it's all the same to me now. I wonder what sort of God I am. Old Athenodorus used to explain to me the Stoic idea of God: God was a perfectly rounded whole, immune from accident or event. I always pictured God as an enormous pumpkin. Ha, ha, ha! If I eat any more of this goose and drink any more of this wine I'll become pumpkinified too. So Messalina's dead! A beautiful woman, my friends! But bad!'

'Beautiful but bad, Caesar.'

'Carry me up to bed, someone, and let me sleep the blessed sleep of the Gods. I'm a blessed God now, aren't I?'

So they took me up to bed. I stayed in bed until noon the next day, fast asleep all the time. The Senate met in my absence and passed a motion congratulating me on the suppression of the revolt, and another expunging Messalina's name from the archives and removing it from every public inscription, and destroying all her statues. I rose in the afternoon and resumed my ordinary

Imperial work. Everyone whom I met was extremely subdued and polite, and when I visited the Law Courts nobody, for the first time for years, attempted to bustle or browbeat me. I got through my cases in no time.

The next day I began to talk grandly about the conquest of Germany; and Narcissus, realizing that Xenophon's medicine was having too violent an effect – disordering my wits instead of merely tiding me gently over the shock of Messalina's death, as had been intended – told him to give me no more of it. Gradually the Olympian mood faded and I felt pathetically mortal again. The first morning after I was free from the effects of the drug I went down to breakfast, and asked: 'Where's my wife? Where's the Lady Messalina?' Messalina always breakfasted with me unless she had a 'sick headache'.

'She's dead, Caesar,' Euodus answered. 'She died some days ago, by your orders.'

'I didn't know,' I said weakly. 'I mean, I had forgotten.' Then the shame and grief and horror of the whole business came welling back to my mind, and I broke down. Soon I was babbling foolishly of my dear, precious Messalina and reproaching myself as her murderer, and saying that it was all my fault, and making an almighty fool of myself. I eventually pulled myself together and called for my sedan. 'The Gardens of Lucullus,' I ordered. They took me there.

Seated on a garden bench under a cedar, looking across a smooth green lawn and down a wide grassy avenue of hornbeams, with nobody about except my German guards posted out of sight in the shrubbery, and with a long strip of paper on my knee and a pen in my hand, I began solemnly working out just where and how I stood. I have this paper by me as I now write and will copy out what I put down exactly as I find it. My statements fell, for some reason or other, into related groups of three, like the 'tercets' of the British Druids (their common metrical convention for verse of a moralistic or didactic sort):

> I love liberty: I detest tyranny.
> I have always been a patriotic Roman.
> The Roman genius is Republican.
>
> I am now, paradoxically, an Emperor.
> As such I exercise monarchical power.
> The Republic has been suspended for three generations.

The Republic was torn by Civil Wars.
Augustus instituted this monarchical power.
It was an emergency measure only.

Augustus found that he could not resign his power.
In my mind I condemned Augustus as hypocritical.
I remained a convinced Republican.

Tiberius became Emperor. Against his inclination?
Afraid of some enemy seizing power?
Probably forced into it by his mother Livia.

In his reign I lived in retirement.
I considered him a blood-thirsty hypocrite.
I remained a convinced Republican.

Caligula suddenly appointed me Consul.
I only desired to be back at my books.
Caligula tried to rule like an Oriental monarch.

I was a patriotic Roman.
I should have attempted to kill Caligula.
Instead I saved my skin by playing the imbecile.

Cassius Chaerea was perhaps a patriotic Roman.
He broke his oath, he assassinated Caligula.
He attempted, at least, to restore the Republic.

The Republic was not then restored.
Instead there was a new Emperor appointed.
That Emperor was myself, Tiberius Claudius.

If I had refused I should have been killed.
If I had refused there would have been Civil War.
It was an emergency measure only.

I put Cassius Chaerea to death.
I found that I could not yet resign my power.
I became a second Augustus.

I worked hard and long, like Augustus,
I enlarged and strengthened the Empire, like Augustus.
I was an absolute monarch, like Augustus.

I am not a conscious hypocrite.
I flattered myself that I was acting for the best.
I planned to restore the Republic this very year.

Julia's disgrace was Augustus's punishment.
'Would I had never wed, and childless died.'
I feel just the same about Messalina.

I should have killed myself rather than rule:
I should never have allowed Herod Agrippa to persuade me.
With the best of intentions I have become a tyrant.

I was blind to Messalina's follies and villainies.
In my name she shed the blood of innocent men and women.
Ignorance is no justification for crime.

But am I the only guilty person?
Has not the whole nation equally sinned?
They made me Emperor and courted my favour.

And if I now carry out my honest intentions?
If I restore the Republic, what then?
Do I really suppose that Rome will be grateful?

'You know how it is when one talks of liberty.
Everything seems beautifully simple.
One expects every gate to open and every wall to fall flat.'

The world is perfectly content with me as Emperor,
All but the people who want to be Emperor themselves.
Nobody really wants the Republic back.

Asinius Pollio was right:
'It will have to be much worse before it can be any better.'
Decided: I shall not, after all, carry out my plan.

The frog-pool wanted a king.
Jove sent them Old King Log.
I have been as deaf and blind and wooden as a log.

The frog-pool wanted a king.
Let Jove now send them Young King Stork.
Caligula's chief fault: his stork-reign was too brief.

My chief fault: I have been far too benevolent.
I repaired the ruin my predecessors spread.
I reconciled Rome and the world to monarchy again.

Rome is fated to bow to another Caesar.
Let him be mad, bloody, capricious, wasteful, lustful.
King Stork shall prove again the nature of kings.

By dulling the blade of tyranny I fell into great error.
By whetting the same blade I might redeem that error.
Violent disorders call for violent remedies.

Yet I am, I must remember, Old King Log.
I shall float inertly in the stagnant pool.
Let all the poisons that lurk in the mud hatch out.

I kept my resolution. I have kept it strictly ever since. I have allowed nothing to come between me and it. It was very painful at first. I had told Narcissus that I felt like the Spanish sword-fighter whose shield-arm was suddenly lopped off in the arena; but the difference was that the Spaniard died of his wound, and I continue to live. You have perhaps heard maimed men complain, in damp, cold weather, of sensations of pain in the leg or arm they have lost? It can be a most precise pain too, described as a sharp pain running up the wrist from the thumb, or as a settled pain in the knee. I felt like this often. I used to worry what Messalina would think of some decision I had taken, or about what effect a long boring play in the theatre was having on her; if it thundered I would remember how frightened she was of thunder.

As you may have guessed, the most painful consideration of all was that my little Britannicus and Octavia were perhaps, after all, not my children. Octavia, I was convinced, was not my child. She did not resemble the Claudian side of the family in the slightest. I looked at her a hundred times before I suddenly realized who her father must have been – the Commander of the Germans under Caligula. I remembered now that when, a year after the amnesty, he had disgraced himself and lost his position and finally sunk so low that he became a sword-fighter, Messalina had pleaded for his life in the arena (he was disarmed and a net-man was standing over him with his trident raised) – pleaded for the wretch's life against the protests of the entire audience, who were yelling and booing and turning their thumbs down. I let him off, because she said that it would be bad for her health if I refused: this was just before Octavia's birth. However, a few months later he fought the same net-man and was killed at once.

Britannicus was a true Claudian and a noble little fellow, but the horrible thought came into my mind that he resembled my brother Germanicus far too closely. Could it be that Caligula was really his father? He had nothing of Caligula's nature, but heredity often skips a generation. The notion haunted me. I could not rid myself of it for a long time. I kept him out of my sight as much as possible without seeming to disown him. He and Octavia must have suffered much at this time. They had been greatly attached to their mother, so I had given instructions that they should not be told in detail about her crimes; they were merely to know that their mother was dead. But they soon found out that she had been executed by my orders, and naturally they felt a childish resentment of me. But I could not yet bring myself to talk to them about it.

I have explained that my freedmen formed a very close guild and that a man who offended one of them offended all, and that a man who was taken under the protection of one enjoyed the favour of all. In this they set a good example to the Senate, but the Senate did not follow it, being always torn into factions and only united in their common servility to me. And though now, three months after Messalina's death, a rivalry started between my three chief ministers, Narcissus, Pallas, and Callistus, it had been agreed beforehand that the successful one would not use the strong position that he would win by pleasing me as a means of humiliating the other two. You would never guess what the rivalry was about. It was about choosing a fourth wife for me! 'But,' you will exclaim, 'I thought you gave the Guards full permission to chop you in pieces with their swords if you ever married again?' I did. But that was before I took my fateful decision, sitting there under the cedar in the Gardens of Lucullus. For now I had made up my mind, and once I do that, the thing is fixed with a nail. I set my freedmen a sort of guessing-game as to what my marital intentions were. It was a joke, for I had already chosen the lucky woman. I started them off one night by remarking casually at supper: 'I ought to do something better for little Octavia than put her in charge of freedwomen. I hanged all the maids who understood her ways, poor child. And I can't expect my daughter Antonia to look after her: Antonia's been very poorly ever since her own baby died.'

Vitellius said: 'No, what little Octavia needs is a mother. And so does Britannicus, though it's easier for a boy than a girl to look after himself.'

I made no answer, so everyone present knew that I was thinking of marrying again, and everyone knew too how easily I had been managed by Messalina, and thought that if he were the man to find me a wife his fortune was made. Narcissus, Pallas, and

Callistus each offered a candidate in turn, as soon as a favourable moment came for talking to me privately. It was most interesting to me to watch how their minds worked. Callistus remembered that Caligula had forced a Governor of Greece to divorce his wife, Lollia Paulina, and then married her himself (as his third wife) because someone had told him at a banquet that she was the most beautiful woman in the Empire: and he remembered further that this someone had been myself. He thought that since Lollia Paulina had not lost any of her looks in the ten years that had passed since, but had rather improved them, he was pretty safe in suggesting her. He did so the very next day. I smiled and promised to give the matter my careful consideration.

Narcissus was next. He asked me first who it was that Callistus had suggested and when I told him 'Lollia Paulina', he exclaimed that she would never suit me. She cared for nothing but jewels. 'She never goes about with less than thirty thousand gold pieces around her neck in emeralds or rubies or pearls, never the same assortment either, and she's as stupid and obstinate as a miller's mule. Caesar, the one woman for you really, as we both know, is Calpurnia. But you can hardly marry a prostitute: it wouldn't look well. My suggestion therefore is that you marry some noble-woman just as a matter of form, but live with Calpurnia, as you did before you met Messalina, and enjoy real happiness for the rest of your life.'

'Whom do you suggest as my matter-of-form wife?'

'Aelia Paetina. After you divorced her she married again, you remember. Recently she lost her husband, and he left her very badly off. It would be a real charity to marry her.'

'But her tongue, Narcissus?'

'She's chastened by misfortune. That legal tongue of hers will never be heard again, I undertake that. I'll warn her about it and explain the conditions of marriage. She'll be paid all the respect due to her as your wife, and as your daughter Antonia's mother, and have a large private income, but she must sign a contract to behave like a deaf-mute in your presence, and not to be jealous of Calpurnia. How's that?'

'I shall give the matter my careful consideration, my dear Narcissus.'

But it was Pallas who made the correct guess. It was either extraordinarily stupid of him or extraordinarily clever. How could he suppose that I would do anything so monstrous as to marry my niece, Agrippinilla? In the first place, the marriage would be incestuous; in the second place she was the mother of Lucius Domitius, to whom I had taken the most violent dislike; in the third place, now that Messalina was dead, she could claim the title of the worst woman in Rome. Even in Messalina's lifetime it would have been a very nice question how to decide between these two: they were equally vicious, and if Messalina had been more promiscuous than Agrippinilla, she had at least never committed incest, as Agrippinilla, to my own knowledge, had. But Agrippinilla had one lonely virtue – she was very brave, while Messalina, as we have seen, was a coward. Pallas suggested Agrippinilla, with the same proviso that Narcissus had made, namely, that it need only be a marriage of form: I could keep any mistress I pleased. Agrippinilla, he said, was the only woman in Rome capable of taking over Messalina's political work, and would be a real help to me.

I promised to give the matter my careful consideration.

I then arranged a regular debate between Callistus, Narcissus, and Pallas, after first giving them time to sound the willingness of their candidates to stand for the office of Caesar's wife. I called in Vitellius as umpire and the debate took place a few days later. Narcissus, in recommending Aelia, argued that by resuming an old connexion I should introduce no innovation into the family, and that she would be a good mother to little Octavia and to Britannicus, to whom she was already related by being the mother of their half-sister Antonia.

Callistus reminded Narcissus that Aelia had long been divorced from me, and suggested that if she was taken back her pride would be inflamed and she would probably revenge herself privately on Messalina's children. Lollia was a much more eligible match: nobody could deny that she was the most beautiful woman in the world, and virtuous too.

Pallas opposed both choices. Aelia was an old shrew, he said, and Lollia a vacant-minded simpleton who went about looking like a jeweller's shop and would expect a whole new set of gewgaws, at the expense of the Treasury, as regularly as the sun rose. No, the only possible choice was the Lady Agrippina. [It was only I who still called her by the diminutive 'Agrippinilla.'] She would bring with her the grandson of Germanicus, who was in every way worthy of the Imperial fortune; and it was of great political importance that a woman who had shown herself fruitful and was still young should not marry into another house and transfer to it the splendours of the Caesars.

I could see Vitellius sweating hard, trying to guess from my looks which of the three it was that I favoured, and wondering whether perhaps it would not be better to suggest a quite different name himself. But he guessed correctly, perhaps from the order in which I had given my freedmen leave to speak. He took a deep breath and said: 'Between three such beautiful, wise, well-born, and distinguished candidates, I find it as difficult to judge as the Trojan shepherd, Paris, between the three Goddesses Juno, Venus, and Minerva. Let me keep this figure, which is a helpful one. Aelia Paetina stands for Juno. She has already been married and had a child by the Emperor; but as Jove was displeased with Juno, though she was the mother of Hebe, for her nagging tongue, so has the Emperor been displeased by Aelia Paetina, and we want no more domestic wars in this terrestrial Heaven of ours. It is claimed for Lollia Paulina that she is a very Venus, and certainly Paris awarded the prize to Venus; but Paris was an impressionable young swain, you will remember, and beauty unallied with intelligence can have no appeal for a mature ruler with great marital as well as governmental experience. Agrippinilla is Minerva, for wisdom, and she yields little, if anything, to Lollia for beauty. The Emperor's wife should have both good looks and outstanding intelligence: my choice is Agrippinilla.'

As though I had only just considered the matter I protested: 'But, Vitellius, she's my niece. I can't marry my niece, can I?'

'If you wish me to approach the Senate, Caesar, I can undertake to obtain their consent. It's irregular, of course, but I can take the same line as you took the other day in your speech about the Autun franchise: I can point out that the marriage laws at Rome have become more and more plastic in course of time. A hundred years ago, for instance, it would have been considered monstrous for first cousins to marry, but now it is regularly done even in the best families. And why shouldn't uncle and niece marry? The Parthians do it, and theirs is a very old civilization. And in the Herod family there have been more marriages between uncle and niece than any other sort.'

'That's right,' I said. 'Herodias married her uncle Philip, and then deserted him and ran off with her uncle Antipas. And Herod Agrippa's daughter Berenice married her uncle Herod Pollio, King of Chalcis, and now she's supposed to be living incestuously with her brother, young Agrippa. Why shouldn't the Caesars be as free as the Herods?'

Vitellius looked surprised but said quite seriously: 'Incest between brother and sister is another matter. I cannot make out a case for that. But it may well be that our very earliest ancestors allowed uncle and niece to marry; because there is nowhere any disgust expressed in ancient classical literature for Pluto's marriage with his niece Proserpine.'

'Pluto was a God,' I said. 'But then, it seems, so am I now. Pallas, what does my niece Agrippinilla herself think about the matter?'

'She will be greatly honoured and altogether overjoyed, Caesar,' said Pallas, hardly able to conceal his elation. 'And she is ready to swear that she will faithfully devote herself as long as she lives entirely to you, your children, and the Empire.'

'Bring her to me.'

When Agrippinilla arrived she fell at my feet; I told her to rise and said that I was prepared to marry her, if she wished it. She embraced me passionately, for answer, and said this was the happiest moment of her life. I believed her. Why not? She would now be able to rule the world through me.

Agrippinilla was no Messalina. Messalina had the gift of surrendering herself wholly to sensual pleasure. In this she took after her great-grandfather, Mark Antony. Agrippinilla was not that sort of woman. She took after her great-grandmother, the Goddess Livia: she cared only for power. Sexually, as I have said, she was completely immoral; yet she was by no means prodigal of her favours. She only slept with men who could be useful to her politically. I have, for instance, every reason to suspect that she rewarded Vitellius for his gallant championship of her, and I know for certain (though I have never told her so) that Pallas was then, and is now, her lover. For Pallas controls the Privy Purse.

So Vitellius made his speech in the Senate (having first arranged a big public demonstration outside) and told them that he had suggested the marriage to me and that I had agreed about its political necessity, but had hesitated to make a definite decision until I had first heard what the Senate and People thought of the innovation. Vitellius spoke with old-fashioned eloquence. '... And you will not have long to search, my Lords, before you find that among all the ladies of Rome this Agrippina stands pre-eminent for the splendour of her lineage, has given signal proof of her fruitfulness, and comes up to and even surpasses your requirements in virtuous accomplishments: it is indeed a singularly happy circumstance that, through the providence of the Gods, this paragon among women is a widow and may be readily united with a Person who has always hitherto been a model of husbandly virtue.'

You can perhaps guess how his speech was received. They voted for his motion without a single dissentient voice – not by any means because they all loved Agrippinilla, but because nobody dared to earn her resentment now that it seemed likely that she would become my wife – and several senators sprang up in emulous zeal and said that if necessary they would compel me to bow to the consentient will of the whole country. I received their greetings and pleadings and congratulations in the Market Place and then proceeded to the Senate, where I demanded the passing of a decree permanently legalizing marriages between uncles and fraternal nieces. They passed it. At the New Year I A.D. 49 married Agrippinilla. Only one person took advantage of the new law, a knight who had been a Guards captain. Agrippinilla paid him well for it.

I made a statement to the Senate about my temple in Britain. I explained that my deification had come about accidentally, and apologized to my fellow-citizens. But perhaps they would forgive me and confirm the incongruity in view of the political danger of cancelling it. 'Britain is far away, and it is only a little temple,' I pleaded ironically. 'A tiny rustic temple with a mud floor and a turf roof, like the ones in which the Gods of Rome lived, back in Republican times, before the God Augustus rehoused them in their present palatial splendour. Surely you won't object to one little temple, so far away, and an old priest or two, and an occasional modest sacrifice? For my part I never intended to be a God. And I give you my word that it will be my only one. ...' But nobody, it seemed, grudged me the temple.

After closing the census I had not taken on the office of Censor again, but as a prelude to my restoration of the Republic had given the appointment to Vitellius. It was the first time for a century that the control of public morals had been out of the hands of the Caesars. One of Vitellius's first acts after arranging my marriage with Agrippinilla was to remove from the Senatorial Order one of the first-rank magistrates of the year, none other than my son-in-law, young Silanus! The reason he gave was Silanus's incest with his sister Calvina, who had been his own daughter-in-law, but had lately been divorced by her husband, young Vitellius. Vitellius explained that his son had surprised the two in bed together some time before and had told him of it under the bonds of secrecy; but now that he had become Censor he could not conscientiously conceal Silanus's guilt. I examined the case myself. Silanus and Calvina denied the charge, but it seemed proved beyond all dispute, so I dissolved the marriage-contract between Silanus and my daughter Octavia (or rather Messalina's daughter Octavia) and made him resign this magistracy. It had only a single day to run, but to show how strongly I felt I gave someone else the appointment for the last day. Of course Vitellius would never have dared to reveal the incest if it had not been for Agrippinilla. Silanus stood in the way of her ambitions: she wanted her son Lucius to become my son-in-law. Well, I had been fond of Silanus, and, after all, he was a descendant of the God Augustus; so I told him that I would postpone judgement in his case – meaning that I expected him to commit suicide. He delayed for some time, and eventually chose my wedding-day for the deed; which was not inappropriate. Calvina I banished and advised the College of Pontiffs to offer sacrifices and atonements at the Grove of Diana, in revival of a picturesque institution of Tullus Hostilius, the third King of Rome.

Baba and Augurinus were in great form about this time. They parodied everything I did. Baba introduced three new letters into the alphabet: one to stand for a hawk of phlegm, one for the noisy sucking of teeth, and the third for 'the indeterminate vowel halfway between a hiccup and a belch'. He divorced the enormous negress who had hitherto acted the part of Messalina, whipped her through the streets and went through a mock ceremony of marriage with a cross-eyed albino woman whom he claimed to be his fraternal niece. He took a census of beggars, thieves, and vagabonds and removed from the Society all who had ever done a stroke of honest work in their lives. One of his jokes was resigning his censorship and appointing Augurinus as his successor for the unexpired period of his office – exactly one hour by the water-clock. Augurinus boasted of all the glorious things that he professed to do in the hour. His one complaint was that Baba's water-clock didn't keep good time: he wanted to go off and fetch his own, which had hours that lasted at least three times as long. But Baba, imitating my voice and gestures, quoted a phrase I had recently used in the law-courts, and was rather proud of, 'One can expect agreement between philosophers sooner than between clocks', and refused to let him go. Augurinus insisted that fair was fair; if he was going to be Censor, he needed a full hour of regulation size and weight. They carried on the argument hotly until Augurinus's term of office ended suddenly with nothing done. 'And I was going to dip you in boiling tar and then fry you within an inch of your life, according to a picturesque institution of King Tullus Hostilius,' Augurinus grieved.

I allow Baba and Augurinus perfect freedom to parody and caricature me. They draw great audiences in their performances outside the Temple of Mercury: Mercury is, of course, the patron of thieves and practical jokers. Agrippinilla was highly offended by the insult to her of Baba's marriage to the albino, but I surprised her by telling her firmly: 'So long as I live Baba's life is to be spared, understand – and Augurinus's too.'

'Exactly so long, to the very hour,' Agrippina agreed in her most unpleasant tones.

There was a plague of vipers this year: I published an order informing the public of an infallible remedy against snake-bite, namely, the juice of a yew-tree. Augurinus and Baba republished it with the addition of the phrase 'and contrariwise', which, it seems, is recognized as one of my stock expressions.

Chapter 31

I AM near the end of my long story. I have now been five years married to Agrippinilla, but they have been comparatively uneventful years, and I shall not write about them in too great detail. I have let Agrippinilla and my freedmen rule me. I have opened and shut my mouth and gestured with my arms like the little jointed marionettes they make in Sicily: but the voice has not been mine, nor the gestures. I must say at once that Agrippinilla has shown herself a remarkably able ruler of the tyrannical sort. When she comes into a room where a number of notables are gathered, and looks coldly around her, everyone quakes and springs to attention and studies how best to please her. She no longer needs to pretend affection for me. I soon made her realize that I had married her purely on political grounds; and, physically, she was repulsive to me. I was quite frank about it. I explained: 'The fact is, that I got tired of being Emperor. I wanted someone to do most of the work for me. I married you not for your heart but for your head. It takes a woman to run an empire like this. There's no reason for us to pretend amorous devotion to each other.'

'That suits me,' she said. 'You're not the sort of lover one dreams about.'

'And you're not quite what you were twenty-two years ago, my dear, when you were a bride for the first time. Still, you'll last a little longer if you continue with that daily facial massage and those milk baths: Vitellius pretends to find you the most beautiful woman in Rome.'

'And perhaps you'll last too, if you don't exasperate the people you depend on.'

'Yes, we two have outlasted all the rest of our family,' I agreed. 'I don't know how we've done it. I think we ought to congratulate each other, instead of quarrelling.'

'You always begin it,' she said, 'by being what you call "honest".'

Agrippinilla could not understand me. She soon found that it was unnecessary to coax or cheat or bully me if she wanted things done her way. I accepted her suggestions on almost every point. She could hardly believe her luck when I consented to betroth Lucius to Octavia: she knew what I really thought of Lucius. She could not make out why I consented. She was emboldened to go further and suggest that I should adopt him as my son. But that was already my intention. She first let Pallas sound me on the subject. Pallas was tactful. He began speaking fondly of my brother Germanicus and of his adoption by my Uncle Tiberius at Augustus's request, though Tiberius had a son of his own, Castor. He enlarged on the remarkable brotherly love that had sprung up between Germanicus and Castor and the generosity that Castor had shown to Germanicus's widow and children. I knew at once what Pallas was driving at, and agreed that two loving sons were better than one. 'But remember,' I said, 'that was not the end of the story. Germanicus and Castor were both murdered; and my Uncle Tiberius in his old age, as it might be myself, named another pair of loving brothers as his joint heirs – Caligula and Gemellus. Caligula had the advantage of being the elder. When the old man died Caligula seized the monarchy and killed Gemellus.'

That silenced Pallas for a while. When he tried a slightly different line, this time telling me what fast friends Lucius and Britannicus had become, I said, as if quite irrelevantly: 'Do you know that the Claudian family has kept its descent direct in the male line, without adoptions, ever since the day of the original Appius Claudius, five whole cycles ago? There's no other family in Rome can make the same boast.'

'Yes, Caesar,' Pallas said, 'the Claudian family tradition is one of the least plastic things in a remarkably plastic world. But, as you wisely point out, "all things are subject to change".'

'Listen, Pallas. Why do you go on beating about the bush? Tell the Lady Agrippinilla that if she wishes me to adopt her son as my joint-heir with Britannicus I am ready to do so. As for plasticity, I've gone very soft in my old age. You can roll me in your hands like dough and fill me with whatever stuffing you like and bake me into Imperial dumplings.'

I adopted Lucius. He is now called Nero. Recently I married him to Octavia, whom I had first, however, to let Vitellius adopt as his daughter, to avoid the technical crime of incest. On the night of their marriage the whole sky seemed on fire. A.D. 50 Lucius (or Nero as he was now called) did his best to win Britannicus's friendship. But Britannicus saw through him and haughtily rejected his advances. He refused at first to address him as Nero, continuing to call him Lucius Domitius until Agrippinilla intervened and ordered him to apologize. Britannicus replied: 'I shall apologize only if my father orders me to do so.' I ordered him to apologize. I still saw very little of Britannicus. I had fought down my morbid suspicions about his being Caligula's bastard – and loved him now as dearly as ever before. But I concealed my true feelings. I was determined to play Old King Log, and nothing must hinder my resolution. Sosibius was his tutor still and gave him an old-fashioned education. Britannicus was accustomed to the plainest foods and lay at night on a plank bed like a soldier. Horsemanship, fencing, military engineering, and early Roman history were his chief studies, but he knew the works of Homer and Ennius and Livy as well as or better than I did. In his holidays Sosibius took him down to my Capua estate, and there he learned about bee-keeping, stock-breeding, and farming. I allowed him no training in Greek oratory or philosophy. I told Sosibius: 'The ancient Persians taught their children to shoot straight and speak the truth. Teach my son the same.'

Narcissus ventured to criticize me. 'The sort of education that

Britannicus is being given, Caesar, would have been all very well in the old days when, as you are so fond of quoting,

> Under the oak sat Romulus
> Eating boiled turnips with a will,

or even a few hundred years later when,

> Called to fight his country's foemen
> Cincinnatus left the plough.

But surely in this new ninth cycle of Roman history it is a little out of date?'

'I know what I am doing, Narcissus,' I said.

As for Nero, I provided our young King Stork with the most appropriate tutor in the world. I had to send all the way to Corsica for this prodigy. You will guess his name, perhaps: Lucius Annaeus Seneca, the Stoic – that flashy orator, that shameless flatterer, that dissolute and perverted amorist. I pleaded before the Senate myself for his forgiveness and recall. I spoke of the uncomplaining patience with which he had borne his eight years of exile, the rigorous discipline to which he had voluntarily subjected himself, and his deep sense of loyalty to my house. Seneca must have been astounded, after the two false moves he had recently made. For shortly after the publication of his *Consolation to Polybius*, Polybius had been executed as a criminal. Seneca had then tried to remedy the mistake by a panegyric on Messalina. A few days after it was published at Rome, Messalina followed Polybius into disgrace and death, and it was hurriedly withdrawn. Agrippinilla was quite ready to welcome Seneca as Nero's teacher. She valued his talents as a teacher of rhetoric and took all the credit for his recall.

Nero is afraid of his mother. He obeys her in everything. She treats him with great severity. She is certain that she will rule through him after my death, just as Livia ruled first through Augustus and then through Tiberius. I can see farther than she can. I remember the Sibyl's prophecy:

> The hairy Sixth to enslave the State
> Shall give Rome fiddlers and fear and fire.
> His hand shall be red with a parent's blood.
> No hairy seventh to him succeeds
> And blood shall gush from his tomb.

Nero will kill his mother. It was prophesied at his birth: Barbillus himself prophesied it, and Barbillus never makes a mistake. He was even right about the death of Messalina's husband, was he not? Agrippinilla, being a woman, cannot command the Roman armies or address the Senate. She needs a man to do that for her. When I married her I knew that I could count on surviving so long as Nero was too young to step into my shoes.

Agrippinilla asked me to persuade the Senate to give her the title of Augusta. She did not expect me to give her what I had refused Messalina, but I did. She has taken upon herself other unheard of privileges. She sits on the tribunal beside me when I judge cases, and drives up the Capitoline Hill in a chariot. She has appointed a new Guards Commander to supersede Geta and Crispinus. His name is Burrhus and he is Agrippinilla's man, body and soul. (He served with the Guards at Brentwood and there lost three fingers of his right hand to a British broad-sword.) Rome's new Augusta has no rivals. Aelia Paetina is dead, perhaps poisoned: I do not know. Lollia Paulina was also removed: her champion, Callistus, having died, the other freedmen made no objection to her removal. She was accused of witchcraft and of circulating an astrological report that my marriage to Agrippinilla was fated to be disastrous to the country. I was sorry for Lollia, so in the speech that I made to the Senate I merely recommended her banishment. But Agrippinilla would not be cheated. She sent a Guards colonel to Lollia's house and he made sure that she killed herself. He duly reported her death, but Agrippinilla was not satisfied. 'Bring me her head,' she ordered. The head was brought to her at the Palace. Agrippinilla took it by the hair and, holding it up to a window, opened the mouth. 'Yes, that's Lollia's head, all right,' she said complacently to me as I came into the room. 'Here are those gold teeth that she had put in by an Alexandrian dentist to fill out her sunken left cheek. What coarse hair she had, like a pony's mane. Slave, take this thing away. And the mat too: have the bloodstains scrubbed out.'

Agrippinilla also removed her sister-in-law Domitia Lepida, Messalina's mother. Domitia Lepida was very attentive to Nero now and used to invite him frequently to her house, where she caressed and flattered him, and gave him a good time and reminded him of all that she had done for him when he was a penniless orphan. It was true that she had occasionally taken charge of him when her sister Domitia went out of town and could not be bothered to take the child with her. Agrippinilla, finding that her own maternal authority, which was based on sternness, was being threatened by Domitia Lepida's auntish indulgences, had her accused of publicly cursing my marriage-bed and also of failing to restrain the slaves on her estate in Calabria from dangerous rioting: a magistrate and two of his staff who attempted to restore order there had been set on and beaten, and Domitia Lepida had locked herself up in the house and done nothing. I allowed her to be sentenced to death on these two charges (the first of which was probably a fabrication) because I was now aware of the assistance she had given Messalina in the Appius Silanus affair and other deceptions practised on me.

One act only of Agrippinilla's I found it hard to take philosophically. When I heard of it I confess that tears came into my eyes. But it would have been foolish for old King Log to have gone back on his resolution at this point, and roused himself and taken vengeance. Vengeance cannot recall the dead to life again. It was the murder of my poor Calpurnia and her friend Cleopatra that made me weep. Someone set fire to their house one night and the two were trapped in their beds and burned to death. It was made to look like an accident; but it was clearly murder. Pallas, who told me about it, had the insolence to suggest that it was done by some friend of Messalina's who knew the part that Calpurnia had played in bringing her to justice. I had been most neglectful of Calpurnia. I had not visited her once since that terrible afternoon. At my private order a handsome marble tomb was erected for her on the ruins of the burned villa, and on it I put a Greek epigram. It was the only one that I have ever composed except as a school exercise: but I felt that I had to do something out of the ordinary to express my great grief for her death and my gratitude for the love and devotion she had always shown me. I wrote:

> 'A harlot's love, a harlot's lie' –
> Cast that ancient proverb by.
> CALPURNIA's heart was cleaner far,
> Roman matrons, than yours are.

Last year, the year of Nero's marriage, was marked by a world failure of crops * that all but exhausted our granaries. This year, though the harbour of Ostia was now completed, a strong northeast wind blowing for weeks on end prevented the Egyptian and African corn fleets from making our shores. The Italian harvest promised well, but was not yet ready to cut, and at one time there

* See Acts xi. 28. – R.G.

was only a fortnight's corn supply left in the public granaries, though I had done everything possible to fill them. I was obliged to reduce corn rations to the lowest possible level. Then, as though I was not doing and had not always done everything possible to keep my fellow citizens well fed (building the harbour, for instance, in the face of general discouragement, and organizing the daily supply of fresh vegetables), I suddenly found myself regarded as a public enemy. I was accused of purposely starving the City. The crowd groaned and howled at me almost whenever I showed myself in public, and once or twice pelted me with stones and mud and mouldy crusts. On one occasion I narrowly escaped serious injury in the Market Place: my yeomen were set upon by a mob of 200 or 300 persons and had their rods of office broken over their own backs. I only just managed to get safely into the Palace by a postern gate not far off, from which a small party of armed Guardsmen dashed out to my rescue. In the old days I would have taken this greatly to heart. Now I just smiled to myself. 'Frogs,' I thought, 'you are getting very frisky.'

Nero put on his manly-gown, in the year after his adoption by me. I allowed the Senate to vote him the privilege of becoming Consul at the age of twenty, so at sixteen he was Consul-Elect. I awarded him honorary triumphal dress and appointed him Leader of Cadets, as Augustus had appointed his grandsons, Gaius and Lucius. In the Latin holidays, too, when the Consuls and other magistrates were out of the City, I made him City Warden as Augustus had also done with his grandsons, to give them a first taste of magistracy. It was customary to bring no important cases before the City Warden, but to wait for the return of the proper magistrates. Nero, however, managed a whole series of complicated cases which would have tested the judgement of the most experienced legal officers in the City, and gave remarkably shrewd decisions. This gained him popular admiration, but it was perfectly clear to me, as soon as I heard about it, that the whole affair had been stage-managed by Seneca. I do not mean that the cases were not genuine, but Seneca had reviewed them carefully beforehand and arranged with the lawyers as to just what points they should bring out in their speeches, and had then coached Nero in his cross-examination of witnesses and his summing-up and judgement. Britannicus had not yet come of age. I kept him from the society of boys of his own age and rank as much as possible: he only met them under the eye of his tutors. I did not wish him to catch the Imperial infection to which I was purposely subjecting Nero. I let it go about that he was an epileptic. Public flattery was all concentrated now on Nero. Agrippinilla was delighted. She thought that I hated Britannicus for his mother's sake.

There was a big riot about the sale of bread. It was a quite unnecessary riot, though, and according to Narcissus, who loathed Agrippinilla (and found to his surprise that I encouraged him in this), it was instigated by her. It happened when I was suffering from a chill, and Agrippinilla came to my room and suggested that I should issue an edict to reassure and quiet the populace. She wanted me to say that I was not seriously ill and that, even if my illness took a serious turn and I died, Nero was now capable of conducting public affairs under her guidance. I laughed in her face. 'You are asking me to sign my own death warrant, my dear? Come on, then, give me the pen. I'll sign it. When's the funeral to be?'

'If you don't wish to sign it, don't,' she said. 'I'm not forcing you.'

'Very well, then, I won't,' I said. 'I'll inquire into that bread riot and see who really started it.'

She walked angrily out. I called her back. 'I was only joking. Of course I'll sign! By the way, has Seneca taught Nero his funeral oration yet? Or not yet? I'd like to hear it first, if none of you mind.'

Vitellius died of a paralytic stroke. A senator who was either drunk or crazy, I can't say which, had suddenly accused him before the House of aiming at the monarchy. The charge appears to have been directed at Agrippinilla, but naturally no one dared to support it, much as Agrippinilla was hated, so the accuser was himself outlawed. However, Vitellius took the matter to heart and the stroke followed soon after. I visited him as he lay dying. He was unable to move a finger but talked quite good sense. I asked him the question that I had always meant to ask: 'Vitellius, in a better age you would have been one of the most virtuous men alive: how was it, then, that your upright nature acquired a sort of permanent stoop from playing the courtier?'

He said: 'It was inevitable under a monarchy, however benevolent the monarch. The old virtues disappear. Independence and frankness are at a discount. Complacent anticipation of the monarch's wishes is then the greatest of all virtues. One must either be a good monarch like yourself, or a good courtier like myself – either an Emperor or an idiot.'

I said: 'You mean that people who continue virtuous in an old-fashioned way must inevitably suffer in times like these?'

'Phaemon's dog was right.' That was the last thing he said before he lapsed into a coma from which he never recovered.

I could not be content until I had hunted down the reference in the library. It appears that Phaemon the philosopher had a little dog whom he had trained to go to the butcher every day and bring back a lump of meat in a basket. This virtuous creature, who would never dare to touch a scrap until Phaemon gave it permission, was one day set upon by a pack of mongrels who snatched the basket from its mouth and began to tear the meat to pieces and bolt it greedily down. Phaemon, watching from an upper window, saw the dog deliberate for a moment just what to do. It was clearly no use trying to rescue the meat from the other dogs: they would kill it for its pains. So it rushed in among them and itself ate as much of the meat as it could get hold of. In fact, it ate more than any of the other dogs, because it was both braver and cleverer.

The Senate honoured Vitellius with a public funeral and a statue in the Market Place. The inscription that is carved on it reads:

LUCIUS VITELLIUS, TWICE CONSUL,
ONCE CENSOR.
HE ALSO GOVERNED SYRIA.
UNSWERVINGLY LOYAL TO HIS EMPEROR

I must tell about the Fucine Lake. I had lost all real interest in it by now, but one day Narcissus, who was in charge of the work, told me that the contractors reported that the channel was dug through the mountain at last: we had only to raise A.D. 53 the sluice-gates and let the water rush out, and the whole lake would become dry land. Thirteen years, and 30,000 men constantly at work! 'We'll celebrate this, Narcissus,' I said.

I arranged a sham sea-fight, but on a most magnificent scale. Julius Caesar had first introduced this sort of spectacle at Rome, exactly 100 years before. He dug a basin in Mars Field, which he flooded from the Tiber, and arranged for eight ships, called the Tyrian fleet, to engage eight more, called the Egyptian fleet. About 2,000 fighting men were used, exclusive of rowers. When I was eight years old Augustus gave a similar show in a permanent basin on the other side of the Tiber, measuring 1,200 feet by 1,800, with stone seats around it like an amphitheatre. There were twelve ships a side this time, called Athenians and Persians. Three thousand men fought in them. My show on the Fucine Lake was going to dwarf both spectacles. I didn't care about economy now. I was going to have a really magnificent show for once. Julius's and Augustus's fleets had been composed of light craft only, but I gave orders for twenty-four proper war vessels of three banks of oars each to be constructed, and twenty-six smaller vessels; and I cleared the prisons of 1,900 able-bodied criminals to fight in them under the command of famous professional sword-fighters. The two fleets, each consisting of twenty-five vessels, were to be known as the Rhodians and the Sicilians. The hills around the lake would make a fine natural amphitheatre; and though it was a very long way from Rome, I was sure that I could draw an audience there of at least 200,000 people. I advised them by an official circular to bring their own food with them in baskets. But 1,900 armed criminals are a dangerous force to handle. I had to take the whole Guards Division out there and station some of them on shore and the rest on rafts lashed together across the lake. The line of rafts was a semicircle which made a proper naval basin of the southwestern end of the lake, where it tapered to the point at which the channel had been cut. The whole lake would have been too big: it spread over 200 square miles. The Guards on the rafts had catapults and mangonels ready to sink any vessel that tried to ram the line and escape.

The great occasion finally came; I proclaimed a ten-days' public holiday. The weather was fine and the number of spectators was more like 500,000 than 200,000. They came from all over Italy, and I must say that it was a wonderfully well-behaved and well-dressed gathering. To prevent overcrowding, I divided up the lake-shore into what I called colonies and put each colony under a magistrate; the magistrates had to make arrangements for communal cooking and sanitation and so on. I built a large canvas field-hospital for the wounded survivors of the battle and for accidents on shore. Fifteen babies were born in that hospital and I made them all take the additional name of Fucinus or Fucina.

Everything was in position by ten o'clock on the morning of the fight. The fleets were manned and came rowing up in parallel lines towards the President, namely, myself, who was sitting on a high throne dressed in a suit of golden armour with a purple cloak over it. My throne was at a point where the shore curved out into the lake and gave the widest view. Agrippinilla sat beside me on another throne, wearing a long mantle of cloth of gold. The two flagships came close up to us. The crew shouted: 'Greetings, Caesar. We salute you in Death's shadow.'

I was supposed to nod gravely, but I was feeling in a gay humour that morning. I answered: 'And the same to you, my friends.'

The rascals pretended to understand this as a general pardon. 'Long live Caesar,' they shouted joyfully. I did not at the moment realize what they meant. The combined fleets sailed past me cheering and then the Sicilians formed up on the west and the Rhodians on the east. The signal for battle was given by a mechanical silver Triton that suddenly appeared from the lake-bottom, when I pressed a lever and blew a golden trumpet. That caused huge excitement among the audience. The fleets met, and expectation ran high. And then – what do you think happened then? They simply sailed through each other, cheering me and congratulating each other! I *was* angry. I jumped down from my throne and rushed along the shore shouting and cursing. 'What do you think that I got you all here for, you scoundrels, you scum, you rebels, you bastards? To kiss each other and shout loyal shouts? You could have done that just as well in the prison-yard. Why don't you fight? Afraid, eh? Do you want to be given to the wild beasts instead? Listen, if you don't fight now, by God, I'll make the Guards put up a show. I'll make them sink every one of your ships with their siege-engines and kill every man Jack who swims ashore.'

As I have told you, my legs have always been weak, and one is shorter than the other, and I am not accustomed to use them much, and I am old and rather stout now, and besides all this I was wearing an extremely heavy corselet, and the ground was uneven, so you can imagine what sort of a figure I cut – stumbling top-heavily along, with frequent falls, shouting at the top of my not very melodious voice, red and stuttering with anger! However, I succeeded in making them fight, and the spectators cheered me with, 'Well done, Caesar! Well run, Caesar!'

I recovered my good humour and joined in the laugh against myself. You should have seen the murderous look on Agrippinilla's face. 'You boor,' she muttered as I climbed back on my throne. 'You idiotic boor. Have you no dignity? How do you expect the people to respect you?'

I answered politely: 'Why, of course, as your husband, my dear, and as Nero's father-in-law.'

The fleets met. I shall not describe the battle in much detail, but both sides fought splendidly. The Sicilians rammed and sank nine of the big Rhodian vessels, losing three of their own, and then cornered the remainder close to where we were sitting and boarded them one by one. The Rhodians repelled them time and time again, and the decks were slippery with blood, but finally they were beaten and by three o'clock the Sicilian flag was run up on the last vessel. My field hospital was full. Nearly 5,000 wounded were carried ashore. I pardoned the remainder, except the survivors of three big Rhodian vessels who had not put up a proper fight before being rammed, and six of the Sicilian lighter craft who had consistently avoided combat. Three thousand men had been killed or drowned. When I was a lad I couldn't bear the sight of bloodshed. I don't mind it at all now: I get so interested in the fighting.

Before letting the water out of the lake I thought that I had better satisfy myself that the channel was deep enough to carry it off. I sent out someone to take careful soundings in the middle of the lake. He reported that the channel would have to be dug at least a yard deeper if we were not to be left with a lake a quarter of its present size! So the whole spectacle had been wasted. Agrippinilla blamed Narcissus and accused him of fraud. Narcissus blamed the engineers who, he said, must have been bribed by the contractors to send in a false report as to the depth of the lake, and protested that Agrippinilla was being most unjust to him.

I laughed. It didn't matter. We had witnessed a most enjoyable show and the channel could be dug to the proper depth within a few months. Nobody was to blame, I said: probably there had been a natural subsidence of the lake-bottom. So we all went home again and in four months' time back we came. On this occasion I did not have enough criminals available for a big sea-battle, and did not wish to repeat the spectacle on a smaller scale, so I had another idea. I built a long, wide pontoon-bridge across the end of the lake and arranged for two forces of two battalions apiece, called Etruscans and Samnians, appropriately dressed and armed, to fight on it. They marched towards each other along the bridge, to the accompaniment of martial music, and engaged in the centre, where the bridge widened out to 100 yards or so, and there fought a vigorous battle. The Samnians twice took possession of this battle-field, but Etruscan counter-attacks forced them back and eventually the Samnians were on the run, losing heavily, some run through by bronze-headed Etruscan lances or chopped down by two-headed Etruscan battle-axes, some thrown off the bridge into the water. My orders were that no combatant must be permitted to swim ashore. If he was thrown into the water he must either drown or climb back on the bridge. The Etruscans were victorious and erected a trophy. I gave all the victors their freedom, and a few of the Samnians, too, who had fought particularly well.

Then at last the moment came for the water to be let out of the lake. A huge wooden dining-hall had been erected close to the sluice-gates and the tables were spread with a magnificent luncheon for me and the Senate, and the families of senators, and a number of leading knights and their families, and all senior Guards officers. We would dine to the pleasant sound of rushing water. 'You're sure that the channel is deep enough now?' I asked Narcissus.

'Yes, Caesar. I've taken the soundings myself.'

So I went to the sluice-gates and sacrificed and uttered a prayer or two – they included an apology to the nymph of the lake, whom I now begged to act as guardian deity of the farmers who would till the recovered land – and finally lent a hand to the crank at which a group of my Germans was posted, and gave the order, 'Heave away!'

Up came the gates and the water rolled crashing into the channel. An immense cheer went up. We watched for a minute or two and then I said to Narcissus: 'Congratulations, my dear Narcissus. Thirteen years' work and thirty thousand – –'

I was interrupted by a roar like thunder, followed by a general shriek of alarm.

'What's that?' I cried.

He caught me by the arm without ceremony and fairly dragged me up the hill. 'Hurry!' he screamed. 'Faster, faster!' I looked to see what was the matter, and a huge brown-and-white wall of water, I wouldn't like to say how many feet high, on the model of the one that runs yearly up the Severn River in Britain, was roaring up the channel. *Up* the channel, mark you! It was some time before I realized what had happened. The sudden rush of water had overflowed the channel a few hundred yards down, forming a large lake in a fold of the hills. Into this lake, its foundations sapped by the water, slid a whole hillside, hundreds of thousands of tons of rock, completely filling it and expelling the water with awful force.

All but a few of us managed to scramble to safety, though with wet legs – only twenty persons were drowned. But the dining-chamber was torn to pieces and tables and couches and food and garlands carried far out into the lake. Oh, how vexed Agrippinilla was! She blazed up at Narcissus, telling him that he had arranged the whole thing on purpose to conceal the fact that the channel was still not dug deep enough, and accused him of putting millions of public money into his own pocket, and Heaven only knows what else besides.

Narcissus, whose nerves were thoroughly upset now, lost his temper too and asked Agrippinilla who she thought she was – Queen Semiramis? or the Goddess Juno? or the Commander-in-Chief of the Roman Armies? 'Keep your paws out of this pie,' he screamed at her.

I thought it all a great joke. 'Quarrelling won't give us back our dinners,' I said.

I was more amused than ever when the engineers reported that it would take two more years to cut a new passage through the obstruction. 'I'm afraid that I'll not be spared to exhibit another fight on these waters, my friends,' I said gravely. Somehow, the whole business seemed beautifully symbolic. Labour in vain, like all the industrious work that I had done in my early years of monarchy as a gift to an undeserving Senate and People. The violence of that wave gave me a feeling of the deepest satisfaction. I liked it better than all the sea-fighting and bridge-fighting.

Agrippinilla was complaining that a precious set of gold dishes from the Palace had been carried away by the wave and only a few pieces recovered: the others were at the lake-bottom. 'Why, that's nothing to worry about,' I teased. 'Listen! You take off those beautiful shining clothes of yours – I'll see that Narcissus doesn't steal them – and I'll make the Guards keep the crowd back and you can give a special diving display from the sluice-gate. Everyone will enjoy that tremendously: they like nothing so much as the discovery that their rulers are human after all. ... But, my dear, why not? Why shouldn't you? Now, don't lose your temper. If you can dive for sponges, you can dive for gold dishes, surely? Look, that must be one of your treasures over there, shining through the water, quite easy to get. There, where I'm throwing this pebble!'

To console Agrippinilla for her losses, I gave her, some days later, a very valuable present – a snow-white nightingale, the first ever reported of that colour. Narcissus, as an apology for his rudeness, gave her a talking blackbird. The blackbird talked almost as well as a parrot, and the white nightingale sang quite as well as the ordinary brown sort. Agrippinilla could not easily conceal her delight in these birds. My family, by the way, has always shown a weakness for pet animals. There was Augustus with his watchdog, Typhon; Tiberius with his wingless dragon; Caligula with the horse Incitatus. My sister Livilla kept a thievish, mischievous marmoset; my brother Germanicus a black squirrel, and my mother Antonia a large pet carp. This fish would answer to its name, which was 'Leviathan', swimming up from its lair among the water-lilies in its pool and allowing my mother to feed and tickle it. It was a present from Herod Agrippa, who had fixed a little pair of jewelled ear-rings in its gills. She used to claim that when it opened and shut its mouth it was addressing her, and that she understood it. I never had a pet myself. I have always felt that in these cases one gives more than one gets, and there is a temptation to believe the creature both more affectionate and more sagacious than it really is.

Chapter 32

IT is now September in the fourteenth year of my reign. Barbillus has lately read my horoscope and fears that I am destined to die about the middle of next month. Thrasyllus once told me exactly the same thing: for he allowed me a life of sixty-three years, sixty-three days, sixty-three watches, and sixty- A.D. 54 three hours. That works out to the thirteenth of next month. Thrasyllus was more explicit about it than Barbillus: I remember that he congratulated me on this combination of multiplied seven and nines: it was a very remarkable one, he said. Well, I am prepared to die. In court this morning I begged the lawyers to behave with a little more consideration for an old man; I said that next year I shouldn't be among them, and they could treat my successor as they pleased. I also told the court, in the case of a noblewoman charged with adultery, that I had now been married several times, and that each of my wives in turn had proved bad, and that I had showed them indulgence for a while, but not for long: so far I had divorced three. Agrippinilla will get to hear of this.

Nero is seventeen. He goes about with the affected modesty of a high-class harlot, shaking his scented hair out of his eyes every now and then; or with the affected modesty of a high-class philosopher, pausing to ponder privately, every now and then, in the middle of a group of admiring noblemen – right foot thrown out, head sunk on breast, left arm akimbo, right hand raised, with the finger tips pressing lightly on his forehead as if in the throes of thought. Soon he comes out with a brilliant epigram or a happy couplet or a profound piece of sententious wisdom; not however his own – Seneca is earning his porridge, as the saying is. I wish Nero's friends joy of him. I wish Rome joy of him. I wish Agrippinilla joy of him, and Seneca too. I heard privately, by way of Seneca's sister (a secret friend of Narcissus's who gives us a lot of useful information about the nation's latest darling), that the night before Seneca received my order for his recall from Corsica he dreamed that he was acting as schoolmaster to Caligula. I take that as a sign.

On New Year's Day this year I called Xenophon to me and thanked him for keeping me alive so long. I then fulfilled my promise to him, though the agreed fifteen years' term is not yet over, and won from the Senate a perpetual exemption from taxes and military service of his native island of Cos. In my speech I gave the House a full account of the lives and deeds of the many famous physicians of Cos, who all claim direct descent from the God Aesculapius, and learnedly discussed their various therapeutic practices; I ended up with Xenophon's father, who was my father's field-surgeon in his German wars, and with Xenophon himself, whom I praised above them all. Some days later Xenophon asked permission to remain with me a few years longer. He did not put his request in terms of loyalty or gratitude or affection, though I have done much for him – what a curiously unemotional man he is! – but on the grounds of the convenience of the Palace as a place for medical research!

The fact was that when I paid Xenophon this honour I was counting on him to help me carry out a plan that called for the utmost secrecy and discretion. It was a debt that I owed to myself and to my ancestors: it was nothing less than the rescue of my Britannicus. Let me now clearly show why I deliberately preferred Nero to him, why I gave him so old-fashioned an education, why I guarded him so carefully from the infection of the court, from contact with vice and flattery. To begin with, I knew that Nero is fated to rule as my successor, carrying on the cursed business of monarchy, fated to plague Rome and earn everlasting hatred, to be the last of the mad Caesars. Yes, we are all mad, we Emperors. We begin sanely, like Augustus and Tiberius and even Caligula (though he was an evil character, he was sane at first) and monarchy turns our wits. 'After Nero's death surely the Republic will be restored,' I argued; and it was my intention that Britannicus should be the one to restore it. But how was Britannicus to live through the reign of Nero? Nero would surely put him to death if he remained at Rome, as Caligula had put Gemellus to death. Britannicus must be removed, I decided, to some safe place where he could grow up virtuously and nobly like a Claudian of ancient times, and keep alight in his heart the fire of true liberty.

'But the world is now wholly Roman, with the exception of Germany, the East, the Scythian deserts north of the Black Sea, unexplored Africa, and the farther parts of Britain: so where can my Britannicus be safe from Nero's power?' I asked myself. 'Not in Parthia or Arabia: there could be no worse choice. Not in Germany: I have never loved the Germans. For all their barbaric virtues they are our natural enemies. Of Africa and Scythia I know little. There is only one place for a Britannicus, and that is Britain. The northern Britons are racially akin to us. Queen Cartimandua of the Brigantians is my ally. She is a noble and wise ruler and at peace with my province of South Britain. Her chieftains are brave and courteous warriors. Her young stepson, who is her heir, is coming here in May, accompanied by a band of young nobles and noblewomen, as my guests at the Palace. I shall make Britannicus his host and secretly bind the two together in blood-brotherhood, according to the British rite. These Brigantians will remain here for the entire summer. When they sail back (and I shall send them back by long sea, from Ostia direct to their port in the Humber) Britannicus will go with them in disguise. He will have his face and body stained blue, and will be dressed in the red smock and tartan trousers of a young Brigantian nobleman, with gold chains around his neck. Nobody will recognize him. I shall load the Brigantian prince with gifts and bind him with the holiest possible oaths to keep Britannicus safe, and to hide his identity from everyone but the Queen. He will bind his companions with the same oaths. At Cartimandua's court Britannicus will be presented as a young Greek of illustrious birth, whose parents have died and who has been left penniless and who has come to seek his fortune in Britain. At Rome he will not be missed. I shall give out that he is unwell, and Xenophon and Narcissus will assist me in the fraud. Presently I shall announce his death. Xenophon has a written order from me giving him the right to claim the body of any dead slave in the hospital on the island of Aesculapius for use as a subject for dissection. (He is writing a treatise on the muscles of the heart.) He can surely find a suitable corpse to offer as Britannicus's. At Cartimandua's court Britannicus will grow to manhood: he will teach the Brigantians the useful arts that I have been at pains to have him taught. If he bears himself modestly he will never want for friends there. Cartimandua will permit him to worship his own gods. He will avoid the society of Romans. On Nero's death he will reveal himself and return as the saviour of his country.'

It was an excellent plan and I did all I could to put it into execution. When the Brigantian prince arrived, Britannicus was his host, and formed a close friendship with him. Each taught the other his own language and the use of his country's weapons. They worked and played together all summer long. They bound themselves by the blood-rite, unprompted by any suggestion of mine, and exchanged gifts. I was pleased that things were going so well. I told Xenophon and Narcissus of my plan. They undertook to help me. They made all arrangements. But see what has happened! All my ingenuity has been wasted.

Three days ago Narcissus brought Britannicus to me, very early in the morning, when all the Palace was asleep. I embraced him with a warmth that I had abstained from showing him for years. I explained to him why it was that I had treated him as I had done. It was not cruelty or neglect, I said, but love. I quoted to him the Greek line that Augustus had quoted to me just before his death: 'Who wounded thee, shall make thee whole.' I told him of the prophecy and of my desire to save from the wreckage of Rome the person whom I most loved – himself. I reminded him of the fatal history of our family and begged him to fall in with my plan, in which lay his only chance of survival.

He listened attentively and finally burst out: 'No, Father, no! Father, I confess that I have hated you ever since my mother's death. I thought the very worst of you. To me you were a pedant, a coward, and a fool, and I was ashamed to be known as your son. I see now that I misjudged you and I ask your pardon. But no, I cannot do what you ask me to do. It is not honourable. A

Claudian should not paint his face blue and hide away among barbarians. I am not afraid of Nero: Nero is a coward. Let me put on my manly-gown this New Year. I will still be only thirteen, but you can forgive me the extra year: I'm tall and strong for my age. Once I am officially a man I'll be a match for Nero in spite of the start you've given him, and in spite of his mother. Make us your joint-heirs and then we'll see which of us two gets the upper hand. It is my right as your son. And I don't believe in the Republic, anyway. You can't reverse the course of history. My great-grandmother Livia said that, and it's true. I love the days of old, as you do, but I'm not blind. The Republic's dead, except for old-fashioned people like you and Sosibius. Rome is an Empire now and the choice only lies between good Emperors and bad ones. Make me joint-heir with Nero and I'll defy the prophecies. Keep alive a few years longer, Father, for my sake. Then when you die, I'll step into your shoes and rule Rome properly. The Guards love me and trust me. Geta and Crispinus have told me that when you're dead they'll see that I become Emperor, not Nero. I'll be a good Emperor, just as you were until you married my stepmother. Give me proper tutors. My present ones are no use to me. I want to study public speaking, I want to understand finance and legal procedure, I want to learn how to be an Emperor!'

He was not to be dissuaded by anything that I could say, nor even by my tears. Now I have abandoned all hope of his rescue: no doctor can save a patient's life against his determined will to die. Instead, I have done all that he asks of me, like an indulgent father. I have dismissed Sosibius and the other tutors and appointed new ones. I have promised to let him come of age this New Year and am altering my will in his favour: in my previous will he was hardly mentioned. To-day I have made the Senate my farewell speech and humbly recommended Nero and Britannicus to them, and given these two a long and earnest exhortation to brotherly love and concord, calling the House to witness that I have done so. But with what irony I spoke! I knew as certainly as that fire is hot and ice cold that my Britannicus was doomed, and that it was I who was giving him over to his death, and cutting off, in him, the last true Claudian of the ancient stock of Appius Claudius. Imbecilic I.

My eyes are weary, and my hand shakes so much that I can hardly form the letters. Strange portents have been seen of late. A great comet like that which foretold the death of Julius Caesar has long been blazing in the midnight sky. From Egypt a phoenix has been reported. It flew there from Arabia, as its custom is, followed by a flock of admiring other birds. I can hardly think that it was a true phoenix, for that appears only once every 1,461 years, and only 250 years have elapsed since it was last genuinely reported from Heliopolis in the reign of the third Ptolemy; but certainly it was some sort of phoenix. And as if a phoenix and comet were not sufficient marvels, a centaur has been born in Thessaly and brought to me at Rome (by way of Egypt where the Alexandrian doctors first examined it), and I have handled it with my own hands. It only lived a single day, and came to me preserved in honey, but it was an unmistakable centaur, and of the sort which has a horse's body, not the inferior sort which has an ass's body. Phoenix, comet, and centaur, a swarm of bees among the standards at the Guards Camp, a pig farrowed with claws like a hawk, and my father's monument struck by lightning! Prodigies enough, soothsayers?

Write no more now, Tiberius Claudius, God of the Britons, write no more.

The Near East in the Time of the Emperor Claudius, A.D. 41 to 54.

Three Accounts
of Claudius's Death

I

AND not long after this he wrote his will and signed it with the seals of all the head-magistrates. Whereupon, before that he could proceed any further, prevented he was and cut short by Agrippina, whom they also who were privy to her and of her counsel, yet nevertheless informers, accused besides all this of many crimes. And verily it is agreed upon generally by all, that killed he was by poison, but where it should be, and who gave it, there is some difference. Some write that as he sat at a feast in the Capitol castle with the priests, it was presented unto him by Halotus, the eunuch, his taster; others report that it was at a meal in his own home by Agrippina herself, who had offered unto him a mushroom empoisoned, knowing that he was most greedy of such meats. Of those accidents also which ensued hereupon the report is variable. Some say that straight upon the receipt of the poison he became speechless, and continuing all night in dolorous torments died a little before day. Others affirm that at first he fell asleep, and afterwards, as the meat flowed and floated aloft, vomited all up, and so was followed again with a rank poison. But whether the same were put into a mess of thick gruel (considering he was of necessity to be refreshed with food being emptied in his stomach), or conveyed up by a clyster, as if being overcharged with fullness and surfeit he might be eased also by this kind of egestion and purgation, it is uncertain.

His death was kept secret until all things were set in order about his successor. And therefore both vows were made for him as if he had lain sick still, and also comic actors were brought in place colourably to solace and delight him, as having a longing desire after such sports. He deceased three days before the ides of October, when Asinius Marcellus and Acilius Aviola were consuls, in the sixty-fourth year of his age and the fourteenth of his empire. His funeral was performed with a solemn pomp and procession of the magistrates, and canonized he was a saint in heaven;* which honour, forelet and abolished by Nero, he recovered afterwards by Vespasian.

Especial tokens there were presaging and prognosticating his death: to wit, the rising of a hairy star which they call a comet; also the monument of his father Drusus was blasted with lightning; and for that in the

* I.e. officially deified. – R.G.

same year most of the magistrates of all sorts were dead. But himself seemeth not either to have been ignorant that his end drew near or to have dissembled so much; which may be gathered by some good arguments and demonstrations. For both in the ordination of Consuls he appointed none of them to continue longer than the month wherein he died, and also in the Senate, the very last time that ever he sat there, after a long and earnest exhortation of his children to concord, he humbly recommended the age of them both to the lords of that honourable house; and in his last judicial session upon the tribunal once or twice he pronounced openly that come he was now to the end of his mortality, notwithstanding that they that heard him grieved to hear such an osse, and prayed the gods to avert the same.

Suetonius *Claudius*
Tr. Philemon Holland (1606)

II

In the midst of this vast accumulation of anxieties Claudius was attacked with illness, and for the recovery of his health had recourse to the soft air and salubrious waters of Sinuessa. It was then that Agrippina, long since bent upon the impious deed, and eagerly seizing the present occasion, well furnished too as she was with wicked agents, deliberated upon the nature of the poison she would use, whether, 'if it were sudden and instantaneous in its operation, the desperate achievement would not be brought to light: if she chose materials slow and consuming in their operation, whether Claudius, when his end approached, and perhaps having discovered the treachery, would not resume his affection for his son'. Something of a subtle nature was therefore resolved upon, 'such as would disorder his brain and require time to kill'. An experienced artist in such preparations was chosen, her name Locusta; lately condemned for poisoning, and long reserved as one of the instruments of ambition. By this woman's skill the poison was prepared: to administer it was assigned to Halotus, one of the eunuchs, whose office it was to serve up the emperor's repasts, and prove the viands by tasting them.

In fact, all the particulars of this transaction were soon afterwards so thoroughly known, that the writers of those times are able to recount, 'how the poison was poured into a dish of mushrooms, of which he was particularly fond; but whether it was that his senses were stupefied, or from the wine he had drunk, the effect of the poison was not immediately perceived': at the same time a relaxation of the intestines seemed to have been of service to him; Agrippina therefore became dismayed; but as her life was at stake, she thought little of the odium of her present proceedings, and called in the aid of Xenophon the physician, whom she had already implicated in her guilty purposes. It is believed that he, as if he purposed to assist Claudius in his efforts to vomit, put down his throat a feather besmeared with deadly poison; not unaware that in desperate villainies the attempt without the deed is perilous, while to ensure the reward they must be done effectually at once.

The senate was in the meantime assembled and the consuls and pontiffs were offering vows for the recovery of the emperor, when, already dead, he was covered with clothes, and warm applications, to hide it till matters were arranged for securing the empire to Nero. First there was Agrippina, who feigning to be overpowered with grief, and anxiously seeking for consolation, clasped Britannicus in her arms, called him 'the very model of his father', and by various artifices withheld him from leaving the chamber; she likewise detained Antonia and Octavia, his sisters; and had closely guarded all the approaches to the palace; from time to time too she gave out that the prince was on the mend; that the soldiery might entertain hopes till the auspicious moment, predicted by the calculations of the astrologers, should arrive.

At last, on the thirteenth day of October, at noon, the gates of the palace were suddenly thrown open, and Nero, accompanied by Burrhus, went forth to the cohort which, according to the custom of the army, was keeping watch. There, upon a signal made by the praefect, he was received with shouts of joy, and instantly put into a litter. It was reported that there were some who hesitated, looking back anxiously, and frequently asking, where was Britannicus? but as no one came forward to oppose it, they embraced the choice which was offered them. Thus Nero was borne to the camp, where, after a speech suitable to the exigency, and the promise of a largess equal to that of the late emperor his father, he was saluted emperor. The voice of the soldiers was followed by the decrees of the senate; nor was there any hesitation in the several provinces. To Claudius were decreed divine honours, and his funeral obsequies were solemnized with the same pomp as those of the deified Augustus; Agrippina emulating the magnificence of her great-grandmother Livia. His will, however, was not rehearsed, lest the preference of the son of his wife to his own son might excite the minds of the people by its injustice and baseness.

Tacitus, *Annals*
(Oxford translation)

III

Claudius was angered by Agrippina's actions, of which he was now becoming aware, and sought for his son Britannicus, who had purposely been kept out of his sight by her most of the time (for she was doing everything she could to secure the throne for Nero, inasmuch as he was her own son by her former husband Domitius); and he displayed his affection whenever he met the boy. He would not endure her behaviour, but was preparing to put an end to her power, to cause his son to assume the *toga virilis.* and to declare him heir to the throne. Agrippina, learning of this, became alarmed and made haste to forestall anything of the sort by poisoning Claudius. But since, owing to the great quantity of wine he was for ever drinking and his general habits of life, such as all emperors as a rule adopt for their protection, he could not easily be harmed, she sent for a famous dealer in poisons, a woman named Locusta, who had recently been convicted on this very charge; and preparing with her aid a poison whose effect was sure, she put it in one of the vegetables called mushrooms. Then she herself ate of the others, but made her husband eat of the one which contained the poison; for it was the largest and finest of them. And so the victim of the plot was carried from the banquet apparently quite overcome by strong drink, a thing that had happened many times before; but during the night the poison took effect and he passed away, without having been able to say or hear a word. It was the thirteenth of October, and he had lived sixty-three years, two months and thirteen days, having been emperor thirteen years, eight months and twenty days.

Agrippina was able to do this deed owing to the fact that she had previously sent Narcissus off to Campania, feigning that he needed to take the waters there for his gout. For had he been present, she would never have accomplished it, so carefully did he guard his master. As it was, however, his death followed hard upon that of Claudius. He was slain beside the tomb of Messalina, a circumstance due to mere chance, though it seemed to be in fulfilment of her vengeance.

In such a manner did Claudius meet his end. It seemed as if this event had been indicated by the comet, which was seen for a very long time, by the shower of blood, by the thunderbolt that fell upon the standards of the Praetorians, by the opening of its own accord of the temple of Jupiter Victor, by the swarming of bees in the Camp, and by the fact that one incumbent of each political office died. The emperor received the state burial and all the other honours that had been accorded to Augustus. Agrippina and Nero pretended to grieve for the man whom they had killed, and elevated to heaven him whom they had carried out on a litter from the banquet. On this point Lucius Junius Gallio, the brother of Seneca, was the author of a very witty remark. Seneca himself had composed a work that he called 'Pumpkinification' – a word formed on the analogy of 'deification'; and his brother is credited with saying a great deal in one short sentence. Inasmuch as the public executioners were accustomed to drag the bodies of those executed in the prison to the Forum with large hooks, and from there hauled them to the river, he remarked that Claudius had been raised to heaven with a hook. Nero, too, has left us a remark not unworthy of record. He declared mushrooms to be the food of the gods, since Claudius by means of the mushroom had become a god.

At the death of Claudius the rule in strict justice belonged to Britannicus, who was a legitimate son of Claudius and in physical development was in advance of his years; yet by law the power fell also to Nero because of his adoption. But no claim is stronger than that of arms; for everyone who possesses superior force always appears to have the greater right on his side, whatever he says or does. And thus Nero, having first destroyed the will of Claudius and having succeeded him as master of the whole empire, put Britannicus and his sisters out of the way. Why, then, should one lament the misfortunes of the other victims?

> Dio Cassius, Book LXI
> as epitomized by Xiphilinus and Zonaras (tr. Cary)

The Pumpkinification of Claudius

A SATIRE IN PROSE AND VERSE

By Lucius Annaeus Seneca

I MUST here put on record what took place in Heaven on the thirteenth day of October of this very year, the year that has ushered in so glorious a new age. No malice or favour whatsoever. That's right, isn't it? If anyone asks me how I get my information, well, in the first place if I don't want to answer, I won't answer. Who is going to compel me to do so? I am a free man, aren't I? I was freed on the day that a well-known personage died, the man who made the proverb true, 'Either be born an Emperor or an idiot'. If I do, however, choose to answer, I shall say the first thing that springs to my lips. Are historians ever compelled to produce witnesses in court to swear that they have told the truth? Still, if it were absolutely necessary for me to call on someone, I would call on the man who saw Drusilla's soul on its way to Heaven; he will swear that he saw Claudius taking the same road, 'with halting gait' (as the poet says). That man simply cannot help observing everything that goes on in Heaven: he's the custodian of the Appian Way, which of course is the road that both Augustus and Tiberius took on their way to join the Gods. If you ask him privately he will tell you the whole story, but he will say nothing when a lot of people are about. You see, ever since he swore before the Senate that he saw Drusilla going up to Heaven, and nobody believed the news, which was certainly a little too good to be true, he has solemnly engaged himself never again to bear witness to anything he has seen – not even if he sees a man murdered in the middle of the Market Place. But what he told me I now report, and all good luck to him.

> Great Phoebus had drawn in his daily course,
> And longer stretched the darksome hours of sleep.
> The conquering Moon enlarged had her domain
> And squalid Winter from rich Autumn now
> Usurped the throne. To Bacchus the command
> Was 'Grow thou old!' and the late vintager
> Gathered the few last clusters of the grape.

You will probably understand me better if I say plainly that the month was October and the day the thirteenth. I cannot, however, be so precise about the hour – one can expect an agreement between philosophers sooner than between clocks – but it was between twelve noon and one o'clock in the afternoon. 'You're not much of a poet, Seneca,' I can hear my readers say. 'Your fellow-bards, not content with describing dawn and sunset, work themselves up about the middle of the day too. Why do you neglect so poetical an hour?' Very well, then:

> Phoebus had parted the wide heavens in twain
> And somewhat wearily 'gan shake the reins,
> Urging his chariot nightwards: down the slope
> Of day the grand effulgence, waning, slid.

It was then that Claudius began to give up the ghost, but couldn't bring the matter to a conclusion. So Mercury, who had always derived great pleasure from Claudius's wit, took one of the three Fates aside and said: 'I consider, Madam, that you are extremely cruel to allow the poor fellow to suffer so. Is he never to have any relief from torture? It's sixty-four years now since he first started gasping to keep alive. Have you some grudge against him and against Rome? Please let the astrologers be right for once: ever since he became Emperor they have laid him out for burial regularly once a month. However, they can't really be blamed for getting the hour of his death wrong, because nobody was ever quite sure whether he had really been born or not. Get on with the business, Clotho:

> Slay him, and in's stead let a worthier rule.'

Clotho replied: 'I did so wish to give him just a little longer, just enough time to make Roman citizens of the few outsiders who still remain: he had set his heart, you know, on seeing the whole world dressed in the white gown – Greece, France, Spain, even Britain. Still, if you think that a few foreigners ought to be kept for breeding purposes, and you really order me to put an end to him, it shall be done.' She opened her box and produced three spindles: one was for Augurinus, one for Baba, and the third for Claudius. 'These are to die in the same year quite close to each other, because I don't want him to go off unattended: it would be very wrong for him to be suddenly left alone, after always having had so many thousands marching before him and trailing behind him, and crowding up against him from either side. He will be grateful for these two friends of his as travelling companions.'

> She spoke, and round the ugly spindle twined
> The thread of that fool's life, then snapped it close.
> But Lachesis, her tresses neatly prinked
> And on her brow Pierian laurel set,
> Plucks from a fleece new threads as white as snow
> Which, as she draws them through her happy hand,
> Change hue. Her sisters at the marvel gaze.
> Not common wool, this, but rich thread of gold,

That runs on, century by century,
Termless. They pluck the fleeces with good will,
Rejoicing in their task, so dear the wool:
Nay, the thread spins itself, no task for them,
And as the spindle turns, drops silken down,
Passing Tithonus' lengthy count of years
(Aurora's husband) and old Nestor's count.
Phoebus attends, and from a hopeful breast
Chants as they work, and plucks upon his lyre
And otherwhiles himself assists the task.
Thus the Three Sisters hardly know they spin:
Too close intent on the sweet strains they hear,
And rapt with praise of their great brother's song,
They spin more than the fated human span.
Yet Phoebus cries: 'My Sisters, be it thus:
Cut no years short from this illustrious life,
For he whose life you spin, my counterpart,
Yields not to me either in face or grace
For beauty, nor for sweetness in his song.
He is it, who'll restore the age of gold
And break the ban has silenced all the laws.
He is sweet Lucifer who puts to flight
The lesser stars; or Hesperus is he
Who swims up clear when back the stars return;
Nay, rather he's the Sun himself, what time
The blushing Goddess of the Dawn leads in
The earliest light of day, dispersed the shades –
The Sun himself with shining countenance
Who pores upon the world, and from the gates
Of his dark prison whirls his chariot out.
A very Sun is NERO and all Rome
Shall look on NERO with bedazzled eyes,
His face a-shine with regal majesty
And lovelocks rippling on his shapely neck.'

Apollo had spoken. But Lachesis, who had an eye for a handsome man herself, went on spinning and spinning and bestowed a great many years more on NERO as her own personal gift.

As for Claudius, they tell everyone to

> Be of good cheer, and from these halls
> Speed him with not impious lips.

And he really did bubble up the ghost at last, and that was the end even of the old pretence that he was alive. (He passed away while listening to a performance given by some comedians, so now you know that I have good cause to be wary of the profession.) The last words that he was heard to utter in this world followed immediately upon a tremendous noise from the part of his body with which he always talked most readily. They were: 'O good Heavens, I believe I've made a mess of myself!' Whether this was actually so or not, I cannot say: but everyone agrees that he always made a mess of things.

It would be waste of time to relate what afterwards happened on earth. You all know very well what happened. Nobody forgets his own good luck, so there's no fear of your ever forgetting the popular outburst of joy that followed the news of Claudius's death. But let me tell you what happened in Heaven; and if you don't believe me, there's my informant to confirm it all. First, a message came to Jove that someone was at the gate, a tallish man, with white hair; he seemed to be uttering some threat or other because he kept on shaking his head; and when he walked he dragged his right foot. He had been asked his nationality and had answered in a confused nervous manner, and his language could not be identified. It was not Greek or Latin or any other known speech. Jove told Hercules, who had once travelled over the whole earth and so might be expected to know all nations in it, to go and find out where the stranger came from. Hercules went, and though he had never been daunted by all the monsters in the world, he really got quite a shock at the sight of this new sort of creature, with its curious mode of progression and its raucous inarticulate voice, which was like that of no known terrestrial animal but suggested some strange beast of the sea. Hercules thought that his Thirteenth Labour was upon him. However, he looked more closely and decided that it was some kind of a man. He went up to it and said what a Greek naturally would say:

> Most honoured stranger, let me now demand
> Thy name, thy lineage, thy paternal land.

Claudius was pleased to find himself among literary men. He hoped to find some niche in Heaven for his historical works. So he replied with another quotation, also from Homer, which conveyed the fact that he was Claudius Caesar:

> The winds my vessel bore
> From ravaged Troy to the Ciconian shore.

But the next verse was much truer and just as Homeric:

> And boldly disembarking there and then,
> I sacked a city, murdering all its men.

And he would have made Hercules, who is not particularly bright-witted, take this literally, if there had not been someone in attendance on Claudius – the Goddess Fever. She alone of the Gods and Goddesses of Rome had left her temple and come along with him. And what she said was: 'The man's lying. I can tell you everything about him, because I have lived with him for very many years now. He was born at Lyons, a fellow citizen of Marcus's. Yes, a native Celt, born at the sixteenth milestone from Vienne: so of course he conquered Rome, as any good Celt would. I give you my honest word that he was born at Lyons – you know Lyons, surely? It's the place where Licinus * was king for so long. Surely you know Lyons, you who have covered more miles in the course of your travels than any country carrier? And you must know, too, that it's a long way from the Lycian Xanthus to the Rhône.'

This stung Claudius, and he registered his anger in the loudest roar he could command. Nobody could make out exactly what he was saying, but as a matter of fact he was ordering the Goddess Fever to be removed from his presence and making the customary sign with his trembling hand (always steady enough for that, though for practically nothing else) for her head to be cut off. But for all the attention that was paid to this order you might have thought that the people present were his own freedmen.

Hercules said: 'Now listen to me, you, and stop making a fool of yourself. Do you know what sort of place this is? It's where mice nibble holes in iron, that's the sort of place it is. So let's have your story straight, or I'll spill some of that nonsense from a hole in the top of your head.' To impress his personality on Claudius still more strongly, he struck a melodramatic attitude and began rolling out the following lines:

> Quick, the whole truth! Where were you born and why?
> Tell me at once, or with this club you die,
> That's cracked the skull of many a dusky king.
> (What's that? Speak up! I can't make out a thing.)
> Where did you get that wiggly-waggly head?
> Is there a town where freaks like you are bred?
> But stay, once in the course of my tenth quest
> (I had to travel out to the far West
> And bring back with me to a town of Greece
> The oxen of three-bodied Geryones),
> I noticed a large hill, which when he rises
> The very first thing that the Sun God spies is.
> I mean the place where headlong-tumbling Rhône
> Is met by shallow, wandering Saône,
> Most vague of streams – the town between these two,
> Tell me, was it responsible for you?

His delivery was most bold and animated, but all the same he had little confidence in himself and feared the 'fool's blow', as the saying is. However, Claudius, finding himself face to face with a big hero like

* An unpopular governor of Augustus's. – R.G.

827

Hercules, changed his tone, and began to realize that what he said here did not have anything like the same force as at Rome; that a cock, in fact, is worth most on its own dung-hill. So this is what he said, or at least what he was understood to say: 'O Hercules, bravest of all the Gods, I had hoped you would stand by me; and when your fellow Gods called for someone to vouch for me, you were the person I was going to name. And you know me very well really, don't you? Think for a moment. I'm the man who used to sit judging cases in front of your temple, day after day, even in July and August, the hottest months of the year. You know what a miserable time I had there, listening to the barristers talking on and on, all day and night. If you had fallen among that lot, though you're the strongest of the strong, I'm sure you'd have much preferred to clean out the Augean stables again. I reckon that I drained away far more sewage than you did. But since I want ...'

[*Some pages are missing here. A group of Gods all talking together are now addressing Hercules: he has forcibly introduced Claudius, whom he has consented to champion, into the Heavenly Senate.*]

'... You even burgled Hell once and went off with Cerberus on your back: so it's not surprising that you managed to burst your way into this House. No lock could ever keep you out.'

'– But just tell us, what sort of a God do you want this fellow to be made? He can't be a God in the Epicurean style: for Diogenes Laertius says: "God is blessed and incorruptible and neither takes trouble *nor causes trouble to anyone.*" As for a Stoic God, that sort, according to Varro, is a perfectly rounded whole – in fact completely globular without either a head or sexual organs. He can't be that sort.'

'– Or can he? If you ask me, there *is* something of the Stoic God about him: he has no head, and no heart either.'

'– Well, I swear that even if he had addressed this petition to Saturn instead of Jove he would never have been granted it – though when he was alive he kept Saturn's All Fools' Festival going all the year round, a truly Saturnalian Emperor.'

'– And what sort of a chance do you think he has with Jove, whom he as good as condemned for incest? I mean, he killed his son-in-law Silanus just because Silanus had a sister, the most delightful girl in the world, whom everyone called Queen Venus, but he preferred to call Juno.'

Claudius said: 'Yes, *why* did he do it? I want to know *why*. Really, now, his own sister!'

'– Look it up in the book, stupid! Don't you know that you may sleep with your half-sister at Athens, and that at Alexandria it can be a whole one?'

'Well, at Rome,' said Claudius, 'mice are just mice. They lick meal. ...'

'– Is this drawing-master teaching us to improve our curves? Why, he doesn't even know what goes on in his own bedroom.'

'– And now he's "conning the secret realms of sky" and wanting to be a God.'

'– A God, eh? I suppose he isn't satisfied with his temple in Britain where the savages worship him and humbly pray "Almighty Fool, have mercy upon us!" '

It occurred to Jove that senators were not allowed to debate while strangers were present in the House. 'My Lords,' he said, 'I gave you permission to cross-examine this person, but by the noise you are making anyone would mistake this for the cheapest sort of knocking-shop. Please observe the rules of the House. I don't know who this person is, but whatever will he think of us?'

So Claudius was taken out again and Father Janus was called upon to open the debate. He had been made Consul for the afternoon of July 1st next, and was a brilliant fellow, with a pair of eyes in the back of his head. He had a temple in the Market Place, so naturally he made a splendid speech: but it was too fast for the official recorder to take down, so I will not attempt to report it in full, not wishing to distort anything he said. At any rate, his theme was the Majesty of the Gods and that one ought not to cheapen Godhead by random distribution of the honour. 'It was a great thing once to be a God,' he said, 'but now you've brought it down to the level of jumping-beans. I don't want you to think that I am speaking against the deification of any one particular man; I am speaking quite generally; and to make this clear I move that, from now on, Godhead be conferred on none of those who, in Homer's phrase,

eat the harvest of the field,

nor yet of those whom, again in a phrase of Homer's,

nourishes the fruitful soil.

After my motion has been voted on and pronounced law, it should be made a criminal offence for any man to be made, displayed, or portrayed as a God, and any offender against the law should, I suggest, be handed over to the Hobgoblins and at the next Public Show be flogged with a birch among the new sword-fighters.'

The next to be called upon was Diespiter, the Underground God, son of Vica Pota, the God of Victory. He had been chosen for the Consulship and was a professional moneylender: he also used to sell citizenships in a quiet way. Hercules went up to him with a friendly smirk and whispered something in his ear, so he came out with the following speech: 'The God Claudius is related to the God Augustus. The Goddess

Augusta, whom he deified himself, is his grandmother; so, as he is by far the most learned man who has ever lived, and since as a matter of public policy someone ought to join the God Romulus in

eating boiled turnips with a will,

I propose that the God Claudius be regularly enrolled among the Olympians and enjoy the privileges and perquisites of Godhead in its fullest traditional sense, and that a note to that effect be inserted in Ovid's *Metamorphoses*.'

The House was divided, and it looked as though Claudius would carry a majority of votes; because Hercules saw that he had a good chance now and went rushing about from one bench to another saying: 'Now, please don't oppose me. I am personally interested in this measure. If you vote my way now, I'll do as much for you some other day. You know the proverb, "*Hand washes hand*."'

Then the God Augustus arose, for it was now his turn, and spoke with the greatest eloquence. 'I call on you, my Lords, to witness that ever since the day of my official deification I have not uttered a single word. I always mind my own business. But now I cannot keep up the pretence of impartiality any longer, or conceal the sorrow which shame makes deeper still. Was it for this that I made peace over land and sea, and put a truce to Civil War, and endowed Rome with a new constitution, and embellished her with stately public buildings, that ... that ... that ... Words fail me, my Lords. Nothing that I might utter could possibly match the depth of my feelings in this matter. In my indignation I must borrow a phrase from the eloquent Messala Corvinus: he was elected City Warden and resigned after a few days, saying "I am ashamed of my authority". I feel the same: when I see how the authority that I established has been abused I am ashamed of ever having exercised it. This fellow, my Lords, who looks as though he hadn't guts enough to worry a fly, sat in my place and called himself by my name and ordered men off to execution just as easily as a dog squats. But I won't speak of all his victims, fine men though they were: I am so preoccupied with family disasters that really I have no time to waste over public ones. I'll only speak about family disasters, then, because "a radish * may know no Greek, but I do": I at least know one Greek proverb, "The knee is nearer than the shin." This impostor, this pseudo-Augustus, has done me the kindness of killing two great-granddaughters of mine, Lesbia with the sword and Helen by starvation. And one great-

* The manuscript reading is *sormea*, which is meaningless; and editors suggest *soror mea*. But Augustus, whose style is here reproduced, could certainly not have been credited with the expression, '*My sister* may know no Greek, but I do.' His only sister was the learned Octavia. I suggest the better and simpler reading of *surmea*, which is the Egyptian radish, used by the Romans as an emetic. – R.G.

grandson, Lucius Silanus. (Here I expect you, my Lord Jove, to be fair in a bad cause, which after all is your own.) Now answer me, you God Claudius, why did you condemn so many men and women to death without first calling on them to defend themselves? What sort of justice is that? Is it the sort that is done in Heaven? Why, here's Jove has been Emperor all these centuries and never did more than once break Vulcan's leg:

> Whom seizing by the foot, his anger high,
> He flung over the threshold of the sky,

and once lose his temper with his wife and string her up. Did he ever actually kill a single member of his family? But you, you killed Messalina, your wife, whose grand-uncle I was as much as yours. ("Did I really?" you ask. A thousand plagues on you, of course you did! That makes it all the more disgraceful: you go about killing people and don't even know it.) Yes, my Lords, and he went on persecuting my great-grandson Gaius Caligula even when he was dead. It's true that Caligula killed his father-in-law, but Claudius, not content with following his example in that, killed a son-in-law too. And whereas Caligula would not allow young Pompey, Crassus Frugi's son, to take the title 'The Great', Claudius gave him his name back, but took off his head. In that one noble family he killed Crassus Frugi, young Pompey, Scribonia, the Tristionias, and Assario: Crassus, I own, was such a fool that he might almost have been made Emperor instead of Claudius. Do you really want this creature made a real God? Look at his body, born under the wrath of Heaven; and when it comes to that, listen to his talk! Why, if he can say as many as three words on end without stuttering over them, he can have me for a slave! Who is going to worship a God of this sort? Will anyone believe in him? If you turn people like him into Gods, you can't expect anyone to believe in *you*. In brief, my Lords, if I have earned your respect, if I have never given any mortal too definite an answer to his prayer, I count on you to avenge my wrongs. So my motion is' – he read it out from his notes – 'that insomuch as a certain God Claudius has killed his father-in-law Appius Silanus; his two sons-in-law, Pompey the Great and Lucius Silanus; his daughter's father-in-law Crassus Frugi (a man who resembled him as closely as one egg resembles another); Scribonia, his daughter's mother-in-law; his wife Messalina; with others too numerous to mention – I hereby move that he should be prosecuted with the utmost rigour of the law, that he should be refused bail, that he should be sentenced to immediate banishment, being allowed no more than thirty days to leave Heaven, and thirty hours to leave Olympus.'

A division was hurriedly taken and the motion carried. As soon as the result was known Mercury seized Claudius by the throat and dragged him off to Hell,

> Whence none, 'tis said, returns to tell the tale.

831

As they came down along the Sacred Way, Mercury asked what all those crowds of people meant. Surely it wasn't Claudius's funeral? It was certainly a most marvellous procession and no expense had been spared to show that it was a God who was being buried. Flute music, blaring of horns, a great brass band made up of all sorts of instruments, such a terrific noise, in fact, that even Claudius was able to hear it. Every face was wreathed in smiles: the whole Roman populace was walking about like free men again. Only Agatho and a few amateur barristers were in tears, and for once really meant it. The professional lawyers were slowly crawling out of dark corners, pale and gaunt, hardly alive, but reviving with every breath they drew. One of them, when he saw Agatho's group condoling with one another, came up to them and said, 'I told you so. This All Fools' Festival had to come to an end some day or other.'

When Claudius saw his funeral go by, he understood at last that he was dead. A great choir was chanting his dirge in antiphonal chorus:

> Weep, O Roman, beat thy breast,
> Mournful be thy Market Place,
> We bear a wise man to his rest,
> The bravest, too, of all thy race.
>
> With swift foot he could outrun
> Any courser in the land:
> He could the rebel Parthian stun,
> No Persian might his darts withstand.
>
> With steady grasp he bent his bow:
> Away they streamed in headlong packs.
> Slight was the wound, yet the Medes show
> In rout their ornamental backs.
>
> He sailed across an unknown sea
> And into Britain's island strode:
> He battered down the shields, did he,
> Of the Brigantians, blue with woad.
>
> He chained them with a Roman chain,
> Then with the Roman rods and axe
> He disciplined the Ocean main
> And took its terror for a tax.
>
> Mourn for the judge who could provide
> Quick sentences to marvel at:
> Who only listened to one side,
> Who could dispense with even that.

Where shall another such be found,
  To sit and judge the whole year through?
Minos the Cretan, underground,
  Must now resign his bench to you.

You barristers, who have your price,
  Weep, and all small poets, weep,
And weep, you rattlers of the dice
  Whom cogging does in plenty keep.

Claudius was charmed by this panegyric and wanted to stay to see the show through to the end. But Mercury, the trusted messenger of the Gods, pulled him away, first muffling his head so that nobody should recognize him, and took him across Mars Field and finally down to Hell between the Tiber and the Subway. His freedman Narcissus had gone down ahead by a short cut, ready to receive him on his arrival, and now came smiling forward, fresh from a bath and exclaiming: 'Gods! Gods come to visit us mortals! What may I have the honour...?'

'Go and tell them that we're here. And hurry up about it.'

At this order of Mercury's Narcissus darted off. The road to Hell's gate is all downhill and, as Virgil remarks somewhere, very easy going; so though Narcissus was suffering from gout it only took him a moment to arrive. Before the gate lay Cerberus or, as I think Horace calls him, 'the five-score-pated beast'. Narcissus was no hero: he was used to a little white lapdog bitch, and when he saw this enormous shaggy black cur, not at all the sort of animal you would like to meet in a dark place like Hell, he was thoroughly scared. He gave his message, 'Claudius is here,' in a loud yell.

For answer there came a burst of cheering and out marched a troop of ghosts. They were chanting the well-known song:

He's found, he's found!
Let joy resound!
O clap your hands,
The lost is found!

The choir included Gaius Silius, Consul-Elect, Juncus the ex-magistrate, Sextus Traulus, Marcus Helvius, Trogus, Cotta, Vettius Valens, Fabius – Roman knights whom Narcissus had ordered for execution. Mnester the comedian was there, whose appearance Claudius had improved by the removal of his head. Hell was buzzing now with the news of Claudius's arrival and everyone ran for Messalina. His freedmen, Polybius, Myron, Harpocras, Amphaeus, and Pheronactus were the first. Claudius had sent them all on ahead here, not wanting to be unescorted anywhere. Then came two Guards Commanders, Catonius Justus and Rufrius Pollio. Then his friends Saturninus Lusius, Pedo

833

Pompey and the two Asinius brothers, Lupus and Celer. Finally came Lesbia, his brother's daughter, and Helen, his sister's daughter, and sons-in-law and fathers-in-law and mothers-in-law – the entire family in fact. They formed up and marched off in a body to meet Claudius. Claudius stared at them and exclaimed in surprise, 'Why, what a lot of friends! How in the world did *you* all get here?' Pedo answered: 'How did we get here indeed, you bloodthirsty villain! How dare you ask us that? Who sent us here but you yourself, the man who kills all his friends? We're going to prosecute you now, so come along. I'll show you the way to the Criminal Courts.'

Pedo brought him into Aeacus's court; Aeacus was the judge who tried murder cases under the Cornelian Law. Pedo requested him to take the prisoner's name and then filled in the charge-sheet:

Senators murdered: 35.

Knights, Roman, murdered: 221.

Other persons: impossible to keep accurate records.

Claudius applied for counsel, but nobody volunteered to act for him. At last out stepped Publius Petronius, an old drinking friend who could talk the Claudian language quite well, and claimed a remand. Aeacus refused to grant it, so Pedo Pompey began his speech for the prosecution, shouting at the top of his voice. Counsel for the defence attempted to reply, but Aeacus, who is a most conscientious judge, ruled him out of order, and summed up on the case as presented by the prosecution. Then he pronounced:

> As the rascal did, he must
> Himself be done by. And that's just.

An extraordinary silence followed. Everyone was amazed at the decision, which was considered to be entirely without precedent. Claudius himself, of course, could have quoted precedents, but thought it monstrously unjust nevertheless. Then there was a long argument about the sort of punishment he ought to be awarded. Some said that Sisyphus had been rolling his stone up that hill quite long enough now, and some said that Tantalus ought to be relieved before he died of thirst, and some again said that it was time for a drag to be put on the wheel on which Ixion was perpetually being broken. But Aeacus decided not to let off any of these old hands for fear Claudius might count on getting a similar respite himself some day. Instead, some new sort of punishment had to be instituted: they must think of some utterly senseless task conveying the general idea of a greedy ambition perpetually disappointed. Aeacus finally delivered the sentence, which was that Claudius should rattle dice for ever in a dice-cup with no bottom to it.

So the prisoner began working out his sentence at once, fumbling for the dice as they fell and never getting any further with the game.

Ay, for so often as he shook the cup
And ready sat to cast them on the board,
The dice would vanish through the hole beneath.
Then would he gather them again, and seek
To rattle them and cast them as before.
But still they cheated him, and cheated him,
Retiring through the bottom of the cup.
And when once more he stooped to pick them up
They slipped between his fingers and escaped,
And endlessly continued to escape –
As when his rock with labour infinite
Sisyphus rolls unto Hell's mountain-peak
But down it comes, rebounding on his neck.

Suddenly who should come in but Gaius Caligula. 'Why, that's a slave of mine,' said Caligula. 'I claim him!' He produced witnesses who testified that they had often seen him flogging Claudius with whips and birch-rods, and knocking him about with his fists. So the claim was allowed, and Claudius was handed over to his master. However, Caligula made a present of him to Aeacus, and Aeacus handed him over to his freedman Menander, who set him the task of keeping the court records.

[Trans. by R.G.]

SEQUEL

Seneca was forced to commit suicide in A.D. 65 at Nero's orders. He survived most of the other characters in this story. Britannicus was poisoned in A.D. 55. Pallas, Burrhus, Domitia, the surviving Silanuses, Octavia, Antonia, Faustus Sulla – all met violent deaths. Agrippinilla lost her hold on Nero after the first two years of his reign, but regained it for a while by allowing him to commit incest with her. He then tried to murder her by sending her to sea in a collapsible ship which broke in two at a considerable distance from the coast. She swam safely ashore. Finally he sent soldiers to kill her. She died courageously, ordering them to stab her in the belly which had once housed so monstrous a son. When in A.D. 68 Nero was declared a public enemy by the Senate and killed by a servant at his own request, no member of the Imperial family was left to succeed him. In A.D. 69, a year of anarchy and civil war, there were four successive Emperors: namely, Galba, Otho, Aulus Vitellius, and Vespasian. Vespasian ruled benevolently and founded the Flavian dynasty. The Republic was never restored.

THE
ROYAL FAMILY
OF THE
HERODS

HEROD THE GREAT, son of Antipater, Governor of Judaea, and an Arabian Princess (mentioned in St Matthew ii)

married 1. Doris
2. MARIAMNE I, granddaughter of King Hyrcanus
3.
4.} Two nieces, names unknown
5. Mariamne II, daughter of Simon, the High Priest
6. Malthace, a Samaritan
7. Cleopatra of Jerusalem
8. Pallas
9. Phaedra, mother of one Roxana
10. Elpis, mother of one Salome

and had children

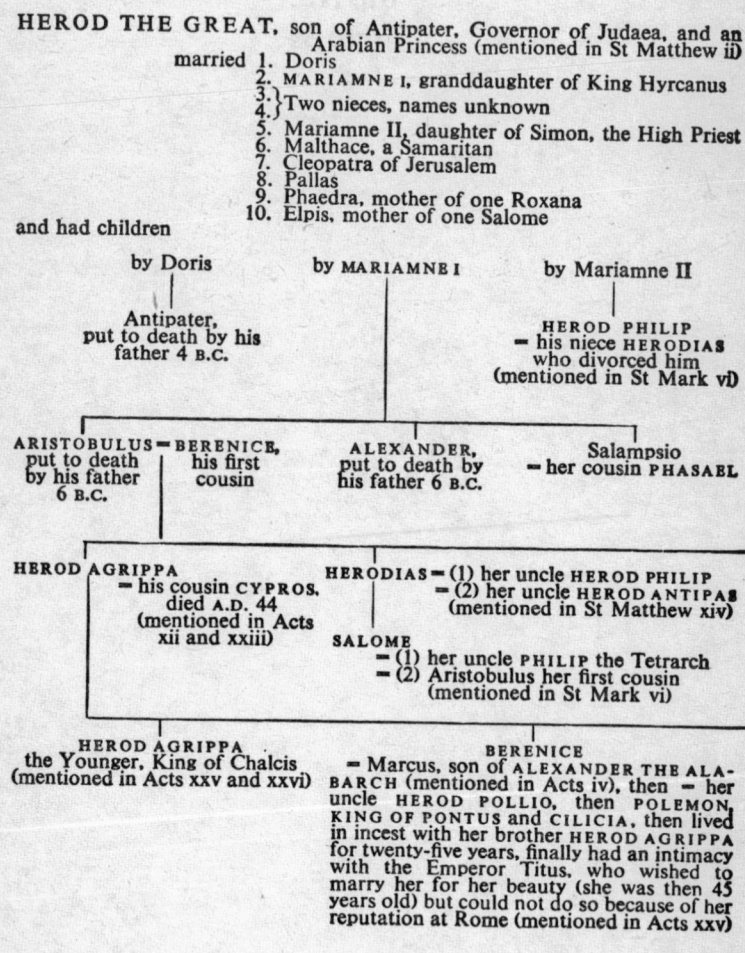

by Doris

Antipater,
put to death by his
father 4 B.C.

by MARIAMNE I

by Mariamne II

HEROD PHILIP
— his niece HERODIAS
who divorced him
(mentioned in St Mark vi)

ARISTOBULUS — BERENICE,
put to death   his first
by his father   cousin
6 B.C.

ALEXANDER,
put to death by
his father 6 B.C.

Salampsio
— her cousin PHASAEL

HEROD AGRIPPA
— his cousin CYPROS,
died A.D. 44
(mentioned in Acts
xii and xxiii)

HERODIAS — (1) her uncle HEROD PHILIP
— (2) her uncle HEROD ANTIPAS
(mentioned in St Matthew xiv)

SALOME
— (1) her uncle PHILIP the Tetrarch
— (2) Aristobulus her first cousin
(mentioned in St Mark vi)

HEROD AGRIPPA
the Younger, King of Chalcis
(mentioned in Acts xxv and xxvi)

BERENICE
— Marcus, son of ALEXANDER THE ALA-
BARCH (mentioned in Acts iv), then — her
uncle HEROD POLLIO, then POLEMON,
KING OF PONTUS and CILICIA, then lived
in incest with her brother HEROD AGRIPPA
for twenty-five years, finally had an intimacy
with the Emperor Titus, who wished to
marry her for her beauty (she was then 45
years old) but could not do so because of her
reputation at Rome (mentioned in Acts xxv)

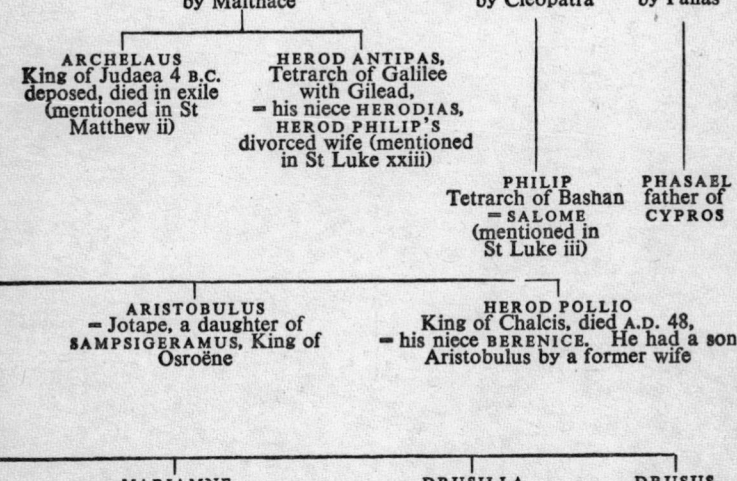

by Malthace   by Cleopatra   by Pallas

ARCHELAUS
King of Judaea 4 B.C.
deposed, died in exile
(mentioned in St
Matthew ii)

HEROD ANTIPAS,
Tetrarch of Galilee
with Gilead,
= his niece HERODIAS,
HEROD PHILIP'S
divorced wife (mentioned
in St Luke xxiii)

PHILIP
Tetrarch of Bashan
= SALOME
(mentioned in
St Luke iii)

PHASAEL
father of
CYPROS

ARISTOBULUS
= Jotape, a daughter of
SAMPSIGERAMUS, King of
Osroëne

HEROD POLLIO
King of Chalcis, died A.D. 48,
= his niece BERENICE. He had a son
Aristobulus by a former wife

MARIAMNE
= (1) Archelaus, son of Helchias,
Master of Horse
= (2) Demetrius the Alexandrian
Alabarch

DRUSILLA
= (1) the King of Homs
= (2) FELIX, Governor of
Judaea (mentioned in
Acts xxiv)

DRUSUS
died young

FOR THE BEST IN PAPERBACKS, LOOK FOR THE 🐧

In every corner of the world, on every subject under the sun, Penguin represents quality and variety – the very best in publishing today.

For complete information about books available from Penguin – including Puffins, Penguin Classics and Arkana – and how to order them, write to us at the appropriate address below. Please note that for copyright reasons the selection of books varies from country to country.

In the United Kingdom: Please write to *Dept E.P., Penguin Books Ltd, Harmondsworth, Middlesex, UB7 0DA.*

If you have any difficulty in obtaining a title, please send your order with the correct money, plus ten per cent for postage and packaging, to *PO Box No 11, West Drayton, Middlesex*

In the United States: Please write to *Dept BA, Penguin, 299 Murray Hill Parkway, East Rutherford, New Jersey 07073*

In Canada: Please write to *Penguin Books Canada Ltd, 2801 John Street, Markham, Ontario L3R 1B4*

In Australia: Please write to the *Marketing Department, Penguin Books Australia Ltd, P.O. Box 257, Ringwood, Victoria 3134*

In New Zealand: Please write to the *Marketing Department, Penguin Books (NZ) Ltd, Private Bag, Takapuna, Auckland 9*

In India: Please write to *Penguin Overseas Ltd, 706 Eros Apartments, 56 Nehru Place, New Delhi, 110019*

In the Netherlands: Please write to *Penguin Books Netherlands B.V., Postbus 195, NL-1380AD Weesp*

In West Germany: Please write to *Penguin Books Ltd, Friedrichstrasse 10–12, D-6000 Frankfurt/Main 1*

In Spain: Please write to *Longman Penguin España, Calle San Nicolas 15, E-28013 Madrid*

In Italy: Please write to *Penguin Italia s.r.l., Via Como 4, I-20096 Pioltello (Milano)*

In France: Please write to *Penguin Books Ltd, 39 Rue de Montmorency, F-75003 Paris*

In Japan: Please write to *Longman Penguin Japan Co Ltd, Yamaguchi Building, 2-12-9 Kanda Jimbocho, Chiyoda-Ku, Tokyo 101*

A CHOICE OF PENGUIN FICTION

Stanley and the Women   Kingsley Amis

Just when Stanley Duke thinks it safe to sink into middle age, his son goes insane – and Stanley finds himself beset on all sides by women, each of whom seems to have an intimate acquaintance with madness. 'Very good, very powerful . . . beautifully written' – Anthony Burgess in the *Observer*

The Girls of Slender Means   Muriel Spark

A world and a war are winding up with a bang, and in what is left of London all the nice people are poor – and about to discover how different the new world will be. 'Britain's finest post-war novelist' – *The Times*

Him with His Foot in His Mouth   Saul Bellow

A collection of first-class short stories. 'If there is a better living writer of fiction, I'd very much like to know who he or she is' – *The Times*

Mother's Helper   Maureen Freely

A superbly biting and breathtakingly fluent attack on certain libertarian views, blending laughter, delight, rage and amazement, this is a novel you won't forget. 'A winner' – *The Times Literary Supplement*

Decline and Fall   Evelyn Waugh

A comic yet curiously touching account of an innocent plunged into the sham, brittle world of high society. Evelyn Waugh's first novel brought him immediate public acclaim and is still a classic of its kind.

Stars and Bars   William Boyd

Well-dressed, quite handsome, unfailingly polite and charming, who would guess that Henderson Dores, the innocent Englishman abroad in wicked America, has a guilty secret? 'Without doubt his best book so far . . . made me laugh out loud' – *The Times*

A CHOICE OF PENGUIN FICTION

The Enigma of Arrival V. S. Naipaul

'For sheer abundance of talent, there can hardly be a writer alive who surpasses V. S. Naipaul. Whatever we may want in a novelist is to be found in his books . . .' Irving Howe in *The New York Times Book Review*. 'Naipaul is always brilliant' – Anthony Burgess in the *Observer*

Only Children Alison Lurie

When the Hubbards and the Zimmerns go to visit Anna on her idyllic farm, it becomes increasingly difficult to tell which are the adults, and which the children. 'It demands to be read' – *Financial Times*. 'There quite simply is no better living writer' – John Braine

My Family and Other Animals Gerald Durrell

Gerald Durrell's wonderfully comic account of his childhood years on Corfu and his development as a naturalist and zoologist. Soaked in Greek sunshine, it is a 'bewitching book' – *Sunday Times*

Getting it Right Elizabeth Jane Howard

A hairdresser in the West End, Gavin is sensitive, shy, into the arts, prone to spots and, at thirty-one, a virgin. He's a classic late developer – and maybe it's getting too late to develop at all? 'Crammed with incidental pleasures . . . sometimes sad but more frequently hilarious . . . *Getting it Right* gets it, comically, right' – Paul Bailey in the *London Standard*

The Vivisector Patrick White

In this prodigious novel about the life and death of a great painter, Patrick White, winner of the Nobel Prize for Literature, illuminates creative experience with unique truthfulness. 'One of the most interesting and absorbing novelists writing in English today' – Angus Wilson in the *Observer*

The Echoing Grove Rosamund Lehmann

'No English writer has told of the pains of women in love more truly or more movingly than Rosamund Lehmann' – Marganita Laski 'She uses words with the enjoyment and mastery with which Renoir used paint' – Rebecca West in the *Sunday Times*. 'A magnificent achievement' – John Connell in the *Evening News*

The Greek Myths
(in two volumes)

Not for over a century, since Smith's *Dictionary of Classical Mythology* first appeared, has the attempt been made to provide for the English reader a complete 'mythology', in the sense of a retelling in modern terms of the Greek tales of gods and heroes. In the two volumes of this book Robert Graves, whose combination of classical scholarship and anthropological competence has already been so brilliantly demonstrated in the *The Golden Fleece*, *The White Goddess*, and his novels, supplies the need. In nearly two hundred sections, it covers the Creation myths, the legends of the birth and lives of the great Olympians, the Theseus, Oedipus, and Heracles cycles, the Argonaut voyage, the tale of Troy, and much else.

All the scattered elements of each myth have been assembled into a harmonious narrative, and many variants are recorded which may help to determine its ritual or historical meaning. Full references to the classical sources, and copious indexes, make the book as valuable to the scholar as to the general reader; and a full commentary to each myth explains and interprets the classical version in the light of today's archaeological and anthropological knowledge.

Count Belisarius

The Sixth Century was not a peaceful one for the Roman Empire. Invaders threatened on all frontiers; Huns, Vandals, Goths, Saracens, Moors, Persians. But they grew to fear and respect the name of Belisarius, horseman, archer, swordsman and military commander of incredible skill and daring. Belisarius led the Imperial armies wherever the Emperor Justinian sent him; to the Eastern Frontier on the Euphrates, across the Mediterranean to Carthage, and to Rome.

In his palace at Constantinople, Justinian plotted and intrigued, dominated by his wife Theodora whose spies were everywhere. Justinian hated Belisarius for his success, his nobility and his universal popularity. But Belisarius was the one man who could save the Empire . . .